LAWANA BLACKWELL

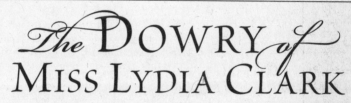

The DOWRY *of* MISS LYDIA CLARK

THE GRESHAM CHRONICLES | BOOK THREE

BETHANYHOUSE
Minneapolis, Minnesota

The Dowry of Miss Lydia Clark
Copyright © 1999
Lawana Blackwell

Cover design by Jennifer Parker

The Story of Little Sarah and Her Johnny-Cake and the poem *Hot Apple Pie* are from *Pictures and Stories From Forgotten Children's Books,* by Arnold Arnold (Copyright 1969) and granted permission by Dover Publications, Inc., New York.

Published by Bethany House Publishers
11400 Hampshire Avenue South
Bloomington, Minnesota 55438

Bethany House Publishers is a division of
Baker Publishing Group, Grand Rapids, Michigan.

Printed in the United States of America

ISBN 978-0-7642-0269-8

The Library of Congress has cataloged the original edition as follows:

Blackwell, Lawana, 1952-
     The dowry of Miss Lydia Clark / by Lawana Blackwell.
        p.   cm. — (Gresham chronicles ; bk. 3)
     ISBN 0-7642-2149-3
     I. Title. II. Series: Blackwell, Lawana, 1952-   Gresham chronicles ; bk.3.
PS3552.L3429   D69   1999
813'.54—dc21   99-6390
                                                                                          CIP

This book is lovingly dedicated
to my sister,
Lynn Wolverton,
who is a delightful mixture
of warmth, beauty and wit.

THE GRESHAM CHRONICLES

The Widow of Larkspur Inn
The Courtship of the Vicar's Daughter
The Dowry of Miss Lydia Clark

TALES OF LONDON

The Maiden of Mayfair
Catherine's Heart
Leading Lady

A Table by the Window

LAWANA BLACKWELL has eleven published novels to her credit including the bestselling GRESHAM CHRONICLES series. She and her husband have three grown sons and live in Baton Rouge, Louisiana.

www.lawanablackwell.com

April 8, 1872

Mealtimes in the dining room of the vicarage behind Saint Jude's were often noisy events, but Julia Phelps could not bring herself to scold the children for it. Not when her husband of sixteen months was one of the chief contributors to the chatter that accompanied clinks of silver against china and muffled thumps of glassware against the linen-draped tabletop.

It was obvious that Vicar Andrew Phelps, having spent his childhood in boarding schools or under the supervision of nannies, now relished having a brood about him. And as he had told Julia many times, he and Laurel would have been terribly lonely these past eight months since his older daughter Elizabeth's wedding were it not for his new wife and three stepchildren.

"But no knowledge is ever wasted," he was saying over breakfast to fourteen-year-old Aleda, who had expressed dismay that Miss Clark was planning to introduce algebra to the seventh standard students at the *Octavia Bartley School for Advanced Learning*. "And she'll explain it one step at a time."

"Yes," Philip agreed between bites of toast. At sixteen years of age, he and stepsister Laurel had only one more year of secondary school remaining. "It's just an introduction, you know. She won't have you factoring polynomials with summer break only two months away."

Grace, who turned nine a little over a fortnight ago, screwed up her heart-shaped face. "What does that mean?"

"Polynomials?" Laurel replied. "They're—"

"Not that. What does it mean that no knowledge is ever wasted?"

Andrew paused from cutting his bacon. "Why, because learning makes our minds grow."

"Bigger?"

"I shouldn't think so, Gracie. Or else our skulls would have to expand

5

as well." He winked at her. "And that would be a sight now, wouldn't it?"

"Miss Clark would have to stoop to come through the schoolroom door," Laurel said, touching her own blond head for emphasis. "She practically has all of the textbooks memorized."

"Jonathan is bright too," Grace asserted. She was the only child in the household who still attended the village grammar school, where Elizabeth's husband was schoolmaster. And while she referred to him as Jonathan in the family setting, he became Mr. Raleigh as soon as she set foot on school property. "He can spell words backward."

"Children?" Julia was forced to give a reminder from her place at the foot of the table. "You don't want to be tardy, do you?" This directed their attention back to the task at hand—breakfast. She met Andrew's apologetic smile with an indulgent one of her own. Another reason she did not scold was that she herself enjoyed the chatter. For the sake of her lodgers at the *Larkspur*, she had had to insist that her children speak only occasionally at the long dining table, and then only after asking for her permission. She was acutely aware, with Elizabeth now married, and Philip and Laurel leaving for the university in little over a year, that there would be future days when she would sorely miss young voices around the table.

It was only after Grace had obediently finished her coddled eggs and bacon that she ventured forth on the previous subject. "But what if someone decided to memorize the name of every person in Spain?" she inquired meticulously. "Wouldn't that be wasted knowledge?"

Her stepfather cocked his head at a thoughtful angle and dabbed his mouth with a napkin. "Does this particular person ever intend to visit Spain, Gracie?"

"No, sir."

"Or perhaps author a book on Spanish genealogy?"

"No book."

"Then indeed that would be wasted knowledge. So you've proven the old adage to be false."

Grace nodded solemnly, signifying that she did not take lightly the responsibility of being an adage-disprover. But her composure was disrupted when Aleda sent her a wry smile and asked, "And what about the ability to spell words backward? Isn't that wasted knowledge?"

After a second of tight-lipped concentration, Grace replied, "That's not the same thing."

"Then how is it useful?" Philip asked, not to be left out of the teasing.

"It just is." Clearly outnumbered, Grace called for reinforcement from the head of the table. "Isn't it, Papa?"

A smile warmed Andrew's expression. She had started addressing him as Papa instead of the more formal Father only weeks ago, and knowing how much it pleased him, Julia reckoned he would defend her position if she maintained that cows had green spots.

"Does it make you smile when Jonathan spells words backward, Gracie?" he asked.

"Yes, sir. Everyone in the whole schoolroom."

"Then I would consider that extremely useful knowledge."

After the children had left for school, Julia and Andrew took their second cups of tea in the parlor so that Dora's cousin Wanetta, the housemaid hired shortly after their honeymoon, could clear the table. Andrew, dressed in his black suit for making calls, looked dignified, as befitting his station. Only the crinkles at the corners of both hazel eyes and the dimples faintly visible beneath his blond beard would suggest to a stranger that he was capable of playfulness as well as piety.

And Julia looked the part of a minister's wife in a green-and-white striped silk, its overskirt draped in back to form a modest train. Only her auburn hair, falling to her waist behind her shoulders, still needed arranging into a chignon upon which to anchor a pert straw hat trimmed with ribbons and flowers. She enjoyed making calls with Andrew and would have joined him today were it not for the meeting of the Women's Charity Society held on the first Monday of every month.

"Mrs. Paget asked me to remind you to stop by the kitchen," Julia told her husband as they sat on the sofa with teacups and saucers. One of Andrew's usual Monday errands, after conducting chapel at the grammar school, was to call upon seamstress Mrs. Ramsey and her mother, Mrs. Cobbe, for prayer and a condensed version of the sermon that Mrs. Cobbe's frail health had prevented them from hearing at Saint Jude's the previous day. As Mrs. Paget usually began her baking for the week on Monday mornings, she often had a treat to send along for the two to enjoy.

"And please don't let anything happen to whatever she sends with you," Julia felt compelled to add, for Andrew had a habit of misplacing things whenever he was in deep thought.

He nodded sheepishly. "I'll have to remember not to leave it in the schoolroom."

"Pray do, or Jonathan will assume it's for him." Their son-in-law's sweet tooth was notorious, especially for baked items from Mrs. Paget's kitchen. "But why can't you just leave it in the trap?"

Lowering the teacup from his lips, he replied, "Because I'm not taking the trap, dear. Don't you remember—your meeting?"

"Oh, but Mrs. Bartley is hosting it today. The manor house isn't that far."

"Neither are any of my calls."

Sighing, because she was aware that any argument she could present

7

would not pierce his stubborn chivalry, Julia nonetheless made an attempt. "Andrew, how do you think I managed my way around Gresham before we married?"

He simply gave her a maddening grin. "You walked, of course. And a handsome sight you were. I used to go out of my way down Market Lane in the hopes you would be on your way to *Trumbles* or somewhere. Remember the time we both slid and almost collided on the ice?"

It was unfair that he could coax a smile out of her even when she was exasperated with him. "Yes, I remember."

"You had on those outlandishly huge boots," he said with a chuckle.

"And your hat flipped right into my hands." She forced herself out of the pleasant reverie. "Your calls are much farther away than my meeting, Andrew."

He set his empty cup and saucer on the tea table, then took hers from her hands and did the same. "I'll not ride when my wife is walking, Julia Phelps. And I must leave soon, so we're wasting valuable time arguing that could be spent more profitably."

"More profitably, Vicar?"

His arm cradled her shoulders. "A kiss, dear wife! Two if there's time."

———————

As it turned out, there was time for three, but that meant Andrew had to grab his bowler hat and hurry out the door. Just as he was unlatching the garden gate, Dora came rushing outside with a basket upon her arm. "Mrs. Paget says not to let this out of your sight this time," she said, indicating the bundle wrapped in a white towel tucked inside.

Andrew winced, recalling the reproachful looks the cook had given him for days just last month after it was discovered that an apple pie had grown stale in the boot of his trap. Mrs. Paget, good soul that she was, did not appreciate having the fruits of her labor wasted. "I've already been warned," he replied, and as the delicious aroma wafted up to his nostrils, he added hopefully, "Fig bread?"

"With walnuts, too," the maid replied with a knowing smile.

"Perchance she's keeping some aside for us?"

"Oh, you know how Mrs. Paget is when she gets to baking. She's set aside a loaf for the missus to take to Miss Elizabeth and put two more to the cupboard."

A breeze scented of apple blossoms from the squire's orchards met Andrew in the vicarage lane, quivering the new leaves of the aspens to his right like harp strings. Beyond, the village green was sprinkled with yellow cowslips, blue and pink wild forget-me-nots, and ragged robin. He could faintly hear the moving waters of the River Bryce and, farther in the distance, the exquisitely soothing sound of a cowbell. *Oh to be in Gresham now that April's here!* he thought, taking liberty with Robert Browning's poem. As much as he looked forward to heaven, he was grateful to God for the bits of heaven on earth he had experienced in his lifetime.

A quarter of an hour later he reached the steps of the mellow brick building in which many of Gresham's inhabitants had first learned their alphabets and numbers. Faintly he could hear youthful voices trailing off with the final notes of "We Bless the Name of Christ the Lord." Andrew was reaching for the doorknob when he remembered the basket upon his arm. The heavenly aroma was still noticeable, so there would be no hiding that he carried baked goods with him. Being an adult, Jonathan would understand—albeit reluctantly—that the treat was intended for someone else. But how could Andrew justify tempting thirty-three children when he had not the liberty to share? In one fluid motion, he set the basket down on the stoop behind him and advanced on into the classroom.

"Good morning, ladies and gentlemen," he greeted the schoolchildren after Jonathan's nod to indicate that he was finished leading hymns.

"Good morning, Vicar Phelps," a chorus of voices returned.

Andrew's message centered around the parables of the lost sheep and the lost coin, for he could not stress enough to the children how precious even the most seemingly insignificant life was to their heavenly Father. He labored as diligently on his school messages as he did on his Sunday sermons—he would not justify appearing at the school once weekly just for the sake of a ritual. And he received occasional encouragement that his ministry was bearing fruit, such as the conversions of two of the most irascible students, Jack and Edgar Sanders, now faithful members of the Wesleyan chapel.

Coming to faith seemed to have made them only slightly less irascible, but Andrew had to remind himself that even Saint Peter had had a few rough edges to his personality. Thinking about the Sanders brothers caused him to notice, as he concluded his devotion, that their back row desks were empty. And at that same moment, the door opened slowly, and two boys with sun-bronzed faces shuffled into the room.

"We're sorry we're late, Mr. Raleigh," Edgar, the oldest, mumbled to the floorboards. "A wheel broke off the wagon, and Harold made us fix it."

"He wouldn't even get down to help," Jack threw in.

"Well, take your seats," Jonathan told them with a glance in Andrew's direction.

Andrew nodded that he understood and waited until the two empty desks were filled before directing the students to bow their heads for prayer.

Back on the front stoop, Andrew noticed two speckled drays pulling the Sanders wagon away from the stand of elder trees in front of the school yard. Shocks of straw-colored hair peeked from under the driver's felt cap. Just before another tree blocked Andrew's view of him, the man turned in his seat and they locked eyes. It was Harold, the oldest son, Andrew realized. With courtesy usually found lacking in most Sanders males, he sent Andrew a cheery wave. Andrew raised his arm to return the greeting, then bent down to pick up the basket—which felt considerably lighter. He gaped down at it for several seconds before his mind would accept that it was indeed empty.

Indignation quickening his pulse, he tightened his grip around the basket handle and considered giving chase. He would certainly do so if he had the trap. But there were certain restraints imposed upon him by his vocation, and one was that vicars did not sprint down village lanes trying to outrun a pair of horses—much less pull young men from wagon seats to throttle them for some offense.

Sighing, he stepped down into the school yard and considered facing Mrs. Paget straightaway to confess how he had not kept the basket in sight at all times. It was usually better to get unpleasant tasks over with rather than dread them all day. And being that there were two more loaves in the cupboard, surely she wouldn't mind sending another. *Would she?*

He scratched his bearded cheek and thought of the lecture she would deliver. In the bounds of the kitchen, it was easy to forget that he was the master of the house and Mrs. Paget the servant, for she had cooked at the vicarage for years before his arrival and had the knack for making him feel like a small boy at times.

And then an idea rescued him from his dilemma. *Bakery.* And Mrs. Paget wouldn't even have to know. He hushed the little twinge in his conscience by reminding himself that the cook's intent was that Mrs. Ramsey and her mother receive a loaf of fig bread. And he would carry out that intent to the best of his ability.

The bell over the door tinkled a welcome as Andrew entered *Johnson's Baked Goods,* a red brick building with cheerful sash windows on Market Lane. Josiah Johnson ceased wiping the counter with a rag and lifted in greeting the one dark eyebrow that slashed across his beefy face. "Good mornin' to you, Vicar."

"And to you, Mr. Johnson," Andrew replied, removing his hat. He set the basket upon the counter. "I would like a loaf of fig bread, please."

"Haven't any," the baker replied with a shake of the head.

"Couldn't you bake some?"

"If you've a mind to pick it up this afternoon."

"That long?"

10

"Yeast has to rise, you know, Vicar." The baker grinned. "To my way of thinking, some nice pear tarts would be just what you're needing."

"I can't wait until this afternoon." He would see Mrs. Paget at lunch, and without doubt she would ask him if he had made the delivery. Andrew scrutinized the pastries and cakes behind the glass counter, as if he could make a loaf of fig bread materialize if he looked hard enough.

When one didn't, he frowned. "What is the closest thing you have to fig bread?"

"Blackberry?"

He frowned again. While he had rationalized that one loaf of fig bread could take the place of another with no explanations necessary, he could not in good conscience pass off blackberry bread for fig. But surely it would mollify the cook somewhat if he was able to report to her that he had brought Mrs. Ramsey and Mrs. Cobbe *something*.

"Blackberry will be fine."

Leaving the bakery, he made his way over to Thatcher Lane and the vine-covered cottage with its gray stones brightened by blue morning glories. Mrs. Ramsey answered his knock with her usual welcoming smile. She was a plain woman with pockmarked cheeks, but according to local historians her late husband, who was considered one of the most handsome men in Gresham, had doted upon her their whole married life.

"The dear woman!" she gushed, scooping out the loaf from the proffered basket. "Always so thoughtful of others. It'll be just grand with our lunch."

Guilt swept through Andrew, but since he had not actually *said* who had baked the bread, he told himself that there was no deliberate deception. It was one thing to have to confess to his cook that he had not kept the basket in sight, but he did not care to allow the incident to become a topic of conversation over every garden gate. Not that Mrs. Ramsey was malicious, but gossip in a small village was almost impossible to stem.

"Would you care to have a slice with some tea now, Vicar?" Mrs. Ramsey asked apologetically, as if she had mistaken his silence for disappointment that the treat was to be set aside for later.

He thanked her but refused the offer. Even though he happened to like blackberry bread just as well as fig, he wanted no part of it.

———

After Julia finished dressing, she took up her reticule, notebook, and a towel-wrapped loaf of fig bread for Elizabeth and went out front where Luke had hitched Rusty to the trap.

"Handsome day for taking a drive, ain't it?" the caretaker asked as he took her parcels so she could step up into the seat. He was a tall man of about thirty, with curly brown hair and a gap between his teeth that made words like *handsome* come out in a whistle. Many an unmarried woman in Gresham had set her cap for him, including Wanetta, but aside from an infatuation with Fiona three years ago, he seemed content in his bachelorhood.

"It is a fine day at that, Luke," Julia replied, taking up the reins. She bade him farewell after he handed her things over, and just a flick of the reins was all Rusty, the blue roan, needed to be set in motion. Julia had asked Andrew to teach her how to drive on a whim one day and found that she enjoyed it very much—especially on mornings like this one, for spring air bathed her cheeks as the trap carried her along. At the end of the vicarage lane she reined Rusty to the west for twenty yards or so, to where a half-timbered, two-story cottage sat at the corner of Church and Bartley Lanes. The cottage had once belonged to Captain and Mrs. Powell, until the former schoolmaster transferred to Shrewsbury for his position with Her Majesty's Inspectors.

Hilda Casper, employed as Elizabeth and Jonathan's housemaid, welcomed Julia into the parlor. She seemed even younger than her eighteen years, with a boyishly thin figure and transparent lashes and brows. For three years she had milked cows on a dairy farm before deciding housework was more to her liking. "Good morning, Mrs. Phelps," the girl said. "Mrs. Raleigh is still upstairs. I'll let her know you're here."

"Please tell her not to hurry," Julia said. "I'll just put this loaf in the kitchen." As Hilda went to the stairs, Julia crossed the parlor and walked through the dining room toward the kitchen. The cottage was narrow but well built and cozy. Combining Jonathan's wages with what Elizabeth earned for organizing and copying Mr. Ellis's and Mr. Pitney's archeological notes, they were able to afford a cook and housemaid and still put some savings aside for the future. Jonathan was determined not to have to ask his family back in Kensington for financial assistance. Still, in his eagerness to provide Elizabeth with as good a life as possible, he had gratefully accepted their offer to purchase the cottage and furniture as a wedding gift last June. The couple could have lived in the *Larkspur*'s vacant family quarters free of charge, but Julia could well understand their desire for a home of their own.

As Julia entered the kitchen, the cook was seated at the worktable peeling potatoes over a dishpan. "Keep your seat, Mrs. Littlejohn," Julia told her when she made a move to push out her chair. "I'll just leave this on the cupboard shelf. How are you keeping?"

"Right well, Mrs. Phelps," the older woman replied with a smile. She had a squarely proportioned face under a topknot of dark brown hair that resembled one of the unpeeled potatoes. For some twelve years she had worked in the squire's scullery, until Mrs. Bartley—formerly Mrs. Kingston—recommended her for the position with Elizabeth and Jonathan. "Won't you be wantin' to return the towel to the vicarage?"

"I'll just collect it on my way home after the meeting."

"No use in going to all that fuss. Just pull out that drawer behind you and take a clean one. Every kitchen in Gresham has the same ones anyway—threepence a bundle at *Trumbles*."

Julia did as she was told. When she turned around again, the cook nodded toward the door she had entered. "Mrs. Raleigh's still going with you?"

"Why, yes. As soon as she comes downstairs."

"Oh. Well, a little sunlight is good for a body."

Mrs. Littlejohn began peeling potatoes again, but her preoccupied expression worried Julia. Stepping closer to rest a hand on the back of a chair, she asked, "Is there something wrong with Elizabeth, Mrs. Littlejohn?"

"Well . . ."

"Please tell me if there is."

The cook darted a glance up at the ceiling, as if she could see Elizabeth moving about upstairs, before saying, "Hilda heard her being sick a little while ago. And it weren't the first time."

"Being sick?"

She touched her lips. "Heaving up her breakfast."

"Oh dear." Julia glanced at the ceiling as well. "Is there any stomach powder in the house? I could dash over to *Trumbles* . . ."

An enigmatic smile curved the corners of the cook's lips. "I don't believe stomach medicine will be of any use to the missus."

It took Julia a second before the meaning of the cook's observation sunk in. Pulling out the chair, she sank into it. *Is it possible?* Even though Elizabeth was a woman of twenty-two, it was so easy to forget that she wasn't still the insecure girl she had first met weeping in the vicarage garden three years ago. "Are you positive?"

"Fairly. She's gotten sick a couple of other mornings lately."

"Have you asked her about it?"

Mrs. Littlejohn shook her head. "I didn't know if it was my place to, Mrs. Phelps. Seems that if she wanted me and Hilda to know, she would have told us."

"I wonder if she knows it herself?" Julia wondered out loud. *She didn't have a mother for so long.* And the subject of childbearing wasn't considered appropriate conversation for polite society, so she could understand how Elizabeth could be in the dark about it. *You should have prepared her better,* she chided herself. Beyond a private talk on the eve of Elizabeth's wedding, when she answered her stepdaughter's timidly stated questions as forthrightly as possible, she had not thought of the months beyond the honeymoon. She thanked Mrs. Littlejohn for confiding in her, rose from the table, and returned to the parlor. Elizabeth was just coming down the staircase.

"Julia! Thank you for waiting," she said, a smile dimpling both cheeks. She looked quite becoming, her slender frame draped in a silk gown of blue and sage green. From under her Maltese lace morning cap the wheat-colored hair fell upon her neck in looped braids, and her fringe had been given the attention of a curling iron. She did not address Julia as Mother, as did Laurel—not from any lack of affection but simply because she was twenty years old when Julia married her father. "We aren't late, are we?"

"Not at all." Julia motioned toward the kitchen with the folded towel in her hand. "Mrs. Paget sent some fig bread."

"Jonathan will be glad. Please thank her for us."

When she reached the bottom of the steps, Elizabeth gave her a quick embrace. *It can't be so!* Julia thought as they drew apart, then reminded herself, *You were eighteen when Philip was born.* Noticing faint shadows under her stepdaughter's eyes, she asked, "How are you feeling, Elizabeth?"

The dimpled smile wavered. "I'm not quite sure, Julia. I've had spells of queasiness for the past few mornings. I haven't mentioned it to Jonathan because he has so much on his mind with the archery tournament coming up. And just when I start thinking about seeing Doctor Rhodes, the nausea passes. I've barely slept the past two nights for worrying about it."

"Let me see." Julia pressed a hand against the young woman's forehead and cheek. "No fever."

"See? If it wasn't for the morning spells, I would feel fine."

"Hmm. Why don't we sit for a minute or two?"

"Sit?" Elizabeth glanced at the long case walnut clock against the wall, a wedding gift from Andrew and Julia. "But it's almost half past. You shouldn't be late."

"Mrs. Bartley is very capable of beginning without me," Julia said, gently taking her arm. "She's the real leader of the society anyway."

When they had settled on the Chesterfield sofa, Elizabeth eyed her curiously. "Are you all right, Julia?"

"Oh, I'm quite well, thank you." But she was finding it most difficult to keep a serious expression upon her face. "Do you mind if I ask you some questions, Elizabeth?"

"Questions? No, of course not."

Elizabeth's subsequent replies, delivered with flushed cheeks, removed all doubt. And the joy of it made Julia seize her stepdaughter's hand.

"Silly me . . . I should have expected this!"

"What is it, Julia?" Elizabeth asked with a worried crease between her brows.

"You haven't any idea?"

14

After a puzzled silence, her mouth gaped slightly. "You mean the nausea is normal when . . ."

"Not in every case, but more often than not."

"Oh, Julia!" Elizabeth exclaimed and caught her up into another embrace. "I can scarcely believe it! How wonderful!"

When they drew apart, the sight of tears in her stepdaughter's brown eyes made Julia's water as well. She wiped them with a corner of the towel and offered the other end to Elizabeth as she prayed silently, *Father, you're so good!* To be a wife and mother was what Elizabeth had wanted most for her life, and now both prayers would be answered.

Words began tumbling from Elizabeth's lips as she nervously tapped the fingertips of her hands together. "I'll have to tell Mrs. Littlejohn and Hilda. I know they've heard me being sick and are probably worried. Oh, but Jonathan must hear it first! I wonder if I should meet him at school for lunch? But he has to watch the children, so it would be hard to get him away. Perhaps I should wait until he gets home. Anyway, I should think it would be hard for him to concentrate on teaching after hearing such news."

"And Papa . . ." she went on after pausing for a deep breath. "I would like him to hear the news from both Jonathan and me, so please don't tell him." She gave Julia an apologetic look. "It's just that I'd like to see his face when he hears it. Do you understand?"

"Of course," Julia assured her.

"Perhaps the two of you could come over this evening after I've told Jonathan? Oh . . . but what about the children? Should we tell them?"

"Your father and I will come after supper. That way you'll give your husband time to absorb the news. And as for your sisters and brother, it might be best to wait a bit, if Mrs. Littlejohn and Hilda will agree to keep it quiet."

"Thank you, Julia. I'm glad one of us has a clear head right now." Elizabeth put her hands to her flushed cheeks and took in another deep breath. "I don't think I could concentrate on anything else today. Do you think the other ladies would mind if I—"

"Stayed here?" Julia smiled. "My dear, I insist upon it. We're going to be discussing the new pulpit—nothing terribly urgent. Go upstairs and get some more rest."

Years of feeling responsible for setting a good example as the vicar's daughter, however, were not easily suppressed. "But what will you tell them?"

"I'll simply inform anyone who asks that you weren't able to come." Patting her shoulder, Julia said, "Today is a milestone for you, Elizabeth. Stay home and make plans for your baby."

*F*iona Clay stepped back from the dressing table in the apartment over the *Larkspur*'s stables to adjust the angle of the leghorn Spanish hat over her coal black ringlets. Her cashmere gown flowed gracefully over the curves of her petite figure like water over a stone, and its shades of mauve and violet made her eyes seem the color of ripe mulberries. From her ears dangled a pair of onyx earrings set in gold, and at her throat hung a matching pendant. She was still self-conscious about going anywhere in Gresham decked in such finery, but because her husband, Ambrose, insisted upon pampering her, finery was all she owned. In London she had no qualms about wearing them, for there she was known only as the wife of actor Ambrose Clay. But there were few people in Gresham who did not remember when she was the *Larkspur*'s housekeeper.

Not that anyone had ever been less than gracious to her. But she couldn't help but wonder if people outside her immediate circle of friends thought she was putting on airs. *And it's your own pride that makes you even wonder!* she scolded herself silently, crossing the bedroom to the window that looked out over the carriage drive. Mr. Herrick, caretaker of the *Larkspur*, was hitching Donny and Pete to the landau to deliver her, Mrs. Durwin, and Mrs. Latrell to the meeting of the Women's Charity Society. *Pride and self-absorption,* she sighed. For who but a prideful woman would assume others had nothing better to do than think critical thoughts about her?

She pulled on a pair of white gloves, took her velvet reticule from the foot of her bed, and walked into the parlor. Ambrose sat at a window, still in his velvet dressing gown, staring at the view opposite from the one she had surveyed. In the near distance the Anwyl rose abruptly—boasting its five hundred feet of red sandstone, green grasses, wildflowers, footpaths, and tenacious trees—crowned by the ruins of a second-century Roman fort. From the faint droop of her husband's posture, Fiona could tell that the dark mood was still upon him. She walked closer and touched one shoulder.

"Fiona . . ." he said, as if startled out of a daydream. He turned to look at her, the pallor of his aristocratic face lightening just a bit. "You're so beautiful."

Fiona smiled and leaned down to kiss his forehead. "I don't have to go, Ambrose," she said in her soft Irish brogue.

"Oh, but I wish you would." Raising his hand to cover hers upon his right shoulder, he said, "It'll be good for you to be involved with something other than nursemaiding me."

"Nursemaiding you, Ambrose? That's not what I do, and you know it. If anything, you've been the one to take care of me."

"A responsibility I do not take lightly," he teased.

It was so encouraging when Ambrose could find his sense of humor even when in the grip of despondency. Coming home to the *Larkspur* four days ago had been the wise thing to do. He had finished the twenty-month run of *The Barrister* at the Prince of Wales Theatre with the usual glowing reviews. But in the latter months of the performance, his vacillating moods, coupled with the demands of the stage, had proved so taxing upon his strength that taking up another role immediately afterward was unthinkable. They were exceedingly blessed in that wise investments made during his earlier years made it possible for him to take long stretches of rest, even to retire if he wished. This welcome interlude would last until February of next year, when he was committed to begin rehearsals for Byron's *Sardanapalus* at the Princess's Theatre.

"But what will you do while I'm away?" she asked. "Sit at this window all morning?"

"No, of course not."

"Well, I'm relieved to hear—"

"I may move to the other window."

Frowning, Fiona said, "Ambrose . . ." He chuckled, a welcome sound to her ears.

"Or rather, I'll dress and see if Mr. Durwin is up to a game of draughts, seeing as how his wife will be away as well."

A knock sounded at the door. "That will be Mr. Herrick," Fiona told him. She kissed his forehead again and left, looking back once from the doorway just to reassure herself that his urging her to go had not been just a noble act. Had there been tears shining in his slate gray eyes, she would have stayed, but he was smiling with his hand lifted to bid her farewell.

———

Andrew spent almost an hour with Mrs. Ramsey and Mrs. Cobbe, then returned to Market Lane and headed north. While passing the *Larkspur*, he set the basket down over the wall to be collected on his way home. His next visit would be with Mrs. Perkins, who was recovering from an attack of ague. He paid attention only to the lane directly in front of his steps, grateful that no passersby were out with whom he would have to stop and make small talk. *Why didn't you simply tell her where the bread came from?* he asked himself. Lies told by omission were just as sinful as those spoken aloud.

He had just raised a lethargic fist to knock upon Mrs. Perkins' cottage door when his left ear caught a series of dull raps and a male voice shouting something that sounded suspiciously like an oath. Andrew stepped back into the lane and peered toward the stone bridge over the River Bryce. The Sanders wagon sat motionless, still hitched to the pair of speckled drays, and listing to the left where a familiar figure was bent over a wheel, banging at it with a hammer.

"Thank you, Father!" Andrew muttered as he hurried up the lane with fists balled at his sides. At least he would have the opportunity to give Harold Sanders the rough side of his tongue for all the trouble he had caused! But that righteous indignation began to fade with every step. One of the consequences of spending hours each week in Bible study was that scriptures having to do with returning good for evil and turning the other cheek now nudged themselves into his mind uninvited. He unclenched his hands, and when he was within hearing distance, he called out, "Broke again, did it?"

Harold twisted his body only long enough to send a scowl over his shoulder, then raised the hammer again. "It's a piece of rubbish, this old wagon!"

Stepping closer, Andrew could see the problem. The wheel had apparently hit a rock, which caused the seam in the iron rim to separate, breaking the wood felly and two spokes. "Couldn't have happened in a better place, you know." When Harold looked at him again, Andrew motioned toward a stone cottage and wheelwright's shop at the entrance to Worton Lane. "Mr. Mayhew's. I don't see how you can fix it yourself without the proper tools."

Harold's scowl grew even more sour. "Can't take it there."

"Why not?"

"My papa—" he began, then shrugged.

It was easy for Andrew to supply the rest in his imagination, for it seemed that either Willet Sanders or one of his older sons had feuded with every man in Gresham. Even easygoing Mr. Trumble had banned Harold's brother, Dale, from his shop for several months for insulting one of his customers.

"Well, if you'd like to unhitch one of the horses and go home for help, I'll stay with the other one."

18

"Can't. My papa and Dale are in Grinshill lookin' at some cattle. Won't be back 'til afternoon milking. And Fernie and Oram are as useless as Jack and Edgar."

Why don't we try being a little more negative? Andrew thought. "What if I spoke with Mr. Mayhew? I'm sure he would allow your father to pay him later."

The man got to his feet and turned around to face him. One eyebrow lifted over a deep-lidded moss green eye. "You would do that, Vicar?" He motioned toward the bed of the wagon and at least had the decency to blush. "You know I stole your cake."

And I've half a mind to bring you to Mrs. Paget and let her deal with you! Andrew thought. "It's fig bread. And yes, I would do that, Harold."

Both eyes narrowing with suspicion, the man asked, "How did you know my name?"

"The same way you know mine, I expect. Small village."

"You ain't gonter make me promise to go to church, are you?"

"I can't make you promise anything," Andrew replied. "But I confess it would please me if you did."

He shifted his feet. "Well, I'm Wesleyan."

Andrew did not contradict the man by pointing out that having a sister and two younger brothers in the Wesleyan faith did not make one a Wesleyan any more than having a brother in the Royal Navy made one a sailor. "You can find God at the Wesleyan church, too, Harold. Or I can tell you about Him now, if—"

"We'd best get on over there if you're gonter talk with Mr. Mayhew," Harold cut in. "But it won't do no good."

With a quiet sigh, Andrew replied, "Well, you never know until you ask."

As it turned out, Mr. Mayhew declared he could get to the job within the hour and didn't seem to mind that it was a Sanders wheel he would be repairing. He even offered to allow Harold to leave one of the horses in his paddock so he could go home on the back of the other one and tend to some chores. After thanking Mr. Mayhew, Andrew walked with Harold back to his wagon and helped him unhitch the horses.

"Here, this is for you," the man said, avoiding Andrew's eyes as he scooped a towel-swathed bundle from the bed of the wagon and thrust it at him. He shrugged again. "I just wanted to see if I could get away with it anyway."

It was on the tip of Andrew's tongue to tell Harold to keep the loaf, but then it didn't seem right that thievery should be rewarded—even when the thief offered to return his bounty. So he tucked it under his arm and caught up the reins of the horse that he would be walking over to Mr. Mayhew's.

"Think about church, now. Reverend Seaton would be happy to see you."

Harold mumbled something in reply that could have been either affirmative or negative—or perhaps simply a grunt—as he hoisted himself onto the bare back of the other horse. He took up the reins, lifted a hand in farewell, and rode off across the bridge.

Just as Andrew was leaving the wheelwright's shop, it dawned upon him that he could now right the wrong he had perpetrated earlier. He would have to confess all to Mrs. Ramsey, of course, but it would be better than living with the guilt that had returned in full force to nag at him. And how could Mrs. Paget hold it against him if the proper loaf of bread had eventually found its way to the Ramsey cottage?

He took the back way down Walnut Tree Lane, eager to have it done with before making the rest of his calls. Recrimination no longer clouded his senses, enabling him to appreciate the coolness of the tree-shaded lane and the varied colors of newly blooming gardens in front of half-timbered and stone cottages. Within minutes his spirits were fairly soaring.

And then his eyes caught motion in the distance ahead. Mrs. Ramsey, wearing a bonnet and carrying a shopping basket, was walking briskly toward Market Lane. *Must be going to Trumbles*, he thought, hurrying to narrow the distance between them so he could call out to her. But then an idea insinuated itself into his mind, causing him to return to a slower pace.

She only leaves when her mother is napping. And their kitchen was located in front of the cottage. He had never actually mentioned to Mrs. Ramsey what *kind* of bread he had brought her. What if he slipped inside and switched the loaves? It would be such a relief not to have to worry about this whole affair becoming fodder for gossip.

Shame! he told himself. No decent Christian would even consider such a thing, much less a man of the cloth. But then another thought nudged the first one aside. *Is it so wrong to want to undo what I've done?* True, it would require a certain unpalatable stealth, but hadn't Joseph once surreptitiously hidden a silver cup in his brother Benjamin's sack? Who would argue that Joseph was not a righteous man!

And what about Harold Sanders? Now that was something to consider. If word reached the young man's ears that the vicar had spread tales of his misdeed, he might never darken the door of a church!

"Good mornin' to you, Vicar!"

Andrew fairly jumped at the booming voice of Doctor Rhodes' gardener, who raised his clay pipe in greeting. "Good morning, Mr. Blake,"

Andrew returned when his pulse slowed to normal again. "A fine day for gardening, isn't it?"

"Ah, but it is at that!" The gardener's grin stretched wide above a red beard. "And a fine day to be out walkin'. Men are gettin' too soft these days, forgetting what the Almighty made feet for!"

"Yes, that's true," Andrew agreed, but with much less enthusiasm than Mr. Blake's, seeing as how he would be riding in his trap if Julia hadn't needed it. He passed six more cottages and then turned onto Thatcher Lane, all the while almost hoping someone would be in the lane or out in a garden to stop him. When he reached the Ramsey cottage, shaded by the meandering branches of a sentinel oak, he stopped and sent a look in all directions. There was no one in sight. *I'm simply correcting myself*, he rationalized. If he had accidentally walked away with Mrs. Ramsey's umbrella instead of his own, there would be nothing wrong with switching them in her absence.

With heart pounding he opened the front door—he would not ease it open as a thief. *You're not a thief*, he reminded himself. If Mrs. Cobbe woke, he would just have to explain his actions. He could see a white, familiar shape upon the table and drew closer. Incredulously, Mrs. Ramsey had wrapped the loaf in a towel identical to the one Mrs. Paget used—white cotton with yellow binding. And so the task was easier than he had imagined, a simple matter of switching bundles and heading out the door again.

He had to retrace his steps up Walnut Tree Lane, in case Mrs. Ramsey should be on her way home. If only the hard knot in the center of his chest would go away! With everything put to rights again, surely he should be feeling as cheerful as he had this morning when he left the vicarage. *It's this loaf!* he thought, glancing down distastefully at the blackberry bundle under his arm. Like Achan's gold, it was a symbol of what happens when one takes that first step on the downward path of deception. He had to be rid of it as soon as possible!

Turning onto Church Lane, he could see the Worthy sisters across from the *Larkspur*'s carriage drive, sitting in a patch of sunlight in their garden between a pear and yew tree. The lap cushions upon which the white-haired women pinned their lace-spinning patterns were so much a part of their frames that it always seemed unusual to Andrew to see the two seated in church without them. As he moved closer, the two bade him good day in unison. Andrew returned the greetings. His steps finally felt a little lighter.

"How are you keeping this morning?" he asked the two, who were actually sisters-in-law, not siblings by birth.

Jewel, the more outspoken of the two, nodded as her gnarled fingers continued to weave threads through the pins on her cushion. "Got more orders than we know what to do with, Vicar."

"But we're making a tablecloth now," Iris told him in her soothing voice. "To send to the queen. Her birthday is next month, you know."

"And ye may as well nail us in our coffins with our cushions and pins when the time comes for us to go," Jewel added. Her voice resembled metal grating against a file. "Because our old fingers ain't going to know how to stop spinnin'."

Giving her sister-in-law a stern look, Iris reproved, "You shouldn't be talking about our coffins like that, Jewel."

"And why not?"

"Because it's inviting trouble. Remember old Mr. Summers who lived on Short Lane? He was forever telling folks that—"

"He lived on Thatcher Lane," Jewel interrupted as Andrew waited for a pause in which to remind them gently that he had delivered a forceful sermon against superstition just last month. "In that old stone cottage with the dirty windows. It were before the lanes was cobbled, and folks was always havin' to clean dust from the windows so's they could see out. But his wife, Mrs. Summers, she didn't—"

Iris, whose lips had drawn together tightly during Jewel's narrative, finally cut in. "But that wasn't the old Summers place, Jewel. That was their son Rowan's. Old Mrs. Summers used to give us pears from her tree, and her windows were as clear as well water."

In an effort to change the subject, Andrew leaned closer to inspect the band of lace trailing from Iris's pillow and quipped, "Isn't it narrow for a tablecloth?"

The tactic worked, for they stopped arguing and stared up at him as if he had lost all his faculties. "We sews 'em together, Vicar," Jewel explained in the tone one would use to tell a child why he mustn't eat peas with a knife.

"Yes, of course." He drew the loaf from under his arm. "Would you care for some blackberry bread?"

Both wrinkled faces wreathed in smiles. He was clearly forgiven for his attempt at humor. "Why, how good of you, Vicar!" Iris exclaimed. "And Mrs. Paget, too, of course."

"Oh, but this came from the bakery just a couple of hours ago," Andrew was quick to make clear. "I'll just need to take the towel with me."

"We're right fond of bakery bread too," Jewel reassured him. But then she looked helplessly at her spinning fingers, as if not quite sure how to command them to stop.

"We'll have it with our tea later," said Iris.

But when she also seemed hesitant to take the loaf from him, Andrew nodded understanding. "Shall I bring it inside for you?"

Relief washed across both aged faces. "Would you, Vicar?" Iris asked. "We shouldn't want to get any crumbs on the queen's lace."

"I don't mind at all," Andrew replied. He felt so much better as he crossed the garden that he found himself whistling one of his favorite hymns, "Blest Be the Tie." The wattle-and-daub cottage consisted of two rooms, the front serving as a parlor, dining room, and kitchen. Andrew went straight to the bread box sitting on a dresser and opened its lid.

"Blest be the tie that binds . . ." he sang softly while unwrapping the towel. And then he froze. A slice had been cut from one end of the loaf.

"No!" he groaned. How would he explain that? When did the day begin to unravel for him? If only he could start it over again! With clenched teeth, he took a knife from a crock of cutlery.

"I pray you don't mind . . ." Andrew said on his return to the sisters. Showing them the thin slice of bread resting upon the folded towel in his hand, he added sheepishly, "I took the liberty of helping myself."

Of course they assured him that they didn't mind. He felt shamed by their graciousness and took a bite because he knew it would please them. "Very tasty," Andrew said after swallowing. Ordinarily he was fond of blackberries, and this bread was heavy with the moist fruit. But guilt made it as palatable as sawdust. "And now I must finish my calls."

He didn't have the heart to reprove them for the coffin comment. After his actions for the past two hours, a little superstition seemed a mild thing. It was only after Mrs. Perkins had welcomed him into her cottage that the thought struck Andrew of how Mrs. Ramsey would soon be unwrapping the loaf in her kitchen.

*A*s Rusty pulled the trap at a spanking pace down Bartley Lane, Julia realized that she was still smiling. *A grandchild!* Jonathan would be so delighted to find out he was going to be a father! He was so good with children in the classroom, and now there would be a little one at home as well. And Andrew! He would be beside himself with joy! It was going to be difficult to keep the secret, but Elizabeth was right—she and Jonathan should be the ones to tell the new grandfather-to-be.

She rode past the new red brick building that housed the *Octavia Bartley School for Advanced Learning* and scanned the four front windows, though she knew Aleda, Laurel, and Philip would be busy at their desks. A stab of memory found her heart of how her first husband had swung her up into his arms and laughed when she shyly told him she was carrying their first child.

At only seventeen, Julia had still been a child herself during the pregnancy. Little did she know that in addition to his long days as a surgeon at London's *Saint Thomas Hospital*, Dr. Philip Hollis was already finding another outlet for his time—the gaming halls. When he died of a heart attack fourteen years later, he left a wife and three children who barely knew him, as well as debts that cost them everything they owned. *Except the Larkspur*, Julia thought. A loan and some wise advice from her butler, Mr. Jensen—now the *Larkspur's* manager—combined with hard work and the grace of God had enabled her to turn the abandoned coaching inn into a successful lodging house.

And God had been faithful to send many people along the way, whose generosity of spirit and encouragement fortified her when she needed it most. Former housemaid, Fiona O'Shea, now Mrs. Ambrose Clay, who insisted on moving to Gresham with her, working at first without wages. Mr. and Mrs. Herrick, whose caretaking and cooking freed Julia to learn the business aspects of running the inn. Even her first lodger, Mrs. Kingston, now Mrs. Bartley, taught her not to rush to judgment of other people. *And of course, Andrew*, Julia thought. *Dear Andrew*. He had given her a love based upon friendship and respect—as well as romance—and was a caring father for her children.

The manor house loomed in sight, a high-gabled, red sandstone building set in a framework of pine and deciduous trees on manicured lawns. It was owned, along with a good deal of the farmland in Gresham, by Squire Bartley, founder of *Anwyl Mountain Savory Cheeses.* The old squire was showing increasing signs of mellowing since his marriage last year. He actually smiled whenever people greeted him and Mrs. Bartley in the course of their daily walk. It was he who had constructed the secondary school in honor of his wife.

Empty carriages in the gravel drive stood as evidence to Elizabeth's prediction that Julia would be late. Gratefully she turned her reins over to a young groomsman, Silas Reed, lingering only long enough to compliment his clear tenor voice, heard every Sunday in the chancel choir at Saint Jude's. A maid ushered her into the house and to the drawing room, where twenty or so women sat upon velvet-upholstered Queen Anne furniture and were thankfully still occupied with socializing. Near one oak-paneled wall a table boasted a silver tea service and dishes of sponge cakes covered with chocolate sauce.

Julia spotted Fiona right away and they exchanged smiles. Her dear friend shared a sofa with Mrs. Durwin and Mrs. Latrell, the *Larkspur*'s newest lodger. Fiona had expressed an interest in becoming involved with the community while in residence but confided to Julia at church yesterday that her husband was suffering another dark mood. Knowing Ambrose's gallant nature, Julia was certain that he had urged her to attend today's meeting anyway.

"Well, Mrs. Phelps, you managed to show yourself after all!" Mrs. Bartley, a commanding gray-haired presence, rose from a chair, her voice carrying over the hum of conversation. Three years ago Julia would have wilted at the woman's tone, but now she knew well the warm heart inside that forbidding exterior. She simply walked over to plant a kiss upon her former lodger's wrinkled cheek.

"And I'm terribly sorry, Mrs. Bartley. Have I missed anything important?"

"Nothing earth shattering, I suppose," she replied in a voice considerably warmer. She sent a worried glance past Julia's shoulder. "I trust Mrs. Raleigh is well? Several ladies noticed your trap at her cottage."

But of course they would, Julia thought, for there were few secrets in Gresham. With truthful evasiveness she replied, "Elizabeth was feeling a little out of sorts, so I urged her to stay home and rest."

"I pray it's nothing serious. And you gave her very astute advice. It's always best to stay in when there is the possibility one may be carrying something contagious."

"My thoughts exactly."

Mrs. Bartley took her arm. "And so now why don't you go ahead and have some tea and cake so our meeting can begin?"

Having had two cups at the vicarage as well as a hearty breakfast, Julia declined politely, opting to call the meeting to order as soon as the others had served themselves. She crossed the room, exchanging greetings along the way, and took a place near the marble fireplace in which a low fire snapped in the grate to break the morning chill. When everyone's attention was directed her way, she expressed appreciation to Mrs. Bartley for hostessing the meeting and led the group in prayer.

The Women's Charity Society's main concern was raising money to help provide food and other necessities for Gresham's poor. But Saint Jude's centuries-old pulpit had needed replacing for years, and just because it hadn't actually crumbled apart when given a good pounding during a heated sermon, the diocese was dragging its collective feet in replacing it. Mrs. Derby, the cobbler's wife, was first to raise her hand when Julia asked for suggestions.

"We could sew quilts and sell them." That idea was swiftly and tactfully put to rest because of the time such a project would require—not to mention that several of the members, Julia included, had never sewn a stitch beyond needlepoint.

The most impractical suggestion came from Mrs. Bartley, yet it drew spirited applause—muffled by gloves. "We drag the pulpit out to the green and make a bonfire."

"Mrs. Bartley," Julia was compelled to respond while constraining a smile, "how would that help the matter?"

A coy smile curved under the elderly woman's hawkish nose. "The diocese would have no choice but to give us a new one, now would they? They couldn't very well expect Vicar Phelps to prop his prayer book and Bible on the floor."

Again there was applause, with Mrs. Bartley soaking it up like the sponge cakes soaked up chocolate sauce. "Aye, but they jolly well might if we burnt our own pulpit," Mrs. Sykes argued, as if she believed Mrs. Bartley actually intended to carry out her plan.

It was timid Mrs. Durwin who started everyone down the path toward a solution. "Why not sell sandwiches and lemonade on May Day?"

"That's a fine idea!" Mrs. Sway, wife of the greengrocer, enthused. "We could ask the vicar to announce it in church. But would that raise enough money?"

"Why not have a pantomime too?" Mrs. Johnson suggested. "We could charge admission."

"But May Day is less than a month away. Would we have time to arrange it?"

Mrs. Bartley got to her feet again. "Instead of a pantomime . . ." She looked across at Fiona, who stared back at her with growing caution upon her oval-shaped face. "Why not real theatre! After all, one of our parishioners is a famous actor. And his one-man show two years ago was the talk of Gresham."

The muffled claps were louder this time, intermingled with excited chatter. Intercepting Fiona's panicked look, Julia raised a hand for attention.

"Ladies . . ." she said when silence finally arrived. "I must remind you that Mr. Clay is here for a much needed rest."

Mrs. Bartley was the first to retract. She had once been Ambrose's walking partner and felt great affection for the man. "That's true," she declared. Resuming her chair, she sent Fiona a look filled with regret. "I quite forgot myself."

"It was a good idea, Mrs. Bartley," Fiona replied calmly, smiling to show that she understood.

A moment or two of collective thoughtful silence had lapsed, when Mrs. Latrell had a suggestion. "We auctioned box lunches on May Days back in Faversham. You know, for the unmarried couples? Couldn't we do that here as well?"

This plan was seized upon eagerly. Mrs. Bartley was nominated, seconded, and then voted unanimously to head the project. When the business part of the meeting was concluded, Julia slowly made her way over to Fiona. Every woman she passed complimented her on her husband's sermon yesterday or asked about Elizabeth, and it would have been rude not to linger and chat for a minute.

"How is Ambrose?" Julia asked her friend when they finally had the opportunity for private conversation. She wasn't quite sure when friendship between the Phelps and Clays had evolved into a first-name basis, but it seemed perfectly natural to her now.

Taking her hand, Fiona replied, "The same. Thank you for coming to his rescue. He insisted that I attend today."

"I assumed as much. Your happiness is so important to him."

"I would have been just as happy to stay with him." She flashed a guilty glance to the nearest circle of chatting women. "Not that I'm not having a lovely time."

"I understand," Julia assured her.

"Anyway, he mentioned challenging Mr. Durwin at the draughts board. And Mr. Bancroft from London has asked him to read a couple of plays to keep in mind for the future. So at least he has things to do with his time besides stare out the window."

"And besides pamper his wife?" Julia asked with an affectionate squeeze of her friend's hand.

A spark warmed Fiona's violet eyes. "We wouldn't want to get *too* carried away, would we now?"

————

"And so who can give us an example of *iambic pentameter*?" Lydia Clark asked the seven girls and five boys at their desks, students of the *Octavia Bartley School for Advanced Learning*. As usual, Helen Johnson's arm shot up immediately, while other students rustled through the pages of their anthologies. Lydia simply sent the girl a smile that said, *Let's give someone else a turn this time, shall we?*

"Ben?" she said after an appropriate amount of time had passed.

The wheelwright's son looked up from his text. "Uh . . . *The Eve of Saint Agnes?*"

"A very good example. John Keats used iambic pentameter more than any other form. Read us a line, please."

Ben, whose dream was to be an architect in a big city, cleared his throat. *"The owl, for all his feathers, was a-cold."*

"Can you hear the five soft and strong rhythms?"

Twelve heads nodded, and Lydia stepped over to the blackboard. "For this next exercise, I would like you to pretend you're writing the body of a letter to a friend, using iambic pentameter. It should be at least eight lines."

The faces of all five boys filled with panic, as if she had asked them to prepare a dissertation in Latin. "It isn't that difficult once you get in the habit of thinking in rhythm," she reassured them. "You may even enjoy it."

If any believed that, it didn't show by their expressions. Billy Casper's arm shot up, prompting Lydia to add, "An *imaginary* friend will be fine." The arm lowered.

"Write your letter in iambic pentameter, telling your friend anything you wish." When three more hands were thrust into the air, she added, "And no, it doesn't have to rhyme."

It wasn't that she was clairvoyant, but after teaching school for over sixteen years, Lydia had developed an instinct for anticipating the questions that would accompany any new assignment. She pointed to the blackboard. "I've written some sample sentences. Let's read them together."

"My *Fa*-ther *took* us *to* the *shop* for *treats*" was delivered by twelve young voices in unison. Three minutes later, the only sounds in the room were scratchings of pencils upon paper and the occasional creak of wood as a student shifted in his chair. Lydia went to her own desk and started marking arithmetic papers. She looked up presently and frowned. In the front row, Phoebe Meeks was rubbing her eyes. Lydia rose from her chair and went over to her.

"Let's go to the cloakroom, Phoebe," she said softly. Eleven sets of eyes sent curious looks her way, but at a warning lift of Lydia's brows, they all darted back down to the task at hand. Painfully shy during her own school years, Lydia had too much empathy to scold or even counsel a student in front of his classmates. In the cloakroom she smiled at the thin, brown-haired girl to reassure her that she wasn't about to be reprimanded.

"You've been rubbing your eyes quite often today. Have you another headache?"

"Yes, ma'am," the girl murmured. Phoebe was not pretty like the children who graced the labels of bottles of castor oil and tins of cocoa, but she possessed a fine bone structure that would change into beauty when her face reached maturity.

"Did you tell your mother about them?" Lydia asked.

Phoebe's green eyes evaded hers. "I thought it wouldn't happen any more since you moved my desk."

"Will you tell her today? She needs to know."

"But I can see much better. . . ."

"If your eyes aren't causing the problem, an oculist will rule that out. But we need to find out, Phoebe." She put a hand lightly on the narrow shoulder. "And if you won't tell your mother, I shall be forced to pay her a call."

Receiving a reluctant assurance from the girl that she would talk to her mother this evening, Lydia allowed her to return to the classroom. She couldn't fault Phoebe for not wanting to wear spectacles. Those who wore them were not considered attractive by most people, no matter how clear the complexion or finely carved the bone structure. A terrible thing for a girl, for in every generation there seemed to be a certain number of healthy-sighted individuals who took it upon themselves to remind those less fortunate ones of just how unattractive spectacles were.

Lydia scanned the three rows of desks to monitor her students' progress, then fed the two goldfish in a bowl on top of the bookcase. The breeze had teased loose one of the curtains at a front window, and she went over to tie it back more securely. She had been spared the humiliation of eyeglasses. It was as if God had decided that natural plainness was enough of a burden. Taller than most boys during her school days, she walked with slumped shoulders until it dawned upon her that it was just as ridiculous to look like a question mark as to be overly tall. And one day she decided that the curls she labored over with a curling iron to camouflage her prominent ears consumed a fair amount of time that could be more enjoyably spent in the pages of a book. After thirty-four years of spinsterhood, romance was surely out of the question.

She had learned not to mind it so much. At least she had had children—more than two hundred over the past sixteen years. Fourteen of those years were spent at a boarding school for girls in Glasgow. No matter the gender or location, the students brought her joy and frustration, laughter and sometimes sorrow, but they gave her a worthy reason to get out of bed every morning.

Sounds in the lane interrupted her reverie. She peered out of the window to the left. Three women in Sunday dresses and bonnets were being driven in a landau toward Church Lane. Behind followed a parade of other horses, carriages, and wagons. Her mother had mentioned a meeting at the manor house this morning, so she would be passing by as well. Lydia turned to look at her students—most were twisted in their chairs in an effort to observe the scene behind them.

"There was a meeting of the Women's Charity Society at the manor house," she explained, for it was unfair that she enjoyed the privilege of investigating from the window when they did not. "And may I assume that you've finished your assignment?"

Only Helen Johnson nodded proudly while pencils started moving furiously against papers again. Lydia walked behind the last row, glancing over shoulders to see how her students were progressing. At Ben Mayhew's desk she stopped, her eye having caught a familiar name. She kept reading:

> When I sit at my desk to start the day
> I pray that Laurel Phelps won't look my way
> It's not because I think that she is plain
> But her brown eyes are harmful to my brain
> I suddenly cannot add three plus three
> Who went to war with Prussia? Don't ask me!
> I think if I'm to ever finish school
> I should wear blinders like my father's . . .

She waited until the boy had put the period behind the final word, *mule*, then tapped him on the shoulder. He started and gaped up at her in horror.

"The cloakroom," Lydia whispered.

With a worried expression he turned his paper facedown, left his desk, and accompanied her as if on the way to his own funeral. When they were alone, she asked, "Are you aware that we'll be reading the compositions aloud?"

Color seeped from the roots of his carrot-red hair down to his chin, blending his mass of freckles into one rosy glow. "We will?"

"Wouldn't another topic be more appropriate?"

"I'm sorry, Miss Clark. I just got carried away."

"Well, you'd best get started on something else now. You haven't much time."

"Yes, ma'am!"

She had to linger in the cloakroom for a second longer, for the struggle to keep from smiling had been intense. Fifteen minutes later, all pencils in the class had stopped moving. "And now, who would care to read first?" Lydia asked, leaving her desk again for the back of the classroom.

Of course Helen Johnson's hand stabbed the air first, but since none of the five male hands were raised, there wasn't as much competition. This time Lydia granted her permission to proceed. Hurrying to the front of the classroom to stand next to Lydia's empty desk, the girl arranged both dark brown braids to fall over her shoulders, cleared her throat delicately, and read in a dramatic voice:

> On Saturday I penned a page of prose
> So beautiful the angels quit their horns
> to listen. Then arose a wondrous sound;
> The flutterrings of a thousand mighty wings!
> As they paid tribute to my humble words
> I smote my quill upon my chest and cried,
> It was not I who stirred your heartstrings so!
> For talent is a gift from God, you see.

"Thank you, Helen," Lydia said as the baker's daughter lowered the page. And because she always attempted to find something to compliment whenever a student put some effort into an assignment, she added, "You maintained the iambic pentameter perfectly through every line."

"Thank you, Miss Clark," Helen said, beaming all the way back to her desk.

Lydia could only pray that one day the girl would recognize the pride behind such a declaration of humility. It was one thing to give God credit for assigning talent, and quite another to suggest He had authored the poem himself. That was a lesson each of her students would have to learn for themselves—as it would have to come from a heart closely attuned to the Father and eyes that sought out wisdom from the Word. And as her students were still very young, there was always hope that that would happen.

One by one, she called upon others to read. The topics ranged from Christmas memories to learning to ride a horse to gathering wildflowers on the Anwyl. Ben Mayhew stood and delivered a poem about fishing that was adequately structured but not nearly as amusing as the one Lydia had read over his shoulder. She called upon Philip Hollis last. Reluctantly he walked to the front of the classroom, his auburn hair almost dull compared to his friend Ben's cap of flame.

And like Ben, Philip maintained he had no use for poetry. "*What good will it do a doctor to know the difference between trochees and dactyls?*" he had once asked her in frustration when he was having a particularly tough time completing an assignment. He held his paper at chest level with both hands and began:

> *At River Bryce a tortoise bit my toe*
> *I danced and roared but it would not let go*
> *And so I hobbled home, at least a mile*
> *Attached to that cantankerous reptile*
> *The cook saw my predicament and cried,*
> *"I have the kettle boiling—come inside!"*
> *That night I said to family as we dined*
> *"If there's a toenail in your soup, it's mine.*

Youthful laughter filled the classroom as Philip lowered his paper, his face fairly glowing with surprise and pleasure. Lydia smiled too. To know that she had had a hand in helping him discover this latent talent filled her with a wondrous awe. A familiar scripture came to her mind regarding children. *Happy is the man that hath his quiver full of them.*

She asked Philip to read his poem again and thought, *Happy also is the woman whose days are full of them.*

The Dowry of Miss Lydia Clark *Chapter 4*

After taking a shortcut across the green, Andrew was just unlatching the vicarage gate when he heard the trap being pulled up the lane. Just the thought of spending a little time with his wife was enough to lighten the doldrums that had afflicted him all morning. It seemed that at every call he made after leaving the Worthy sisters, people had looked at him curiously. Even the occasional passersby with whom he traded greetings in the lanes. Was he that transparent, his guilt so easily readable across his face? *I'll never do anything like that again, Father,* he vowed.

Again he set the basket down, this time over his own garden wall, and turned to wait for Julia. Only it was Mrs. Hayes, one of his parishioners, sitting at the reins of a runabout being drawn by a chestnut-colored bay. *Of all mornings!*

"It looks like that Missus Hayes again." Luke's voice came from behind his shoulder, unmistakable for the whistled "s."

"I'm afraid so," Andrew was unable to restrain himself from saying, even while he raised a listless hand to greet his visitor.

"You should'ha stayed away a little longer, Vicar."

Andrew turned his head to grin at the caretaker and was dismayed to receive the same look that had haunted him from other faces for most of the morning. *At my own home too?* he thought. But the trap had come to a halt, and he stepped forward to assist Mrs. Hayes as Luke took charge of the horse.

"I want you to talk with my Luther!" the woman declared before her feet had even touched the ground. She was a waspish little woman in her late forties, with hair drawn back into a severe knot under a little straw bonnet and a high-pitched, whining voice.

"Mrs. Hayes, this is not a convenient—"

"He said he was just going to deliver the morning milk to the factory . . . *four hours ago!*" The veins in her forehead stood out in livid ridges. "Well, sure enough, he's been at the smithy all morning, trading lies with that other lot of slackers!"

"Now, Mrs. Hayes, just because they like to visit—"

But she continued on as if he hadn't attempted to speak. "You don't find me wasting time at those charity women's teas and such nonsense!"

And they thank you for that, Andrew thought.

"And when I went there to fetch him, he sent me away! I want you to go over there and tell him his duty is to be at home with his wife!"

"I cannot do that, Mrs. Hayes."

She fixed Andrew with a look that would curdle milk. "Well, I don't see why not! You're the vicar. He listens to you."

"Then I'll pay a call later when he's at home. I'll not embarrass him in front of his friends."

"Well, he didn't mind sending me away in front of his friends!"

"Two wrongs don't make a right, Mrs. Hayes." Taking her gently by the arm, he guided her toward the runabout, which Luke had had the good sense to abandon after tying the reins. "I'll be over this afternoon. Until then, why don't you find a good book to read or sit in your lovely garden with a cup of tea? You'll find Mr. Hayes will be home before you know it."

By the indignant primp of her mouth, Andrew could tell the woman wasn't favorable toward his advice. But she allowed herself to be assisted into her carriage. As he handed her the reins, she lifted her chin and allowed two parting remarks to drift down to him.

"Vicar Wilson would have come at once, you know. And *he* conducted himself with dignity!"

Wounded by the implications of both statements, Andrew watched with gaping mouth as she drove back down the lane. Then he turned and walked woodenly through the garden. He was at the door when the sound of another approaching carriage caught his ears. He turned, his heart sinking. Apparently, Mrs. Hayes had thought of more insults to fling at him.

But when he reached the bottom step, he realized that it was his wife at the reins. He hurried out to the drive. Luke appeared again from wherever he had gone to hide.

"Was that Mrs. Hayes who turned down Church Lane?" she asked as Andrew helped her from the trap. "I only saw her from the back."

"Then you had the best vantage point, didn't you?"

She gave him a worried look. "Oh dear."

"It's nothing—all that matters is that you're home." He held her hand as if it were spun of fine glass and thought he had never appreciated her so much. Should the whole world turn against him, here was the one person who would stand by his side, no matter what! Holding the gate open for her, he asked, "How was the meeting?"

"Very pleasant, but it went a little long."

Feigning a shudder, he said, "That's the trouble with meetings—they always go too long. It seems that about seventy percent of the discussion of any given subject is superfluous."

They had reached the steps leading up to the stoop, and she paused to level her eyes at him. "Are you implying we women talk too much?"

"Not at all, dear wife. We do the same in our diocese meetings. Every minute point has to be discussed *ad nauseam*. It's as if the vicars are paid by the . . ."

His voice trailed off as he realized she was not paying attention. Or rather, not to his *words*, for his face had her full bemused scrutiny. *Oh no!* he groaned under his breath. *Not you too!*

She tapped her upper lip. "You have something . . ."

"Here?" he asked, touching his blond mustache.

"No, between your teeth in several places. Something dark."

Using his tongue, he pried away something hard and round. It sent a mildly bitter taste through his mouth when he crunched it between his back teeth. "Oh." Andrew shrugged. "Seeds. I had a slice of blackberry bread at the Worthy sisters'. I'll clean my teeth inside."

"You mean they actually stopped spinning long enough to offer you refreshment?"

"Well, not quite." Taking her by the elbow, he said, "Here, careful with those steps. So tell me . . . how did the discussion commence about the pulpit? I want to know every word that was said."

She gave him a sidelong look as they climbed the steps. "After what you said about meetings, don't you think that would bore you?"

He reached for the doorknob. "I can't think of any subject that would fascinate me more right now, Julia."

However successful he was at steering Julia away from the unpleasant subject of his misspent morning, he could not avoid Mrs. Paget's query after she served them bowls of wild mushroom consommé.

"Did my fig bread make it over to Mrs. Ramsey's?" she asked.

"Absolutely, Mrs. Paget." Though wounded at the shade of doubt in her tone, Andrew flashed her a seedless smile. "This soup is quite tasty. Do I detect fresh basil?"

She shook her head. "Thyme." She was a graceful, thickset woman in her midfifties, with graying blond hair and fine wrinkles webbing her eyes. "Queer little woman, that Mrs. Ramsey."

"Why do you say that, Mrs. Paget?" Julia asked.

"Why, it *is* thyme after all." Andrew took another bite and smacked his lips appreciatively. "I was so certain it was basil. Not that I'm disappointed, mind you."

For a second both women stared at him with expressions that were becoming all too familiar. "Thank you, Vicar," Mrs. Paget said presently.

And then to Julia she replied, "Well, I had Dora nip over to *Trumbles* this mornin' for lard. And she met up with Mrs. Ramsey. Only the woman was gushing on about the blackberry bread I'd sent her, telling Dora to make sure she told me it was the best she'd ever tasted."

"Yes?" Julia shook her head. "That *is* a little odd. But I sometimes say one thing when I mean the other, don't you?"

Bless you, wife! Andrew thought. "I've done that countless times myself."

"You'll find yourself doing that more and more as you get older," the cook conceded. "I'm forever callin' my daughters by each other's name."

"And I mistook the thyme for basil," Andrew reminded her.

"That's so, Vicar." Empty tray in hand, Mrs. Paget turned to leave the dining room. Only she paused at the door and turned toward them again. "Funny thing is, Dora said it looked like she had blackberry seeds in her teeth."

Andrew met his wife's puzzled look with a sheepish one of his own. It was so tempting to shrug his shoulders and change the subject again, but he couldn't bring himself to do it. He sighed, just as the cook was turning to the door again. "Mrs. Paget, will you please sit with us?"

She stared at him as if his brains had been coddled, for it was very likely that she had never lowered her stout form into one of the dining room chairs in her thirty-four years of service at the vicarage. "Begging your pardon, Vicar?"

Andrew rose to pull out the chair adjacent to his left and across from Julia. "Please? I have a confession to make." He glanced at his wife again, who was observing him with a worried expression. "To both of you."

"Very well." She reluctantly allowed him to take the tray from her and place it at the other end of the table. When they were all seated, Andrew cleared his throat.

"I've not been truthful," he said, spreading his hands upon the cloth on both sides of his bowl. He took another deep breath and dove into an account of how he had left the basket on the schoolhouse stoop, ending with his return to the vicarage with purple teeth.

He was not prepared for the reaction he received, for after a second of uncertain silence, Mrs. Paget convulsed into such violent laughter that Andrew feared she would rupture something.

"Oh, Vicar!" she exclaimed between gulps of air. "That's rich, it is!"

Andrew turned a concerned face toward Julia and was startled to see her shoulders shaking as well. Any hope of decorum vanished, for the two women fed upon each other's mirth and could not look at him without bursting into laughter. Finally Andrew gave up and joined them, smiling self-consciously at first, and then chuckling to the point that he had to wipe tears from his face with his napkin.

"You won't tell anyone . . . will you?" he asked when Mrs. Paget finally pushed herself to her feet, jovially declaring herself almost too weak to walk.

"Why, no, Vicar," she assured him. Her dancing eyes became shrewd. "But you know . . . I could use an extra day off to visit me daughters next week. Nettie just had another little boy, and of course I can't be neglecting Myra's little ones."

Shock rendered Andrew speechless for several seconds. When he found his voice, it was to say, "Blackmail, Mrs. Paget?"

"Why, Vicar!" She raised a hand to her bosom and said with an injured tone, "I was going to ask you after supper tonight anyway. Just figured now would be a better time, seeing as how you're in such a jolly mood."

Andrew looked at Julia, who appeared suspiciously close to laughter again, and then back at the cook. "Have I ever refused you anything, Mrs. Paget?"

"Now, that you haven't, Vicar," she replied with a shake of her head.

"Well, take your extra day. Take two, in fact, and we'll have our meals at the *Bow and Fiddle* while you're gone."

Clasping both hands together, she cried, "Oh, bless you, Vicar!"

"But I would rest more comfortably if I had your assurance that you'll forget about what happened to that fig bread."

"Fig bread?" Mrs. Paget took the tray from the table and raised her eyebrows innocently. "Why, yes . . . we do have some loaves in the cupboard, Vicar. However did you know?"

"Ambrose?"

Ambrose Clay smiled at Fiona, who had just greeted him from the midst of the garden at their London townhouse. *How nice it is to come home to her.* As he reached the gate, a rustling sound drew his attention to one of the shrubberies near her. From behind it slunk a large rat with beady, malevolent eyes. Desperately Ambrose fumbled with the gate latch and tried to alert his unsuspecting wife, but his throat would not obey. *No!*

"Ambrose?"

He became aware of a gentle but insistent pressure upon his shoulder. Turning his head upon the pillow, he opened his eyes. Fiona was seated upon the side of the bed, watching him. Ambrose took a deep breath and felt his racing heartbeat. "Fiona."

She smiled, unaware that she had just snatched him from the jaws of a nightmare. "You asked me to wake you in an hour?"

"Yes." Raising himself upon an elbow, he rubbed his eyes with his other hand. "It seems I just fell asleep."

"Would you like to rest a little longer?"

"I don't know if I can stand any more rest like that."

"I beg your pardon?"

Ambrose grimaced self-consciously. "A nightmare."

His wife combed her fingers through his dark hair. It made him feel like a small boy being comforted—not an unpleasant sensation.

"Would you care to tell me about it?" she asked.

"I would just as soon forget about that one," he said. "You don't believe dreams are prophetic, do you?"

"Surely some are. But you mustn't take bad dreams too much to heart, Ambrose. If most foretold anything, I would have shown up at church in my nightgown by now."

Ambrose chuckled. "You consider that a nightmare? Wearing your nightgown to church?"

"I suppose you have to be a woman to understand it," she said, smiling. "Why don't we take our walk now?"

Physical exertion of any kind was the last thing he desired during such times as today, but thanks to Fiona, Ambrose had learned that exercise helped to lighten the despondency. Being accompanied by the person dearest to him didn't hurt either. He quickly dressed again, and minutes later they were strolling up Market Lane.

"How many matches did you and Mr. Durwin manage to finish?" Fiona asked after sending a wave to Mrs. Summers, who, though bent with age, was briskly sweeping the stoop of the lending library.

"Three," Ambrose replied. "We were just about to start a fourth when Mrs. Beemish announced lunch."

"And?"

"I won all three, of course." He gave her a little sidelong grin. "I'm telling you, he holds back when I'm out of sorts like this. Or why else would he manage to win other times?"

"Then why don't you just ask him to stop?" she asked, threading her arm through his.

"Because it obviously gives him pleasure to do so. Or perhaps he fears I'll become suicidal if I lose?"

"Ambrose." A little furrow appeared in her brow. "Don't joke about such things."

"Forgive me. Of course I didn't mean that." It struck him then that he was being very self-centered. Mrs. Beemish had called everyone to lunch as soon as the three women returned from the meeting, and then Ambrose took his nap without thinking to ask Fiona about her morning.

"And I must beg your pardon again. How was your meeting?"

"Interesting. You were almost committed to another one-man drama."

He grimaced. "Almost, did you say?"

"To raise money for another pulpit. The present one's about to fall apart from age."

"I can identify with that," Ambrose quipped, but then felt a stab of guilt for not having the energy to involve himself in such a project.

"Anyway, Julia came to your rescue," Fiona continued.

"I'll have to be sure to thank her."

They became silent upon reaching the blue waters of the Bryce. A benign east breeze carried with it the nectarlike aroma of golden catkins frosting the willow trees along the riverbank. Among their branches hovered and darted legions of bees collecting pollen. By the end of the month, their humming would be replaced by youthful laughter and banter as the Irish Keegan children gathered the limber twigs for their father's baskets.

After they had crossed the bridge, Ambrose continued as if no time had lapsed. "You know, this village has been good to us. We could donate funds for a fine pulpit."

"That's very generous of you, Ambrose. But the idea is to allow as many people as possible to have a part in it. That way, every worshiper can look at the pulpit and feel a sense of ownership."

"Hmm. That makes sense." He still couldn't let go of the guilt. "But can your ladies raise enough that way?"

She squeezed his arm. "Just be sure to buy your sandwiches from me, Ambrose Clay, and I'll see that you pay dearly for them."

———

Fiona and Ambrose went to supper in the *Larkspur*'s dining room that evening, as usual. It was good for Ambrose to be in the company of other people who understood his mood swings. Fiona could recall when he arrived in Gresham in the grip of severe depression three years ago. Julia had wisely insisted that he could stay only if he came to the dining room for meals with the other guests. It was to save the servants from having to run up and down stairs with trays, but joining the others had also kept him from becoming totally reclusive during his dark episodes.

And Fiona enjoyed mealtimes as well. Some of the faces around the table had changed since the last time she lived here, but the atmosphere was one of mutual affection, and interesting conversation flowed as freely as did food from the sideboard. That evening over roast trout with beetroot sauce, the subject drifted to the Roman ruins atop the Anwyl. This was to be expected with two archeologists lodging under the same slate roof. Mrs. Dearing, who had followed her late husband to the California gold fields and wore her white hair in a long braid, asked if any treasures were uncovered today.

"Actually, a very exciting find," Mr. Ellis, in charge of the excavation commissioned by the British Archeological Association, replied. He would have been perfectly cast if he were an actor *playing* the role of an archeologist, for his tall, slightly stoop-shouldered frame and graying beard lent him a scholarly and occasionally preoccupied appearance. "A Celtic hand mirror that likely predates the Roman fort."

"How can you tell that it's Celtic, Mr. Ellis?" asked Mrs. Durwin. Petite and soft-spoken, with gentle gray eyes and soft wrinkled cheeks, she enjoyed helping the servants lay the table for supper. She and seventy-three-year-old Mr. Durwin, founder of *Durwin Stoves*, had been married in Saint Jude's less than two years ago. "And was the glass still intact?"

"We can tell its origin chiefly by the design on its back, Mrs. Durwin. And the face is actually of polished brass, not glass. We haven't packed it up for shipping yet, so I'll bring it up from the cellar later if any of you would care to see it."

Mrs. Latrell nodded. "Please do, Mr. Ellis." The head movement caused her to raise a hand to hold her wig in place. It was of a style popular a decade ago, parted in the center with corkscrew curls over both ears. The stark black tresses leeched the color from her face, for her eyelashes and brows were still white. Vain though she was, the widow had traveled the world extensively on her own and possessed an unwaveringly cheerful outlook on life. "But do tell us, when did glass mirrors come to be?"

Fiona met her husband's eyes and smiled, for they were both aware of what was coming next. Mr. Ellis did not allow a conversation regarding his profession to continue for too long without generously including his assistant. Sure enough, Mr. Ellis pointed his butter knife at the younger man. "Would you say fourteenth century, Mr. Pitney?"

If dark-haired Jacob Pitney were to play any role, it would have to be of a plowman in the fields. Big-boned and awkward, he towered over everyone in the lodging house. It was not surprising that in his midthirties he had not married, for to court a woman would require him to actually *speak* to her, and he was one of the most timid people Fiona had ever known. Only when answering a query about his beloved vocation did his brown eyes light up and he seem able to find his tongue.

"Yes, fourteenth-century Venice," he replied with a serious little nod. "Only the technology was crude, so for the next three hundred years or so the images were blurred and distorted."

"Fascinating, Mr. Pitney," Ambrose commented, in spite of his dark mood. "But tell me, why would anyone tolerate mirrors with such imperfections? And for three centuries?"

A corner of Mr. Pitney's mouth twitched timidly. "Those early mirrors were expensive and therefore symbols of wealth."

"Some even wore them as jewelry, didn't they, Mr. Pitney?" was Mr. Ellis's rhetorical question.

"They did. On small chains. Some men even had them set in the hilts of their swords. For practical usage, though, I believe many continued to use the metal mirrors until the technology advanced."

The conversation went on to Mr. Jensen's recollection of something from the book of Exodus, where Moses commanded the women of Israel to surrender their "looking glasses," to be melted down into a brass ceremonial washbasin for the tabernacle. This information was received with great interest, so the manager of the *Larkspur* offered to show everyone the exact location of the passage in his Bible after supper.

Even Georgette and Sarah, maids standing at the sideboard to refill dishes and teacups, listened attentively—whether it was because they were also interested in historical antiquities or in studying Jacob Pitney's handsome face, Fiona wasn't sure, but she certainly couldn't fault them. But there was one person in the room who almost never contributed when the conversation drifted over to archeology—Miss Rawlins. In fact, the gray eyes behind her spectacles almost seemed to glaze over during such times. Her silence was a mystery to Fiona, because one would think a writer of historical novelettes would be taking notes on such valuable information, at least mentally.

Julia had once confided to her that she believed Mr. Pitney to be infatuated with Miss Rawlins. Now that she had had occasion to observe the two, Fiona was sure she was correct. They were almost the same ages, and though she supposed Miss Rawlins would not be considered a beauty in the classical definition, the coffee brown hair falling just below her chin flattered an angular, interesting face, and the wire spectacles served to accent large eyes of smoky gray. How odd, that a woman who spent hours daily writing about romance would be so immune to it in actual life.

Perhaps it's because he's not like the heroes of her stories. Fiona had read most of Miss Rawlins' novelettes because she had not the heart to refuse when the author pressed them upon her. *Other than being tall, that is,* she thought, for without exception every hero was as tall as every heroine was slender. And Mr. Pitney's dark hair and eyes would put him in the same category with about ninety percent of the writer's heroes.

But that was where the similarities ended, for the archeologist was not a "mysterious rogue with a heart of gold" who meets his match in a "fiery-tempered woman with a mane of wild tresses." He was just a considerate man who loved his work, opened doors for women, and attended church every Sunday. Not very exciting compared to the men who swashbuckled their ways through Miss Rawlins' fictitious world.

Chapter 5

I'll be glad to see the back of this day," Andrew groused to Julia as they climbed the stairs together to hear the children's bedtime prayers.

Julia couldn't help but smile to herself, for if everything went according to plan, his day would soon improve greatly. They went down the corridor to Philip's room first. The sixteen-year-old, who had once declared himself too old for such things, seemed to enjoy the nightly ritual. But back then, he had felt pressured to be the man of the family. Now that he had surrendered that responsibility to Andrew's capable hands, he could relax and be a boy again. Julia noticed he had tacked a copy of his poem, which the family had coaxed him into reciting three times during supper, to the wall just above his night table.

"I think I'll send a copy to Gabriel too," her son said, leaning upon an arm propped upon his pillow. Philip had befriended Gabriel Patterson during his ill-fated months at *The Josiah Smith Preparatory Academy* two years ago.

"He'll be happy to learn you've become a fellow writer," Julia said from his bedside.

"I'm not nearly as good as Gabriel. It was just a poem. And I still want to be a doctor."

"Perhaps you'll do both," Andrew told him. "Look at Saint Luke. He was a doctor and wrote two books of the Bible."

The boy smiled. "And if I've paid attention in church, he had some help."

"Absolutely so, my literate son. But since you pay attention in church so admirably, you know that God still helps us."

Julia then had to remind both that the girls were waiting to be tucked in as well. She was very grateful that Andrew took the time to chat with Philip and seemed to enjoyed their discussions. That was something the boy's own father had never made time to do. They listened to his prayer, and Julia kissed his forehead while Andrew extinguished the lamp.

The girls' room was the largest in the vicarage. After Elizabeth's wedding, Laurel had asked to move in with Aleda and Grace, so the upstairs sitting room was transformed into a bedroom. Soft laughter drifted from under the door as Julia and Andrew paused outside. "What mischief are they up to now?" Andrew whispered with his hand upon the knob.

"Surely you're aware that girls don't need to be up to mischief to giggle," Julia whispered back.

"Ah, but those definitely sound like 'up to mischief' giggles to me."

Andrew opened the door and followed Julia inside. They were met with an abrupt silence from the three girls who smiled at them from beds covered with pink organdy coverlets. But then Grace hiccuped loudly, which caused the usually somber nine-year-old to smother a giggle with her hand. The older girls sent her warning looks from both sides.

"What's going on in here?" Andrew demanded with eyes narrowing.

"Nothing, Papa," came a threefold reply, expressions smug with the knowledge that they were being teased. Grace hiccuped again, and this time Aleda pushed her face into her own pillow with shoulders shaking.

"We were just talking," Laurel explained while a suspicious tint crept into her cheeks.

"Hmm." With a look at Julia, Andrew went over to Grace's bed and motioned for her to move over so he could sit next to her. "Let me count those hiccups for you, Gracie."

She leaned up on her pillow. Within seconds another erupted in the silent room.

"That's one," Andrew said. He held up two fingers. "Now, let's hear number two. And quickly, please. We haven't all night."

As she watched the girl screw up her face in concentration, Julia realized that she was holding her own breath. Aleda and Laurel stared from either side. But presently Grace shrugged her narrow shoulders and smiled.

"They're gone."

"Good!" Andrew patted her shoulder and returned to where Julia stood at the foot of the middle bed. "Then shall we pray now?"

All heads bowed reverently. Laurel, the oldest, went first, asking God to bless and protect the family, including Elizabeth and Jonathan and their grandmother in Cambridge, as well as the servants. Aleda added the people living at the *Larkspur* to her prayer, which took a little longer. Grace's prayer was almost word for word the same as Aleda's except for the addition of an unusual postscript. Her hands pressed together piously and eyes shut tight, she concluded, "And please don't let Laurel marry Ben, because I don't want her ever to leave Gresham."

"Grace!" Laurel exclaimed, staring daggers at her, while Aleda sought refuge in the pillow again.

"But I didn't say anything about *it*," Grace defended.

"What is *it*?" asked Andrew.

Laurel blew out her cheeks, her expression still stormy. "A poem Ben gave me after school today."

"He did?" Alarm and despair mingled in Andrew's hazel eyes. "Little Ben Mayhew?"

"He's sixteen years old, Papa. Just like me."

"What kind of poem?"

"Just . . . a poem."

Julia touched her husband's arm. "Why don't we allow them their sleep, dear?"

For a second he stared at her, as if needing reassurance that everything familiar had not been taken from him. "Very well," he finally agreed. Both went from bed to bed, kissing foreheads, and then Andrew put out the light before they went back out to the corridor.

"Ben Mayhew?" he said as soon as the door closed behind them. "I've already lost one daughter, and now a boy with cheeks still too smooth for a razor is writing love poems to my Laurel?"

"Sh-h-h. Let's go downstairs."

He obliged halfheartedly, and it was only when they were standing inside the doorway of the parlor that Julia attempted to reassure him. "You can expect when girls and boys that age go to school together, they'll have infatuations. It doesn't mean they're courting."

"But they're both sixteen. And you were seventeen when you married."

Julia shook her head. "That was different, Andrew. I was smitten by an older man who knew how to charm me out of seeing his faults. Ben is a decent boy, and he'll be off to university in another year, so I'm sure you have nothing to worry about."

Finally he drew in a deep breath. "You're right, of course. I suppose I overreacted a bit."

"I think you were just fine. After all, you didn't demand to see the poem, did you?"

"No, of course not." He gave her a sad little smile. "But I would have if you hadn't been there to calm me."

"Well, knowing Ben, it will probably have something to do with architecture." Julia put a hand upon his arm and decided it was time. "Let's go for a little ride, shall we?"

"A ride? But it's almost nine."

"Let's visit Elizabeth and Jonathan. I'm sure they haven't retired for the night." *How could they, with so much to discuss!*

"Would you mind if we put it off until tomorrow?" He sent a wishful look up at the ceiling, as if he could see their bedroom above it. "This has been a day I'd like to put behind me as soon as possible."

"Has it been that terrible?" she asked sympathetically.

"Considering that I slipped around like a thief, was told off soundly by Mrs. Hayes and then had to counsel her husband to pay her a little more attention—when I don't blame him for spending time away from her—made a fool of myself in front of you and Mrs. Paget . . . and then found out that a young man is writing poems to my daughter, I would say so."

Julia willed herself to keep from smiling at his doleful tone. For all their strength, men were sometimes like little children. "We wouldn't have to stay long."

After a sigh for her benefit, he agreed, as Julia knew he would. He was fortunate that her wants were few, she teasingly reminded him sometimes. For like Ambrose with Fiona, he loved indulging his wife.

"But what reason will we give?" her husband asked as the trap rattled down the dark vicarage lane under a cloudless, starry sky.

"Why must we have a reason to call on family?" Julia answered evasively, then changed the subject. "Can you smell the apple blossoms? Flower scents are so much more intoxicating at night, don't you agree?"

"Ah . . . certainly," he said with a curious sideways glance at her.

Minutes later they were standing at the cottage door. Jonathan answered Andrew's knock almost right away, his aristocratic face wearing the same grin Julia was certain she had worn earlier.

"Please, do come in," he greeted them, gesturing past himself with a flourish. "Elizabeth is in the kitchen putting the kettle on. We gave Mrs. Littlejohn and Hilda the evening off."

"You were expecting us?" Andrew asked with brow furrowed.

"Family should always be expected, don't you think? Why don't we visit in the kitchen so we can be close to the kettle?"

"This is very odd, Julia," Andrew whispered as they followed their son-in-law through the house. "Is there something you're not telling me?"

"I can keep secrets too, Vicar," she whispered back.

He gave her a stricken look. "They aren't moving away, are they?"

"No, of course not."

"And here they are, Beth!" Jonathan announced grandly at the kitchen doorway.

As they entered, Elizabeth, wearing an apron over her dress, looked up from spreading a cloth upon the table. "Hello, Papa. Julia."

And then Andrew did a curious thing. "You're going to have a child?" he asked in a voice filled with wonder.

Julia shook her head at Elizabeth's questioning glance, then asked her husband, "How did you know, Andrew?"

"It's so, then?" He went around the table and took Elizabeth in his arms. Julia blinked away tears for the second time that day, and when she looked at Jonathan beside her, his gray-green eyes were glistening as well.

"I'm going to be a grandfather!" Andrew exclaimed when he finally released his daughter. "Imagine that!"

This time it was Elizabeth who asked, "But how did you know, Papa?"

Andrew looked at Julia with what seemed to be a plea for understanding before replying in the tenderest of voices, "Because you look just like your mother did . . . when she told me that she was carrying you."

Julia and Andrew stayed for another half hour, visiting over fig bread and tea at the table and chuckling over Elizabeth's confession that she had feared that she was suffering some mysterious disease. They agreed that it would be best to tell the children later, as Mrs. Littlejohn and Hilda could be trusted to keep the secret. Occasionally Julia's eyes met her husband's, and she detected worry in his. When they finally took their leave, they rode in silence until he reined the trap to a halt halfway up the vicarage lane.

"I have something to ask you that can't wait," he said before she could wonder why they were sitting in the dark. "And if I get too close to home, Luke will come out for the horse, and then Dora will be asking if we'd like some cocoa, and then one of the children might—"

Julia put her fingers up to his lips. "You're worried that I might be hurt because of what you said about Kathleen."

Taking her hand from his lips to press it against the coat lapel over his heart, he replied, "I fear I was grossly insensitive."

"You weren't insensitive at all, Andrew. You have some wonderful memories of your first marriage. Why should you never mention them?"

Perhaps if Andrew were not so loving and attentive to her, she would feel differently. But God had supplied her with the grace to regard Kathleen as someone she would have liked to have known as a friend. After all, they had both fallen in love with the same wonderful man.

His voice thickened with emotion. "I just don't want you to ever doubt that I love you more than life itself."

Leaning her head against his sturdy shoulder, she told him, "I have never doubted that for one moment, Andrew." They sat in that comfortable silence for a little while until Rusty, anxious to be in his stable, took a few tentative steps forward, then several more. He obviously regarded Andrew's inattention to the reins as permission to proceed and delivered them back to the vicarage at a brisk trot.

"Did I mention what a wonderful day this has been?" Andrew asked as they held hands and ascended the steps to their home.

Though he knew he would regret it sorely at six o'clock the next morning when Mr. Ellis knocked upon his door, Jacob started reading another chapter of *Rachelle of Chamonix*. He had endured Miss Rawlins' indifference for almost two years now and was eager to hurry up and finish the novelette so that they would finally have something to discuss beyond the weather.

At first he had assumed that she suffered from the same timidity that plagued his life, but he had come to realize that her silence was the result of having no interest in his occupation. While the other lodgers inquired often of the latest findings on the Anwyl, she seldom joined in the discussions. Often she even seemed bored.

The realization had disturbed him until he forced himself into seeing the situation from her point of view. Just because he was curious about how people of past civilizations lived their lives didn't mean everyone felt that way. When had he expressed any interest in *her* occupation?

And he did enjoy reading in his spare time, so this would be a pleasant way to develop a friendship. Writers such as Sir John Barrow, Daniel Defoe, and James Fenimore Cooper had carried him off to many an adventure since his early school days. He almost identified with them, for every piece of the past that he held in his hand from his findings atop the Anwyl represented a story.

But there was one thing he didn't understand about Miss Rawlins' novelette, and it worried him a little. He frowned as he began another paragraph:

> *Rachelle de Beaufort's full lips formed a pout as she stamped her satin-covered foot. "Just because you've conquered the Russian Army, General Massena, doesn't mean you can march back here to Chamonix and expect me to fall at your feet like the rest of France! If the Alps couldn't tame me in three years, what makes you think you can in one week?"*

"But she *likes* him," Jacob mumbled. Hadn't Rachelle dreamed about the handsome general just two chapters earlier? True, he paid some attention to her cousin Fleurette during a dinner party. But it was at the Bonaparte estate, and he had no choice in the seating arrangement.

And General Massena had apologized for that. Why, then, was Rachelle behaving as if she despised him? Surely one little dinner party couldn't have caused her to change her mind so completely. Even more perplexing, Jacob discovered as he read further, was the way the general reacted to her outburst of temper. He had carried a lock of her flaxen hair in his breast pocket into battle, so clearly he loved her as well. But rather than defend himself and explain the position he had found himself in at dinner, he simply turned on his heel and walked away!

Does that mean they'll never be together? But with five chapters remaining, *something* had to happen. A yawn seized him, and then another. No matter what lay in store for Rachelle de Beaufort and General Massena, he had a responsibility to the British Archaeological Association and to Mr. Ellis to keep his mind sharp. He closed the book, resisting the temptation to peek ahead at the last page to see how the story would be resolved.

THE DOWRY OF MISS LYDIA CLARK *Chapter 6*

*T*he sun was just peeking above the treetops of Gipsy Woods the next day when Lydia Clark stepped out of her parents' door with satchel in hand. Wisps of remaining fog reflected the early light, giving an ethereal glow to cottage gardens and causing shafts of trees flanking the lane to appear like the columns of an ancient ruin. It was her favorite time of day, which was why she chose to prolong the experience by walking to school. And the exercise was a tonic for her after having contracted pleurisy almost two years ago.

Even though she was now in good health and feeling back to full strength, her past bout with the illness had served to make her parents overly protective, even at her age. At the least hint of inclement weather, her father insisted upon delivering and fetching her in his trap. She couldn't fault him for that, for she supposed she had given them both quite a fright.

She turned the corner to walk eastward down Church Lane. To her right the Worthy sisters' garden was vacant, but light shone from their kitchen window, and she knew they would be at their posts as soon as the sun rose a little higher. Ahead of her on Market Lane several red-and-white cheese wagons were rumbling southward with their morning deliveries to the Shrewsbury railway station. And to her left, the crunching of gravel announced the archeologists on their way to the Anwyl.

"Good morning, Miss Clark!" Mr. Ellis, the older of the two, greeted with a tipping of his hat. The same was echoed by Mr. Pitney, who had to switch the leather sack—which presumably carried their lunches and whatever else an archeologist would need—to his other shoulder so that he could pay the same courtesy.

"Good morning, Mr. Ellis . . . Mr. Pitney," Lydia returned with a smile and nod. It was as much conversation as they ever exchanged, though sometimes comments were made concerning the weather. Always from Mr. Ellis, for Mr. Pitney seemed quite bashful.

Mr. Raleigh was just opening the door of the grammar school as she passed. When he turned to look at her, his face wore the grin of a boy harboring a wonderful secret. "Delightful morning, isn't it?" he hailed.

"Yes, delightful." Lydia had consulted with him several times over school matters and appreciated his dedication to education. His students who went on to secondary school were more than ready for advanced studies. "Are your children excited about the tournament?"

The archery tournament, to be held on the twenty-fifth of May, had grown considerably in just the three years since its inception. Now four grammar school teams would be competing—Gresham, Prescott, Clive, and Lockwood. Affecting a grimace, the young schoolmaster replied, "Too much so, Miss Clark! With that *and* summer just around the corner, I'm finding it most difficult to keep their noses pressed to the books."

He reminded her then that afternoon practice would begin in another week. "You may wish to remind those with siblings on the team. We're going to keep it down to an hour, so it shouldn't be too much of a hardship."

"I'll remind them," she promised, as if he hadn't made the same request last week. Clearly his mind was occupied with something else, but at least it had to be something pleasant, judging by the grin that had taken over his face again. Lydia wondered if Elizabeth Raleigh could possibly be expecting a child. She hoped so, for two people who so enjoyed children should have some of their own.

The morning progressed well. After prayer and scripture readings were completed, she continued the poetry lesson, then introduced prime numbers to her first-year students without causing too much angst. During the lunch break the students hurried through their sandwiches so that they could divide into teams to play "rounders," a game similar to American baseball. It moved along much faster than cricket, which was important when less than an hour was left to them. They placed bases made of sacking in the field next to the schoolhouse and used a cricket ball with a bat Tom Keegan had fashioned out of ash wood.

Lydia settled into a chair well out of harm's way and divided her attention between the game and a novel from the lending library, Trollope's *Barchester Towers*. Eleanor Harding was just arriving at the Stanhopes' when Lydia looked up from the page and watched Phoebe Meeks being handed the bat. The girl swung once, twice, and then by some miracle on the third pitch, the dull crack of wood rang out in the spring air. By an even greater miracle, the ground ball eluded both pitcher and third baseman, George Coggins and Aleda Hollis, who apparently both assumed the other would go after it.

"Run, Phoebe!" her teammates cried, excitable Bessie Worthy leaping up and down. After a split second of dazed inaction, Phoebe started running with skirts flowing behind her. George had left his post to fetch the ball after all, confusing Phoebe, who aimed herself in the direction of second base. She ignored the frantic admonitions from her teammates as she ran across the pitcher's mound. It was only when George tagged her with the ball just inches away from the base that Phoebe discovered her error and burst into tears.

While children of both teams sent perplexed looks to one another, Lydia hurried from her chair and toward the field. Only Billy Casper jeered, but she silenced him with a look. "There, there now," she comforted the girl, gathering her into her arms.

"I got confused in all the excitement," Phoebe blubbered.

"Of course you did." Lydia led her back toward the schoolhouse, and when they had crossed the baseline, she turned her head to tell the others that they could resume their game. "She'll be fine," she added. She brought the girl into the schoolroom, sat her on a bench at the science table, and wiped her face with a dampened handkerchief.

"Won't it be nice when you won't have to worry about seeing anymore?" she said gently when the tears were finally abated, for Phoebe had told her this morning that her mother had agreed to have her eyes examined as soon as possible.

The girl stared down at the floor as if she wished it would open up and swallow her.

"Phoebe?"

"I lied to you, Miss Clark. I'm sorry."

"Lied?"

Her bottom lip quivering, she confessed, "My mother said I would have to wait, since it's almost summer anyway."

"But you can't see now."

Finally Phoebe raised her head to regard Lydia with a pair of frank green eyes. "She says we haven't the money now, Miss Clark."

"Oh." Embarrassed for the girl, Lydia thought, *Why didn't I consider they might have financial troubles?* She was aware that Phoebe's father had died from a fever four years ago, leaving a wife and four children. But she had paid visits to the family's small dairy farm and assumed it produced a fair income. Phoebe's clothing was as nice as any of her schoolmates', and she wore shoes even in the warm months.

Lydia's ignorance was to be expected, for she had inherited her parents' repugnance for talebearing. *"Noble minds dwell upon ideals, and small minds upon rumors,"* she had heard her father state more than once. And so most villagers had learned to take their seeds of gossip to more fertile ground.

"May I walk home with you?" she asked after sending up a quick prayer for wisdom. It was out of courtesy that she asked, for she had the authority to accompany the girl if she pleased. "I would like to speak with your mother."

Worry and shame mingled in the girl's expression. "Will you tell her I lied?"

"I don't suppose that's necessary, Phoebe, since you admitted it. You've always been truthful before."

"Thank you, Miss Clark."

"You're welcome." Folding her arms, Lydia added, "Just bear in mind that integrity is worth more than anything money can buy, and you don't want to go throwing it away out of pride."

"Yes, ma'am," Phoebe murmured.

When the school day was over, Lydia gathered papers into her satchel to mark while Phoebe cleaned the blackboard and Tom Keegan swept the porch. As they left the schoolhouse, Lydia found herself wishing she had taken her father's trap this morning, for the Meeks lived across the Bryce.

Exercise is as good for the soul as it is for the body, she reminded herself.

Phoebe wasn't her most talkative student, so Lydia did not attempt to prod her into conversation as the two walked in silence. The parade more than doubled when the girl beckoned to her brothers and sister, who were standing in a queue of children near the grammar school's merry-go-round. The group also became noisier, for Mark, Trudy, and Lester were not as reticent as their older sister, especially when they crossed Church Lane and caught sight of two men giving chase to a litter of squealing piglets escaped from a pen behind one of the cottages bordering the green. The knot of women at the pump had ceased their gossiping to watch, and some schoolboys abandoned their cricket match to join in the chase with shouting and laughter.

"Will they ever catch them, Miss Clark?" asked seven-year-old Lester, clearly wishing to give chase himself. He was a hardy-looking boy with at least three cowlicks swirling his blond hair. Trudy, his twin, resembled Phoebe more than him with her brown hair and slight build.

"I would imagine so, Lester," Lydia replied.

"Maybe someone told them where bacon comes from," ten-year-old Mark suggested in a droll voice. He had brown hair like both sisters, but with Lester's sturdier build.

"And sausages and ham," offered Trudy.

Lester shook his blond head. "Pigs can't understand words, can they, Miss Clark?"

"I shouldn't think so."

"May I carry your satchel, Miss Clark?" Mark asked, switching his lunch pail to his left hand.

"Thank you." Lydia handed it over.

"What do you carry in there, Miss Clark?" asked Trudy.

"Papers to mark."

"What sort of papers?" asked Lester.

"Geography and arithmetic today." Lydia sent Phoebe an understanding smile. No wonder the girl wasn't talkative, with so many competing for attention. Finally she and the children reached the Meeks farm, the first on Arnold Lane. The one-story cottage was made of weathered stone with a thatched roof, as were most farm cottages north of the river. To the east were the milking and hay barns, and to the west a hedged pasture from which a half dozen cattle cropped grass or raised placid heads to stare. In front of the cottage grew a large and tidy vegetable garden. Lydia had not noticed the lack of flowers, save wild violets sprinkled in the yard, on her two previous visits with the family. She realized now that if finances were tight, growing food would have priority over decoration. The children ushered Lydia into a front parlor filled with worn furniture.

"She's likely in the kitchen," Mark said, motioning for her to continue through the cottage. But Lydia shook her head.

"I'll wait here. She's not expecting me."

"Children?" came a voice through the doorway, and Mrs. Meeks entered the room wearing an apron over a faded blue calico gown. Younger than Lydia by a couple of years, she was as petite as Lydia was tall and would have been beautiful had not the weight of the burdens she carried settled into the lines of her face. She gave a nervous pat to her chignon, from which strands of light brown hair had worked themselves loose. "Why, Miss Clark . . ."

"I pray you'll forgive me for showing up uninvited like this."

"You're welcome here anytime." Turning to the children, she said, "Go outside and play." When they had reluctantly obeyed, she offered Lydia a chair and apologized for being out of tea. "But I've got some cocoa powder and fresh milk."

"No, thank you," Lydia told her, settling on a chair covered with peach-colored cloth frayed at the arms. "I've come to speak with you about Phoebe. Have you a minute?"

Mrs. Meeks took a seat at the end of a threadbare horsehair sofa and folded her work-worn hands. "Is this about the spectacles, Miss Clark?"

"It is, Mrs. Meeks." Concerned that she would think she had come here to censure her, Lydia hurried on. "I'd like to ask your permission to purchase them for her myself. As you know, I've no children to spend my wages on, and I live with my parents, so my expenses are minimal. Please allow me to do this."

Her offer was met with silence, as Mrs. Meeks simply stared straight ahead. Lydia waited, deciding it best not to pressure her. When the woman finally spoke, Lydia heard the strain in her voice.

"It's just so hard to keep takin' and having naught to give back. What with parish assistance helping pay our rent, and the Women's Charity Society buyin' the children's school clothing and shoes."

"I didn't realize that."

"You didn't?" Mrs. Meeks looked surprised and just a little disbelieving.

"My family is the last to hear what's going on in Gresham." Lydia gave her a tentative little smile. "It's actually a blessing most of the time."

The woman actually smiled back, lightening the careworn expression of her face. "I see." But then a sigh escaped her lips. "It ain't that I don't appreciate the help, Miss Clark. I thank the good Lord for the folks who've been so decent to us. But I weren't raised that way, and I don't want the children thinking it's proper to go about with their hands held out all of the time."

"I understand," Lydia said, though up until this minute she had blithely assumed that the worse part of being poor was the lack of material things. She had never considered how humiliating it would be to have to ask for assistance. And now she felt embarrassed for barging in and thinking she could wipe away a problem with the loosening of her purse strings. "Please forgive me, Mrs. Meeks. It seems I've led a sheltered life."

"Oh, Miss Clark, there's naught to forgive. It's so good of you to offer." She pressed her lips together for a moment and then added, "And for Phoebe's sake, I have to accept. I suppose I just needed time to grieve over it."

Lydia decided she liked this woman for her honesty. "I appreciate that. May I bring her to Shrewsbury on Saturday morning?"

"Yes, thank you. Will you come early and have breakfast with us?"

Lydia's immediate thought was that she didn't want to take anything from people who had little enough for themselves, but then she understood it was the woman's way of retaining a remnant of dignity. Graciously Lydia accepted, stifling the impulse to offer to bring something from the bakery. Mrs. Meeks walked her to the door, but before going through it, Lydia turned to say, "Phoebe has impressed me with her self-discipline and character, Mrs. Meeks. I've even noticed it in your younger children. And you're seeing to it that they have an education and spiritual upbringing. I daresay you won't have to worry about their futures."

"Thank you," Mrs. Meeks whispered with brown eyes clouding.

In the yard again, Lydia bade farewell to the children outside, answering more questions from the younger ones as they escorted her to the lane. Henry Temple happened to be passing by in his delivery cart and paused to give her a ride as far as his father's butcher shop. She thanked him, walked another half block, and even though the afternoon was being rapidly swallowed up by eventide, she stopped for her usual brief chat with the Worthy sisters.

"What did ye boys and girls learn today?" Jewel asked while her nimble fingers wound threads around pins.

"I'm introducing the younger ones to algebra," Lydia replied.

"Alge—?"

"Algebra. It's—"

Before Lydia could explain, a "Humph!" of disapproval rasped from the elderly woman's throat. "Now, where are they going to talk that? It's just like them French lessons Mr. Raleigh brought here with his high-town ways. Do you know anybody in Gresham who'll ever see the likes of France?"

"Jewel," said Iris in a long-suffering voice when her sister-in-law's tirade was finished. "It's not a language, dear. It's the green we see growing on the bridge stones when the Bryce is low."

Again Lydia was opening her mouth to provide tactful contradiction, when Jewel subjected her to the scrutiny of two faded blue eyes.

"You know, Ezra Towly was askin' about you in *Trumbles* today, accordin' to Mrs. McFarley."

Lydia recalled a leathery-faced dairy farmer receiving condolences in the churchyard some three months ago. "Mr. Towly? But we've never even met, aside from his wife's funeral. Why would he be asking about me?"

"He was speculating on the size of your dowry, if you were to marry," Iris said with a little frown of disapproval.

"My *dowry*?"

"Talk is that he's considering courtin' you . . . and doubling the size of his herd."

Jewel made several tsks of disapproval and grumbled, "And the grass not yet covering Willa's grave! He should'ha least waited six months."

"Jewel!" her sister-in-law exclaimed.

"That's my way of seeing it," Jewel said with stubborn defensiveness.

"But you've said yourself many times that anything less than a year is a disgrace."

"Well, there's the fact that he needs a wife right now for those five young'uns and that farm to tend. And Lydia ain't gettin' any younger. Mayhap she needs to think about findin' a hus—"

"Excuse me!" Lydia interjected when she could bear it no longer. Both women stared up at her again, clearly stung by the sharpness of her voice. She forced herself to take in a deep breath before saying in a calmer, but no less insistent, tone, "I'm not interested in Mr. Towly."

Jewel's eyes fluttered in her parchmentlike face. "I were just sayin' that—"

"I know what you were saying, and I appreciate your concern about my future. But there are worse things than being a spinster. And at the very *top* of this list I would put being married to a man who would walk into a public place and ask about someone's dowry . . . and only three months after the mother of his children has died."

She bade them good-day and turned to leave before the subject could be discussed any further. The anger that hastened her steps toward home was not at the Worthy sisters, for Lydia allowed them the same indulgence one would give to beloved aunts—even though their words could sometimes make her cringe. *How dare he ask about me in public!*

The sight of her family's two-story stone cottage on Walnut Lane gave her some comfort. Her mother's sunflower blossoms had not yet attained enough height to peer over the picket fence, but they would be radiant in late summer. Pots of red geraniums sat in every windowsill. As she opened the gate, she could see her father sitting with his chair propped back against the trunk of the elm tree with Jeanie the cat curled in his lap. His mouth was gaped slightly, producing contented snores that stirred his white beard with the rise and fall of his chest.

Lydia smiled at the realization that both of his feet, planted beside the book that had fallen to the ground, were bare. Amos Clark believed in comfort, which was why five years ago he turned over control of his iron foundry to Lydia's older brother, Noah. He had worked hard for most of his sixty years, he declared back then, and would spend his later years doing the things he had never seemed to have enough time for. His days were now primarily filled with reading, painting, and walking to the smithy to sit and reminisce about earlier years in the village with some of his longtime friends.

Jeanie woke, stretched, and jumped weightlessly down to follow Lydia into the house, causing her father to stir slightly and alter the rhythm of his snoring for a second or two. Lydia let herself in the door and into a front parlor filled with overstuffed furniture around a colorful rug. Her father's easel was set up in a corner near the large, east-facing windows that allowed the best sunlight to filter in each morning. Walls displayed the landscapes he finally had time to paint. Her mother looked up from her perch at the edge of the sofa, where she was sorting fabric quilting squares onto the tea table.

"Lydia." The matronly voice was a verbal caress. "You're home. I was beginning to worry."

Lydia walked over to kiss the top of her mother's head. She had to lean down quite a bit to reach the graying brown hair. It was as if her typical selflessness had compelled Oriel Clark to ask God to give height and lean-ness to the rest of her family, while she gladly took the leavings. "What a day," Lydia sighed, tossing her satchel into a chair and dropping down beside her mother on the sofa.

"What's wrong, dear?"

"Oh, the Worthy sisters tell me Mr. Towly was in *Trumbles* apparently telling anyone who would listen of his intention to court me."

Her mother's hand went up to a plump cheek. "Oh my."

"*If* my dowry is adequate enough to buy some cattle, that is."

"But his wife . . ."

"I know." A little shudder snaked down Lydia's spine. "If that odious man comes calling here, you won't ask him in, will you?"

"Absolutely not! Anyway, after I tell your father about it, he'll not be welcomed beyond the gate."

Lydia breathed a sigh of relief. "That's good to hear."

"But I'm still curious as to why he would take it upon himself to court someone he only met briefly at his wife's funeral."

Her mother could be a little naive at times, Lydia thought. "He obviously assumes that plainness and desperation go hand in hand." Banishing Mr. Towly from her mind, she picked up a square of blue calico. "I remember this. You made Mrs. Tanner an apron from the rest, didn't you?"

Mrs. Tanner was their cook, their only servant, because even though the iron foundry provided a good income, Lydia's mother's greatest joy was tending her own house. Her only other concession to convenience was having the clothes and linens sent to Mrs. Moore's to be laundered.

"I did." Her mother took the square from her and set it back on the table. Mahogany-colored eyes looking into hers, she said, "You know, most women with gardens pride themselves on their roses, but I've never cared to grow them. To me, my sunflowers are far more beautiful."

"Yes?" Lydia had no idea what this had to do with Mrs. Tanner's apron, but her mother usually had a plan in mind when she strayed so far from a subject.

"There is beauty in all God's creation, Lydia. You mustn't think of yourself as plain. And if you would have stayed here instead of spending fourteen years isolated at that girls' school, you would have been long mar-ried by now." There was no recrimination in her tone, just a statement of what she perceived to be fact.

"Thank you for saying that, Mother."

"Well, it's the truth."

Lydia squeezed her hand. "Then I'm happy to be one of your sun-flowers."

That night as she lay in that tranquil space between prayer and sleep, Lydia thought of the fair portion of her life spent at *Saint Margaret's*. It had seemed to her more of a ministry than a vocation. Though her students came from the wealthiest families, they had been little more than orphans, shuttled away to boarding school so that their parents could take grand tours without the encumbrance of little ones to distract them. Lydia, with no family to tend and little interest in the gossip cliques of the other schoolmistresses, had given every scrap of free time to her girls. And it seemed what they had needed most was someone to offer them a listening heart and ear.

God had spoken to her at the end of those fourteen years, impressing upon her that it was time to come home to stay. Her aging parents would not be around forever. Once she arrived, her availability had hastened the founding of a secondary school. Two very good reasons for her to be in Gresham again.

And yet sometimes she caught glimpses of a vision that God had something else planned for her. She couldn't begin to explain it, even to herself, but occasionally she sensed that the road ahead of her would take some unpredictable turns. God had been good to her, and she was willing to set out in whatever direction He determined was necessary for her life to continue to have meaning.

But please, Father . . . she prayed. *Don't let it be in the direction of Ezra Towly!*

THE DOWRY OF MISS LYDIA CLARK   *Chapter 7*

*E*arly Wednesday afternoon, Julia accompanied Andrew to pay calls on the Fletchers, Putnams, and Sloanes across the Bryce. On their return down Market Lane, they could see Ambrose and Fiona entering the *Larkspur*'s garden up ahead. The couple turned to wave as the trap drew closer, and Andrew reined the horse to a stop.

"Have you time for a visit?" Ambrose asked after greetings were exchanged, to which Julia and Andrew agreed. With an hour and a half still remaining in the children's school day, they were glad to have some time to spend with their dear friends.

Julia was happy to observe that the actor, flush from his walk, appeared in brighter spirits than he had so far since arriving from London.

"You're looking well, Ambrose," she commented when the two couples had settled into adjacent willow benches in front of a young May tree on the verge of blooming.

"Thank you," he replied and drew in a deep breath appreciatively. "I feel as if I could run all the way up the Anwyl today."

"It seems the bad spell is over for now," said Fiona, smiling and looking lovely in a two-piece costume of mauve and white patterned chintz.

"I'm glad to hear it," Andrew said. "I only wish your good days would last forever."

"That would be nice, old friend," Ambrose agreed. "But you know, every cloud has its silver lining, as the saying goes. With Fiona's help, I've learned something through all of this. Remind me to tell you about it one day."

"Why not now?"

"Because I don't want to spend the first decent chance we've had for a chat droning on and on about myself. Tell us, Julia, how are the children?"

"Very well, thank you," she replied. "They've adjusted to combining the families with remarkable ease."

"Of course it helped that they were already friends before the marriage," Andrew added.

"And the newlyweds?" asked Fiona.

Julia wished they were free to share the news about Elizabeth, but she had to respect her stepdaughter's desire for secrecy until the pregnancy was further along. "Very happy. And Jonathan loves his teaching position. I doubt they'll ever leave Gresham."

Andrew smiled at Mr. Clay. "And now that we've brought you up to date with the vicarage clan, I'd really like to hear what you've learned, Ambrose. You know I'm always looking for insights to enhance my sermons."

"Tell them, Ambrose," Fiona urged, touching his elbow.

"It seems you're outvoted," Julia added. "I'd like to hear it too."

Smiling, the actor shrugged. "If you're quite sure. But I'm trusting you not to allow me to become a bore." He sat back in the bench and steepled his fingers upon a crossed knee. "Have you ever been to the Cotswolds?"

Julia and Fiona shook their heads. Andrew replied that he believed he had as a boy on a rare family holiday to visit relatives.

"Well, the roads are quite hilly." Ambrose moved a hand sideways in an undulating motion. "The horses have a time of it. And Fiona has helped me to realize that life is like those roads. And not just my life, although my condition makes mine a little more hilly than most."

"In other words, we each have our hills and valleys," said Andrew.

"Exactly. But in my young adulthood, I spent the hilltop days cramming as much activity into them as possible, not allowing myself to think about the coming valleys. But they came anyway, accompanied by crushing disappointment. I've now learned to take a pause to look back, every time life becomes good again."

"Back?"

"Over the road I've already traveled. My life so far, if you will. It's simple to do so when you're standing on a hilltop, but nearly impossible from a valley. While I can see all the low places, I can also see the elevated ones. And then I turn to look at the road ahead of me. It's the same. And I tell myself, 'Ambrose, this happiness won't last. It hasn't before. But neither will the darkness, for I can see the hills rising up for miles and miles.' So when the low days come, and my heart is telling me I'll never be happy again, my mind takes me back to the view I saw from the last hilltop."

He shrugged again, a little self-consciously. "It helps. Tremendously, in fact."

"I can see how," Andrew said. "*Weeping may endure for a night, but joy cometh in the morning.* We seem to remind ourselves of that passage only while in the dark of night, don't we? But that is also when it's hard to see the joy that's ahead through the tears." He leaned forward a bit, warming to the subject. "What you've done, Ambrose and Fiona, is pile up stones."

"I beg your pardon?"

The clattering of wheels and hooves that had sounded unobtrusively in the distance grew loud enough to prevent him from answering without shouting. Three red-and-white cheese factory wagons, drawn by pairs of dray horses, were returning from their afternoon deliveries to the Shrewsbury railway station. When he could be heard again, Andrew said as if the interruption had never occurred, "After the Israelites crossed the Jordan on dry land, they piled up twelve stones on the riverbank as a memorial, a reminder for future generations of how God had led them through the wilderness to the Promised Land. When you're standing in a high place, as you are now, you pile up stones. And you can look back and see them from the next low place."

Ambrose slapped a knee with his hand and smiled. "And *I* see a sermon on this in the near future."

"Missus Phelps?"

Everyone looked to the right, where Sarah stood holding a tray about three feet away. Julia wondered how she could have approached so soundlessly until she remembered the cheese wagons. With a smile she said, "Good afternoon, Sarah."

"Good afternoon, missus." The maid advanced to place the tray on the seat beside Julia. "Mr. Jensen saw you through the window and thought you'd be wantin' some refreshment. He also asks if you've time to speak with him before you leave."

Julia assured her that she would be inside as soon as their tea was finished, then took charge of pouring cups and handing out the small dishes of ginger biscuits. The day she married Andrew, the *Larkspur* became his as well as hers. Because he had such extensive duties to parish and family and no experience with running a lodging house, he had gratefully accepted Julia's offer to take care of any matters that should arise. Those were few and far between, with Mr. Jensen so capable a manager.

Some twenty minutes later Julia excused herself and stepped inside the hall. Mrs. Dearing, white braid trailing gracefully down her back, turned to smile from the bench of the pianoforte.

"Good afternoon, Mrs. Dearing."

"And good afternoon to you, Mrs. Phelps. Is the good vicar not with you?"

"He's in the garden with the Clays. I just stepped in to see Mr. Jensen." She looked around at the empty sofas and chairs. "Where is every-one?"

"Mr. and Mrs. Durwin are visiting with the Sykes, Mrs. Latrell is up-stairs, and Miss Rawlins is working on her latest manuscript." Mr. Ellis and Mr. Pitney, of course, would be atop the Anwyl. "I've noticed that every-one seems to have reasons to absent themselves from the hall every day just about the time I'm due to practice."

Suppressing a smile because it was likely true, Julia walked over to stand beside the piano. A book of scale exercises was propped upon the ledge. "Now, Mrs. Dearing. Aleda tells me you're progressing very well." Aleda still gave the woman lessons on Tuesday and Thursday afternoons.

"A gracious young lady, that daughter of yours." The levity in her tone was a sure sign that Mrs. Dearing took no offense at the emptiness of the room. "But had I the mastery of Clara Schumann, repetitive scales could still become tedious to the ears. So you had best go find Mr. Jensen before you become a captive audience."

The notes of the f-major scale followed Julia down the corridor to Mr. Jensen's office. Knowing that he was expecting her, she gave a light knock and eased open the door. The former butler immediately started getting to his feet, but she waved him back into his seat, closed the door, and slipped into the chair in front of his desk.

"Thank you for coming, Mrs. Phelps," Mr. Jensen said.

"But of course, Mr. Jensen. How are you today?"

A smile deepened the lines of his sixty-five-year-old face. The former butler was a courtly looking man, with thinning, iron-gray hair. Even seated, his posture was as perfect as a dowager's. "As I am every day in Gresham. Most content."

"I understand." It was here under the *Larkspur*'s roof that Julia had learned the true meaning of contentment herself. "And you deserve it, I might add."

"That would be debatable, but it's kind of you to say it."

"I say it only because it's true."

How strange it still seemed to Julia to be so beholden to the person she had considered her worst enemy back in London. From the day she crossed the threshold of surgeon Philip Hollis's home as a seventeen-year-old bride until shortly after her husband's death three years ago, this same man had treated her with just enough politeness to keep from losing his position. It was clear that he considered her, and later the children, im-positions to his well-established routine.

And so it would have seemed that Mr. Jensen would have been ecstatic to learn that his former master's gambling debts had left Julia penniless. But incredibly, he had advised her to transform her only asset, an abandoned coaching inn, into a lodging house—and then insisted on lending her the money for refurbishing and to cover her living expenses until rents from the *Larkspur*'s lodgers could be counted upon.

Julia was well aware that God had sustained her family in those days, and she still thanked Him daily for His benevolence. Even so that knowledge did not lessen her gratitude to Mr. Jensen, for he could have hardened his heart to the Father's suasions. God would have likely provided another way, but she was glad that had not been necessary, because the man had proved himself to be a good friend as well as a capable manager.

"Thank you for sending tea," Julia went on, changing the subject in deference to Mr. Jensen's embarrassment when being complimented too effusively.

"You're welcome, Mrs. Phelps." Mr. Jensen folded his hands upon his desk and assumed a businesslike demeanor. "I will try not to keep Vicar Phelps waiting too long. This morning, Mrs. Latrell received a wire from her widowed sister in Northumberland. I gather the sister is lonely, for she has asked Mrs. Latrell to move in with her as soon as possible. The chambermaids are assisting her in packing, and Mr. Herrick will deliver her to Shrewsbury in the morning."

"I see." Julia was not as well acquainted with Mrs. Latrell as with the other lodgers, simply because she had married and moved out before the woman's arrival. But she could understand how a sister would find solace in her cheerful disposition. "Of course she must go. I'll slip upstairs and speak with her as soon as I leave you."

"She has offered to pay next month's lodgings for having given such short notice."

"Do you think that is necessary?" Julia asked him. "We still have those other inquiries, haven't we?" They were responses to the advertisements that had been posted in several English newspapers almost a year ago when Mrs. Kingston was on the verge of becoming Mrs. Bartley. Mrs. Latrell's letter had arrived first. After it was arranged that she would take the room, Mr. Jensen had sent at least two dozen letters of regret, but surely one of those who had inquired would still be interested in the *Larkspur*.

"We have indeed, Mrs. Phelps," Mr. Jensen replied. He picked up a sheet of stationery and leaned forward to hand it across the desk. "But I would like you to see a letter that arrived only yesterday."

Julia set the fine vellum paper on the desk in front of her to smooth out the folds, then held it out in front of her to read the bold script:

Dear Mr. Jensen,
    I am a solicitor, practicing in London. One of my clients is the Long & Currier Publishing House, which I have learned represents one of your

*lodgers, a Miss Eugenia Rawlins. I obtained your address from the pub-
lisher in the hopes that you would have a vacancy at present for another
client of mine, a Mrs. Somerville.*

*Mrs. Somerville is a widow with a sterling reputation who is sadly
still grieving the loss of her husband two years ago. Her family feels that
a change of location and an extended stay in the country would benefit
her enormously. Would you happen to have a room available?*

*Enclosed you will find reimbursement for a wired reply, if you would
be so kind.*

Very truly yours,
Osbert Radley

"How sad," Julia said as she lowered the page. She could certainly feel
empathy for a woman still so newly widowed.

"He enclosed two pounds."

"Two pounds? And with no guarantee of a room? His client must be
desperate."

"Apparently so, judging from what was not said."

Julia gave him a questioning look. "What do you mean?"

"Do you not detect that there is far more to this story than meets the
eye?"

Scanning the letter again, she experienced a vague uneasiness but attributed it to the notion that they would be exchanging Mrs. Latrell for a
stranger. And she had learned in recent years that feelings were sometimes
a poor barometer of reality. "I can understand anyone needing to get away
from familiar surroundings after losing a loved one." It had certainly done
her a world of good to move to Gresham after her husband's death—even
though the circumstances were not of her choosing.

"Then we should wire Mr. Radley in the affirmative?"

Still, a faint doubt nagged at her. "It doesn't quite seem fair, putting
this one ahead of the others. Wouldn't you agree?"

"If you will pardon my bluntness," he replied, "the *Larkspur* is yours
to do with as you wish."

"Granted. But it's your decision as well. After all, you have more contact with the lodgers than I have."

She knew what Andrew would advise. Take some time to pray before
making a decision. But judging from Mr. Radley's letter, time on that end
was in short supply. And it would be nice to have an immediate lodger,
instead of having to wait for Mr. Jensen to send out letters and then receive
replies. She prayed daily that the *Larkspur* would run smoothly. Wouldn't
such a prayer encompass this situation as well?

Mr. Jensen's voice broke into her thoughts. "May I offer a suggestion,
Mrs. Phelps?"

"Please do."

"I could wire Mr. Radley, with the understanding that Mrs. Somerville must be interviewed before we can guarantee her the room."

Of course that was the perfect solution—and fair, because Julia had made a policy of interviewing potential lodgers from the beginning. She nodded. "Then send your wire, Mr. Jensen."

———

"Remember the arithmetic test on Friday," Lydia reminded her younger students before dismissing school that afternoon. She saw panic wash across Aleda Hollis's face and added, "And there will be no algebra on it this time. Just long division."

When the students were gone, Lydia took up her satchel and stepped out into an unseasonably warm afternoon. The sound of an approaching wagon met her ears, not a rare occurrence, considering that the manor house was just down the lane. But as she crossed the school yard, an odd quirk of dread made her consider retreating for the schoolhouse again. By the time a vaguely recognizable face came into view, it was too late. She fastened her eyes on the side of the lane ahead of her and prayed that by some miracle the driver had an appointment with the squire.

But this was not the case, for Mr. Towly reined to a halt a disinterested-looking dray horse. The poor beast's red coat was flecked with bits of dried mud, in spite of the fact that the last rain had fallen a week ago.

"Afternoon, Miss Clark!" he greeted.

"Good afternoon, Mr. Towly." It was a strain to keep just the proper tone in her voice. Too friendly would only serve to encourage the man, too distant would be rude. A lifetime of caring about manners could not be shaken easily, even though rudeness would likely serve her best in this situation.

The man removed his felt hat, revealing greasy brown hair molded against his head. Small hazel eyes were set in a weathered face. "Lovely day, ain't it?"

"Indeed." Lydia allowed just enough of a smile to be pleasant. "And I must be on my way. Good day to you, Mr. Towly."

But he was not so easily swayed. She had only managed a step or two when he said, "But I've come ter offer you a ride home, Miss Clark."

She looked up at him again. The mental picture of a certain headstone in the churchyard made it easier to put a chill in her voice. "Thank you, but I prefer to walk."

"Oh, come now. It's got ter be a mile, at least."

"I enjoy walking, Mr. Towly. Good day to you."

To his credit he did not argue but shrugged and turned the wagon around. He sent her a friendly wave as he passed, as if she had not just spurned his company. Lydia ignored the wave and walked faster. *Forgive me if this sounds disrespectful, Father*, she prayed, recalling the many requests she had sent heavenward in her earlier years for a husband. *But all those prayers, and this is how you choose to answer?*

Under a sky of pure lucid blue that same afternoon, Jacob Pitney knelt among the ruins and carefully brushed dirt from the area that had already produced a hardened leather shoe and a broken perfume container. A bit of metal caught the sunlight and his attention at the same time. He concentrated his brush in that one particular spot and held his breath as more of the metal—gold, he realized—was revealed.

"Have you something interesting there, Mr. Pitney?" asked Mr. Ellis, who was also on his knees some six feet away.

Jacob smiled. "You might want to come and see this."

With the older archeologist at his elbow, Jacob brushed the last bit of dust from what he knew now to be a bracelet. Carefully he picked it up. Several chips of what appeared to be jade were missing from an ornamental design, but it was in good shape otherwise.

He handed it to Mr. Ellis, who removed his spectacles and held it close to his eyes. "Must have cost a tidy sum back then."

Jacob nodded. "Probably belonged to one of the senior officer's wives—or more likely, a daughter. It's small for a woman's wrist."

"I agree. Unless she was unusually small boned." Bringing it again to his eyes, Mr. Ellis squinted. "Why, there appears to be a name among the jade leaves."

"May I have a look?" Jacob asked. Mr. Ellis surrendered it with relief in his expression. Jacob knew that his senior partner was sensitive about his difficulty with reading items close up, and tried to spare him embarrassment whenever possible. The Latin word etched into the metal was so delicately scrolled and worn by time that he also had to squint. Presently he smiled and looked at Mr. Ellis. "Didn't Cerealis have a daughter named Vernita?"

"Vernita." Mr. Ellis tilted his head thoughtfully. "Meaning, *born in the spring*. His only daughter after five sons." Replacing his spectacles, he said, "And his family accompanied him when he assumed governorship of Britain England. But it has always been assumed that he never traveled west of the River Trent."

Jacob looked over the ruins—their workplace for the past two years. So far their careful, back-wearying brushing away of barely a quarter-inch of dirt at a time had yielded the usual artifacts—pottery, combs, spearheads, and the like. Interesting and important, but nothing as promising as this find. For if they gathered enough evidence to prove that the Roman Commander Cerealis, generally regarded as complacent, had at least attempted a push toward Wales, history texts would have to be rewritten.

It never ceased to amaze him that the earth could yield such clues about civilizations long dead for centuries. Before archeology had become his passion, one mound of dirt looked like another to Jacob. Now he was consumed with knowing what lay beneath it waiting to be discovered. If only he had a better command of the English language, he would be able to explain to Miss Rawlins that his life was occupied with fascinating stories too. *But it probably wouldn't matter*, he thought sadly. He realized then that Mr. Ellis had spoken. "I beg your pardon?"

Mr. Ellis, wrapping the bracelet reverently in a handkerchief, was smiling. "And to think my father wanted me to be a chemist."

Jacob smiled back, grateful for this reminder that at least there was one love that remained constant in his life—archeology. "Mine is still waiting for me to come to my senses and work at the family bakery."

"Why did I teach in Scotland?" Lydia repeated the question she had been asked by Phoebe Meeks, who was seated beside her in the trap on Saturday morning. She had enjoyed a breakfast of sloeberry scones and tea with the girl's family earlier, and now they were on their way to Shrewsbury. "Well initially, Gresham already had teachers for the grammar and infant schools. And having never traveled outside of Shropshire, I was anxious to see a bit of the world. But I never intended to stay there for fourteen years."

"Then why did you?" Phoebe asked in a hesitant voice, as if she feared Lydia would consider her cheeky for asking so many questions.

"I was needed." She smiled. "It's a long story. And I did come home for Easter and Christmas every year, mind you. But it's good to be here to stay."

And it was good to be under the sun that morning and holding the reins to her father's high-spirited chestnut hunter, Wellington, who was feeling his morning oats and pulled the trap along the macadamized roadway as easily as if it were a paper kite. On impulse Lydia had put on one of her favorite Sunday dresses, a sea green organdy, and fastened a straw bonnet with a little sprig of silk forget-me-nots over her chignon. She pointed to a large field at their right at the foot of the Anwyl, carpeted with dewy pink knapweed and playing host to hundreds of butterflies. "Now, doesn't a sight like that make it worth getting out in the morning?"

"It's all beautiful," the girl replied while admiring the scene, then admitted, "I've never been outside of Gresham."

"You haven't? Then today will be an adventure, won't it?"

"Yes, ma'am."

They rode in silence for some five minutes longer, until Lydia caught sight of a figure up ahead. "Can you tell who that is?"

The girl sat up and squinted short-sighted eyes in that direction. "Where?"

"Never mind." Lydia could tell now that the person was a man, walking toward Shrewsbury with his hands in his pockets. He turned to wave at her, so she reined Wellington to a walk, then a halt.

"I see him now, Miss Clark," Phoebe whispered as the man approached. "It's one of the Sanders."

Of course Lydia recognized the strapping build, the shock of straw-colored hair jutting around his ears from under his cap, and the deep-set forest green eyes. Harold Sanders was about three years younger than was she, but the sun combined with a boisterous lifestyle had aged his face considerably. He had not attended the grammar school or Saint Jude's during their childhoods, but Lydia had seen him in town now and then over the years. And she knew of his family's reputation—one didn't have to indulge in gossip to gather that most of the males were as rough as a rat-catcher's dogs.

"Will you give me a lift to Shrewsbury?" the man asked upon reaching Lydia's side of the carriage.

Lydia replied that she supposed she could. While he and his brother Dale were brawlers, they had never assaulted any woman to her knowledge. She motioned for him to go around to the other side, while Phoebe sidled over to the middle of the seat.

"I'm Harold Sanders," he said when Wellington began moving again. "You teach at that new school?"

"I do," Lydia answered with a polite smile directed toward the horse's tail. "I'm Lydia Clark. And this is Phoebe Meeks."

"Your papa has the foundry, don't he?"

"Yes. But my brother, Noah, runs it for him now."

"Noah Clark," the man mused. "Can't recall ever fightin' no Noah Clark."

"You haven't," Lydia told him.

"No? How do you know that?"

"You're still alive, aren't you?" She regretted saying it as soon as the words left her mouth. All Noah needed, with all his other responsibilities, was to have a Sanders following him around intent on defending his reputation as a brawler. With a sigh she leaned forward a little to look past Phoebe. "That was a joke, Mr. Sanders."

He grinned back at her. "That was a good one, Miss Clark. You know, I said to myself that you was jokin', but being as we've never talked before, I weren't sure." With an appreciative chuckle he added, "And I know a good joke too. You wanter hear it?"

"Is it fit for decent company, Mr. Sanders?"

"Oh." He sat in silent disappointment for a few seconds, then brightened again. "This one is—I made it up myself last year. When is a merry-go-round most like a spinnin' jenny?"

"When they're both going in circles?" Lydia guessed at length.

"No, that's not it," Mr. Sanders chortled with a pleased tone, then asked the girl in the middle, "Do you know?"

"No, sir." Phoebe moved just a little closer to Lydia.

"When the merry-go-round is . . . a-spinnin' *Jenny!*"

"That's very clever, Mr. Sanders." Lydia sent another polite smile toward Wellington's hindquarters. *Why was he walking anyway?* For just a half-shilling, a person could ride on one of the cheese wagons on one of its twice-daily rounds.

"I suppose you're wondering why I was walkin'," he said, as if he had read her mind.

"Why, no," Lydia lied, loathe to admit that any facet of her passenger's life held any interest for her. An immediate stab of conscience compelled her to admit, "Actually, the question did occur to me."

"I had a ride on a cheese wagon, but the driver put me out."

"He did?"

"We hit a bump, and I bit my tongue and let out a swear word. I didn't know the driver was a Baptist. They've got no humor about such things."

Wonderful! Lydia thought. She leaned forward again to send him a meaningful look. "I'm not Baptist, but I'm inclined to be that way too, Mr. Sanders."

"Oh, but you don't have to fret yourself about that," he assured her after a chuckle. "I don't swear in front of women and girls. Used to around my sister, Mercy—only if I was galled about something, mind you—until she married that horse farmer, Seth Langford. He won't allow us to say so much as a—"

"Mr. Sanders . . ." Lydia warned, tightening her hands around the reins.

Harold Sanders' ruddy face assumed a wounded expression. "I weren't gonter swear, Miss Clark."

"That's good to hear, Mr. Sanders." Lydia relaxed, sat back, and hoped for silence for the rest of the ride. But within seconds Mr. Sanders leaned forward again.

"I s'pose you're wondering why I'm going to Shrewsbury."

"I wasn't wondering that at all," Lydia replied, this time in all honesty.

This did not discourage him. "Well, our wagon's been patched to death and ain't reliable for making milk deliveries to the factory, so my papa is sending me to see if he can get a new one made cheaper down there than he can from Mr. Mayhew. He'll waste a whole day o' my time just to save tuppence." He gave another little chuckle. "If he knew how tickled I am to get out of milkin' cows, he'd send one of the others."

"Hmm," was Lydia's only response.

"That's the trouble with working for your own papa," he sighed. "Mine kicks us out of bed at the break o' dawn. I'd give anything to have the money to get my own place." They happened to be passing a large stone farmhouse with thatched outbuildings and vast hedged pastures. Harold gestured toward it. "Like that one. And I'd have enough workers so's I could take it easy onest in a while."

"Indeed?"

While the man's attention was still drawn covetously toward the farm, Lydia sent Phoebe a wink, which caused the girl to bite her lips to keep from smiling. Harold went on, pointing out that life was unfair, that he worked just as hard as any worker on any dairy farm, and should be rewarded accordingly.

Some three-quarters of an hour after taking Mr. Sanders as passenger, they rode down Berwich Road into northern Shrewsbury. It was a jewel of a large country town, nestled on a peninsula of rising ground formed by a loop of the River Severn. The steep, winding cobbled lanes were flanked with angular black-and-white half-timbered Tudor shops and dwellings, symmetrical buildings of red Georgian brick, and modern Victorian gingerbread houses. Each dwelling had its own small garden plot, with spring flowers blooming among early vegetables. The shops also boasted flowers in window boxes and in any available inch of ground. Beside her, Phoebe took in as much as her weak eyes would allow. *I should bring her sister and brothers here one day*, Lydia thought. *Mrs. Meeks too*, she added mentally, for surely there had not been much time for leisure in the woman's life.

"You can put me out here," Mr. Sanders said after Castle turned into Saint Mary Street.

By now, Lydia knew more than she cared to know about how unfairly life had treated him, so it was with great relief that she reined the horse to a stop. He jumped down from the carriage.

"Thank you kindly, Miss Clark. When will you be passing back this way?"

"I beg your pardon?"

"My business won't take too long, I shouldn't think."

As much as Lydia revered courtesy, she had also absorbed from her parents that in matters that weren't life-and-death, one had to put limits upon how far one must allow oneself to be imposed. And she had had quite enough of the man.

"Mr. Sanders, I've no idea how long *our* business will take. So I suggest you ride back on one of the cheese wagons."

"But they won't—"

"Not all the drivers are Baptists, Mr. Sanders. But it might behoove

71

you to watch your language, in any case."

She gave him a nod and snapped Wellington's reins, leaving the man standing in the street. Moving back into the space he had vacated, Phoebe twisted around to squint in that direction. "I think he's still watching us, Miss Clark."

Lydia felt compelled to explain her harshness. "He'll find a ride easily enough if he minds his manners. That's how the cheese wagon drivers make a little extra money, you know."

"But what will you do if he's there when we leave?"

"Oh my." Lydia hadn't considered this. "I couldn't very well pass him by. We'll just have to loop around to Dogpole Street on our way out."

Doctor Rhodes had recommended an oculist on High Street, a German by the name of Mr. Rosswald. "You'll pay more than at some places, but his spectacles are custom made," Doctor Rhodes had said. This sounded good to Lydia, who had only known of shops with racks of spectacles from which one could only choose the pair that worked best.

As it turned out, Mr. Rosswald had built up a reputation. A dozen somber-looking people were already seated in ladder-back chairs against the walls of his waiting parlor. Phoebe began to look a little pale after about fifteen minutes of waiting, and Lydia asked her if she felt ill.

"No, ma'am," the girl answered, but shortly afterward she turned to her and whispered, "It won't hurt, will it?"

"No, not at all," Lydia whispered back. "And I'll go with you."

That seemed to reassure her somewhat, for the tenseness drained from her expression. An hour later Lydia accompanied her young charge into a long, narrow room. Attached to the far wall was what the oculist explained as the *Snellen Chart for Distance Testing*. Mr. Rosswald, a bespectacled, bearded man with only a faint trace of accent, had Phoebe read the letters to him as he covered alternating eyes with squares of dark pasteboard. It was no surprise to Lydia, who sat in a corner chair out of the way, when the girl could not read the bottom three rows. The oculist then used a retinscope and looked into each of Phoebe's eyes to determine if she suffered from an astigmatism.

"She has the astigmatism," Mr. Rosswald said when the examination was finished. "Her eyeglasses will correct that as well. You must bring her back here in two weeks to have them fitted."

"I'll be able to see?" the girl asked.

"You'll be able to count the leaves on the trees, Fraulein," he said, patting her shoulder.

They lunched on fidget pies at the *Lion Hotel*, which was crowded with patrons, giving them ample opportunity for people-watching without being rude. Lydia bought her father some paints and linseed oil afterward in a dusty little art supply shop. To her disgust, her conscience would not allow her to bypass Saint Mary Street on her way out of town again, but at least her conscience did not prick at her when she did not rein Wellington over to wait in case Mr. Sanders was to show. They rode in silence for a quarter of an hour, and then Lydia turned to Phoebe. "You're not looking forward to the eyeglasses, are you?"

"But I am, Miss Clark," Phoebe replied while aiming her eyes just under Lydia's eyebrows. "I'll be able to see everything. Thank you for buying them for me."

"I'm asking you to be honest with me, Phoebe."

When the girl did not speak right away, Lydia turned her attention back to the horse and road to give her some time.

Finally a small voice replied, "No, ma'am." She sent a worried look sideways to Lydia. "But it's still very kind of you, Miss Clark."

Lydia had to smile at her. "Some favors we can do without, yes?"

Phoebe's green eyes clouded. "I'll be ugly."

"That's not so. Do you really think a bit of wire and glass could detract from such a lovely face?"

"I'm not lovely. And everyone will laugh."

Please help me again with this, Father, Lydia prayed while drawing in a quiet sigh. She wouldn't lie to the girl, for even though she didn't allow her students to ridicule one another, she couldn't monitor them every hour of the day. And children nowadays were no different from when she was in school.

"It's not fair," the girl whispered.

Lydia nodded. "I know, Phoebe. And if it were in my power to change that, I would. But you can't allow this to ruin your life." She let go of the reins with one hand long enough to touch the girl's shoulder. "Every person has his own burden to carry. Remember Captain Powell? He didn't allow the loss of an arm to hinder him."

"But he was an adult. I'm the only one in the school with a burden."

"Some burdens you can't see, Phoebe—and some will come later. That's the way of life. But God helps us to bear them, if we ask Him. And we can still have happiness in spite of them."

"Did you have a burden when you were a girl?" Phoebe asked after a thoughtful hesitation.

"Oh, I thought I did. My height and ears."

The girl gave her a blank look. "Your ears?"

"Don't tell me you haven't noticed."

"But I haven't. Honestly, Miss Clark. You're almost as beautiful as Miss Raleigh."

Lydia remembered then that the girl was short-sighted and smiled. "Thank you, Phoebe."

A silence lapsed between them for several minutes, and then Phoebe turned to her again. "People teased you?"

"Oh, unmercifully."

"What did you do about it?"

"Somehow I realized that my height and ears weren't all there was to me—if they had been given to someone else, that person would have suffered the same teasing. That helped me not to take it so personally. And by the way, when the teasing stopped mattering so much to me, it eventually faded away."

"Have you a burden now?"

As unfair as it was that she should hear the girl's innermost angst and then not confide her own, Lydia could not go burdening a child about the ache that sometimes stabbed her heart at the sight of a happily married couple, like the vicar and his wife. She replied lightly instead, "I have a dear student who would rather go through life running to second base and bumping into things than wear a pair of spectacles on her *lovely* face."

Finally a smile touched the girl's lips. "I've never bumped into anything, Miss Clark."

Lydia smiled back. "Well, it was just a matter of time."

*T*he following Sunday, Jacob Pitney mustered up enough courage to plant himself two rows behind Miss Rawlins during the morning worship service at Saint Jude's. Vicar Phelps delivered a fine sermon centered around the parable of the laborers in the vineyard, but sitting so close to the object of his affection made it difficult for Jacob to keep his attention from straying to the back of Miss Rawlins' head.

During the closing prayer Jacob added a petition of his own that she would walk back to the *Larkspur* unaccompanied. He pretended to fuss with the cuff-fastener of his tweed coat while she passed his pew on her way toward the front, counted fifteen silent seconds as planned, then stepped out into the aisle himself.

But he hadn't planned on Mr. Trumble cornering him in the vestibule.

"I've been meanin' to ask you about a collection of marbles I've got from the ruins uphill." The shopkeeper held up both palms as if to head off any accusation. "I got them before you and Mr. Ellis started your *escallation* up there, mind you."

Escallation? A fraction of a second later it dawned upon Jacob that *excavation* was likely the intended word. He darted a helpless glance in the direction of the open front door, where the vicar was shaking hands with Miss Rawlins. "Why don't you bring them over this afternoon and we'll have a look?"

"You sure it's no *incompetence?*"

"Incompetence?"

"You know . . . too much trouble?"

"I would be very interested in seeing them," he assured the shopkeeper before bidding him good-day and exiting the church. He sent a silent *thank you* heavenward at the sight of the writer strolling along the willows alone.

"Miss Rawlins?"

Jacob was chagrined to hear his own voice break as he spoke—like a half-grown schoolboy's, but she turned and smiled. His breath caught in his throat. She looked so elegant with her salmon-colored gown billowing about her slippers in the breeze.

"Mr. Pitney," Miss Rawlins said as he caught up to her. "Where is Mr. Ellis?"

This deflated his confidence. Did she only see him as part of a team? *We work together, we're not married,* he thought but of course did not say. "He's visiting his family in Bristol and should return by late afternoon." Jacob had carried on as usual atop the Anwyl yesterday, because they did not normally take Saturdays off unless visiting their families.

"Would you mind if I accompanied you?" he asked, holding his breath.

He let it out again when she replied, even pleasantly, "That would be nice."

This encouraged him to press on in his quest to deepen their nonexistent relationship. "I've recently finished reading *Rachelle of Chamonix.*"

"Indeed?" Looking at him with new appreciation in her expression, she said, "Tell me, what did you think of it?"

"I liked it."

"You *liked* it?"

Jacob wondered if he had imagined the little edge to her voice. *What did I say?* Perhaps *like* was too weak a word. Too late to take it back now, but he could amplify it. "*Very* much, I meant to say. I liked it very much."

He didn't imagine the sigh that came from her rose-colored lips. "But how did it make you *feel,* Mr. Pitney?"

How did it make me feel? Clearing his throat, he replied, "Uh . . . good?"

She stared at him as if he had belched. "And that's all you came away with after reading it? You felt *good?*"

Jacob could feel his cheeks getting warm. "Rachelle and General Massena ended up marrying. Shouldn't I feel good about that?"

"But did you understand any of the symbolism?"

"Symbolism?"

"The bowl of chrysanthemums at the table . . . the sudden hailstorm on the night Rachelle wrote in her diary . . . the rip in the scullery maid's apron . . ." She lifted a slender hand in a helpless gesture, then allowed it to drop to her side. "I could go on and on, Mr. Pitney. Didn't you see anything below the surface?"

"Well, of course." Though an indulgent mid-April sun sent down only mild rays, he was beginning to sweat beneath his tweed coat. He tried to think fast, for he could sense her opinion of him diminishing every second that he delayed his reply. Finally an answer popped into his head and came to his rescue. "I learned that one shouldn't pay attention to other people at dinner parties, if one is in love with someone else. But then Rachelle de

Beaufort was at fault too, because she didn't give the general an opportunity to explain."

"And *that* is what you consider symbolic, Mr. Pitney?"

"Well, yes." He ran a finger along the inside of his collar. "Shouldn't a person know how to behave properly at dinner parties?"

"Oh, unequivocally. Proper etiquette at the dinner table is the foundation of our empire."

Was she being sarcastic? Jacob had dug a hole so deep with his answers that he decided silence was now his safest defense. Apparently she did not mind, for she did not speak to him again until he held the *Larkspur*'s door open for her.

"Thank you for the company, Mr. Pitney," she said politely before retiring to her room. She did not come down for lunch, which wasn't unusual when she was finishing a manuscript. Miss Rawlins had donated copies of her two dozen or so novelettes to the inn's library, so Jacob picked up a copy of *Jewel of the Empire* and took it up to his room. He resolved he wouldn't make the same mistake twice. He would study this story as thoroughly as if it were an archeology text and be prepared the next time with the right answers.

And the next time, she would look at him with awe—not as if he had egg in the corner of his mouth.

———

The following Sunday, Vicar Phelps delivered a stirring message on the memorial of twelve stones on the banks of the Jordan. Still, Lydia could barely keep her eyes focused on the minister. *You've the self-discipline of a gnat!* she lectured herself.

She would not think of showing up at school too groggy to perform her duties competently, yet she had come to church in that condition, as if God didn't matter as much as her occupation. Yesterday Mrs. Summers had informed her that Thomas Hardy's *Under the Greenwood Tree* had just arrived by post at the lending library, and Lydia could be the first to borrow it. She had not intended to stay up all night reading, but one chapter led to another, and then another, until she became aware of the downstairs clock chiming four in the morning.

She found herself almost nodding off while standing during the closing prayer, which was mercifully brief. All she could think about during the hymn, "Now Thank We All Our God," was the comfort of her bed and the softness of her pillow.

Outside the church, she and her parents were approached by her brother, Noah, and his wife, Beatrice. They always sat in the second row with Beatrice's mother, Mrs. Temple, who was hard of hearing and needed to be close to the pulpit. Noah and Beatrice's marriage had been childless for eighteen years, and then, like Hannah, Beatrice gave birth to a son they appropriately named Samuel. A daughter, Mary, followed a year later. So in their early forties, the couple had two children not even old enough for grammar school. And they delighted in this new stage of their lives.

"Mother is asking us all to lunch," Beatrice said. She was a handsome woman, with jet black hair still showing no signs of gray. "Will you come?"

Lydia's parents readily agreed. Sundays were Mrs. Tanner's day off, so they usually had their noonday meal at the *Bow and Fiddle*. But Lydia begged off. "I just want to sleep all afternoon," she told them apologetically. Fortunately she had an understanding family. Her brother, one of the few people in Gresham who towered over her in height, even squeezed her shoulder. "Stayed up all night reading again, did we?"

"What do you mean . . . *again*?" Lydia demanded with an affectionate smile. "I haven't done that since I was a girl."

"Not counting last night?"

She covered a yawn. "Not counting last night."

Bidding them farewell, she started across the green alone. Dark clouds loomed overhead, and the air smelled heavy with rain. She reached Market Lane and was just passing in front of the *Larkspur* when she noticed the wagon coming from Church Lane and pausing in the crossroads ahead. Mr. Towly sat at the reins, clad in a black suit that looked newly tailored. But even a suit of golden armor wouldn't have impressed Lydia.

"Good day to you, Miss Clark!" the man boomed. Apparently not used to courtesies, he forgot to remove his hat this time. He could have removed it a hundred times, and still, Lydia wouldn't have been impressed.

"Good day, Mr. Towly," she mumbled as she continued her walk along the low stone wall of the *Larkspur*'s garden. The crossroads were getting nearer, as was her opportunity to turn to the right and head for home.

"I was wonderin' if you wanted to have some lunch at the *Bow and Fiddle*—as long as you don't spend more than half-a-crown."

Lydia halted in her tracks. The man, horse, and wagon were only ten feet away from her now. "Mr. Towly," she said wearily, "where are your children?"

"Why, I sent them on home."

"And what do you plan to give *them* for lunch?"

He sat a little straighter and replied, "We've a cook, Miss Clark. I had to hire one when the missus passed on. . . ." Now at the mention of his wife, he thought to remove his hat. "God rest her soul."

And she's likely enjoying that rest, Lydia thought. Sighing, she looked about her. Families strolled toward cottages, but no one appeared near enough to witness their discourse. *Best get it over with now.*

"Mr. Towly," she said.

"Yes?" he replied hopefully.

"Your children need you. They aren't so quick to get over the loss of their mother as you obviously are. And while I'm flattered by your attention, I'm not interested."

His stubbled jaw dropped. "Huh?"

Sighing again, Lydia said, "I presume you wish to court me, Mr. Towly. But I do not wish to be courted by you."

"But you don't know aught about me. If we had lunch—"

When cows write poetry, she thought. "I prefer to keep it that way, sir. Please pay me the courtesy of leaving me alone."

The man's face mottled with anger. "Oh, I'll pay you that courtesy, all right. And I don't expect I'll be changin' my mind, even if you was to beg me!"

That was the best news Lydia had heard all day. "Thank you, Mr. Towly."

Clearly taking offense at the relief in her voice, he continued in an injured tone, "But as I hear it, there ain't any other men givin' you the time o' day. I was willing to overlook your homeliness, but there ain't many as willin' to do so."

With that, he snapped the reins unnecessarily hard, prodding the ill-groomed horse north up Market Lane. And when the wagon moved away, a tall, broad-shouldered figure stood watching Lydia with a perplexed expression. Mr. Pitney. Tears blurred Lydia's eyes. No matter how little she cared about Mr. Towly, the words had stung. And much more so, now that she knew they had been witnessed.

She started again for the crossroads, but Mr. Pitney moved rapidly across the lane and came to her side.

"Miss Clark?" he began in a hesitant voice, as if he was unused to confronting women who had just been insulted in the center of town. "Are you all right?"

"I'm fine, thank you." Lydia increased her pace, but the long legs of the man beside her did the same. She sent a nod in his direction while chiding herself for not bothering with carrying a reticule, as did other women, for she was in dire need of a handkerchief. "Really."

"You don't look fine, if you'll forgive me for saying."

"Why not say it? It's been said before."

"No, I meant . . ." From the corner of her eye Lydia watched him withdraw a handkerchief from the breast pocket of his tweed coat. "Please, take this."

She had reached Church Lane and turned westward, and still he accompanied her. Practicality soon overcame Lydia's pride, and she stopped to take the handkerchief from his hand. He was gentlemanly enough to look elsewhere as she blew her nose into it. Lydia felt grateful for that, and especially thankful that the Worthy sisters had not yet returned from church and did not spin lace on Sundays.

"Thank you," she said as she folded the handkerchief.

He turned to look at her again. She had never really noticed how handsome he was, with his dark brown hair and eyes. Not that it mattered. She was the last person to judge a book by its cover. True, Mr. Towly's cover had not impressed her, but she could have possibly overlooked it had the book been worth reading.

"Are you better now?" Mr. Pitney asked.

"Much better. I'm just mortified about the little scene."

"Please don't be. The man was rude."

She didn't want to think about Mr. Towly anymore. "May I return the handkerchief when I've had it cleaned? I don't think you want it back in your pocket."

He smiled, somewhat bashfully. "Of course. But there's no hurry, mind you. My mother gives me three dozen every Christmas. She's certain that digging about in damp ruins causes head colds—never mind that I've not had one in years."

Lydia suspected that he was attempting to cheer her. And it worked, for she found herself returning his smile. "It must be very interesting work."

A spark lit his brown eyes. "Actually, I seldom think of it as work. Is teaching like that for you?"

"From the first day, Mr. Pitney. So we're both blessed in that regard." She realized his dinner was waiting, so she offered her hand in farewell. "And it was very kind of you to see about me."

"You'll be all right, then?" he asked as they shook hands.

"Yes, thank you."

They wished each other good-day, and Lydia turned to continue her walk home. Even when she was a schoolgirl, a frank acceptance of reality had kept her from being schoolgirl-*ish*, with a head full of romantic notions. And at the age of thirty-four, romance seemed as unattainable to her as the moon. But it was quite a while before she could drift into sleep that afternoon, for she could not stop imagining a pair of kind brown eyes.

————

Good—she's here, Jacob Pitney thought, pausing in the doorway leading into the hall that evening. Miss Rawlins, looking like an Egyptian princess in her beige gown and straight, short dark hair, sat in one of the chairs.

At half-past ten, the Clays and Mr. Ellis had retired to their chambers for the night, but Mrs. Dearing and the Durwins were usually inclined to visit in the hall until later. Miss Rawlins had no set pattern for appearances—when she tired of sequestering herself in her room, she came downstairs for some companionship.

But not *his* companionship, Jacob was sadly aware. That would soon change, however. He had just finished reading *Jewel of the Empire* not only for content, but he had studied every phrase, every word. And he had routed out every symbol as meticulously as if it were a buried artifact waiting to be discovered.

"Why, good evening, Mr. Pitney," Mrs. Dearing greeted from the sofa as he walked into the room. "Did you have trouble sleeping?"

The motherly concern in her voice put him more at ease, and he smiled back at her.

"I was just upstairs reading." He casually folded his limbs into the chair beside Miss Rawlins' as if it was the most convenient one—when in fact, he had to cross the carpet and pass five other empty ones to reach it.

"Some archeological text, no doubt?" Mr. Durwin queried.

"A novelette, actually."

"Well, the mind needs recreation as well as the body. Although I was never fond of novels. Nonfiction has always been my cup of tea, such as *The Stones of Venice* by John Ruskin." The elderly man inclined his head toward Miss Rawlins. "No offense to you, Miss Rawlins."

"None taken," she replied, smiling. "My father happens to be of the same persuasion."

Jacob sat in silence, hoping the conversation would drift back to the subject they had been discussing when he stood in the hall doorway—the properties of the catmint plant and its fascination to felines. He could have kissed Mrs. Durwin when she said, "I just don't understand. Why will a cat avoid catmint if it's planted from seed? And how does he know the difference?"

"That's a mystery all right," replied her husband. "But I've noticed it myself. Surely you've heard the old axiom . . . *If you sow it, the cats won't know it.*"

"Then why would anyone care to plant it?" Mrs. Dearing asked. "Of what use is it, if not recreation for one's cat?"

Mr. Durwin smiled, clearly in his element. "Because the tea is an effective remedy for stomach upsets and children's colic."

To Jacob it seemed a perfect time to draw Miss Rawlins into a discussion. "*Jewel of the Empire* was the book I just finished," he told her quietly.

The author turned her attention from the ensuing conversation and raised an eyebrow. "Yes?"

"I was in complete awe over the symbolism."

"Such as. . . ?"

Shaking his head at the wonder of it, Jacob said, "Where do I even begin? I must confess—I've been grossly imperceptive not to notice such things before now."

She actually straightened in her chair, and it seemed that a flicker of interest flashed in her smoky gray eyes.

He went on. "When the butler had to use three matches to light the drawing room lamp, I could tell right then that the courtship of Jewel Stuart and Major Adams was doomed to failure because he hadn't told her about the three years he spent in indentured servitude in the States as a young man. And the ruby pendant the evil Lady Beatrice refused to remove from her neck—that one was the most difficult to figure, but I understand now that it was a symbol of the hardness of her heart."

He thought he should pause and allow her space to comment. It had been worth it, staying up until the wee hours every night last week until the words on the pages ran together in front of his eyes. For her eyes now studied his face intently.

"Incredible."

Jacob lowered his chin modestly. "Thank you."

"I'm inclined to believe that imagery is wasted on certain readers who lack imagination."

"Ah . . . I beg your pardon?"

Drawing in a deep breath, Miss Rawlins said, "The butler needed three matches because the room was damp. Remember, it was the monsoon season? I simply wanted to remind the reader of that dampness, so later, when Lord Helmsly announces he must transfer to a drier climate because of his gout, the reader is not taken completely by surprise. It's a writer's technique called foreshadowing. And as for the ruby pendant . . . Lady Beatrice wore it constantly because she did not trust the Indian servants. Criminals are very suspicious of others' motives, you know. That was the only reason."

Jacob refused to give up. He had labored too hard at this and had to redeem himself. "The four out-of-tune keys on the piano—"

"The dampness, remember?" she cut in wearily. "Simply a vehicle to introduce Kalari, the piano tuner who unwittingly saves Jewel's life later. What did you think the out-of-tune keys meant, Mr. Pitney?"

What he had *thought* after several hours of deliberation was that because the keys were the notes g-a-c-e, which rearranged formed the word *cage*, they were a clear signal that Lady Beatrice would be going to prison—which indeed happened near the end of the story. Aware that the three other lodgers were now blatantly eavesdropping, he mumbled, "Never mind."

Jacob felt very much like a child who has been chastened by his mother for tracking mud into the house, for he had sullied up Miss Rawlins' story with ridiculous assumptions. He needed an escape now and covered a feigned yawn with his hand. "Well, morning arrives early," he said for lack of anything better and then winced at the inaneness of that statement. *Stupid, stupid, stupid!* he told himself under his breath.

"Good night, Mr. Pitney," the elderly lodgers said as he got to his feet and walked across the carpet. And when Miss Rawlins bade him the same, he knew he had not imagined the relief in her voice.

*O*n Monday the twenty-third of April, twenty-one-year-old Noelle Somerville paced the floor of her Compton Street flat in London, alternately staring out the parlor window and appraising herself in her bedroom full-length mirror. The image peering back at her met with her approval every time, from the mass of strawberry-blond ringlets to the silver gray silk gown that complemented the jade green of her eyes—but still she felt compelled to reassure herself again and again.

He has to come today. She had taken great pains to dress herself this morning in addition to having to teach the new girl Quetin had hired for her how to tighten the stays of her corset without cutting her in two, and how to apply the curling iron without burning her scalp. How someone so featherbrained could even negotiate the streets of London without ambling into the path of a hansom was beyond her. *And she's likely hiding somewhere now to keep from working.*

As if to prove her wrong, the girl eased the door open and stuck her head tentatively through the opening. Hope quickened Noelle's pulse. "Yes, Zelda?"

"Beggin' yer pardon missus, but me name's Nelda. Named after me papa's sister that lives in Stepney on the east—"

"Fine!" Noelle snapped, then drew in a deep breath to calm herself. "Nelda. What is it you want?"

"Would missus care for a cuppa?"

"No," she replied, irritated that the girl wasn't announcing Quetin's arrival. "And what have I told you about knocking?"

The girl rolled her eyes sheepishly. She was thin as a cat's elbow, with stringy ginger-colored hair—most of which hung loosely about a topknot. "I do beg pardon, missus. I tries to remember, really I do. But me missus I had afore, Missus Farris, never wanted me to knock, with her havin' such frightful headaches all the time. So's I sometimes fergets it's you I'm seein' about and not—"

"That's enough! *Mercy*, you do go on and on!" Noelle felt an acute throb in her temple and wondered if the reason this Mrs. Farris had been afflicted with headaches was because of the frowzy girl standing at her door. Ignoring the wounded expression on the maid's face, she said, "Yes, I'll have some tea. And remember to send Lord Paxton up here as soon as he arrives."

"Yes, missus."

Before the door could close all the way, Noelle thought to add, "And do pin up your hair before you tend to my tea."

She was in no hurry for refreshment—indeed it was only to provide a distraction that she had even agreed to take some—and she couldn't stomach the idea of finding another red hair in the leavings of her cup. A half hour later she sat perched in the window seat, weary of haunting the mirror, when a familiar set of footsteps sounded on the stairs. Resisting her initial impulse to fly to the door, Noelle took another sip from her cup and waited for the knock. "Who's there?" she asked unnecessarily, because the knock was as familiar as his footsteps.

"As if you have to ask," a masculine voice exclaimed as the door opened and the Honorable Lord Quetin Paxton, Member of Parliament, entered. Noelle forgot her resolve at once, set her half-filled cup precariously on a tuft of the velvet cushion, and flew to meet him. Their embrace lasted several seconds, and then she pressed kisses upon his cheek until he laughingly pushed her away to hold her at arm's length.

"Now let my sore eyes have a look at you," he ordered. He let go of her shoulder just long enough to toss his silk top hat on the nearby settee. "How do you manage to grow more beautiful with each passing day?"

"You don't see me every day, so how would you know that?" she replied with just enough pout to show she wasn't so easily pacified by his compliments.

A smile curled under his dark mustache, and he tapped his jutting chin with a forefinger. "You forgot a spot."

Obediently Noelle planted a kiss, and then another upon the face she had come to know so well. It wasn't a handsome face. The azure pupils of his oversized eyes were so transparent that they made him appear almost blind, and a once strong jawline was beginning to soften with his forty-two years. But the power and vitality behind his features more than made up for any lack of aesthetic proportion. And as Quetin had always maintained that a well-cut suit could make even a troll look attractive, he paid his tailor well to perform miracles—such as the frock coat of fine-milled wool he wore over a waistcoat of gold and black brocade.

"Now, why has it been a whole week?" she asked him.

"Parliament is as demanding a mistress as you are, my dear." There was a slight irritation to his voice, though his arms still encircled her.

"Surely your friends keep you busy enough so that you aren't pining away for me."

"One can only play so many games of *Speculation* before it becomes a bore."

"But I take it shopping isn't quite so boring?" An eyebrow arched over a pale eye. "If the bills your dressmaker sends me are any indication."

Noelle did not look for any hidden resentment in his statement because he had never begrudged her anything in the three years they had been together. "Do you like this one?" Stepping back from his arms, she flounced a ruffle on the pagoda sleeve. "I thought I would wear it to the theatre."

"Yes, it's fine." But an odd discomfort crossed his face, and he stepped back to lower himself onto the settee. "We must talk, Noelle."

"Now?"

"I can't stay."

"Quetin! You promised . . ."

He patted the seat beside him. "Sit down."

The tone of his voice did not invite argument. Reluctantly she settled next to him, raising a hand to trace the lion design on one of the brass buttons of his coat. He took the hand in his and sighed heavily.

"What's wrong, Quetin?"

"It's Averyl. Now that the girls are all married off, she wants to start spending the seasons here in London. In fact, she's due to arrive in another three days."

The very mention of that name was enough to cause a vein to throb in Noelle's temple, but since he did not usually care to discuss his wife with her, she restrained from making a scene.

Their arrangement had been so perfect. She and Quetin were able to be together often during the season when Parliament was in session from March through mid-August, even though for appearance' sake he had to maintain his own flat on Grosvernor Street as well. And when Parliament wasn't in session, his home in Reading was only two hours away by railway. Quetin's position in government gave him more than enough excuses to visit the city during the off-season to see Noelle. *Why can't she stay in Reading and crochet or something?*

"Can't you talk her out of it?"

He shook his head. "She won't listen to reason. She's even considering looking for a townhouse."

Noelle pressed her lips together. Her most fervent wish was that Lady Paxton would die. It was obvious that the former widow had married Quetin only for his title, and she held her vast fortune over him like a carrot dangled before a donkey. What right did she have now to demand his company, when she had spent the fifteen years of their loveless marriage doting over her four spoiled daughters, excluding him so that he was forced to seek companionship elsewhere.

At least the odious woman had never had children by Quetin. That would greatly hamper the divorce he promised Noelle as soon as his private investments brought in enough to keep her in the lifestyle to which she had become accustomed. She had assured him many times that the money didn't matter, just because she knew he liked to hear it. But they were both very aware that it did.

"What are we going to do?" she asked as the tears in her eyes blurred his image.

"There, there now." He kissed her hand. "I've already taken care of that, my sweet. We must move you out of the city for a while."

"Leave London? But—"

"Just until August or so. Or until Averyl discovers that she has no liking for the social life here. And we certainly can't afford to be seen together while she's here. People will turn blind eyes to certain things when the wife is away, but if she discovers evidence to divorce me on grounds of adultery, I'll lose everything."

Noelle knew next to nothing of the law, even after spending three years as a lawmaker's courtesan, but that sounded likely. Especially considering that Quetin was bankrupt at the time he married his much-older wife.

"When? And where?"

"You'll be out in the country where no one knows either of us. It's a charming little village, Mr. Radley tells me."

"Who?"

He sighed. "My solicitor, Noelle. You've met him several times. You know, it's an irritating habit you have, forgetting names."

Her little memory lapses had nothing to do with the devastating news he had just dropped into her lap, so why did he feel compelled to deliver another lecture at this moment? But in the interest of harmony, she merely replied, "I never forget the name of anyone who's important, Quetin."

"But you never know when someone might turn out to be important."

"I'll try to do better," she promised, not for the first time.

"Good." He glanced away for a fraction of a second. "And you'll leave Wednesday."

Noelle's breath caught in her throat. "In two days? But I can't possibly be packed by—"

"I'll have a trunk sent around. Just pack what you can. Four months isn't forever, you know."

"My furniture?" She had just refurbished the flat only six months ago, filling the four rooms with elegant Louis XIII reproductions.

"You'll have no need of it in the lodging house where I've made arrangements for you to board. I'm keeping the flat, so it'll be here waiting for you." His brow furrowed thoughtfully. "But perhaps you should give me your jewelry to store in my safe. You'll have scant need for it in a country village, and you don't want to concern yourself about some chambermaid rummaging through it when you aren't in your room."

Noelle lovingly touched the emerald bracelet on her wrist, a birthday gift from Quetin just three months ago. The gold metal felt lustrous against her skin. Give up her jewelry, even for four months? "I could bring a box and key . . ."

"Too risky. Just keep out the costume pieces, if you wish. That's all you'll need." He narrowed his eyes with mock severity. "Unless you plan to bedeck yourself with jewels and flirt with other men while you're there."

"I just may," she murmured coyly, wishing she felt as lighthearted as the tone of her words. She could tell by his expression that he was growing weary of having to reassure her. He would leave if she became too taxing. *You have to be brave*, she told herself. Well, she could do that. She managed to give him a smile. "I'm sure it will work out just fine, Quetin."

Cocking an eyebrow again, he said, "You mean that?"

Would it do any good if I didn't? "Yes. I suppose one can endure almost anything for four months." But a little sigh escaped her. "Did Mr. Radley tell you the name of this . . . this village?"

Quetin nodded. "I believe it's called Gresham."

———

"Well, I think it's ludicrous," Valerie Bradburn, tall, pale and lithe, said as her red-tipped fingers snapped and shuffled the playing cards that evening. "So she expects to waltz into town and become a grand dame of society? I've seen the woman before—she's a cow!"

Gathered at Noelle's dining table for a game of *Speculation* were her only female friends, each who had arrangements with other members of Parliament. Of the three, only Valerie had once been married. Titian-haired Geneva Hunt, who sometimes drank too much wine and then wept over her mistreatment by the aunt who raised her, actually kept company with a member of the House of Commons, but Noelle thought no less of her for that. In fact, the only one of the three she had less than amiable feelings for was Meara Desmond, seated across from her. Dark and full-figured, with the amber-spoked eyes of a cat, the Irishwoman now wore the infuriating expression of someone who is harboring an amusing secret and not inclined to share it.

One would have assumed that Meara wouldn't feel so smug, since her benefactor, Lord Ogden, was stricken with palsy and had to leave London for Norwich. No doubt he still provided for her financially, but the word was that his health was failing rapidly, and Noelle couldn't imagine his widow continuing Meara's support.

Just the notion of Lady Ogden writing out monthly cheques for her husband's former mistress made Noelle smile to herself. But then considering the fact that Lord Ogden was a repulsive-looking man with foul breath and a ridiculous powdered wig, perhaps Lady Ogden would feel beholden to Meara after all.

"Noelle, what's the name of that town?" Geneva asked while peering thoughtfully at the three playing cards fanned covertly in the palm of her hand. Her words were already beginning to slur. Another half hour and she would be relating how she was forced to scrub chamber pots or polish floors because her aunt considered her no more than an unpaid servant.

Not tonight, Noelle pleaded silently, in spite of her fondness for Geneva. There was enough misery in the present to be mulling over the pain of the past. In reply to her friend's question she said, "Gresham."

"Gresham." Valerie shook her head and snapped a card, facedown, upon the table. "How far away is it?"

"About eight hours I suppose, taking into account stops at every little depot along the way." She sighed. "Quetin has promised to visit as often as he can get away, but it's going to be at least August before I see any of you again. I'll be so lonesome!"

Over the rim of her wine glass, Meara's cat-eyes gave her a genuinely sympathetic look. In her soft Irish brogue she said, "There, there, Noelle. You'll have your fellow lodgers to keep you company."

"Well, the very thought of it makes me want to weep," Valerie declared loyally. "I wish we had more time to spend with you before you leave. But Lord Paxton will want you all to himself tomorrow, no doubt."

Noelle, in fact, did have doubts about that, for he had not mentioned doing so. But she could not admit those doubts, even to Valerie and Geneva. They were friends, yes, but still practiced a good deal of one-upmanship over who was pampered the most. How could she now admit to them her fears of late that he was growing bored with her? *It'll be good, my being away*, she tried to reassure herself while staring blankly at the trio of cards in her hand. In her absence he would see just how tightly their lives were connected and how much he needed her.

As Noelle had feared, Quetin did not come the next morning when the trunk he sent for her arrived. She had little opportunity to brood over it though, as she had to keep a constant eye on Nelda to see that she folded her clothes correctly. Only a half dozen times did she peer out the window and try to catch sight of Quetin through a drizzling rain.

By midafternoon she knew with all certainty that she would not see him until tomorrow. She dismissed Nelda for the day—not out of consideration, but because she feared the girl would attempt to lift something from the trunk if left alone. Exiting the apartment building, Noelle scanned both directions for a passing hansom. Finally she gave up and walked a quarter of a block to a hansom stand. "Cheapside," she told the driver. "The cigar store across from the Bow Church."

The horse worked its way methodically down the cobbled streets in a tedious file of carriages, cabs, omnibuses, and carts. It seemed that everyone in London but her had some purpose to attend of his own choosing. She, on the other hand, felt like a leaf at the mercy of a capricious wind. She had no more control over the events that were now propelling her toward an unknown future than did the horse in harness over which direction he would take. It was an unsettling and frightening place to be.

As the hansom carried her past Sir Robert Peel's statue where Newgate flowed into Cheapside, she could see the steeple of Saint Marylebow's off to her right, soaring above the rows of houses huddled against it on either side. The driver reined the horse in front of *Wetherly's Imported Cigars*, as instructed, and hopped down from his precarious perch behind the passenger seat to assist her to the walkway. For that courtesy Noelle added threepence to the two-shilling fare and then walked over to stand under the awning of the cigar shop. Better to stay in the shadows, even though the street traffic constantly interfered with her view of the narrow, three-story brick building to the right of the church. The vicarage looked the same with its wrought-iron fence separating the walkway from a tiny garden. The shutters were new, yet still the same olive green as before. It

90

seemed to Noelle that if a person were to have to replace shutters, one would want to try a different color. But then, there was the risk that some of her father's parishioners would disapprove of the change.

To say that the church was important to her family would have been an understatement. Just as it towered over their home physically, it overshadowed every waking moment and activity. Plans were made with the unsaid understanding that her father may or may not be present. Countless times his place at the dinner table had been empty because he was off ministering to some other family. Usually it was to provide solace during time of illness or bereavement, for the parish of Marylebow was an old one, with many elderly parishioners. Noelle spent her childhood envying the members of her father's congregation for their access to him—she was twelve or thirteen when it occurred to her that she also was a member. That revelation had only intensified the abandonment she felt.

Fat, sparse raindrops began pelting the canvas above her. She was glad for the rain, for that lessened the chance that someone would leave the house and spot her. Of course it would take a blizzard to stop her father from his missions of mercy. She had heard that Aaron, her older brother, married last year. And Oswald married three years ago. That left only two sisters and a brother at home. Young or old, they were cut from the same cloth. Pious and industrious, content with their Sunday leg-of-lamb and Wednesday roast beef, piano lessons and choral practices, latest issues of *Sunday at Home* and, for the younger ones, *Sunday Scholar's Reward*.

The cobbler's children have no shoes, Noelle thought, for most activities even bearing the name "Christian" had not provided the spiritual nurturing she had thirsted for after coming to a personal faith at the age of eleven. *Be a good example* was the only catechism she absorbed. So when she found that harder and harder to do, it became easier and easier to push God to the back of her mind.

She had never felt she fit in her family anyway. And especially not after she left home three years ago—only weeks after she had met Quetin in a millinery shop, where he was purchasing a hat for a woman who would soon become his former mistress.

The notion that one of their daughters was a *kept woman* was too much for Noelle's parents. When her father stoically informed her that she was no longer welcome beyond the threshold, the reason he gave was that she would be a bad influence upon her younger sisters. But Noelle suspected the chief reason was fear that his parishioners would find out and perhaps demand of the diocese a less tainted-by-scandal minister.

"Do you require assistance, miss?"

Noelle turned to the man standing in the doorway behind her. *Mr.*

Wetherly, she recognized, the proprietor of the cigar shop. "No, thank you."

Instead of returning to his business as she hoped he would, he raised his balding head to peer at her through the spectacles perched upon the tip of his nose. "Miss Somerville? Is that you?"

"I'm afraid you're mistaken." Noelle turned her attention again to the building across the street. She heard the door close behind her. The thickening rain blended outlines of the passing vehicles with the gray of the street. Still, her eye caught movement at a second-story window. The drapes were parted, a shadowy figure lowered the glass and then disappeared as the curtains fell back into place. A lump welled in her throat. It could have been anyone—a housemaid, her mother, or one of her siblings. Whoever it was, Noelle had the feeling this person was the last tenuous link she would ever have with her family.

A hackney cab approached. The mackintosh-clad driver spotted the handkerchief she waved, reined his horse to a stop, and held an umbrella over her as he assisted her from the walkway to the carriage.

Back at her flat, Noelle stood on tiptoe and stretched to reach into the back of her armoire. She brought down a biscuit tin she had taken a fancy to as a young girl. It had been given to her by their housekeeper when the last of the *PEEK, FREAN & COMPANY ANGEL CAKES* were consumed. A classroom setting was portrayed upon the lid in vivid colors and gilt, showing students studying a map that illustrated that four hundred million *Peek, Frean & Company* biscuits and pastries touching each other would stretch from pole to pole.

She went to the window seat and opened the lid for the first time in over a year. Inside were such treasures as a redbird feather she had found in the vicarage garden, assorted Sunday School merit ribbons for memorizing scripture passages, a pair of velvet doll slippers, a paper doll of a much younger Queen Victoria, a needlepoint bookmark her sister had given her for a birthday, and a tarnished silver whistle from a Christmas stocking.

Carefully Noelle unfolded a yellowing advertisement she had cut carefully from a discarded magazine at the age of nine or ten. Above the words touting the merits of *TRUESDALE & COMPANY, Tea, Coffee & Colonial Merchants* was an idyllic portrait of a family gathered in a cottage garden. The father was playfully hoisting a young child above his head while at his side a boy patted the family dog. Before the wooden gate stood the smiling mother, arm outstretched to receive a posy from her little girl.

It was a scene Noelle had studied often during her childhood. She had envied the little girl holding the posy, and even the rosy-cheeked boy with the dog, for they appeared to be so cherished and happy. Children were listened to in that cottage garden, and not only when they were reciting, but also when they wished to talk about the happenings of their day, their fears and friendships, likes and dislikes. Many daydreams had carried Noelle to that special place, which she came to think of as Truesdale.

But as she grew older, she came to understand that Truesdale did not exist. She would never visit there. The parents and children and even the garden were created by an artist's brush. As cynicism began to take root in her heart, she wondered if the artist had even known such a family. Perhaps the reason he had managed to portray them so skillfully was because he, like Noelle, had wished such people to be real.

Because she was allowed only one trunk and would be returning within four months, she had not thought it important to bring the tin with her. But now she couldn't imagine leaving it behind. If she had to live among strangers, at least she would have something of the familiar with her.

Wrapping her arms around her knees, Noelle turned to the window and watched rivulets of water join other rivulets to run down the pane. Beyond, she could see umbrellas bobbing up and down on the walkway. People hurried beneath them to homes and shops and businesses, unaware that they were being stared upon from a third-story window by the loneliest woman in London.

———

"But surely he could have managed an hour," Noelle sniffed Wednesday morning to the man seated across from her in the private coach moving toward Paddington Station. Mr. Radley was one of the last people she would choose to confide in—his bulbous nose had pores the size of billiard pockets, and his small weasel eyes seemed to be constantly watching for an opportunity to advance his own interests. But he was the only available ear, and her disappointment was so overwhelming.

"There, there now. Some unexpected debate on Irish land reform came up. The Irish Republican Brotherhood are making threats again." The solicitor reached forward to pat Noelle's knee. "I assure you that he was just as crushed as you are. And he'll certainly visit you as soon as possible."

Noelle wiped her eyes with her handkerchief again. "So you saw him this morning?"

The weasel-eyes blinked. "This morning?"

"When he said he couldn't get away."

"Oh yes. This morning." Changing the subject, he said, "By the way, the proprietor of the lodging house, a Mr. Jensen, assumes you are a widow."

"I beg your pardon?"

He waved a hand. "Just a little invention to evoke sympathy for your cause, Miss Somerville. There was no guarantee that we could procure a room on such short notice, you see."

"*And* . . . " he went on with a leer in his little eyes, causing Noelle to turn her knees sharply to the side against the seat when he seemed to be on the verge of patting them again. "People in villages tend to be more straightlaced than Londoners. Were they to know your real . . . ah, situation, they would likely invite you to leave. So I would advise keeping up the charade."

Noelle steamed inside at the whole notion, but it would do no good to complain to the man across from her whose company was becoming increasingly more disagreeable. She would certainly complain to Quetin on his first visit about his choice of a solicitor. Surely with the whole of London's legal expertise from which to choose, he could do better than Mr. Radley!

A more practical matter suddenly occurred to her. "Quetin didn't give me any money last time we spoke. How am I to pay for my lodgings?"

"That has been taken care of for the next four months, Miss Somerville."

"And what about the other things I'll have need of?"

"I'll make mention of it to Lord Paxton. Surely he'll send a cheque by and by." Leaning forward again, he told her, "But *I* might be inclined to lend you a bit, if you're in desperate straits."

A shudder of revulsion snaked down Noelle's spine. "I will never be that desperate, Mr. Radley."

He grinned and settled back into his seat. Noelle actually found herself relieved when the coach reached its destination and she was able to set foot on the ground. Paddington's platform was a sea of people boarding and detraining, meeting and seeing off, while behind it a great black locomotive bearing the title *London & Birmingham Railway* in silver letters sent a blast from its shrill whistle.

"Your train should arrive in half an hour," Mr. Radley said when the whistle was silent again. Behind them, the solicitor's coachman had set down her trunk and was now engaged in seeking out a porter. When he returned with one some five minutes later, Noelle held out a gloved hand to her obnoxious companion.

"Thank you, Mr. Radley, but you needn't wait."

He shook his head while clasping her hand. "Lord Paxton has commissioned me to take care of you, Miss Somerville. I cannot in good conscience shirk my duty."

"Oh, but I insist," Noelle said, pulling her hand away. "And I'll certainly explain that to Lord Paxton." *Along with some other things, you knee-patting toad.*

"Fine, then," he replied while a smug smile spread itself under the cratered nose. "We'll see just how well you can take care of yourself."

"What do you mean by that?"

The weasel eyes narrowed as his mouth opened to give reply. But he snapped it shut again, and his face assumed a blank expression. "I only meant that you could accidentally board the wrong train, Miss Somerville. Have a pleasant journey." He turned on his heel and was off, threading his way through the press of people with his coachman following in his wake.

———

Four hours later the train screamed to a halt at Birmingham Station, where Noelle would disembark and wait for the *Severn Valley Railway* for the next leg of her journey. While waiting for a porter to open the door of her first-class coach, she used the time to bid farewell to the Shipleys, a mother and daughter who had been her traveling companions all the way from London. That way she wouldn't have to spend any time with them on the platform, meeting family members who surely would be just as boring as those two had been.

"You'll be sure to visit us soon, Mrs. Somerville?" Mrs. Shipley's irritatingly shrill voice gushed in the sentimental tone one would use when parting from a lifelong friend.

"I'll be looking forward to it," Noelle replied, adding under her breath, *Then you can tell me again every detail of the wedding plans.*

Mrs. Shipley's daughter, Amelia or Abigail or something like that, bobbed her too-giggly-to-be-marrying head. "Do come, Mrs. Somerville! I would love to show you my gown."

I'll see your gown every time I close my eyes for the next week, Noelle thought while gracing the girl with a warm smile. She had spent the better part of an hour hearing about satin fabric, Belgium lace, and seed pearl trimming. When the porter finally came around to release her from her prison, Noelle snatched up her reticule, gave the two a wave, and stepped out of the coach.

Fortunately the platform wasn't nearly as crowded as Paddington's had been, giving Noelle reason to hope that she would have a coach all to herself when her train arrived. Behind her, she could hear Mrs. Shipley trill to a group of waiting relatives, "And her husband lost his life saving the queen from an assassin! He was a captain in the Royal Guard, you see . . ."

Noelle smiled to herself. At least traveling with the Shipleys had given her an opportunity to rehearse the details of her new identity. If she had to be a widow, she would at least invent an interesting reason for being one. She was hungry, having had only tea for breakfast, and went inside the depot's refreshment room to see what was being offered. Other passengers had the same idea, and some fifteen or so were queued up at the counter before her. *All this trouble for food that smells like shoe leather?* Abandoning her meal plans, she freshened up in the accommodations room and then found a bench and watched porters unload trunks as effortlessly as if they were bed pillows. Some quarter of an hour after the *London & Birmingham Railway* had switched tracks for its return trip to London, the Severn Valley train came in sight, shrilling and belching smoke.

Chapter 12

*M*ay I be of assistance, miss?" a burley porter asked Noelle after the first boarding whistle had sounded and people were scurrying for the different coaches. She shook her head, then thought again and motioned toward a huddle of luggage that had been taken from the earlier train.

"I'm going on to Shrewsbury. You're positive my trunk will be in there too?"

"Oh yes, miss." He gave her a sociable grin, exposing two missing top teeth. "But that won't do ye any good if ye ain't on the train, now will it?"

"I'll be along, thank you," she responded with a polite chill, for familiarity irritated her when coming from people in servile positions. Especially if such people were unattractive. The man shrugged and went on about his business. When it appeared that most people had boarded, Noelle got to her feet and walked toward the front of the train. There were only four first-class coaches—none of them vacant. As she had not realistically expected the situation to be otherwise, her disappointment wasn't overwhelming. At least she wouldn't be forced to listen to wedding plans, for she could see through the open door of the third coach from the engine that the lone occupant, a sandy-haired gentleman seated at the opposite window, was staring intently at a book he held open before him. He looked over at her as she stepped through the doorway.

"Good afternoon," Noelle said, taking the seat facing his but just inside the door.

"Good afternoon," he returned in a pleasant baritone.

He appeared to be about her age and was exceedingly handsome, with Nordic blue eyes and a tall, athletic frame clothed in a black suit. But Noelle's heart was still raw and aching from missing Quetin, so she was not disappointed when the man returned his attention to the book. Resting her head against the back of the leather seat, she closed her eyes. The train began moving shortly afterward, lulling her into a dream in which she and Quetin were walking in Kensington Gardens. An abrupt crunching sound brought her back to the present.

"I beg your pardon," apologized the sandy-haired man as Noelle looked over at him. He held up a large red apple with one bite missing. "I didn't realize . . ."

Noelle couldn't help but smile, for his clean-shaven cheeks were stained pink with embarrassment. "Please, enjoy your apple."

"Would you care for one?" he asked after a moment's hesitation.

As if on cue, her stomach made a sound like a coiled spring, which he either didn't hear or was too gentlemanly to give sign of doing so. "You have another?"

"Yes." He set the open book upside down upon his knees and reached into a leather satchel on the seat beside him. Handing the apple across to her, he said, "They're last year's, but still quite good. My parents have an orchard."

"How convenient." She took a bite, and the fruity aroma filled the coach. When she had finished half, she said, "You know, I've never been overly fond of fruit. But this is delicious."

He looked up from his book again and smiled. "Thank you."

"No, thank *you*." Extending her free hand, she said, "My name is Noelle Somerville."

"Paul Treves," he said and shook her hand. "I'm pleased to make your acquaintance."

Suddenly loathe to slip back into her lonely retreat, Noelle asked, "What are you reading?" He picked up the cover to show her the title, which did no good because the imprint was small against the leather cover.

"*Journal*, by John Wesley," he said, then lowered the book again. "Have you read it?"

"Not that I recall."

"Oh, but you should treat yourself to it sometime. Fifty years ago, I would have been afraid to show this in public."

This took Noelle by surprise. He seemed too unworldly for the type of licentious books Quetin kept on a shelf in her parlor—for fear that his wife would accidentally come across one in his own flat. "Is that so?"

"Most definitely," the man said. "He was considered such a renegade during his lifetime. But now his commentaries are much admired, even by the Church hierarchy."

This conversation was becoming too complex for Noelle. But her ears had caught a word that was all too familiar to her. "Are you a minister, Mr. Treen?"

"It's Treves, actually," he corrected in a friendly tone while wrapping his apple core in a handkerchief to stash back into his satchel. "And yes, I'm in the ministry."

Wonderful! Noelle thought, now regretting her choice of this particular coach.

"I was assigned to Lockwood just last year after being promoted to vicar," he continued. "I don't suppose you've ever been there?"

"I've never been outside of London."

"Oh. Do forgive me." Now another flush tinted his face. "I've been trying to break the habit of monopolizing conversations."

In spite of her misgivings about his vocation, she found herself amused again at his embarrassment. Had her father ever been this unsure of himself at any time in his life? "But I started it by asking you about the book, remember?"

He gave her a grateful smile. "So you did. And may I inquire as to your destination?"

"Shrewsbury. Or at least that's where I leave the train. My final destination is a village called Gresham." She could tell he recognized the name by a subtle shift of his expression. "Have you been there?" she asked.

"Many times." The smile faded, but still he spoke in a friendly tone. "In fact, Lockwood is just eight miles to the east."

"Indeed? What's it like?"

"Gresham?"

"Well, both," Noelle said, remembering her manners, when in actuality she had no interest in Lockwood because it didn't affect her life.

"Green and pleasant—both places." He smiled again. "And inhabited by people who are the salt of the earth."

"How reassuring."

Now it seemed that she had given something away in her expression, for he studied her face and said, "You're not happy about going there?"

The concern in his voice caused tears to sting her eyes, but she blinked them away and pretended nothing was amiss. *Quetin would be ashamed of you for being so weak*, she scolded herself. That spurred her on to muster a smile. "Just a bit anxious. But my . . . mother and father insisted that the change of scenery would be good for me. I find myself unable to cope with London's frantic pace since my husband passed away two years ago."

She didn't understand why she felt compelled to pretend that she had normal family ties in front of this man, clergy or no clergy. In all likelihood she would never see him again. And her lifestyle had ceased to cause her shame—at least in the presence of her friends and acquaintances. The quiet of night was sometimes another story, but one that she didn't like to think about during the day.

"I'm so sorry," Mr. Treves was saying, his blue eyes filled with sympathy.

"Thank you." Noelle allowed herself a brave little sigh. "But life must go on, mustn't it?"

"Yes, it must. Even through the times we wish it wouldn't."

"You've lost someone as well?"

He shook his head in an almost imperceptible motion. "Not the way you have. Your situation is far worse."

The drift of the conversation was only adding to Noelle's melancholy, so she decided against relating the story of her fictitious husband's heroism and guided the subject back to less emotional ground. "Perhaps my parents are right about my getting away from London. But I won't know a soul in Gresham."

"You'll find yourself well received, I can assure you." He also seemed relieved at the change of subject. "Will you be staying for a while?"

Ages and ages. "A few months. I'll be lodging at an inn called the *Larkspur.*"

"I know it well. At least from the outside."

There was a hiss of steam as the train started reducing its speed. Noelle peered out the window at the approaching platform for any sign of where they happened to be.

"Albrighton," Mr. Treves supplied. When she looked at him again he said almost apologetically, "I'm very familiar with this route. I visit my family every six weeks or so—they live in King's Heath, a few miles south of Birmingham."

It was touching, the way his voice warmed at the mention of his family.

"I'm sure they're happy to see you," Noelle found herself saying.

"Well, they claim to be." He smiled again. "That's the nice thing about family, isn't it? No matter what, there is always someone happy to see you again."

"Yes," Noelle agreed just before turning her face to resume her stare out the window.

———

Why do you always speak before thinking, Paul Treves chastised himself as Mrs. Somerville still stared out the window, even though the train had come to a stop. Hadn't his failure with Elizabeth taught him that? And a minister was supposed to be sensitive to people's needs. He had gone blathering on about how wonderful his family was, when she was still mourning the loss of her late husband.

Any opportunity of apologizing was ruined when a gentleman who introduced himself as Mr. Weston boarded with his wife and two young sons.

Mr. Weston, a banker from Shrewsbury, was clearly infatuated with the sound of his own voice, for it filled the inside of the coach with meaningless chatter. After a while, Mrs. Somerville rested her head against the narrow window ledge and closed her eyes. Noticing the thick lashes resting against her clear cheeks, Paul thought she was quite beautiful, and she seemed much too young to have been widowed two years ago. He realized he was staring and happened to glance at the loquacious Mr. Weston, who gave him a knowing wink. Cheeks flaming, Paul opened his book again.

The train pulled into Shrewsbury station two hours later. Mrs. Somerville sat up immediately, as if she had not been sleeping after all, and was the first to exit the coach. Paul was the last, his progress hindered by the Westons, who gathered parcels and moved as slowly as cold treacle. Finally stepping onto the busy platform, he spotted her standing only ten feet or so away, looking very vulnerable and alone.

"May I be of assistance, Mrs. Somerville?" he asked upon reaching her.

Her smile did not soften the apprehension in her green eyes. "Someone will be meeting me here. I just won't know how to recognize him."

"Then I'll wait with you." When she started to protest, he said, "My churchwarden will be waiting for me with his carriage. If there was a misunderstanding of your schedule, we'll deliver you to Gresham."

"That's very thoughtful," she said with an easing of her posture. "I suppose it would have been wise to write what I would be wearing, but there was no time."

"I'm sure they'll find you."

Just as the words had left his mouth, from his right came a voice with a heavy accent. "Frau Somerwheel?"

They both turned in that direction. For a fraction of a second Paul thought it was a child who stood there, but then recognized the man from the days when he was courting Elizabeth Phelps. "Aren't you caretaker of the *Larkspur?*"

"*Ja,*" he replied, doffing his corded cap. "I am Karl Herrick."

"Paul Treves." He leaned down to shake Mr. Herrick's hand. "And this is Mrs. Somerville."

Mrs. Somerville merely nodded with a tight smile, but then she had had a long journey and was now plunged into unfamiliar surroundings. *Everything will be all right,* he wanted to reassure her but feared he had acted with too much familiarity already. And since there was no more use for him, Paul took his leave. "I wish you well in Gresham," he told her in parting.

"Thank you, Mr. Treen."

He did not correct her this time but shook her offered hand and moved on toward the front of the depot where his churchwarden would be wait-

101

ing with his carriage. Paul always insisted that Mr. Lawson not venture out onto the platform on account of the man's advanced years, but in truth he had another reason as well. It would shame him greatly to be seen traveling first-class. Not only was it wasteful on a young vicar's salary, but as many of his parishioners would not be able to afford such a luxury, he never wanted to appear to hold himself above them. And had not Saint Paul written that Christians should strive for moderation in all things?

But the Scriptures were also adamant about honoring one's father and mother. And Paul's parents not only insisted upon purchasing his round-trip ticket every time he visited, but they turned unheeding ears to his assurances that he was happy to travel second-class.

The thought occurred to him that had he done so today, he would not have met Mrs. Somerville. Was it more than just chance that caused her to pick his particular coach? Was it possible that God had arranged it so that he could somehow help her?

Immediately he discounted that notion, for she would be residing in Vicar Phelps' parish. Whether it was his maturity or because he had suffered the loss of his first wife—or simply because his heart was as attuned to the Almighty as Paul longed his own to be—Vicar Phelps was infinitely more skilled at counseling. The best Paul could do would be to pray that Mrs. Somerville find the rest and solace she was seeking. And as there were people with needs in Lockwood as well, it was time to direct his energies toward them.

———

"You vill come with me to the carriage *bitte*, Frau Somerwheel?" the dwarf asked Noelle, who realized oddly enough that she had been staring at Mr. Treen's departing back. She turned to the little man again. Clad in a brown coat and trousers, he was old, perhaps fifty, with gray sprinkled through his brown hair. His head, shoulders, and upper torso were almost normal proportions, but the arms and legs were as short as a child's.

"It's Somer-*ville*," she corrected. *How in the world does he buy clothes?* Motioning toward the train, she said, "My trunk?"

"I vill attend to that as soon as you are safely in the carriage."

He was the only person she knew in the whole of Shropshire, excluding Mr. Treen, who was well on his way by now, so she had no choice but to follow—close enough to keep sight of him when he occasionally wove around knots of people, but far enough away so as not to give those who stared the impression that she was with him. At least the landau was impressive, black and polished, behind a pair of well-groomed red cob horses.

"Frau Herrick has packed some sandwiches and lemonade, in case you are hungry," he said after he had provided a step and an outstretched hand to assist her into the landau. "I vill return to you shortly."

Noelle noticed the large cloth-covered basket on the seat beside her and wondered if this Frau Herrick had mistakenly assumed the dwarf was fetching four people instead of one. And then the name registered in her mind.

"Didn't you say your name was Herrick as well?" she asked just as he was turning to leave.

He turned back to her and nodded. "*Ja*, Frau Somerwheel. She is my vife of twenty-three years and the *Larkspur*'s cook."

"Is she . . . like you?" A small chagrin came over her after she allowed the blunt query to escape her lips. *But someone who gets stared at surely is used to personal questions*, she told herself. And besides, he was only a servant.

Still, she was somewhat relieved when he gave her an understanding smile. "She is not like me, Frau."

"Indeed?"

"She is English, and I am German."

With that he left for the platform, leaving Noelle wondering at the glint in his brown eyes just before he turned away. After a few seconds she dropped the matter and took a sandwich from the generous basket. It was roast beef, cooked just the way she liked it with a hint of garlic, spread with a deliciously tangy mayonnaise. At least the meals would be adequate, if this was any indication. She settled back into her seat, dabbed a bit of mayonnaise from the corner of her mouth with the cloth, and watched people and trunks being loaded into other carriages and coaches. Presently the dwarf returned, directing a porter pulling a loading truck to the boot of the landau. He then climbed up into the driver's seat and turned to nod at her before he took up the reins.

Soon the streets of Shrewsbury gave way to a long macadamized road. Noelle looked out at thatched-roof farmhouses and barns, along with pastures seamed with hedgerows in which black-and-white cattle grazed. Her heart sank as even these signs of civilization grew farther apart. *What have you done to me, Quetin?*

*N*oelle breathed a little easier when the wheels of the coach touched cobbled stones again. This Gresham wasn't London or even Shrewsbury by any stretch of the imagination, but it wasn't a cave somewhere either. Cottages were clean and well kept, with budding gardens. In the shaded streets she caught sight of signboards on shops—only a handful, but enough to reassure her that the inhabitants did not barter animal pelts or pouches of corn by way of commerce.

Soon the horses were pulling the landau into a carriage drive between a large building of weathered stone and some stables. "Velcome to the *Larkspur*, Frau Somerwheel," the dwarf said after jumping from his seat and coming around to assist her.

"Thank you," Noelle replied. She had the feeling it would be useless to continue correcting his pronunciation of her name. From her beaded reticule she withdrew two shillings and offered them to him.

He looked at her palm and spoke with a dignity disproportionate to his small stature, "That is not necessary, Frau."

"Very well." She shrugged and dropped the coins back into her reticule.

"If you vill come vit me, please," he said with a nod toward a courtyard. They had only taken a couple of steps when a voice, as dry as a bundle of sticks, hailed her.

"Are ye Mrs. Somerville?"

Noelle stopped and looked to her right, where two white-haired women who looked as old as Christmas nodded at her from chairs in a garden across the lane. Oddly enough, they both held what appeared to be cushions in their ancient laps.

"The Verthy sisters," the dwarf said in a low voice in response to her puzzled glance. "They spin lace."

He did not move, which made Noelle realize he was waiting for her to answer the woman's query. "Yes I am," she called back politely.

"We would'ha gone inside a half hour ago, but we wanted to get a look at you."

"Well, now you see—"

"You're from London, aren't you?" asked a much more pleasant voice, coming from the woman on the left.

Noelle glanced longingly back toward the inn. She had awakened earlier this morning than she had in years, in addition to getting little sleep the past two nights. Every inch of her being longed for a glass of sherry and a bath. "Yes, I am."

"We're Iris and Jewel Worthy."

"I'm pleased to make your acquaintance. Well, good—"

"Perchance you know our niece, Lucille Forster?"

"No, I'm afraid—"

"Her husband's name is Roderick Forster," said the raspy-voiced woman on the right. "He's a tailor, and they live on one o' the main streets—Picolo-dally, I believe."

"I'm certain you mean *Piccadilly*," Noelle corrected, though she didn't know why she took the trouble. She motioned to the caretaker that she would like to go inside.

But before setting out again the man raised an arm to the two women. "Good evening to you, fraus."

"And to you, Mr. Herrick . . . Mrs. Somerville," both voices responded. Behind her Noelle could hear a mild argument break out—one woman saying something to the effect that a picolo was a flute-like instrument, and the other insisting that it was a relish one ate with fish. She followed Mr. Herrick across a flag-stoned courtyard, shaded by an enormous oak, then to the heavy wooden door. Turning to give her a nod, the man opened it for her. Noelle stepped into the corridor, took five steps, then nearly collided with a body nipping around the corner.

"Oh! Excuse me," apologized a girl clad in the black alpaca, white apron, and lace cap of a servant.

"That's quite all—"

"Would this be Mrs. Somerville?" the maid asked Mr. Herrick while peering owlishly at Noelle through thick spectacles.

"*Ja*. You vill show her to Mr. Jensen?" There was relief in the man's voice, as if he was glad to be shed of her.

Noelle resented being discussed in her presence as if she were mute and cleared her throat. "And who is this Mr. Jensen?" she demanded. She heard the sound of the door closing behind her and glanced over her shoulder. Mr. Herrick was gone.

"Why, he manages this place, ma'am," the girl answered. She dipped into a curtsy. "I'm Georgette. The *Larkspur* belongs to Mrs. Hollis—I mean, Mrs. Phelps—but since she married the vicar, she don't live here. But Mr. Jensen was in the hall, last time I looked. Shall I fetch him?"

"No, just show me the way," Noelle replied wearily. She followed the girl around the corner down a longer corridor, heard kitchen sounds behind a closed door on her left, and caught the aroma of food being prepared. Soft piano notes grew in volume as she passed a staircase on her right, and on her left was an open door through which she could see a long dining table.

Finally the maid paused at an arched, open doorway and turned to her. "This is the hall, ma'am."

"Well, go on."

She followed the girl into a room as large as her whole flat—where she would give anything to be at the moment. At the piano sat an elderly woman playing a tune Noelle recognized from *Don Carlos*, one of the tedious operas Quetin insisted upon having her attend with him. A braid of white hair draped over one shoulder, and from her ears dangled a pair of turquoise and silver earrings. Lips were pressed in a straight line, as she was concentrating on a sheet of music before her and had not noticed Noelle.

Which was fine with her, for the aged sisters outside had been enough for one evening. Noelle did not consider herself a snob, but she found old people depressing reminders that beauty and youth eventually faded, and there was nothing she could do about it. And judging from countless parishioners who had sat to tea in the vicarage parlor as she was growing up, they seemed to have a morbid fascination with their own and with each other's aches and pains.

A sound from one of two facing sofas caught her attention, where a white-haired man and woman were engaged in conversation with a man seated facing them. Noelle could not see his face because his back was to her, but the strands of iron-gray hair combed over a pink scalp indicated he also was elderly. In fact, besides the maid, Noelle had not seen any person since the carriage drive who looked to be under fifty years old. *I've been sent to a pension home*, she fumed. She hoped Mr. Radley was enjoying a good chuckle from this, for she certainly intended to wire Quetin in the morning and tell him about the cruel joke his solicitor had played.

The maid approached the man with the iron-gray hair. "Mr. Jensen?"

"Yes, Georgette?"

"Mrs. Somerville is here," she said with a motion toward Noelle.

The man turned to look over his shoulder at her, then rose to his feet. "Mrs. Somerville," he said, walking around the sofa. He carried himself with the erectness of a palace guard but smiled warmly. "Welcome to the *Larkspur*."

"Thank you," Noelle replied but did not offer her hand. He was, after

106

all, just the manager. But since she couldn't in all fairness fault him for Mr. Radley's incompetence, she did manage a strained smile as the piano grew silent behind her. "May I see my chamber now?"

"Why, of course." He sent an uncertain glance back toward the couple on the sofa, who watched her with curious expressions. "But wouldn't you care to meet—"

"Later, I'm sure that would be lovely," Noelle said, sweeping an apologetic smile around the room.

"Very well, Mrs. Somerville."

They were only a couple of feet from the doorway when Noelle felt a hand touch her lightly upon the back of the shoulder. She turned to find the piano player standing there, her face wreathed in a smile.

"We've been so curious about you, Mrs. Somerville. That's the only reason those two are sitting down here enduring my piano practice."

"Now, that's not true, Mrs. Dearing," the man protested from behind her.

"You play lovely," said the man's elderly companion.

Mrs. Dearing winked at Noelle, as if to indicate she realized she was being flattered. She thrust out a hand, which Noelle had no choice but to take. "I'm Blanche Dearing. Forgive my bluntness, but we certainly didn't expect you to be so young."

And I didn't expect everybody to be so old, Noelle thought, even as she shook hands and returned the smile. "Thank you, Mrs. Dearling. . . ."

"Forgive me, but it's Dearing," the woman corrected in a pleasant tone.

"Mrs. Dearing. And now if you'll forgive—"

"Mrs. Somerville?" This came from the woman on the sofa, who was now being helped to her feet by her husband. Heart sinking, Noelle had no choice but to wait for their approach. The woman, who had pleasant enough gray eyes, came barely to Noelle's chin, while the man was tall and looked surprisingly fit for his advanced years. "We're Mr. and Mrs. Durwin. We gathered the periwinkles you'll see on your bureau up on the Anwyl."

Noelle had no idea what the Anwyl was, nor did she care. There was no way on earth she could consider staying in a place like this until August, no matter how hospitable its inhabitants. Again she stretched her lips into a smile, though the effort was becoming wearisome. "Thank you. I'm sure they're lovely."

"Oh, they're more than just ornamental," the man said with a knowing nod at his wife. "Periwinkle, or *Vinca major*, if you will, is of great medicinal value. A fresh leaf inserted into the nostril will stop a nosebleed immediately."

"How . . . interesting." Noelle thanked the couple and turned to follow Mr. Jensen out of the room and to the staircase she had passed in the corridor. He allowed her to take the steps first, and they climbed in silence. She was grateful that he wasn't fawning and prone to small-talk. On the first landing, he motioned toward an open door.

"This is the sitting room," he told her, taking a step toward it. But Noelle shook her head.

"I'll see it later, please. I would rather go to my room now."

"Right away, Mrs. Somerville."

But he did not stop walking. Noelle heard him speak to someone inside the sitting room, and then a rounded woman, with graying dark hair drawn back into a knot, accompanied him out into the corridor.

"This is Mrs. Beemish, our housekeeper," Mr. Jensen said.

The woman dipped into a quick bob. "Welcome to the *Larkspur*, Mrs. Somerville."

"Thank you," Noelle replied with what she considered heroic restraint.

"Mrs. Beemish will assist me in showing you to your chamber."

Assist you? Noelle caught on then and had to clear her throat to cover a smile. The old fossil was concerned about propriety! Did he really think she was worried that he might attempt to take advantage of her? She walked with the couple down a corridor, pausing again only to be shown the location of the water closet and lavatory.

Noelle decided that the chamber was adequate for the short amount of time she intended to spend here, with its attractively papered walls, rugs on the floor, and comfortable looking—though too heavy for her taste— furniture. She was surprised to see her trunk already on the floor at the foot of her bed. And on the bureau, indeed, sat a vase bursting with purple-blue flowers with triangular petals. *Enough to take care of all the nosebleeds in London*, she thought while tossing her reticule into the upholstered chair by the window. "This will be fine, thank you."

"You have a couple of hours until supper, if you'd like to rest," the housekeeper suggested meekly.

"Actually, I would rather have a bath. Will you have someone draw me one? And I'll take my supper on a tray, as I will be retiring for the night shortly." The manager glanced at the housekeeper and was opening his mouth to reply when Noelle thought of her most pressing concern. "Do send up a sherry first, will you?"

Mr. Jensen cleared his throat. "I'm afraid that is not possible, Mrs. Somerville. This is a temperance establishment."

"Surely you jest."

"Were you not informed by your solicitor?"

"He somehow neglected to mention that part." *Mr. Radley, you'll never practice law again when Quetin finishes with you.* Noelle shrugged. "When will my bath be ready?"

"I'll see to that right away," the housekeeper offered.

"Wait please, Mrs. Beemish," Mr. Jensen said to her before turning again to Noelle. "Now that you have approved of the room, Mrs. Somerville, there is the matter of the interview. I believe we will be more comfortable in the sitting room."

Noelle blinked. "Interview, Mr. Jensen?"

"I take it that your solicitor . . ."

"He's not *my* solicitor," she protested but then sighed. "Very well." She had to spend the night *somewhere*. But first thing in the morning she would wire Quetin and tell him this place was unacceptable. *Surely a person can send a telegraph somewhere in this village.*

As she accompanied Mr. Jensen and the housekeeper back to the sitting room, Noelle thought that it would be best not to advise the manager of her plan to leave as soon as possible. It would surely take Quetin a few days to find her another place to stay or, better yet, come back to his senses and allow her to go back home. Until then, she had no other place to go, and not enough money to pay even if there was one. She sat down on the settee that Mr. Jensen offered.

"You see, Mrs. Somerville, we do not consider the *Larkspur* merely a business," he began after he and Mrs. Beemish had lowered themselves into chairs. "For the welfare of all our lodgers, we strive for harmony . . . not unlike a large family."

"I strive to be agreeable to everyone, Mr. Jensen," Noelle informed him.

"I'm pleased to hear that, Mrs. Somerville. But it is my duty to inform you that we extend that courtesy to the servants as well. And while any of the chambermaids will be only too happy to draw a bath, we do not require them to carry trays up and down the stairs unless a guest is ill. I believe you will find the fellowship in our dining room much to your liking, as I do not boast when I say that the *Larkspur* has the most congenial people you will find at any lodging house."

But of course they would be, Noelle thought, for what was there to argue about once one became old? Which liniment was most effective upon rheumatic joints? "Very well," she replied. "I can live with those conditions." *As long as I don't have to live with them for long.*

Later, Noelle was relieved when one of the chambermaids who introduced herself as Ruth not only drew her a nice warm bath, but hung her clothes in the wardrobe and even offered to press a fresh gown for her. After Mr. Jensen's little speech, she had wondered if she could expect the servants to do anything. With Ruth's assistance, she slipped into a dress of violet percale with tiny black dots. "That will be all," she told the maid, then, remembering Mr. Jensen's comments, added, "Thank you."

"Oh, you're welcome, ma'am," the girl replied from the doorway with a smile across her freckled face. "We hate to see folk leave, mind you, and Mrs. Latrell was a dear lady. But it's exciting to see who comes."

I would imagine anything would be exciting in this place, Noelle told herself as she twisted her waist-length strawberry blond hair into a loose chignon and fastened it with a comb. She felt no need to take great pains with her appearance, for there was not one person under the *Larkspur*'s roof—or in the whole village—whose opinion mattered. That was a depressing thought, and once her hair was arranged, she closed her eyes and allowed her imagination to carry her back to her London flat. She was at her own dressing table preparing for an evening with Quetin. Perhaps they would go to the *Grand Hotel* after the theatre and have lobster.

A lump thickened her throat. If only she could *will* herself home! But when she opened her eyes, the same unfamiliar room was reflected in the mirror in front of her. Sighing, she pulled herself to her feet and thought about how much she hated Averyl Paxton.

*O*ut in the corridor, yet another elderly man was passing by. He stopped to speak with Noelle. "Good evening. Allow me to introduce myself—I'm Randall Ellis." He was scholarly looking, stoop-shouldered with flecks of gray in his beard. "I presume you are Mrs. Somerville?"

Extending her hand, she gave him a polite smile. "Yes, I am."

"May I show you the way to the dining room?" he asked as they shook hands.

It was on the tip of her tongue to reply that she already knew the way. That was the only trouble with being beautiful. Men of all ages, physiques, and professions presumed that the pains she took with her appearance gave them open invitation to flirt. But because she did have to live in harmony with her fellow lodgers for the next few days and happened to be on her way to the dining room anyway, she replied instead, "That's very kind of you, Mr. Elkins."

"Ah . . . it's Ellis."

"Do forgive me." She gave a sheepish little shrug. "I'm afraid I've never been good with names."

"Oh, but you must use my wife's little technique," he said as they walked toward the staircase side by side. "Whenever she meets someone new, she repeats the name under her breath seven times. It's very effective."

"Indeed? Why seven?"

"She read somewhere that it takes seven repetitions of any action to form a habit. And she has always been quite adventurous about trying new ideas."

It was a relief to Noelle that he would mention his wife at length, for men entertaining the illusions of a romance never mentioned their wives unless in the negative sense. "Is your wife downstairs?" she asked.

"Alas, but she resides in Bristol, where our home is. I'm on assignment for the Archeological Association, you see. But I try my best to go home one weekend every month. I do miss her terribly in between times."

The sentiment in the old man's voice was touching, yet it sent a stab of pain through Noelle's heart. Would Quetin miss her as much? A year, or even six months ago she wouldn't have had to ask herself that question. She lapsed into a melancholy silence as they walked downstairs. At the dining room door he courteously stood aside to allow her to enter. A long table stretched out before her, covered with a white cloth and set with Blue Willow china. Most of the chairs on either side were filled with people engaged in chatter. Noelle recognized, besides Mr. Jensen at the head of the table, the three people she had met in the hall—though she couldn't recall their names. And she was surprised to discover two people closer to her own age, sitting on opposite sides of the table and four chairs apart. One was a giant of a man with dark hair, and the other a curiously short-haired woman wearing eyeglasses over an angular face.

"Good evening, everyone," Mr. Ellis said from Noelle's elbow. "Have you met Mrs. Somerville?" This brought conversation to a pause. Faces turned her way, and the men pushed out their chairs to stand.

"Not all of us," Mr. Jensen responded, stepping aside from his chair. He introduced her to Mr. Pitney, the giant, and Miss Rawlins, the bespectacled woman. After Noelle had returned their greetings, the manager led her to an empty chair between the woman who had played the piano and the man who had advised her to stuff periwinkle leaves up her nose should it bleed. The dark-haired giant was directly across from her. Remarkably, besides sending her a bashful smile as she took her chair, he did not attempt to flirt with her.

"Did you find your room agreeable, Mrs. Somerville?" the woman with the braid asked from beside her.

"Quite so," Noelle replied. It was a lie though, not because the room was lacking in comfort, but because it wasn't home.

"Tomorrow you must acquaint yourself with Gresham. It's a charming little village."

"Is there a place from which I could send a wire? I would like to inform my parents that I've settled safely."

"*Trumbles* general merchandise shop," Mr. Jensen offered from the head of the table. "If you care to write your message, I shall be happy to have it delivered over there first thing in the morning."

"That's very kind of you, but I'm looking forward to exploring," she lied again. She certainly didn't want to have anyone read what she would have to say to Quetin.

"Have you lived in London long, Mrs. Somerville?" the periwinkle-gathering woman asked from Noelle's left, leaning forward a little to see past her husband.

112

"All my life," Noelle replied cordially, while wondering exactly when these people intended to eat. In spite of the sandwich she had consumed three hours ago, the aromas wafting from the sideboard were becoming irresistible. She glanced to her left and noticed that two places farther down on the opposite side were still empty.

"Do forgive me for asking, dear, but you're so young . . ." said the woman with the braid, studying her with sympathetic eyes. "How did your husband pass away?"

All attention was focused somberly upon her, even from the two maids flanking the sideboard. Noelle decided that if she was unable to eat, she could at least attempt to chase away the melancholy by amusing herself. With a brave little smile she replied, "John—Major John Somerville—was assigned to the Royal Guard." She had told the Shipleys on the train that he was a captain but decided the story could use some embellishing. "Almost two years ago a man armed with a pistol somehow managed to slip into Buckingham Palace. John discovered him in the corridor just outside the Queen's bedchamber."

"My goodness!" The short-haired woman, who had not spoken except to greet her, raised a hand to her collar. "He shot your husband?"

"Yes, as they struggled for the pistol. John was attempting to disarm him without using his own pistol, you see, for fear of stray shots causing harm to Her Majesty or any of her children."

"What happened to the murderer?" Mrs. Periwinkle asked from her husband's other side.

Noelle allowed herself pause, noting with satisfaction that no one seemed to breathe while waiting for her answer. "Even though wounded, John did manage to wrestle the gun away and shoot the man through the heart. But my husband passed on an hour later." She looked wistfully just over the giant's shoulder, as if her imagination was taking her back to the scene. "Only minutes after I was brought to his side. It was as if he was hanging on to life until he could say good-bye."

A couple of dinner napkins were raised to eyes, so Noelle decided it would be a nice touch to raise her own. "We had only been married three months when it happened."

She was sent pained and sympathetic looks from all directions as a hush settled over the room. From one of the maids Noelle heard a sniff. And then a voice with the faint trace of a Cornish accent came from the doorway, "Please forgive us for keeping you."

Noelle looked to her right. An aristocratically handsome man had just entered the room with a beautiful dark-haired woman upon his arm. As they walked toward the two empty places, he explained, "We were reading and didn't think to mind the time, I'm afraid."

The men at the table rose until the woman was seated. "We didn't mind waiting, Mr. Clay," Mr. Jensen assured him in a somber tone, then gestured toward Noelle. "Have you met Mrs. Somerville?"

"Why, no, we haven't," the man answered, sending a warm smile across the table while the woman with him did the same.

Noelle searched her mind for when she would have seen the man before, for he looked incredibly familiar. *Did he call him Mr. Clay?*

"Ambrose Clay, Mrs. Somerville," the man said. "And this is Fiona, my wife."

"Welcome to the *Larkspur*, Mrs. Somerville," his wife said in a soft Irish lilt.

"Ambrose Clay?" Noelle was stunned silent until she became aware that her mouth was gaping in an unladylike fashion. Quetin was as fond of the theatre as he was the opera, and she could very well recall seeing Mr. Clay onstage. "You're the actor?"

"Guilty," he replied, still smiling.

"Why, I saw you in *The Barrister*."

"Yes? How delightful. I'd like to hear your impression of it." He sent a guilty glance around the room. "But as I tend to wax verbose when discussing theatre, perhaps we shouldn't allow the food to get cold."

Why is he here? Noelle wondered.

Meanwhile, the male lodgers who had stood for Mrs. Clay began assisting the women from their chairs. Mr. Periwinkle pulled out Noelle's chair after helping his wife to her feet. But still no one made a move toward the sideboard. "Mr. Durwin, would you lead us in prayer this evening?" Mr. Jensen asked.

Noelle bowed her head and squeezed her eyes shut. Of course her family had prayed before meals when she lived at home, but it had been so long ago that she had almost forgotten that people did this.

"Our Heavenly Father," the man next to her began, just as Noelle was beginning to wonder if he had heard Mr. Jensen's request.

"We thank Thee for this food and ask that you bless the hands that prepared it. May it nourish our bodies, providing strength to do Thy will. Forgive us where we've failed Thee, and we give thanks that Mrs. Somerville's journey was a safe one. In the name of Jesus Christ our Savior, amen."

"Amen," was echoed softly by the others at the table, and then the men allowed the women to queue up first at the sideboard. As the newest lodger, Noelle was urged to take the lead. Her protests were to no avail.

"Now, enjoy being pampered while you can, dear," the soft-eyed woman said with a pat to her shoulder.

Durwin, Noelle thought, recalling that Mr. Jensen had addressed her husband by such when asking him to pray. Not that it mattered.

"We fairly trample over each other most other times."

"As if you would trample anyone, Mrs. Durwin."

This was said by the Irish woman, Mr. Clay's wife. Noelle found herself a little envious of the camaraderie of these people. There was no evidence of the one-upmanship that permeated her own friendships. Even the two maids were asked about their families as they helped to serve plates. After taking servings of medallions of beef with wild mushrooms and vegetables, Noelle went back to her chair, which Mr. Ellis stepped away from the queue to pull out for her.

When the meal was finished, topped off with an almond-and-caramel tart, Noelle was invited by one and then another to join them in the hall. As weary as she was, she decided that it wouldn't hurt to show a little cordiality. And besides, it would take her mind off Quetin for a while.

"Here, come sit with us," the braided woman invited, taking her arm and leading her to a place on a sofa between her and the bespectacled woman. On the facing sofa sat the periwinkle-gatherers and Mrs. Clay, while the men settled into the chairs close by. The giant had quietly slipped away.

"Mrs. Somerville was telling us about her late husband's untimely demise two years ago," the braided woman said quietly to the Clays. "Before you came to supper." She turned to Noelle. "Still, it must comfort you that he gave his life so courageously."

"Oh, it does," Noelle assured her, eyes wide with sincerity.

"He saved the queen's life." Mrs. Periwinkle's eyes were as wide as Noelle's as she related the whole story to the Clays.

"How terribly tragic that he had to lose his own," Mrs. Clay said in the soft brogue while her husband nodded somberly from the chair beside the sofa.

Noelle noticed how they managed to hold hands upon the upholstered arm between them. A twinge of envy pricked at her. Though Quetin had been good to her, he never displayed affection in public like that, even with a simple gesture such as holding hands. Noelle found herself resenting the delicate beauty of the woman across from her. *No doubt she's been pampered and doted upon her whole life.*

"Did he receive a medal, Mrs. Somerville?" Mr. Jensen was asking. "Posthumously, I mean?"

Noelle nodded, ignoring an annoying little warning voice that told her she was taking her story too far. "A beautiful gold one in the shape of a star. I sleep with it under my pillow."

"May we see it, do you think?" Miss Rawlins asked from Noelle's left, with admiration in her voice. "Forgive me for saying so, but Major Somerville is the embodiment of the courage and dashing that I attempt to portray in my heroes. I compose novelettes, you see, and would love to base one on the events of your husband's life."

"I'm flattered, but I'm afraid I left the medal in my father's safe in London. I feared I would lose it somehow while traveling."

"I wonder why the incident never made the newspapers," Mr. Clay commented. His expression gave no sign of his having misgivings about her story. "Surely this would have been front-page news all over England."

"Why, in every newspaper in the world!" Mr. Durwin corrected.

That reptile Mr. Radley couldn't leave well enough alone, Noelle fumed. He *had* to go and present her as a widow, and now she was forced to invent a past that was beginning to sound overbaked even to her own ears, never mind that Miss Rawlins was staring at her with awe.

What does it matter? You'll be leaving as soon as Quetin finds another place. "It was kept quiet by request of the Queen," she replied finally. "Her majesty didn't want it made known that security could be breached so easily."

"Well, I would hope precautions were taken so that it doesn't happen again," Mr. Ellis declared.

Noelle nodded. "The guard was doubled that very same day, in fact."

Mr. Durwin made a tsking sound. "The man must have been out of his mind."

"Or a political zealot," Mr. Jensen offered.

"He was a member of the Irish Republican Brotherhood," Noelle said. She had heard Quetin mention the terrorists once or twice and could not resist the covert little stab at Mrs. Clay, sitting there so doted upon by the man who any woman in London would give anything to have holding her hand. But she was also careful to send the woman a meaningful look that said, *But, of course, I don't judge you by your nationality.*

For all the discomfort in the Irish woman's expression, Noelle could have declared that the would-be assassin was a leprechaun. In fact, Mrs. Clay gave Noelle a grateful little smile, as if she appreciated her feigned reluctance to spare her feelings. Was she really so naive? Didn't she realize that by being so beautiful and beloved she would immediately incur the dislike of any other beautiful woman in her vicinity?

"Every cause seems to attract its extremists," the braided woman was commenting from Noelle's left. "Why, just look at Mary, Queen of Scots."

Talk ventured in that direction, and Noelle found herself at a loss. If the queen of Scotland was burning people at the stake, shouldn't she be stopped somehow? The world outside London was just too complicated. Her earlier fatigue returned, and she excused herself to retire for the evening.

"Will you remember the way to your room, dear?" Mrs. Durwin asked after the others bade her good-night. "I'll be happy to accompany you upstairs."

Noelle's irritation at the implication that she was simple-minded evaporated as she realized the elderly woman was genuinely concerned about her. These were peculiar people who seemed to have no hidden agendas behind their words. "No, thank you," Noelle replied, even giving her a smile. She went upstairs to find the bed sheets turned down for her and a low lamp burning on her night stand.

Perhaps I should wait before sending that wire, she told herself after changing into a nightgown and slipping into bed. She wouldn't want Quetin to think she was a spoiled child who couldn't at least give the place a chance.

"Well, what did you think of Mrs. Somerville?" Ambrose asked Fiona as he stood behind her at the dressing table and brushed her hair. Fiona wasn't sure when it had become a nightly ritual, but she liked it very much.

"I thought she was pleasant," she replied.

"I suppose."

"Suppose?" He had been in a good mood for the past week, so she hoped this wasn't a sign that the despondency was returning. "You've some doubts about her?"

He pulled the brush gently through her hair again. "The remark about the Irish Republicans. Surely she could tell that you are Irish."

"But if it's the truth, why shouldn't she say it?"

"I hope I'm mistaken, but it seemed to me she rather enjoyed giving out that tidbit of information."

"Ambrose." Fiona directed a reproving look at him through the mirror. "She was describing the person who murdered her husband, and only because we asked. No woman would enjoy speaking of such matters."

"All I'm saying is that I thought I caught something in her expression that made me think she wanted to hurt you."

"She doesn't even know me."

"She knows you're more beautiful than she is."

"But I'm not—"

"Oh yes, you are," he said in a tone that made it clear any further debate would be useless. The brush flowed through her hair again. "That's enough to make her dislike you."

"That would be so shallow," Fiona protested. "Even if that were the case."

"You've never met any shallow people in your twenty-eight years?"

Before she could answer, her husband put the brush upon the table and added, "I'll grant I very well may be wrong. But you, my raven-haired beauty, are too noble for your own good. You assume everyone is as decent as you are, so you're blinded by their faults."

"You exaggerate, you know." Fiona rose from the bench, turned, and put her arms around his shoulders. Raising an eyebrow, she said, "And I do seem to recall certain scriptures warning against judging others."

"Touché, dearest," Ambrose grinned as his arms went about her waist. "But I also recall one about being as wise as serpents and harmless as doves."

"Then I won't lend her any money until I know her better."

"It's not your money I'm worried about." He brushed a kiss upon the tip of her nose. "It's your heart."

Kissing his clefted chin, Fiona smiled. "I'll not be lending my heart to anybody, Ambrose Clay. It belongs entirely to you."

I don't like my eggs runny," Harold Sanders complained Thursday morning to Mrs. Winters, the cook they had hired when his sister, Mercy, married and moved down the lane. Though she didn't take meals with Harold or his father and five brothers, Mrs. Winters had no qualms about using the foot of the table for a work space, even while the family was seated to eat. *Especially* while they were eating lately, for she was determined to torment Papa until he built the little worktable she insisted she needed.

"You'll eat 'em or do without," Mrs. Winters replied gruffly, her broad shoulders bent over the lump of dough she was kneading. With her every motion the table rocked, and the undercooked yokes of his four eggs quivered upon Harold's plate.

"Papa . . ." he whined, only to be silenced by a severe look from the head of the table. His father had determined that a worktable was a waste of time and money and had yet to yield an inch. It was a wonder that the woman had stayed this long with Papa so stubborn, but then there were likely not many families in Gresham who would put up with Mrs. Winters' bossy ways.

"Fernie, you sluice out the milking barn," his father said after crunching down on a piece of overcooked bacon. Mrs. Winters had prepared bacon perfectly until she got the notion for the worktable in her head. Turning to Harold, he said, "I want you and Dale to haul thet load of manure behind the haybarn over to the turnips." The turnip patch was in the back pasture, surrounded by a wood rail fence to keep the cattle from eating until they bloated and died. Most of the vegetables would be stored to provide winter forage along with the hay.

"We'll have to wait for the wagon," twenty-eight-year-old Dale replied, for Oram would soon be delivering milk to the cheese factory and then driving Edgar and Jack to school.

"No need to put more wear on the wagon 'til we get another made. Use the wheelbarrow."

After an exchange of outraged glances with Dale, Harold protested, "But it'll take all day!"

Their father ignored the loud thump from the foot of the table, where a tight-jawed Mrs. Winters had just slapped down the mound of dough. "Not if you put your backs into it."

Later, after Harold had heaved what had to be his hundredth shovelful of manure into the barrow, he paused to wipe his brow with a grimy sleeve. "Papa ain't got the right to treat us like this."

"No, he don't," Dale agreed but kept on shoveling. "Come on, let's get it done with. I don't wanter be here all day."

Now Harold was interested. Of the two, he was considered the fighter and Dale the lover. At least that was what *they* considered themselves. "You seeing somebody later?"

A grin spread under Dale's forest green eyes, so like Harold's own. "Lucy Bates. She works on a pig farm in Myddle. She's got a sister who ain't too rough on the eyes. Wanter come along?"

Just days ago the idea would have been tempting, but then Harold reckoned he had gained some maturity over the past few days. He was thirty-one years old, with nothing to show for it. Yes, the farm would go to him when his father passed on, but the man was strong as a stump and would likely outlive all of them. If he didn't take hold of his life and make some plans for the future soon, Harold could easily see himself drifting along year after year, slaving for his father and having to put up with Mrs. Winters' vinegary comments.

It was his chance meeting with the schoolmistress, Miss Clark, that gave him a little ray of hope for the future. Schoolmistresses were paid wages, and besides that, her father owned the iron foundry. That meant there would likely be a good-sized dowry if she ever wed. He lifted another shovelful. *Her papa's likely wondering if he'll ever marry her off.* Why, a decent dowry would give him the funds to get his own farm. *And nobody to tell me what to do.*

"What are you grinnin' at?" his brother asked, leaning on his shovel to wipe his nose with the tail of his shirt.

"Just thinking about Miss Clark."

"That school lady?"

"I'm thinking about courtin' her."

"*Her?*"

Harold felt his temperature rising. "What's wrong with that?"

"She looks like a monkey for one thing, with those ears. And she's tall as a maypole."

"But she don't slop pigs for a livin'," Harold shot back. "Looks ain't everything, you know. She's got a nice voice . . . and besides, her ears don't stick out as much as Constable Reed's."

"Well, I wouldn't court Constable Reed either."

Just as he was on the verge of throwing down his shovel and taking Dale by the throat, Harold forced himself to calm down. He couldn't fault his brother for having no idea about planning for the future. Dale wasn't the brightest one in the family.

With a grunt Harold hefted another load. "If she helps me get away from this place, it don't matter what she looks like."

They both shoveled in silence for a few minutes, topping off the barrow. It was Dale's turn to haul it across the barnyard and pasture to the turnip patch. He wiped his face with his shirt again and glanced at the cottage. "This is stupid . . . not bein' able to use the wagon. We would'ha been finished by now."

"Maybe when I get my own place you can come work for me."

An eyebrow cocked on his brother's grime-smeared forehead. "You think that schoolmistress will help you do that?"

Harold nodded. "She still lives at home, so she must have a fair amount of wages saved up." He mentioned his hopes for a dowry as well.

Finally Dale seemed impressed. Picking up the barrow by both handles, he said, "Well, you'd best make sure you court her the right way."

"What do you mean?"

His younger brother actually wore an expression of wisdom. "I learnt with Mary, over to the *Bow and Fiddle*, that you can't just go tellin' a woman you want to court her. You have to make her want to court you too."

"How do you do that?"

Dale raised a hand to scratch his head, which was a mistake because the top-heavy barrow tipped over to the right, dumping its contents to the ground. He let out a curse that would have curdled even Papa's ears and righted the barrow again. Any other day Harold would have found some shade and sat out his brother's refilling of the barrow, but curiosity led him to pick up both shovels.

"Here," he said, handing one over to Dale. They began shoveling again. "How do you make a woman *want* to court you?"

"Well, I ain't exactly sure when it comes to somebody like Miss Clark. All I had to do was whistle and wink at Lucy, but proper women don't like that."

"Then how am I gonter know what to do?"

Dale raised a hand again, but this time he wasn't holding the barrow's handles, so no damage was done. After a second or two of serious head scratching, he gave Harold a self-satisfied smile. "You ask Mercy."

Four hours later when the work was finished, Harold and Dale slipped off to bathe in the creek behind the pastures. Harold didn't mind grime on his clothes and skin—a fellow couldn't very well farm without it—but some grime was worse than others. They hadn't thought to bring a change of clothes, so they beat their soiled shirts and trousers against the trunk of an apple tree on the bank.

He couldn't wait to get over to Mercy's to ask her advice, but then lunchtime was upon him, and of course his papa had thought up other chores. "Scrub out the water troughs," he told Harold around a mouthful of pork-and-turnip stew. "And have it done by milking."

That gave him only two hours until time to bring the cattle from pasture for the afternoon milking, but Harold worked harder than he had ever worked. When the chore was done he still had an hour remaining. He changed his clothes and ran the half mile to Seth Langford's horse farm, thoughts of Miss Clark and her handsome dowry giving him speed. Panting, he let himself in the gate in front of the two-story stone cottage. His sister, Mercy, lived here with her husband, Seth Langford, stepson Thomas, who was nine and would be at school now, and baby Amanda. Harold heard his name and waved a greeting to Seth, who was leading a horse and newborn colt into one of the paddocks in front of the stables.

He liked Seth. Everyone had thought the Londoner was daft when he first came to Gresham with the intention of raising horses, but he had shown them all. At last count he had three dozen well-bred Cleveland bays, not counting the recent batch of colts. And the word around Shropshire was that his stock was far superior than any animal a person could get in Wolverhampton.

And Seth Langford wouldn't allow Papa to boss him around, which made Harold admire and envy him all the more. Only two other people had managed to do that in Harold's lifetime—Mrs. Winters, and that Mrs. Kingston, who was now Squire Bartley's wife, who had persuaded Papa to send Jack and Edgar to Mr. Raleigh's school. He had to add his sister, Mercy, to that list, he supposed, though she had only stood up to their father during her last few months at home.

He opened the door and walked on into the tidy parlor. "Mercy?"

From above him came a muffled "Help!"

Harold bounded up the staircase, two steps at a time, and found Mercy in her room bending curiously over the bed. He recognized Amanda's gurgling chatter from beneath his sister's long curly hair, then saw a little foot move. Mercy, whose face was hidden from him, said, "Seth?"

"It's me—Harold."

She gave a little laugh. "Help me get my hair loose. Every time I pry one hand open, she grabs another handful."

"All right." Chuckling at the notion of a grown woman being trapped by a six-month-old, he sat on the edge of the bed and reached for a little hand. "Can't you just pull it out?"

"It might cut her. Just untangle that hand and I'll get the other."

Soon his sister was freed, and Amanda, who must have thought it was a fine game, kicked her hands and feet and made cooing noises at Harold. She wore a pink flannel gown, and her soft fair hair quivered on her head like thistles in a breeze every time she moved. "Whew!" Mercy exclaimed, raising herself again. "I'll know not to change a nappie halfway through repinning my hair again." She handed him a cloth, rolled into a ball. "Would you toss that in the pail in the corner?"

"Ugh!" Harold shied away as if she held a snake.

"Sissy," she teased and did it herself. Harold would have thrashed on the spot any *man* who dared to call him that, but now he just shrugged. Mercy had changed so much since her marriage to Seth, losing the tired, worried look she had worn at home all the time. Why, she even seemed younger to him now.

"Hold Amanda and let me tend to my hair, will you?" she asked him.

He picked up the baby and sat her on his knee, facing her mother, who sat only a couple of feet away. Amanda immediately twisted around and attempted to push her fingers in his mouth, so that he had to raise his chin to talk. "I come to ask you about Miss Clark. You know, the schoolmistress."

"Yes?" Mercy turned to him, hairpins between her teeth. "What about her?"

"I want to court her, but Dale says you have to court women like her different."

"Different-*ly*."

"What?"

"Never mind."

Still facing him, she wove her hair with both hands behind her head. It wasn't until after her marriage that Harold realized his sister was comely to look at, somehow having escaped all the male Sanders' deep-lidded, froglike eyes. Her eyes were a calm hazel, set over a slightly upturned nose in a serious face that could break into a smile at any minute. *She looks like Mother*, Harold thought with a little lump in his throat. Only their mother hadn't smiled much.

"I have to wonder . . . why Miss Clark?" Mercy was saying as she stabbed hairpins into the knot. "You've never shown interest in anyone like her before."

You too? Harold thought. He surely didn't expect Mercy to be as snooty as Dale had been. "Just because she's homely don't mean she ain't nice."

His sister shook her head, her mouth a straight line. "She's not homely at all, Harold. That's not what I meant. But to put it bluntly, she has high moral standards."

"I like women with high moral . . . what did you say?"

"Standards."

"I like women with those," he defended, though he still wasn't quite sure what that last word had meant.

"Yes? Name one that you've ever courted."

That hurt. "A man can change, Mercy."

"Yes, Harold. But usually not overnight."

"Weren't overnight. I've been feelin' this way since the Saturday before last. And by the way, Miss Clark gave me a ride to Shrewsbury in her papa's trap, and we got along real good."

"You did?" His sister stretched forward to take the wiggling Amanda from his arms. "My mistake, then. But the way to get any decent woman interested in you would be to be decent yourself."

"How do you do that?"

Now it was Mercy who tried to talk around the busy little fingers at her lips. "Any other time I would urge you to become a Christian, Harold. But not just so you can attract a woman. God's salvation isn't to be treated frivolously."

Harold hated it when she used big words, but he was relieved when she did not go on, for he had heard enough of Mercy's sermons. "Is there anything else, then?

"Well, church certainly wouldn't do you any harm. And it just may happen that—"

"I can't do that."

"Fernie went last Sunday."

"Only because Jack beat him at mumblety-peg." He shuddered. He had only been in church twice in his life—his mother's funeral at Saint Jude's, and Mercy's wedding at the Wesleyan chapel. They were both depressing places, with folks wearing dour faces that would dry the cows right up if they wore them to milking. And they talked about God too much. God was equally depressing, to Harold's way of thinking, because He didn't want people to have any fun.

"But He changes your notion of what fun is when you give Him control of your life," Mercy had argued once when he stated that opinion to her.

Well, the last thing Harold wanted was someone else controlling his life. Papa was bad enough.

"Well, what's next on the list after church?" he asked, as if he was reconsidering that step.

She rested her chin lightly atop Amanda's little head. "I like it when Seth brings me flowers and leaves little notes where I'll find them . . ."

"Flowers and notes," Harold said under his breath. He couldn't read or write, but Jack and Edgar could. In fact, Papa complained that going to school had ruined them, for they always seemed to have their noses stuck in books lately. Just last week Jack had gotten the strap for balancing a book upon his knees as he milked a cow, getting more milk on the outside than the inside of the pail.

" . . . and when he asks my advice," his sister went on.

This took him by surprise. Big strong Seth Langford asking advice of a woman? "About what?"

"About anything. It makes me feel he thinks that I'm intelligent."

"What?"

"Bright."

"Women like to feel bright?"

"Why, yes," she replied, giving him a curious look. "Don't you?"

No one had ever accused Harold of being bright, so he wasn't quite sure. From downstairs the cabinet clock, a gift from the squire's wife to Seth and Mercy on their first anniversary, sent up two chimes. He jumped from the bed. "Got to go, or Papa will skin me alive."

———————

Later that afternoon when the two youngest boys had returned from school, Harold took Edgar aside by the well and said, "I want you to write me a note."

Immediately the fourteen-year-old balked. "I got the strap last time I did that."

"This ain't to Mr. Pool." It was just like Edgar to bring that up again, even after so many months. That plan would have worked, if only the innkeeper hadn't known that Papa couldn't read or write. Fortunately, Edgar had not dragged Harold down with him but owned up to asking for the bottle of gin on credit himself.

"Why don't you get Jack to do it?" Edgar asked.

" 'Cause you write better."

"How do you know if you can't read?"

Weary of his brother's uppityness, Harold seized him by the shoulder. "I hear talk. Now, are you gonter do it, or do I have to . . ."

"All right, then," Edgar cut in, frowning and pulling away. "What do you want me to write?"

He hadn't considered that. "Put down . . . 'Miss Clark, I'm fond of you, you have a pretty voice.' "

The boy's eyes widened. "You like Miss Clark?"

Harold gave him a warning scowl. "What's wrong with that?"

"Nothing," Edgar said hastily. "I'll write it after supper. Do you want me to sign your name?"

Harold nodded and went on to finish up his chores. Now all he had to do was get some nice flowers, but with a village full of gardens that wouldn't be too difficult.

———

The next morning Lydia left her parents' cottage with Mr. Pitney's handkerchief in her satchel, having received it back from Mrs. Moore with the rest of the laundry yesterday afternoon. She expected that she would see the archeologists, for she had passed both every morning since Sunday. Each time Mr. Pitney had given her a smile that, though retaining the same timidity as before, was altered somewhat by a slight lift of the brows. It was as if he wondered if she was completely recovered from Sunday's humiliation at the crossroads, yet dared not embarrass her by asking in front of Mr. Ellis.

And every morning Lydia had returned the smile with a little nod, which was her own unspoken message, *Yes, I'm fine . . . thanks to your chivalry and kindness.* She hoped that he would not mind her handing over the handkerchief in this manner as he was leaving for his work. It seemed too ceremonious for her to deliver it to him at the *Larkspur*, but too ungrateful simply to ask one of the inn's servants to give it to him.

Hearing the familiar crunches of gravel, Lydia paused at the end of the carriage drive. She was surprised when a lone figure came around the wing from the courtyard. She returned Mr. Pitney's smile and reached into her satchel.

"Good morning, Miss Clark," he said when she raised her head again.

Lydia returned the greeting, followed by, "I hope Mr. Ellis isn't ill."

"Quite the contrary, thank you." Mr. Pitney stopped a respectable two feet in front of her, his leather sack hanging from one broad shoulder. "He'll be joining me later. An old chum from his university days is passing through Shrewsbury later this morning, and they arranged to meet between trains."

As he spoke, Lydia noticed Mr. Herrick leading one of the horses from the stables. The caretaker raised a hand to Lydia, and she waved back with the same hand that held the handkerchief.

"It's clean now," she told Mr. Pitney as she handed it over, thinking how ludicrous that sounded. Would he have expected her to return it in any other condition? "I do appreciate your lending it to me."

"You're welcome." After tucking the cloth into his coat pocket, he looked at her as if he wanted to say more. Indeed, his dark eyebrows lifted slightly.

"I'm fine," Lydia volunteered impulsively.

"Yes? I wanted to ask, but . . . ."

"I know."

Relief washed over his darkly handsome face. "It's as my mother said to my sister, Gloria, when she went through the same unfortunate situation—*time heals all wounds*. And now Gloria is married to a very decent—"

It was at his point that Lydia stopped smiling blankly and gasped, "You thought that Mr. Towly was breaking courtship with me?"

"Well, uh, wasn't that...?"

She recalled being uncertain of exactly how long Mr. Pitney had stood on the other side of Market Lane on Sunday past. Truly, someone hearing Mr. Towly's parting remarks could have drawn an incorrect conclusion. She shook her head with the same fervor she'd use if someone had asked if she were an anarchist. "I was informing the man that I would not be courted by *him*, Mr. Pitney."

Color flooding his cheeks, he sent a quick glance full of longing toward the Anwyl's crest. "Please forgive me, Miss Clark. I fear I jumped to the wrong—"

"Indeed you did, Mr. Pitney." And the very notion that all week he had assumed that she was pining away for Mr. Towly's removed affections suddenly struck her as funny. So much so that she let out a little chuckle.

Mr. Pitney's eyes widened. "Miss Clark?"

"Oh, Mr. Pitney!" She covered her mouth with her hand as waves of mirth shook her shoulders. When she could speak again, she said, "Forgive me, but that's rich!"

"It is?" Tentatively he smiled. "I confess he didn't seem well-suited to you, Miss Clark."

"But he considered himself well-suited to my dowry."

"Indeed?" The archeologist directed a frown toward the crossroads, as if he could still see the dairy farmer in his wagon. "Well, you were well-rid of him then, weren't you?"

"Like the whale was well-rid of Jonah, Mr. Pitney."

Now it was he who chuckled, and so heartily that Lydia found herself caught up in another spate of laughter. When their mirth was spent, they stood there smiling until Lydia remembered that she had duties to attend, as did he. She moved her satchel to her left hand and held out her right. "I do appreciate your concern, Mr. Pitney."

Still smiling, he took her hand. "And I appreciate your not being angry with me."

"Not at all, Mr. Pitney."

They bade each other good-day, and as she walked to school, her mind summoned up the whole exchange twice—as one would call for an encore to a particularly enjoyable performance. *I wonder why such a nice man hasn't married yet?* But as her steps were turning onto Bartley Lane, she made herself turn her mind to the day ahead of her.

Should try to finish reading Lorna Doone so we can start something else Monday, Lydia thought as she switched her satchel to her left hand and opened the schoolhouse door. *Something short so we'll have time to finish*. It was hard to believe that April had only four more days remaining. Summer would be upon them before they knew it.

With the door open, she set the satchel down just inside and started drawing drapes and opening windows, her first duty of the day because one must have air and light before anything else could be accomplished. One of the windows on the north side was proving a bit stubborn, so she had to put her shoulder into it before it raised with a spine-chilling squeak. *I'll have to ask Mr. Sykes to have someone fix it*, she told herself. Had the day been rainy, she might not have been able to raise it at all.

The Luck of the Roaring Camp suddenly popped into her mind. She was positive Mrs. Dearing would lend it to her again. The collection of short stories by a San Franciscan news editor, Bret Harte, would not only acquaint the children with a time and way of life different from their own, but she could definitely finish it by the end of May.

Perfect, she thought, smiling as she raised the second north-facing window. It never ceased to amaze her how God had created the mind to continue working when a question had been posed to it, even when the person has gone on to think about other things. A fitting scripture came to her mind: *I will praise thee; for I am fearfully and wonderfully made.*

When she had made the full circle of the room raising windows, she collected her satchel from the door. That was when she noticed the bouquet of daisies in a canning jar upon her desk. *Mr. Pitney* was her immediate thought, irrational that it was. She quashed it immediately, for fantasies were for schoolgirls. "Please Lord, not Mr. Towly," she prayed on her way across the room. She set her satchel on the edge of the desk and picked up the folded sheet of paper propped against the jar.

Dear Miss Clark,
I am mean as a snake and stupid as a box of rocks.
Will you marry me?

With fondest regards,
Harold Sanders

"Obviously he didn't write this himself," her father said that evening at the supper table, trying to compose himself after a good chuckle. He squinted at the neatly printed note. "I don't think any of those Sanders can read except for the two in school."

"And the daughter," Lydia's mother reminded. "She married that horse farmer, Mr. Langford."

"I would assume one of his younger brothers played a trick upon him," Lydia ventured. She did not tell them that it had stung a little, for it was a variation of a game that had been played occasionally in the school yard back when she was head and shoulders taller than all of the boys her age. When a boy wanted to tease another into trading fisticuffs, all he had to say was, "You're going to marry Lydia Clark." The Sanders boys had reputations as pranksters. She did not appreciate being the ammunition one used to play a prank on another.

But by the time Mrs. Tanner had served a dessert of chestnut pudding, Lydia had consoled herself with the thought that it was far preferable to be ammunition for a prank than the object of Harold Sander's affection.

Chapter 16

$\mathcal{M}$r. Trumble tells me you've assisted him with donating his marble collection to the British Museum," Mr. Durwin said to Jacob and Mr. Ellis Friday night over a supper of stuffed breast of wood pigeon with marsala sauce. "I must say he's excited about it."

First dabbing his mouth with his napkin, Mr. Ellis replied, "We shipped them off with our last batch of artifacts—except for a handful that have sentimental meaning to him."

"Have you found any more uphill?" asked Mr. Clay.

"Dozens, actually. It was a popular game among the Roman children."

"And to think . . . I thought marbles were a new invention when my brother brought some home as a boy," Mrs. Dearing declared, shaking her head with wonder.

Mr. Ellis chuckled. "They would have been had you lived in Egypt three thousand years before Christ, Mrs. Dearing."

"Three *thousand* years?"

"B.C.," he reminded her.

Even Mrs. Somerville, who was rather quiet most of the time, looked interested. "But how can you tell by looking at a marble how old it is?"

"That would fall under the realm of Mr. Pitney's expertise," Mr. Ellis replied with a smile in Jacob's direction.

Jacob had long ago figured out that this was the older man's way of graciously drawing him into the discussions. And it had been effective over the past two years, for Jacob found himself far more at ease among his fellow lodgers than he had been during those first few months. *Except for Miss Rawlins.*

But even she was looking at him expectantly now. He cleared his throat and prayed he didn't have food between his teeth. "The oldest set we're aware of was found buried with an Egyptian child in a grave site at Nagada. And once the date of the grave was determined by translating the hieroglyphics, it was simple to determine the age of the marbles."

"Were they of glass, Mr. Pitney?" Mrs. Durwin asked.

Jacob smiled at her. He liked Mrs. Durwin, recognizing in her the same timidity that had plagued him all of his life. "They were carved of semiprecious stones, Mrs. Durwin. But marbles have been made of all sorts of materials through the ages—clay, hazelnuts, even ordinary stone."

"Then how did they come to be named marbles?"

This question was posed by Miss Rawlins, incredibly enough. With his heart beating a little faster in his chest, he replied, "It was the Greeks who named them thus—or rather, *marmaros*, which was their term for the polished white agate they used."

The sweet that followed the meal was apple-and-raisin pie, Jacob's favorite, but in his state of happiness he could scarcely taste it. At last he had found a subject that interested Miss Rawlins besides her books, which he was sadly ill-qualified to discuss.

He dawdled as the lodgers left the dining room, staying behind to help Sarah carry an overloaded tray to the kitchen. By the time he reached the hall, everyone had settled into chairs and sofas save the Clays and Mrs. Somerville, who had retired for the evening. Gratefully Jacob noticed that Miss Rawlins had taken her usual seat by the fireplace, in which a hearty fire snapped and hissed against the evening chill.

She glanced at him as he ambled over to take the chair next to hers but turned her attention back to the discussion among Mr. Durwin, Mrs. Dearing, and Mr. Ellis over the identities of the "giants of the earth" in the sixth chapter of the book of Genesis. Jacob listened with only rudimentary attention, his mind consumed with how to initiate another conversation with Miss Rawlins. Finally a lull occurred in the discussion—apparently the three different opinions had reached an impasse. Jacob saw his chance and seized it.

"Miss Rawlins?"

She turned to look at him. "Yes, Mr. Pitney?"

The light from the fireplace reflected in her spectacles and shielded her eyes, which unnerved him a bit. Still he ventured forth. "Would you be interested in knowing how marbles were used for divination purposes by ancient priests in the Near East?"

He was encouraged when she smiled. But his own smile grew stiff upon his face as he listened to her reply.

"No doubt it's a fascinating story, Mr. Pitney. But I had just a moment ago decided to retire for the night. I'm quite fatigued." She covered a yawn with her hand as if to give proof.

"I . . . I pray you rest well," Jacob managed.

"Thank you."

After bidding everyone a pleasant night she was gone, leaving Jacob feeling twice the idiot because the others present had probably eaves-dropped upon another fumbling attempt at conversation. He felt his cheeks flame and wondered bitterly why they were so wont to betray him— weren't blushes only supposed to occur on female faces?

He couldn't get up and leave, or it would appear that he was following Miss Rawlins. And so he stared miserably into the fire. After a little while had passed, Mrs. Dearing walked over to sit in the chair beside him.

"I wish I had a daughter, Mr. Pitney," she said kindly. "I wouldn't rest until you and she were courting."

Jacob shook his head. "No doubt she would find me a bore, Mrs. Dearing."

"You? Heaven forbid! Why, you're one of the most interesting people I know."

Of course she was only trying to cheer him, but he gave her an appreciative smile. "Thank you for saying that."

"Oh, but it's true." She glanced over at the others, now discussing whether they preferred broiled or baked fish, and lowered her voice. "Miss Rawlins loves to discuss her novelettes. I realize that your occupation consumes enormous amounts of time, but perhaps if you were to read some of them?"

"I've already done so. And she despises me the more for it. It seems I can't recognize the most obvious of symbolism."

"Yes? Well, you mustn't fault yourself. Clearly your mind is more scientific than perspicacious."

"Perspi—"

"Discerning. At least in the case of fiction." Mrs. Dearing pursed her lips thoughtfully for several seconds, then smiled. "I believe I have a solution, Mr. Pitney."

"You have?"

"Miss Clark."

"I beg your pardon?" Jacob said. "You mean the schoolmistress?"

"I have spoken with her on many occasions at the lending library. She's the most well-read woman I've ever met. If she can't ferret out the symbolism in Miss Rawlins' books, no one can."

"But I hardly know her. And certainly not well enough to ask a favor."

"I'm not suggesting you do that, Mr. Pitney. What I'm suggesting is that you offer to commission her services."

"Hire someone to read books?"

"Why is that so strange? People are hired every day to exercise their particular skills. Summer is fast approaching, and I daresay she would enjoy the task."

The whole notion seemed so hopeless that Jacob felt emotionally drained. "I don't know, Mrs. Dearing . . ."

The elderly woman's lips tightened, giving her the appearance of a stern schoolmistress. "Mr. Pitney, the American poet John Greenleaf Whittier had something to say about this situation."

"He did?"

She lifted her chin and quoted softly:

> Of all sad words of tongue or pen,
> The saddest are these: "It might have been!"

Resuming her "stern schoolmistress" expression, she asked, "Will you ask yourself twenty years from now, when it's too late, if you could have won Miss Rawlins' hand with just a little more effort?"

Her argument crumbled his defenses so completely that all he could do was mumble, "I suppose it wouldn't hurt to speak with Miss Clark."

She smiled, reached over, and patted his cheek as if he were but seven years old. "Such a bright young man you are, Mr. Pitney."

The quarterly regional meeting of the diocese was to be held in Lockwood on Saturday, which would be Vicar Paul Treves' first time to host it. For that reason Andrew prepared to leave Gresham a half hour earlier than necessary to see if he could lend assistance in any way. "But won't you hinder him from dressing?" Julia asked while he ate a quick breakfast of toast and jam with his tea.

"If I know Paul, he dressed himself hours ago," was Andrew's confident reply. For the young vicar reminded him so much of himself in his early years—so unsure of himself among his peers, and so conscious of crossing every *t* and dotting every *i* correctly.

At least Paul had shed some of the stuffed-shirt notions he had held two years ago while courting Elizabeth. A wise old bishop had once remarked to Andrew that a minister was of no earthly use until his heart had been broken. Well, that had certainly occurred when Elizabeth broke off their courtship. Since being assigned to the neighboring village, Paul looked to Andrew as a mentor, often asking advice about how to minister to his own parishioners. Evident in the young man's character now was more empathy and more patience with people's shortcomings.

Just a quarter of a mile east of the vicarage lane, the wheels of Andrew's trap left cobbled stones for the macadamized roadway leading eight miles through Gipsy woods so embowered with trees that it resembled a pleasantly cool green tunnel. It had been little more than a dirt path until five years ago when Squire Bartley expanded his cheese factory and began purchasing milk from the neighboring village. Of course Lockwood's dairy farmers needed a good road for making deliveries.

The village broke into Andrew's vision as soon as his horse and trap left the woods. Sequestered in a gradual hollow, it was a pleasant hamlet where black-and-white friesians grazed in hedged pastures, and weathered buildings of stone, brick, half-timbering, and wattle-and-daub rubbed shoulders together in an amiable fashion. The fine fifteenth-century tower of the red sandstone church of Saint Luke's roosted on a little knoll overlooking the village. Andrew tied Rusty's reins to the picket fence surrounding the half-timbered vicarage, opened the gate, and walked the path through the garden.

Fine day for a meeting, he thought, but carried his umbrella crooked over one arm just in case the smell in the air of forthcoming rain wasn't his imagination. There was no bell chain at the door, so he knocked four times in a row. After at least two uneventful minutes had passed, Andrew gave a much stouter series of knocks while wondering if Paul had gone ahead to the town hall. *Of course.* Be it like him to hover over the women trying to set up tables and refreshments.

He had just turned to leave when the squeak of the doorknob roused his attention. The door opened several inches, and Paul Treves' face appeared, blinking and slack-jawed.

"Vicar Phelps?"

This is the twenty-seventh? Andrew asked himself. But of course it was, for all of his absent-mindedness, he had yet to forget an important date. The door opened wider, exposing a wrinkled flannel dressing gown and bare feet.

"Paul?" Andrew said. "Why aren't you dressed?"

The young man blinked again. "What time is it?"

"Half-past eight," Andrew replied after fishing his watch from the fob pocket of his trousers.

"Oh no!" Paul backed away from the door. "Come in, please. I was up all night with the Gripps, and—"

"You're ill?"

He shook his head and started for the staircase, motioning for Andrew to follow. "The Gripps—Stanley Gripp is a carpenter. Doctor Rhodes had to amputate his foot yesterday from gangrene."

"I'm so sorry," Andrew said, jogging up the steps behind him.

"Me too. But to hear Mr. Gripp joke about it beforehand, it was all a lark. He was making all sorts of plans for the wooden foot he was going to carve himself."

Andrew winced. "Well, a merry heart and all that . . ."

"He wasn't so merry afterward, I'm afraid. But he'll rouse himself in good form."

They had reached a bedroom, where the young vicar hurried over to the washstand. "Still a little warm," he said, dipping fingers into the pitcher. "Israel must have filled it this morning. I wonder why he didn't wake me?"

"Where is everyone?"

"Mrs. Coggins would be at the hall helping lay out refreshments. And no doubt Israel has been put to arranging chairs." He poured some of the water into the bowl. "You know, I do seem to recall his speaking to me sometime this morning. But it's all fuzzy."

"Shall I make you some tea?"

"No, thank you. The shock has me well awake now." He turned from the mirror while vigorously banging the sides of a shaving brush against the inside of a mug. "But I would have been suicidal if you hadn't shown up and got me on my feet. Oh . . . do have a seat, will you?"

Andrew pulled out the chair from a writing table and watched the young man spread lather all over his face. "Your clothes?"

"Mrs. Coggins will no doubt have them laid out in the room next door. Will you get them for me?"

"But of course." Leaving the chair he had just settled into, he went into the corridor and on into another bedroom, where a black suit and white shirt lay across the bed. Paul was already drying his face when Andrew returned with the clothes over his arm. "That was fast."

"Hit or miss." The young man turned to him again and raised an anxious eyebrow. "You won't tell anyone about this, will you?"

"I suppose I could keep it quiet for a couple of years."

"I beg your pardon?"

"Time has a way of bringing out the humor of circumstances." Andrew smiled. "Trust me, in two years you'll be telling people about it yourself."

After a bemused pause, the young man returned his smile. "I wish I had your maturity, Vicar Phelps."

"In due time, my friend. And with it come the gray hairs and wrinkles, so don't wish too hard."

The young man looked doubtful as he shrugged off his dressing gown and picked up the white shirt. "Youth isn't always all it's touted to be."

"Now, there's a truth," Andrew had to agree. There was something to be said for the calm waters of maturity, as opposed to the turbulent currents of youth. But both had their purposes, and he would not presume to improve upon the way God had designed His creation.

They walked over to the town hall, situated on the green just as Gresham's. Just stepping down from the portico was Israel Coggins, vicarage caretaker and son of vicarage housekeeper, Mrs. Coggins. Thin as a lath and white as an altar sheet under a mop of unruly brown hair, the seventeen-year-old was the most timid creature Andrew had ever met. He rarely even looked anyone beside Vicar Treves or his mother in the eyes.

"Mother says I must have not woke you good," he said to Paul with halting speech. "But I did, didn't I?"

"You did fine, Israel," Paul said, patting the boy's arm. He motioned toward Andrew with his other hand. "You remember Vicar Phelps, don't you?"

"Rusty is your horse's name," the boy recalled, turning his head to stare at some point over his own left shoulder.

Andrew chuckled. "That's right. And he remembers you, too, I've no doubt."

"That's because I give him apples." He smiled and asked Paul, "May I give him one now, Vicar?"

"Of course. If your mother is finished with you in there, that is."

"She said to see if you was awake and needed anything."

"Well then, I suppose I need Vicar Phelps' horse watered and given some oats."

The boy hurried away in a shambling gait, and Andrew accompanied the young vicar into the town hall. Mrs. Coggins returned Andrew's wave from the far end of the room, where she and two other women were arranging refreshments on a cloth-covered table. Only two other vicars had arrived—Vicar Wright from Myddle and Vicar Nippert from Prescott were drinking tea and engaged in conversation among the dozen chairs that had been grouped together. Or rather, Andrew realized as he drew closer, Vicar Nippert was extolling the talents of his daughter Ernestine into the other vicar's captive ear.

"I had half a mind to bring her with me today," Vicar Nippert enthused. "Everyone so enjoys her singing. But Vicar Treves being so young and all . . . I feared he would take it as a reflection upon his—"

"Good morning, gentlemen," Andrew cut in after a conspiratorial wink at Paul.

The two turned to look at him. Both rose to their feet and held out hands. Vicar Nippert's smile exposed two rows of prominent teeth, and Vicar Wright's face wore an expression of relief. Other clergymen began arriving shortly. Cups of tea were passed out by the women, who left the hall when white-haired Bishop Edwards stood to call the meeting to order. After an hour of old and new business had been discussed, the women slipped back into the room with fresh pots of tea, and Paul nervously invited everyone to avail themselves of the refreshments upon the table.

"Everything is going well," Andrew reassured him while their fellow clergymen chatted and stacked sandwiches and small cakes on their plates.

"You don't think I should have held it in the vicarage, do you?" Paul looked around him. "I thought my parlor would be too small, but this room is so overwhelming . . ."

"It's fine, really." He caught sight of some unruly brown hair on the other side of the refreshment table, where Israel was assisting his mother. An idea crossed his mind. "But why don't you ask Israel to play?"

He blinked, uncomprehending. "Play?"

"During the break. None of the others have heard him, and I believe they would enjoy it."

"Do you think the bishop would mind?"

"Not at all. But I'll ask him while you speak with Israel, if you'd rather." *After all, he's sat through Ernestine Nippert's song after song.* Which reminded Andrew. "Just make sure you warn him to stop after one song."

And so five minutes later, Israel Coggins had seated himself with his beloved stringed dulcimer on his knees. With his face turned to the left, so he did not have to look at his audience, he began fingering the rich strains of "Come Thou Fount of Every Blessing." A hush fell over the gathering. From the serving table Mrs. Coggins beamed with pride.

And the silence did not break when the last notes had resonated through the room, until Bishop Edwards stood and said, "You have a rare gift, son. I have read of the dulcimer in the Bible but have never seen nor heard one. Will you play another song for us?"

The boy looked to Paul for permission and received a smile and nod. He played "Amazing Grace" so sweetly that Andrew noticed Vicar Stillman of Bomere Heath wiping his eyes. "Do you know any more?" the bishop asked Israel in the reverent silence that followed.

"Yes, sir," Israel mumbled bashfully to that point over his left shoulder.

Paul Treves stood to say, with a considerable lessening of anxiety in his young face, "He can play any hymn he has ever heard. Just tell him what you would like to hear."

The bishop asked for "Abide with Me," which the boy played without a sour note, though he never looked down at the fingers that traveled the delicate chords. Others asked for songs, and Israel delivered them expertly. It was with a regretful expression that Bishop Edwards finally rose to his feet again. "We must resume our meeting, but I could listen to you all day, son. Will you accompany your fine Vicar Treves to visit me one day to play for my family?"

"Y-yes, sir," the boy answered without looking at the bishop.

When the meeting was over and all the visiting clergymen besides Andrew were on their way home, Paul walked Andrew back to the vicarage where Rusty and the trap waited. "I'd say that turned out rather well, wouldn't you?" the young vicar asked in an exuberant tone that suggested he couldn't quite believe it himself.

"Very well," Andrew agreed.

"I can't thank you enough for suggesting that Israel play."

"That was entirely selfish of me, I assure you. I enjoy hearing him myself."

Paul shook his head. "You wanted to help me make a good impression, Vicar. I hope I can be as selfless as you are one day."

It was embarrassing to hear Paul speak of him so, when Andrew was painfully aware of his own faults. "I wish that was entirely true. Just like Saint Paul, I have to strive with the old 'self' daily." He smiled. "But it's a noble battle, isn't it?"

"Indeed." A companionable silence developed as they walked past the imposing tower of Saint Luke's, along the stone fence surrounding the headstones of the churchyard, and then on to the vicarage. Andrew was loosening Rusty's reins from the fence when the young man asked, "How is Mrs. Phelps?"

"Very well, thank you."

"And the children?"

"Eager for summer. Except for Grace, who thrives upon school."

The young vicar smiled, but his blue eyes betrayed a question still in his mind.

"And Elizabeth is fine," Andrew added, giving him an understanding smile.

His face altered marginally. "I'm glad."

"I know you are." After a pause Andrew continued. "God has someone for you, Paul." And it was a little surprising that he had not found someone else yet, for with his blond Nordic looks, Paul Treves was considered by even the women of neighboring villages to be the most handsome vicar to ever put on a vestment.

The answer came in the young man's thickened voice. "Not like Elizabeth."

"No, not like her," Andrew agreed. "But you have to stop looking for Elizabeth. I would have never married again had I determined to find someone exactly like my first wife."

"And you're just as happy as you were . . . before?" There was apology in his expression for asking such a personal question, mixed with a longing to understand.

"Absolutely. I have been twice blessed, Paul. It's possible to find that great love again. But it won't happen while you're still living in the past."

"That's just it," Paul said miserably. "I don't know how to stop living there."

Now Andrew felt the need to be blunt for the young man's sake. Kindly but with insistence he said, "We can control our thoughts to a great degree, my young friend. When you find yourself dwelling upon memories that only make you feel miserable, force yourself to think of something else. You can't think of two ideas at once, see?"

"And if they keep returning. . . ?"

He didn't say *to Elizabeth*, but it wasn't necessary for Andrew understood his meaning. "You have to be persistent. Habit is one of the strongest forces, and it can be used for or against us. Let it work for you in this case."

"I'll try," Paul promised, but then frowned slightly, a furrow denting his brow. "My father despises the word 'try.' "

"Wise man, your father."

"I'll *do* it, is what I meant to say. With God's help."

Andrew smiled and clapped him on the shoulder. "Yes, *you* will. And *He* will help you."

*H*ave you tried some of Mrs. Herrick's strawberry jam?"
Mrs. Durwin timidly asked Noelle at the breakfast table on Sunday morning, leaning forward to see past her husband while holding the crystal serving dish in case she should be called upon to pass it.

"I don't care for fruit," Noelle replied without thinking and mentally kicked herself for causing the embarrassment on the older woman's face as the dish was lowered to the table again. Then she chastized herself mentally again for caring, when these people meant nothing to her. But it was hard to stay aloof when surrounded by such relentless warmth. "Most fruit, that is," she amended quickly. "But strawberries—well, that's another story. Will you pass it, please?"

Her aged face beaming, Mrs. Durwin handed the dish over to her husband, who passed it to Noelle. Noelle spread as little as possible on a toast point and took a bite. It was surprisingly good, so she nodded at Mrs. Durwin and said, "Very nice," and received a grateful smile in return.

"No doubt you've gathered by now that Mrs. Herrick indulges us almost sinfully," Mrs. Clay added.

Noelle had gathered that by her second day. Spreading a liberal amount of jam on a second toast point, she said, "My clothes are already feeling a little snug. I'm going to have to start cutting back on portions, or Quetin won't allow me back to London." Her spoon stopped moving as she realized her slip of the tongue. Surely no one had noticed?

"Quetin?" asked Mr. Ellis.

"My brother. He teases me constantly about my appetite." Congratulating herself on her quick thinking, she sent a smile down the table. "I don't suppose any of you grew up with siblings who were lovingly insufferable."

"Oh, dear me!" Mrs. Dearing chuckled. "My brother, Martin—the one who brought home the marbles when I was a child—knew I was terrified of insects. I learned never to put on my shoes in the mornings without shaking them."

That set in motion a discussion about other notorious siblings. Even Mr. Pitney mentioned unobtrusively that his brothers and sister labeled him "Jake the Giant" when he started outgrowing them. Everyone chuckled at this except for Miss Rawlins, whose contribution to the conversation was that she was an only child.

"You should come down for breakfast more often, Mrs. Somerville," Mrs. Dearing told her. "See how you've already brightened our day?"

Noelle thanked her. She could hardly believe that she had risen early and dressed for church, but after four days of venturing no farther than *Trumbles* to see if a letter or wire from Quetin had arrived, she was desperate for something to do. Besides, it seemed a waste to have a trunk of such beautiful clothes—such as the white poplin sprigged with little mauve and burgundy flowers that she was now wearing—and no place to show them off.

She had decided to tough it out and stay in Gresham. True, the village was about as exciting as a monastery, but she had begun to wonder if Quetin might be testing her somehow by choosing such a place. He had accused her of being a malcontent more than once in the past, when she complained about servants or pressed for a more spacious flat. Wouldn't he be surprised, when he came for a visit, to find her participating in the community like one of the natives? She would show him that she had more mettle than he suspected!

And besides, as enamored as she was with Quetin, she enjoyed being in the company of Mr. Clay. Even if that necessitated including his dull, ever-amiable wife. He was witty and handsome, with certainly a most interesting profession.

She was a little piqued later to learn that the lodgers walked to Saint Jude's when weather permitted, except for Mrs. Dearing, who went to the Baptist chapel with the Herricks and one of the parlormaids. Noelle was no great judge of distance, but it looked to be at least a half mile across the green. Didn't these people know what carriages were for?

She supposed she could have asked Mr. Jensen to have the little man drive her there, but then she would look like a spoiled city girl to everyone else. And it had dawned upon her that she *cared* what the other lodgers thought. Not that they were anything special, except for Mr. Clay, but they made up the little world that she inhabited at present. They didn't necessarily have to *like* her, but for some inexplicable reason, she was uncomfortable with the thought of them talking about her in derogatory ways.

So as the bell broke solemnly from the stone tower of Saint Jude's, Noelle walked across the green with the group consisting of lodgers, Mr. Jensen, and even three of the maids, whose names she still confused one for another. The vicar stood beside the open doorway greeting worshipers.

Blond-bearded and broad-shouldered, he was a little shorter and certainly more robust than the clergymen who had been her father's associates. His hazel eyes crinkled at the corners as Mrs. Durwin introduced them.

"Mrs. Phelps has been most anxious to meet you," the vicar told Noelle, "but thought she should give you some time to settle in before rushing over."

"Well, I'm quite settled now," Noelle said, offering her hand. *Any more settled and I would sprout roots.*

"You know, she lived in London most of her life. No doubt you'll have much to discuss."

So why isn't she there now? Surely no one *purposely* chose this place as opposed to the most exciting city on earth. From bits and pieces of conversation that had drifted her way, she had gathered that even the Clays were here only for a respite from the demands of the theatre.

"I look forward to meeting her," Noelle lied, for she had no use for anyone so overly pious as she would imagine his wife to be. As she moved on through the vestibule, the familiar aromas of candles and polished old wood greeted her in the sanctuary. Rows of bench pews faced an altar with a decorative frontal cloth, and brightly colored stained-glass windows depicted Biblical scenes. A choir of a dozen or so robed people were filing into the chancel, and at the west end a woman sat behind a pipe organ while a man standing nearby tightened the strings on a violin.

For a second Noelle faltered and considered making some excuse and turning back for the *Larkspur.* She had assumed that because Saint Jude's was a village church it would be different enough from Marylebow so as not to bring back any painful memories. But the atmosphere was the same—hushed, august, reverential. Closing her eyes, she could almost imagine her father stepping up to the pulpit.

She felt a light touch upon her sleeve.

"Are you all right, dear?"

Noelle turned to find Mrs. Durwin peering up at her with concern in her soft eyes. *I'm so sorry, but this beastly headache has come upon me.* But for some reason the words would not form. "I'm just wondering where to sit."

"Why, you'll sit with us, won't you?"

This invitation was echoed by Mr. Durwin, with Miss Rawlins nodding at his elbow, so she really had no choice. The group from the *Larkspur* seemed so tightly knit that she was surprised to see them separate. She would have much rather sat with the Clays, but they had gone off to sit on the opposite side of the church. Once she was established in a pew between Mrs. Durwin and Miss Rawlins, Noelle looked around and was amused to notice that many sets of eyes were studying her, only to dart away when she looked at them directly. Newcomers were likely rare in a place so off the beaten path, so she could not blame anyone for staring.

Anyway, she rather liked to be noticed. She certainly was a step above the other women in fashion, excluding Mrs. Clay, whom she grudgingly conceded had looked stunning this morning in a gown of green brocaded silk with a collar and cuffs of Maltese lace. Many of the women still wore the sausage curls of the sixties peeking from the sides of their outdated bonnets and wide skirts without a hint of a bustle. Didn't they have access to fashion magazines? Surely *Godey's Lady's Book* was available by post.

The reverent atmosphere in which she was seated was beginning to have some influence over her, for she found herself feeling a little ashamed for being uncharitable. This was a dairying village, and it was likely that most of these woman spent a good portion of their time milking cows. Who would have time to keep up with fashion, in that case? She rather liked the strange inner glow that those magnanimous thoughts produced, so she took them one step further. *And not everyone has as generous a benefactor as Quetin.*

Her feelings of good will—the first she had experienced since coming to this dreadful town—grew even stronger during the song service. For a congregation made up of mostly country people, their voices harmonized nicely, and the organ and violin accompaniment was surprisingly polished.

The choir sang next, also accompanied by both instruments.

> *Near the cross, a trembling soul*
> *Love and mercy found me;*
> *There the Bright and Morning Star*
> *Shed his beams around me . . .*

Noelle found herself so moved by the words, by the pure adoration evident on the face of each singer, that tears stung the corners of her eyes. If only it were that simple! She had never stopped believing in God, but when guilt over her relationship with Quetin threatened to consume her in the early days, she had had to push Him out of her mind or lose her sanity. It became easier and easier to do so as time passed, especially with Quetin assuring her that guilt was a tool that the church hierarchy had used to control the populace since medieval times. And because he was so well educated and able to reason away her misgivings, it was easy to trust him.

It was only during the space between wakefulness and sleep each night that she sometimes wondered if she had hardened her conscience irreparably. Even if she were to end her relationship with Quetin—which even the thought of filled her with panic—would she ever have the same longing for God that she had as an eleven-year-old girl?

The vicar stepped up to the pulpit when the music was finished. Noelle shifted in her seat and wondered again why she had talked herself into coming. *What was his name . . . Philips?* After prayer he began telling a story that was all too familiar to Noelle—of how King David had committed adultery with Bathsheba, then caused her husband's murder when his attempt to cover their sin failed.

Noelle's heart began to pound in her chest so violently that she feared Mrs. Durwin and Miss Rawlins could hear it. *But Quetin and I haven't hurt anyone,* she rationalized. From the corner of her eye, she noticed Miss Rawlins studying her curiously, which made her realize she was tapping her foot. She stopped and shifted in her seat again. She certainly had never taken anything away from Quetin's wife, for his duties would have taken him to London whether she spent time with him or not. And while Bathsheba's husband had apparently been the decent sort, Averyl Paxton was a nagging shrew. If she were any kind of a wife, her husband wouldn't feel the need to stray.

She had just convinced herself that David and Bathsheba's situation had nothing to do with her when the vicar looked out across his congregation and, it seemed, directly at her. "Never assume that because God is patient, He has turned a blind eye to your sin. The consequences of David and Bathsheba's moment of pleasure plunged his family and, eventually, an entire nation into generations of conflict. Is the pleasure you derive from your hidden sin worth the price you will have to pay for it one day?"

Heat rose to Noelle's cheeks. She was certain that the eyes of every person behind her were trained upon her at that very moment. How did he know? *Mr. Radley wrote and told him.* That was why he was so smug at the station! She wished he were sitting beside her right now—she would gladly slap a whelp upon his leering face. Why, she would deliver it to him in London, for Averyl or no Averyl, she was determined to leave this village as soon as she could procure a ride to Shrewsbury. She reckoned she had just enough money for a ticket—if not, she would ask Mr. Jensen to refund the rest of her lodgings.

And then you'll make Quetin furious, she told herself, trying to calm down. Where could she go if he decided she wasn't worth the trouble anymore?

Her thoughts were in such a tumult that she could no longer concentrate upon what the vicar was saying. But between catching occasional familiar words like *propitiation* and *atonement,* she took three deep breaths and forced herself to sort out the situation. Mr. Radley, reptile that he was, surely wouldn't do anything to cause her to leave Gresham after he had gone to the trouble of manufacturing a background for her that would evoke sympathy so she could stay. And as Quetin's solicitor, he had not the liberty to act upon his own dislikes.

She breathed easier now. She of all people knew that ministers were still human. There was no way Vicar Phelps could have known her situation. If he had happened to look her way while stressing a point, well, she noticed that he looked out to the congregation through his whole sermon. And he certainly couldn't help making eye contact—what was he to do, stare at the back wall?

Her self-reassurances were realized at the end of the service when he again clasped her hand warmly at the door. "Mrs. Phelps will want to meet you. Would you mind waiting a minute? It takes her a little time to make her way from the front."

That's it—Phelps. "I'm afraid I'm in rather a hurry to get back to the *Larkspur*," Noelle replied, bestowing upon him a chaste smile. It was enough that she had agreed to attend church in an attempt to fit into village life. She certainly had no desire to stand in front of the church and make small talk with the vicar's wife. "I have this beastly headache, you see."

———————

Something's rotten in Denmark popped into Andrew's head as Mrs. Hayes regarded him with tight-lipped disapproval, while offering her hand as stingily as if it held gold in the palm. And Mr. Hayes, standing beside her with a pained expression on his ruddy face, looked as if he wished the smithy shop opened on Sundays.

The couple sat in a back pew and usually were among the first to exit, but they had apparently stayed on purpose until no more parishioners waited to shake his hand at the door.

"I pray you have a pleasant afternoon," Andrew told them both in spite of his apprehension.

Mr. Hayes held out a work-worn hand. "And you as well, Vi—"

"We wish to speak with you, Vicar," Mrs. Hayes' high-pitched voice cut in.

Andrew's smile did not fade. He reckoned he could smile while being horsewhipped after over two decades in the ministry. "Very well. Why don't I stop by tomor—"

But she was shaking her severely combed head. "This can't wait. I spent the whole sermon looking through the hymnal for that choir song, and it wasn't in there."

"You mean 'Near the Cross.' " Relieved that this issue was a relatively minor one, Andrew nodded understanding. "That's because I happened upon it in a recent issue of *Christian Observer*. It was written by an American woman, a Fanny Crosby. Very moving, wasn't it?"

"And what's wrong with the old hymns, pray tell?" the woman demanded. "Vicar Wilson never brought newfangled songs into the church. *He* understood the importance of tradition!"

The two turned to leave then, Mr. Hayes sending an apologetic look back over his shoulder. Struck speechless, Andrew could only stare after them until he felt a touch upon his left sleeve and turned to rest his eyes upon more pleasant scenery.

"I'm sorry I was held up," Julia said. "Mrs. Rhodes has asked us to supper tomorrow—she had to leave out the side door to assist with a calving." She looked past him, out into the yard where several of the congregation were still milling about. "I hope Mrs. Somerville doesn't think me terribly rude. Will you show her to me?"

"She asked me to give you her apologies. She was suffering a headache." Rubbing a spot that had begun to throb over his right eyebrow, Andrew added, "I never realized they were contagious."

"Oh dear," Julia said sympathetically. "But surely you don't think you caught a headache from Mrs. Somerville."

He gave her a wry smile. "No . . . not from Mrs. Somerville."

*L*ater that afternoon, Jacob took a leisurely stroll up Walnut Lane. He was relieved to see that the Worthy sisters weren't in their usual spot in the sunlight—they didn't spin on Sundays, he supposed. Had he seen them, he would have altered his route accordingly.

Behind a white picket fence sat the two-story Clark cottage, built of the same sandstone and slate as the *Larkspur*. A sixtyish woman answered the door, short and rounded, with gray hair and serene brown eyes.

"Mrs. Clark?"

"Yes," she replied with a smile. "And who might you be, young man?"

He swept the hat from his head. "Jacob Pitney, Mrs. Clark."

"Ah . . . you're one of those archeology men." A contemplative frown furrowed her brow. "Am I saying that correctly?"

"Actually, it's archeologist. But either title is fine with me."

"Yes? Well, I do like people who are easy to please. What might we do for you, Mr. Pitney?"

Suddenly the nature of his call seemed ludicrous. But it was too late to excuse himself without appearing more foolish, and he couldn't think of any other reason to give for knocking on the door of virtual strangers. "I was wondering . . . ah, may I speak with Miss Clark?"

"Why, certainly." Thankfully, she didn't look at him as if he was odd but ushered him on in through the doorway into a parlor of overstuffed chairs set about a multicolored oval rug. Landscapes and still life portraits hung from every wall, and near an open window a bearded man stood in front of an easel holding a palate of paints. Over his shirt and trousers he wore an apron spattered with every color imaginable. There was even a tiny streak of blue in his long gray beard.

"This is Mr. Pitney, Papa," Mrs. Clark said to the man, though it was obvious from their ages that he was her husband and not her father. "One of the . . . ar-che-o-lo-gists."

She looked at Jacob for approval after sounding out the last word, and he smiled and nodded.

"Lydia is upstairs. I'll fetch her." She was gone before Jacob could apologize for troubling her.

"Archeologist, eh?" Mr. Clark angled a curious look at him. "Lodging at the *Larkspur*?"

"Yes, sir." A nutmeg-colored cat came from seemingly nowhere and began rubbing its fur against Jacob's trousers' leg. He reached down to stroke its back, but the animal apparently thought little of this familiarity and went in the direction Mrs. Clark had gone.

"Nice house, the *Larkspur*," Mr. Clark was saying. He held up a paint-stained hand holding a brush. "I'd offer to shake hands, but . . ."

"That's all right, sir." Jacob had never been adept at small talk, so the only thing he could think of to say next was, "I didn't know that you painted."

"Well, being as how we just met, anything I do would be a surprise to you, now wouldn't it?"

Feeling the warmth rising to his cheeks, Jacob stammered, "Uh . . . y-yes, sir."

Mr. Clark gave him a mirthful wink. "Just funning with you, young man. Would you care to have a look?"

"I would, thank you," Jacob replied and relaxed a little. The man stepped back from the easel as he approached. On the canvas was portrayed a wattle-and-daub cottage with a thatched roof and cheery garden. One of the several trees surrounding the cottage had yet to be filled in with leaves, and in front was a small expanse of blank canvas.

"I'll be putting my grandmother there, washing clothes in a kettle," Mr. Clark said, nodding toward the white space. "People are the most difficult, so I save them for last."

"They are?"

"Why, yes. You can paint the eaves of a cottage an inch longer than it should be, and no one will be the wiser. But a chin or nose, well . . ."

Jacob could see his point. "Is that your grandmother's home?"

"Aye, but I'm forced to go from memory. It was torn down some thirty years ago. The greengrocery now sits on the plot. Cyril Sway is my cousin, you see."

"It's remarkably good," Jacob told him.

"Thank you." The elderly man stepped forward and began dabbing green leaves upon the unfinished tree. "Talent's a gift, though, so I can't rightly take all the credit."

"But you use your gift. Some people don't, I expect."

"Now you sound like the vicar." The man grinned, though he didn't take his eyes off the canvas. "But that's true. I had scarce time to devote

148

to it over the years until my son took over the foundry. Feeding the family had to come first, you know."

"Of course."

"Have to confess I don't know anything about archeology. What sort of things are you finding up there?"

While watching the foliage of the tree take shape, Jacob told him about some of the artifacts he and Mr. Ellis had uncovered. Presently he heard footsteps and female voices on a staircase he could see just outside the parlor door. The two women entered the room and smiled at him.

"Mr. Pitney," Miss Clark said, stepping forward with hand outstretched. "How nice to see you again."

"Thank you," Jacob replied as they shook hands. Now that Miss Clark stood close, he realized her right cheek was scarred with a pattern, as from the texture of a bedspread. "I've awakened you from a nap?" he asked and then felt his face flame again, for a gentleman wasn't supposed to point out physical flaws to a lady, even temporary ones, and he was almost certain that napping was also an inappropriate subject.

But she smiled and touched her cheek. "Does it show? I was just resting my eyes, so you didn't wake me."

Her mother spoke up. "Mrs. Tanner—she's our cook—made some wonderful cinnamon scones this morning, Mr. Pitney. Would you care for some, with tea?"

"No, thank you," Jacob told her. Such warm hospitality to a stranger who had knocked upon their door uninvited was unexpected and gratifying. He was reminded of his own family in Dover.

"Then why don't you two visit in the back parlor?"

"Uh . . . fine," he replied to Miss Clark's questioning look. He followed her through the house to a smaller room that was more a library than a second parlor, for the shelves against three walls were practically groaning with books. *I've come to the right place*, Jacob thought. He waited until she had seated herself on an overstuffed green sofa before taking a seat in a nearby chair.

"You must be wondering why I'm here," he told her.

She was seated with the prim posture that Jacob imagined was required of every English schoolmistress—carriage erect and hands folded in her lap. Yet a mischievous little smile curved her lips.

"You aren't here to console me again over Mr. Towly's removed affections, are you?"

Jacob returned her smile, the shared humor calming his nerves somewhat.

"Not that, I promise. You're acquainted with Mrs. Dearing, aren't you?"

"From the *Larkspur*." Miss Clark nodded. "We've enjoyed several book discussions at the library."

"She suggested that you might. . ." Jacob became aware that he was drumming his fingers on a chair arm as the nervousness returned full force. This was just a potential business transaction, as Mrs. Dearing had explained it. So why couldn't he simply say what was on his mind?

"Might what, Mr. Pitney?"

Just say it. He cleared his throat. "I wonder if you would help me to understand some books—for pay, of course. I do realize that your school duties take up most of your time, so if you have to decline I'll take no offense."

"I make time to read no matter how busy I am, Mr. Pitney. But I'm afraid I would be lost in an archeology text."

"Oh, not that. These are stories or novelettes, as they're called. Have you heard of Miss Rawlins? She writes under the name Robert St. Claire."

"I've seen her at church. She also lives at the *Larkspur*, yes?"

"Yes." He noticed that he was drumming his fingers again and moved his hands to his knees. "It's her books I would like to have explained to me."

"I see," she said with a nod.

Mercifully she spared him further embarrassment by refraining to ask his reason. He had a feeling she had already figured it out anyway.

A slight wariness crept into her expression. "Forgive me for saying this, Mr. Pitney, but I would want no part of any deception."

"Deception?"

"Again, forgive me, but you're not asking me to tell you the plots so you can pretend you've read the books, are you?"

"Oh no," he hastened to reassure her. "I would read them first, then pass them on to you. I've already finished two, so I could deliver those to you first, if you were agreeable."

"And what is it that you didn't understand about those two?"

Jacob raised a hand and let it fall back to his knee. "Everything, apparently. The symbolism in particular. I'm quite dense when it comes to all of that."

She smiled. "I never realized density was a prerequisite for becoming an archeologist."

It took him a second to realize that she had given him a compliment. Returning her smile with a grateful one of his own, he said, "I suppose a female author would be better understood by women."

"In which case I qualify. Would you want to meet weekly to discuss the stories?"

Jacob raised his eyebrows hopefully. "You'll do it?"

"It sounds intriguing."

"Thank you." Remembering that he had yet to discuss compensation, he asked, "Would one pound per book be satisfactory?"

"Didn't you say these were novelettes?"

"Yes."

"Half-a-crown would be more than enough. As I said, I make time to read anyway."

Jacob asked if she was sure, and she replied that she was quite sure. He was about to thank her and stop imposing upon her time, when one more thought occurred to him. "Uh . . . about our meetings. . . ?"

"Yes, Mr. Pitney?"

"Is it possible we could hold them in the evenings?" Now he became aware that he was drumming his fingers upon his knees. He considered sitting upon his hands but discarded that notion right away. Focusing his eyes somewhere in the vicinity of her chin, he said, "Sundays are my days off, but people are sure to notice if I come here every week in broad daylight. I don't intend to deceive Miss Rawlins, but I'd rather her not find out that I'm being tutored. Her opinion of me is low enough as it is."

"I see."

Miss Clark was thoughtfully quiet for a second. Jacob looked at a potted geranium in one window, the bookshelves, anywhere but her intelligent green eyes.

"Then how about Monday evenings after supper, Mr. Pitney? Excluding tomorrow, of course."

"After supper? Wouldn't that be too late for you?"

"Not at this house," she assured him, smiling. "We tend to stay up later than what most people would deem sensible."

He returned her smile and let out a relieved breath. "That would be fine, thank you."

———

"What did the young man want?" Lydia's mother asked as soon as the door closed behind Mr. Pitney.

The hope in her expression saddened Lydia, for she knew what was going on in her mind. For it was the same thought that had occurred earlier in her own mind—that Mr. Pitney was calling upon her simply because he had enjoyed their exchange of conversation at the end of the carriage drive on Friday past. It was a silly notion, she realized now, because she had never before had a gentleman caller. And as it turned out, he was only seeking help in impressing the writer, Miss Rawlins. Lydia couldn't help but wonder why he thought it necessary to go to all that trouble. Surely his thoughtfulness and obvious decency were enough to impress any woman.

"He has hired me to read some books for him," Lydia replied.

"Surely he can read, if he's an archeologist," her father said, his eyes fixed upon the canvas as his brush moved with confident strokes.

"Not read *to* him, Papa." She decided she would have to tell the whole story if Mr. Pitney would be showing up here every Monday. Of all people, she knew she could rely upon her parents' discretion. And she certainly didn't want them to get their hopes up by assuming that this business arrangement was anything resembling a courtship. For the only men who seemed to have an interest in her were a widower looking for a sizable dowry and a brawler with a prankster in his family.

"Mrs. Herrick tells me you haven't asked her to prepare baskets for tomorrow," Mrs. Dearing said to Noelle and Miss Rawlins at supper Tuesday night, the eve of May Day. "Surely you'll want to take part in the auction."

Noelle exchanged amused glances with the writer before replying, "It would be too embarrassing, I think. What if no one bid on mine?"

"That's very unlikely," Mr. Ellis spoke up while cutting his roast beef with a fork and knife. "I daresay there are several young swains who are counting on sharing lunch with either of you."

He was probably correct, Noelle thought, at least concerning herself. But there was no man in this village whose company she desired, even just to share a lunch. Her heart was still heavy for Quetin, who had yet to send a letter or wire, though she had been here a whole week. "I believe I'd rather watch the goings-on," Noelle demurred.

On second thought, she didn't think she would mind a friendly chat with Mr. Clay, but of course that was impossible with his Irish wife always clinging to his side like a barnacle. She glanced over at the couple now. It was odd, how the actor was less than his usual self tonight. Shadows lurked beneath his slate gray eyes, as if he were feeling out of sorts. Perhaps he was dying, she thought, but discounted that notion, for how would that explain the energy and gregariousness he had displayed up until now?

Miss Rawlins' voice cut into her thoughts. "There aren't any *swains* in Gresham with whom I would care to keep company," she was saying to Mr. Durwin with a trace of disdain in her voice.

For all her talent, Noelle thought the woman foolish for not giving Mr. Pitney at least a little encouragement, for he was clearly infatuated with her. She was certainly not attractive, with those sharp cheekbones and spectacles and awful mop of short hair. Noelle would have imagined the writer to be grateful to have any man interested in her.

While reaching for the salt cellar, Noelle glanced at Mr. Pitney and felt a little sorry for the hurt evident upon his handsome face. Why, she would consider him for herself, if she were not so attached to Quetin, and if archeologists commanded much higher wages than she suspected they did.

———

May Day dawned cool and breezy, with benign white clouds like lace curtains against the blue sky. On the green, a Maypole, decorated with daffodils, bluebells, cowslips, and violets rose up between two long tables, garlanded with flowers and bearing punch, cake, and biscuits. Near the platform for the brass band—in which her father played trombone—stood a table of picnic baskets that would be auctioned. Mrs. Raleigh, Vicar Phelps' daughter, sat in a chair at one end with a stack of little cards and pencils as one by one some blushing milkmaid, farmer's daughter, or factory worker brought over a basket to be labeled.

And Lydia could not blame them for their self-consciousness, for some eight feet away a gang of male wagsters from the cheese factory nudged one another into calling out comments such as, "Does a kiss come with that lunch, Nellie?" and "Will you give us a peek at what's in the basket, Abigail?" until Mrs. Raleigh shooed them away.

Mrs. Trumble, the former Miss Hillock, who still taught at the infants' school since her marriage to the shopkeeper last September, had asked Lydia's assistance in posing the children for the photographer. Excusing herself from her family, Lydia queued some three dozen freshly scrubbed children in rows from shortest to tallest. Her secondary school students fancied themselves too old for such goings-on, but she noticed that a handful watched younger brothers and sisters from a distance with traces of envy in their expressions.

After the photograph was taken and the odor of sulfur hung heavy in the air, the children assembled under the direction of Mrs. Trumble and several mothers to begin their procession. They would take turns carrying a garland of flowers fixed to a light circular frame—crafted by grammar schoolchildren the day before—and a box in which money would be collected for the poor of the parish.

Lydia watched the giggling and singing group start off toward the vicarage. She turned to rejoin her parents and nearly bumped into Harold Sanders.

"Pardon me, ma'am," he said, jumping backward.

Lydia wondered how long he had stood there at her elbow. "That's quite all right, Mr. Sanders." But there was little chance of passing him by, for he seemed determined to speak with her. She was a little amused to note that the straw-colored hair showing beneath his cap was plastered so thickly with macassar oil—or at least she hoped it was macassar oil and not bacon grease—that the comb marks resembled a plowed field. The stubble was gone from his cheeks, leaving a nick on one jaw to which a dried drop of blood clung. A new-looking tweed coat topped a pair of checked trousers in a curious combination of chartreuse green and tomato red.

He doffed his felt cap, causing several strands of oiled hair to spring apart from the others. "Mrs. Raleigh says you've no basket on the auction table, Miss Clark."

"No, I haven't."

"Oh." His deep-lidded eyes glanced down at a rock he was pushing with the toe of his shoe. "Well, are you gonter?"

"No, Mr. Sanders," she replied with a polite smile. "But there are several others from which you can choose. Now if you'll excuse me—"

But he simply turned to accompany her. "I bought this suit in Shrewsbury yesterday," he declared. "There is a shop with clothes ready-made."

"It's very original," Lydia told him.

"Thank you." Setting his cap back on his head, he continued, "I were thinking about getting some new working clothes too, but since I only get 'em dirty, I couldn't decide if it would be a waste of money or not. My papa fusses if we ask for too much money."

"Indeed?"

"What do you think I should do?"

Lydia paused, her mother in sight chatting with Noah and Beatrice. She certainly didn't care to have him follow her to them, for her mother would give him a gracious smile and ask about his health or some such pleasantry, and then Mr. Sanders would presume that he was welcome to spend the rest of the day with her family. Turning to the man beside him, she said, "What should you do about what, Mr. Sanders?"

"Should I buy some more working clothes?"

"Why are you asking me this?"

"Because I figgered a woman as bright as you would give good advice."

Stifling a sigh, Lydia said, "Then buy a set to have ready when you need to go to town and don't want to dress up, but keep using the others for work until they wear out."

After a thoughtful purse of his lips, he grinned and bobbed his head up and down. "That's real bright of you, Miss Clark. I'll do that!"

"Ah . . . good. Now if you'll excuse me . . ."

"Did you like the flowers?"

Lydia's breath caught in her throat. "*You* put them on my desk?"

He actually blushed. "I went to the schoolhouse before milking, when I knew nobody would be there."

"And the note?"

"Edgar. Mercy says he has the best penmanship. But I told him what to write."

Now Lydia had to restrain herself from smiling. While a prank was still involved in the whole situation, it had not been intended as a reflection on her undesirability as a sweetheart. "The flowers were beautiful, Mr. Sanders. Thank you. But may I ask why you brought them?"

He stared down at the toe of his shoe again. Off to the east, Lydia could hear young voices singing for a penny at the vicarage door. "I thought you might be willin' to court me if you liked them."

"I see." Drawing in a sigh, Lydia wondered at the irony of going thirty-four years with no man showing interest in her, and then having two men, whose company she did not desire, pursuing her at the same time. But because Harold Sanders was a human being with feelings—at least she supposed he was capable of sentiment—she attempted to soften the blow she was about to deliver with an understanding smile.

"Mr. Sanders . . ."

"You can call me Harold if you like," he offered hopefully.

That was going a bit too far. She shook her head. "Mr. Sanders. It was kind of you to bring me flowers, but I'm sure there is some nice girl who would love to spend time with you." She winced inside after the words left her mouth, for it was highly unlikely that any *nice girl* would be interested. But she certainly couldn't correct herself without damaging his pride even more, so she sent up a quick silent apology to God for not weighing her words.

Anger flashed in his leaf-colored eyes, only to be replaced by determination. "Is there someone else?"

"No, there isn't." *But ask me next week*, she thought wryly. *Perhaps an ax murderer will escape from prison and propose to me.* "It's just that we are totally incompatible, Mr. Sanders."

"Incom . . ."

"We have absolutely nothing in common."

Now it was Mr. Sanders who sighed. After the third sigh, Lydia wondered if she should slip away and leave him to himself.

"You won't change your mind?" he asked with surprising meekness.

This time Lydia was determined to weigh her words. It would be kinder to nip any feelings this man had for her in the bud than to give him false hopes of any chance at a relationship. "We can be cordial when we happen to see each other, Mr. Sanders. That's all I can promise."

He seemed poised to ask her something else but then shrugged. "I expect you wanter go back to the picnic?"

"Yes, Mr. Sanders," Lydia answered frankly. She extended her hand and bade him a pleasant day. After shaking her hand, he mumbled a fare-well and turned away from the picnic to hurry off in the direction of Mar-ket Lane.

"Well, at least that's over with," she said to herself. And she could go to her grave with the knowledge that even though she was a spinster, she had broken two men's hearts in her lifetime—or at least bruised them a little.

———

There was only one thing Harold knew to do—find the brightest man in Gresham and ask whether or not he still had any chance of courting Miss Clark. And of course that man would be Mr. Trumble, who could sling big words around as easily as Papa could swear. And he was likely in his shop waiting for the children to come by.

He frowned at the thought of Jack and Edgar and his nephew, Thomas, parading around carrying flowers. *Foolishness*, he thought, shoving both hands into his trouser pockets as he walked across the green. They wouldn't be singing and carrying on so happily if they had an inkling of how soon they would be grown and doomed to lives of drudgery like his own.

Even the bell's merry tinkle over Mr. Trumble's door irritated Harold. The shopkeeper turned from a table where he was straightening some bolts of cloth and smiled. "We're closed today, Mr. Sanders. I just came back to hand out pennies and treats."

"I don't wanter buy anything," Harold told him. "I came to ask you something."

"Yes?" Mr. Trumble leaned against the table edge and hooked both hands under his armpits. "Well, then I'll answer if I can."

Rubbing his forehead, Harold tried to recollect exactly what Miss Clark had said. When it came to him, he nodded. "What does 'coor-dile' mean?"

"Coordile . . . hmm." Mr. Trumble blew out his clean-shaven cheeks, quivering the hairs of his walrus mustache. "I have to confess I don't rightly know, but I do know how we can find out."

"You do?"

The shopkeeper was already on his way to the curtained door leading to the back. He returned with a thick book of some sort in his hands and set it on the counter with a thud. Motioning Harold over, he told him, "My wife says I should try to improve my vocationary." He rolled his eyes and grinned. "That's what happens when you marry a schoolmistress."

I wish that would happen to me, Harold thought on his way to the counter.

Tapping the lettering etched into the leather binding, Mr. Trumble went on. "*A Dictionary of the English Language*, by a Mr. Samuel Johnson." He looked up at Harold. "No relation to Josiah Johnson, I don't think."

"And this book will tell you what *coor-dile* means?" Harold asked warily. He didn't really have the time or inclination to stay and listen to a whole book being read.

The man chuckled and opened the cover. "It has in here every English word ever spoken from the time of Adam and Eve on." For several minutes he rustled through the thin pages, occasionally licking his thumb. And then when he seemed to have found the page he wanted, he ran his forefinger slowly down it.

"Hmm," Mr. Trumble finally murmured.

"What is it?"

The shopkeeper leaned closer to the open book, squinting his eyes. "I don't see a *coordile* here. But here's a *corrigible*." He looked up. "Could it be that's the word you're wanting to know about?"

That sounded about right, so Harold nodded.

"Capable of being corrected, reformed or improved."

"What does *that* mean?" Harold asked, leaning over to look at the upside-down page as if the mystery would somehow show itself to him.

Mr. Trumble raised himself again and rubbed his chin. "Well, I believe it means it could be better. Whatever it is that's *corrigible*, I mean."

"So if a woman says you and her could be *corrigible*, what's she really saying?"

"Why, it means she wishes you and she was better friends."

"Better friends." Casually, Harold asked, "What if she was someone you wanted to court?"

"Well, you can't court a woman who doesn't want to be your friend, Mr. Sanders."

He raised a hopeful eyebrow. "So *corrigible* is good?"

Giving another chuckle, the man closed his book. "Sounds good to me."

*T*heir duty of dispensing a penny to the youthful parade finished, Andrew and Julia strolled back to the green from the vicarage. Julia had joined the others from the Women's Charity Society in the manor kitchen to assemble sandwiches yesterday and would be taking her turn at the refreshment table after the auction.

"Of course, Grace had the sweetest voice of the whole group," Andrew commented.

"But you wouldn't be prejudiced, would you?" Julia gave him an indulgent smile, although she had always thought Grace had a melodious little voice.

"Why, not at all. Just because she's my daughter doesn't mean I have to overlook her talent."

Moving her hand from the crook of his arm long enough to flick a grasshopper off the sleeve of her cream-colored organdy gown, Julia said, "You know who you sound just like, don't you?"

"Don't say it, Julia." He gave her a sidelong look. "Don't even *think* it."

Julia smiled again, not shaken over his mock severity. "Very well. There are worse vices, I suppose."

"And how would you know that, Mrs. Phelps?" he teased. "You've never even put a stray toe off the path of righteousness."

"You're speaking about Fiona now." And just as she said her friend's name, she looked ahead and spotted the Clays among the assemblage, spreading a picnic quilt upon the grass. Fiona fairly glowed in a pearl-gray silk gown, but as Julia and Andrew drew closer she could tell from Ambrose's shadowed eyes that he was in the grip of the despondency that had so marked his adult life. After they exchanged greetings, Julia impulsively embraced the actor. "You'll get through this, you know."

"I know, Julia," he responded with a wan but affectionate smile when they drew apart. "I just have to wait for that next hilltop."

"It's good that you came," Andrew said as the two shook hands. "The fresh air will do you good."

"I wouldn't want to miss it."

Julia knew Ambrose well enough to know that he would actually prefer to be secluded in his apartment, but he had made this unselfish effort on his wife's behalf. Fiona's expression told Julia she knew as well.

"Won't you join us?" her friend asked. "We've time for a nice visit before our turns to serve."

Andrew nodded at the glance Julia sent him and excused himself to fetch the quilt he had spread earlier on the far side of the Maypole.

When he returned and the two quilts were side by side, Ambrose said, "Why don't we save yours for the children? There is more than enough room on ours. Speaking of the children, where are they?" he asked when the four had settled upon the Clays' quilt.

Julia returned the waves of Elizabeth and Jonathan, still overseeing the table of lunches to be auctioned, and nudged Andrew to do the same. "Elizabeth is helping Jonathan with the auction." As her stepdaughter's nausea was limited to early mornings, she had declined Julia's offer to have Laurel and Aleda take her place. "Philip went fishing for a little while with his friends, and Laurel and Aleda are following the children's parade—to keep an eye on Grace, they say."

Andrew blew out a breath. "And I'm exhausted from just hearing their whereabouts, so you can imagine what it's like to keep up with them physically."

"And you love it . . . both of you," Ambrose smiled.

"Yes, of course," Julia replied quietly, remembering that the couple would likely never have children. But God had given them an extra measure of grace in this regard, for they had never shown any sign of jealousy. In fact, they had become like an aunt and uncle to Julia and Andrew's children.

The brass band Mr. Durwin had assembled several months ago began tuning their instruments on the platform, producing inharmonious but not unpleasant little sounds. While Andrew and Ambrose discussed Saturday's Rugby match in Queensferry between England and Wales, as reported in yesterday's *Shrewsbury Chronicle*, Julia moved closer to Fiona to ask about the new lodger. "I haven't been over to meet her because I didn't want her to be overwhelmed by so many new faces. I hoped to see her Sunday, but Andrew says she went home with a headache."

"I don't think it lasted long," Fiona said. "She was in good spirits at lunch."

"What's she like?"

"Very agreeable. At times she seems a little sad, but no doubt she still misses her husband." Fiona craned her neck to look past Julia's shoulder. "Why, there she is now. She wasn't down for breakfast, so I wasn't sure if she would be here."

Twisting around, Julia scanned the people gathered in groups to chat or lounging upon quilts on the grass. The only new face belonged to a young woman speaking to Mrs. Sykes across the lemonade table. She was fashionably dressed in a dress of white piqué sprigged with small bouquets of brown and pink. After accepting a cup from the churchwarden's wife, she sipped it while looking about her as if a little lost.

"That's not her, is it?" Julia asked, motioning discreetly. Because most of her lodgers were elderly, she had assumed Mrs. Somerville would be as well. And Andrew, having never been one to comment on other women's appearances, had not said anything about her age.

"We were surprised as well." The young woman looked in their direction, and Fiona raised herself to her knees. "You don't mind my asking her to join us, do you?"

"Of course not."

Mrs. Somerville, first looking to both sides as if unsure if Fiona had meant her, smiled and handed her cup back to Mrs. Sykes. "Mrs. Somerville is coming over," Julia leaned over to tell Andrew and Ambrose at the first pause between talk of place kicks and scrummages. The two men made moves to get to their feet, but by that time the young woman had reached them and held up a hand for them to stay put.

"Please, don't get up," she said. She was quite attractive, with strawberry-blond curls straying from a narrow-brimmed straw bonnet. "I'm staying but a minute. I just wanted to see what was going on."

"We're glad you came," Fiona said, smiling. "Will you join us?"

"Oh, no thank you." Mrs. Somerville gave a sheepish little shrug that looked charming on her. "I don't want to impose on anyone. I thought I would bring a sandwich back to the inn."

"Now, we can't have you doing that," Andrew told her. "We've room enough here to spare."

"But I wouldn't want to intrude. . . ."

She was assured by both couples that she was most welcome. The men moved over to the next quilt, and Julia and Fiona made room for the newcomer between them. "I'm so sorry we didn't have a chance to meet Sunday," Julia told her, extending a hand. "I'm glad your headache went away."

"Oh, I was *crushed*," Mrs. Somerville assured her as they shook hands.

The three women chatted about London for a bit. No matter how happy Julia was to be settled in Gresham, she enjoyed hearing about the city. "It's been a bit over a year since our last visit," she explained. "Fiona tells me it has changed even since then."

"It's dizzying how much it changes," Mrs. Somerville agreed. "Why, there are ready-made clothing shops springing up all over. For women as well as men. It doesn't seem natural, does it? Just walking in from the street and coming out with a gown."

"There is such a shop in Shrewsbury now," Julia told her. "I've never been inside, but our parlormaid bought a dress there just last week."

"Just *one* shop?" The younger woman shook her head sympathetically. "I don't see how either of you aren't terribly homesick."

"What do you mean?" Fiona asked.

"For London." She waved a hand to indicate her surroundings. "Not that this isn't a lovely place, mind you. But the city has so much more to offer."

"We had no choice in the matter," was Julia's honest reply. She smiled at Fiona, whose loyalty and optimism had made those terrible days bearable when her home was foreclosed. "Or at least . . . I didn't."

"I didn't either," Fiona corrected softly.

"Incredible," Mrs. Somerville said at length in a strangely flat voice. "Then that makes three of us."

That was a curious thing to say, Julia thought. According to her solicitor, Mrs. Somerville had applied of her own volition because her family was concerned about her. But then, some families were more insistent than others. She supposed that as long as Mrs. Somerville got along with her fellow lodgers and paid her rent, it was none of her business why she was here.

———————

Noelle leaned back on the heels of her hands and watched a dark-haired young man ask for attention from the platform where a brass band had just finished playing. "The Phelps's son-in-law, Jonathan Raleigh," Mrs. Clay supplied from beside her. "He's schoolmaster of the grammar school. And the young woman handing him a basket is Elizabeth, his wife."

"Thank you," Noelle told her. Sheer boredom had driven her from her room where she had planned to spend the day. If only Quetin would write! Other lodgers received mail, so the postal system had to be aware of this place. *But perhaps mail takes longer to get here*, was her only consoling thought. Surely small villages weren't first priority, with so many people in the cities to service.

As young men, and some old, began taking sheepish steps toward the platform, Noelle breathed in the aroma of freshly cut flowers and had to admit to herself that this was preferable to sulking in her room. Her father's duties had never allowed time for such nonproductive frolic when she was a child, and Quetin certainly wouldn't have taken her to any such celebration in the London parks. He was quick to accuse her of being a snob, but he himself was only interested in events frequented by the *bon ton*, the upper crust. Why, he had even admitted to her once, after several glasses of wine had loosened his tongue, that he actually found opera maddeningly tedious!

She had become a little nervous when children began showing up and dropping themselves down on the vicar's quilt, but they were surprisingly mannerly and didn't whine or pull each other's hair as she imagined most children were wont to do. The youngest, a girl with brown curls, even took a peppermint from her pocket and offered it to her. Noelle would not have taken it had she been starving, for she was dubious about the hygiene of even well-behaved children, but the offer touched her.

"Now, who will bid for this basket, belonging to the lovely Miss Jowett?" the man on the platform was saying, motioning toward a family seated on a quilt who nudged and whispered to a plump, crimson-faced young woman. The first bid—for tuppence—was hooted down. But finally, the basket and Miss Jowett's blushing company sold for a florin to an equally blushing young man.

"What if some baskets aren't bid on?" Noelle asked Mrs. Clay, who looked unsure and repeated the question in a low voice to the vicar's wife.

Mrs. Phelps leaned close enough to reply softly to both of them, "There's scant chance of that, for there are more unmarried men than women in Gresham. But just in case, Jonathan has asked some of the older widowers to step up. You'll notice they haven't made any bids yet because they haven't needed to."

"I see." Though it was no concern of hers, Noelle was relieved to learn that none of the young women would be humiliated. Even having to share a picnic with an old person would be better than not being chosen, especially in front of so many people.

A young woman wearing an obviously home-sewn yellow gingham gown passed within two feet of the Clays' quilt with the young fellow who had placed the highest bid for her basket. His face was tanned from labor in the sun, and his clothes the simple fustian of a farmer, but one might have thought he was Prince Charming for the way the girl looked at him. And his expression plainly said that the affection was reciprocated.

Perhaps they would marry, if they weren't already betrothed. And the girl would spend most of her remaining years bearing and tending children, selling eggs and butter for pocket money, and saving scraps from the clothes she sewed to make quilts to warm their beds. She would likely never wear expensive perfume, experience the richness of fine silk against her skin, or know what it was like to have the waiters at *Gatti's* know without being reminded that she did not care for onions in her *Colin a la Polonaise.*

That's almost how it would have been with me. If Quetin had not held the door for her at that millenary shop. She would have married some young curate or bank clerk—perhaps even another vicar, as had one of her sisters. And not knowing any better, she would have worn the same adoration on her face as the young woman in yellow had just worn.

At least I wouldn't have to be hiding from another man's wife now, she thought. Her eyes stung, but she blinked the budding tears away and made herself focus her attention back on the auction. If crying did any good, she would have been back in London days ago.

———

After the lunches had been auctioned, gallons of lemonade and hundreds of sandwiches consumed, and the brass band had played every song in their repertoire at least six times, Mrs. Bartley ascended the platform and asked for attention. Marriage agreed with Ambrose Clay's former walking partner, for the rough edges to her personality had softened considerably over the past year. *But I'd wager she keeps the squire on his toes,* Ambrose thought, smiling to himself.

"On behalf of Saint Jude's Women's Charity Society, I wish to thank you for participating in our fund-raising effort today. I'm very pleased to announce that enough money has been raised for the church's new pulpit."

The elderly woman beamed with hands clasped through the ensuing applause, and when it died down, she continued. "Mr. Howard Croft has kindly agreed to apply his excellent craftsmanship to the project . . ."

"The coffin maker?" Ambrose whispered to Fiona.

"He says he can do it," she whispered back.

"How long will that take?"

His wife put a finger to her lips and made a slight nod toward the platform where Mrs. Bartley was saying, ". . . which he assures us will be completed by midsummer, if not before."

There were murmurs of disappointment after the announcement. Apparently many in the crowd had expected the pulpit to be in the church by the next service. With a long-suffering smile, Mrs. Bartley explained. "This will be no ordinary pulpit, you understand. And elaborate hand carvings take time."

"Let's just hope he doesn't get carried away and carve R.I.P. on the front," Ambrose couldn't resist whispering.

"Sh-h," scolded Fiona.

A half hour later as they crossed Market Lane from the green, she squeezed his arm happily. "This was such a good idea, Ambrose. Just think . . . every schoolchild who bought a glass of lemonade will feel he had a part in the new pulpit."

"And every husband who paid an exorbitant sum for sandwiches?" he teased.

Smiling, she replied, "At least you're in good company with the squire and Mr. Durwin. I noticed their wives were equally as ruthless."

"You mean our dear little Mrs. Durwin is capable of extortion? What is the world coming to?"

"It's coming along very well," she replied, then gave him an appraising look as they walked along the *Larkspur*'s garden wall on their way to the carriage drive. "And I'm glad you're feeling well enough to make jokes."

"I do feel better," he admitted. "Good company is good medicine."

"But apparently not for everyone." Fiona sent a concerned glance to the *Larkspur*'s second story. Mrs. Somerville had excused herself from the festivities soon after the auction and was likely still alone inside. "The poor woman. So young to be widowed."

"Yes."

"Do you think we should see about her?"

He shook his head. "Perhaps she just wanted some privacy. If not, she'll have plenty of company soon enough."

During the auction he had happened to glance in Mrs. Somerville's direction and noticed her efforts to cover what appeared to be tears. His own bouts with despondency gave him compassion for anyone likewise suffering, and he had considered motioning to Fiona. She could have comforted General Cornwallis at Yorktown.

But he had not allowed himself to do so. Having been surrounded by actors for most of his life, he had a keen sense of when someone was putting on a performance. And he couldn't help but wonder if Mrs. Somerville had done nothing but perform since her arrival. He no longer shared his uncharitable thoughts with Fiona, who, like the other lodgers, had taken to her as if she were a tragic long-lost cousin. There was likely no harm in that, but he intended to keep a wary eye on this newcomer.

Fiona had suffered too many hurts in her life from the hands of unscrupulous people. And he considered it one of his primary missions to see that it never happened again.

Chapter 20

*S*houldn't you see a dentist?" Julia asked Andrew in the vicarage dining room Saturday morning. She was dressed to accompany him on a call but noticed the difficulty he was having chewing his breakfast. "We can be in Shrewsbury in less than an hour."

"I'll drive you," Philip offered.

Andrew shook his head, the swelling in his right cheek obvious even through his beard. With clenched teeth, because drawing in air was painful, he said, "Let's give it a few more days. Monday, if it's no better."

"There is always Mr. McFarley," Wanetta suggested while bringing in a fresh jar of marmalade to empty into the server dish. "He's quick and only charges two-bob."

"I would no more allow a barber to extract my tooth than to amputate my leg," Andrew articulated plainly in spite of the clenched teeth.

"They used to do that, you know," Aleda offered. "Surgeries, I mean. That's why the pole is red and white. People were once given small poles to hold because of the pain, and—"

"Let's discuss that some other time, Aleda," Julia interrupted with a glance at Andrew.

"Are you afraid to go to the dentist, Papa?" Grace asked.

There was a silence of several seconds before he replied. "Terrified. So let that be a lesson for all of you."

"What lesson, Papa?" Laurel asked with a puzzled look.

"Not to take good health for granted. You should get on your knees and thank God every day that your teeth don't hurt. I know I shall when this is over."

A half hour later, Julia and Andrew left the vicarage. As the affliction had come upon him yesterday evening, it caught them with very little salicin in the cupboard. Their first stop would have to be *Trumbles*. Julia drove the trap while her husband sat with his hand pressed against his jaw, letting out a low groan at every bump in the lane. When they reached the shop, Mr. Trumble turned from stocking items upon his shelves to peer sympathetically at Andrew. "Headache?"

"One of his back teeth is hurting terribly," Julia answered as they approached the counter. "We almost sent Philip to wake you last night."

"Yes? Well, I wish you would have. There's no night so long as when you've a toothache."

Andrew made an appreciative groan and motioned toward the shelves.

"He would like a dose of the medicine now, please," Julia translated.

"Right away." Mr. Trumble reached for an amber-colored bottle, pulled out the stopper, and poured out about a tablespoon of the white powder into a square of brown paper. As Andrew tossed it back into his mouth, wincing at the bitter taste, Julia hurried for a dipper of water from the pail at the far end of the counter.

Thoughtfully, the shopkeeper scooped out a peppermint ball from a glass jar and handed it over. "This'll get the taste out. One for you, too, Mrs. Phelps?"

Julia politely declined as Andrew put the candy in his mouth, and resisted the impulse to smile, for the dignified Vicar of Gresham now resembled a hamster with two bulging jaws. The effect only lasted a second before he spat the candy into his hand as if it were poison. "Hurts!"

"Oh, I should have thought about that," the shopkeeper said with a slap on his own forehead. "Sweets can make it worse."

There was nothing Julia could do besides offer sympathetic little murmurings, so she paid for the medicine and put the rest of the bottle into her reticule. Andrew, caught up in his own agony, waited mutely.

"Next time now, be sure to wake me," Mr. Trumble told them as he handed over Julia's change. "I wouldn't want desolation to drive you to the riverbank to chew on a tree."

Julia and Andrew exchanged glances. She understood that he had likely meant *desperation*, but chewing upon a tree?

"Salicin." Mr. Trumble explained with a chuckle at their confused expressions. "It's made from willow bark, you see?"

After expressing appreciation for this bit of information, Julia thanked the shopkeeper and guided her suffering husband back out to the trap. "Andrew, this is ridiculous," she said, picking up the reins again. "It's only going to get worse."

"Can't hurt any more than this."

I'm not too sure about that, Julia thought, but having never had a tooth extracted, she had no choice but to heed his wishes in the matter. "Then you should at least be in bed. We can visit Mrs. Hayes another day. You know all she's going to do is complain about her husband. I'll send Luke to explain."

He shook his head, causing Julia to wonder if all men were this stubborn about their work. "She's likely to show up at the vicarage if I don't come. And I'm feeling better now."

There was nothing to do but drive the trap southward and fume silently, her frustration divided between Andrew and Mrs. Hayes. Some quarter of a mile past the *Bow and Fiddle*, she reined Rusty to the east, down a dirt drive flanked by hedgerows frosted with white hawthorn blossoms. Black-and-white cattle grazed upon grass shiny with dew, and in the near distance sat a cottage and several outbuildings of mellowed stone. A deceptively tranquil scene, Julia thought. Minutes later she was reining the horse to a stop in front of the stables. She turned to her husband and found him fast asleep, his chin touching his chest.

"Andrew?" she nudged after debating whether she should turn the trap around and head back for home.

"Huh?"

"We're here."

"Oh." He blinked and looked sheepishly at her. "The medicine."

"And your tooth?"

"Much better." This time his smile seemed more genuine. He patted her hand. "Thank you for being so patient with me, dear."

"Oh, that's not so difficult," Julia replied, her resentment evaporating.

A ruddy-faced man in work clothes advanced upon them as Andrew was helping Julia from the trap—Luther Hayes. He didn't seem surprised to see them. After they had exchanged greetings, he took the reins from Andrew to loop around a post. "We've some new calves. Would you care to see 'em before we let 'em out to pasture?"

"Yes, that would be lovely," Andrew replied. The three walked some seventy feet to peer over the wide gate leading into the barnyard, where a half dozen calves were either nursing or nuzzled up against their cud-chewing mothers.

"Young animals are so winsome, aren't they?" Julia said to Mr. Hayes as they both watched Andrew hold out a stalk of hawkweed in an attempt to coax a calf closer. The animal did not budge but regarded him with cautious interest in its brown eyes.

"Aye, they are," the man agreed. "And we've four more ready to calve any—".

He was interrupted by a wailing sound from the vicinity of the hay barn so filled with agony that chills pricked Julia's back.

"What was that?" Andrew asked, quickly rejoining her side.

"We've had to pen up one o' the bulls. A bad tooth. Mrs. Rhodes is comin' this morning to pull it."

"Yes?" Another bellow pierced the air. "Does that happen often?"

"Only once here," Mr. Hayes replied. "Some five years ago. He'll have to be put to sleep with some o' that chloroform, of course. They don't take kindly to knives."

"Knives?"

"Why, yes. The gum has to be slit so's pliers can get a better grip."

Andrew's face went pale. Threading an arm through her husband's, Julia said, "We should look in on Mrs. Hayes now. Thank you for showing us the calves."

"Yes, thank you," Andrew echoed in a strained voice. "Will you be joining us inside?"

The dairy farmer shook his head. "With all due respect, Vicar, I would just as soon stay with the bull." And then as if fearing he had offended Julia, he touched the brim of his hat. "Sorry, ma'am."

No ready reply presented itself to Julia, so she just nodded. She was accompanying Andrew up the walkway through a garden, which almost rivaled the squire's in its profusion of well-tended flowers, when the cottage door opened. Mrs. Hayes, framed by the doorway, squinted at them. "I was expecting you last night," she said in a voice laden with umbrage. "Didn't James tell you it was important?" James was one of the farm workers when he wasn't running errands for Mrs. Hayes.

"And good morning to you too, Mrs. Hayes." Andrew doffed his hat. "Your garden is looking especially lovely today."

"You're baiting her," Julia whispered. With a calm smile she explained to the woman as they reached the door, "We were entertaining supper guests when your note arrived and knew you would understand our waiting until this morning."

It didn't matter that the guests were Jonathan and Elizabeth and the Clays. Family members and old friends were due the same courtesies as any other guests. Had there been an actual emergency, Andrew would have left at once. But he had been summoned by Mrs. Hayes enough times in the past to know that this wasn't one.

Mollified only a little, the woman frowned and glanced past them. Her blond hair was drawn back so tightly that the comb marks were visible. "You'll need to fetch Luther, Vicar. He's—"

"Busy in the barnyard," Andrew cut in. "Will you allow us inside, Mrs. Hayes?"

"But—"

"Or shall we stand here and chat?"

The woman looked stunned but stepped back to allow entrance into the parlor. She nodded them toward an austere mahogany-framed settee, the seat upholstered with figured brocatelle, then sat in a matching chair. "I don't see how you can put Luther to rights if he's not here," she whined. "He spent almost all of yesterday afternoon at that smithy's."

"I can lecture him until I'm blue in the face," Andrew replied. "But I can't undo the damage from what goes on here every day."

Julia held her breath. She had never heard him speak so bluntly. *It's his tooth*, she realized, for he kept his jaw almost rigid as he spoke. But why take it out on a distraught woman—even if she was a bit of a nuisance?

"What do you mean, what goes on here?" Mrs. Hayes asked, fingers worrying the ivory cameo pin on her collar. "I'm a God-fearing woman, Vicar. You know that."

With an audible sigh, Andrew answered, "I'm afraid you talk too much, Mrs. Hayes. And most of what you say is of the complaining nature."

She gaped at him while two red spots spread across the severe lines of her cheeks.

"The Scriptures say that it's better to live in the wilderness than with a contentious woman. You must either change your ways or resign yourself to many more years of loneliness in your own cottage."

Julia noticed a slumping of the woman's shoulders and wished she could get up and put her arms around her. But whatever Andrew's mood, she knew his counsel to be good, and she must not interfere.

"H-how?" Mrs. Hayes asked.

Andrew must have sensed that he was pushing too hard, for he sat back a bit and said more compassionately, "Your garden is lovely, Mrs. Hayes. But the most beautiful flowers in the world can't bring you the joy that a good marriage can. I would advise you to put as much time and effort into your marriage as you do your garden."

She asked again, with still a trace of a whine in her voice, "How, Vicar? It's rare that he even listens to me."

"Then listen to him for a change."

"But he hardly speaks to me either."

"Why make the effort if he's only going to be interrupted with some complaint? Conversation—even in a marriage—is not unlike a game of catch, Mrs. Hayes."

"Catch?"

He gave her a grimacelike smile, but his eyes crinkled at the corners. "You played it as a child, didn't you?"

Her expression softened with memory. "Oh yes, Vicar."

"The object of the game was simple, wasn't it? You toss the ball back and forth. A good conversation is built upon the same principles. After you've had an opportunity to speak, you allow the other person the same courtesy. It wouldn't be much fun to play catch with someone who refused to toss the ball back to you, now would it?"

He rose from the settee, so Julia got to her feet as well. "And now we'll leave you to do what you have to do."

"What I have to do?" she asked, looking up at both of them.

"Mr. Hayes is proud of those new calves. I would imagine if you spent a little quiet time at his side, he would be happy to tell you how he's tending to them."

She sat there wrapped in silence while Andrew and Julia started for the door. Julia paused to pat the woman's shoulder before following him out of the cottage. After Andrew had loosened the reins, handed them to her, and settled into the trap beside her, she heard the door open again. Mrs. Hayes was hurrying purposely through the garden in the direction of the barnyard.

"Weren't you a little harsh with her?" Julia asked. The trap gave a slight lurch as Rusty started down the drive. "Her husband has to share some of the fault."

"Her husband isn't the one who sends for me. And I didn't intend to be harsh."

"Is it the tooth?"

Instead of replying, he asked, "Can you drive this all the way to Shrewsbury?"

"Now?"

He groaned when a wheel hit a rock and jarred the trap.

"We're on our way," Julia assured him.

They had traveled but a mile when she caught sight of a figure walking in the road ahead. He glanced over his shoulder and then moved to the side. Julia touched Andrew's sleeve. "Is that—?"

"Harold Sanders," her husband mumbled.

"Are you up to offering him a ride? Surely the cheese wagons have long since passed."

After a slight hesitation, Andrew gave her a pained nod and moved closer. But when Julia reined Rusty to a stop, the man just grinned and made no effort to come closer.

"We're going to Shrewsbury, if you would care for a ride," Julia offered.

He touched the brim of his felt hat respectfully. "No, thank you."

"Are you quite sure? It's a long walk."

"He's sure," Andrew mumbled.

"I'm sure," the man answered.

———

The plan was as good as any that was ever made, Harold thought as he watched the trail of dust following the vicar's trap. It pleased him so much that he chuckled every time it crossed his mind. *And Papa says Mercy and*

Jack and Edgar are the bright ones. All he had to do was saunter up to the oldest Meeks boy during May Day and ask when his sister was going to fetch her spectacles.

Happily he kicked a rock into the hedgerow on his right. A wood pigeon flapped from the spot with angry screeches. He hadn't known what time Miss Clark would be setting out for Shrewsbury, but figured it would be near the same hour she had left the week before last. Just to be on the safe side, he had set out this morning before the sun came up and before his father could wake and put him to work. Even the cheese wagons had rumbled past almost an hour ago. But he didn't want to cover too much distance on foot, for that would mean less time in the carriage with Miss Clark. So he took infant steps and waited.

And it was the second part of his plan that pleased him the most. Hadn't she advised him on May Day to buy another suit of work clothes? Now he had a perfect excuse for going to Shrewsbury, one that would at the same time show her that he thought she was bright. He would ride with her to the spectacle doctor, telling her that he could go to the clothes shop from there. As soon as she and the girl went inside, he would race to the shop, make his purchase, and be back before they could leave. Miss Clark would be too mannerly not to offer him a ride home, and didn't she say she wanted them to be corg-able?

About a quarter of an hour later his ears again picked up the sounds of hooves and wheels, so he hastened his steps so as not to be seen idling— in case it was Miss Clark. It was only when the rumbling was loud enough to be almost upon him that he allowed himself to turn and look.

It was her all right. She was driving a wagon today, not a carriage, and from the bed the four Meeks children were eyeing him curiously. The pair of horses slowed to a stop, and Harold forgot about the children at the sight of the smile on Miss Clark's face. Why, it was as if she was happy to see him!

"Good morning, Mr. Sanders," she greeted him from the seat. "Are you on your way to Shrewsbury?"

"Uh-yes," he replied and glanced at the children again. But perhaps the wagon was better, he told himself, for he would share the narrow seat with only Miss Clark. She would be close enough to smell the hair tonic he had bought from Mr. Trumble, *Sir Lancelot's Fine Grooming Pomade for Distinguished Gentlemen.*

" . . . in the back?"

He realized that Miss Clark had been speaking and blinked at her. "Huh?"

"I said, would you mind riding with the children? We're a bit late, but I can't drive the horses too fast for fear of bouncing one of the little ones out. You could help Phoebe make sure that they don't try to stand up."

There was nothing he could do but nod and climb on in back. The Meeks children stared somberly at him, except for a girl of about seven who gave him a timid smile. He forced himself to smile back and then grabbed at his hat as the horses started off again, this time at a canter. After a while the children grew used to him and began to chatter. He didn't scold when they began kneeling in order to peer out the sides because he was getting bored himself just looking at the bed of the wagon. After enough time had passed for him to be sure that they weren't going to take any risks, he turned and edged closer to the seat.

"It's a nice day if it don't rain."

Miss Clark turned her face only long enough for a quick glance, "I beg your pardon?"

He raised his voice over the rattle of the wagon. "It's a nice day if it don't rain."

"Yes, it is," she said with another backward glance.

"I'm gonter buy that suit of work clothes today. Remember . . . you said it was a good idea? But you don't have to let me out anywhere. I can get there from that spectacle doctor's shop."

Miss Clark turned her face toward him again, but this time wore a little frown. "Mr. Sanders, will you please watch the children?"

With a sigh he resumed his post. Then he paid closer attention to what the youngest girl was sitting on—a large wicker hamper, probably made by those mick Irish who lived down Whorton Lane. *I'll wager there's food in there.* Of course. Why else would all these children be along—for the ride? So if he happened to be hanging about after his quick dash to the ready-wear shop, Miss Clark would have to invite him to have lunch—especially after he had done her a favor by watching the children. And then he would have a chance to chat with her, for surely it would be in a park where the children could play.

It would have to be a park. Or else what were they planning to do? Spread a picnic on one of the storefronts? Or the middle of the street? That notion made him chuckle, and the youngest boy looked at him. Harold grinned back.

You should have reminded her yesterday, Lydia told herself, Mrs. Tanner's admonition echoing in her mind. Then she wouldn't have had to scurry about the kitchen this morning with her mother and the cook, boiling eggs, slicing beef and bread, and squeezing lemons for lemonade. All this caused her to set out for the Meeks' a half hour later than she had planned. And the children, having waited in their school clothes in their tiny garden, felt nature calling the minute Lydia brought the wagon to a stop in front of their cottage.

"Are you sure you wouldn't like to come with us?" Lydia had asked Mrs. Meeks as the children dashed for the privy.

"I believe I would enjoy the peace and quiet more," the woman had answered. "But will you need me to tend them?"

Lydia assured her that she could manage just fine with Phoebe's help. But it was only when they were on the road that she found herself with misgivings over the weak-sighted girl's ability to keep a brother or sister from tumbling from the wagon. She gave the reins another flick, coaxing Wellington and Nelson into a trot. She was actually grateful that Mr. Sanders had been on the road today. If she could make up for some of the lost time, perhaps Mr. Rosswald's office wouldn't be too crowded yet.

The first inkling that this was not to be was when the horses turned onto High Street, and she could find no place to leave the wagon. They had to travel another block before she could finally pull the horses to a halt, which presented another problem. If the street was this crowded, there would surely be no room for the children in the oculist's waiting parlor. And if she managed to squeeze them in a corner somewhere, what fun would that be?

"Well, I'll be off to that shop now," Mr. Sanders informed her from the ground beside the wagon.

Lydia looked over at him while a thought formed in her mind. But dare she? She twisted in her seat to glance at the children, whose saucer eyes took in the shops and bustle of traffic and pedestrians with wonder. *If this impresses them, they'll love the castle.*

This helped her to decide. "Would you mind waiting, Mr. Sanders?"

"Waiting? Uh-yes. I mean, no. Not at all, Miss Clark."

She beckoned to Phoebe and said in a low voice, "You know we have a long wait ahead, don't you?"

"Yes, ma'am," the girl replied. "But what are we going to do with the others?"

"What if we joined them later?"

"Yes, ma'am. But where would they go?"

Whispering that part of the plan to the girl, who gave a hesitant nod, Lydia then turned back to Harold Sanders. "Are you in a hurry to shop, Mr. Sanders?"

"No, ma'am. No hurry at all."

His hopeful expression pricked her conscience in light of what she was about to ask him to do. She smiled. "I'm so glad. May I ask a favor?"

————————

"What does it say, Mr. Sanders?" Trudy Meeks asked Harold as they stood looking at the carved wooden signpost among the flower beds of the castle grounds. The building, of the same red sandstone used throughout most of Shropshire, was imposing even if only three stories high, not counting the high slotted wall around the flat roof. The two towers were a little higher, so of course the children wanted to climb these first.

"Don't you go to school?" Harold asked the girl.

"But I don't know the big words yet."

Fortunately, Mark came to his rescue. "It says the castle was founded in 1070."

"What does *founded* mean?" asked Lester, who had told Harold on the way over in the wagon that he was Trudy's twin.

Now that something had been asked that he could answer, Harold grabbed for it. "You know, they found it."

Mark scratched his head. "I don't think it means—"

"Well, that's what it says, don't it?"

"Who found it, Mr. Sanders?" Trudy asked.

"The folks looking for it, I'd wager. Are we gonter stand here all day or climb that tower?"

They decided upon the east tower first, closest to the River Severn. "Ooh, look, you can see forever," Trudy cried while pointing her finger through one of the gaps used for aiming weapons. After the three children had made a circle, staring from each gap, they were ready for the other tower.

"Don't you want to rest a spell?" Harold asked, having just leaned against the wall with his hands in his pockets. "I'm still winded from the stairs."

"Please, Mr. Sanders?" asked Trudy. "We've never had so much fun."

"Oh, all right," he grumbled.

At the top of the west tower, Harold watched them run from gap to gap, as before. He felt like he had pulled a plow through the pasture, and they weren't even winded. Noticing that Lester was making an attempt to climb up into one of the gaps, Harold left his spot and pulled the boy back by the collar. "Don't go doin' that."

He wasn't exactly sure when his plan started to fail. All he knew was shortly after Miss Clark smiled at him, he was driving the wagon back through the streets of Shrewsbury.

"There are people down there," Mark said with excitement flushing his face. "We could spit and pull our heads in, and they'd think it was birds!"

That sounded like a fine idea to Harold, who craned his head to spot any target below. Then he recalled how the schoolmistress had reminded him that he should set a good example for the children. While she hadn't exactly mentioned spitting, he reckoned she would feel the same way about that as she did about swearing. With a stern voice he said, "Don't go doin' that."

"I wasn't going to do that, Mr. Sanders," the boy turned to him to explain, eyes wide with sincerity. "I just meant it would be funny."

"Well, it ain't. Now just be good whilst I get my wind back."

"But we want to see the main building too," Trudy said.

"Please, Mr. Sanders?" Lester asked.

Rolling his eyes, Harold pushed himself from the wall again. *That's what's wrong with children these days—they don't want to wait for nothing.*

"Is this good enough?" Mr. Pool's nephew twisted around to ask Noelle after reining the horse to a stop in the square. He was a young man, about nineteen, with acne-scarred cheeks. Noelle had forgotten his name almost immediately after the innkeeper introduced them, for all she cared about was transportation to Shrewsbury.

"Yes, that's fine," she told him. When it dawned upon her that the boy didn't intend to assist her from the carriage, she snatched up her reticule, kirtled her skirts around her ankles, and stepped down to the street. "Fetch me here at three."

"That'll be another two bob."

"What?" She took two steps toward the driver's seat. "But I already paid you."

"Aye, for the trip down here. I've got to go all the way back to Gresham and then back here again." He held up four snuff-stained fingers. "You can't expect to pay just two shillings for four trips."

"Very well," she grumbled. "But I won't pay the rest until you return. I don't want to be stranded here while you're in a card game somewhere with my money."

He shrugged agreement and took up the reins again. Noelle's glare followed him as the carriage moved on down the street, but she was just as perturbed at herself. She had considered it beneath her dignity to procure a much cheaper ride on one of the cheese wagons, as it seemed everyone else in Gresham without a carriage did. And if she would have only waited another week as Mr. Jensen had suggested, Mr. Herrick would have driven her down for nothing. But the Herricks were visiting their son in Stafford, where he was a university student or something, and Noelle had thought she would die of boredom if she didn't see something other than sleepy lanes and cows.

———

After what seemed like hours, the door leading into the inner recesses of Mr. Beales' practice opened and the dentist entered the parlor. He was as tall as Mr. Pitney, though slump-shouldered, no doubt from the years of bending over required of his profession. Meeting Julia's questioning look with a nod, he waited until he was closer to say, "Your husband is fine, Mrs. Phelps."

"Thank you." Julia stood and glanced past him at the doorway. But then why wasn't Andrew with him?

Mr. Beales looked over at the two other waiting patients, both men, whose faces wore the same mixture of pain and trepidation that Andrew's had. Lowering his voice, he replied, "The tooth was split down into the root, unfortunately, requiring a slice in the gum. I administered chloroform beforehand, and he's on a cot in my office sleeping it off."

"Oh dear. May I see him?"

"There's nothing that can be done for him now except to allow him his rest. Why don't you come back in a couple of hours?"

Julia wouldn't think of abandoning her husband, even if she couldn't be in the same room. "I'll just wait here—"

But the dentist was propelling her by the elbow to the front door, his voice gently insistent. "It's just a tooth, Mrs. Phelps. We'll take good care of him. Meanwhile, have some lunch, do some shopping."

She had no choice but to leave, and supposed Mr. Beales was right. She could do Andrew no good by wringing her hands in the parlor. It was still such a new experience, having a husband who needed her as much as she needed him. Wandering about in the shops, she had little inclination to buy, and besides, she had not anticipated being in Shrewsbury when they left the house this morning, so carried very little money in her reticule.

The bell above Saint Alkmund's chimed out the eleventh hour. *Another hour*, she thought. She supposed she might as well have the lunch the dentist had suggested. Andrew surely wouldn't have any desire for a meal when she was finally allowed to collect him. She and the children had patronized a cafe on Market Street on a shopping trip last summer. It was a casual place—no maître d', just a dozen tables or so, and a menu limited to soups, sandwiches, and meat pies. She stepped inside and glanced around. As the noon hour drew closer she would likely have to share a table, but as of now, she didn't want to intrude upon any of the handful of patrons who had already staked out places.

She was about to step over to an empty table by the window when she sensed someone watching her. Julia turned to the left and met Mrs. Somerville's eyes—just before the woman's gaze shifted abruptly from her.

She saw me, Julia thought. *But did she recognize me?* Surely if she had, she would have shown some sign. But then, Mrs. Somerville wouldn't have expected to see her in Shrewsbury, and Julia herself had been known to stare past members of even her own family while deep in thought.

It seemed approaching her was the right thing to do. If Mrs. Somerville had indeed recognized her and was merely bashful, it would be snobbish to move on as if they had never made eye contact. Weaving her way over, Julia paused at her table. "Mrs. Somerville?"

The woman looked up again, and this time smiled. She was dressed in a becoming brown spring silk. "Why, Mrs. Phelps. How good to see you."

"Thank you—and the same to you."

"Will you join me?"

Julia smiled. "It would be my pleasure."

A waiter appeared just as she had sat down in the opposite chair. Because Mrs. Somerville had occupied the table first, Julia waited for her to order. But the woman shook her head. "I ordered just before you came in."

So you saw me after all, Julia thought but kept her face impassive as she ordered creamed mushroom-and-leek soup and tea. And as she could think of no reason the woman would have to dislike her, she again attributed her looking away to bashfulness. "Have you been shopping?" Julia asked after the waiter left.

"Looking, mostly. And you?"

"The same. My husband had a tooth removed, and I was ordered not to collect him until noon."

"Oh my." Mrs. Somerville made a sympathetic face. "That sounds serious."

"He was given enough chloroform to put him to sleep," Julia replied. "So at least there's no pain at the moment."

"How are you going to get him home?"

"In our trap. When he wakes up, of course."

"Of course," Mrs. Somerville agreed.

———————

"Please may we have our picnic now, Mr. Sanders?" Lester asked for the third time, when Harold and the Meeks brood were finally back on solid ground. "My stomach is making noises."

"Well, fine then!" Harold snapped. To Mark, he ordered, "Fetch the hamper from the wagon. And stay out of the street."

It'll serve her right if they eat every last bit of it, he told himself. When the boy had returned, dragging the hamper at his side, Harold found a spot under a fir tree, opened the lid, and passed out boiled eggs and sandwiches wrapped in brown paper. The crockery jug of lemonade could wait until after the food was finished. Even though Trudy assured him they could eat and drink at the same time, Harold didn't want them making a mess of their clothes and giving Miss Clark a reason to think he wasn't able to tend children. After all, women likely took note of such things when choosing husbands. Finally the little beggars had filled their stomachs, and Harold his. He took four tin mugs from the basket and poured lemonade.

"What will we do now?" Mark asked after returning the basket to the wagon.

"Yes, what will we do now, Mr. Sanders?" Trudy echoed.

Harold propped himself back on his elbows. "There's naught to do but wait for Miss Clark and your sister."

"But how will they get here?"

"Hire a carriage, most likely."

"Have you a handkerchief?" Lester asked.

"Why?"

"We could play blindman's buff."

"Yes, let's!" Trudy exclaimed.

Anything to keep them from pestering me, Harold thought, leaning to one side to reach the bandana wadded in his back pocket. He reckoned he could buy his own farm today if he had a shilling for every question that had been put to him by the Meeks children.

"Will you play with us, Mr. Sanders?" Mark asked.

"No."

Trudy's gray eyes were pleading. "You can be first."

"No." *If you don't get here soon, Miss Clark, I might just change my mind about marrying you.*

"Please . . ."

Harold motioned for them to leave him alone. "I don't play games!" He hadn't meant for his voice to come out so harsh, but he was tired of playing nanny. And the thought of facing Papa's wrath for slipping away didn't help.

But he had gone and barked at them, and now the children stood staring at him as though they were statues. Trudy's lower lip even trembled. With a weary sigh he pushed himself to his feet. At least he didn't know anybody in Shrewsbury, so there would be no one to laugh at him for wearing a blindfold and playing a children's game. *And if anyone does, I'll knock his head off.*

He realized he was frowning and eased his lips into a halfhearted smile. "Now, don't go lookin' at me like that," he told the children. "I were just joking with you."

Chapter 22

I thought I would go mad from boredom, so I hired a carriage from the *Bow and Fiddle*," Noelle confessed after the waiter had brought identical orders of soup with a server of buns and cups of tea. Now that the discomfort of spotting the vicar's wife at the door and then having to offer to share her table had passed, she found herself relieved to have the company. It wasn't that the *Larkspur* was lacking in that regard, but the only two women near her age were dreamy Miss Rawlins and the tediously perfect Mrs. Clay.

She had been too preoccupied to notice last Wednesday how attractive Mrs. Phelps was—and certainly well-preserved—to have a married daughter. Her burnished red hair—the sides drawn up into a straw hat trimmed with blue ostrich feathers—and fringe, curled above her eyebrows, contrasted her eyes so that they shone like green emeralds.

"It's a pity we couldn't have saved you the trouble and expense," the vicar's wife was saying while spreading butter on one of the rolls. "But we didn't plan on ending up in Shrewsbury when we set out this morning."

Noelle took a spoonful of the soup. It couldn't hold a candle to Mrs. Herrick's but was still warm and filling. "Are there no dentists in Gresham?"

"Mr. McFarley pulls most of the teeth. He's the barber." Mrs. Phelps smiled at Noelle's look of horror. "We're told he's competent, but . . ."

"I understand," Noelle assured her. "But what I still *don't* understand is how you live like that, not when there are churches on practically every corner in the cities." She remembered as the words left her mouth how Mrs. Phelps had said she had no choice in moving there. "Couldn't your husband ask for a transfer?"

"Andrew?" After a moment, awareness cleared her puzzled expression. "Andrew had actually requested somewhere rural, but that's another story. You see, Gresham is where we met. I had moved there with my three children six months earlier."

"You mean he's your . . ."

"Second husband, yes. I was widowed just before we left—" Holding her soup spoon poised over her bowl, Mrs. Phelps stopped abruptly, "Do forgive me."

"For what?"

"I'm sure that's not a pleasant subject for you."

Why would I care if you were widowed? Noelle then realized the vicar's wife was referring to her own fictitious hero-husband. "Well, one must go on," she said bravely. And curiosity compelled her to ask, "But I confess I still don't understand. What *did* force you to move to Gresham?"

"Finances. Our London home was foreclosed after my husband's death. The *Larkspur* was all we had."

"I'm sorry." She really meant it. "And you with three children."

"Thank you. But you know, I treasure the lessons I learned during that time."

"Lessons?"

A self-conscious smile curved Mrs. Phelps's lips. "I was as shallow as a goose spiritually. Oh, I was a believer, but I sent prayers heavenward because I had been taught since childhood that it was what decent people did—not out of any desire for fellowship with God. And then when there was no one to take care of me, I began to realize how much I had taken for granted over the years. I saw how much I really needed Him. And His companionship and guidance became more important to me than even material provisions."

That a vicar's wife could be so transparent about any spiritual failings astounded Noelle. Her parents had striven hard to maintain auras of perfection, never relaxing their guard even in front of their own children— who were constantly reminded that they, too, must be examples.

"Forgive me," Mrs. Phelps said. "I didn't intend to go on and on. I'm just a bit anxious about my husband."

"No, I was interested in hearing it," Noelle told her. But she was morose *enough* about being banished from London—she didn't care to be reminded of her own spiritual emptiness, so she artfully steered the subject back to more comfortable ground. "Speaking of your husband, I hope his recovery is swift. My brother had a tooth pulled when I was a girl, and it stayed swollen for days."

"Oh dear. I didn't think that far ahead, but surely he won't be able to conduct services tomorrow." Mrs. Phelps pushed up her sleeve to glance at a narrow gold watch, then looked up again. "Will you mind if I leave you? It's a bit early still, but I should like to see about him."

"Of course not," Noelle replied, surprised to find herself a little disappointed at the loss of company.

The vicar's wife took a florin from her velvet reticule to leave next to her half-filled bowl of soup. They said their farewells, and Mrs. Phelps wove her way back around tables now filled with patrons. Just as the door closed behind her, some odd impulse seized Noelle. She hastily left some money on the table and hurried through the cafe. Ahead on the walkway she could see the familiar royal-blue dress and auburn chignon showing beneath a straw hat.

"Mrs. Phelps?" she called when she had almost closed the gap between them.

The woman paused and turned, her expression puzzled. "Mrs. Somerville?"

Raising a hand to her chest while she caught her breath, Noelle asked, "May I be of any assistance?"

Mrs. Phelps smiled. "God must have sent you, Mrs. Somerville. I was just wondering if Andrew will be able to sit up in the trap."

"Then let's go, shall we?" Noelle urged when the other woman did not move.

"But I just remembered—what about the carriage you hired?"

"I'll be back before he leaves Gresham." *But I just may not tell Mr. Greedy-pockets.*

They walked together, turning the corner at High Street and arriving at a two-story red brick building connected to a row of other shops and businesses. The signboard boasted a white molar tooth about the size of a hatbox—hideous in Noelle's opinion. The waiting parlor was empty, and after a moment of staring helplessly at an inside door, Mrs. Phelps suggested that they sit. "There were other patients here when I left. Mr. Beales may be with one now."

Mrs. Phelps seemed in no state to chat now, and she kept glancing at the back door as if she were second-guessing her decision to stay put. After ten or so minutes Noelle assured her, "Your husband will be out shortly. It's as you said, the dentist is tending someone else."

Turning a grateful smile to her, Mrs. Phelps replied, "Thank you, Mrs. Somerville. Now I *know* you were sent by God."

"Somehow I doubt that," Noelle told her. She wished God wouldn't keep cropping up into their conversations.

The back door opened and two men came through it—neither was Vicar Phelps, but it was easy to tell which one was the patient, for the shorter of the two held a handkerchief to his mouth. He gave a muffled reply to the taller man's farewell and made for the front door.

"Your husband is just now stirring, but I believe he can walk," the dentist said while approaching Mrs. Phelps, now on her feet.

"May I take him home? I'm sure he'd rather be in his own bed, and our children have no idea where we are."

182

"Is your carriage out front?"

Mrs. Phelps replied that it was, and the dentist asked her to wait there before disappearing through the doorway again. He returned three minutes later. Vicar Phelps, at his side, was indeed walking, but appeared unsteady on his feet and liable to topple over any minute. A strip of white cloth was wound tightly around his head from chin to the crown, the ends tied off at the top and comically resembling a girl's hair ribbon. In his right cheek something bulged.

"I feared he wouldn't keep his jaw closed as he slept," the dentist explained. "He must keep pressure on the cloth in his mouth to stem the bleeding, so I would advise keeping the bandage on during the ride home as well."

He spoke as if his patient wasn't in the room, and judging by the vicar's glassy-eyed expression, Noelle gathered it was a fair assessment. With the dentist holding the door, Noelle took the vicar's left arm and helped Mrs. Phelps walk him through it. Inside the trap, he sat quietly between them with his hands tucked between his knees as Mrs. Phelps reined the horse through Shrewsbury's streets. Occasionally he swayed to one side or the other. The first few times that he leaned against Noelle he righted himself immediately and mumbled an apology. But just as the trap was leaving the city for the road to Gresham, he slumped against her shoulder and stayed there.

"Andrew?" Mrs. Phelps asked in a worried tone.

"He's asleep." Noelle turned her head as far to the right as was possible to look at her, causing the loose bandage ends to brush against her nose. "I don't mind."

"Again, I'm in your debt, Mrs. Somerville." But after a hesitation she added, "Are you positive he's just asleep?"

The chloroform, Noelle thought. With her shoulder held as rigid as possible, she took up one of his hands and found a steady pulse in his wrist. "He's asleep."

"I shouldn't have hurried him," Mrs. Phelps fretted. "We could have even booked a room for the night. I could have asked you to send word to the children."

"Mmm?" the vicar murmured.

"He would want to be at home, as you said," Noelle reminded her.

"Yes . . . thank you."

Their journey to Gresham was tediously slow, and by the time the trap stopped in front of a stone cottage behind Saint Jude's, Noelle's shoulder was aching. A man, presumably the caretaker, gave them a puzzled look from just outside the stable and hurried over.

"What happened to the vicar, Mrs. Phelps?" he asked, a faint whistle trailing his question.

"His tooth, Luke," she replied. "He's been drugged, so do be gentle about him."

Hurrying around to Noelle's side of the trap, the caretaker gave her a somber nod and eased his hand between her shoulder and the vicar's head, allowing her to slip to the ground. "Hmm?" the vicar murmured, blinking.

"You're home now, Andrew," his wife said from the caretaker's elbow. He shook his head as if to clear it. "Home?"

The auburn-haired boy from the picnic appeared out of nowhere and dropped the cricket bat he carried. He helped the caretaker lead the vicar through the garden gate while Mrs. Phelps held it open for them. But the vicar's wife then turned to face Noelle. "Please come inside and have some refreshment, Mrs. Somerville."

Noelle smiled but shook her head. "You have enough to do without entertaining."

"Then at least come inside until Luke can deliver you home."

"I would rather walk, thank you." She had ridden enough for one day. After Mrs. Phelps had thanked her warmly again, Noelle set out across the green. A perplexing sense of well-being accompanied her. She had proved herself useful—and to a vicar and his wife of all people! Wouldn't Quetin chuckle when she told him.

The sight of the *Larkspur* ahead dampered her spirits—even after ten days it was no more of a home to her than it was when she first arrived. But her spirits lifted considerably as she crossed Market Lane, for off to her left she could see a familiar carriage and horse leave the *Bow and Fiddle* to head toward Shrewsbury.

———

"Blindman's buff?" Lydia whispered to Phoebe from where they stood on the castle grounds. She had to smile at the sight of Harold Sanders wearing a bandana over his eyes and attempting to catch the giggling children under his charge.

"They play it a lot at home." Wire-rimmed eyeglasses securely in place, Phoebe watched her siblings without having to squint.

The girl had been almost effusive in her thanks after leaving the oculist's, but Lydia caught a glimpse of disappointment in her reflection as they passed the window of a glover's shop. She decided to allow her to adjust to the new situation without offering any motivational homilies. "He looks as if he's enjoying himself," Lydia said, still smiling.

"Yes, ma'am."

"Well, I suppose it's time to break it up."

She and Phoebe had taken a few steps forward when they were spotted by Lester, who called out "Miss Clark and Phoebe are here!" The bandana was whisked from Harold Sanders' face as quickly as if it were on fire.

"I were just tryin' to keep them from straying all over the place," he explained sheepishly. "Besides, they begged on and on until I feared little Trudy would cry."

"That was very good of you, Mr. Sanders," Lydia told him.

He shoved the bandana into his coat pocket. "It weren't nothing." Then as if grasping for something to steer the conversation away from his frolicking, he said to Mark in a mildly gruff tone, "Well, don't just stand there. Go fetch the basket from the wagon."

"That's not necessary, but thank you," Lydia told them before the boy could obey. "Phoebe had a meat pie on the way here, and I had a big breakfast."

At this point Lester noticed his sister's eyeglasses. "You can see, Phoebe?" he asked, causing the other two to crowd close to Phoebe and ask for turns to try them on. Meanwhile Lydia moved over to Harold.

"I would like to show Phoebe the castle, Mr. Sanders."

A flicker of discouragement crossed his face. "Uh-huh?"

"So why don't you take the wagon to the clothing store? We should be finished by the time you return."

If he seemed disappointed before, he looked crushed now. "It ain't that important that I get them clothes today."

"Surely, it is, if you were prepared to walk all the way to Shrewsbury for them."

"But—"

"Now, now, Mr. Sanders." With an encouraging smile she insisted, "I shall feel simply awful if you don't. Go on and make your purchases."

"Where are you going, Mr. Sanders?" Mark called as the man walked away with hands shoved dejectedly into his pockets.

Harold turned long enough to mutter with as much enthusiasm as if he were heading for his own hanging, "To buy a suit of clothes."

You're a heartless woman, Lydia told herself while herding children toward the castle's main entrance. It had occurred to her, during the long wait in the oculist's parlor, to wonder why Harold Sanders would be walking to Shrewsbury. True, she had come upon him on foot once before, but surely by now he would have learned to watch his tongue in the cheese wagons. What she suspected was that he had somehow found out when she would be traveling in that direction again.

She did appreciate his help with the children. But to allow him to set himself up again for future rejection seemed a poor return for a favor. Best

185

to continue to keep the man at a distance and pray that whatever affection he had for her would wane—and the sooner the better.

Just inside the stairway of the west tower, Phoebe stopped to remove her spectacles and rub her eyes with the heels of her hands. "Are you all right?" Lydia asked, switching Trudy's hand to her left so she could take the eyeglasses.

The girl blinked. "Yes, ma'am. My eyes just feel a little tired."

"Mr. Rosswald said it would take some time to get used to them, remember?" After giving the girl a minute or two she handed the eyeglasses back. "Wear them for now so you don't go taking a wrong step. But on the way home you should take them off and rest your eyes."

Surely Harold wouldn't mind watching the other children in the back of the wagon again.

A pink-cheeked curate, a Mr. Mitten or Mutton, from a village he called Bomere Heath delivered the sermon Sunday morning, which Noelle was relieved to learn was not about David and Bathsheba's adultery—or anyone else's. Actually it was a hodge-podge of subjects ranging from Gideon's faith to Ruth's loyalty, and from Paul's sermon on Mars Hill to Queen Jezebel's treachery. After an hour had passed, Noelle could hear shifting in the pews, mothers whispering admonishments to wiggling children, and from a far corner of the sanctuary, faint snoring. Miss Rawlins, beside her, glanced at her watch every ten minutes or so.

Having been practically raised in church, Noelle was aware of what was going on. Young curates were so pleased to be given the opportunity to preach that they invariably found it difficult to settle on one particular subject. As had happened on Sunday past, Noelle found that the atmosphere of Saint Jude's caused her to feel a little more kindhearted. Perhaps because she bore no grudge against this particular church for intruding into her family. And so for the sake of the poor curate, she sat at attention— though her thoughts strayed often.

During the closing prayer, she found herself adding a silent plea that Quetin would write, but she stopped herself short. To disobey God's law was one thing, but to enlist His aid in doing so was surely a sin worthy of the worst kind of punishment.

Mrs. Phelps drew her aside in the yard while the Durwins and Miss Rawlins were chatting with an elderly couple they had introduced to her as Squire and Mrs. Bartley. "My husband was so grateful when I told him how you helped us. He remembers nothing about the trip home."

Noelle nodded understandingly. "And how is he?"

"Swollen, as you warned. But salicin helps to ease the pain."

"I'm glad." She corrected herself. "About the salicin, not the swelling."

"I knew what you meant," the vicar's wife assured her, smiling. "And

I wonder if you would care to take lunch with us on Saturday? My husband would like to thank you in person."

Immediately Noelle's mind began racing. While she liked the woman standing before her, the fact that she was a vicar's wife made any hope of friendship impossible. Watching her tongue to make sure none of the details of her private life slipped out was taxing enough at the *Larkspur*.

"Surely he'll need more time to recuperate," she hedged when no other excuse came to mind. That was another thing she mentally added to her list of things to dislike about Gresham—there were few activities available for excuses. In London one could always claim to have theatre tickets or an invitation to some social function.

"Doctor Rhodes looked at him yesterday evening and said the swelling should be gone in another three or four days," Mrs. Phelps replied. "Of course we may have something soft for lunch, but Mrs. Paget cooks a wonderful mulligatawny soup."

Just tell her you're too busy, Noelle urged herself. *What does it matter if she's offended? You'll be gone in a few months.*

But much to her disgust, she found herself unable to utter the words. "I would enjoy that," she lied.

———

The familiar pang touched Paul's heart as he tied Caesar's reins to the hitching post outside the vicarage garden on Monday morning. Before a certain face could form itself in his mind, he took Vicar Phelps's advice and forced himself to think of something else. The something else he grasped for happened to be the breaded liver Mrs. Coggins had served along with his breakfast eggs. He despised liver but had not the heart to tell her so, for she was adamant that a weekly dose was good for the blood. Paul reckoned it to be so, or else why would anyone ever eat it?

Dora answered his knock with a welcoming smile, "Why, Vicar Treves, it's been such a long time!"

Returning her smile, he replied, "Yes, it has. And how are you keeping, Dora?"

"Oh, fine and dandy. It's the vicar that's hurting."

Paul winced and dug into his coat pocket for a cloth bag of dried herbs. "I shan't disturb him. But Mrs. Coggins sent some bishopswort to make a poultice."

"Yes? Maybe that means a promotion will be comin' for you soon."

"I beg your pardon?"

"You're delivering *bishops*wort." She shook her head. "I apologize, Vicar, that was a poor joke."

"No, it was a good one," he assured her, smiling. "Do tell the vicar I'm praying for him?"

"Aye, I'll do that, sir. You could tell him yourself if he wasn't asleep. But wouldn't you like to speak with the missus?"

"Oh, I'd really rather not intrude—"

"I'm sure she'd want to see you. And she's just in the kitchen chatting with Mrs. Paget."

Reluctantly Paul allowed the maid to usher him into the parlor. He sat in a chair and eyed the sofa where he had sat with Elizabeth the evening she broke off their courtship. *What a thickskull you were back then*, he told himself. So smug in his convictions and so condescending in the way he spoke to her. How could he fault her for not wanting to spend her future with such an arrogant lout?

"Spinning wool, Vicar?"

The feminine voice snapped him out of his thoughts. Getting to his feet, he smiled sheepishly at Mrs. Phelps, who smiled back at him from just inside the doorway. "Guilty, Mrs. Phelps. But my mother always referred to it as building air castles."

She stepped over to offer her hand. "Well, it's delightful to see you, wool or castles aside. Dora showed me the herbs you brought for Andrew. How did you learn about his tooth?"

"Mr. Mitton was so overjoyed about being allowed to preach that he has no doubt informed half of Shropshire by now." Quickly he added, "Not that I'm faulting him, mind you. I was the same way when I was a curate."

"So was Andrew, to hear him tell it."

"Is he suffering much pain?"

"Considerably less than when the tooth was intact." She gave him an apologetic look. "But I'm afraid he's asleep at the moment."

"I only came to deliver the herbs," Paul assured her.

"You'll stay and have some tea, won't you?"

"No, thank you. I promised Mrs. Coggins I would be back in time for lunch."

Mrs. Phelps smiled and folded her arms. "Tell me, does she rule the vicarage as our Mrs. Paget does?"

"With an iron spoon," he replied, rolling his eyes.

Her laugh was gratifying to Paul's ears. For so much of his life he had held the opinion that sobriety was demanded of ministers of the Gospel. Didn't the Bible state that men would be held accountable for every idle word? He had never admitted as much to Elizabeth, but there was a period of time when he judged Vicar Phelps unfavorably for his lightheartedness. He would have most likely continued in that vein had she not broken off

189

their courtship. The resulting pain set him on a path of prayerful intro-spection, which began revealing to him the serious flaws in his way of thinking.

Though he knew he still had a long path to travel toward maturity, he was learning to appreciate humor as God-given and blessed. For if it was frivolous to laugh, then the Scripture wouldn't abound with passages such as *Eat thy bread with joy,* and *These things write we unto you that your joy may be full.*

Mrs. Phelps accompanied him out to where Caesar was tied, though Paul had assured her it wasn't necessary. Luke, hammering a nail into a loose board in the fence, stopped to wave. "I gave him a bit of oats and water, Vicar Treves."

"Thank you, Luke," Paul called to him. When he turned back to Mrs. Phelps, she was studying him with a bemused expression. He had shaved in his usual hurry this morning but quelled the impulse to raise a hand to explore his face for dried blood.

"Andrew will be so disappointed he missed a chat with you," she said finally.

Breathing a little easier now, Paul replied, "Do tell him I'll return when he's feeling more robust."

She smiled. "Doctor Rhodes has assured us that he'll be himself again by midweek. So why not join us for lunch on Saturday?"

———

"Surely, you didn't," Andrew said thickly from his parlor chair that evening. Wearing a flannel dressing gown over his nightshirt, he propped his right elbow against the chair arm and held the poultice against his cheek. Julia had offered to wind another bandage from chin to crown so it would stay in place without tiring his arm, but when Andrew had sobered enough to get a look at himself in a mirror on Saturday, the dentist's bandage had come off.

"And what is wrong with inviting him?" Julia asked, seated on the ottoman so she could be at his side. They rested their joined hands upon the left arm of the chair. "He said he would be returning to see about you anyway."

"Then why did you wait until everyone was gone to tell me?"

It was true, she had waited until the children were occupied upstairs with homework. But only because it was easier to chat with no distractions, for the girls hovered around their father as if he were a wounded war hero. Only now Julia was beginning to realize what Andrew already suspected—that her procrastination had more to do with not wanting to be accused of matchmaking than any desire for peace and quiet.

"They're both lonely," she said defensively.

A pained expression settled upon his face—either from the missing back tooth or the subject of their discussion. She was just about to ask if he needed more salicin when he explained, "We don't know enough about Mrs. Somerville. Paul was hurt once before."

"Granted. But it's just lunch. And she seems a very decent person."

He merely stared at her, so Julia pressed on. "And they're both adults. If they're not suited for each other, surely they'll realize it. But what if it turns out that they're meant to be together?"

"If they're meant to be together, God will see to it that it happens."

"But God could have given me the idea to invite them here."

After a sigh, he halfway conceded. "Perhaps He did."

Though Julia appreciated hearing this, his earlier argument had planted some seeds of doubt in her mind. Paul Treves was their friend, and friendship obligated the parties involved to certain responsibilities. If Philip were older, would she instigate a possible romance between him and a woman she hardly knew? *Never.*

" . . . Julia?"

She looked up at her husband again. "You were saying something, Andrew?"

"I asked what was wrong."

Sighing, she replied. "I must admit I acted strictly upon impulse. A picture crossed my mind of the two of them together. . . ."

"And it set your romantic heart to beating, didn't it?" His hazel eyes crinkled at the corners. "Well, as you said, they're both adults. And it's just lunch."

"Thank you." She felt somewhat better now. "But you're the romantic in the family, Andrew."

"I think not."

"Oh, but you are. In fact, I never knew a man could be so romantic until we started courting."

The left side of his mouth curled into a pained smile. "Indeed?"

"Absolutely."

Squeezing her hand, he said, "Then you wouldn't mind fetching a romantic old fellow another dose of salicin, would you?"

———

After supper the following evening, Jacob Pitney went upstairs to clean his teeth and give everyone else ample time to take up their usual stations in the hall. He descended the staircase with light steps afterward, turning left and heading past the kitchen door. From the other side the clatter of china and cutlery blended with female voices to produce sounds of comfortable domesticity. But it was the short corridor just past the kitchen that was his destination. He turned the corner sharply to the left, grateful that no one had seen him yet.

Dusk had settled outside when he pushed open the courtyard door, the western clouds stained crimson from the sun hiding behind the Anwyl. The door had no sooner closed behind him when Jacob noticed the two faces turned in his direction from one of the benches.

"Good evening again, Mr. Pitney!" Mr. Clay greeted.

"Uh . . . good evening," Jacob replied. He tipped his hat to Mrs. Clay. "I was just . . . walking about."

The two didn't seem to find anything odd about this. "We're enjoying the evening breezes," Mr. Clay explained. "They're quite refreshing. Will you join us?"

All you have to do is decline politely and walk past, Jacob told himself. But then wouldn't they wonder why he was headed off toward the back lanes at this time of evening? Only Mrs. Dearing, Miss Clark, and her parents knew about the lessons. Too many people for his comfort, but he had no control over that. If Miss Rawlins ever found out, she would despise him so much that he could forget any hopes of courting her.

"Are you all right, Mr. Pitney?" It was Mrs. Clay who asked, her usually serene face wearing a concerned expression. "Perhaps you would care to sit and chat?"

She knows, Jacob thought in a panic. But that wasn't possible. He was just allowing his nerves to overrule his common sense. He cleared his throat and smiled. "I'm fine, thank you. I'll be going inside now."

He would have to leave through the front, which he prayed wouldn't attract too much attention. Fortunately, the hall was almost empty for a change. "I believe I'll take a walk," Jacob mentioned casually on his way past the two facing sofas from which Mr. Jensen and the Durwins were chatting.

Mrs. Durwin looked up from her needlework. "This late, Mr. Pitney?"

"It's only a quarter past eight," he told her, then noticing the defensiveness of his voice, added in a more pleasant tone, "The evening breezes are so refreshing, aren't they?"

"I was always taught that night air was poison for the lungs," Mr. Jensen remarked. "I never saw a firefly until after I went into service. Mother forbade us to go outside after six o'clock."

"Surely you're aware now that that's not true," said Mr. Durwin.

"Yes, but I confess I still find myself taking shallow breaths if I happen to be outside very late. And I cannot bring myself to sleep with an open window."

I should have gone out the back, Jacob thought, waiting with strained patience but unable to leave because the conversation, in a way, still included him.

"My mother believed hot water caused rheumatism," Mrs. Durwin said, smiling. "So our baths were as tepid as possible without actually causing icicles to hang from our noses."

This brought chuckles from the two men. Had Jacob the time he would have been happy to tell them how the Romans heated their baths, but he was in a hurry. Resolved that it was now or never, he gave the threesome a farewell wave as he walked over to the door, took hold of the knob, and was finally on his way.

It took but a few minutes of brisk walking to reach his destination. Mrs. Clark greeted him at the door. "Lydia is in the back parlor," she said, taking his hat. "And did you find some nice things on the hill today?"

"Nothing but dirt, I'm afraid."

"Oh dear," she sighed. "Your whole day wasted."

"Not necessarily," he said with a smile. "You have to move the dirt to find the treasures."

She liked that and laughed. "That's the way to look at it, Mr. Pitney." She led him through the house to the back parlor, where Miss Clark was sitting on the sofa with what appeared to be a school text, and her father sat in the overstuffed chair reading from a newspaper. The old man grinned up at him.

"Evening to you, Mr. Pitney!" He acted as if he were greeting an old friend and not someone who had been to his cottage only once before. "And how's the digging? Find any swords or skulls?"

"Only dirt today, Papa," said his wife. "Come and I'll help you clean your paintbrushes."

"Since when do you care about my brushes?" the man grumbled while easing himself up from his chair. Clearly he would have liked to have stayed and chatted. When they were gone, Miss Clark smiled and put her book aside. He could see now that a cat was curled up in her lap.

"She's asleep," Miss Clark said in response to his gaze. The schoolmistress wore a gray gown, with narrow blue stripes set about an inch apart, and wore her hair in a loose knot. "Jeanie is twelve years old and rheumatic, so I would rather not disturb her. Would you mind getting Miss Rawlins' book from the top shelf? It's off to itself on your right."

"Of course." Jacob went to the bookcase on the wall behind her father's chair and found *The Sandringhams of Longdendale* right away. About a dozen narrow strips of paper stuck between pages fanned out at the top. He turned to hand the novelette to her, but she shook her head.

"You'll need to see the pages too. Perhaps you had best set it here between us."

The sofa was an ugly mustard color and, like the two chairs, did not match anything else in the room. But it made up for its lack of aesthetic beauty with comfort, for its cushions were thick and soft.

"Where did she get the name Jeanie?" Jacob asked, seating himself.

Miss Clark scratched gently between the cat's ears. The animal made a slight movement at this attention but did not open her eyes. "From the song 'Jeanie with the Light Brown Hair.' My father orders sheet music for his trombone and took a liking to it."

"I don't think I've ever heard that one."

Taking the novelette from his hands, she set it between them on the sofa and opened it to the first marker. "Don't say that in my father's hearing unless you're prepared for a concert."

Jacob chuckled, easily able to imagine Mr. Clark performing with no timidity whatsoever. He found that he rather liked the Clark family, so at ease with themselves and visitors. "A concert would be nice, I should think."

Smiling, she turned her attention back to Miss Rawlins' story. "Now in this first chapter, did you understand the significance of the death of the future Lord Sandringham's governess?"

Jake thought for a minute and then shrugged. "I'm afraid I didn't. The governess is never mentioned in the story again."

"That's true. But because the boy's parents traveled a good deal, he was very attached to her. It was like losing a mother."

"Yes, I see."

"So how would that affect his adult years, do you think?"

Brow furrowing, Jacob replied, "Would that be the reason he was afraid to ask for Miss Webb's hand?"

"I believe so," Miss Clark replied. "But please understand that while we can discuss our interpretation of things that happen in the story, we can never know precisely what Miss Rawlins' intentions were."

"We can't?"

"No one can read minds, Mr. Pitney."

He let out a sigh. "Whatever happened to reading for the enjoyment of it? I dig in dirt every day for things hidden. Why must I dig through pages for meanings that may or may not be there?"

Jeanie the cat had somehow sensed his frustration, for she raised her head to give him an appraising look before climbing off her mistress's lap. Miss Clark lowered the animal to the carpet, then gave Jacob a sympathetic smile. "The lament of every university student, Mr. Pitney. But don't lose heart. We can find enough here to impress Miss Rawlins."

"Are you sure?"

"Quite sure."

She spent the next forty-five minutes going over foreshadowing, symbolism, and character development with him, so when it came time to take from his pocket the half-crown they had agreed upon, he felt he had gotten quite a bargain.

"I still feel a bit strange . . . taking money for reading," she told him as they both rose to their feet.

"You performed a worthwhile service, Miss Clark." He pressed the coin into her hand. "But are you sure this hasn't interfered with your teaching duties?"

"The stories aren't lengthy. And this is a pleasant diversion from drawing up lesson plans."

"Then you wouldn't mind reading another?"

"I'll read as many as you would care to discuss. You can drop it off in the morning if you'd like."

"I have it here." With a smile Jacob withdrew *The Marquis' Daughter* from his coat pocket. "As you said, they aren't lengthy."

Setting the book on the arm of the sofa, she led him back through the cottage. Her green eyes had a conspiratorial glint as she turned to face him at the door. "I'm looking forward to hearing what Miss Rawlins thinks of your newfound insight."

So am I, Jacob thought on his way home. But even though he understood one of Miss Rawlins' novelettes, he dared not flaunt that limited knowledge too soon. Memories of how he had made a complete idiot of himself in his earlier attempts still intimidated him. *The more books you understand, the more impressed she'll be*, he told himself, imagining that grand moment when he would become a veritable fountain of knowledge, and she would look at him with awe.

Bless you, Miss Clark, he thought.

*L*ydia walked to school carefully the next morning over cobbled stones glistening from a late-night shower. Tucked in her satchel was *The Marquis' Daughter* to read during her lunch break while her students played. As she passed the *Larkspur*'s carriage drive on her left, she saw no signs of the archeologists. *Perhaps the ground is too wet*, she thought. She wondered if Mr. Pitney had had the chance to chat with Miss Rawlins about *The Sandringhams of Longdendale* yesterday evening. She hoped the writer appreciated it. How many other men would take such pains to win a woman's heart?

You had a man pretend to walk to Shrewsbury to get your attention, she reminded herself. And into her head popped a shocking thought. *If only it would have been Mr. Pitney instead of Harold Sanders.*

"Enough of such foolishness," Lydia murmured, hastening her steps to leave the *Larkspur*'s vicinity, lest Mr. Pitney come around the wing and see her thoughts written upon her face.

At the schoolhouse, she glanced immediately at her desk upon opening the door—as was becoming a habit. She was grateful to see it was just as she had left it yesterday. Perhaps having to ride in the back of the wagon and being asked to tend children had put a damper on Harold Sanders' enthusiasm after all.

The students began arriving three-quarters of an hour later. Phoebe's eyeglasses did not cause the stir Lydia had feared, simply because the girl wasn't wearing them. By midmorning she felt compelled to usher the girl into the cloakroom.

"Where are your eyeglasses?" she asked in a low voice so the others wouldn't decide that eavesdropping was more interesting than the arithmetic word problems in their texts.

"In my lunch pail, Miss Clark," the girl replied. Quickly she added, "Thank you for buying them for me."

"You've already thanked me, Phoebe, and you're welcome. But I want to know why you're not wearing them."

"You haven't written anything on the blackboard yet."

"Has someone teased you about them?"

"No, Miss Clark."

Of course not. She would actually have to wear them first. Lydia sighed. "Phoebe, patterning your life around others' opinions is nothing more than slavery."

Now confusion came to the short-sighted eyes. "Ma'am?"

Sending up a quick prayer for wisdom *and* patience, she explained, "There are eleven other students in this classroom. Each one of them has family, chores, schoolwork, sports, music lessons, and so on. The amount of time that any of them would spend thinking about your eyeglasses is minuscule. Wouldn't you agree?"

"Yes, ma'am," the girl replied after a thoughtful hesitation.

"Then why spend most of the day uncomfortable, just for the sake of what someone may think of you in those few seconds?" She gave her a moment to mull this over, then asked, "Do you understand?"

"Yes, ma'am."

Grateful that her point had been made so easily, Lydia smiled. "Now, go on back to your desk and finish your assignment. With your eyeglasses on, please."

The girl did as instructed, but tucked them away in her lunch box again during the noon break. Passing where Lydia sat on the porch steps with Miss Rawlins' novelette, she explained, "I don't want anything to happen to them."

Oh yes, you do. She didn't reprimand the girl, for one of her father's favorite homilies about leading a horse to water came to mind. Just before dismissing her students that afternoon, she reminded them of an upcoming assignment. "May twentieth is less than two weeks away, and I'm looking forward to seeing your maps."

The bas-relief maps of the British Isles were assigned shortly after the Easter recess. Her ears caught the sound of a low groan—decidedly male—but she pretended not to hear it and even smiled inwardly. How she had made nearly perfect marks during her schooling years never ceased to amaze her, for she had spent so much time reading novels that she was forever playing catch-up with other assignments.

It was Philip and Aleda Hollis's turns to help tidy up the classroom. "What will you do with these this summer, Miss Clark?" Aleda asked as she sprinkled meal over the goldfish bowl.

At her desk, Lydia looked up from fastening the catch to her satchel. "I had planned to take them home. But Mrs. Bartley has offered her pond."

"For the summer?"

"I'm afraid it would have to be for life. They would soon outgrow their bowl after living in a pond." She got to her feet and walked over to where the girl stood. Gently tapping the side of the bowl, she said, "I can't help but think they would enjoy having a lot more space."

Philip came inside holding a broom and wearing an uncertain expression. "Uh, Miss Clark?"

"Yes, Philip?"

"Mr. Sanders is coming up the lane."

"No," she whispered, then held her breath to listen. She could hear wagon wheels—a dreadful sound. *There are more than one Mr. Sanders in Gresham* was the first hopeful thought she could muster. And as most of the village's pastureland was leased from the squire, this person could have some business at the manor house.

Philip walked over to the window. "He's holding some flowers, Miss Clark."

"Oh." There was nothing Lydia could do but send Philip and Aleda home. And since propriety wouldn't allow her to invite a man into the schoolroom, even to stress to him that she wanted to be left alone, she walked out on the porch with the two. In the lane Harold Sanders sat in a new-looking wagon behind a team of speckled drays.

"Hullo, Miss Clark," the man called, wearing his May Day suit of clothes and holding up a bouquet of violets as proudly as a flag-bearer displays his colors.

"Good day, Mr. Sanders."

"Shall we stay with you, Miss Clark?" Philip whispered at the bottom of the steps.

From the boy's other side, Aleda suggested, "Philip could stay while I fetch Papa or Luke."

She gave them both a grateful smile. "Thank you, but I should speak with him." When they looked doubtful, she added, "He's quite harmless. At least around women and children."

Lydia walked over to the wagon as the Hollis children—with several backward glances—cut across the school yard to the north. "Please stay in your wagon, Mr. Sanders," she said when he started looping his reins around the whip socket.

"I just thought you'd wanter ride . . ."

"I'm quite content to walk, thank you."

" . . . in my papa's new wagon," he finished lamely, his heavy-lidded eyes seeming to glaze over.

She didn't have the heart not to make some comment. "It's a fine wagon, Mr. Sanders. But as I said, I will be walking home. And shouldn't you be fetching your brothers anyway?"

"They got archery practice." He shrugged and held out the bouquet to her. "But I brought you some flowers."

The faint pleading in his voice made Lydia feel sorry for him again. She had no experience with these things but sensed there was a delicate line between nipping a romance in the bud and destroying a man's pride. And so she took the flowers and thanked him. "For the students," she made it clear. "They'll enjoy looking at them."

———

Harold had been so confident Miss Clark would accept the ride that he found himself with time on his hands. If he went home, he would just have to turn around and come back to fetch his brothers. *Papa oughter get them their own horses*, he thought. Even Mercy and Seth's Thomas rode a pony to school. But his father had calluses on his thumbs from squeezing pennies, so that wasn't ever likely to happen. It was in a foul mood that Harold reined the wagon to a halt under the elms outside the grammar school yard. Practice took place behind the schoolhouse near the squire's orchard, but he was in no mood to watch. So he sat slumped forward with elbows propped on his knees and tried to figure out where he had gone wrong with Miss Clark.

She took the flowers. That had to mean *something*. Or did it? Why was she so hard to court? Other men weren't queuing up to ask her hand, as far as he could tell. He wasn't the most handsome man in Gresham, but he still had all of his teeth and bathed regularly, sometimes as much as once a week. He didn't get drunk more than once a month either and had never dipped snuff. While he had yet to warm a church pew, as Mercy had suggested, Miss Clark had never mentioned it as a hindrance to their courtship.

Heaving a sigh, he rubbed the back of his neck and pictured himself as an old man, still breaking his back for his father. Presently a child's voice penetrated his thoughts.

"Let's go again, Phoebe."

He edged the team up so he could see past the elm that blocked his view of part of the school yard. The merry-go-round was in motion with a handful of children seated and Phoebe Meeks doing the pushing. When it squeaked to a stop again, he recognized Lester and Trudy among the younger children. *Mark must be at archery practice*, he thought. Not that he cared a lick.

"Again, Phoebe?"

"You'll have to let me rest another spell," the girl panted, sitting down on the edge of the contraption.

I thought she was supposed to be wearing spectacles. Again, it was none of his affair. He tried to peer around the school building for any sign of the archers. Wasn't school the place where a person learned to read and cipher? It was bad enough that he and his brothers had to take up the slack with Jack's and Edgar's chores, but with all the time the archery foolishness took, they were almost worthless around the farm.

The merry-go-round squealed into motion again with Phoebe pumping her feet and trying to hold her skirt about her knees with one hand. It would go much faster had she been a boy, but of course all the grammar school boys of any size were at archery practice.

He went back to cradling his head with his hands.

"Faster please, Phoebe!"

"I'm going as fast as I can."

With a groan Harold whipped the hat from his head and flopped it on the seat beside him. He tied the reins, jumped to the ground, and was across the school yard before Phoebe could push the merry-go-round another turn. "Get on," he ordered.

Straightening, she blinked at him as if he had told her to fly, while the five seated younger children stared with gaping mouths. "Sir?"

Harold heaved another sigh. "Do you want me to push this thing or not?"

"Yes, sir—thank you, sir." She sat and grabbed one of the metal bars.

"Will you go fast, Mr. Sanders?" asked a grinning Lester.

In spite of his sour mood, Harold grinned back at him. "Just hold onter your cap."

———————

That evening after a supper of saveloy sausage and cabbage was served by a sullen Mrs. Winters, Harold took up a lantern and walked down to the cottage at the end of the lane. He gave the door a rap and then let himself in the parlor. "Anybody here?" he called only out of courtesy because light had flowed from the windows.

"We're in here, Harold," his brother-in-law called from the kitchen.

He walked into the room, where Seth and Mercy sat at the table. Seth gave him a nod and went back to penciling something into a ledger book, and Mercy, who was hemming a shirt, smiled. "Would you care for some chocolate biscuits?"

That was one good thing about coming here—his sister didn't mind folks helping themselves in her kitchen. Mrs. Winters, on the other hand, ranted as if the food came out of her wages. He scooped up a handful of biscuits from the crockery jar in the cupboard, heaped them on the table in front of an empty chair, then poured a cup of tea from the pot on the back of the stove. "Anybody else?" he thought to ask.

With cups already before them, his sister and Seth declined. Harold pulled out the chair and crunched his way through a half dozen biscuits while the two continued with their tasks. "Amanda and Thomas asleep?" he finally asked, unsure of how to begin. The last time he had come for advice, he was confident that Miss Clark would be eager for him to court her. It was hard on his pride to admit she might not be as fond of him as he had thought.

"They are," Mercy replied.

Harold crunched down on another biscuit. "Children need their sleep."

"That's true."

"And apples too. Mr. Trumble says that if a body was to eat one every day, he'd never need Doctor Rhodes."

"Indeed? Well, it's good that we have apple trees then, isn't it?"

"That's just what I told Mr. Trumble," Harold nodded. "I said, 'It's a good thing we have apple trees by the creek.' I didn't mention your trees exactly, but if they're good for one body, they oughter be good for everybody . . . right?"

Setting her sewing down upon the table, his sister studied his face. Even Seth looked up, marking his place in the ledger with a finger. "Is there something wrong, Harold?" Mercy asked.

He raked his fingers through his hair, then wiped the excess *Sir Lancelot's Fine Grooming Pomade* on the edge of the tablecloth. "It's that Miss Clark. I tried all the things you told me to do, and they ain't workin'."

"Hmm. Then you've been to church?"

"Well, no. She's said nothing about it though, so that can't be what's wrong. But I gave her flowers—two times—and asked her advice like you said."

"Maybe it's time to give up," Seth advised while making another mark in the book.

"Give up?"

"Sh-h-h," Mercy scolded. "The children."

"Sorry." Harold ate another biscuit. "There's got to be something else that would make her want to marry me." And he was sure if he sat there long enough, the answer would come to him. Or better yet, to Mercy and Seth, so they could explain it to him.

Presently, Seth put down his pencil and closed his ledger. "We'll be turning in soon, Harold. You may sit here and eat biscuits, if you'd like."

Fat lot of good that would do, Harold thought, though the biscuits were better than Mrs. Winters used to bake—back in the days when she made treats for them—before she got it in her mind that she needed a worktable. But since it would do no good to argue with Seth Langford, he let out a long pitiable sigh. "I just figgered if anybody could help me it would be the two of you."

"I gave you a suggestion, Harold," his brother-in-law reminded him. "You said to give up."

"That's your only option at this point. Miss Clark is aware that you're interested in courting her by now, so if she has any feelings in kind, she'll find a way to make them known to you."

Harold sent a helpless look to Mercy.

"He means it's time to step back and see if Miss Clark misses the attention you've been showing her," she explained.

That didn't make sense. If a man wanted to catch a fish, he took his line and bait to the riverside and kept at it. How many fish ever jumped out of the river into a man's arms? He scratched his head. "I don't know . . ."

Now it was Seth who gave a sigh, and by the look on his face, Harold reckoned he would soon be sitting at his sister's table alone.

"That was how Mercy won my heart," his brother-in-law explained.

"It was?"

Seth winked at Mercy, who smiled back. "For some weeks she paid Thomas and me lots of attention, coming over here and cooking Saturday dinner for us. And then suddenly she would hardly speak to me."

"Yes?" Harold looked at his sister with renewed appreciation. Until she set her cap for Seth Langford, she had always been so soft-spoken and meek that he had to wonder how she found the courage to change. "You was uppity?"

"Not at all," she replied. "Just distant."

Distant? But until her marriage, she had never lived anywhere but their father's cottage. "Where did you go?"

Seth shook his head. "She didn't leave Gresham. But when I came across her in town or at church, she was just polite, not overly friendly."

"And that made you want to marry her?"

"Yes." He smiled at Mercy. "There were other reasons as well, but that was what got my attention."

Less than five minutes later, Harold walked back through the night with hope in his heart and chocolate biscuits in his pockets. Why not try something different, seeing as how giving Miss Clark all that attention wasn't working? He could be distant too.

He just had to make sure she noticed.

*N*oelle wasn't fooled by the emptiness of the shop as the door chimed to a close behind her. She had caught sight of Mr. Trumble through the window on her way across the lane. The curtain to the store-room was even swaying a bit. With lips pressed together like a disapproving dowager's, she crossed the room and paused at the counter. "Mr. Trumble?"

She heard movement in the back, and then silence. *This shop wouldn't last a year in London,* she fumed inwardly. "Mr. Trumble, I know you can hear me. Shall I go back there and find you?"

This time the curtain moved, and the round-faced shopkeeper came through it. "Oh, Mrs. Somerville," he greeted, his eyes not quite connecting with hers. "I *thought* I heard someone out here. Fancy meeting you again today."

She was certain he was being sarcastic, but as vexed as she was, she could not afford to get on his bad side. So with a great act of the will, she stretched her lips into a smile. "Forgive me, Mr. Trumble. I'm so very worried that something happened to that letter. It would be from an old friend in London—actually my cousin-twice-removed on my father's side—who has been courting the most charming woman you would ever wish to meet. I introduced them, actually, at a soiree on derby day. My friend promised to write as soon as he's gathered the courage to propose and tell me all about it."

The shopkeeper nodded as she spoke, but with eyes glazed over. Noelle supposed she ought to stop telling him the story, for by now surely he was aware of the letter's importance.

"Anyway, when Mr. Jones had nothing for me today, I wondered if you had received tomorrow's mail yet." She walked over to look behind the postal slots and discovered a canvas sack in the corner, about the size of a bed pillow. "And so you have."

"Now, Mrs. Somerville," he appeased. "I ain't ready to sort it yet. I've a crate of goods just arrived last hour needin' to be stacked on the shelves first."

"Then just allow me to look through the sack. I won't get in your way."

He gaped at her as if she had suggested she douse the sack with kerosene and burn it. "Postal regenerations, Mrs. Somerville."

"Then *I'll* stack the merchandise." She couldn't believe she was offering this, but she had had a strong feeling all day that the letter would come and had spent practically the whole morning in the garden waiting on Mr. Jones. When he had something for almost everyone in the *Larkspur* but her, she could have wept. "Just show me where it goes."

"But I can't allow—"

Noelle rolled her eyes. "Don't tell me postal regulations forbid that as well, Mr. Trumble."

"Well . . ." He raked a hand through his thinning blond hair and, mumbling to himself, went back behind the curtain. The crate he set on the floor at the end of the counter contained what appeared to be about five dozen tins and jars of assorted vegetables, fruits, and meats along with some household supplies. "It ain't as easy as it seems, Mrs. Somerville. You'll have to rotate the merchandise."

"Rotate?"

"The newer things go in back so's everything stays fresh as possible."

"Very well," she said, waving him away. It was a simple task, actually, and gave her something to do besides pace the floor. She just had to move aside the merchandise already on the well-dusted shelves, arrange the newer items behind them, and place the older in the front again. To reach the two highest shelves she used the footstool and resignedly stepped aside twice whenever Mr. Trumble waited on patrons.

The first, a middle-aged woman purchasing a spool of thread and card of buttons, sent so many curious glances in her direction that Noelle finally smiled brightly and held up the jar that was in her hand. "Would you care to buy some *Beetham's Glycerin and Cucumber Lotion*, ma'am?"

"Ah . . . no, not today," the woman replied and did not look at her again.

The second customer was a man of dubious hygiene and stubbled cheeks who bought several items. He stared boldly at her, and after returning to the shop to heft a sack of oats upon his shoulder, he went over to where Mr. Trumble had resumed sorting mail. Stacking tins again, Noelle could not hear the question the man murmured to the shopkeeper, but her ears prickled at Mr. Trumble's reply.

"She's a widow, Mr. Towly."

"And content to stay one!" Noelle snapped so that the odious man was sure to hear. She did not turn to see his reaction, but a few seconds later the bell over the door jingled, followed by a hearty slamming noise. She sent a sharp look over to Mr. Trumble, who shrugged.

"He asked if you was married. What was I to say?"

"You could have told him I was a nun."

The shopkeeper chuckled. "You could do worse. Mr. Towly makes a decent living."

"Then *you* marry him." Noelle went back to stacking tins. But when the task was halfway finished, she stepped down from the stool again and folded her arms. "You know, you have no order here."

"I beg your pardon?"

Making a sweeping motion with her hands, she told him, "Tins of tooth powder standing next to tins of beets, matches shoved in here beside lard . . ."

He stood with his hands on his hips, staring at her with injury across his round face. "But it's all stacked neat."

"It's chaos, Mr. Trumble. I don't see how you ever find anything." Giving a sigh, she asked, "Are you about finished there?"

"Not quite." The injury in his tone matched the look he had given her. "I've had customers, you recall."

Staring up at the shelves again, she asked herself, *What else have you to do today?* She sighed again. "Well, I'm just going to have to put some order here."

"Order?"

"Clearly this place needs a woman's touch. I should wonder why your wife hasn't complained."

"My—"

"Please get on with sorting the mail, Mr. Trumble." Noelle motioned him back toward his postal counter. "Trust me, you'll be glad I came by today."

Pursing her lips, she scanned the rows of merchandise. *Tinned foods should have a shelf of their own.* She had shown heroic patience with the local people's lack of urban sophistication but now felt compelled to bring some light into the darkness. She picked up a tin of stewed apples and mused, "Now let's see. We should start with fruits. Alphabetically, of course."

The project required more stamina then she had imagined, especially with her having to move aside every time Mr. Trumble assisted a customer. "I cannot find anything, Mrs. Somerville," he complained an hour later, surveying with a dazed look upon his face the tins and jars and boxes that covered every inch of his counter.

"Well, I haven't finished." But Noelle was running out of steam and wondered whatever had possessed her to begin in the first place. "And what about the mail?"

Now his expression grew fearful. "I'm sorry—there's no letter for you."

That was enough to sap her strength completely. She sat back on the stepladder, propped her elbows on her knees, and buried her face in her hands. "I just don't understand . . ."

"Mrs. Somerville?" Mr. Trumble came hurrying around the counter. "Are you all right?"

Looking up at him through blurry eyes, Noelle muttered, "May I have some privacy, Mr. Trumble?"

"But this is my shop."

"Oh, very well." She rose to her feet and waved him aside. "If you'll be so kind as to give way."

"Give way?" He blinked several times, his mouth gaping. "Mrs. Somerville, you can't leave me like this."

"Well, I'm sorry, but I'm in no condition to finish. But I've gotten you off to a good start, so—"

"A good start?" Pink spots rose in his cheeks. "I asked you not to go tearin' apart my shelves, Mrs. Somerville. But now that you've started, you'll have to finish."

She could hardly believe he was speaking to her this way—and with her heart broken from the disappointment of no letter. *After I spent all that time trying to help him.*

Before she could remind him of that fact, he drew in two deep breaths that sounded like bellows. "Mrs. Somerville," he said afterward with surprising calm.

"You're still in my way, Mr. Trumble."

He moved aside. "I aim to be a gentleman at all times, Mrs. Somerville. But if you don't put my shelves to order again, I'll not allow you back in my shop."

"But I'm your best patron."

"Patrons spend money, Mrs. Somerville! All you've done since you moved to Gresham is come in here and imitate me, day in and day out."

Noelle was opening her mouth to argue when his words registered in her mind. *Imitate?* The picture that came to her mind was so ludicrous that a little chuckle escaped her.

"And what's so funny?" the man asked suspiciously.

"Nothing, Mr. Trumble." She suppressed her smile and picked up a jar of pickled beets. It was rather cruel of her to leave him to finish alone, she supposed. *And he's likely to pile everything up there every which way.* Besides, she had not thought to brood during the time she had already spent on the task. That in itself was reason enough to continue. Meekly, she asked, "Will you at least help me?"

"I've no choice, have I? If I want to close up shop by suppertime, that is."

"We'll have it done by then," she promised.

They were finished by half-past six. In silence she and the shopkeeper stepped back to survey their work. Noelle had always considered it a matter of pride that she had never spent a day of her twenty-one years laboring with her hands. She had never even swept the floor of her own flat. But the pride she now felt as she looked at the orderly rows of merchandise was inexplicably satisfying.

"Well, what do you think?" she asked Mr. Trumble, whose face wore no expression that she could recognize.

He turned to her and smiled. "It's some change, Mrs. Somerville."

"Does that mean you like it?"

"I like it fine. I'm going to fetch Mrs. Trumble right away, in fact."

"Tomorrow you'll tell me how she liked it?"

"Wouldn't you care to wait and see for yourself?"

Noelle shook her head. "I'm a little tired now."

"Then I'll wait to tell you." Still smiling, he walked her to the door. "I hope you get your letter tomorrow, Mrs. Somerville."

The glow of accomplishment stayed with her all through supper, tempering her disappointment over Quetin's failure to write. She even sat with the others in the hall. But when the discussion drifted over to a book circulating throughout England, written by an American named Charles Russell and stating positively that Christ would return in 1874, she excused herself for her room. Such talk was terrifying—it was easier to store in the back of her mind the notion that one day Quetin would make an honest woman of her and she would reconcile with God. The last thing she wanted to think about was facing Him in the near future.

Oh, Quetin, I need to be with you, she thought, biting her lip as she took pen and vellum paper from her writing table. She needed his soothing assurances that she wasn't a bad woman just because she loved someone.

> *Dearest Quetin,*
> *It has been two weeks now, and I so long to hear from you.*

And then because she knew he would become irritated if she dwelled upon her misery too much, Noelle forced herself to inject some lightness into the letter. She told him of coming to the aid of the vicar and his wife in Shrewsbury, of the May Day auction, and helping Mr. Trumble organize his shelves. She even described the lodgers and the servants at the *Larkspur*.

In closing, Noelle could not resist one more plea.

> *It's not knowing what to expect in the future that casts a shadow over everything. Is Averyl living in London now? When do you expect I can come home? Will you visit soon? I realize that your Parliamentary duties consume large portions of your time, Quetin, but please respond to this letter as soon as possible.*
>
> > With undying affection,
> > Noelle

She folded the pages and was about to put them in the envelope when a more practical matter caused her to pick up her pen again and add a postscript:

> *Forgive me for calling attention to this matter, but I am almost completely out of money.*

The words looked so pathetic, even in her practiced flourishing script, that she felt her eyes begin to burn again. Hastily she folded the letter and stuffed it in the envelope, lest a tear blur the words and give Quetin evidence of how truly desperate she was. Then she recapped the ink and rested her head on folded arms upon the table. Like the proverbial eggs in one basket, her whole emotional and material well-being was in the hands of one person—one who certainly wasn't as dependent upon her.

———

Late the next morning, Fiona accompanied Ambrose to the vicarage, bringing a pan of Mrs. Herrick's butterscotch custard. Though Andrew's cheek was still quite swollen, he was in good enough spirits to sit out in the garden and even told them of a parishioner in Cambridge who had once brought him a cherry pie.

"She was proud of her baking ability and rightly so," he said. "But in this case she forgot to remove the pits. My cook feared one of us would choke or break a tooth, so all we could do was consign it to the dustbin."

Julia slanted a mock suspicious look at him. "I suppose she was one of your pursuers?"

"She was twenty years my senior and happily married, my dear."

"Did I hear *one* of your pursuers?" Ambrose asked with raised brows. "And wouldn't that be pursueresses?"

Giving a crooked swollen grin, Andrew replied, "Two would be more accurate, though I venture if either could catch sight of me now, she would be happy for her lack of success."

"Did the lady who gave you the pie ever ask about it?" Fiona asked the vicar.

"The very next Sunday. And with me standing in the doorway of the church. Of course location has nothing to do with the gravity of a sin, but you can understand that I was at a loss for words."

"What did you say?" asked Julia.

"I finally told her, 'A pie like that doesn't last long at our house.' "

Ambrose chuckled over it again as they strolled arm in arm across the green an hour later. Four women were gathered at the pump, one holding a chubby infant who cackled with delight every time someone worked the handle. "Do you believe laughter is a gift from God, Fiona?"

"Oh, most definitely, Ambrose. And so are tears, I think." Fiona smiled at him. "But I enjoy the laughter most."

"So do I," he agreed.

We've had both in our marriage, Fiona thought. Laughter that could spring from the smallest occurrences, simply because they experienced them together. And prayerful tears—hidden from her husband—during some of his darkest moods. Still, she was content.

They met Mr. Jones opening the letter box at the *Larkspur*'s gate. "Shall I bring those inside?" Ambrose asked with a nod toward the envelopes in his hand.

"Very well, sir." The postman handed them over and touched the bill of his hat to Fiona. "Jolly keen weather we're having, wouldn't you say?"

"Indeed it—"

A slamming sound cut into her reply, and all three heads turned toward the *Larkspur*'s door. Mrs. Somerville, wearing a burgundy silk wrapper and with her hair disheveled about her shoulders, hurried up the garden path. "Oh, Mr. Jones?" she called, waving an envelope.

The postman mumbled something Fiona couldn't decipher, but when she looked at him, he was hefting his satchel upon his shoulder again. She and Ambrose traded curious glances.

"Forgive my dressing gown," the young woman pleaded at the gate, "but I've a letter that simply must go out today."

She was close enough now for Fiona to notice the circles under her eyes. "Have you another headache, Mrs. Somerville?" she asked.

"No, thank you." Mrs. Somerville sent a quick preoccupied smile in her direction while handing the envelope to Mr. Jones. As she watched it disappear into the satchel, she said, "Have you anything for me today?"

"Mr. Clay has all of the *Larkspur*'s mail, madam." There was no mistaking the relief in the man's expression as he touched the bill of his hat again. "I must attend to my rounds. Good day to all of you."

Mrs. Somerville paid him no attention, for she was now at Ambrose's elbow. "Are you going to stand there holding them all morning, Mr. Clay?"

"Be my guest," he offered affably, handing over the stack of envelopes.

She scanned each address, her face losing a little of its composure with each that was flipped to the back. Then she sorted through them again. "It's not here."

"Well, perhaps tomorrow—"

Face clouding, she shoved the envelopes back into his hands. "Yes, perhaps." She turned and hurried back to the house with her wrapper flowing about her ankles.

Fiona took a step in that direction but felt Ambrose's hand upon her arm.

"You don't want to get involved, Fiona."

"But she's upset, Ambrose."

"Then she'll have to find solace from someone else. The house is full of people." He gave her a tender smile, but his gray eyes were serious. "I still have an uneasy feeling about her."

Though she trusted his instincts, Fiona had to wonder if he was over-reacting. "We practically live in the same house."

"I don't propose that we ignore her completely." Ambrose glanced at the *Larkspur* and then lowered his voice. "Please. She's been here only a fortnight. Let's wait a little while longer before you go reading each other's diaries and all that."

Though she felt much sympathy for the lonely young woman, her first loyalty was to her husband. She resolved to pray that Mrs. Somerville would find the solace she needed, then said, "Reading each other's diaries, Ambrose? First I would have to write one."

Offering his elbow, he walked her along the garden wall again, around the corner, and toward the carriage drive. "Surely you kept one when you were a girl. I thought young ladies liked that sort of thing."

"I didn't learn to read until I was eighteen. But perhaps I'll start one someday."

"You'll mention me every now and then, won't you?"

Pretending to think this over, Fiona replied, "I suppose I would have to. After all, I do see you fairly often."

He chuckled. "And what will you write, pray tell?"

"Ah, but diaries are supposed to be secret, Ambrose."

"That's so, Mr. Clay," came a grating voice from across the lane.

A sweeter voice added, "I've even heard of some with locks and keys."

Caught up in each other's company, they had forgotten about the dear old village sentries. They turned to greet the Worthy sisters across the lane, and Ambrose asked them, grinning, "Surely you don't believe a wife should keep secrets from her husband, do you?"

Jewel Worthy nodded enthusiastically. "Indeed she should. I didn't tell my Silas every thought that rattled through my head. A woman's got to have a little mystery about her if she wants to keep her man interested."

"Why, Mrs. Worthy." Ambrose cocked his head to study her. "There is more to you than meets the eye, isn't there?"

Giving him a beatific smile, the elderly woman replied, "Begging your pardon, Mr. Clay, but if I didn't tell my husband all there was to me, I'll not be telling you."

Jewel's dry laughter filled the air, and soon Fiona and Ambrose and Iris were joining in. Minutes later, when Fiona and Ambrose had reached the staircase leading up to their apartment, her husband realized the letters were still in his hand. "Go on up, why don't you?" he said. "I'll bring these inside."

"See if there's anything for us first," Fiona suggested.

"Certainly."

As it turned out there was one for her from Ireland, addressed in the uneven print of her sister, Breanna. She went upstairs and sat down on the parlor settee, broke the seal, and straightened the page.

Dearest Fiona,
  Aileen is soon to be marrying the Mooney boy who tends sheep. Our mother longs to see you, as we all do . . .

"Mother . . . Ireland," Fiona murmured.

*T*here was no sign of Mrs. Beemish or Mr. Jensen as Ambrose walked up the back corridor, and the noises from the doorway suggested that the kitchen servants were too busy with lunch preparation to be troubled about letters. He walked on to the hall, exchanged greetings with Mrs. Dearing, who was squinting at an open exercise book at the piano, and fanned the envelopes out on a tea table where they could be seen.

"I believe there is a magazine here for you," he said to the elderly woman. "Would you like it now?"

"I'll see to it later, thank you." Mrs. Dearing glanced toward the corridor doorway and lowered her voice. "Have you happened to see Mrs. Somerville this morning?"

"Why, yes. Just a little while ago."

She hesitated before continuing. "I was just upstairs when she came bounding up the steps with her face flushed as if she'd been crying. But when I asked about her, she ignored me, went into her room, and slammed the door."

After sending a look to the doorway himself, Ambrose said, "I'm certain it had nothing to do with you, Mrs. Dearing. It seems she was expecting an important piece of mail."

The older woman breathed a sigh of relief. "Here I've been wondering if I've done something to offend her. Hopefully she'll get her letter tomorrow."

"Yes, hopefully." On his way back down the corridor, Ambrose thought about the woman who was no doubt weeping upstairs. He could not help but feel sympathetic, his having had more than a nodding acquaintance with despondency. But when weighed against his wife's welfare, Mrs. Somerville's troubles did not even make the scale.

And he was positive by now that the *Larkspur*'s newest lodger had something against Fiona. More than once Ambrose had caught a look of contempt in her eyes when she looked at his wife. Whether from jealousy or prejudice against the Irish, he didn't know or particularly care. He only knew that if Fiona allowed her innate compassion to draw her close to this woman, she would eventually be hurt.

His wife was standing at the window when Ambrose walked into the parlor of their apartment.

"You've delivered the letters?" she asked.

"As far as the hall. They'll find their way to the owners soon enough." He noticed the creased page on the settee. "How is your family?"

"Very well. There is to be a wedding in four weeks—my sister Aileen."

She turned back to the window, prompting Ambrose to walk over to stand behind her and put a hand upon her shoulder. "You want to go, don't you?"

"No, of course not." But then she turned, and he could see the sheen in her eyes. "I never thought I would, after what my father did," she murmured.

Ambrose knew the story. At the age of fourteen Fiona was married off to a cruel older man. Bartered, actually, because her father gained a horse and wagon from the arrangement. But he understood how enduring family ties could be. Though his father's drinking and mood swings and his mother's complacency had strained their relationships, he would want to see them were they still living.

"It's been ten years since I left Ireland," she went on with the most melancholy of expressions. "I've nieces and nephews I've never seen."

"Then we'll go, Fiona."

"I don't see how."

"Why, we simply take the train to Bristol and catch a boat," he teased.

Her eyes were still somber in spite of a grateful little smile. "May I be perfectly honest with you, Ambrose?"

"When have you ever been otherwise?"

She sighed. "You would despise every minute of it. Whether we stayed with my family or Breanna, there are too many people living in too close quarters to allow for any privacy. Especially with the wedding. I daresay we wouldn't have a room to ourselves."

"Surely there is an inn. . . ."

"Not for thirty miles. What if you slipped into a dark mood while sharing a room with some of my brothers or Breanna's boys?" She shook her head and said in a resigned tone, "It's just too impractical to consider."

"I'm sorry," Ambrose told her, stepping back a bit with a heavy heart. Over the two years of their marriage, she had almost convinced him that it wasn't weakness which made him the way he was. What a vain fool he had been to ignore the facts. For she was right. Such a situation would be sheer torture for him. Just imagining it made the back of his neck break out into a sweat.

But even more agonizing was the thought of her going there alone. True, she had emigrated from Ireland alone at the age of eighteen without incident, but she hadn't been his wife then, and he hadn't yet made it his life's mission to protect her.

There was no reproach in the violet eyes that sought his. "You're my family too, Ambrose."

That wasn't enough and he knew it. How much longer would her parents be alive? Would she resent him, even unwittingly, when they were gone?

The solution that suddenly entered his mind was so simple, so reasonable, that he took her hands and smiled. "We'll send them the money to come here."

"The money—"

"All of them. Surely they could use a holiday. And what better place to have a wedding?" Warming up to the idea, he made plans. "There are plenty of beds at the *Bow and Fiddle*, and—"

She took a hand from his and reached up to put a finger to his lips. "They can't leave their crops, Ambrose. And likely wouldn't come if they could. My folks are old and set in their ways. Besides, there is the young man's family to consider as well. Will you have the whole of Kilkenny here?"

He didn't know how to respond except for an unimaginative, "Oh."

After lunch they sat in rocking chairs in the *Larkspur*'s library to read— or at least *she* read, from Charlotte Bronte's *Villette*, while Ambrose merely stared at the same page of Disraeli's *Felix Holt* until the print wavered as if underwater—when another solution occurred to him. A much more difficult one, at least for him. Dare he mention it? *You have to*, he told himself.

"Fiona."

"Yes, Ambrose?" she said, looking up from her book.

"What is that oldest Keegan boy's name?"

"You mean Tom?"

"Yes. How old is he?"

"Sixteen, I believe. He's still in secondary school."

"Which lets out in June. And the willow-gathering season should be over by then."

She studied him curiously. "Are you suggesting that Tom accompany me?"

"Surely he would be willing to earn some money and see a bit of his homeland again at the same time." He was a strapping lad as well, who looked older than sixteen. His presence in Fiona's company would surely discourage anyone with less than honorable intentions. And as the Keegan family had seven children in their small cottage, he would most likely not balk at being asked to share a bed with any of Fiona's brothers or nephews.

Ambrose couldn't stop himself from harboring a selfish hope that she would decline the proposed arrangement. He felt shamed when relief flooded her face.

"Oh, Ambrose, that's a wonderful idea." With the book still open in her lap, she pressed her palms together and rested her fingertips against her chin. "And I wouldn't worry about your being lonely with so many of our friends here."

"Why, I'll hardly know you're gone," he quipped in a performance worthy of any stage.

"Ambrose." She straightened in her chair, violet eyes appraising him frankly "I'm not so foolish as to believe that. But you can bear it for a fortnight, can't you?"

A fortnight? He had had in mind a week or less when he suggested the Keegan boy. But he had to remind himself that it would take about three days to get to Kilkenny, and the same amount of time to return. *Two weeks without her?*

"Because if you don't think . . ."

Mustering a little smile, he replied, "I'll miss you terribly, Fiona Clay, but it's important that you go. I would rather suffer for two weeks now than live with guilt years later that I kept you from your family."

As she settled back into her chair, her eyes took on a luster again. "Thank you, Ambrose," she said quietly.

The love in her expression made it all worthwhile. Ambrose's smile became more genuine. "I suppose we should be calling upon the Keegans this afternoon, shouldn't we?"

————

The sky was an inverted bowl of perfect Wedgwood blue as Noelle set out on foot for the vicarage two days later. She scarcely noticed, for her thoughts centered feverishly around Quetin, as usual. There had to be a reason he had yet to write. Perhaps Averyl had grown suspicious and was having his every move watched? She certainly had the means with which to do so.

Or could it be that Quetin felt she would reconcile herself to Gresham more easily if he gave her some time without news from home? He was so much wiser than she. Was this silence for her welfare? She could bear that, if she could only be sure.

Think about something else, she commanded herself, rubbing her temple hard with a gloved hand as if to aid her mind in doing so. She was actually glad she had accepted the invitation, for she feared she would go mad from worry if she didn't find a distraction. The Phelps were pleasant company—even if he was a vicar—and besides, she couldn't afford any more shopping trips to Shrewsbury. And as much satisfaction as rearranging Mr. Trumble's shelves had given her, she had no inclination to rearrange the rest of his shop, as he had jokingly suggested when she asked about the mail yesterday.

The vicarage came into her sight after she passed the town hall. Mrs. Phelps, looking youthful in a yellow gingham gown, waved to her from the garden. Noelle returned the wave and inquired about her husband's health when she reached the gate.

"Much improved, thank you," Mrs. Phelps replied, holding the gate open for her. "He'll be back in the pulpit this Sunday. However he's not quite ready for rib roast or anything of that sort, so Mrs. Paget is preparing baked trout for lunch."

"I'm glad he's better." Noticing the scissors in Mrs. Phelps's hand, Noelle asked if she could be of any assistance.

"I've just finished, thank you." She picked up a basket lying on the ground near a wicker chair and showed Noelle the purple English irises she had just picked. "For the table."

"Very lovely. You do your own gardening?"

"Just since I married Andrew." They strolled together toward the porch. "I started out by helping our caretaker, and gradually it became a hobby. I've discovered there is something immensely soothing about putting your hands in the dirt."

"Perhaps I should bathe with it, then," Noelle said dryly before she could stop herself. She was startled when Mrs. Phelps laughed.

"Forgive me, but you have such a droll way about you sometimes," the vicar's wife said. "It's quite charming."

"No one has ever said that to me." Not even Quetin, but then he could be downright miserly with compliments.

"No? I'm very surprised." Near the foot of the steps Mrs. Phelps turned to her, concern replacing the levity in her green eyes. "You're still homesick, aren't you?"

Noelle answered with a casual shrug but had to glance away for a second.

"You poor dear. Forgive me for offering unsolicited advice, but why don't you go back to London? Not that we don't enjoy having you in Gresham, but if it's only making matters worse . . ."

Tears stung Noelle's eyes—not so much from homesickness as from the compassion in the other woman's voice. She blinked them away and thought, *If you knew the truth about me, you wouldn't even have me in your home.* "I can't go back yet. But I do appreciate your concern."

The sound of an approaching horse gave her an opportunity to change the subject. Turning toward the lane, she said, "I believe someone's coming this way."

"That would be Paul Treves," Mrs. Phelps told her. "He's vicar of Lockwood, the neighboring village. You won't mind his joining us for lunch, will you?"

There was no mistaking the faint tension in the older woman's voice. Sighing inwardly, Noelle supposed it was inevitable that someone would try to initiate a romance between her and one of the locals. A lonely young *widow* would be too much of a temptation for Mrs. Phelps's compassionate nature. So instead of expressing resentment at this intrusion into her affairs as she might have just weeks ago, she shook her head and commented casually, "We've met."

Mrs. Phelps blinked at her. "Indeed? You and Vicar Treves?"

"We shared a train compartment when I came from London."

"Why, that's remarkable. I had no idea."

At least Noelle supposed he was the same man, though she seemed to recall his name being Treen. A carriage came into view, and she recognized the face.

"Andrew has been a mentor to him this past year," Mrs. Phelps said, lifting a hand to wave. "And we've been intending to invite him over for some time now. . . ."

"I'm sure I'll enjoy renewing my acquaintance with him," Noelle assured her.

Only the vicar wasn't alone, but accompanied by an odd-looking young fellow with a pale face and disheveled brown hair, who headed immediately for the paddock beside the stable when the carriage stopped. Vicar Treves, strikingly Nordic-looking in spite of his black suit, came through the gate wearing an expression of pleasant surprise. "Why, Mrs. Somerville. How good to see you."

"Good morning, Vicar Treves."

"How are you finding Gresham?" he asked as he shook the hand she had offered.

"Green and pleasant, as you said." Or at least she *thought* he had said something to that effect.

"I'm so glad to hear it." He then turned to Mrs. Phelps and shook the hand she offered as well. "And, Mrs. Phelps. Thank you for inviting me. How is the vicar?"

"So much better, thank you. I left him in his study just a little while ago, jotting down some sermon notes."

"I take that to mean he'll be preaching tomorrow?"

"Wild horses couldn't keep him away."

"I understand," Vicar Treves said, smiling. He glanced over his shoulder to where his young companion appeared to be feeding something to Vicar Phelps's horse. "I pray you don't mind my bringing along Israel Coggins. It occurred to me this morning that you and the children have never heard him play, and the vicar enjoys it so."

"How thoughtful," Mrs. Phelps replied. "Andrew speaks so highly of his talent. I'll just ask Dora to set another place. Surely he'll want to be with you."

He gave her a grateful smile. "Thank you. As you can see, he's terribly shy. I'm afraid he'll panic if I'm out of his sight for too long." That settled, Vicar Treves excused himself and went to the gate to wave him over.

"Who is he?" Noelle whispered to the woman beside her.

"Vicar Treves' caretaker. I believe his mother is the cook."

And he's to sit at the table with us? Noelle thought, then remembered that Mrs. Phelps owned the *Larkspur*, where a paying lodger could be asked to leave for not being considerate of the servants. She supposed it was all well and good to extend Christian charity to those less fortunate, but she would be relieved to return to London, where the class lines were comfortingly rigid.

"Thank you for waiting," Vicar Treves said, returning with the boy at his side.

At least Noelle assumed he was a boy, judging by the guilelessness in his face. But had she to pinpoint his age, she would have guessed anywhere from sixteen to thirty. Fastened to a cord that hung across his body from the opposite shoulder was a stringed instrument of some sort. She gave him a polite nod when he doffed his cap but did not offer her hand. If the Phelps wanted to be democratic, that was their business.

Mrs. Phelps not only offered a hand, but a compliment as well. "Bishop Edwards visited us Thursday, Mr. Coggins, and praised your music highly."

Ignoring her hand, the boy stared at the ground and mumbled, "Thank you. Bishop is a nice man. His horse is named Mordecai."

He's feeble-minded, Noelle realized. Surely Mrs. Phelps would change her mind about seating him at the table. It was one thing to show kindness to someone less fortunate, but another to subject one's guests to him. What if he drooled, or slurped his soup? Just the thought was enough to ruin Noelle's appetite.

But Mrs. Phelps clearly had not considered that, for she simply smiled and said, "Shall we go inside?"

Vicar Phelps was descending the staircase just as they passed through the vestibule. He greeted them warmly and assured them he was in no more pain. Israel, he clapped upon the back. "Why, the Bishop and I were talking about you just two days ago, and I had a longing to hear you again."

"I gave Rusty an apple," Israel replied. He still stared down at his feet but smiled this time. "He liked it."

The vicar chuckled. "I'm sure he did."

"If you'll go on into the parlor," Mrs. Phelps invited, raising the basket upon her arm, "I'll put these in water and fetch the children."

"I've already told them to wash up," her husband said, then explained to his guests, "The older three are working on some map projects for school, and Grace is advising."

Noelle glanced at the staircase in wonder, recalling the many times she and her siblings had donned starched ruffles and lace for the purpose of being presented to guests in the parlor, only to be consigned to the nursery five minutes later for their meal. Heaven forbid that guests should be exposed to the not-so-polished table etiquette of children, with the constant threat of spilled milk or crumbs upon one's bodice.

She was even more bemused when, after the children had joined them in the parlor, it was pointed out by one of the girls that Philip wore a spot of green paint upon one earlobe. Everyone simply laughed—even Israel Coggins—as the boy grinned and excused himself to tidy up. The formality that so pervaded the vicarage beside Saint Marylebow was absent, replaced by a camaraderie that was difficult to fathom. Had she not watched Vicar Phelps in the pulpit she would have questioned his dedication to the ministry, for wasn't sobriety a requirement for a man of the cloth?

In the dining room, she was given the seat across from Vicar Treves. She wondered if he also suspected that Mrs. Phelps had ulterior motives for inviting them both on the same occasion. He was certainly handsome and mannerly enough, but even if her heart were not already fixated upon Quetin, she had no interest in becoming romantically involved with a minister. Childhood memories were still too fresh. It was commendable that people like the Phelps were more relaxed than her parents had been, but the thought of living in a vicarage again—being at the beck and call of a congregation—was too horrendous to consider.

From the corner of her eye she watched Vicar Treves tuck Israel's napkin into his collar after the boy's attempt to do so had failed. He was quietly solicitous, acting as if he did this sort of thing every day. And a disconcerting thought occurred to Noelle. Here she had been mentally listing reasons why she could never consider a future with a man of the cloth, when it was highly likely that someone like Vicar Treves had his own list of women he wouldn't consider. And prominent on that list would be someone who was a kept mistress.

Not that it matters to me, she told herself, turning her attention to the meal placed before them.

*I*f he were any fresher, he would be winking at you," Andrew said in response to Mrs. Somerville's compliment on the tastiness of the trout. "Laurel and Philip caught a nice string of fish this morning."

"Laurel?" Vicar Treves asked, giving the girl a smile. "I thought our Mrs. Miller was the only woman who fished."

"Mrs. Miller?" asked Andrew.

"My churchwarden's mother. She says she has fished almost every Saturday morning, weather permitting, of her seventy years."

"She has a dog named Copper," Israel offered. "She says it's because he's red. But she hasn't a horse."

"I only go fishing now and then," Laurel confessed. "Most of the time I would rather read."

"We're all fond of reading," Aleda told the young vicar. "Once when Mother brought home *An Old Fashioned Girl* from a bookseller in Shrewsbury, Laurel and I were so desperate to get to it that we wound up reading it together."

"However did you manage that?" Mrs. Somerville asked.

"Well, first we tried to sit side by side and look at the same pages, but that didn't work very well. So we took turns reading aloud to each other."

"It must have been a good story."

"Oh, it was wonderful," Laurel exclaimed. "We've each read it again since then."

"Speaking of Shrewsbury . . ." Julia turned to Vicar Treves in an effort to prod him into a conversation with the woman across from him. "I never would have gotten Andrew home last week if Mrs. Somerville hadn't been there."

It worked, for the man looked across at Mrs. Somerville and smiled. "Indeed?"

"I'm afraid we ruined her outing," Andrew said apologetically while mashing butter into his boiled potatoes with his fork. "Chloroform destroys a man's dignity, trust me."

Julia sent him a look that meant, *Let them talk to each other*, but he simply gave her a maddeningly blank smile and went on mauling his potatoes.

"My day wasn't ruined at all," Mrs. Somerville protested. "In fact, it turned into an adventure."

"Like Alice's?" Grace asked her.

"Alice?"

"She means Alice in *Through the Looking Glass*," Aleda explained with a hint of long-suffering in her tone. "That was just fantasy, Grace."

"I know that," Grace defended. "I meant that Mrs. Somerville had an adventure, just like Alice did."

"I'm afraid I haven't read the story," Mrs. Somerville replied. Giving the nine-year-old a wry little smile, she asked, "Has it anything to do with dental surgery?"

"No, ma'am," Grace said over chuckles from everyone else at the table—everyone but Julia.

We should have done this yesterday, she told herself, for the children would have been at school. She and Andrew had definitely been lax about their chatting at the table. With fewer people present, surely Vicar Treves and Mrs. Somerville would be more inclined toward conversation with each other.

"Tell me, Mr. Coggins, how did you become interested in the dulcimer?" Andrew asked.

The boy looked at Vicar Treves as if asking permission to answer, then encouraged by his nod stared again at his plate and replied, "My mother bought it for me from a peddler last year."

"Had you any instrument before then?"

Israel simply shook his head, prompting Vicar Treves to say, "Israel has never even taken a music lesson."

"It must be a miracle," Grace said with awe in her voice. Aleda nodded in wide-eyed agreement. Julia could feel knots in her stomach. She looked helplessly again at Andrew, who this time sent her an unmistakable message with his eyes.

Calm down.

For the first time since their guests' arrival, Julia realized she was acting as if the fate of the whole world hinged upon a romance developing between Vicar Treves and Mrs. Somerville at lunch today. She drew in a deep breath. What had Andrew said? *If they're meant to be together, God will see to it that it happens.* Since when did the Almighty require her help?

Taking in a deep breath and holding it, she willed her tensed muscles to relax. She had given the two an opportunity to renew their acquaintance. The rest was up to them and God. And as for her first attempt at

221

matchmaking—she had had enough of it. From now on, she hoped she would have the sense to leave it to people like Mrs. Bartley, who had stronger nerves.

Feeling as if a weight had been lifted from her shoulders, Julia smiled at Israel. "Your mother must be very proud of you."

———

After the meal, which Noelle had actually enjoyed because she didn't think of Quetin even once, Vicar Phelps suggested that they sit out in the garden. The wicker chair offered to Israel Coggins was turned to face the others, and more chairs were carried from the dining room. "May I invite Elizabeth and Jonathan?" the auburn-haired Aleda asked her mother.

Mrs. Phelps hesitated, seeming to struggle over what seemed to Noelle should be a simple reply. In that space of silence Vicar Treves said to her, "Please do, Mrs. Phelps."

The glance the two exchanged was rapid but fraught with meaning. Noelle realized the "Elizabeth and Jonathan" in question were the couple she had met at the May Day picnic. *The vicar's daughter and son-in-law.* Raleigh was their name, she actually remembered. Why weren't they invited to lunch? *Of course.* Vicar Treves had said something on the train about losing someone in the past, but not to death. *You should be a detective*, Noelle told herself.

While Philip was commissioned to hurry over to the Raleighs, Vicar Phelps sent the youngest girl inside to invite the servants, resulting in more chairs being brought outside. Meanwhile, Israel Coggins sat in his chair and stared at his hands.

"It's a wonder he has the nerve to play in front of people," Noelle said in a low voice to Vicar Treves, who amazingly enough had asked permission to share her bench after lending a hand with hauling chairs.

Noelle assumed it was for Elizabeth Raleigh's benefit, if her supposition about the two of them was correct. But she didn't mind and even took it as a compliment. If a man wanted to make another woman jealous, or at least prove to her that he wasn't miserable without her, he would of course pay attention to the most beautiful eligible woman in the vicinity.

"The music does something remarkable to him," the young vicar said in response to her comment. "It's as if God gave him the talent to compensate for his lack of conversational ability."

The compassion in his voice made her a little ashamed of her earlier discomfort at sharing the same table with Israel. *Well, he could have drooled*, she rationalized. "What do you think would have happened if his mother hadn't bought him the dulcimer?"

"I suppose we would have all missed out," Vicar Treves replied. He shook his head. "You know, until his talent was discovered, he was dubbed the village idiot."

"How cruel," Noelle said, ignoring the little stab in her own conscience.

"I'm afraid I was just as uncharitable with my thoughts."

"At least you didn't voice them."

"But it was wrong, just the same. Judgment is judgment, whether it's spoken or thought." With a self-conscious little smile, he added, "Forgive me, Mrs. Somerville. I sometimes forget I'm not in the pulpit."

She was strangely moved that he would allow himself to be so transparent. "I can't imagine you being anything less than kind," she told him in all honesty.

"Thank you, but if only that were so. Unfortunately, there was a time when I was full of myself just because I had so much Scripture committed to memory. I didn't realize God still had much to teach me through other people." He shook his head ruefully. "And I'm afraid I have a habit of monopolizing the conversation when I'm in your company."

"I like people who will speak up," Noelle confessed. "Unless they're describing wedding gowns."

"I beg your pardon?"

She smiled. "I was thinking of a couple of women I met on my first train from London. If the person I'm with will talk, I don't feel so pressured to tax my brain for something intelligent to say."

"Why would that pressure you?" he asked, giving her a curious look. His voice was frank, with no hint of flirtatiousness. "You're an intelligent woman."

For the first time in her near memory, Noelle felt a blush steal across her cheeks. Odd that the compliment would please her, when she had always considered beauty her most important quality. Didn't every woman wish to be beautiful? How many heroines of songs or fairy tales were described as intelligent? Not only had she never minded that Quetin treated her as if she were a simple child, but it had never occurred to her to question that it should be any other way. He was older and wiser and definitely more experienced with the ways of the world. What did she know?

"You're too kind," was all she could think to answer.

"Truthful, you mean." And then, as if concerned that he had overstepped his bounds, he became silent until Vicar Phelps, seated on the bench beside him with his wife, asked him if he had received a recent copy of a diocese newsletter. Behind Noelle the servants chatted, and presently the Raleighs arrived with the older girls and two women wearing aprons over their dresses.

"Mrs. Somerville, how good to see you again," Elizabeth Raleigh said as she approached Noelle's bench. "Are you enjoying your stay in Gresham?"

"Very much so," Noelle responded automatically before realizing that it was true, if only for the past couple of hours.

"I'm so glad to hear it." Then with just enough nervousness to confirm Noelle's earlier suspicions, Mrs. Raleigh looked at the man beside her and said, "It's good to see you again, Vicar Treves."

At his feet now, he took her offered hand. "You're looking well, Mrs. Raleigh," he said warmly, with no trace of artificial exuberance.

"Thank you." She beckoned to Mr. Raleigh, who had stopped to speak with Vicar Phelps. "May I introduce you to my husband, Jonathan?"

"But, of course."

The man walked over, and after making a little bow over Noelle's hand and exchanging pleasantries with her, he shook hands with Vicar Treves. "I'm so pleased Lockwood has decided to participate in the tournament this year."

"Our students are almost beside themselves," Vicar Treves replied. "And according to our schoolmistress, Mrs. Mobley, their marks rose dramatically when the team was formed."

"I'm pleased to hear that," Mr. Raleigh said, a glint of humor in his gray-green eyes. "Archery saved my sanity during my first year as schoolmaster. I shall have to tell you that story one day."

"I look forward to hearing it," Vicar Treves replied, smiling, but when the Raleighs had moved on to settle into chairs on the other side of the Phelps, his hands were trembling slightly.

As Israel Coggins began strumming the first chords, she felt compelled to lean closer and whisper, "You handled that very well."

"Thank you," he whispered back.

The strains of "Abide with Me" were surprisingly sweet and fluid. Closing her eyes, Noelle rested her head against the high wicker back of the bench. The story of young David came to her, how his lyre music soothed King Saul's tormented mind. If only Israel Coggins could play his music for her every day. Perhaps then her own mind could find such solace, instead of having to work so hard to keep at bay a growing suspicion that she had given up her family and her God for a security that was beginning to feel nebulous.

Without missing a stroke of the strings, Israel began playing "Rock of Ages, Cleft for Me." One of the maids seated behind Noelle began humming. Grace Phelps started singing softly in a pure little voice, and before long it seemed as if everyone was singing. Even Vicar Treves, in a pleasant baritone. For all his earlier nervousness, he seemed at peace.

Archery practice was the best thing ever invented, Harold Sanders decided. For by bullying Fernie, Dale, and Oram out of their turns to collect Jack and Edgar, he had a reason to be in the grammar school yard every time Miss Clark came walking by on her way home. He had failed the first couple of times by getting so involved with spinning children on the merry-go-round that he forgot to keep watch for her. Now he had formed the habit of taking a few steps to peer down Church Lane every time he stopped to collect his breath.

And she would be by any minute now, he thought as he took another look that Monday afternoon of May twentieth. The lane was still empty. He felt a tug at his cuff and looked to his right.

"Mr. Sanders?" Timmy Casper said through a gaping tooth.

"Give me a minute," Harold told him sternly on his way back to the half dozen children who waited for siblings at practice. "I've told you how taxin' this is to a grown man's body."

"Yes, let him rest," Phoebe Meeks scolded.

"Why don't we give you a turn, Mr. Sanders?" asked Lester from the merry-go-round.

"Give me a turn?" Harold chuckled. Wouldn't that be a sight? "I'm too heavy for the likes of you."

"No, you ain't, Mr. Sanders." Lester let go of the iron bar and let himself to the ground. "We're strong enough. Do get on."

"Please?" another child pleaded. "You don't have to be afraid. It won't hurt you."

Hurt me? Did they really think he was afraid? Throwing up his hands, Harold declared, "All right. You can give me a spin."

There was much giggling as children scattered from the contraption and took up positions at the bars. Trudy looked for a place from which to push but was admonished by Phoebe to move out of the way lest she get trampled. That led to tears, so Harold intervened.

"Here, now," he said. "You can ride with me." So when he was satisfied that the giggling girl's arms were securely wrapped around a bar, he made a face at the children waiting to push. "Go ahead—if yer able, that is."

With a whoop they were at it, their legs pumping slowly at first as the merry-go-round squeaked into action. "I told you I was too heavy," he taunted. But in just a few seconds they had built up a surprising speed. The school building, trees, his papa's horse and new wagon—they all whizzed by him. He clutched the bar a little tighter, while beside him Trudy squealed and begged to go faster.

Why do they like this so much? he wondered as queasiness rolled up in waves from his stomach to the top of his head. He thought that maybe the scenery flying past was the problem, so he closed his eyes. That made it even worse.

"Wheee!" Trudy cried.

"Stop!" Harold shouted.

When the contraption was mercifully still again, Harold flung himself out of it. Only the ground was spinning just as fast, and he pitched forward to his hands and knees.

"Mr. Sanders?"

The little monsters were all around him now, staring with wide eyes.

"I'm all right," he muttered.

"Shall I fetch you some water, Mr. Sanders?" asked Phoebe.

"No. Just leave me alone."

"Miss Clark is coming," Lester warned.

"Oh." Harold pushed himself to his feet. He took a few unsteady steps to look past the corner of the schoolhouse. Sure enough, she was walking up the lane. With his stomach still in his throat he wove toward the wagon and shimmied up into the seat.

"Good afternoon, Mr. Sanders," he heard a minute later.

He tore his eyes from the fingernails he was pretending to study, looked down at the lane beside him, and replied nonchalantly, "Oh . . . good afternoon, Miss Clark, I didn't know you was there."

As usual she did not stop to chat, but he was positive that her steps slowed a little. Was she hoping he would chat some more? *You're supposed to be distant,* he reminded himself. So he gave his attention again to his fingernails. He did not look up again until she had had time to go beyond the crossroads, for it would ruin his plans for her to look back and catch him staring at her.

The children were still milling about the merry-go-round and sent him remorseful looks as he approached.

"We're sorry for making you sick, Mr. Sanders," Timmy apologized.

"I weren't sick. I just didn't care for it." And Harold couldn't see how anyone in his right mind would want to spend one minute spinning around like a top. But as the children about him were fond of the contraption, and he had nothing better to do, he asked in a gruff voice, "Well, are you gonter stand there all day or get aboard?"

*T*he Worthy sisters were not alone in their garden when Lydia crossed Market Lane. Her father, wearing a paint-spattered smock over his clothes, stood in concentration behind his easel about six feet away from their chairs.

Iris noticed her first and gave her a serene, if rather stiff, smile while her fingers continued to spin lace on the cushion in her lap. "Good afternoon, Lydia."

At the sound of her name, Lydia's father looked up from his canvas long enough to salute her with his brush. "Hello, daughter."

"Good afternoon," Lydia said to all three as she drew closer.

"Did all the children bring their maps to school today?" Iris asked.

"What maps?" Jewel asked before Lydia could reply.

"The paper-mache ones. You remember Ben Mayhew showing us his just this morning, don't you?"

Jewel frowned. "That were a map?"

"What did you think it was?"

"Ladies, please," Lydia's father interrupted. "Will you look this way again?"

Meekly, both obeyed. Lydia went around to her father's side of the canvas. True to his habit, he had painted the wattle-and-daub cottage and the garden first. A surprisingly good likeness of Jewel stared back at her while he filled in the finishing touches to Iris's black lace bonnet. "Very nice," Lydia said.

"Thank you." And without missing a brush stroke, he lowered his voice to ask, "Did Harold Sanders snub you again today?"

Lydia glanced at the sisters, whose expressions had become decidedly more attentive. "Papa . . ."

He grimaced. "Sorry."

"Well *I'm* not," she was unable to resist saying with a little smile before bidding farewell to the three of them.

Five minutes later as she unlatched the gate in front of the cottage, she saw her mother sitting in the long shade of the elm tree, squinting at a familiar-looking book held close to her face. *Countess Lucinda's Journey*, the novelette she and Mr. Pitney would be discussing tonight for their third discussion meeting. "You'll ruin your eyes," Lydia warned after leaning down to kiss the proffered soft cheek.

"The book isn't *that* bad, dear."

"No, I meant the lighting." Realizing her mother was teasing, she smiled and shook her head. "You and Papa are just alike, you know?"

"Yes? Is that a terrible thing?"

"It's wonderful." She put her satchel on the ground, and her mother gathered aside the skirt of her gingham gown to make room for her on the bench. "How did he convince the sisters to sit for him?"

"Oh, they were delighted to do so after your father offered to make them another washpot." Her mother returned the wave of Doctor Rhodes passing by in his trap and asked, "Will your Mr. Pitney be here again tonight?"

"He's not *my* Mr. Pitney, Mother," Lydia replied, surprised by the bitterness in her own voice. "Miss Rawlins holds claim to his heart—even though she doesn't realize it—nor deserve it."

"It's not like you to speak that way, Lydia." Her mother gave her a pained but understanding smile. "You've grown fond of him, haven't you?"

Very fond of him, Lydia thought, but replied, "It doesn't matter how I feel about him. But it grieves me to see a man practically have to memorize her little stories to get her to see his worth."

Patting her hand, her mother said, "Infatuation is a strange thing, Lydia. It's like a spell we cast on ourselves. If he's so ill acquainted with her, then Mr. Pitney has obviously fallen in love with love itself."

"He's too intelligent for that," Lydia protested.

"Unfortunately, that has little to do with infatuation. But sometimes intelligence will bring it to an end, in due course."

"How?"

"If his knowledge of Miss Rawlins' books does indeed bring them together, he'll be forced to contend with her true personality instead of the myth his mind has created. Perhaps he'll find himself suited to her—or perhaps not."

Lydia couldn't help but feel hopeful at the *perhaps not*. Not because she entertained any hope that he might turn his affections in her own direction. But at least he wouldn't continue offering his heart to someone unable to see that it was made of gold.

———

That evening, Jacob's knock upon the Clark cottage door was answered by Mr. Clark himself. "And so you've come for some more book talk, have you?"

Though there was no mockery in the elderly man's voice, still Jacob found himself stammering his reply. "Uh . . . yes, sir."

"Well, come inside, then," he said, stepping out of the way. "Lydia's fetching my pipe. You've time to compliment me on my latest project."

Jacob was motioned to an easel set up before the fire screen. "Why, it's the Worthy sisters."

"Don't see how you can tell. I ran out of daylight."

Incredulously Jacob looked up at him, for even if one face was unfinished, any resident of Gresham could tell their identities by the lace-spinning cushions and cottage in the background. He realized then, by the glint in the man's eyes, that he was teasing. Jacob smiled. "This is very good. But didn't you say people were difficult to paint?"

"Aye, they still are." He cocked a white eyebrow meaningfully. "And catching them is even more so."

A vision of Mr. Clark chasing down one of the Worthy sisters flashed before Jacob's eyes. "Sir?"

"Cost me a washpot, just to get those two to sit in their garden and do what they would be doing anyway. And I won't be surprised if they up their fee when I go back to finish tomorrow."

From the open doorway leading into the rest of the cottage called a familiar voice. "You left it in the kitchen, Papa! Mrs. Tanner says you ought to keep one in every room so we aren't always . . ." Miss Clark entered the room and paused at sight of Jacob. "Oh, good evening, Mr. Pitney," she greeted with a sheepish little smile.

"Good evening," Jacob replied, returning her smile.

She handed her father his pipe and then offered her hand. She was clothed in a simple blue dress, and her brown hair drawn back loosely into a knot. Jacob was surprised at himself for not noticing before now that she was almost as tall as he. Or that her ears were slightly prominent. He rather admired that she didn't try to conceal them with curls or ribbons or such.

"I wouldn't have bellowed like a fishwife had I realized you were here, Mr. Pitney," she apologized. "I'm afraid we're used to shouting at each other, especially when Papa misplaces his—"

"Amos—it's not upstairs!" another female voice called through the doorway, just before Mrs. Clark stepped into the room. Her plump cheeks pinked. "Oh, Mr. Pitney. How rude you must think us."

"Actually, you make me feel quite at home," Jacob confessed. "We've a bakery connected to our house back in Dover, and our father would often have to shout through the doorway for another hand if business was brisk. My sister and brothers and I could each mix dough and serve customers by the age of ten."

"That's a far step, isn't it?" asked Mr. Clark. "From baking to archeology."

"Amos . . ." cautioned his wife.

"I don't mind." Not only did Jacob not mind, but he found himself enjoying the exchange. "I actually spent my first year at Oxford studying to become an engineer. My mother's brother was an engineer, and I admired that he got to travel and build bridges. But I happened upon a book titled *Nineveh and Its Remains* in the library one day—"

"And Nineveh won out over bridges!" Mr. Clark exclaimed. "What an interesting story, Mr. Pitney. I do so admire folks who aren't afraid of change."

"Amos," Mrs. Clark said again, yet with affection in her voice as she took his arm. "We should allow Mr. Pitney and Lydia time to chat."

The old man looked disappointed but shrugged. "Very well. I suppose I'm to find something useful to do."

"I could use some help with untangling a skein of wool upstairs. Jeanie made a mess of it."

"Oh joy," he mumbled affably.

Seconds later, Jacob was seated with Miss Clark on the sofa in the back parlor. Jeanie, the yarn-tangling cat, jumped to the space between them and curled up for a nap. "You'll have to forgive my father's gregariousness," Miss Clark said while turning pages of the copy of *Countess Lucinda's Journey*. "He forgets that you aren't here just to socialize with him."

"I enjoyed the chat," Jacob assured her. "But I'm afraid I did most of the talking."

"I don't recall your doing that, Mr. Pitney. And I can assure you that my parents enjoyed every minute of it." She ran a finger down a page and stopped. "Now, I suppose we should start with the scar on Count Basil's forehead. The shape of it means something, don't you think?"

"Why, I believe so. Come to think of it, it was mentioned often."

And never without the descriptive *hook-shaped* preceding it. Jacob had even wondered at one point if Miss Rawlins believed her readers unable to remember such a simple detail from one page to another—and then felt guilty for such a disloyal thought.

"But I haven't a clue what it could mean," he confessed. "Have you?"

"Not yet. But it'll come."

"How?"

Miss Clark looked at him again with the same glint of humor in her eyes that he had seen in her father's earlier. "As you mentioned once before, Mr. Pitney. We dig."

After fifteen minutes of exploring possibilities, Lydia helped Mr. Pitney ascertain that the hook-shaped scar surely symbolized the way Count Ferdinando's life would change from misfortune to fortune, culminating with his marriage to Lucinda—who finally discovered her love for him when he rescued her from the Ghibellines. Had the scar turned downward instead, it would likely mean something else.

The rest of the novelette was much easier to decipher. Still, Mr. Pitney took a small notebook and pencil from his breast coat pocket after a while. "I use it while I work," he explained in an apologetic tone. "With so many books to learn, I'm afraid I'll get them confused."

I hope she appreciates all your effort, Lydia thought. Though she wasn't sure she wanted to know the answer, she could not stop herself from asking. "Was Miss Rawlins impressed with your insight of the first two stories?"

"Well . . ." Absently he rolled a pencil against his knee with the palm of his hand. "I haven't drawn her into a conversation about them yet."

"You haven't?"

"I suppose I've been afraid I'll forget everything we've discussed and look like a greater fool."

"Never! A man who can find stories from things pulled out of the ground?"

He gave her a grateful, if surprised, look. "Thank you for saying that."

"Well, it's so." She knew she must sound terribly forward, but if it was forward to tell the truth, then she would just have to accept that. But to take the compliment any further would be downright flirtatious, and so she veered the subject into another direction by asking how the excavation was progressing.

"Very well," he said, animation flooding his expression. "We uncovered something recently that could have significant meaning."

"What did you find?"

He told her about a bracelet that could possibly have belonged to the daughter of Roman Governor Cerealis. "He left Britain in A.D. 74, so it would naturally predate that time."

"What makes you suspect it might have been his daughter's?"

"The workmanship was extraordinarily fine, which would make it beyond the wages of the average Roman legionnaire. And most importantly, the name Vernita was engraved inside." Leaning forward intently, he explained, "You see, it has always been assumed that Cerealis had little interest in expanding Roman territory in Britain. The only fortification he is known to have built is at York. If we can find enough evidence that he initiated a push to the west, it would be quite a revelation. No doubt the Archeological Association would extend our work here indefinitely."

"So you must wonder constantly if this will be the day you find more proof."

"It makes brushing dirt away a little more exciting," he agreed, then frowned. "I wish we hadn't been so hasty about shipping the bracelet to London so I could show it to you."

That he would care to have her see his work brought a small ache to Lydia's chest. If Mr. Pitney was this thoughtful to someone with whom he shared only a business arrangement, what must it be like to be the object of his affection? Afraid that her face was wearing her thoughts, she scooped up the cat just to have something to do. "When you find your other proof, I would enjoy seeing it."

"Absolutely, Miss Clark." With a glance toward the clock, which read half-past nine, he got to his feet. "Forgive me. I didn't realize the time."

Lydia carefully put the cat to the side and rose. "That's not considered late at this house, Mr. Pitney."

He gave her another grateful look as they walked through the cottage together. "Perhaps you would care to watch us work one day when school is out? People come up there every now and then."

"That would be interesting," Lydia told him noncommittally, but smiling. When he was gone, she carried *Veronique and the Highwayman*, her next assignment, upstairs to her room to read for a little while before turning out the lamp. As harsh as her thoughts had been toward Miss Rawlins, Lydia realized she was in the writer's debt. If Miss Rawlins wasn't making it so difficult for Mr. Pitney to initiate a courtship, he would have no reason to call here on Monday nights. And Mondays were becoming more and more special to Lydia.

She thought about his invitation to watch the excavation. She had too much pride to take advantage of any invitation that was extended for politeness' sake. But if he ever mentioned it again, she decided she would make that trek up the Anwyl. What did she have to lose?

———

I'm going to do it today, Jacob thought atop the Anwyl on Tuesday afternoon as he brushed another layer of dirt from the base of what was appearing to be a small urn. When panic quickened his pulse, he reminded himself of Miss Clark's assurance that he wasn't a fool. *A man who can find stories from things pulled out of the ground?* she had even added.

The thought fanned the feeble flame of his self-confidence so much that by the time he sat down at the *Larkspur*'s supper table that evening, he felt a rush of disappointment that Miss Rawlins did not appear. If she was sequestered in her chamber penning a new story, it could be hours before she came downstairs. But he was willing to wait, so after the meal he settled into a hall chair and listened to the other lodgers discuss favorite places they had visited during the courses of their lives.

It was during Mrs. Dearing's account of the days of the California Gold Rush that Jacob's eyelids began to flutter. The voices began to swirl pleasantly about him, just as the gravel and water swirled in the pans of the forty-niners, and he lapsed into a dream about hopeful men standing up to their knees in the American River.

He had no idea of how much time had passed when he heard Mr. Durwin's voice nudging him back into consciousness. "Mr. Pitney?"

Jacob became aware, in that fraction of a second just before opening his eyes, that his jaw was hanging wide open. A snort escaped him as he snapped it shut. He straightened in his chair and blinked at Mr. Durwin's sleep-blurred image.

"You were snoring, Mr. Pitney," he whispered.

"Oh . . . I'm sorry." And that was when he noticed that the chair on his immediate left was filled with the svelte form of Miss Rawlins. Though she appeared to be absorbed in the account Mr. Ellis was giving of the fortnight he had spent at Interlaken with relatives as a boy, Jacob's vision grew clear enough to catch the faint amusement in her expression.

Heat rising to his cheeks, his immediate impulse was to flee the room. Again he had proved himself a total social misfit, so what use was there in attempting to impress her? But Jacob thought then of Miss Clark and how disappointed she would be to learn that he had lost heart again. He cleared his throat and gave a mirthless little chuckle. "I didn't realize I was so sleepy."

Miss Rawlins merely glanced at him long enough to give a quick nod, then turned her attention back to Mr. Ellis. Jacob sighed inwardly and assumed a listening posture that belied the racing of his mind. It wasn't that Mr. Ellis's travelogue of Switzerland wasn't interesting, but he could have been giving the secret of growing gold sovereigns in clay pots, and Jacob couldn't have forced himself to pay attention. He was totally absorbed with waiting for a break in the narrative so that he could speak with Miss Rawlins.

So when it at last came, he was ready. "I enjoyed *The Sandringhams of Longdendale*, Miss Rawlins," he told her in as casual a voice as possible.

She turned to him again with her little smile. "Very kind of you to say, Mr. Pitney."

It appeared she was about to look away again, when he forced himself to say, "A very complex character, Lord Sandringham. It's interesting to

see how the events of our childhoods set the stage for our later perform-
ances as adults."

"Why, that's true," she said, staring as if he had just recited the *Gesta
Romanorum*—in Latin. "And I attempted to portray that in the story."

"As you did so skillfully. Just look at the influence his governess had
over the choices he made, even though she had passed away when he was
just a boy."

A tentative appreciation came into the smoky gray eyes behind her
spectacles. "Thank you, Mr. Pitney."

He decided it was time for a swift *coup de grace*.

"The governess reminds me in a way of the magistrate in *The Marquis'
Daughter*. While her influence was positive, except that her death caused
young Lord Sandringham an insecurity about life, the magistrate's influence on young Nicola is extremely negative—and his death frees her to
live life to the fullest."

She actually blinked. Twice. "Why, Mr. Pitney. I'm flattered that
you've devoted so much thought to my prose."

Returning her smile, Jacob thought, *And I'm grateful that you're so
bright, Miss Clark.*

*O*n Wednesday, May twenty-second, exactly four weeks since Noelle's arrival in Gresham, a letter arrived for her. Only the return address was that of Mr. Radley. A dreadful foreboding accompanied her up the staircase to the privacy of her room, where she broke the seal and pulled out a single folded sheet of paper.

> *Dear Miss Somerville,*
>
> *Please be advised that my client, the honorable Quetin Paxton, M.P., has decided, in the best interests of his marriage, that certain ties with the past must be severed. Therefore Lord Paxton requests that you, Miss Somerville, make no further attempts to contact him.*
>
> *But being that Lord Paxton is a compassionate man, he is not without concern for your situation. He is hereby offering to sponsor your lodgings in Gresham for an indefinite period of time, determined solely upon your willingness to reside there. In addition, he will send a generous monthly allowance of two pounds, the first to be sent as soon as I receive word by return post or wire that this will be agreeable.*

There was more, something to the effect that Lord Paxton wished her health and happiness for the future, but the words became blurred. And they really didn't matter, for the gist of the letter was that he no longer wanted her. Suddenly bereft of strength, Noelle lowered herself to the carpet and wrapped her arms around her knees. The sobs began in the pit of her stomach, growing so much in intensity that she had to press her mouth to one knee to keep from sharing her grief with the whole house.

As it was, a knock sounded at the door.

"What is it?" Noelle managed through a raw throat after wiping her face upon the hem of her gown.

"Are you all right, ma'am?" Sarah's voice, filled with concern, came through the other side of the door.

"I'm fine. Go away, please."

She spent the rest of the day atop the covers of her bed, with no appetite for meals nor company. Mrs. Dearing knocked once and called out to her, and later Mrs. Beemish came to see if she was in need of anything. She ignored both. Her thoughts moved frantically from image to image, her mind a stage upon which scenes of the past three years were played—scenes where she had angered Quetin with some foolish observation or complaint, scenes of his surely being bored to death by her prattling on and on about the latest fashions, and so many images of her holding her hand outstretched for money.

And then another scene took center stage. Herself, playing *Speculation* with her only three women friends. Meara Desmond, with her amber cat-eyes, so smugly solicitous of her predicament. So unruffled, even though her means of support would be coming to an end any day. What had she said? Noelle strained her mind to remember.

"*At least you'll have the other lodgers to keep you company.*"

"How did she know?" Noelle rasped into her sodden pillow. She went over every detail of that night and could not recall mentioning anything about her new living arrangements before Meara made her remark.

With dreadful clarity now, she could see why she was here. Perhaps Averyl Paxton was in London, perhaps not. But Quetin, with his repugnance for altercation, had found a way to cast her aside.

———

Gresham woke to a hazy sky on Thursday, and by noon the first black clouds had begun creeping in from the northwest. Three o'clock seemed more like seven as Harold reined Dan and Bob onto Church Lane, but still he was surprised to find a half dozen carriages and wagons queued in front of the grammar school, and Mr. Raleigh helping children into them.

"What happened to archery practice?" he asked Jack when he and Edgar appeared with lunch pails and books under their arms.

"Just look at the sky," Jack replied, staring as if Harold had said something ignorant, while setting his books and lunch pail into the wagon bed.

That's the trouble with all that schooling, Harold thought. *Too big for their britches.* "Well, it ain't rainin' yet."

Edgar, climbing up the wagon spokes, shrugged. "Mr. Raleigh didn't want us to get caught up in it."

Harold ground his teeth. This wasn't good. Miss Clark wouldn't be by for another half hour yet, and he had no excuse to lurk around the school yard. With the archery tournament in just two more days, these fine opportunities for ignoring her would come to an end. Ignoring the questions of his brothers, he jumped from the wagon seat and stalked over to Mr. Raleigh, who at this time was helping Trudy Meeks into a wagon hitched to his two horses—and already crowded with Meeks and Kerns.

236

"What if it don't rain for hours?" he demanded of the schoolmaster's back.

Mr. Raleigh turned to him with a puzzled look. "I beg your pardon?"

"Hello, Mr. Sanders," Trudy Meeks called from the carriage.

"Hullo yourself," Harold replied over the schoolmaster's shoulder. "How are we gonter win that tournament if we don't practice? It's only two days away."

"I didn't know you were interested in archery, Mr. Sanders," Mr. Raleigh said, crossing his arms.

"Well, my brothers are on the team, ain't they?"

"They're our biggest assets, actually."

Harold narrowed his eyes. His brothers might be full of themselves since they got educated, but nobody who wasn't a Sanders had the right to call them names. Only by the look on Mr. Raleigh's face, he didn't seem to intend any spite.

Warily Harold asked, "What do you mean by that?"

"I mean that they're excellent marksmen." Mr. Raleigh glanced overhead, unfolded his arms, and took a step back toward his carriage. "Look, we'll have to discuss this later, Mr. Sanders. I've still to get to the other school and try to deliver these children home before the sky falls out."

Resignedly, Harold was about to turn to leave when Mr. Raleigh's words found their way through his felt cap. "The other school?" he asked as the schoolmaster climbed into his carriage seat.

Mr. Raleigh picked up the reins. "To fetch Phoebe Meeks. Miss Clark knows to keep her there if the weather is threatening."

"Good idea," Harold declared and took a step closer. "But why don't I take the Meeks? I've got plenty of room in the wagon."

"I don't think—"

"That way mebbe we both can get back home before the rain."

"May we please go with Mr. Sanders?" Lester Meeks asked his schoolmaster.

Harold could have kissed him.

Ten minutes later he was reining the horses to a halt in the lane outside Miss Clark's school. "Want me to fetch her?" Mark asked from the back.

"I'll do it." Harold was already handing the reins to Jack, who sat on the bench beside him. "And you'll have to move when Miss Clark comes out."

"But I thought we were here for Phoebe," Edgar said.

By then, Harold was halfway to the porch. "Her too." Once inside the schoolroom, however, he realized he had forgotten how unreasonable Miss Clark could be.

"Thank you, but my father will be along shortly," was her reply to his offer, even though she had smiled sweetly and thanked him for coming for Phoebe.

"Don't you wonter save him the trouble?"

"He's likely halfway here already. Besides, your taking me home would increase the chances of you getting caught up in it." She actually shooed him out of her schoolroom as if he were a guinea rooster in her garden. "You had best hurry, Mr. Sanders."

Harold's thoughts were as dark as the clouds overhead as he escorted Phoebe out to the wagon. Or rather walked in front of her, for he was so vexed that he took long fast strides.

"Is Miss Clark still coming?" Lester asked, craning his neck to see past Jack's shoulder.

Harold flung the boy a look that silenced him. In fact, none of his passengers said another word until he reined the horses onto Arnold Lane, and then only to reply to his question about the location of the Meeks' cottage.

"It's the first one, Mr. Sanders," Mark offered while from the distance came the rumble of thunder. "I'll show you."

Soon he was letting children out of the wagon in the carriage drive of a weathered cottage. There were no cattle in the pasture, but the barn door was closed, and he reckoned that the children's mother had penned the animals inside for the approaching storm. He didn't think he had ever met her, not even in town. *It's a shame that a woman had to tend children and this farm without a man*, he thought. Dairying was hard work.

"Thank you, Mr. Sanders," the three children said almost at the same time after Jack and Edgar had assisted them to the ground.

Harold merely nodded, but then because Trudy was looking at him with expectant green eyes and it wasn't her fault that Miss Clark was so stubborn, he followed with a gruff, "You're welcome."

The thunder rumbled, this time louder. "Now take yourselves on inside before you get rained on," he ordered.

———

"And there it is," Lydia announced, crossing the front parlor to collect her father's pipe from the criss-cross table that held his palette, assorted jars of paint, a bottle of linseed oil, and brushes and rags smudged with dried paint. Rain beat a continuous tattoo against the windowpanes, which rattled with every clap of thunder. From the easel the Worthy sisters' likenesses stared, as if to say, *We could have told you where his pipe was if you'd only asked.*

Holding the lamp closer to the finished portrait, Lydia wondered where her father would hang it once it was framed. It wasn't enough that the sisters' watchful eyes took in almost everything that went on in the village—now they would gaze at her from one of the cottage walls. *But it could be worse*, she thought as two other faces came into her mind. Immediately she chided herself for the uncharitable thought—for Mr. Towly had left her alone since the altercation at the crossroads, and Harold Sanders, except for today's offer of a ride, had been considerate enough to ignore her for over two weeks now.

She was heading for the stairs when a tentative knock sounded at the door—so low that for a second she panicked, thinking that Jeanie had somehow been let out into the storm. Only she then remembered seeing the cat upstairs, curled in her mother's rocking chair. Crossing the room, she opened the door and raised her lamp. "Mr. Pitney?"

"I realize it's late, and it's not our usual meeting night. . . ." Though the porch provided shelter from the rain, he was holding an umbrella aloft, and his words spilled out in an uncharacteristic rush, as if he feared she would slam the door. "But I saw your lights were still burning, and I remember your saying that you stay up late—"

"Do come in."

"Oh, I shan't stay but a minute. . . ."

"I can barely hear you for the rain, Mr. Pitney." Lydia stepped back to allow him entrance. "Please?"

A blush, obvious even in the lamplight, rose to his cheeks as he closed his umbrella and propped it just outside the door. "I'm not usually so impulsive, Miss Clark."

"Life wouldn't be as exciting if we thought out everything," she offered affably, to show that she wasn't annoyed by his appearance. On the contrary. She just wished she was wearing something besides her faded-but-too-comfortable-for-the-rag-bin chenille wrapper, and that she had not been so hasty about taking down her hair, for she looked like an Amazon woman with it hanging loose about her shoulders.

"Lydia . . . my pipe?"

Begging Mr. Pitney's pardon, she stepped over to the door leading to the staircase and rest of the cottage. "In a minute, Papa!" *No sense in pretending to be genteel in this household*, she thought. In the course of taking the few steps back to her visitor, she realized with an aching heart what this unexpected visit had to be about. *The lessons worked.*

"I couldn't wait to tell you that the lessons were successful," Mr. Pitney declared. "Miss Rawlins and I chatted for what seemed like hours last night about the three novelettes you and I studied. And the reason I couldn't come here earlier is that we sat in the library after supper and continued the discussion. She even apologized for telling me that I lacked imagination."

"That's wonderful, Mr. Pitney," Lydia told him, and in a way she was truly happy for him, for he radiated a confidence that she had not seen during his three visits. But then a sad thought occurred to her. Her services were no longer required. "If you'll wait here, I'll fetch that other book."

Brown eyes uncomprehending, he said, "But we haven't discussed it."

"I thought . . ."

Fear flooded his handsome face. "Oh, but I've already told Miss Rawlins I plan to read every book she's written. I would never be able to understand them on my own. Please, Miss Cl—"

"Very well, Mr. Pitney. I assumed I was being dismissed."

"Dismissed?" He shook his head adamantly. "I should never have had the nerve to speak with her again without your help. You *will* allow the lessons to continue, won't you?"

"Of course."

"Thank you!"

The relief in his voice made Lydia smile. "You're welcome, Mr. Pitney."

"Well, I should go now," he said.

Yet something in his expression seemed to say that he would be content to linger for a while. But of course he had dreamed of winning Miss Rawlins' respect for a long time, Lydia told herself. *Why shouldn't he enjoy speaking about it?*

"Forgive me for taking up so much of your time, Miss Clark," he told her, reaching back for the doorknob.

You could take up the rest of my life, rushed into Lydia's head. She was shocked at herself for the most unschoolmistress-like thought and hoped her expression hadn't given her away. Just to be sure, she shifted her eyes from his face to look down at the pipe in her hand. "No apology is necessary, Mr. Pitney. But I should bring this upstairs before my father becomes apoplectic."

Her father unwittingly came to her assistance then by bellowing out, "Lydia!"

With another apology for the late hour, Mr. Pitney thanked her for her part in his good news and took his leave. Lydia leaned against the closed door and listened to his footsteps on the porch. She could tell when he paused to open his umbrella, and then stepped out onto the sodden steps, making little splashing sounds as he walked down the stone path. And then there was only the sound of the rain. For a second or two, her ears strained for any sound of his turning around to come back, but reason soon prevailed.

As she carried her father's pipe upstairs, she thought about the hundreds of novels she had read over the years. Unrequited love had been the theme of many. Surely one should have warned her of how painful it could be.

————

Having spent the whole morning in the *Larkspur*'s cellar among their latest artifacts, Jacob and Mr. Ellis had to change their dusty clothes for lunch. Jacob was just leaving his bedchamber when he spotted Miss Rawlins farther down the corridor near the staircase. He cleared his throat.

"Uh, Miss Rawlins?" She turned, and her pleased expression caused his heart to make a little leap.

"Mr. Pitney? Why aren't you on the hill?"

"Last night's rain," he reminded her, hurrying to catch up.

"You don't dig when the ground is wet?"

"We can't." He was overjoyed that she was asking him about his work. "You see, we don't actually *dig* for fear of damaging the artifacts. We brush the dirt away, a layer at a time." Mr. Ellis had explained this at least once at the supper table, and Jacob had spent many an inclement day indoors, but he couldn't fault Miss Rawlins for forgetting. After all, her mind was likely overburdened enough with story plots.

They took the first downward steps side by side. "Well, where have you been all morning?" she asked.

"In the cellar. We save days like this for cleaning the most recently found artifacts, then cataloging and packaging them for shipment."

"Oh." She wrinkled her nose. "I suppose that's a bit less tedious than digging in the dirt all day."

We don't actually dig, he started to remind her, but then his heart fell. Not only did she have no interest in his profession, but she found it boring. Misery threatened to overwhelm him, but then he reminded himself that *he* was not his profession, no matter how dear archeology was to him. And hadn't she listened attentively to his every word for the past two evenings?

"Have you been writing all morning?" he asked.

A smile lit her face, and he was proud that he had caused it.

"*Valentina of the Apennines*," she replied. "And as fast as my poor fingers could bear. After mulling all week over how to reconcile Valentina and Count Lobue after their misunderstanding, inspiration struck this morning."

They paused at the foot of the staircase across from the dining room, and she was so caught up in her plot that she absently rested a hand upon his sleeve. He wished he had the courage to put his hand over hers.

"You see," Miss Rawlins went on, "Valentina's cousin, Mercede, has been a minor character so far, but it occurred to me that she could be the instrument to reconcile the two. And you'll never guess how she does it."

Jacob smiled at the excitement in her eyes. "How?"

"She'll forge a letter to each, pretending it's from the other. They'll say basically the same thing, begging for forgiveness and requesting a meeting in Signor Patrizio's conservatory."

"Yes, very good." Jacob nodded. "Just as Aimee did in *Rachelle of Chaminox*. It worked splendidly that time, so why shouldn't it again?"

The smile left her face just as her hand left his sleeve. "It's not exactly the same, Mr. Pitney."

"Oh. I see." But he didn't see, and his mind raced to figure out why.

"In *Rachelle of Chaminox*, Aimee didn't forge letters to Rachelle and General Massena. She sent her lady's maid to deliver the messages in person. And they were to meet at a gazebo, not a conservatory. Really, Mr. Pitney, a child could have seen the difference."

Humbled, he followed her into the dining room, where the others had assembled and were involved in conversation. Even Mrs. Somerville was present after having spent two days in her room with a headache.

"It's good to see you at the table, Mrs. Somerville," Mrs. Dearing said after everyone had filled a plate from the two sideboards. "I hope this means you've recovered."

"Yes, thank you," she replied with a smile that seemed forced to Jacob. In fact, she looked as bleak as he felt.

"Were the herbal teas beneficial at all?" Mr. Durwin asked her.

Mrs. Somerville nodded. "It was very thoughtful of you to send them up."

She was fussed over by other lodgers with advice for warding off any future headaches, from Mr. Jensen's deep breathing exercises to Mrs. Clay's avoidance of highly seasoned foods. Jacob would have suggested his mother's sworn remedy, a daily dose of cod liver oil, but he feared he would somehow say the wrong thing again.

It seemed that the only women, besides his mother and sister, with whom he could share his innermost thoughts were Miss Clark and Mrs. Dearing. He winced inside at the memory of his most recent conversation with Miss Rawlins. Perhaps misunderstandings were usual and even to be expected in all courtships. There was inevitably at least one misunderstanding between the hero and heroine of every one of Miss Rawlins' stories he had read so far, and she was much wiser to the ways of the world than was he.

That reassured him a little. And when the meal was over, he was quick to seek her out in the corridor before she could disappear into her chamber again. "I must beg your forgiveness," he said earnestly. "I spoke before thinking."

She looked up at him with a serious expression, yet her words were kind. "It's not your fault, Mr. Pitney. You wandered in creative darkness for years, so we can't expect enlightenment to come all at once."

Knees weak from relief, he fairly gushed, "Thank you!"

"You're welcome." Incredibly, she smiled. "And you would pay me a courtesy by addressing me as Eugenia, if you wish."

His heart skipped a beat. "I may?"

"Yes, you may . . . Jacob."

Chapter 30

*B*y late Friday morning, enough of the shock had worn off to allow Noelle to draft a reply to Mr. Radley's letter. Only she would have sooner cut off a finger than correspond with the odious toad, so she decided to respond to Quetin directly. Or rather, indirectly through Valerie Bradburn, the closest person to a true friend that Noelle had in the world. Surely she would find a way to get it to him without Averyl Paxton's knowledge.

> *Dearest Quetin,*
> *Whatever I have done to incur your disfavor, I beg of you the opportunity to make amends.*

Her words took much effort and were frustratingly formal. She would have rather poured out her angst and told him of the sleepless nights and how her heart felt like a gaping wound in her chest. But Quetin would take one glance at such a letter and toss it away.

> *Sending me here to Gresham was a wise action, I can now see. My character has matured over the past four weeks. I have learned not to complain so much and to appreciate all the things I have.*

The latter part wasn't quite true, for she still had some concern about her belongings. Especially tormenting was the thought of Meara Desmond bedecked in her jewelry. But mentioning that would cause him to think she was more concerned about the financial loss than the loss of his affection, which was certainly not the case.

> *If you would just allow me one more opportunity to see you, I am certain you would agree that I have become a much more agreeable companion.*

"Keep it brief," she murmured, forcing herself to close the letter with a simple *Very truly yours* and sign her name. Of all times, she couldn't afford to try his patience now.

She penned a letter to Valerie next. This time she poured out her heart, having to stop to wipe her eyes and blow her nose several times. On the way to take the envelope—addressed to Valerie—to the letter box, she came across the Durwins and Clays in the hall. The men sat on opposite sides of the draughts table, and the women were chatting while walking toward the front door. All faces turned in her direction when Mr. Durwin spoke.

"Good morning, Mrs. Somerville. We missed you at breakfast."

"Thank you," Noelle replied. "I'm afraid I overslept."

"You haven't another headache, have you?" asked Mrs. Durwin with a concerned expression.

Noelle was growing weary of that question, especially considering that she could recall having had only one actual headache since her move to Gresham. But she supposed it was her own fault for overusing such a convenient excuse. And she supposed she should be grateful *somebody* cared about her well-being. "I'm quite well, thank you," she replied.

"Would you care to take a stroll with us to *Trumbles*?" Mrs. Clay asked. "We can wait if you'd like to fetch a hat."

Noelle wondered exactly how many Parisian gowns the actor's wife owned, for she couldn't recall having seen the day dress of figured grenadine with fluted green trim she now wore. She swallowed her envy to reply, "No, thank you. But will you mind giving this to Mr. Trumble?" It would not reach London any sooner than the mail Mr. Jones would collect in the letter box today, but at least it would *seem* to be starting its journey sooner. She would take any condolence where she could find it, no matter how small.

———————

"Surely he was jesting," Ambrose said as he brushed his wife's hair at the dressing table that night. "You know how fond Mr. Trumble is of a good chuckle."

"No, Ambrose. He said rearranging the shelves took her most of a day, too."

"*Our* Mrs. Somerville?"

Fiona stared at him in the mirror. "Why do you say it like that?"

"I just can't imagine her taking the time to do a good deed for anyone, to be honest."

"Even after she helped Julia get Andrew home from the dentist that day?"

He opened his mouth to argue but found himself at a loss for words. *I know I'm not imagining the way she looks at Fiona*. But he hadn't realized until just recently how prone to headaches the young widow was. Could he, in his desire to protect his wife, possibly have misinterpreted physical discomfort in Mrs. Somerville's facial expressions for dislike? He reckoned anyone looking at his own face during one of his dark moods would assume he hated the whole world.

Father, forgive me if I've judged her wrongly, he prayed while pulling the brush through Fiona's raven hair. *But please grant me discernment to know for sure.*

"I'm sorry for saying what I did," he finally told Fiona, setting the brush upon the table. "A wise person once admonished me to be more charitable with myself. I should extend that charity to others as well."

"Oh, Ambrose." She rose from the bench and turned to him, her violet eyes serious. "You're one of the most charitable people I know."

"How can you say that, after—"

Smiling, his wife put a finger up to his lips. "I didn't say you were perfect, Ambrose. And I adore you even more for your little imperfections, if the truth were to be known."

"You do?"

"I do."

Gathering her into his arms, he held her snugly while she rested her head upon his shoulder. "You know, I occasionally forget and use the wrong fork," he murmured into her freshly brushed hair.

"Mmm?"

"And I've been known to dog-ear the page of a book. . . ."

———

Swallowing hard, Kermillie lifted her chin and boldly met his gaze. "You may own all the land in Keswick, Lord Wilffrith, but you will never own me!"

There was derision and sympathy mingled in his dark eyes. "So you'll allow your father to rot in debtor's prison rather than marry—"

"A man I do not love!" she finished for him. "And never will!"

Lord Wilffrith took a step closer to whisper, "But you love your father, don't you?"

Jacob was so caught up in reading *Kermillie of Keswick* in the sitting room Friday night that he didn't hear the next set of footsteps until they were almost upon him. He jumped from the sofa and went to the doorway, holding his place in the book with his hand. But it was only Mrs. Beemish, the housekeeper, walking up the corridor with a stack of freshly laundered towels in her arms. She stopped to smile at him.

"Would you be wanting anything sent up, Mr. Pitney? Some hot chocolate?"

"Oh, no, thank you." Then wondering if he should explain, he said, "I just felt like reading in here tonight."

"Ah," she said with a knowing nod that made him blush. "Well, I'll leave you to your reading."

He thanked her and went back to the sofa. Surely Miss Rawlins—he couldn't quite refer to her as Eugenia yet, even in the privacy of his mind—would happen by soon, if only to bid good-night to the lodgers still sitting downstairs in the hall. It would be so much simpler to knock upon her door and ask to speak with her, but had he the courage of Marc Anthony, he still couldn't bring himself to step over the bounds of propriety.

The story claimed his attention again. He hoped with all his heart that Kermillie wouldn't be forced to marry the brooding, mysterious Lord Wilffrith. What did it matter that he was wealthy and tall and darkly handsome, if she didn't love him?

It's the same situation Rosemarie found herself in, Jacob mused, though he didn't think he should share that observation with Miss Rawlins. After all, there were important differences between this story and *Rosemarie of Roubaix*. It was Rosemarie's brother, not father, facing debtor's prison, and she was being pressured to marry a tall, wealthy, darkly handsome French marquis instead of an English lord. At least there was a ray of hope for Kermillie, for in the latter novelette Rosemarie had ultimately fallen in love when she realized that inside the marquis' cynical chest beat a compassionate heart.

He heard footsteps again and went to the doorway. This time his surveillance was rewarded, for Miss Rawlins was coming down the corridor. She looked wonderful in a loose-flowing beige gown, her short hair slightly tousled. Jacob broke out into a smile. "Miss Rawlins."

She walked over to him, returning his smile. "I was under the assumption our friendship had graduated to given names, Jacob."

"Forgive me," he said as another blush warmed his cheeks. "Eugenia."

"Forgiven. Especially when I see you reading another one of my stories."

"Oh, I can scarcely put it down."

"I'm flattered." She looked past him. "Do you always come in here to read?"

"No . . . I . . . uh . . . actually was hoping to speak with you."

"Yes?"

Shifting his weight to his other foot, he said, "The Anwyl is still muddy, you see, and we shipped out the artifacts from the cellar this morning, so Mr. Ellis plans to visit his family tomorrow. I would visit mine, but Dover is too far away to allow me to return Sunday, and besides, I spent Easter week there."

Her eyes seemed to glaze over a bit, and Jacob realized he was rambling. *Get on with it*, he told himself. "Anyway, I was wondering if you would care to accompany me to the tournament tomorrow."

"The tournament?"

"You know, the school archery teams."

"Yes, of course." Miss Rawlins shook her head. "I'm afraid I haven't the constitution for crowds, Jacob."

"I'm sorry."

"Oh, please don't be. It's just that an artist's soul is best nurtured by solitude."

"Well, you should have plenty of it," he assured her through his disappointment. "Almost everyone here is planning to go."

"Yes, I would imagine," she replied with a preoccupied little frown.

"Is something wrong, Mi—Eugenia?"

"Why, no." But then she shrugged. "Actually, I was just thinking that I should like to have your opinion of a scene in *Valentina of the Apennines*."

"You were?" Jacob knew he was grinning like a gargoyle, but he could not help himself. "Why don't you bring it in here now?"

"Because I'm not quite finished writing it. But I should be by morning." Pursing her lips thoughtfully for a second, she then said, "You know, I hardly ever sit in the garden because there are so many distractions that interrupt my train of thought. Passersby wishing to engage in small talk, Mr. Herrick planting and weeding, and so on. But tomorrow morning would be a lovely time, with everyone away."

But then she gave him a quick apologetic look. "How terribly selfish of me, Jacob."

"Selfish?"

"It quite slipped my mind that you plan to attend the tournament."

He had to think hard to understand what his attending the tournament had to do with her enjoying solitude in the garden. *Could it be?*

"You're inviting me to sit in the garden with you?" he scarcely dared ask for fear of being presumptuous.

"No, of course not." But before Jacob's hopes could go crashing down about him, she added with a dreamy cast to her expression, "It would be a lovely setting in which to read those scenes aloud, mind you. But I wouldn't dream of asking you to miss the tournament."

He had never felt so flattered and was even comfortable enough to risk making a joke. "Tournament?" he asked, smiling. "What tournament?"

The next morning Jonathan Raleigh determined that the green was still too damp for holding the tournament. Fortunately he had considered an alternate plan in advance, and so the targets were set up on the cobbled stones of Bartley Lane in front of the secondary school, out of the way of village traffic. By ten o'clock, carriages and wagons from Prescott, Lockwood, Clive, and even Gresham lined both sides of the lane, stopping at the roped area in which the teams would compete. Misters Johnson and Pool of the bakery and the *Bow and Fiddle,* having been also warned in advance that their potential customers would be moved to the east side of the village, had hastily assembled food stands already in place and were conducting business at the corner of Church and Bartley Lanes.

All of this served to irritate Harold Sanders. He had looked forward to a fine opportunity to be distant with Miss Clark, but her family had already found places to stand directly behind the rope stretched from sawhorse to sawhorse across the lane—giving her no reason to look back and notice him. He craned his neck to send a glare down the lane at Mr. Raleigh, who was queuing his team in front of the rope. Did the schoolmaster have to invite practically all of Shropshire to compete?

"Fernie says you can see the target and everything better from back there," Oram said from Harold's elbow. The sixteen-year-old pointed back to where their team and wagon waited. Fernie, standing in the bed, waved. But Harold shook his head. Though he would be standing above the people assembled in the lane, Miss Clark would have no reason to look back over her shoulder at him back there.

"You go on then," he told his brother. There was but one thing he could do—make a place to stand at the rope. Close enough for Miss Clark to notice him, but not close enough as to appear he was trying to be noticed.

Elbowing his way through the spectators, he staked a place for himself up front, just four or five feet down from Miss Clark. A pair of elderly women made loud remarks to each other about rudeness, so Harold turned to one and offered an apologetic, "Beg pardon, but I have to stand in front. I'm feeling out o' sorts and don't wanter chuck-up on nobody."

He shrugged when the two hurried away to find other places to stand. Presently the tournament began, with the youngest members of the four teams alternating the first turns at the targets. All eyes were on the competition, but Harold kept his trained on Miss Clark. And occasionally, she did look in his direction. He was quick to jerk his face in the other direction every time. *That'll show her.*

But after a good half hour of this, his neck began to ache. His stomach sent up rumbles too, for all Mrs. Winters had prepared for breakfast was porridge. He figured he had ignored Miss Clark enough for a little while, and judging by the number of people standing in wagon beds, the porch of the secondary school, and in the lane behind the rope, Mr. Johnson would soon run out of meat pies. If he hurried he could make it back in plenty of time to watch Jack and Edgar take their turns.

Not that he gave a farthing about archery, except for the excuses it had given him to ignore Miss Clark. But the two had pleaded with him this morning. With Papa still bitter about anything having to do with the school, and Dale having unhitched one of the horses to slip off to Myddle and visit Lucy Bates, Harold supposed it was his duty to watch. It was easier to make his way to the back of the spectators than it had been to get up to the rope. To his disgust, he could see a queue of about two dozen people in front of Mr. Johnson's stand. *Aren't they supposed to be watching the shooting?* He was just about to hurry on over when he felt a tug at his sleeve.

"Mr. Sanders?"

He turned to look at Lester Meeks, who stood there grinning at him as if he were Father Christmas. Impulsively Harold reached out to tousle the boy's cowlicked blond hair. "Hullo, Lester."

"Hullo, Mr. Sanders. We came to watch Mark."

"Well, that's good." He realized then that the boy wasn't alone. Besides Trudy, there was a woman who was even smaller than his sister, Mercy, with light brown hair showing from under a faded rose-colored bonnet. She had a nice smile, but in her brown eyes he could see traces of that worried look that his sister used to wear before she married Seth.

"Mr. Sanders," she said. "I'm Hannah Meeks. It was so kind of you to bring the children home Thursday. I was in the barn haying the cows or I would'ha come out to thank you."

"Aw, it weren't nothing," he told her while working loose a rock in the lane with the toe of his boot. He wasn't used to folks, especially women, saying nice things about him.

"Mr. Sanders played blindman's buff with us at the castle," Trudy told her mother.

Now Harold could feel his cheeks grow hot. "They made me," he explained right away, wishing he had stayed up by the rope.

But Mrs. Meeks laughed—not like she was making fun of him, but like she appreciated the predicament he had found himself in. "They talked of little else for a whole week," she told him.

Unsure of how to reply and eager to forget all about playing blindman's buff, he looked about him and asked, "Where's Phoebe?"

"She's watching from Mr. Mayhew's wagon with some of her class-mates."

"Humph," Lester snorted. "Not if she takes off her spectacles."

"She takes them off all the time," Trudy added, nodding. "Even when we remind her not to."

"Now, you're not to be carrying tales against your sister," their mother scolded mildly. "She's got to have time to get used to the idea." With an apologetic look at Harold, she said, "Forgive us for keeping you, Mr. Sanders. It was good to meet you, finally."

"The same here," Harold told them. With a farewell wave he turned to resume his walk to the bakery stand. *Nice folks*, he thought, happening to glance back over his shoulder. He stopped and turned.

Now, how are they supposed to see? he asked himself, for they had made no moves to push their way for the rope. Instead they craned their necks, Mrs. Meeks even hefting Trudy up in her arms. He thought about the meat pies being sold behind him, sighed, and walked back to where the family was standing.

"Mrs. Meeks?" he said just as cheers were going up all around him for the finishing third standard students. She did not hear him, so he reached up a hand to tap her shoulder, then reconsidered. Mrs. Meeks was one of those decent women Dale had mentioned, and he didn't think a fellow was supposed to touch a decent woman without her permission. He tapped Trudy's shoulder instead. From her mother's arms the girl looked back at him, smiled, then whispered something in her mother's ear.

"You can see better from my wagon," Harold almost shouted when the woman turned.

"I beg your pardon?"

He motioned behind him. "My wagon."

"It's very nice, Mr. Sanders," she said with a friendly, albeit puzzled, nod.

"No, you can—" Realizing the cheering had quieted down for the moment, he lowered his voice. "My brothers say you can see the whole thing just fine from our wagon."

Now Mrs. Meeks nodded understanding. "We wouldn't be imposing?"

"No, ma'am," he said, taking Trudy from her arms. "But we'd best hurry if you want to see Mark."

The meat pies were likely cold by now anyway, he told himself.

*D*amp were the grasses and blooms of the *Larkspur*'s garden, and droplets of water beaded the leaves of the shrubberies and trees. Still, Jacob and Miss Rawlins were comfortably situated in a willow bench, thanks to Mr. Herrick's kindly draping it with a thick carriage blanket before leaving for the tournament.

"And here is my favorite passage of all," Miss Rawlins was saying above the cheers drifting over from Bartley Lane. She looked lovely in a pink gown with tiny white dots and a narrow-brimmed straw hat over her short hair. Jacob was glad he had dressed up in his Sunday tweed and a new royal-blue cravat, for he wouldn't want her to be ashamed to be seen with him.

Lowering her gaze to her manuscript again, she read:

> *Valentina Fabroni's tiny nostrils flared with fury, her sapphire blue eyes clawing across the handsome officer's face like talons. "Just because you've driven out the Austrians, Count Lobue, doesn't mean you can march back up here to Pontremoli and expect me to fall at your feet like the rest of Italy! If the mountains couldn't tame me in eight years, what makes you assume you can in two weeks?"*

"Well, what do you think?" she asked, watching him with anticipation in her gray eyes behind the spectacles.

It's very nice, were the first words to form themselves in Jacob's mind, but he knew better than to speak them. And he certainly knew better than to tell her that the passage sounded vaguely familiar. If only Miss Clark were here, she would help him to find a satisfactory and honest answer. *But she's not, so you have to think*, he told himself.

"I like the eyes raking across his face like talons," he ventured cautiously. "It's very good . . . imagery."

"Thank you. It makes one think of a fierce bird, doesn't it?"

"Like a hawk. Or an owl."

"I prefer the hawk image. Owls are not as romantic."

"They're not?"

Miss Rawlins shook her head but gave him an understanding look. "It takes an artist's eye to discern such things, Jacob. Certain animals lend themselves more suitably to romantic prose than others. For example, you can imagine a dashing hero riding a thoroughbred horse, but never a donkey."

"I see," he acknowledged with a nod. "Even though the two are related—just as are the hawk and owl."

"I'm impressed with how quickly you learn," she said, smiling.

He felt the blush steal across his cheeks and wondered if it were possible to die of happiness. "Thank you for saying that, Eugenia."

"You're welcome, Jacob. And the same applies to human characters. I'm sure you've realized from my stories that certain types of people are more romantic than others."

"Attractive people are more romantic," came to his lips at once, for which of her heroes and heroines had not been so?

"Of course." Placing her manuscript in her lap for the first time since they seated themselves an hour ago, she peered at him seriously through her spectacles and explained, "But it goes beyond mere attractiveness, Jacob. The heroine must be young and beautiful, of course, but she should also be titled, or at least related to someone of the peerage. If she lives in poverty, as Kermillie does, it must always be because the family fortune was somehow lost or stolen in the past."

"Why is that?"

She shrugged. "There are some things I can't explain. A writer just knows them instinctively."

"Instinct," Jacob echoed thoughtfully. Though he admired Miss Rawlins' immense talent, he was glad he had decided upon archeology as his life's work and not writing, for he would have never figured out the rules on his own.

"The man is always older," Miss Rawlins went on, "and if he is to be romantic, he must be tall. That's practically set in stone."

"But wasn't Napoleon short?" Jacob asked before thinking, then winced. "Forgive me. I just assumed he was thought of as a romantic figure—but I'm sure I'm mistaken."

"Don't apologize, Jacob. It's good that you have a questioning mind. Someone such as Napoleon would be an exception because of his military and political power. If I ever write about a short hero, he will have to be extremely powerful to make up for his lack of height."

She gave him a frank smile. "But to be truthful, Jacob, I can never see myself doing that. Why write about a hero for whom you have to compensate? A tall man is simply more romantic."

Being well above average in height himself, Jacob was overjoyed to hear those words stated so adamantly. He straightened his shoulders and sat a little taller. "Yes, of course."

"Especially if he has dark eyes."

His heart leapt in his chest just as another cheer came from Bartley Lane, for surely she had noticed that he had brown eyes, and hadn't his sister, Gloria, always told him that he should have been a girl, with his dark eyelashes?

"He should also have a mysterious, quiet way about him," Miss Rawlins continued.

That was a bit discouraging, for Jacob reckoned there was nothing mysterious about himself. But he had always been on the quiet side. And as he had three of the romantic qualities—tall, dark-eyed, and quiet— wouldn't they make up for the lack of mystery? He wished he had the nerve to ask without revealing it was himself about whom he was concerned.

Suddenly a way presented itself to him. Jacob cleared his throat. "If the man—in one of your stories, of course—isn't particularly mysterious, but is tall and quiet with dark eyes, may he still be considered romantic?"

"Hmm." Pursing her lips, she stared out at something in the distance. "I've never written about a hero who wasn't mysterious. But as would be the case of great power compensating for Napoleon's short stature, I suppose some other quality could be substituted for a lack of mystery."

Almost afraid to breathe, Jacob asked, "Such as. . . ?"

"A poetic soul, I should think."

"Poetic soul?"

"If such a hero were well-versed in poetry, I should think he would be extremely romantic." After more seconds of thoughtful silence, in which she pressed a fingertip against her chin, she mused aloud, "I wonder why it has never occurred to me to do that? I should definitely give my next hero the soul of a poet. Women just adore men who can quote poetry."

"My, my," Jacob said weakly.

She turned her face toward him again, and it seemed her gray eyes could see into his poetry-deficient mind. "Forgive me, Jacob," she said, sighing. "This will never do."

"It won't? But—" In a panic, he strained to recall a poem he had memorized in grammar school. *How did that go? Water, water everywhere, and all the boards did—*

"You passed up the archery tournament to listen to my manuscript, and here I am going on and on about characterization. You must be bored silly."

"Never," he assured her while relief poured through him like a tonic. "I enjoy listening to you talk about writing as well as hearing you read."

"How very kind of you to say." She smiled, lifting her manuscript again.

Jacob let out a quiet, long breath. But he couldn't afford to relax totally. Just because he was granted a reprieve did not mean the subject wouldn't come up again.

"*The tears in Valentina's sapphire blue eyes were gone, as if evaporated by a rushing wind,*" Miss Rawlins read.

Jacob smiled at the drama she infused into her voice, making the scene come alive. He would simply have to memorize some poetry, in addition to studying the novelettes. He could do that. She was worth all the trouble, for he had never met anyone like her. He even dared to imagine the two of them in later years, sitting in front of their own cottage while she read her latest stories to him.

"*But the vow her father had made before she was even born weighed upon her, choking her . . .*"

He just had to find out which particular poems would impress her. Certainly nothing related to shrinking boards and albatrosses. He let out another relieved breath. Maybe he didn't know where to look, but he knew whom to ask.

———————

Standing in back of the wagon belonging to Mr. Lawson, his churchwarden, Paul Treves clapped his hands and sent out a long whistle as eleven-year-old Bobby West lowered the bow and turned from the target. The boy had scored only thirteen points with his six arrows, but archery was new to Lockwood, and the team had come more for the practice of competing than with hopes of winning. "Just give us another year or two," he told Mr. Lawson.

"Aye, another year or two," the churchwarden agreed.

"Vicar Treves?"

Paul looked down at Holly Wingate, who smiled up at him from under a lace-edged parasol, though the sun had hidden behind clouds all morning. "Good morning, Miss Wingate," he greeted above the cheers for a girl from Clive who had just stepped up to the target. "Are you enjoying the tournament?"

"I'm afraid I'm having trouble seeing it," she replied with a helpless little smile.

"Oh, I'm sorry to hear it."

Sending a sideways glance to Mr. Lawson, Paul received a raised eyebrow in return, while Israel Coggins continued to stare past him, mesmerized by the competition. Indeed, the boy had cheered for every child who had raised a bow so far, no matter which team.

Paul looked down again at the woman standing in the lane. A girl, really, though many in Lockwood married even younger than Miss Wingate's seventeen years. She was lovely to look at, with shiny auburn hair and a fair complexion. And it was clear that she wouldn't mind his courting her, from the way she smiled at him through lowered lashes every time she offered her hand at the church door. He supposed he should start thinking about courting again if he were ever to have the wife and home he longed for. Most men were settled with families by age twenty-four.

But you don't want to court anyone just for the sake of courting, he reminded himself. And certainly not just because a woman was comely. Fair looks didn't last forever, and even if they did, he figured he would grow weary of even the most beautiful face if there was no substance behind it.

He understood now the reason he had become so enamored with Elizabeth Phelps and why she still crossed his mind—though with much less frequency now that he was heeding Vicar Phelps's counsel about taking control of his thoughts. Elizabeth not only possessed beauty but an intelligent, questioning mind. And a sense of humor like her father's. How painfully ironic it was that his inability to appreciate those latter qualities in a woman had ultimately led to the end of their courtship.

Paul realized he was ignoring Miss Wingate. "You can see everything from up here," he told her, hitching a knee over the side and jumping to the ground. He took her parasol and reticule to hand up to Mr. Lawson, then walked to the back of the wagon to remove the plank from between the stakes and prop it against the side. When he turned, Miss Wingate had followed and was standing only two feet away. Paul cleared his throat. "With your permission. . . ?"

Giving him a demure smile, she moved her arms from her sides so that he could put both hands at her narrow waist. Quickly he hoisted her to sit on the floor of the wagon bed, then stared gentlemanly at the ground while she swung her covered limbs inside. When Mr. Lawson had helped the girl to her feet, and she was staring down expectantly at him, Paul tipped his hat to her.

"I believe I'll walk about a bit," he said with delicate politeness and a smile. "And you'll all be more comfortable if you aren't crowded."

"But don't you want to watch the match?"

"I have height to my advantage. I'm sure I'll be able to see."

As he walked toward the standing spectators, he hoped he had not hurt her feelings. There was no sense in giving the girl false hopes if he did not intend to court her. And he certainly didn't want to provide any other Lockwood residents with fodder for gossip. They were good people, but they would have the two of them practically betrothed by the time the last arrow hit the target.

"Does that mean we're winning?" Noelle asked Mr. Clay after a lad with brown hair scored an impressive nineteen points. She stood on the porch of the schoolhouse with the Clays, Mrs. Phelps, and Elizabeth Raleigh along with about a dozen other spectators. The vicar and Mr. Raleigh were inside the roped area with Gresham's team.

Had anyone but the Clays invited her to accompany them, Noelle would have demurred. But the actor had been in a charming, animated mood at the breakfast table, and the thought of spending another day in her room brooding over Quetin was immensely depressing.

"We won't know that until it's over and the scores are tallied up," Mr. Clay explained.

He spoke to her with much more warmth than at any time since her arrival in Gresham. At first Noelle wondered if he and Mrs. Clay were at disagreement over something and he was attempting to make her jealous, but that notion was put to rest when she saw them holding hands as they left the dining room. She supposed she must resign herself to the idea that the two were a package. One had to put up with pits if one wished to enjoy plums, and with thorns to enjoy roses. And Mrs. Clay's company was certainly more tolerable than Meara Desmond's had been.

Just the thought of the woman's treachery was enough to increase the ache in the lump that had lodged itself inside her chest since Wednesday. She had to think about something else, or she would dissolve into tears and make a scene, so she turned her attention back to the match. Another boy was just stepping up to the shooting line. "Where is he from?" she asked Mrs. Raleigh, standing at her right.

"Prescott," the vicar's daughter replied with a smile. "They've won for the past two years. Papa was almost beside himself with anxiety this morning."

"I would think your husband would be anxious as well, being the schoolmaster."

Mrs. Raleigh and Mrs. Phelps exchanged quick glances. Leaning closer, Mrs. Raleigh lowered her voice to explain, "It's more personal with Papa, you see. A certain vicar lords it over him whenever Prescott wins."

"Elizabeth . . ." cautioned her stepmother.

"Your secret is safe with me," Noelle said, giving a conspiratorial smile to both. "I know just how it is. Vicarage walls are made of glass."

She had slept only fitfully for the past three nights, so her mind was not functioning as well as it should have been. She did not realize her slip of the tongue until Mrs. Phelps asked with a surprised expression, "Why, Mrs. Somerville. Is your father a vicar?"

The mind that had betrayed her couldn't think fast enough to provide her with an escape. And the Clays were watching her curiously now as well. "He is," she replied in an off-handed manner, hoping that by going ahead and admitting it the subject would wear itself out soon.

But it was not to be, for Mrs. Phelps was smiling at her as if she had just discovered they were twins who had been separated from birth. "Andrew is well acquainted with several London vicars. I can't wait to tell him. Perhaps he knows your father."

"Wouldn't that be something?" Noelle agreed halfheartedly.

"Perhaps we've even attended his church," said Mrs. Clay with the same pleased expression. "Which one is it?"

Finally Noelle's mind decided to function. "Oh, but my father hasn't preached in London for years. I lived there because that was my husband's post of duty, you see. My family lives in . . . Truesdale."

It worked, for even if such a town existed outside the advertisement in her biscuit tin, no recognition came across any of the faces about her. She felt safe enough to add, "It's no wonder you haven't heard of it. It's a small village in Humberside, smaller than Gresham, actually. But it's a charming place, and they are very happy there."

She was rescued from any further inquiry by Mr. Clay, who pointed out at the match and said, "It looks as if Grace will be next."

All eyes in the Clay-Raleigh-Phelps party turned back in that direction. Even Noelle was interested in seeing how the girl performed and not just because of the fortunate timing. The girl reminded her of herself as a child—quiet and thoughtfully somber. But she didn't think the Phelps's child's quiet temperament stemmed from loneliness, as had her own. People were born with different natures, else how could she explain why she was never able to content herself with the upbringing her siblings had apparently thrived upon?

Grace's first shot landed in the blue ring to score five points, which brought applause from all over. Most enthusiastic was from the group on the porch, with Noelle contributing as well. One of the girl's six arrows missed the target completely, but one scored a nine, and so her final tally was eighteen. Not the most impressive score, but still applause rippled through the assemblage.

The vicar's two other daughters appeared on the steps from wherever they had been watching the match with faces beaming. "Did you see her, Mother?" Aleda asked unnecessarily.

"She didn't look nervous at all," declared the blond-haired Laurel.

Both nodding, Mrs. Phelps and Mrs. Raleigh agreed that she had performed well. Noelle imagined their smiles would be no less broad if Grace had scored the lowest of all. Their enthusiasm seemed to be based on the girl being a beloved part of their family rather than on her performance. How strange and wonderful to be accepted and cherished for simply being alive. Would Quetin's attentions have found their way into her own eighteen-year-old heart so completely had she not been so starved for indications that she mattered to someone?

When Noelle realized Mrs. Phelps was speaking to her, the two girls were gone from the steps, and a brown-haired lad had taken Grace's place in front of the target.

"I beg your pardon?" she said to the vicar's wife.

"Will you join us for lunch afterward?" Mrs. Phelps asked. "The Clays have agreed, and Elizabeth and Jonathan are coming as well. I know Andrew would enjoy trying to figure out if you have any mutual acquaintances in the ministry."

Though she had nothing else to do but pace the floor of her room to wait for a letter—which may or may not ever come—Noelle could not afford to accept. For if Mrs. Phelps ever realized she had not been straightforward about her background, she would surely demand she leave the *Larkspur*. She was a kind woman, but even kind people could be maddeningly stubborn about sticking to their principles.

Where else could you go? Noelle asked herself. Even if she happened to have enough money left for a ticket to London, she had no place to stay. Though Valerie and Geneva would extend sympathy, there was little else they could do, being the paramours of Quetin's fellow Members of Parliament.

It was an odd twist of fate that she found herself clinging to the place she once loathed. But cling she would have to do, until Quetin came to his senses. Noelle smiled gratefully at the vicar's wife. "It's so kind of you to ask, but I'm rather fatigued."

"Oh dear." Mrs. Phelps gave her a sympathetic look. "You haven't a headache, have you?"

"Not at all," Noelle was quick to assure her. She was quite pleased with herself when a different one came to mind. "I'm embarrassed to admit I spent most of the night reading. I lose all track of time when I'm in the pages of a good novel."

"You too?" Mrs. Phelps looked past her at Mrs. Clay. "I can recall when Fiona would stay up for hours to read. Do you still do that, Fiona?"

"Oh, sometimes," was the Irish woman's smiling reply. "Though I inevitably regret it the next morning. What were you reading, Mrs. Somerville?"

Berating herself for her usual fallacy of not leaving well enough alone, Noelle waved a hand. "Oh, one of those Dickens stories. Look, isn't that another Gresham child at the target?"

$\mathcal{T}$he distraction worked. This time Noelle decided not to tempt good fortune. Pressing hands about her, she murmured farewells and stepped down from the porch. She had woven her way around at least two dozen knots of spectators when she looked to her left and discovered she was passing directly behind Vicar Treves. By his stance she could tell he was totally absorbed by the match, which was fine with her because she had socialized enough for one day.

She was turning her eyes to the front when a flash of movement startled her, just before she collided with something. She let out a gasp, lurched sideways, then found herself sitting on the damp cobbled stones, rubbing a throbbing chin and clamping the other hand over the skirt covering her left knee. Before her stood a brown-haired girl of about fifteen, surprisingly petite for the impact her skull had made upon Noelle's chin.

"I'm sorry, miss," the girl cried. "I didn't see you!"

Vicar Treves came to kneel beside her. "Are you hurt, Mrs. Somerville?"

Having not yet collected her wits, Noelle could only gape at him.

"Is she all right?" asked one of the several people standing and staring.

"The girl ran right into her," said another.

"Shall we fetch the doctor?" someone offered after another round of cheering had abated. "I saw him but a minute ago."

"I think I'm all right," Noelle finally said. Allowing Vicar Treves to take her arm, she attempted to ease up to her feet, but winced at the pain that shot through her knee and sat back down.

"Will someone please find Doctor Rhodes?" the vicar asked. Two young men nodded and moved away. Noelle looked up again and realized the girl with whom she had collided stood as if frozen in place.

"Is she hurt badly?" the girl asked with lips trembling. She blinked her eyes often as if she was weak-sighted.

"I'm sure it's nothing that Doctor Rhodes can't mend," Vicar Treves told her. "How about yourself? Are you all right?"

"Yes, sir. I'm so sorry, miss. I was looking for my mother."

"I wasn't paying attention either," Noelle felt obliged to admit. She felt ashamed that her most immediate impulse upon hitting the cobblestones had been to scold the lass, who looked as if she would crumble at the first harsh word. "And I'll be fine."

"You will?"

"Yes." She even mustered a strained smile. "Why don't you run along now?"

"Thank you, miss," the girl said in a relieved voice before turning to sprint away.

"That was terribly kind of you," Vicar Treves told her, his blue eyes sympathetic.

"Is my chin bruised?" Noelle asked.

"Just a little red. You didn't bang it against one of the rocks, did you?"

"Her head. What are they feeding children these days? They're certainly sturdy." She wiggled her knee a fraction of an inch. "I believe I can walk now."

"Please wait. You could do yourself more damage. The doctor should be here shortly."

"Will you be all right, dearie?" an elderly woman wearing a stuffed redbird on her hat leaned down to ask.

"Yes, thank you," Noelle replied. To Vicar Treves she said, "It's just embarrassing, sitting in the lane like this."

"Only the people in the immediate vicinity are even aware. And I'm down here with you."

"And I appreciate it," Noelle said sincerely.

They were soon joined by a gray-haired man with wiry muttonchop whiskers. "Good morning, madam," he said, crouching down to look Noelle in the eyes. "I'm Doctor Rhodes."

"Noelle Somerville." Noelle could only hope he was a bona fide doctor and not a barber or blacksmith or something of the sort. "It's my knee."

"I see." He raised a broad hand. "Can you tell how many fingers I'm holding up?"

"Three. I didn't hit my head, doctor."

"It's very fortunate that you didn't. Where do you live, Mrs. Somerville?"

"The *Larkspur*."

"Indeed? We're practically neighbors." Doctor Rhodes turned to Vicar Treves, who had moved back a bit to allow him room. "You're a strapping lad, Vicar. Can you carry Mrs. Somerville to my trap? It's a fair distance past the refreshment booths, I'm afraid."

"Yes, of course." Vicar Treves looked at Noelle, his expression uncertain. "With your permission . . ."

She had no choice but to grant it, and so after gathering her skirt close, she was swooped up into his arms. Her lips tightened as pain caught her again.

"Your knee?" he asked, brows drawn together.

"It's not so bad if I hold it steady." Like a child she was carried, her left arm hooked around his neck as he followed the doctor. Practically everyone they passed turned to stare, but there was nothing she could do about that. "Am I too heavy?" she asked when his breathing began to sound a little labored.

"Not at all," he replied in a huff of breath, then gave her a quick smile. "I could carry two of you twice as far."

She had to smile at that notion. "I'm sorry you're missing the match."

"That's all right. I'll hear all the details this afternoon."

"There are other people here from . . ."

"Lockwood," he supplied. "Of course."

"You're not worried about their disapproving?"

"Of what?

"You know . . ."

He shook his head, paused to hoist her up higher, and resumed walking. "I'll grant you rumors will fly that I've gotten myself engaged. But as long as I'm conducting myself morally, I don't worry excessively anymore over my parishioners' approval or disapproval."

This surprised her, because she had seen traces of self-consciousness in him. And wasn't the approval of the congregation the primary concern of all men of the cloth? "Why not?"

"Because I would go mad if I tried to appease every whim and wish. Vicar Phelps helped me see that. So I strive to please God . . . and sleep the better for it."

He was a stronger man than she had assumed on their first two meetings, Noelle thought, and not just physically. She envied his uncomplicated philosophy. If only her life could be that simple. But she had strayed so far from what was acceptable to God that the way back seemed hopelessly insurmountable. She had learned enough scripture as a child to know that repentance was the first step. How could she venture forth when in her heart of hearts she knew that if Quetin were to send for her, she would go?

Just ahead Doctor Rhodes was climbing into a trap hitched to a piebald horse in the lane outside the Raleighs' home. "Just put her here beside me," he ordered, taking up the reins.

"Shouldn't I come along as well?" Vicar Treves asked as Noelle was hefted gently into the seat.

"You'll just be underfoot, Vicar," the doctor replied. "Mrs. Rhodes and the servants are at home. I just came to the tournament to be on hand in case someone caught an arrow the wrong way. We'll see that Mrs. Somerville is delivered safely to the *Larkspur*."

He snapped the reins, and the trap lurched into motion, sending shooting pains up Noelle's knee. But when they had traveled some forty feet, she realized she had not thanked Vicar Treves. She twisted in the seat to look behind her, certain that he would be hurrying back to the tournament. But he still stood there, staring. When she lifted a hand to wave, he waved back.

"Now, that was a lark, wasn't it?" Amos Clark enthused as Wellington pulled the trap at a snail's pace up Church Lane after Gresham's archers were declared victors of the tournament for the first time. On either side people were returning to carriages and wagons or cottages.

"Yes, a lark," Lydia's mother agreed.

Lydia waved at the Keegan family members walking along the lane in front of the grammar schoolhouse. "And winning was the frosting on the cake."

"The plum in the pudding," Papa said. "Your turn, Oriel."

After a thoughtful second, her mother tentatively offered, "The cheese in the rarebit?"

"Aye, that's a good one. But all this talk of food is making me hungry."

"Mrs. Tanner left a soup on back of the stove, dear." She turned to Lydia. "Why hasn't your school an archery team, dear?"

"I expect we will sometime," Lydia told her. "Especially as more and more of Mr. Raleigh's graduates come our way. But with so few villages having secondary schools, competition may have to wait a bit longer."

"Well, I'm looking on starting a team for old men," Papa declared. "There are more than enough of us around."

Lydia smiled. "Wouldn't you actually have to *learn* archery first?"

"A minor complication," he replied, waving a hand. "But I could if I were to put a mind to it. I learned to paint, didn't I?"

"That you did, Amos," Mother agreed.

"Ah, but then I wouldn't have time to paint and read and swap jokes at the smithy's, would I?" he mused as they stopped at the crossroads to yield for a cheese wagon lumbering up Market Lane.

"That's something to consider, dear."

"But it's still an interesting sport, you have to admit. Hmm . . . look who's taken a day off for a change," he said and suddenly reined Wellington to the right instead of continuing across the lane.

"Where are you going, Amos?" Lydia's mother asked, but the words had no sooner left her mouth when they were stopped in front of the *Larkspur*.

"Hello, Mr. Pitney," Papa called, already tying the reins around the whip socket.

Lydia leaned forward to look past her parents and was struck by dread. Mr. Pitney was indeed in the garden, handsome in his Sunday tweed and a blue cravat. And he wasn't alone. "Papa!" she whispered fiercely, but he was already halfway out of the trap.

"It's too late, dear," Mother whispered, her brown eyes sympathetic. "But we'll try to get him away as soon as possible."

"Couldn't I just slip out and walk home?"

"Not without seeming rude, I'm afraid."

"Are you coming or not?" her father asked while holding the garden gate. Turning again to Mr. Pitney, who had taken a few steps away from a blanket-draped bench in which Miss Rawlins was seated, he enthused, "You should have been there at the tournament, Mr. Pitney. We edged past Prescott with eleven points to spare."

"Yes?" The archeologist actually looked pleased. "Good day, Mrs. Clark . . . Miss Clark," he said as they walked past her grinning father, whom Lydia could have gladly strangled. "You've met Miss Rawlins, I presume?"

"Not personally," Papa supplied.

The writer set aside some papers from her lap and rose to her feet. "I'm charmed," she said, smiling and offering a hand first to Lydia's mother as introductions were made. But the gray eyes behind the spectacles showed clear signs of annoyance. "We would offer you a seat," she said apologetically. "But the other benches are too damp for comfort."

"We could sit inside," Mr. Pitney suggested.

"The soup?" Lydia murmured at her father's side. "Remember you're hungry?"

Coming to her aid, Mother added, "And they'll be having their lunch here soon as well."

Papa looked disappointed. "I didn't think about that."

"But not for at least a half hour," Mr. Pitney assured him. "Do come inside, won't you?"

"Yes, do come inside," Miss Rawlins echoed with considerably less enthusiasm.

"Only if you'll promise to chase us out when it's time for us to leave," Lydia's father replied.

The archeologist chuckled. "I'll leave that to Mrs. Herrick, sir."

Two minutes later they were settled upon facing sofas in the hall. Along with Mr. Pitney and Miss Rawlins sat Mrs. Dearing, whom Lydia had met at the lending library. The elderly woman had offered to leave the hall but was assured by all that her presence would be most welcome. Too discomfited to stare across at Mr. Pitney and Miss Rawlins, Lydia allowed her eyes to wander as much as possible. As a girl she had accompanied her parents two or three times to visit Mr. Ethan Banning, the *Larkspur*'s former owner. Nothing seemed to have changed, from the cavernous fireplace to the multicolored carpets on the floor and the pianoforte against one wall.

"They conducted themselves like proper young gentlemen . . . and gentlewomen," Papa was saying. "All four teams. Archery is such a civilized sport, isn't it?"

"Only it didn't start out as a sport," Mr. Pitney tactfully reminded him. "And it's still used in intertribal fighting in Africa and South America, and even some places in the Far East."

"When did we stop using bows and arrows, Mr. Pitney?" Mrs. Dearing asked. "For fighting, I mean."

"Why, Mrs. Dearing, who have you been fighting?" Lydia's father demanded with raised eyebrows, though he hardly knew her.

I'm adopted, Lydia thought.

But Mrs. Dearing laughed. "By *we*, I mean England, Mr. Clark. I suspect you know that anyway. Do tell us, Mr. Pitney."

It was touching to Lydia how Mr. Pitney's face glowed, like that of a well-rehearsed soloist about to perform. "In 1588, Mrs. Dearing. Ten thousand English troops, experimentally equipped with firearms, defeated the Spanish Armada. The Spanish still relied heavily upon archers, you see."

"Fascinating, Mr. Pitney," commented Lydia's mother.

"Yes, fascinating," Miss Rawlins said with a wooden smile as she rose from the sofa, her papers in hand. "But I'm afraid I've tons of work to attend upstairs."

"Why don't you wait?" Mrs. Dearing asked. "You'll just have to stop for lunch before you get good and started."

"That's all right. I seem to have little appetite at the moment."

She bade everyone good-day and crossed the room, the hem of her pink and white gown whispering against the carpet. Lydia observed Mr. Pitney's face as he watched her leave. Gone was the confident glow. In fact, his face resembled Billy Casper's the day she had come upon him in the cloakroom putting a toad in Helen Johnson's lunch pail.

"This has been such a pleasant visit, but we'll be running along now," Lydia's mother said with a quiet forcefulness that Lydia had seen only a

265

few times in her life. Her father, also recognizing her change of tone, did not argue. Mr. Pitney's smile returned as good-days were exchanged, but he could not mask the worry in his brown eyes.

"What was wrong with stopping?" Lydia's father asked defensively as he drove the trap on down Church Lane. "Mr. Pitney was glad to see us."

"Because he was with Miss Rawlins," Mother explained in that same insistent tone, while Lydia wished the whole matter could be dropped.

"Well, I know he's fond of her, or he wouldn't have Lydia helping him read all those books. But surely that doesn't mean he wants nothing to do with nobody else when—"

"Amos," Mother cut in.

"Yes?"

"This hasn't to do with Mr. Pitney or Miss Rawlins or us. Lydia wasn't comfortable there."

"Mother . . ." Lydia interrupted.

Her mother took her hand and squeezed it.

"And why not, pray tell?" Father demanded. "Why, she and Mr. Pitney get along just famously, like two peas in—" But this time he stopped himself, saying not another word until the trap came to rest in the carriage drive of their cottage. "Daughter?" he said, his aged brow furrowed as he leaned forward to look past his wife.

"Yes, Papa."

"You've grown fond of Mr. Pitney, haven't you?"

She had kept very few things from her parents. Tears stung the corners of both eyes. "I have."

Wellington snorted and stamped a foot, ready to be let out of the traces, but still her father sat and stared. "I'm an old fool, aren't I? I never even realized . . ."

"It's all right, Papa," she said, mustering a reassuring smile for his sake. "He doesn't know."

"Mayhap you should tell him. Could be he's smitten with this writer woman because he thinks he can do no better."

"Papa, I'm not any better—"

"In a pig's eye, you're not! You know how I hate to be judgmental, but she sat there looking like she'd been weaned on vinegar."

He would get no argument about that from Lydia, for that was exactly what had happened. But she shook her head. Society had changed considerably since she was a child. Most people considered it just as important to educate girls as boys, and now women could be secretaries and even doctors. But some things had not changed, and a woman just couldn't go telling a man how she felt about him. Especially when that feeling was not reciprocated. "You know I can't do that."

"Well, why not?"

Her mother finally spoke again. "She just can't, Amos. And don't you go doing it for her."

———————

"It was so good of you to bring us home, Mr. Sanders," Mrs. Meeks told him at her cottage door. "But you really didn't have to. We're used to walking everywhere."

"It was on my way anyway," Harold told her. And it was mostly true, for Arnold Lane was just a little detour off North Market Lane. He had not meant to stay so long, but the children had begged, and their mother offered tea and egg sandwiches. And his brothers weren't there to pester him about getting home, for he had made them get a ride with Mercy and Seth when he decided to make the offer to Mrs. Meeks. Glancing at the barn, he asked, "How do you get milk to the factory?"

"Mr. Fletcher is kind enough to help with that. With us only having five cows, there's room for our cans in his wagon."

"Oh. And you milk them all yourself?"

She smiled, lightening the overworked look of her face. "There are helpful hands a-plenty here. All of the children can milk, as I'm sure you could do at an early age."

"Now there's a truth. When I learnt to walk, my papa shoved a bucket in my hands."

"Did he really do that, Mr. Sanders?" A wide-eyed Trudy asked, standing at her mother's side with her skinny arms wrapped around her waist.

"Well, mebbe not that early." Harold winked at the girl and grinned.

About a dozen chickens scattered when he neared the wagon after bidding the family farewell. He hadn't noticed them before, but it eased his mind that the food in his belly hadn't caused too much of a hardship. As he sat alone in the moving wagon, Harold wondered at the odd feeling that had overtaken him at some point today. Peaceful—as if he was sitting on a cloud. All his life he had sneered at folks who helped others, like Mercy helping Mrs. Brent when the old woman was dying, but he was beginning to understand it a little better. Because if it made folks feel good to do such things, why wouldn't they keep it up?

He was feeling so at peace with the world that by the time he reached home, he had decided that when he got his own place, he would do more for Mrs. Meeks and that brood of children. He didn't think Miss Clark, who would be his wife then, would mind their spending a little money on a poor family. After all, she had bought spectacles for Phoebe.

*G*ood evening, young man!" Mr. Clark greeted from his cottage doorway Monday night. "Were you able to work on the hill today?"

"Yes, thankfully," Jacob replied, smiling as he entered the cottage. His spirits were lighter than they had been since Saturday, for finally this evening Eugenia had come down to supper in a talkative mood, even telling him about a plot she was spinning for her next novelette.

"And what did you find, pray tell?" Mr. Clark asked.

He had anticipated that question from at least one of the three Clarks and dug into his pocket. "We found a number of these in the remains of a wooden box."

"Why, it's a spoon!" Mr. Clark exclaimed, closing one eye and holding it away from his face. "It's hard for me to see up close anymore. Bronze, isn't it?"

"It is. The upper classes used silver, but we've found but two of those so far."

"What did the poor use?"

"They carved them from wood, usually."

"How fascinating." Turning to take four paces back toward the other door, he called out, "Lydia! Oriel!"

Jacob smiled again. He could imagine his own father calling out for help from the bakery counter. Presently the two women came into the room with warm greetings for him. Mr. Clark had no sooner given them a chance to admire the spoon when he handed it back to Jacob and said, "Well, Oriel and I have chores to attend. You'd best get on with your book meeting."

Soon Jacob was seated on the sofa with Miss Clark, the cat dozing between them, and a copy of *Venitia and the Highwayman* in her lap. "Do you think I could examine the spoon for just a moment?" she asked. "My father sort of whisked it away in there."

"But of course." Jacob took it from his pocket again and handed it to her. "We found several today."

"How exciting," she said, turning the spoon to catch the lamplight. "I can just imagine a Roman soldier sitting down to have his . . . whatever he ate with this. But no forks?"

"They weren't used until the eleventh century. And only rarely then. Those early ones had only two prongs, by the way."

"But how did people manage before forks? Not all foods can be eaten with a spoon."

Jacob smiled, held up his hands, and wiggled his fingers.

"I should have guessed," Miss Clark said, returning his smile. Her expression then altered, as if she were weighing a question.

"Is there something else you'd like to know?" Jacob asked her. He could talk about antiquities for hours on end. It was only fear of becoming a bore combined with his natural timidity that restrained him.

She hesitated. "We're having our last week of school, Mr. Pitney. My students would enjoy seeing this. Do you think. . . ?"

"But of course. Take it with you tomorrow, if you like. I know Mr. Ellis would concur. We're delighted to show off our finds." Frowning, he added, "We shipped our most recent batch this morning, or I would offer some other items as well."

"There is always next year, if the offer still stands," she told him with a hopeful expression.

"Absolutely."

"Thank you. I can't think of a more interesting way to supplement a history lesson."

"Your students enjoy history?"

"I've some very motivated students, but most would rather be outside playing a game of rounders, I fear."

"How do you keep them dedicated to their studies?"

"By making the subject matter relate to their own lives as much as possible. And yet also attempting to expand their horizons so that they'll develop a thirst for new ideas and experiences."

"You must be a very good teacher," Jacob said. Anyone whose eyes lit up like hers just did had to have a passion for her profession, he thought.

"Thank you, Mr. Pitney." She smiled again as she set the spoon down on the sofa arm. "I do give it my best. As you do." As if suddenly remembering the reason he was there, she picked up the book from her lap. "But we're wasting your time, aren't we?"

Jacob hadn't thought so, but he had to remind himself that he was there to study novelettes and not waste Miss Clark's time. So he turned his attention to the passages she had marked with slips of paper. And when they had ferreted out any potential symbolism, he cleared his throat and gathered up the courage to make another request.

"Would you consider teaching me poetry, Miss Clark?"

"Poetry?" she repeated, tilting her head as if she hadn't heard correctly.

He cleared his throat again. "Romantic poetry is what I'm chiefly interested in."

A corner of her mouth twitched, yet it seemed as if a shadow had passed across her face. "*Chiefly* interested in, Mr. Pitney? Along with what other kind?"

"I beg your pardon?" But then the meaning of her question dawned upon him. "Well, no other kind, actually. So it would be only romantic poetry." He had trouble looking into her green eyes for some reason, so he stared at the cover of *Venitia and the Highwayman* and counted the ticks of the chimneypiece clock.

"I'll not be able to help you with that, Mr. Pitney," she said at length, folding her hands upon the closed novelette.

Perhaps she had mistakenly assumed he would not offer compensation, he told himself. "I would pay you extra, of course."

She gave him a little smile but shook her head. "I'm sorry."

"I understand," Jacob assured her, although he didn't, for he had the uneasy impression that her declining had more to do with disapproval than disinterest. But surely a person who taught poetry in a classroom wouldn't disapprove of anyone wishing to learn it. He wished he had the nerve to ask her if he had somehow offended her. *Just ask*, he urged himself. *She won't be angry.* Indeed, he was beginning to consider Miss Clark a good friend, and couldn't one friend be frank with another?

But years of timidity were not easily shaken, so he nodded and said he should be leaving. He held out a hand to assist her to her feet, and she accompanied him through the cottage. "Good night, Miss Clark," he said at the door. Remembering the copy of *Madeleine's Quest*, he dipped his hand into a coat pocket. "Oh, and here's the next one. You still wish to continue, don't you?"

"Of course, Mr. Pitney."

She looked as if she wished to say something else, or was he just imagining it? He shifted his weight upon his feet. "Thank you. Well, good night, Miss Clark."

"Good night, Mr. Pitney."

Jacob had only gone three steps across the porch when he stopped abruptly. *You have to know*, he told himself, turning.

She answered his knock almost immediately. "Did you forget something, Mr. Pitney?"

"What is wrong with my studying poetry, Miss Clark?"

With no expression that he could fathom, she stared at him for a second or two, then took a step backward. "Do come inside, please."

The door closed behind Jacob. "Correct me if I'm mistaken," he said in a humble tone. "But I have the distinct impression you disapprove."

"May I ask why you wish to study poetry?"

"Why, yes." He could feel warmth in his cheeks, even though she was already aware of why he studied the novelettes so carefully. "Eugenia . . . Miss Rawlins . . . mentioned that men who quote poetry . . ."

"I see," she said, sparing him from having to explain further.

"What do you see, Miss Clark?"

With quiet frankness she replied, "I see a man having to jump through hoops like a circus pony to gain the favor of a woman who can't appreciate him for the decent, kind person he is. And that is why I'll have nothing to do with your poetry quest, Mr. Pitney. It's bad enough that I'm party to studying the novelettes."

Jacob's jaw dropped. "But, Miss Clark, why is it so wrong to try to please the person you—" He meant to say *love* because that was what he felt for Eugenia in his heart. But his tongue would not cooperate, so he finished with, "care for?"

"It just is, if you have to become a completely different person to do so, Mr. Pitney. And now I'm quite fatigued, so I must bid you good-night."

In less than a minute he was crossing the porch again, both hands in his trouser pockets. The sun had been completely swallowed up by the Anwyl, and he was glad for it, for any passersby would surely notice his flaming cheeks.

By the time he reached the *Larkspur*'s courtyard door, he had realized that he held no resentment toward Miss Clark. Indeed, he appreciated her frankness and that she had even called him decent and kind. But he was embarrassed that he had even mentioned the poetry, for the notion now seemed foolish.

Not foolish enough to deter his plan, however. There was one thing Miss Clark didn't understand—how the happiness he felt when Eugenia looked at him with approval was worth any amount of trouble.

———

Harold spent all Wednesday morning waiting for a chance to slip away to the horse farm at the end of the lane, but his papa seemed determined to watch his every move. And it was Dale's fault, for he had snipped most of Mrs. Winter's sweetbrier roses on Saturday past to bring to his girl in Myddle. The cook was so furious upon making the discovery that she threatened to pack up and leave, until Harold's father had had to promise to build her that worktable.

But Harold couldn't hold too much of a grudge against Dale, for the meals had suddenly taken a turn for the better. At lunch, Harold barely dared look at the head of the table for fear some new chore would be laid upon his back. With the archery practices at an end and school almost over, he needed advice in the worst way.

"Harold," Papa grunted around a mouthful of buttered rhubarb.

Harold held his breath.

"Nip over to Seth's and borrow his bench claw when you finish. We need to get started on thet table."

Letting out his breath again, Harold nodded. "That's a right good idea, Papa."

"Aye, and you'll be sure to make it so's the legs is even," Mrs. Winters called out from the stove. Another good thing about her and Papa settling their differences was that she had stopped pounding bread dough and chopping onions at the table during meals. "I can't abide a table what rocks to and fro."

"You'd best get his level too," Papa said with a weary expression.

Harold hurried through his lunch and took off on foot. He walked through the Langford cottage calling his sister's name, but no one answered. Just in case, he decided to check the stables, and there he found Seth using a hoof hook on the hoof of a yellow Cleveland bay about sixteen hands high.

"Afternoon, Harold," his brother-in-law greeted, looking up for a second.

"Where's Mercy and Amanda?" Harold asked, for Thomas would be at school.

"Shopping in Shrewsbury with Mrs. Bartley."

It didn't seem fitting that his sister would run off with the squire's wife and leave her husband to starve. "Well, what about your lunch?"

Seth looked up again. "She left me some sandwiches. Women need to do things with other women sometimes, Harold."

He shrugged. "That a new horse you got there?"

"Bought her yesterday from a fellow in Whixall who wanted to sell off his stock. I've put the word to Mr. Trumble that we're looking for a couple of stable hands, if you know anybody interested."

Harold was interested himself. If he had to break his back working, it might as well be for wages. But he knew what his papa would say to that, which was another reason he had to get his own place. He sure envied Seth Langford's freedom to run his farm according to his own wishes.

"You'll make a good profit?"

"A decent one," Seth replied, still working on the hoof.

"That's good." Running his hand along the animal's velvet flank, Harold asked impulsively, "If I ever marry and get my own place, will you sell me a team cheap?"

His brother-in-law sent him an understanding smile. "I'll give you a team as a wedding gift. How about that?"

"Truly?"

"Truly."

"Why would you do that?" he had to ask, considering how hateful he and his papa and brothers had been to Seth before he married Mercy.

"Because you're family, Harold," Seth replied, back to work at the horse's hoof. "Families don't profit from each other."

Harold was touched, and searched for the words to tell him so. When they wouldn't come, he simply said, "That's right decent of you, Seth."

"You're welcome."

He remembered then that Papa was waiting and got to the most important reason for his visit. "I tried what you said about being distant with Miss Clark. It didn't work."

"Then I expect you should give up."

That was the last thing he wanted to hear. "Don't you have any other ideas?"

Letting down the hoof again, Seth hung the hook on a nail. "Why do you even ask, when you ignore the most important advice we've given you?"

Harold winced. "You ain't gonter go on about church again, are you?"

"Nope." Seth unlatched the stall door and slapped the horse's flank, sending it into the paddock where several others were gathered. "I'd just as soon waste my breath talking to a hitching post."

"Now, that ain't a nice thing to say, Seth."

Turning to him, his brother-in-law crossed his arms across his thick chest. "Harold, I've work to do, as you can see. So I'm going to say this just once. If you aren't willing to endure an hour of church every week for Miss Clark, maybe you had better ask yourself if your feelings for her are genuine."

"Genu . . ."

"If they're real, Harold. And if they're not, you'd be doing yourself a favor by forgetting about her."

Though he was fuming inside, Harold couldn't bring himself to stand his ground. Not after what Seth had said about giving him a team of horses. "Got to get back home," he mumbled with a halfhearted wave of the hand. He had gotten halfway before remembering the tools. By the time he reached home and had to endure his papa's swearing fit for taking so long, he was in such a foul mood that his teeth began to ache from the grinding.

It was during the afternoon milking that Harold's temper finally took a turn for the better. He sat on a stool beside Juneberry, who delighted in whipping her tail back to slap his face, and recalled the many times he had happened to be in the vicinity of Saint Jude's just as Sunday morning services let out. Folks milled around the grounds visiting afterward—dozens and dozens of them. If he happened to be there too, dressed in his new tweed coat and checkered trousers, who was to know that he hadn't been in church?

Just then Juneberry let fly with her tail again, but it didn't wipe the grin from Harold's face.

———

Should I? Paul Treves asked himself again as his train left Birmingham Station on Thursday morning. Sunday activities and his scheduled visit home the next day had prevented him from seeing how Mrs. Somerville was faring. But he was glad for the hindrances, for he needed some time to think. Had he not realized at the archery tournament how much he enjoyed her company, he would have had no inner struggle. It would be a simple matter of paying a courtesy call.

The fact that he and she were both eligible, however, complicated matters. For a visit, combined with the fact that he rather liked her, could be the first step on the road to a courtship. Providing she showed some sign of interest in him, of course. And he believed even that first step should not be taken lightly, for the road ended in marriage. The farther down it a person walked, the more difficult it was to turn aside—or the more painful it was when the other person chose to do so, as had been the case for him with Elizabeth.

He had prayed for direction for the past four days, but with no clear answer. That evening as he readied himself for bed, his prayer changed. If for some reason God chose not to reveal His wishes in this, Paul could accept that. God saw the entire picture—even how the picture would alter in years to come, and sometimes silence was His instrument. *But, Father, if Mrs. Somerville would be adverse to my calling on her now and then, please have her give me some sign.*

He didn't want to make a fool of himself, and he surely didn't want her having to endure his company only for the sake of politeness.

———

On Friday, Julia and Andrew joined the squire and Mrs. Bartley for lunch in the manor house garden. They sat at a wrought-iron table, surrounded by a kaleidoscopic mixture of blue delphiniums, scarlet Oriental poppies, mauve and white foxgloves, and golden feverfew, as they feasted on an excellent *Filet de Porcelet aux Pois Nouveaux*, along with herbed cucumber-and-tomato salad.

"Well, I don't see what you have to worry about," Mrs. Bartley was saying as she refilled Andrew's teacup. She waved away a curious bee, causing the gold bracelet on her wrist to flash with reflected sunlight. "Ben Mayhew is a fine young man."

"He's a dear boy," Julia agreed. "And if God means for them to be together, we'll accept that. But he has such ambitious plans for his career. We hate the thought of having Laurel move away."

"Perhaps he'll live in Shrewsbury," the squire said by way of consolation, his hatless head shining almost as much as his wife's bracelet. A pat of butter had melted and formed a little pool in the center of his porridge. Unfortunately, his stomach could not abide the rich foods that he was proud to serve at his table. "That's not so far."

Andrew shrugged. "I would settle for that. But I fear Shrewsbury isn't what he has in mind."

"You have to consider that the church could very well move *you* one day." Mrs. Bartley's pause to press her lips together evidenced that she did not care for this possibility. "And once the children are settled with families, it would be almost impossible to uproot them."

That faint possibility Andrew did not care to dwell upon. He had found his paradise-on-earth. And for the time being, all of his ducklings were happily in the nest. *You're borrowing trouble anyway*, he told himself, echoing Julia's admonition last night. So what if Ben Mayhew had given Laurel another note . . . had Andrew himself not attended an all-boys' school, perhaps he would have been a notorious note-passer.

But the thought of Laurel's interests growing beyond dolls and storybooks was depressing. He had already blinked once and found Elizabeth grown up. How did one stop time?

His eyes met Julia's across the table. *Are you all right?* was the message in hers.

He smiled back and gave a slight nod. While his mind searched for another subject, Mrs. Bartley obliged him unwittingly by saying, "Speaking of romance, have you heard about Vicar Treves carrying your Mrs. Somerville in his arms at the tournament?"

Of course they had heard. Who in Gresham had not? Even Mrs. Somerville's understandable absence from church on Sunday past had sparked rumors that she was attending Saint Luke's in Lockwood. Andrew knew this not to be the case, for when he and Julia called upon the young woman on Monday, she was having to walk with a cane. "She injured her knee," Andrew reminded the good woman, a little alarmed at the pleased glint in her blue eyes.

Not to be dissuaded, Mrs. Bartley chuckled. "Marriage hasn't caused you to lose your sense of romance, has it, Vicar?"

"It has not," Andrew stoutly assured her. "But you know what happens to those who feast upon rumors."

The squire raised both bushy white eyebrows while his spoon made swirls in his porridge. "What happens, pray tell?"

"I don't quite remember," Andrew had to confess after a moment's thought. He made a sheepish grin. "It was something one of my schoolmasters used to say. Anyway, I would rather feast upon this excellent pork. I do wish you could join us."

"Thank you. But I've gotten used to my gruel," the older man assured him with a smile.

Andrew was mentally patting himself on the back for a clever change of subject when Mrs. Bartley continued.

"Well, I don't see why we can't hope for a romance between the two of them. I rather like Vicar Treves. And they both look lonely, you have to admit."

Please don't say anything was the message Andrew hoped Julia could read in his eyes. She winked back and speared a cucumber slice with her fork.

But the squire was beaming happily. "If anyone can get two people together, my Octavia can. Why, thanks to her, that young Sanders woman had Mr. Langford headed for the altar before he knew what hit him!"

Mrs. Bartley's modest flush did not quite match the proud smile under her hawkish nose. Raising a butter knife as a conductor raises a baton to begin the symphony, she mused aloud, "Now, let me think. We'll invite the two here for lunch—when Mrs. Somerville is recovered, of course."

"Of course," her husband agreed with a nod so enthusiastic that his eyebrows quivered.

It appeared that marriage had infected him with the same fervor that Mrs. Bartley had for pairing off the population of Gresham.

And now Lockwood as well, Andrew told himself.

———

"Were you really worried that I might add fuel to their fire?" Julia asked her husband as he drove the trap up Bartley Lane.

"Not worried, just cautious," he answered. "You know how our dear Mrs. Bartley has a way of influencing anyone in the vicinity."

"Why didn't you attempt to dissuade her?"

"For the same reason I don't demand the River Bryce to change its course. The idea is obviously set in her mind." He feigned a shudder. "I'm reminded of my mother, trying to push all those eligible widows in my direction back in Cambridge."

"They're simply wanting to offer them an opportunity to interact socially again. And remember, they did get along well at the vicarage."

"Julia, Paul is our friend. I don't like to see him treated like some pawn in a game of chess."

"Neither should *you* treat him as one."

Giving her a sidelong look, Andrew asked, "Why did you say that?"

"Because you act as if he has no mind of his own," she stated frankly. "You can't expect to shield him forever. He has some discernment about what makes a decent woman, or he wouldn't have fallen in love with Elizabeth."

She expected him to argue, but he looked at her again and smiled.

"I suppose you're right. I've been a bit overprotective of him. And Mrs. Somerville seems a decent woman."

Julia returned his smile. "And we know how special vicars' daughters are, don't we?"

"Indeed we do."

After a brief silence during which Julia's glance at the secondary school windows did not reveal any familiar faces, she turned to him again. "You know, something occurred to me while we were discussing the children staying put."

"Yes?"

"Why would Mrs. Somerville's family send her here—a village they've never visited? To hear her describe it, Truesdale is just as peaceful."

"Perhaps they hope she'll marry again. If the place isn't on any map, the prospects of making a good marriage would surely be limited."

"So Mrs. Bartley may be on the right path after all," Julia teased. "Are you certain you can't recall meeting Mrs. Somerville's father?"

He shook his head. "I've been acquainted with two Vicar Smiths in my lifetime. But one passed away two years ago, and the other is a bishop in Nottinghamshire now."

"Hmm. Well, perhaps her family will come visit her one day, and you can discover if you've any mutual friends."

"That would be interesting." He reined Rusty to a stop at the crossroads and turned to give her an apologetic look. "Are you anxious to get home?"

"Not particularly," Julia replied, already knowing what he would ask.

"I wonder if you wouldn't mind . . ."

"Dropping in on Elizabeth?" she finished for him. As all thought of Mrs. Somerville was replaced by the thought of a coming grandchild, she replied, "Let's do."

Sixth loop and then under, Noelle told herself on Friday afternoon, her teeth pressed against her lips in concentration as the slender hook moved awkwardly in her unskilled fingers. Sheer boredom from being confined indoors, as well as a need for distraction from thoughts of Quetin, had led her to accept Mrs. Durwin's offer to teach her some simple crochet stitches. Now that the dresser scarf had reached about six inches in diameter, Noelle could measure her progress and found herself eager to see the results of the hours she had poured into it.

"Come in," she called when a knock sounded at the door. Not the door of her regular bedchamber, but of the one formerly occupied by Mrs. Phelps, for Doctor Rhodes had given strict orders that Noelle was to avoid the stairs for a fortnight. Usually Noelle practiced her crocheting in the hall where others could admire her progress and inquire about her strained knee.

At the moment, however, Aleda Hollis was teaching Mrs. Dearing a particularly difficult piano piece, Schubert's *Unfinished Symphony*—which was actually a complete composition, according to the Hollis girl. Complete perhaps, but painful to the ears at this stage of Mrs. Dearing's tutelage. It had not taken long for Noelle to decide to quit the hall for her temporary bedchamber. The Durwins and Mr. Jensen had managed to find excuses to leave as well, so Noelle didn't feel she was being rude.

Sarah, one of the parlormaids, eased open the door. "You've a caller, missus. It's that Vicar Treves from Lockwood."

"Thank you, Sarah." Noelle was finding gratitude easier and easier to express, for the *Larkspur*'s servants had not begrudged her the extra work she had caused them by moving downstairs, and were even extra-solicitous, appearing at her door often to ask if they could fetch her anything. Reaching for the cane Doctor Rhodes also insisted she use, Noelle began slowly getting to her feet.

"Shall I help you, missus?" Sarah asked, stepping inside.

Noelle shook her head and said, "I can manage, thank you. Is the library occupied?"

"I can nip down there and have a look."

Noelle smiled at her. "If you wouldn't mind."

While the girl was gone, Noelle went over to her dressing table mirror and combed her fingers through the curled fringe above her eyebrows. She looked nice, she thought, but almost wished she didn't. For she had been expecting Vicar Treves' call. A little sooner, perhaps, but in that instant she had looked back from the doctor's trap and locked eyes with him, she had known.

The knowledge pained her. He was a decent person who deserved a decent woman. And he would surely find that woman, but not for a long time if he occupied himself with chasing rainbows. He had been hurt once before by a courtship that had gone on too long. As her painful experience with Quetin had taught her, one heartbreak was enough for a lifetime.

"The library's empty, missus," Sarah declared in a breathless voice.

"Did you *run*, Sarah?"

"Just a bit, ma'am."

Noelle shook her head. "You pamper me shamelessly, you know. I'll be tempted to bang my knee again for the extra attention."

After covering a smile with her hand, the maid asked, "Shall I show Vicar Treves to the library?"

"Please do."

He was standing at a row of bookshelves with hands clasped behind his back when Noelle stopped in the doorway, his blond features a striking contrast with his black suit. "Good morning, Vicar Treves."

Turning his face toward her, he smiled. "Mrs. Somerville," he said and started walking toward her. "Please forgive me for not calling earlier. I've just returned from King's Heath yesterday. It's so good to see you up and about."

"There are no apologies necessary," she told him as she offered him her left hand, for the right still held the cane. "I trust you had a pleasant visit?"

"Very pleasant, thank you." Gently he took her hand and sent an anxious glance toward her right side. "You're having to use a cane?"

Noelle lifted the ivory handle to show him. "Mr. Jensen lent it to me."

"But you're better, aren't you?"

"Much better," she assured him. "Doctor Rhodes says I should be completely recovered in another week."

"Thank God for that."

"Yes." With a nod toward the chairs she took her hand from his. "Would you care to sit? Sarah is getting some tea for us."

"Will you be able to manage?"

"Yes, I'm just fine," she replied and sat down. He was still hovering near her, so she handed him the cane, just so he would feel useful. Through the open doorway drifted in the notes of Mr. Schubert's curiously titled composition, mingled with gaps of silence, which reminded Noelle somehow of a picket fence with stakes missing.

"I had hoped to bring you some apples," he told her when he had finally settled into the nearest chair. "Unfortunately, my mother says the remainder of last year's crop are fit only for tarts."

Then I would qualify, flashed across Noelle's mind. Frowning, she tried to push the gloomy thought aside.

Vicar Treves apparently mistook her frown for disappointment. "But this year's will be in before you know it."

"You're very kind," she told him, adding under her breath, *But I wish you weren't.* Because it only made what she knew she would have to do more difficult.

Sarah brought in a tray of tea and shortbread, and it took some time to pour and serve the two little plates. When the maid was gone, Vicar Treves took a sip, crossed his knees, and settled back into his chair. He seemed more at ease and asked how Noelle managed to fill her days while being homebound.

"Well, I've started crocheting."

He smiled. "Yes? Do you enjoy it?"

"More than I thought I would."

"One of my parishioners in Lockwood just learned how last month, and he crochets almost every waking minute now."

"Well, I hope I never get *that* carried away. But did you say *he?*"

"Mr. Gripp is his name. He's recovering from a foot amputation. His wife finally insisted he learn to crochet because all he had to keep his mind occupied was to comment on how she tended house."

Unable to restrain a smile, Noelle told him, "I know I shouldn't say this, considering he lost his foot, but that's rather funny."

"Oh, Mr. Gripp would be the first to agree," he said, returning her smile. "You should see him. He's as huge as an oak trunk, and the crochet hook looks lost in his giant hands. He made me a lovely table scarf, by the way."

Now Noelle had to laugh. The two spent some ten minutes occupied with similar small talk, which she would have enjoyed much more had not the shadow of what was likely to come hovered over her. And then Mr. Treves unwittingly ruined his own day.

"Have you ever heard of well-dressing?" he asked.

"I always try to dress well," she replied with a bemused look at him.

Surely he wasn't implying her wardrobe was lacking in some way.

He chuckled and shook his head. "Forgive me, not that kind of dressing. It's a festival held in Waverly to celebrate Christ's ascension. The villagers decorate their wells with biblical scenes. Some are quite elaborate, I've been told. And it's only about an hour's drive from here."

For a second or two he paused, probably hoping she would respond in some manner. But Noelle didn't, for she was unsure of what to say. She couldn't very well turn down an invitation that had not yet been extended.

"They press flower petals and other natural objects into clay to form the pictures, you see," he finally continued. "Would you care to accompany me there, Mrs. Somerville? The outing would be well-chaperoned, of course. Mrs. Coggins and Israel—"

"It sounds very interesting, but I'm afraid I cannot accept, Vicar Treves."

"Very well," he said with an understanding nod, as if he wished to show that he wasn't as disappointed as his blue eyes hinted. But then a ray of hope seemed to fill them. "I neglected to mention that it's not until mid-June. The festival, that is. In case you're concerned about your injury."

Noelle shook her head, wishing now she had asked Sarah to tell him she was resting or unable to receive callers. How could she have imagined how disconcerting this would be? But as she wasn't quite vain enough to believe he felt anything more for her at this stage than infatuation, she thought it better to hurt him a little now than allow him to think there could be any sort of a courtship between them. It would be far less painful to pull out a splinter than to have to amputate a limb later.

"Vicar Treves," she said quietly, hoping he could tell by the way she looked at him that she actually considered him a pleasant, even interesting, person. "Are you aware that my father is a vicar?" There was no use attempting to keep that quiet since her slip of the tongue Saturday past. And perhaps he already knew.

But he raised both eyebrows, even smiled. "Indeed?"

"Indeed."

"Where?"

"Truesdale. A tiny place, not even on the map." Despising the insensitive act she was going to have to present, she nonetheless went on. "And the reason I'm not there with them is that I disliked growing up in a vicar's household. Actually, *loathed* would be a more appropriate word."

A ripple of shock passed across his face. "What have you against vicars, Mrs. Somerville?"

"Less than before I moved here," she had to confess. "I'll grant you that Vicar Phelps and you have not fit the mold I took for granted was required of men of the cloth. But you're still married to the church."

"What do you mean, *married to the church*?"

"Being at the beck and call of every parishioner who has a complaint or simply wishes to take up your time. Having to be pleasant to people who are often not the same to you—*especially* if they are generous tithers." She shuddered. "And for that, you're allowed to live in a vicarage that isn't your own and watch your pennies so that there will still be meat in the pot by the end of the month."

"It isn't quite that drastic, you know." It seemed Vicar Treves was almost amused, for the corners of his mouth curved faintly. "Most of my parishioners have scant time of their own to be taking up mine. I've discovered that being pleasant takes much less energy than being otherwise. My fireplace is just as warm, even if it doesn't belong to me. And I've yet to go a day without meat." And before Noelle could summon a reply, Vicar Treves stood and gave her a polite smile. "But I'm fatiguing you, when you should be resting. I will continue to pray for your full recovery."

"Thank you," was all she could say. He was correct about her being fatigued, for she suddenly felt drained of strength. Quetin had made bluntness appear to be so effortless that Noelle had not realized how taxing it could be.

"May I assist you to your feet?" he asked.

She shook her head and touched the handle of the cane he had propped against the arm of her chair. "No, thank you. I'll just sit here awhile."

"Very well. Good day, Mrs. Somerville."

When he was gone, she stared blankly at rows of books and wondered if she had hurt him terribly. Even if their acquaintance was too new for him to feel any sort of deep affection for her, men had their pride. *Father, please comfort him*, she prayed before realizing what she was doing. Then she felt worse, for the prayers of a kept women surely went only as far as the slate roof above her.

———

At least she had the decency not to lead me along, Paul told himself as he rode Caesar through Gipsy woods toward Lockwood. He had planned to call upon the Phelps if they were at home, but his heart was no longer in it. Fortunately his heart wasn't shattered, as it would have been had he allowed his thoughts to dwell upon Mrs. Somerville any longer than they had. Another week or two and he would probably forget what she looked like.

———

"I do hope you'll continue reading over the summer," Lydia said that same afternoon to her dozen students sitting at freshly scrubbed, empty desks. It was unnecessary counsel, of course, for the majority were avid readers and did not need encouraging. The few who despised books would be glad for the reprieve. But there were certain things every conscientious teacher was required to say before turning loose the brood whose minds she had nurtured for the past nine months, and that was one of them.

Another was, "I have enjoyed having you in my classroom, and I will continue to pray for each of you every day."

"Thank you, Miss Clark," twelve voices murmured in unison.

She smiled and delivered the last statement, without which the summer could not officially begin. "After we've finished sorting and packing up the textbooks, we'll have punch and cake."

"To hear from thy lettuce . . ."

On the Anwyl Saturday morning, Jacob Pitney frowned down at the bronze ax head he was in the painstaking process of unearthing from the hard ground. *Lettuce? She'll think you're an idiot for certain.*

He gave it another try, mumbling softly so as not to be heard by Mr. Ellis, who was propped upon a huge stone and scribbling notes some twenty feet away.

" . . . from thy *lattice* breathed, the word that shall grant . . . *give* me rest."

"I beg your pardon?" Mr. Ellis said for the third time that morning.

Jacob looked over at him and for the third time replied, "Sorry. Just talking to myself."

His colleague returned to his notes, but not before giving him a curious look. Jacob decided it would be best to practice the lines in his mind, without even moving his lips, but he found the process much more difficult.

It was Mrs. Dearing who had helped him find a poem in the *Larkspur*'s library that would prove to Eugenia that he had the soul of a poet. "*You can almost feel the sultry desert night air,*" Mrs. Dearing had enthused. He would have to memorize other works as well, but not before Bayard Taylor's *Bedouin Song* was cemented as firmly in his mind as the tool in the earth below his fingers. And he believed himself almost ready, in spite of the occasional slip, to impress Miss Rawlins with his poet's soul. The late hours spent in study for the past week had not been in vain.

That evening Jacob dressed quickly for supper, giving himself time to read *Bedouin Song* aloud—or at least a shade above a whisper—six times. He could hardly taste Mrs. Herrick's excellent steak-and-kidney pie, he was so nervous, and while watching Eugenia mash butter into her boiled potatoes, he wondered if it would be unseemly of him to ask her to sit in the courtyard with him. *You sat in the garden together*, he reminded himself. But that had been in the daytime, and where any passerby could see that nothing inappropriate was taking place.

Yet he quailed inside at the very thought of reciting like a schoolboy in front of his fellow lodgers—especially a poem having to do with love.

Perhaps tomorrow would be a better time, while we walk home from church. What was one more night of fitful sleep, haunted by dreams of himself spouting nursery rhymes or the alphabet or some such foolishness? But what if the Durwins accompanied them, as they had just Sunday past?

He drew in a deep breath to calm his racing pulse. Why anyone cared for poetry was a mystery to him, if learning it caused so much anxiety.

"I felt compelled to scold Mr. Trumble for selling the horrible stuff," Mrs. Dearing was saying, making Jacob curious enough to snap out of his self-torment and pay attention to the ensuing discussion. "Why, it's almost criminal!"

To the best of Jacob's knowledge, Mr. Trumble was a good Christian man. What could he possibly sell that would raise affable Mrs. Dearing's ire?

"One can hardly pass a group of children without being reminded of cows working at their cuds," she went on.

"But how can we expect them to do otherwise?" Mr. Jensen suggested tactfully. "Look at the example adults have set over the years with their snuff-dipping."

"Well, I think it's even nastier than snuff-dipping," Eugenia entered into the discussion, her spectacles shifting as she wrinkled her elegant nose. "I actually stepped in a wad of it on my way to the barber's Tuesday. It was murder to get off my shoe."

Her hair. Jacob had *thought* she looked different lately. Without being obvious, he looked across at her again and realized about two inches had been shorn. *You have to be more observant*, he lectured himself.

"And *that's* only when they have the good sense to spit it out," Mr. Durwin added. "Imagine what it does to the intestines of those who simply swallow it."

"But isn't chewing supposed to be good for the teeth?" queried Mrs. Durwin in her usual meek manner. "Dogs chew bones to keep theirs clean."

"Yes, but bones do not adhere to the teeth as chicle does."

"What exactly *is* chicle?" Mrs. Somerville asked.

Mr. Jensen patted his mouth with his napkin before replying. "It is the dried milky sap of a Mexican jungle tree, the sapodilla. There was a most enlightening article about it just last month in the *Saturday Review*."

"But I believe Mrs. Durwin has something there," Mr. Clay said with a wry smile that alerted all lodgers that the next words from his lips would not be serious. "All we have to do is convince Mr. Trumble to sell *bones* to the little ones instead of gum."

"The bigger task would be convincing the little ones to *buy* them," said Mr. Ellis, bringing chuckles from everyone but Jacob, who was still trying to find a foothold in the subject of conversation.

Gum? What was that?

Mrs. Clay, apparently believing him to be too timid to speak, turned to him and smiled. "What are your thoughts on the matter, Mr. Pitney?"

All Jacob could do was confess his inattention. "Forgive me, but I'm afraid I didn't hear the first part of the conversation."

"Woolgathering, Mr. Pitney?" Mrs. Dearing asked.

Sheepishly he replied, "Ah . . . a little."

"About archeology?" Mr. Durwin asked. Before Jacob could reply, a positively mischievous look passed over the elderly man's face. "Or perhaps about a particular young wo—"

"Bertram!" Mrs. Durwin interrupted in a surprisingly forceful whisper.

"Oh, do forgive me, Mr. Pitney," her husband said after a second or two of stunned silence. "I let myself get carried away."

Jacob forced his lips into a smile. "Think nothing of it." But he did not look at Eugenia to see her reaction. As heat stole through his cheeks, he concentrated on his steak-and-kidney pie and hoped no one noticed.

His first inclination was to flee to his room when the meal was finished. But as he stood near the doorway with the other men to allow the women to exit first, he felt a touch upon his elbow. He turned to find Eugenia smiling up at him. "According to Mrs. Clay, the breezes are quite pleasant this evening. I thought I might sit in the courtyard for a little while. Would you care to join me?"

"I . . . uh . . . yes, would be delighted," he stammered, pretending not to notice Mr. Clay's wink over her shoulder.

The evening breezes were indeed pleasant, and more so because Eugenia shared the bench with him. In the west, a faint orange glow of setting sun made the Anwyl stand out in bas-relief against a sky of deep purple. The aroma of white jasmine wafted over from the Worthy sisters' garden, reminding him of his mother's garden at home. If only his family could meet Eugenia! They would be as enchanted as he was, he had no doubt.

Eugenia gave a little sigh of contentment beside him, which he wished he could save and press into a memory book. And her words made him even happier.

"I wanted to speak with you privately because I realized today how much I appreciate you, Jacob."

"You do?" he said, wondering if he had heard correctly.

Her gray eyes shone even in the evening dimness. "It dawned upon me while I was laboring over a particularly difficult scene involving Valentina and Count Lobue. After a half hour of scratching out sentences so that my page resembled an ink blotter, I simply forced myself to stop and conjure up a mental picture of myself reading the scene aloud to you. I even imagined the thoughtful angle at which you hold your head as you listen."

Jacob's heartbeat against his chest almost drowned out her words as she continued.

"And before I knew it, I was writing madly. Your enthusiasm for my stories has unleashed a wonderful new creativity in me."

"I'm honored that you would say so," he told her while barely daring to breathe.

"Well, I believe in giving credit where it is due." She smiled. "And so I told myself today that it would be unforgivable of me not to tell you how much your friendship has meant to me."

Friendship? Jacob's smile stayed locked in place as his heart broke up into pieces inside his chest. He was like a man pushed from a cliff, desperately flailing his arms for anything solid to grasp. And the only thing that met his fingers was *Bedouin Song.*

Clearing his throat, he forced himself to look into her eyes and recite softly:

> *From the Desert I come to thee*
> *On a stallion shod with fire;*
> *And the winds are left behind*
> *In the speed of my desire.*

Her mouth gaped as she stared at him in much the same manner Mr. Durwin had looked at Mrs. Durwin when she corrected him at the supper table. That could either mean she was impressed or thought him odd, but he could not allow himself to ponder that or he would forget his lines. He continued:

> *Under the window I stand,*
> *And the midnight hears my cry:*
> *I love thee, I love but thee,*
> *With a love that shall not die . . .*

"Oh, Jacob!" she cried after the final stanza. "You *are* romantic after all!"

He felt almost faint from happiness. "Do you really think so?"

"Yes, I do! Why have you been hiding it from me for so long?"

A little stab came to his conscience with the thought that *for so long* was actually only a matter of days. But she was looking at him with such admiration that he could only think to reply, "Well, just because."

She giggled at that. "You're too modest, Jacob."

Together they gazed at the first emerging star against the darkening sky, while she recited, with a breathy voice, her favorite poem—a rather melancholy one—by Elizabeth Browning titled *Go From Me*.

But Jacob was not melancholy. In fact, he wondered as she allowed him to hold her hand if it were possible to die from happiness. If only Miss Clark could be here now! Good friend that she was, she would be overjoyed to see that she was wrong about the poetry.

THE DOWRY OF MISS LYDIA CLARK — *Chapter 35*

*T*he stone of Saint Jude's north wall was cool against Harold's back the first Sunday morning in June as he waited outside the building, occasionally peering around the corner for the first sign of worshipers. His plan was so clever that he wondered what he could have done with himself if he had gotten an education. *Maybe Prime Minister*, he thought. Just let Papa try to boss him around then! He reckoned the prime minister didn't have to answer to anybody but the queen, and that wouldn't be so bad because she likely wasn't nearly as unreasonable as his papa was.

The first sounds that caught his ears were children's voices. Turning again, he smiled at the sight of about a dozen boys spilling out onto the green like prisoners escaped from jail. Following them were some more orderly children—girls, of course. He cupped his hands on both sides of his mouth to call out to Phoebe and Trudy but lowered them again as he realized he would be giving himself away and needed to wait until more people were outside. As fond as he was of the Meeks, he had to remind himself it was for Miss Clark's sake that he was here.

A few minutes later, when the green was freckled with knots of visiting people and playing children, he spotted the Clarks emerging from the church. Harold adjusted the collar to his tweed coat, counted to ten, and just to be safe, counted again before abandoning his hiding place.

"Miss Clark?" he said, walking up behind her.

She turned, as did her father and mother. All three wore expressions of surprise. "Mr. Sanders?" said Miss Clark.

"That were a lovely sermon, wasn't it?" he asked them, shaking his head at the wonder of it. "The best I've ever heard!"

The three glanced at one another. For just a second her papa looked as if he was trying hard not to laugh at something, which was odd, considering he had just been to church. Surely Vicar Phelps didn't tell jokes up in the pulpit.

"Yes, lovely," Miss Clark answered. Then as if remembering her manners, she introduced him to her parents. Harold shook the hands they offered.

"It's good to see you at church, Mr. Sanders," her mother said to him, smiling warmly.

Harold nodded and thanked her. "I should'ha done this a long time ago. It's about time I behaved like proper folk do, I figger."

"Well, good for you!" the old man boomed, even clapped him on the back. "Then we can expect to see you next Sunday?"

"I wouldn't miss it," Harold replied with a grin.

Bidding him farewell, they walked over to join some people Harold gathered was Noah Clark and his family. Harold wondered if he should stroll along with them. Perhaps they would even invite him to lunch. *What would Mercy tell me to do?* Having his answer, he sighed and turned to where Dan was tethered to a young elm outside the churchyard. The horse had just lowered a hoof onto the cobbled stones of Market Lane when Harold glanced to his right and spotted Mrs. Meeks and her children walking across the green. He reined Dan back onto the green and waved.

"Mr. Sanders!" Trudy squeaked, just as she did while riding the merry-go-round. The girl and Lester began running toward him, while the rest of the family sent waves from behind. Figuring it would be more polite to leave the saddle, Harold swung himself to the ground and stepped out in front of the horse.

"Hey, Trudy!" He chuckled at the force with which she threw her skinny arms around his waist. Lester, a little more bashful, stopped just short of him and grinned. And soon, Mrs. Meeks, Mark, and Phoebe—wearing her spectacles for a change—caught up with them.

"You were in church, Mr. Sanders?" Mrs. Meeks asked after greetings had been exchanged and they inquired about each other's health. She didn't look so weary today. In fact, her cheeks fairly bloomed to match the pink calico gown she was wearing. She could have been mistaken for a schoolgirl with the little straw bonnet upon her head and her long brown hair tied behind her neck with a pink ribbon.

Harold wondered if it was church that made the change in her appearance. If it was, he supposed it was a good thing—for some people. "Yes," he lied and felt an odd little stab for doing so. Steering the subject away from himself, he asked, "You *walk* here and back every Sunday?"

"Unless the weather's bad," she told him, smiling. "The Fletchers kindly come for us in that case. But it ain't so far. The children walk it almost every day."

She was right—the Meeks' cottage was half the distance of his father's place. But it didn't seem fitting, with her and Phoebe and Trudy being so small. He reckoned Mark and Lester could bear it much easier. Thoughts of the children made him turn to make sure none were too near Dan's hooves. He was satisfied to see that they were taking turns feeding handfuls of grass to the animal. "Well, why don't they give you a ride every Sunday?" he asked, frowning.

"Don't be angry, Mr. Sanders." She pointed off toward the church, several yards away, where a group of about eight people was walking in their direction. "The Fletchers also walk most days—see?"

"Oh."

"Will you come see us this summer, Mr. Sanders?" Trudy stepped around to ask. "We won't be on the merry-go-round until school starts again. We have to help Mother tend the garden and cows."

"Mr. Sanders has his own work to do, Trudy," Mrs. Meeks said before Harold could even think of how to answer. She gave him an apologetic smile. "It was good seeing you, Mr. Sanders. I'd best get the children home and fed."

Harold nodded and bade her farewell, smiling at the way the children had to tear themselves away from Dan. He wondered if they had ever ridden a horse. Perhaps one day he would drop by and give them each a turn. If he had the time, between breaking his back for his papa and courting Miss Clark.

"You've a letter, Mrs. Somerville," Georgette announced after a knock on the door of the room in the family quarters late Monday morning.

Noelle suffered no more pain, and the cane was more nuisance than necessity. But as she didn't want to go through the inconvenience again, she thought it best to obey Doctor Rhode's orders. "Thank you, Georgette," she said, calmly winding her crochet hook through the last loop of her dresser scarf so it wouldn't unravel before taking the envelope from the silver tray. When the maid was gone, she tore open the seal with pulse racing. Her heart fell when two one-pound notes fluttered down to land on the crocheting in her lap. And even more so when she recognized Mr. Radley's handwriting.

> *Dear Miss Somerville,*
>
> *My client, the honorable Quetin Paxton, M.P., has instructed me to inform you that any further attempt at communication from you will result in an immediate cessation of financial support.*
>
> *Cordially,*
> *Osbert Radley*

Though Mr. Pitney had sent her and her parents a friendly wave across the green after church Sunday, Lydia was still a little surprised when he showed up for their Monday night meeting. He did not mention last week's disagreement, nor did she. But judging by the way Miss Rawlins had clung to his arm yesterday, she could only assume that he had gotten hold of some poetry and impressed her.

"There must be some significance to the crock of herbs in the parlor," she told him from the sofa of her own parlor as she held *Madeleine's Quest* open between them. Jeanie, having gotten used to this frequent caller, actually dozed in his lap instead of hers this time. But then, he had tempted the feline by arriving with a cloth bag of catmint he had picked upon the Anwyl just hours earlier.

"Wouldn't you agree?" Lydia asked.

Mr. Pitney nodded, but the line between his dark eyebrows gave evidence to some doubts. And after a thoughtful second or two, he replied, "I just wonder why the crock appears only once. Usually when something is intended to be symbolic, she mentions it so many times that you want to rip the page from the—"

He stopped short, gulping audibly. To save him from further embarrassment, Lydia pretended not to notice and jumped to another subject, the crack in the Dresden China vase—which was mentioned some dozen times in the novelette. She was convinced the crock of herbs meant something significant, but Mr. Pitney had studied more than enough symbolism to fan Miss Rawlins' ego and could allow that one to pass.

The cottage was quiet as she walked with him to the front a short while later. Her parents had again absented themselves soon after his arrival. At the door he reminded her of his earlier invitation to visit the ruin. "You have time, now that school is out, haven't you?" he asked. "I would escort you, of course. And tomorrow would be a good day for it, weather-wise."

"I have time," she replied, surprised that he would reissue the invitation. Wouldn't Miss Rawlins mind? But of course, Lydia was painfully aware that she wasn't exactly a threat to other women. "And I would be delighted to watch you and Mr. Ellis at work." But as setting a proper example to Gresham's schoolchildren was also important to her, she added, "You won't mind if my father comes along, will you? We've hiked the Anwyl before, so you wouldn't have to come down and meet us."

"Yes, do invite him," Mr. Pitney replied with a pleased expression. "And your mother as well."

"I shall, but don't expect her. She's not fond of hiking and will be content to hear all about it when we return."

He smiled. "I didn't even consider that your father would be interested, but he seems to be interested in just about everything, doesn't he?"

"Everything," Lydia agreed. "Life is never dull around here."

"I suppose you're aware of how blessed you are in that regard, Miss Clark. The closeness of your family, I mean."

"I am. And from the way you describe your family, so are you."

"Absolutely." Brown eyes crinkling at the corners, he said, "That makes two blessings we have in common. Beloved families and beloved vocations."

Three, Lydia thought. *We're both in love. Only not with each other.* And on second thought, her love for him couldn't be considered a blessing as long as she had to keep it buried like a smoldering lump of coal under ashes. She realized he was waiting for her to speak. "Why don't you allow us to bring a picnic?"

"Oh, but you're to be our guests," he replied with a shake of his head. "And Mrs. Herrick has already assured me she doesn't mind packing extra. I'll just have to let her know that your father will be joining us."

Lydia was flattered that he had already taken some pains to plan out the day. If he was this considerate to her, someone he simply paid to tutor him, he must treat Miss Rawlins like a princess. But she couldn't allow envy to spoil the special moments that did come her way. They were all she had, and in years ahead she would ponder them by her quiet fire.

Later in the front parlor, as her father dabbled paints on his canvas to put the fine finishing touches on the Worthy sisters' portrait and Lydia and her mother sat on the sofa with cups of cocoa, she related to them Mr. Pitney's remark about the symbolism and tearing out the pages. "It was very much unlike him. Why, he seemed almost angry."

"He *is* angry," her mother declared after a sip of cocoa.

"I don't think so. It was just an impulsive comment—for which he apologized right away."

But her mother shook her head. "He isn't aware of his anger yet, Lydia. But you can be assured that little impulsive spark was just the beginning."

"Angry at what, Oriel?" Lydia's father asked while frowning studiously at his work as it progressed. "I'll warrant Mr. Pitney doesn't know the meaning of the word."

"At having to study all those shallow little stories as if they are university texts. Wouldn't you be?"

"Raging. But then, I'm known far and wide for my fiery temper."

"Yes, Amos." She smiled at Lydia over the rim of her cup. "Everyone knows what a bear you are. Anyway, Mr. Pitney will resent one day that he has to manufacture such enthusiasm for her occupation, while she has none for his."

This wasn't like her mother, who usually had a charitable word for everyone. "We don't know that for certain, Mother," Lydia told her.

"Then I assume that she'll also be touring the ruins tomorrow?"

"Why, I don't think so. But she has to write, remember? And perhaps she has already been up there."

"Perhaps." Setting her cup and saucer on the teatable, Lydia's mother reached down to scoop Jeanie up into her plump lap. "But I doubt it very much."

————

Under a sky of pure lucid blue, Lydia and her father were given a guided tour of the ruins by Mr. Pitney. Mr. Ellis, who chatted affably with them when they first arrived, asked to be excused. "Making the climb every day is strenuous enough," he explained. "Once I'm here, I generally plant myself in one spot and allow Mr. Pitney the heavy labor."

"And you consider showing us about the place heavy labor, Mr. Ellis?" Lydia's father asked with a glint of mischief in his eyes.

"Only if he takes a notion to carry you at the same time, Mr. Clark," Mr. Ellis replied dryly, but with a teasing look in his own eyes as well.

Mr. Pitney first took them to a large weeded area bordered by crumbling stone walls overgrown with brambles and ivy. "This was most likely a common dining area," he said. "As you can see, we've yet to get to it."

The archeologist appeared more at ease than Lydia had ever seen him. She realized it was because he was at home on top of the hill. Pushing back her straw hat to hang by its ribbons, she looked about her. Only an area about thrice the size of her schoolroom showed signs of recent digging. Mr. Pitney had warned her that the work was painstakingly slow, but after two years of excavation work, she had half expected to see the whole ruin laid open, with artifacts glistening in the sun.

"Why would the Society only send two people?" she asked him, quickly qualifying that with an added, "Not that you're not doing a good job of it."

He smiled. "Mr. Ellis and I are what you could term a *scouting party*. Our duties are to collect artifacts, yes, but also to find proof that this ruin is of significant value. If it turns out to be so, this hill will be swarming with archeologists."

"Just like a giant ant bed, eh?" Lydia's father suggested, tugging absently at his beard. "The jade bracelet wasn't enough proof? Lydia told me about it."

"Not enough, I'm afraid," Mr. Pitney replied with a glance in her direction. He looked both surprised and pleased for some reason. Because she discussed his work with her father? But why wouldn't she?

"Nonetheless, the bracelet was exciting to Mr. Ellis and me," he went on. "And highly motivating. For who knows? One of us could be standing directly over the proof we need."

Lydia instinctively took a step backward, causing the two men to laugh. She smiled a little sheepishly. "It makes you treat the ground with a little more respect, doesn't it?"

"It does at that," Mr. Pitney agreed.

They resumed their tour of the ruins, then Mr. Ellis joined them under a hardy sycamore tree for an excellent lunch of cold roasted chicken, cheese, bread, and marmalade. Afterward, the older archeologist asked if Lydia and her father would care to look for artifacts.

"You'll allow us to dig?" her father asked with raised eyebrows. "I mean . . . brush?"

Mr. Ellis smiled. "Allow you to assist us with our work? Certainly."

"We'll team up then, shall we?" Papa said, then turned to Lydia and Mr. Pitney with a face as innocent as a choirboy's. "I'll work with Mr. Ellis. And you two youngsters can work together."

And so Lydia was led by Mr. Pitney to an uneven, man-made depression about three feet deep, bordered on three sides by the remains of a wall. Mr. Ellis and her father began work on the other side of one of these walls, some eight feet away.

"What do you do with the dirt you collect?" Lydia asked.

Mr. Pitney nodded over to a mound outside the wall area. "That's the most tedious part, having to sprint over there to empty our pails. This whole area was a part of some family quarters—someone of the upper class, probably an officer."

"Possibly General Cerealis?" Lydia asked.

"That's what we're hoping." Glancing down at the pit, he looked at her again and said, "Hmm . . . I may need to assist you."

"Yes, of course." By sheer will, Lydia kept her cheeks from blushing, for he was only being polite, as he would be to any visitor who happened to be wearing a gown and wished to maintain some modesty.

"You should sit first," he suggested after jumping down into the depression. He turned his back to her, giving her opportunity to do so.

"I'm ready now," Lydia told him, making sure her gown entirely covered the lower legs she dangled over the side.

Taking a step toward her, he said with an apologetic look, "This will take some planning."

It isn't far from the bottom of my feet—I can just jump, she started to assure him. But then some wicked impulse, perhaps springing from her mother's observations last night, caused her to say, "Just show me how Miss Rawlins got down here, and I'll do the same."

"Miss Rawlins?"

They locked eyes, and she knew from the sadness that passed across his that the writer had not yet bothered to allow him to show her his world. *See? Don't you understand now?* she wanted to shout at him, but of course could not. Instead, she smiled and beckoned him a step closer. "If you'll just stand right there and allow me to put a hand on your shoulder, I can jump quite easily."

"You'll injure—"

"Nonsense. I'm almost as tall as you are." And before he could say another word, she was standing next to him. "It does jar the teeth a bit, doesn't it?"

"A bit," he agreed. "But I still have all of mine after all these years of hopping into pits, so fortunately no damage is done."

From the other side of the crumbled wall came the sound of shared laughter.

"My father has found another soul mate."

"I had a feeling they would get along well," Mr. Pitney replied, smiling and reaching for a short broom made of sedge on the bank of the depression.

"What is this?" Lydia asked him.

"It's your brush." He picked up another. "We go through them quickly, so we've always plenty on hand. The Keegan family makes them for us—you know the basket weavers?"

"But I was expecting . . ."

"Something like a hairbrush?"

"A paint brush, actually."

"We do use brushes when we actually come across a relic. But to use them for moving away all of the dirt would be expensive and even more time consuming."

"I see." She looked down at the earth below her. "Perhaps you should show me where to begin."

"You may turn up something over here," he pointed to his left, showing her a hole the size of a loaf of bread where he had unearthed an urn just last week. "Often when you uncover one thing, there will be others close by."

"I hope so." Figuring her poplin gown would have to be laundered anyway, she got to her knees and brushed the broom lightly against the earth. There was no sign of an artifact, so she repeated the action. She heard a faint chuckle and looked up at Mr. Pitney, standing with his arms akimbo.

"You may move an inch of dirt a month at that rate, Miss Clark."

"But I don't want to damage anything."

"You won't. If being buried for centuries hasn't hurt them, a more vigorous application of the broom won't either. And we'll switch to the brush when you do find something."

"Very well." But she found herself too intimidated by the value of what could possibly be under the earth to allow herself to continue. She held the broom hovered over the earth for a second, then looked at him again. "Will you show me?"

"Of course."

He set his broom down on the ground, which surprised her because she had meant that he should use it to demonstrate how she should proceed. Before she could explain that to him, he had knelt down beside her and covered her hand over the broom handle with his.

"Imagine sweeping ashes from a stove," he said, helping her guide the broom briskly to the left and right. "You've done that before, haven't you?"

"At school."

"Only, I like to alternate directions every so often and crisscross," he explained as he guided her broom out away from her, and then toward her. "Would you care to guess why?"

She had to ponder that one, which was very difficult, when all she could think about was his hand over hers. "So you can detect the first sign of an artifact more easily?" she finally ventured out of lack for any other guess.

Smiling, he shook his head. "It makes patterns . . . see? When you have to do this several hours a day, it breaks up the monotony a bit."

"I see," she told him. *And this is anything but monotonous, Mr. Pitney.*

He moved to a spot about three feet away and went to work with his broom. Comfortable silence settled about them as they listened to the two older men joking and reminiscing about the good old days. A robin fluttered down to perch himself upon a section of wall still standing, angling his head to watch them curiously while spurting out his brilliant little fountain of sound. Lydia worked hard, daydreaming of uncovering the artifact which the archeologists were so intent upon finding that would prove once and for all their theory about Governor Cerealis. How nice it would be to watch Mr. Pitney's face as she told him!

But dirt led only to more dirt. It was her father who finally found something, letting out a whoop as he did so. Mr. Pitney helped Lydia up from their pit to join the older men, and they watched as Mr. Ellis used a brush to uncover the rest. The find turned out to be a drawstring pouch, the leather blackened and as hard as flint, with the outlines of several coins entombed inside.

"I'm afraid we'll not be able to open it up without destroying it," Mr. Ellis explained apologetically. "We'll have to send it to the Society and allow them to decide whether they want to keep it intact or have a look at the coins."

"But you did an outstanding job, Mr. Clark," Mr. Pitney assured him.

Lydia's father gave him a delighted smile. "I did, didn't I?"

Two hours later, after Lydia had whispered to her father that perhaps they had imposed upon Mr. Ellis's and Mr. Pitney's indulgence long enough, they bade the archeologists farewell.

"It was a pleasure working with you," Mr. Ellis told them. "Mr. Pitney and I get along like peas in a pod, but the company has been good for both of us. Feel free to join us anytime."

Mr. Pitney smiled and nodded agreement. "Yes, anytime."

"Did you hear that, daughter?" her father asked as they walked down one of the footpaths. "He enjoyed your company."

"Of course he enjoyed my company," she told him. She could still feel the touch of Mr. Pitney's hand upon hers. "Just as he enjoyed yours. We're all sociable people."

"Well, why not put it to good use? We could come back up here tomorrow."

"I'll not be chasing him, Papa."

"Why not? Your mother chased me."

Lydia sent him a smile. "Mother knew you wanted to be caught."

"Well, mayhap our Mr. Pitney wants to be caught."

"I'm sure he does. But not by me." She could no longer ignore the bruising little pain in one foot and motioned for her father to halt. With her hand upon his shoulder to steady herself, she leaned down to dispose of a troublesome pebble from her shoe. "Next time remind me to wear boots."

He raised white eyebrows hopefully as they continued walking. "So there'll be a next time, then?"

"It was just a figure of speech, Papa."

"But you heard what your mother said," he told her with a frown. "He's not suited to this writer-woman, and you know it. It's just a matter of time before he knows it too."

Lydia gave a quiet sigh of regret that she had ever let her feelings be known to her parents. Not because of any exasperation for having to try to get them to understand how the situation actually stood, but because they had allowed their hopes to be raised so high. She felt guilty for constantly dashing them against stones.

"Papa, whether or not he does know has nothing to do with me. Miss Rawlins and I aren't the only two women in England."

Now it was he who stopped walking, and she had no choice but to do the same.

"Papa?" He looked at her, his aged eyes frank, but mingled with such pure affection that a lump came to Lydia's throat.

"Aye, daughter, but two of the three best women in England live in Gresham. I married one. And when our Mr. Pitney takes his blinders off, he'll know who the other one is."

He was just being a father, but Lydia appreciated his words nonetheless. She slipped her hand into his as they continued the path. "*Two* of the three best women?" she asked. "And who would be the third?"

"Why, the queen, of course," he replied with a sidelong grin. "But she's a mite too old for Mr. Pitney, so you've nothing to worry about on that account."

*E*arly Thursday morning, Ambrose stood at the Shrewsbury's busy platform holding both of Fiona's hands, trying not to think about how much he would miss her. The Keegans were involved in their own farewells a few feet away. Not only was sixteen-year-old Tom accompanying her, but also Mrs. Keegan, who would be traveling on with her son to visit family in Dublin once Fiona was deposited safely in Kilkenny with hers. Figuring there was safety in numbers, Ambrose had been so happy to hear of it that he insisted on financing Mrs. Keegan's trip as well.

"You'll be careful?" he asked Fiona. It was an unnecessary request, for his wife had her feet planted more firmly on the ground than did he, but he needed her assurance anyway.

"Very careful," Fiona promised, her violet eyes a mixture of excitement and sadness. "And you'll not hide yourself away the whole fortnight?"

He winked. "My social calendar is already filling. In fact, I'll be lunching with the squire and Mrs. Bartley tomorrow, and the Phelps the next day."

That made her smile. "I'll write to you," she promised, the *you* being almost drowned out by the locomotive's shrill whistle.

"You'll be back before your letter would have time to reach me. Just concentrate on spending time with your family."

So you won't have to do this again for a long time, was the thought that guiltily crossed his mind.

———

What to do? Noelle asked herself in her chair on Friday afternoon. For three days she had alternated her time between chair and bed, her crocheting abandoned and her knee providing excuse to have meals—which she merely picked at—brought to her on a tray. But Mrs. Beemish and the servants were beginning to look at her with concern in their eyes, and she could not fault them for that, for she lived in her nightgown and wrinkled wrapper. She had not even the energy to clean her teeth or brush her hair. Why trouble herself? She was twenty-one years old, and her future had been snuffed out like one of Quetin's cigar stubs.

The worst part was having no one in whom she could confide her fear and anguish. There was no crime in grieving over a lost love, but she had woven around herself the illusion of the grieving widow. Her lies were so precariously dependent upon each other that she could not afford to have even one taken up and examined more closely, for the others would come tumbling down like a house of cards.

A knock at the door interrupted her self-pity. "Yes?" she called out.

"It's Mr. Clay, Mrs. Somerville. May I speak with you?"

Mr. Clay? Pushing herself to her feet, she padded in her felt slippers over to the door and leaned against it. "Mr. Clay? What is it?"

"I was just at lunch at the manor house, and the Bartleys asked me to give you this invitation personally."

"Who are the Bartleys?"

"The squire and his wife, Mrs. Somerville. Haven't you met them?"

Vaguely she recalled meeting an elderly couple on the green her first Sunday in Gresham. "I remember them now." Accepting social obligations was the last thing she cared to do. But it was good to have a distraction from wallowing in her loneliness, so she wanted to keep him talking for as long as possible. "An invitation to what, Mr. Clay?"

"To lunch."

"But they hardly know me."

"They wish to remedy that, Mrs. Somerville."

She could think of nothing less appealing than spending the afternoon with virtual strangers—and elderly ones at that. "I don't think I'll be able—"

"I would strongly advise you to accept."

"Why?"

She could hear his sigh even through the door. "I'm not at liberty to go on about it, but they're arranging for you to meet someone there."

"Meet someone? Who?"

"That's all I can tell you. But I think you'll be pleasantly surprised."

"Will you and Mrs. Clay be there?"

"My wife is in Ireland, Mrs. Somerville. Weren't you aware?"

Noelle remembered some talk about that at the dinner table before her self-imposed confinement to her room. "Yes, forgive me. I quite forgot."

"Shall I leave it here by the door?" he asked with impatience creeping into his voice.

For the fraction of a second she had the impulse to fly to her dressing table and repair her appearance. But running her tongue over her chalky, neglected teeth, and feeling the heaviness of her oily hair upon her scalp, she knew she would need half a day to make herself look like a human being again. "Yes, please," she replied.

"Very well. Good day, Mrs. Somerville."

"Good day."

She listened to his footsteps against the flagged stoned of the corridor, then eased open the door, bent down, and snatched up the envelope. It was of fine linen vellum, which was not surprising, considering its source. The seal was fresh and easy to break. She took out the single sheet of paper, unfolded it, and read the slightly unsteady script.

> Dear Mrs. Somerville,
>   You are cordially invited to a luncheon to be held in the garden of the Manor House on Saturday, June fifteenth. We will send a driver and carriage for you at half-past twelve upon the date aforementioned.
>   Very truly yours,
>   Squire and Mrs. Thurwood Bartley

Noelle read it again, puzzled at the commanding tone. There were no instructions for responding with either acceptance or refusal. Granted, a squire was an important person, but to the best of her knowledge, serfdom had been done away with years ago.

But two reasons kept her from consigning the invitation to the ash bin. The first was a faint voice of reason. Unless Quetin had a change of heart, which was becoming more and more unlikely as time passed, Gresham was to be home for an indefinite amount of time. There was simply no other place for her to go. Why incur the displeasure of Gresham's most promi-nent citizens?

Curiosity was the second. Why would people she had met only once, and briefly at that, go to the trouble of arranging for her to *meet someone*? She knew instinctively this person would be a male. Who was he?

Returning to her chair, she leaned her head against the high back. *Mr. Clay was just there.* The actor had become much more sociable to her dur-ing the past couple of weeks. And why had he not gone with his wife to Ireland? Could there possibly be trouble in paradise?

Having learned firsthand, and through the experiences of her friends, the intrigue necessary for a relationship with a married man, she became suspicious that Mr. Clay had a part in this. He certainly couldn't express any romantic interest in her here at the *Larkspur* with so many people un-derfoot. Perhaps these Bartleys were his best friends, whom he could trust with any secret.

The more Noelle convinced herself, the more tumultuous her thoughts became. She had hated Averyl Paxton for two years, but now she was experiencing how cold-hearted and ruthless Quetin could be. Was it possible that he was at least partly responsible for the sad state of their marriage? He had led her to believe his wife was a cold, demanding woman who cared only for her daughters. What if, instead, she loved him intensely and was hurt by his infidelities? He had complained of her lack of physical beauty, yet no one had forced him to marry her. Could the reason have been the same money she now claimed she held over his head so that he would do her bidding?

Noelle's thoughts turned inward. Though she had had a longtime affair with a married man, she had held herself much higher on the social scale than the common women who lurked about on certain London streets—sometimes even in broad daylight. Being kept by one man was not the same as being kept by many. But by going from one married man to a second, would the gap between her and those haunted women not be quite so vast? And when the second man tired of her, and all prospects of a decent marriage were lost, would she have to seek the arms of a third, and then a fourth?

And then what? She was already finding faint little lines at the corners of her eyes, no doubt from weeping long nights over Quetin. How much longer would she be beautiful and desirable to men?

I'm so sick of this!

The intensity of the thought startled her. But her sudden revulsion for the path she had chosen in life was at odds with a more compelling force— the terrible, relentless, soul-aching loneliness. And she knew she would be at the squire's luncheon.

———

"Dale! Papa says it's time to get up!" Harold said for the second time, leaning on one elbow on the featherbed they shared and shaking his brother roughly by the shoulder.

"Mmmph," came from the blond head buried in the pillow.

"Come on now. You don't want to start the day by gettin' him all riled up! You should'ha known better than to stay out all night anyway." He had been asleep when Dale slipped into bed, but then, Myddle was almost an hour away by horse, even longer in the dark of night.

"Mmm?"

That was all Harold could take. Flinging back the covers, he hopped out of bed and took his trousers from the back of the chair and pulled them on over his linens. "Serve you right if Papa puts an end to your courtin'!"

Finally Dale raised his head from the pillow and muttered, "All right. You ain't got to go on and on about it."

"Then just lay there all—" Harold began while buttoning his shirt but then bit off his sentence in midair. For the left side of his brother's bleary-eyed face wore an angry red scratch from cheekbone to jaw. Stepping closer, Harold asked, "What happened to you?"

Dale grinned, pushed back the covers, and sat up. "I had to break up a fight between Lucy and Dorene, and got in the way of a fingernail."

"You did? Who's Dorene?"

"Lucy's friend. Or at least she was 'til the fight."

Harold was stunned. Dale had courted some rough women in the past, but he had never heard of any carrying on like men. "Why were they fighting?" he asked.

After a wide yawn that showed all his crocked teeth, Dale snickered. "Because I were talkin' to Dorene, and Lucy thought we was being a little too friendly."

That made Harold suspicious. "All you were doin' was talking?"

"That's all."

"I can't see the harm in talking."

"That's 'cause you're a man, and we have a mite more sense than women. Women get jealous at the drop of a hat."

"Well, are Lucy and you finished?"

"Finished?" Dale gave another snicker as he looked around on the floor for his trousers. "Lucy's wantin' me to marry her now. It's the jealousy that does it, see? Makes 'em scared of losing you."

Harold was so busy digesting this bit of information at the breakfast table—along with his eggs and sausage and bread—that he didn't notice Mrs. Winters had spoken until Oram elbowed him.

"Uh-what?" he said, blinking up at where the cook stood behind Fernie's chair.

She crossed her beefy arms and gave him a thunderous look. Her good mood over getting the worktable had lasted about as long as one of Dale's sober spells. "I said, eat them crusts."

"But they're burnt."

"They're just a bit sooty, that's all. I don't work my fingers to the bone so's you can toss out good bread."

When Fernie snickered, she cuffed him on one ear. "And you—don't lick your fingers at the table! You wasn't reared in a barn, was you?"

"No, ma'am."

Harold picked up a crust of bread. He had learned not to appeal to Papa, who was heaping spoonfuls of sugar into his tea at the head of the table, so he sopped the crusts in his egg yolk and ate them. At least the yolks weren't runny anymore, so he expected the worktable was good for something.

"My plan is to fill my days with as much activity as possible," Ambrose Clay told Julia and Andrew in the vicarage parlor on Saturday afternoon after a simple but hearty meal of fish chowder and crusty brown bread. "The fortnight will drag on forever if I spend it moping in the apartment."

"That's an excellent idea," agreed Julia from the sofa while handing the cup she had just poured over the tea table. The children had resumed their own activities—Philip, fishing the Bryce with Jeremiah and Ben; Laurel and Aleda, helping to compose a play at Helen Johnson's; and Grace, entertaining little Connie Jefferies and their dolls in the garden.

"It was Fiona's idea, actually. She made Mr. Durwin promise to challenge me to as many draughts matches as I could stand."

"And you're to come here for supper on Monday and Wednesday, remember?" Andrew asked as he took his cup and saucer from Julia's hands. "The following week as well."

"You don't have to coddle me like a colicky child, you know," Ambrose said. "I'll manage just fine."

"But of course you will," Julia assured him. "We would still enjoy your company."

With a nod, Andrew added, "Some people save up a week's wages just to see you, Ambrose. All we have to do is put a little chowder and bread before you."

"How can I refuse such gracious invitations? Between you and the Bartleys and Mrs. Herrick, I should expect to put on a stoneweight before Fiona returns."

"I'm surprised Mrs. Bartley hasn't talked you into moving out to the manor house so she can mother you every day," Julia told him while her teaspoon clinked delicately against the side of her own cup as she stirred in the sugar.

"Actually, she did suggest that yesterday—four times, I believe."

Andrew smiled. "Life would be dull around Gresham without our dear Mrs. Bartley."

"I'll say. And she has a new matchmaking project. I had to deliver an invitation yesterday so she could get a certain couple together for lunch. Care to guess who they are?"

"Paul Treves and Mrs. Somerville?" Andrew ventured as he rolled his eyes.

"Very good!" Sitting back against the chair cushions, the actor took a thoughtful sip of his tea. "They would make an attractive couple, don't you think?"

"Et tu Brute!" groaned Andrew.

"Well, you have to admit they're both lonely. I have to confess I was unfairly harsh in my judgment of Mrs. Somerville at first, but she seems a decent woman. And a vicar's daughter . . . what better choice for a young minister?"

"Andrew still has nightmares about the way his mother tried to marry him off," Julia explained.

"Nightmares," her husband agreed dolefully.

"And which one of those women did you marry?" Ambrose asked with raised eyebrows.

Andrew tilted his head as if he hadn't heard correctly. "Marry? Why, none."

"Then, just because your mother paraded the lot in front of you didn't mean you were forced to marry one. Mrs. Bartley isn't going to wrap the two of them in chains and drag them to the altar, you know."

"You *are* referring to our Mrs. Bartley, aren't you? She's perfectly capable of doing just such a thing."

"But being that you're the vicar," Julia told him, "you could simply refuse to marry them in that case."

"Refuse to marry whom, Mother?" came Grace's voice from the doorway as the girl walked into the room with little Connie Jefferies trailing shyly behind.

Sending mirthful glances to the two men, Julia shook her head. "No one, Grace. We're just being silly."

"Oh." The girl's sober expression did not change. "May we have some biscuits for a tea party outside?"

"You'll have to ask Mrs. Paget. But don't trouble her if she's still having her lunch."

"Yes, Mother."

When the girls had left the room, Mr. Clay said, "I can assure you both of one thing . . . your daughters will have no lack of suitors knocking at your door one day."

A sad smile touched Andrew's lips. "The time may come sooner than we're prepared for it. Ben Mayhew has passed Laurel a couple of notes."

"Indeed? *Our* little Laurel?"

"I'm afraid so." Narrowing his eyes, Andrew took on a mock, threatening manner, "So if Mrs. Bartley ever asks you to deliver a luncheon invitation to *her* . . ."

On Sunday morning, Harold told Jack and Edgar that he would be using the horses. "But we need them to get to church," they whined.

"You can stand out front and fetch a ride with Mercy and Seth."

They went to their papa to complain, but the only good thing about being the eldest was that Harold usually got his way when it came to disagreements with his brothers. He made Oram hitch Bob and Dan to the wagon while he put on his good suit and combed some *Sir Lancelot's Fine Grooming Pomade for Distinguished Gentlemen* into his hair. Upon reaching Saint Jude's, he tethered the horses to a post outside the town hall, where Miss Clark would be sure to see them. Then he walked around the corner of the building and waited. Presently the green was filled with worshipers. Upon seeing a familiar figure wearing a blue dress, he raked his fingers through his hair and slipped from his hiding place.

"Mrs. Meeks?" he called, coming up behind her.

She turned and smiled. "Why, Mr. Sanders. How good to see you again."

"Thank you. It's good to see you too."

Trudy, smiling happily, lunged toward him, but Mrs. Meeks caught her shoulder. "Don't, Trudy."

"Aw, I don't mind," Harold said.

"But I'm trying to teach her to be a lady. It's naught against you, Mr. Sanders. You understand, don't you?"

He didn't. "A lady? But she's just a girl."

"We mold the clay before it's set, Mr. Sanders."

That he did understand, and he was a little surprised at himself for doing so. If Trudy, who likely threw herself at him because she didn't have a father, didn't learn to stop while she was young, who knew what trouble it could get her into later? "Yes, ma'am," he replied. "That makes sense to me."

"But I'm glad she's fond of you," Mrs. Meeks said, smiling again. "At least she knows kindness."

"Hello, Mr. Sanders," the girl said from her mother's side.

His cheeks warm from Mrs. Meeks' unexpected compliment, Harold reached out to pat the top of the girl's ribboned brown hair. "Hullo, Trudy."

From the corner of his eye he could see Miss Clark and her parents, which made him remember exactly why he was there. "I brought the wagon today. Can I offer you a ride home?"

"Why, that's good of you. But we don't mind walking."

"But I pass right by your lane," he insisted with another glance in the Clarks' direction. "Seems a shame to waste a whole wagon and team on just me."

"Well, if you're sure you don't mind."

When he assured her that he didn't, Mrs. Meeks sent Trudy to round up the other children. Soon the four had settled into the bed of the wagon. Harold helped Mrs. Meeks up to the driver's bench to sit beside him.

"Will you make them run, Mr. Sanders?" Lester asked from behind as Harold picked up the reins.

Harold sent an apologetic look over his shoulder. "Can't do that. Too hard on the horses."

"Don't they ever run?" asked Mark.

"Out in the pasture. Now, settle down back there so's you don't go fallin' out."

"Yes, settle down, children," Mrs. Meeks said, then turned to Harold with a trace of worry in her expression. "Perhaps I should sit back there with them?"

Harold could see Miss Clark and her parents making their way across the green. He smiled at the woman beside him and shook his head. "We'll go slow. They'll be fine."

———

"Now, who in thunderation would be driving on the green?" Amos Clark muttered, taking Lydia and her mother by their elbows as he looked over his shoulder.

Lydia peered back as well. Harold Sanders sat in the seat of his father's wagon, looking proud as a housecat with Mrs. Meeks seated beside him. Lydia and her parents returned their waves as the wagon passed alongside them, then those of the Meeks' children from the wagon bed. When all the waving was finished, they resumed walking, and Lydia's father grinned at her.

"Ignoring you didn't work out according to plan, so now I suppose he figures to make you jealous."

"Perhaps he is really fond of her," Lydia said hopefully, watching the wagon turn from the green onto Market Lane to head north. "He's been very good to her children."

"That would be a remarkably swift change of heart, dear," her mother pointed out. "I suspect the same as your father."

"So *are* you jealous, daughter?" her father asked in a droll voice.

With a little mock sigh, Lydia replied, "I'll survive, I expect." She glanced to her right in the distance, where Mr. Pitney and Miss Rawlins strolled along the willows arm in arm. *Terribly jealous! May God forgive me.* Even though the jealousy gnawing at her insides was sinful and destructive to her own peace of mind, she could not make it go away. And reminding herself that she had never had Mr. Pitney's affection in the first place did not lessen the pain.

How ironic that she practically lived for Monday evenings, during which she helped him win the affections of another woman. *Perhaps they'll name their first daughter after you*, she told herself bitterly. She glanced to her right again and felt the sting of tears in her eyes. *This has to stop or you'll drive yourself mad.*

———

"It's a shame you missed such a lovely service, dear," Mrs. Durwin said to Noelle at the lunch table after Mr. Jensen had delivered the prayer and plates were filled with servings of shoulder of lamb with soubise sauce, celery a la creme, and stuffed tomatoes.

"Thank you," Noelle told her.

"Are you better now?" asked Mr. Ellis.

She smiled at him. "Yes, much." Though her knee had not pained her in days, it had developed imaginary *twinges* overnight, which prevented her from leaving with the others for worship. That was what she told everyone at breakfast, and it had generated the expected sympathy. And she was half-truthful, for she had been afflicted with twinges. Only of the conscience, or what little of it remained. She simply could not bring herself to sit in a church service, knowing how frequently Mr. Clay had been in her thoughts since he delivered that invitation.

But however wrong she knew her attraction to him to be, she could not will herself to stop thinking about him. That a man with Mr. Clay's wealth and fame might possibly be interested in her made her feel for the first time since being ground underfoot by Quetin that she did have some value after all.

Sending a covert glance down the table, she wondered at the animated way he discussed with Mr. Jensen and Mr. Ellis the results of last week's Derby at Epsom Downs just outside of London. If he missed his wife, he certainly didn't show it. *Why are you tormenting yourself?* some cynical, almost bitter voice said in her mind. Any woman who would leave such an attractive man for any length of time deserved whatever happened in her absence.

She was seated in the empty hall the next afternoon, resuming the crocheting she had abandoned, when Mr. Clay walked in, as she had hoped he would if she was patient enough. They exchanged greetings, and then he asked if she had seen Mr. Durwin.

"Why, yes," Noelle replied with a nod toward the front door. "He mentioned something about the barber. But Mrs. Durwin is in the garden with Mrs. Dearing, if you wish to speak with her."

The actor glanced at the door but shook his head. "No, thank you. Mr. Durwin owes me a draughts match, but I'll just—"

Don't let him turn away. Noelle sat up attentively. "You know, I haven't played draughts since I was a girl."

"You haven't?" he said, giving her a polite smile.

"If you enjoy winning, I would be a more suitable competitor than Mr. Durwin. I'm sure I'm terribly rusty."

He actually chuckled. "I enjoy winning *honestly*, Mrs. Somerville. I've just now managed to get Mr. Durwin past thinking he has to hold back."

"If I promise to try with all my might?" She held up her unfinished dresser scarf and smiled helplessly. "I've been crocheting until my fingers are beginning to ache."

It appeared that he was about to decline, but then he shrugged and stepped over to assist her to her feet. "Very well, Mrs. Somerville. But I warn you, I take the game seriously. You'll not be given leeway for your lack of experience."

"I consider myself forewarned," she replied as he pulled out the chair to the draughts table for her.

"Very well." But for all his stern talk, he removed two of his wooden game pieces before the match ever began. "Just so I can live with myself," he grumbled.

He could have removed half his pieces, and they still would have been woefully mismatched, Noelle realized within seconds. Not that she cared who was winning. But he took time to explain his strategy and to tell her why the moves she had made were not wise ones. "May we give it another try?" she asked when the first match was finished before a half hour had passed.

"Are you sure you want to suffer through that again?"

"How will I learn if I don't practice? And no removing any pieces ahead of time either."

"I do admire your spirit, Mrs. Somerville," he said as he repositioned the pieces on the checkered board.

This time the match moved more slowly, as Noelle thought out her moves and tried her best to remember the strategies he had demonstrated. He would win again, of course, but at least she could show him that she appreciated his spending time with her enough to pay attention. "How did you become skillful at this?" she asked when he had scooped up another of her game pieces.

"Backstage, when my father was an actor. And later, when I was assigned bit parts. There was nothing to do in between my brief appearances onstage, and I proved to have no skill at cards, so . . ."

She asked him to tell her more about his experiences in the theatre. And judging by the glint in his gray eyes, she could tell that he enjoyed relating them to her. She was a bit surprised and disappointed when he declined a third match. When he said, "I believe I'll trot along to the barber's and see what's keeping Mr. Durwin," she wondered if she had only imagined any interest in her on his part.

But as he pulled out the chair for her, he asked, "Have you considered accepting the Bartleys' luncheon invitation?"

Telling herself that the faint disappointment she felt at the actor and even herself was just nervous jitters, Noelle lowered her lashes and pretended to be demure. "I haven't decided yet," she lied. "What would you advise?"

"I would strongly advise you accept, Mrs. Somerville." He smiled knowingly. "Why, your whole future could be affected."

It had been so long since Noelle blushed that she was surprised to feel the heat steal up into her cheeks. "Are you. . . ?"

"Yes?"

But the door opened, and Mrs. Dearing, Mrs. Durwin, and a freshly clipped Mr. Durwin entered with baskets of garden flowers in their arms. Afraid that she would not be able to look at Mr. Clay without revealing her thoughts, Noelle went to her room, which was still downstairs because Mr. Jensen suggested another week to be certain she was completely able to take on the steps. Her crocheting was still in the hall, but she could do nothing but pace her floor anyway.

She wasn't sure why she had even started to ask the actor if he was the *mystery guest*. Of course he was—he had practically said so.

See, Quetin! she thought, wishing she could say the words to his face. *I don't need you anyway.* She couldn't even remember what she had found attractive in the man, with his bulging, pale eyes and arrogant, know-it-all ways. After all her grieving and uncertainty, life was going to be good for her again.

In fact, if she could only sleep nights, and look in the mirror without a brief second's hatred of the image staring back at her, life would be almost perfect.

"You know what occurred to me after you and your father left us last Tuesday?" Mr. Pitney said to Lydia in the back parlor after the two had ferreted out all possible symbolism in *Florentina of Segovia*.

"That we shouldn't give up painting and school teaching?" Lydia suggested with a little smile in spite of the heaviness of her heart. He laughed, which added to her sadness, for she did so enjoy his company.

"I thought that you might care to bring your students up the hill one day when the new school year begins. Children come up there occasionally to watch from a distance, but we can't often take the time to explain what we are doing. But we could easily do so with a group."

Why do you have to be so considerate, Mr. Pitney? Lydia thought. "They would enjoy that. Thank you for suggesting it." *And perhaps by then, the very sight of you won't tear at my heart.* Because she knew what she had to do. *Just give me the strength to do it, Father.*

She looked at Jeanie, dozing contentedly on his knees, and thought of her father and mother, who felt they had to disappear soon after his arrival to keep from monopolizing his time. Mr. Pitney would be missed in the Clark cottage, and not just by her.

Closing the novelette, she handed it to him and said quietly, "I'm afraid this will have to be our last lesson, Mr. Pitney."

Panic flooded his brown eyes. "But why, Miss Clark?"

"It just has to be," was all she could explain.

"If it's a matter of money . . .'"

"Money has nothing to do with it, Mr. Pitney." She was a little hurt that he would even think so. "And I'll not accept payment for this lesson."

His crestfallen expression almost caused her to reconsider.

"Why, Miss Clark?" he asked again.

Because I love you, she thought before replying, "You've become just as adept at discerning the stories as I am. You just needed some confidence in yourself."

He shook his head. "It's you who gives me that confidence, Miss Clark. Just the thought of attempting it without you terrifies me."

And what kind of love makes you terrified? she wished she had the bluntness to ask. But she had already attempted to do so when she refused to teach him poetry, obviously to no avail.

Instead she told him, "You'll do fine, Mr. Pitney. And I've just received some new textbooks I'll need to read over and outline before the coming year, so my summer will be busier than I had planned." There were actually only two new textbooks, but still, she hadn't expected to receive them before fall and would indeed need to study them, so her answer was still truthful.

"I see. Of course." Gently he moved Jeanie to the sofa between them, gave the animal a final stroke on the back, and stood. "May I?" he asked, holding out his hand.

Lydia allowed herself to be assisted to her feet. Mr. Pitney did not let go of her hand but held it and smiled, his eyes a mixture of sadness and warmth. "Perhaps you're right, Miss Clark. I'll try to have more confidence. But I do want to thank you for showing me how to get started. I could have never done this without you."

I changed my mind! I was merely joking! she resisted the impulse to say. Returning his smile, she said, "I wish you all the best, Mr. Pitney."

"And I you, Miss Clark." He let go of her hand, and they walked in silence to the front of the cottage. At the door he turned to ask, "You'll still be bringing your students up to see us work next year, won't you?"

"I will, thank you."

He smiled sheepishly. "But of course, you will. Here I am acting as if we'll never see each other again, but we still live in the same village, don't we?"

"Yes, the same village," she replied. *Just different worlds.*

Chapter 38

I'm trying very hard, Fiona. Ambrose stared out his window at the darkened form of the Anwyl as the clock on his chimneypiece ticked the seconds of the night away. How he wished he could see clear across to Ireland! He was a fool to send her off without him! For he couldn't imagine anything worse than the despondency that had tormented him for the past three days. Even having no privacy and sharing a bed with her brothers couldn't be as miserable as this.

One more week, he told himself. Seven days. Why, she would soon be starting her journey home. A person could live through anything for seven days if he had something to look forward to at the end. *One can even live without sleeping,* he thought as the clock chimed the second hour of the morning.

Dear Lord Paxton,

    I shall not be requiring your financial assistance, as I am keeping company with a gentleman whose name you would recognize immediately if I were to tell you. And I hope that Lady Paxton discovers what a scoundrel you are and divorces you.

                               Disdainfully NOT yours,
                               Noelle Somerville

Mrs. Ambrose Clay would be even better, Noelle thought, flipping over her pillow again in an attempt to chase the sleep that had eluded her thus far. But she couldn't realistically expect Mr. Clay to divorce his wife, no matter that she did go off to Ireland without him.

I would settle for a nice flat in Shrewsbury for now, she thought, closing her eyes again. And then an apartment in London once the actor decided to return to the theatre. Wouldn't she love to show up at *Gatti's* on Mr. Clay's arm! Why, Meara's evil cat-eyes would bulge even more so than Quetin's!

She thought of a good post-script for her imaginary letter to Quetin, which she had amended in her thoughts until her head was beginning to ache.

Your solicitor, Mr. Radley, boasted to me that he has been stealing from you.

That wasn't true, but it was so gratifying to imagine Quetin's reaction. And yet the frantic, shallow activity at which she kept her mind engaged could not drown out the insistent voice that seemed to come from deep within her.

You don't want to do this. You're sick and tired of feeling so dirty inside.
"Yes, I do," she muttered, raising herself enough to pound a dent into her uncooperative pillow with her fist. If Mr. Clay would show her the good times that Quetin used to and would shower her with money and distractions—if she could just live fast enough—she could drown out that voice. She had done it before, so it could be done again.

And what choice have you? Noelle asked herself. But she had cause for worry that the dreams she was spinning would not come to pass, for a change had come over Mr. Clay only hours after Monday's draughts match. The times he had shown up for meals, he had had the animation of a bowl of fruit. Was he simply suffering one of his dark moods, or was he feeling remorse for the plot he had hatched with the Bartleys? If so, it was a simple matter of getting them to withdraw the invitation.

If only he would give her some sign of his intentions. But the few times she had seen him, he had hardly looked at her. Was this because he had lost interest, or because he didn't want their fellow lodgers to suspect anything?

She could hear the faint Westminster chimes of the clock in the library. *How can it be only three o'clock?* Her thoughts were no more settled than when she had first turned down her covers. With a groan of frustration she flung them back again, felt with her toes for her slippers, and lit the candle on her night table. She took her wrapper from where it lay across the bedpost and tied it over her nightgown. No one in Gresham could possibly be awake at this hour. She would sit out in the garden and allow the cool breezes to bathe her face. Perhaps they would soothe her tormented thoughts as well.

The candlelight threw her shadow grotesquely against the wall as she padded down the corridor. Save the ticking of clocks in the library, and then the hall, the house was as quiet as only stone walls could be. How she envied the others their sleep! To lie one's head upon a pillow and simply fade into sweet dreams—when was the last time she had done so?

Halfway across the hall she paused. *The courtyard would be better.* She had no idea how long she would wish to sit outside, and in the back there was no chance of cheese wagons rumbling by before sunrise and disturbing her thoughts. That was reason enough to turn and head in the opposite direction, she told herself, and not because she would be able to see Mr. Clay's apartment. Why in the world would that matter, when he was likely as sound asleep as the rest of Gresham?

The courtyard door was locked, but it was a simple matter of switching the candle holder to her left hand and raising the latch. As soon as Noelle had closed the heavy door quietly behind her, she turned and breathed in the night air. It smelled of impending rain and was indeed fresh upon her cheeks. She almost wished she could bring her pillow and bedclothes outside, for surely she could be lulled to sleep by these gentle breezes.

She walked softly over the flagged stones to sit on one of the benches. A breeze had snatched the flame from her candle, but with the stars visible through the branches of the oak tree, she had no need for it and set the holder down. That was when she noticed the light coming from a window of Mr. Clay's apartment over the stables. Whether candle or lamp, she could not tell because of the curtains. *So he can't sleep either.* Was he thinking of his wife? Or of her?

If only she could talk with him! She would explain how even though she planned to be at the squire's luncheon, she had not set out to become a fallen woman in the beginning. It was simply that once she had stepped across a certain line, there was no going back. For some reason it was important that he understand.

She leaned back and stared at the stars for a while, feeling very small and insignificant. She wondered several minutes later why the light still burned in the window. Had the actor fallen asleep while reading? If so, it was certainly dangerous to keep a lamp burning like that. How could he fault her for showing up at his door with his well-being in mind? And if he took it upon himself to join her outside, perhaps he would rationalize away her guilt as Quetin had so skillfully done, and she would no longer despise herself.

She climbed the staircase on the side of the stables slowly and gave three light knocks upon his door. The door was opened shortly, and he stood there wearing a dressing gown in the glow of a lamp on a table several feet behind him. "Mrs. Somerville?"

"Your light, Mr. Clay," she explained in an apologetic voice. "I was afraid you had fallen asleep."

"Oh . . . that's very kind of you. But I was awake." Glancing out into the night behind her, and then at the wrapper she wore, he asked, "But why are you out here?"

"The same reason you are," she shrugged. "Can't sleep."

In the shadow the lamp made of his face she could see a sad smile.

"I'm sorry," he said. "For both of us."

His sympathy seemed so genuine, and he was treating her with such respect—not like a loose woman—that Noelle found herself saying, "I wonder if you would care to join me in the courtyard, Mr. Clay? The stars are quite beautiful."

After sending an automatic glance skyward, he shook his head. "No, thank you, Mrs. Somerville. Why don't you go on inside? You shouldn't be outside alone this time of night."

Impulsively Noelle said, "If you're concerned about causing any rumors, there's no one else awake."

"Causing rumors? Why, no." The door moved a little as he took a half-step backward. "Again, thank you for seeing about my light, Mrs. Somerville. You really should go on inside now."

The formality that had overtaken his voice startled Noelle. And she knew she would be robbed of even more sleep if she didn't end this confusion once and for all. "Mr. Clay, before I leave I would just like to know if you still plan to be there on Saturday."

"I beg your pardon?"

She took a deep breath. "If you've changed your mind, I would appreciate being told. I can't bear much more of this uncertainty."

"Uncertainty about what?"

He's just pretending not to remember. But why? "Didn't you arrange to . . . meet me at the squire's?"

Mr. Clay stared at her for a couple of long, uncomfortable seconds before replying, "You are obviously mistaken, Mrs. Somerville. And I must bid you good night."

Soon she was facing a closed door. Shame welling up within her as tears welled up in her eyes, she descended the staircase and walked out around the north wing of the *Larkspur* until she met Market Lane. Patches of starry sky between the overhanging branches provided just enough illumination to paint the cobbled stones a ghostly gray as she continued down the lane. The sound and smell of moving water met her ears long before she reached the Bryce. She stood on the bridge and stared down into the dark river, wishing she were much higher up so that she could jump and put an end to the pain. As it was, she would just wash up into someone's pasture down river, wet and cold and even more wretched.

She lowered herself to the cool stones and huddled in a little ball. If the cheese wagons began moving this early, they could run over her and good riddance. Tears ran down her cheeks, dripping from her jaw to the bodice of her wrapper. She had to wipe her nose with her sleeve several times. Her throat was one raw ache. Still worse was the terrible, frightening feeling of having laughed in the face of God too many times. How could He bear to look at her? Was His back turned to her now?

"I'm so sorry," she blubbered over and over between the moans that racked her body. "Please don't leave me alone!"

———————

Rain was softly pelting his windowpanes when Ambrose became aware of the pounding on the door. His most immediate impulse was annoyance, but then he thought that surely Mrs. Somerville wouldn't be foolish enough to return. Swinging his legs from under the covers, he padded barefoot into the parlor and became aware that he was still wearing his wrinkled dressing gown over his nightshirt.

"Yes?" he said at the door.

"Mr. Clay?"

He recognized the voice and opened the door an inch. Georgette stood there underneath a dripping umbrella. "Yes, Georgette?"

"Mrs. Beemish asks if you'll be wanting lunch brought up, Mr. Clay."

"You mean I slept through breakfast?"

"Lunch too. We wasn't sure if you were having it out somewhere or not."

He blinked to clear away the cobwebs in his mind and couldn't recall being invited anywhere for lunch today. Which was good, because he would have been late. And as he hadn't shown up for supper last night, he was suddenly ravenous.

"Is there anything left?"

"Yes, sir. Shall I bring you up a tray?"

He started to agree and then shook his head. No sense in putting an extra burden on everyone else, especially in the rain, just because he wasn't functioning very well. "Have the servants had their lunch yet?"

"We're just about to."

"Then I'll be down shortly, if you'll ask Mrs. Herrick to set another plate in the kitchen."

"In the kitchen, sir?"

Ambrose smiled, in spite of the cloud that still hovered over him. "You don't think I'm going to sit in the dining room alone, do you? And please do tell everyone to start without me if I'm not down yet."

When she was gone, he shrugged out of his nightclothes and bathed and dressed quickly. He would have to wait until tonight to shave. As he stepped out onto the rain-dimpled landing with his umbrella, he recalled how Mrs. Somerville had looked standing there in the darkness just hours ago. *You shouldn't have played draughts with her*, he told himself, for a vague uneasiness had come over him during their second game on Monday past. There was something about the way she looked across at him, her eyes wide with interest while he talked on and on about the theatre.

Fiona was the love of his life, but Mrs. Somerville was beautiful too—and *not* in Ireland. The attention had been flattering. So much so, that when he realized how the atmosphere of the room had changed, he made the excuse to stop after the second game. He had even encouraged her to attend the Bartleys' luncheon, just to make it obvious that he had no romantic interest in her. He tried to recall his exact words and couldn't. Had she assumed he was arranging an assignation between them?

How can I face her? he thought. She had been terribly wrong to turn up at his door, but being almost twice her age, he had to share the guilt. It was unwise to engage in even an innocent activity with an attractive woman other than his wife. Especially with no one else in the hall. Having spent most of his life among actors, he was well aware that most illicit affairs began innocently enough, with shared banter and laughter. How could he have forgotten?

The kitchen was warm, filled with the savory aromas of cottage pie, sausages, pickled beets, and pease pudding. His protests went unheeded by Mr. Herrick, as he was given the chair at the head of the table where the caretaker usually sat on a high stool.

"You shouldn't have waited," he scolded, spooning pease pudding onto his plate after Mr. Herrick had prayed over the meal.

"Ah, but we didn't mind, Mr. Clay," Mrs. Herrick declared with a merry smile. "But we've all decided you'll have to pay penance."

The spoon held over his plate, Ambrose raised an eyebrow. "Penance, Mrs. Herrick? I didn't think that was part of your Baptist doctrine."

"Aye, but it's the doctrine of the kitchen. We voted that you should have to sing for your supper."

"Lunch, you mean," a grinning Mildred reminded her above the chorus of agreement from parlormaids, chambermaids, and kitchen maids.

"I'm sorry, but I'm just not up to singing," Ambrose replied, shaking his head. "And as we're all aware that good Christian people like yourselves won't allow me go hungry anyway . . ."

"A poem then?" chambermaid Ruth suggested.

"Please?" asked Georgette.

"And none o' that Shakespeare," Gertie, the scullery maid, told him with wrinkled nose. "He don't talk like regular folk, and I canno' understand half the words."

Again the others pleaded. Finally Ambrose held up both hands in surrender. "Very well," he said, sighing inwardly. *Can't a man be despondent in peace?* "A short one."

They gave him considerate silence as he inventoried the nonsense

318

verses stored in his mind over the years, which were likely crowding out all common sense. When an appropriate one presented itself, he said, "I learned this one as a child, about stolen pie."

> *As Charles his sisters sat between,*
> *An Apple Pie was brought;*
> *Slyly to get a piece unseen,*
> *The little fellow thought.*

Smiling faces flanked both sides of the table, making him grateful he had turned down the offer of a tray and solitude. He winked at a delighted Gertie and managed to give the next stanza a little more animation.

> *A piece from off Sophia's plate*
> *Into his mouth he flung;*
> *But, ah! Repentance came too late,*
> *It burn'd his little tongue!*

They coaxed him on through three more poems, so by the time he had entertained such an appreciative audience and filled his stomach, his spirits were lighter than when he had gotten out of bed. While his condition was not so simple as could be cured with jests and laughter, the scripture was indeed true that a merry heart was good medicine.

In fact, he almost convinced himself to forget about Mrs. Somerville's early morning visit. She was likely embarrassed and would steer clear of his path from now on. *No, that won't do*, he told himself right away. They lived in the same lodging house and took meals at the same table. It was no good pretending it hadn't happened. And he suspected strongly that his earlier impressions that she had ill feelings toward Fiona were accurate. But speaking with Mrs. Somerville privately—about *anything*—was out of the question. He needed the counsel of his closest friends, next to Fiona. *Please let them be home*, he prayed.

$\mathcal{T}$his is a very grave situation, Ambrose," Andrew told the actor from one of the wooden chairs he had moved to the front of his desk. At Julia's suggestion, the three held their conference in Andrew's study, for the children understood that the closed door—combined with a caller—meant no disturbing unless an emergency presented itself.

"Grave indeed," Julia nodded. But she was unable to surrender her disbelief completely. Not that Ambrose's word wasn't solid gold, but he had admitted staying up until the wee hours. Could he have fallen asleep and imagined the whole thing?

She recalled the young woman who sat with her in the dentist's parlor, reassuring her that Andrew would be all right. And had she uncomplainingly endured his weight on her shoulder during the long bumpy ride home. With an apologetic look at their friend, she said, "Forgive me, Ambrose. But could you have mistaken her intent? I myself would knock on a man's door that time of night if I thought there was danger of fire."

He ran his hand through his dark hair. "At first I believed she was just concerned for my safety." With a look of discomfort, he added, "And you might as well know I paid her some attention Monday afternoon. Innocently I thought, but I had no business doing so. So the fault isn't entirely hers."

"But you didn't show up at her door in nightclothes," Andrew told him.

"She'll have to leave," Julia said reluctantly. "As soon as possible."

Andrew nodded. "I agree."

His brow drawn, Ambrose said, "Surely if you would speak with her . . ."

"We can't have someone behaving that way under the *Larkspur*'s roof, Ambrose," Julia reminded him. "Mrs. Somerville won't be thrown out into the streets. There are other lodging houses in England. And she has family."

A soft knock sounded, and then Dora's voice. "Vicar?"

"Come in, Dora," Andrew said.

The door opened and the maid slipped inside. "Beggin' your pardon, but Mrs. Somerville is in the vestibule in an awful state. I told her you and the missus was in here with Mr. Clay, and she begs to be allowed in."

The three exchanged glances. "Should I leave?" asked Ambrose.

"I think you should stay," Andrew told him. "That way if she contradicts your story, she'll be forced to do so to your face." He turned to Julia. "What do you think?"

"The same, I'm afraid. Will you speak with her, Andrew?" While this had taken place at the *Larkspur*, Andrew was vicar of Gresham, and these were members of his congregation.

"If you wish," he replied, standing. He asked Dora to show Mrs. Somerville in, then went for another chair.

Left alone with Ambrose, Julia watched him frown down at the fingertips he tapped together nervously upon one knee. "We have complete faith in your integrity, Ambrose," she felt compelled to say.

"This would never have happened if I had kept my distance, Julia. And if I hadn't mentioned that luncheon again! I thought it would be amusing to help the Bartleys get them together."

Julia gave him a sad smile. "*Now* I understand Andrew's feelings about matchmaking."

———

Following the maid through the cottage with a thick wool shawl wrapped around her rain-soaked poplin gown, Noelle was still embarrassed that the vicar's son, Philip, had answered her knock at the door. At least the boy had had the presence of mind not to show alarm at her appearance, but calmly asked her to wait in the vestibule, returning two minutes later with the maid and shawl.

The two seconds between the time the maid knocked upon a door and Vicar Phelps opened it seemed like hours. "Come in, Mrs. Somerville," he said cordially, though his expression was somber. As she walked through the doorway, he asked if she would care for tea, but she shook her head. Mrs. Phelps and Mr. Clay were seated in chairs in front of the desk, and two empty chairs faced them. Noelle was surprised when the actor paid her the courtesy of getting to his feet until she was seated across from Mrs. Phelps, when she had no doubt he would rather strike her.

"Are you warm enough, Mrs. Somerville?" Mrs. Phelps asked. "We could light the stove."

That simple consideration caused Noelle a struggle to keep from throwing herself at their feet and sobbing out her utter wretchedness. But she had played the child for too long, surrendering to every impulse. The same inner voice that had urged her to be honest with Vicar Treves had returned to insist it was time to face the consequences of her folly like an adult.

But the voice had not advised her of how to begin, and they were all staring at her. When several seconds of silence had lapsed, the vicar and his wife exchanged glances, then Vicar Phelps turned to her again.

"Mr. Clay has related a disturbing incident to us, Mrs. Somerville."

"Yes," Noelle replied in a thin voice.

"You have the opportunity now to give your side of the story."

She shook her head. "Mr. Clay's account was accurate."

With another glance at his wife, the vicar said, "But you haven't heard his account."

"I went to his door and . . . flirted with him." She could no longer look at the actor, or at any of the faces of the three, so she stared down at her clutched hands.

"And that's all you have to say?"

"No." Taking in a deep breath, she said, "There is more."

Again, silence while they waited. Finally Vicar Phelps asked gently, "What is it, Mrs. Somerville?"

She had thought herself incapable of producing more tears, but one trickled down her cheek to dangle coldly on her jaw until she swiped at it with the back of her hand. Yet she felt an inexplicable relief at putting an end to the lie that had been her life. It was as if she had held an object tightly in her fist for years and was finally allowed to release it. "I'm not *Mrs.* Somerville. I was never married."

———

When Mrs. Somerville—*Miss* Somerville—stopped speaking, Julia felt as drained as the young woman looked.

"Can God ever forgive me?" Miss Somerville asked, wiping red and swollen eyes with Julia's handkerchief.

Andrew nodded. Ambrose had gallantly excused himself as soon as the confession touched upon things not related to her early-morning knock upon his door. "Of course He can. Have you asked?"

"Last night," she told them in a voice becoming increasingly hoarse. "A hundred times."

A soft knock came at the door, and Dora brought tea. "Mr. Clay said you might be needin' this now," she said apologetically.

Thank God for your thoughtfulness, Ambrose. Clearing a space on Andrew's desk, Julia thanked Dora and poured. It was not the time for social pleasantries, so she added sugar and milk to all three cups without asking for preferences. Miss Somerville gave her a grateful nod, held hers between

322

both hands, and gulped half before pausing for breath.

Thank God for milk too, Julia thought, or the young woman would have scorched herself.

"You said you've asked forgiveness," Andrew reminded Miss Somerville after drinking from his own cup. "Surely with your background, you've learned that God forgives when we truly repent."

"Of course," she said, closing her eyes to breathe in a ragged breath. She looked at him again with glistening eyes. "Then, why don't I *feel* clean?"

Julia's husband became thoughtfully quiet for several seconds, and then understanding came into his expression. "Our feelings aren't always true barometers of God's workings, Miss Somerville. But I wonder if there's some unforgiveness on your part that's hindering your fellowship with God?"

"Unforgiveness?" She held up a palm and let it drop again, as if overwhelmed. "Of course I have unforgiveness, Vicar. Lord Paxton and his solicitor . . . Meara Desmond. Look what they've done to me."

———

With a sigh Andrew wondered why anyone under the age of twenty-five was even allowed out-of-doors. But he had much compassion for the young woman in his study. *There, but for the grace of God, sits one of my daughters.* "The people you named, Miss Somerville . . . I'll grant they've treated you wrongly. But they were also the instruments in your finally realizing what you were becoming. And the hatred you're carrying is like a live coal in your heart—far more damaging to yourself than to them."

She was staring back at him, but Andrew couldn't read in her expression whether or not she understood and accepted this. For the sake of clarity he added, "I'm not suggesting that they *deserve* forgiveness, Miss Somerville. And I would strongly advise against contacting them."

"I don't know . . ." she finally said in a faint voice.

"Then think about it. And bear in mind that forgiveness is almost a selfish act because of its immense benefits to the one who forgives." He was about to advise that she meet with Julia and him often until her fellowship with God was restored but realized that he could not. Whether Miss Somerville was allowed to stay at the *Larkspur* was in Julia's hands.

He looked at his wife and nodded.

———

Why did this have to happen? Julia thought. And the day had started out so nicely. The rain had prevented Andrew from making calls and the children from scattering, so they had enjoyed some family time. How could she have guessed that she would soon be evicting one of her lodgers?

"Why did you choose Mr. Clay, Miss Somerville?" she had to ask. "Are you in love with him?"

"Love?" The young woman looked startled. "Why, no. But Lord Paxton didn't want me anymore."

What was it, Julia wondered, that made young women—herself included, at that age—feel incomplete without a man's attentions? She continued in a gentle tone, "We applaud the courage you've shown in coming here, and that you were forthright with us. You didn't have to tell us about your past, and we would never have known."

"Oh, but I did have to, Mrs. Phelps! If you only knew how good it feels to own up to everything."

Julia nodded understanding. While her transgressions had never reached the magnitude of Miss Somerville's stunning confession, sin was sin, and she had experienced the healing of the soul that came from drinking from the cup of mercy. "But I'm afraid it's going to be impossible for you to continue to live at the *Larkspur*."

Miss Somerville went white as a ghost. "But I have nowhere else to go."

"What about your family?" The family Julia and Andrew now knew lived in London, and not in the place of Miss Somerville's own making, Truesdale.

"They disowned me when I first . . . took up with Lord Paxton." She blew into the handkerchief, gave them apologetic looks, and continued. "After three years, I doubt they would even speak to me."

"Even if you told them about your repentance, just as you've told us?"

"It wouldn't make a difference." Again the handkerchief went to her nose. "I embarrassed the family. My returning would only add to that embarrassment."

What should we do? was the message Julia sent Andrew with her eyes. The message in his eyes clearly said, *I don't know.*

She made a slight motion of the head toward the door, and he nodded. Julia rose to her feet and picked up the teapot from the tray on Andrew's desk. "Miss Somerville," she said, handing the young woman her refilled cup. "Vicar Phelps and I will need to speak privately. Will you excuse us?"

"Should I wait outside?" Miss Somerville asked, making a move to rise.

Julia smiled and shook her head. "Just sit there and enjoy your tea. We shan't be long." When the door had closed behind them, they took a few steps down the corridor, and she whispered to Andrew, "What will we do with her?"

"I don't know." The brow over his hazel eyes furrowed. "But you're not thinking of inviting her here, are you?"

The thought actually had occurred to her, but in the fraction of a second after he asked the question, she realized why that couldn't happen. The vicarage was their sanctuary, a place where they could retreat from the responsibilities of the parish. Allowing a troubled young women to stay for a few days would not put a strain upon family harmony, but Miss Somerville required more long-range plans. "No, not here," Julia agreed. "What about moving her to the *Bow and Fiddle?*"

"I don't know about that, Julia. Moving in with us would cause some minor speculation around the village, but people would likely give her the benefit of the doubt. But the *Bow and Fiddle?*" He winced. "The rumors would spread as rapidly as head colds in January."

"Well, we can't do that to her."

"What if she stayed at the *Larkspur* long enough to write to her family and see how they reply?" Andrew asked. "They may miss her more than she thinks, and it's wrong not to give them the opportunity to decide if they wish to take her back. We could warn her to keep her distance from Ambrose."

"I still don't know if that's wise, Andrew. I'll grant you she should contact her family, but why can't she wire them and have it done with in a couple of days or so?"

"Because there is too much she'll need to tell them for a wire. And they'll need some time to think about it before replying—*if* they reply."

With a sigh, Julia looked down the corridor at the closed door to the study. "I wish Ambrose had stayed."

"I have a feeling he has," her husband said. They walked to the parlor. Mr. Clay sat on the sofa, listening to Aleda read aloud a story she had written, while Laurel and Grace sat on the carpet cutting out paper doll clothing. Philip looked up from the fishing lure he was fashioning from feathers and colored pieces of yarn to ask, "Is Mrs. Somerville all right?"

"She will be," Julia replied as Andrew beckoned to Ambrose. *At least I hope so.* The actor accompanied them out into the corridor, near the bottom of the staircase.

"I had an inkling that you might need to speak with me again," Ambrose told them, as if he felt a need to explain his presence.

Julia and Andrew assured him that they were grateful. "We don't know what to do with her," Julia admitted. "I was all set to put her out, but she has nowhere to go. If we allow her to stay at the *Larkspur*—under several conditions—how do you think Fiona will feel about it?"

"And how do *you* feel about it?" Andrew added.

The actor blew out his cheeks. "You know how forgiving Fiona is. And I admire that she chose to come clean with you about her past. I've no doubt she would give my door a wide berth."

"And that would be the major condition," Julia told him.

––––––––––

Noelle had finished her tea by the time the Phelps returned with apologies for leaving her alone for longer than they had anticipated. "Please," she said with a shake of her head. "Don't apologize. You've treated me more decently than I imagined you would."

They sat down across from her, and with kind insistence in her green eyes, Mrs. Phelps said there were several conditions necessary to allow her to stay at the *Larkspur*, at least for a little while. "First, you must write to your parents."

"Yes, of course," Noelle agreed. *They'll throw the letter away, but I'll write.*

"Are you still staying downstairs?"

"Yes. But my knee is fine."

"Good. Ask Mr. Jensen to have you moved back upstairs tomorrow." An understanding little smile touched her lips. "Too much solitude isn't a good thing. We all need accountability to others."

Noelle nodded. "I'm learning that."

The next two conditions were no surprise, yet Noelle's cheeks still warmed when the vicar's wife continued, "Even though I presume you already understand this, I have to warn you against going near Mr. Clay's apartment. And, of course, you're never to be alone in the same room with him."

"I won't," Noelle whispered.

There was still another condition to come. "While you can trust that word of this won't reach anyone else's ears in Gresham, you understand that Mr. Clay will have to tell his wife when she returns. Husbands and wives don't keep secrets of this magnitude from each other. And you'll need to ask her forgiveness."

Noelle's heartbeat quickened. From the start she had disliked Mrs. Clay, who had only been kind to her. She couldn't even recall why. Jealousy? Because she was Irish, like Meara Desmond? Now she dreaded terribly the thought of facing her. Giving Mrs. Phelps a panicked look, she pleaded, "Oh please, Mrs. Phelps. Can't *you* tell her how sorry I am?"

"I'm afraid not, Miss Somerville."

"We aren't trying to be cruel," Vicar Phelps assured her, and the compassion in his hazel eyes bore witness to his words. "But when we hurt someone, it's not enough to ask God's forgiveness. True repentance means making amends with the person when at all possible."

Only for the briefest fraction of a second did Noelle regret making her confession. Had she thought hard enough, she could have invented some believable explanation for the things she had said to Mr. Clay. What was one more lie, after so many?

A little shudder of revulsion snaked down her spine. *God forgive me for even thinking that!* She looked at the vicar and his wife and nodded. "I'll apologize to Mrs. Clay."

They told her again that they admired her courage for being willing to change her ways, and that they would pray for her. The rain had stopped when they walked out onto the porch. At the gate the caretaker waited, while on the other side, the vicar's horse stood hitched to the trap. "Keep it," Mrs. Phelps said when Noelle started to unwind the shawl. "It's an old one, but warm."

"Thank you. It will remind me of how kind you were."

"Reminders are good," Vicar Phelps said, smiling.

She had taken up enough of their time and bade them farewell. But just as she was about to turn away, something occurred to her. "The squire has invited me to a luncheon tomorrow. Should I ask Mr. Herrick to deliver my regrets, or tell their driver when he comes for me?" It occurred to her to wonder who the *mystery guest* Mr. Clay had spoken of would be, but her curiosity wasn't strong enough to compel her to socialize in her current frame of mind.

"We'll ask Luke to do that on his way back." To the man in the garden he called, "Will you take care of that, Luke?"

"Yes, Vicar," the caretaker replied with his faint whistle.

"Thank you," Noelle told him. As the trap carried Noelle down the vicarage lane, the caretaker made small talk about the sun coming out and a visit he planned to see his sister in Crossgreen next Sunday. Noelle responded politely, but her thoughts were heavy. The vicar and Mrs. Phelps had praised her for her honesty. If only they hadn't. For she had not been able to share one detail that they would consider important. She had not admitted that Quetin's solicitor was Mr. Radley, the same person who signed the cheques for her lodging. Truly she had repented of her sinful relationship with Quetin, but as long as she allowed him to support her, she was still a kept woman. How could she begin a new life when she was still attached to his purse strings?

Please help me sort out what to do about that, Father, she said under her breath, hoping her prayer was being heard.

———

"And how do you like the *Chicken a la Marengo*, Vicar Treves?" Mrs. Bartley asked Saturday noon in the Manor House garden.

"Most excellent," Paul replied, smiling. "As is everything else."

"You don't find it too lemony, do you?" asked the squire, who had only a bowl of bread soaked in broth.

"Not at all," Paul reassured him.

The married couple smiled indulgently at him and then at each other. During the next span of silence, Paul wondered again why he had been invited, as he had met the squire and his wife only once since moving to Shropshire. They were so ill-acquainted with one another that he was hard pressed to help keep the conversation going. And he had the strange impression that they were disappointed about something.

He chewed and swallowed another mouthful, then tilted his head thoughtfully. "And I believe I detect a subtle amount of garlic, don't I?"

Josette met the tall man's dark mocking eyes without flinching," Eugenia Rawlins read to Jacob in the *Larkspur's* library on Saturday afternoon.

" 'I would rather have dinner with a petty criminal in a viper pit than with you in your fine château, Colonel Nevelle!' she seethed, tossing her head."

But how did she speak without her head? Jacob asked himself. The picture that his sleep-deprived mind painted of the scene was so ludicrous that he stifled a smile. Or rather, attempted to stifle one, for the next thing he knew, Eugenia was lowering her page with an annoyed expression.

"You find this amusing, Jacob?" she asked.

"Why, no." He shifted his weight in his chair. "I just—"

"Because this is the most intense, heart-wrenching scene in the story, and if it's going to cause people to burst into hysterics—"

"But I didn't—"

"Only because I'm sitting here next to you, I suspect."

You dim-witted ox! Jacob scolded himself. She devoted long hours to her writing, and for him—who couldn't write a line of fiction if his life depended upon it—to sit there grinning like a gargoyle was completely boorish of him.

"Please forgive me," he told her, frowning miserably. "I've not been sleeping well lately and drifted off for a second. It's a marvelous story—your best so far." His words were not flattery because in his opinion it was a marvelous story, in spite of Josette's head-tossing.

Pacified, Eugenia gave him an indulgent smile. "You poor dear. Why haven't you been sleeping?"

The "dear" warming his heart, Jacob reached over to cover the hand she had resting on the arm of her chair. He was still struck with awe that she allowed him to hold her hand almost any time he wished. "I've just been staying up too late, and it catches up with me."

"Well, you'll have to put a stop to that, won't you?" she said in a half-teasing, half-serious manner. "We can't have you dropping off to sleep in the middle of my stories."

"No, we can't," he agreed. If only Miss Clark hadn't decided to discontinue the lessons! Between the excavation and the ever increasing time spent with Eugenia, his late night hours were devoted to poetry—he was now trying to commit to memory *A Love Token* by Adelaide Procter—and studying the novelettes. He did not share Miss Clark's confidence in his ability to find symbolism on his own, so the speed of his work was impeded by more than a few self-doubts.

If only this wasn't so much work! he thought as Eugenia read on. A yawn crept up on him, but practice had made him an expert at yawning with his mouth closed so as not to insult her by making her think he was bored. Were all courtships beset with so many stipulations? He considered the Durwins' marriage. Mrs. Durwin did not attempt to study the herbs that so fascinated her husband, neither did Mr. Durwin show any interest in needlepoint. Yet they got along famously.

But Eugenia was an artist, he had to remind himself. They were different creatures, without whom the world would be a very dull place with no music or paintings, sculpture or stories. She had added color to his life, like geraniums in the windowsill could brighten the barest cottage. He should be ashamed for complaining, even in the privacy of his own thoughts.

He was attempting to concentrate again on Eugenia's *Josette of Manosque* when another scene crossed his mind, of Miss Clark staring at him with a curious hurt in her expression and saying, "I see a man having to jump through hoops like a circus pony to gain the favor of a woman who can't appreciate him for the decent, kind person he is."

Circus ponies have no choice, Jacob told himself to take the sting out of the memory. He, on the other hand, had already won Eugenia's affection and could stop studying so hard any time he wanted to. But why should he, when it made her so happy? Wasn't making the other person happy the meaning of love?

————

Sharing a church pew with the Durwins, Miss Rawlins, and Mr. Pitney—all who treated her as graciously as always—Noelle fully expected to hear a sermon on forgiveness. Perhaps Jesus' parable from Saint Matthew, where a king forgives a large debt of a servant, who in turn will not forgive someone lower than himself a small debt. She was ashamed of her presumption as the sermon progressed, for she should have known that Vicar Phelps would not use his pulpit in a calculating way and aim admonitions at selective members of his congregation.

The theme of the sermon was, in fact, *continuing in the faith even during times of hardship*. As his first example, the vicar cited Joseph's steadfast loyalty to God when sold by his brothers, falsely accused by Potiphar's wife, and thrown into prison. He moved on to the widow who fed the prophet Elijah, but Noelle's thoughts returned to Joseph. She knew the story well. Surely while spending those first menial years in slavery, torn away from his home and a father who doted upon him, he was human enough to have dreamed at least once of extracting revenge upon his brothers. Or later, while in prison. *I certainly would have!*

Would the story have had a different ending if Joseph had allowed bitterness to take root and fester in his heart? Would Potiphar have promoted him to rule over his house had he been a sullen, hate-filled slave? And surely the chief jailer wouldn't have turned the responsibility of the entire prison over to a prisoner who could only rant about the injustice of his sentence.

It was ironic that, as a girl, one of her favorite passages of Scripture was when Joseph granted forgiveness to the brothers who had so abused him. She recalled what the vicar had said just two days ago. *The hatred you're carrying is a live coal in your heart—far more damaging to yourself than to them.*

With a quiet sigh she closed her eyes as the sermon moved on to Mordecai's deliverance from the evil Haman. She had felt the scorch of that live coal, yet it still burned within her. *Father, is your back still turned? Will you distance yourself from me until I forgive Quetin and the others?* She felt the sting of salt tears. *But Joseph was able to forgive because he always had you with him.* Yes, it was she who had been the first to turn away, she freely admitted. But she was trying to make up for it. She had written her family and refused to allow herself to daydream about Mr. Clay. *How can I even begin to forgive without your help?*

It seemed then that the voice she had deafened herself to for so long spoke in her heart. *Help is yours for the asking, My child. But you must take that first step before I can give it.*

When she wanted to protest that it was unfair, a picture came inexplicably to her mind of a boat on rough seas. Two men were huddled together at the mast wearing expressions of terror, yet one man clung to the edge, looking out into the distance. *It wasn't until he stepped out of the boat that Peter was able to walk on water*, the voice seemed to say.

"Will you take lunch with us, Mr. Sanders?" Mrs. Meeks asked after Harold had assisted her from the wagon in front of her cottage. This time Harold was eager to accept, for he was in a fine fettle, and not just because

Miss Clark had again looked at him as he drove the wagon down the green. He had a secret, one that had kept him grinning almost the whole time he waited outside Saint Jude's.

But polite people went through certain motions, he was learning by watching his sister, and so he first replied, "But you haven't got to feed me just because I gave you a ride."

"We would enjoy your company, Mr. Sanders," she told him.

"Well . . . if you're sure—"

"Mr. Sanders, will you catch me?" Lester asked, perched atop one of the wheels. The others had already scrambled down to the ground.

"Lester, Mr. Sanders doesn't want to be pounced upon," his mother scolded.

"I don't mind." Harold turned, took two steps backward, and held out his arms. Hesitating only briefly, as if considering changing his mind, the seven-year-old sailed out into the air and into Harold's arms.

"That was fun!" Lester exclaimed as he was lowered to the ground. "May we again?" he asked, while Trudy and the others looked hopeful.

"No, children," their mother said firmly.

Harold nodded agreement. "You're all too big for the likes of me. But after lunch I'll unhitch Bob and lead you around, if you ain't afraid of riding bareback."

He was almost embarrassed by how happy this made the children, who chattered like rooks and clapped their hands.

"You're too kind, Mr. Sanders," their mother said with her soft brown eyes shining a little in the sunlight.

"Aw, it's nothin'," he replied, ducking his head. But then Harold remembered his delightful secret. Turning to Mark, he said, "Climb back up in there. I've something for all of you."

"There's a sack in here, Mr. Sanders," Mark announced after being directed to open the lid of the supply box behind the wagon seat.

Harold chuckled to himself and hitched his arms over the slats on the side. "Well, hand it over."

With a grunt the boy did his bidding. "It's heavy."

Of course it was, Harold thought happily as he took the drawstring sack from the boy. All of their eyes grew wide as he hefted from it a ham as big as a gourd.

"Mr. Sanders," Mrs. Meeks breathed, her hand up to her collar. "We can't be takin' food from your family."

"It ain't from my family. I bought it with my own money."

"But it's too expensive."

"I got a right fair price," he assured her with a grateful thought toward his brother, who had the good sense to court a woman who worked on a pig farm.

———

Lydia's brother, Noah, along with his family and Beatrice's mother, Mrs. Temple, came for lunch after church. They later visited in the front parlor until the children and Lydia's father grew cranky for need of naps. After the cottage was quiet again, save the click of her mother's knitting needles from the sofa and soft snores drifting from the ceiling, Lydia sat in a chair with William Morris's *The Earthly Paradise*.

She could not absorb herself in the words, however, because her mind continued to dredge up a picture, just as a child wiggles a stubbed toe in his shoe in spite of the pain. Mr. Pitney and Miss Rawlins had walked home from church together several yards in front of her family. The two held hands, and when Mr. Pitney turned to send them a smile and wave, he appeared happier than she had ever seen him.

She closed her book, prompting her mother to lower her knitting to her lap.

"Not a good story, daughter?"

"I'm just not in the mood for reading."

"I could always teach you to knit."

Lydia smiled because the offer was made in jest. It was a family joke that Lydia's domestic tendencies were somehow misplaced when she was created. And her stock answer was, "Perhaps tomorrow, thank you." Setting her book aside, she rose and stretched both arms out in front of her. "I believe I'll take a walk to clear my head."

"Would you like me to go with you?"

Bending down to kiss her forehead, Lydia replied, "No, thank you."

Her intent had not been to hike the Anwyl when she stepped through the cottage doorway. But a half hour later she was walking one of its footpaths. The quarried red sandstone, which had been used to build many of Gresham's cottages, was cool, and the dirt path had dried enough not to be dangerous. Still, Lydia kirtled her dress about her knees so she could see her footsteps. She had no worries about her solitude being invaded, for the dampness would discourage any picnics, and the archeologists did not work on Sunday even when the hill was dry.·

Her lungs filled with air smelling of damp earth and the myriad of tenacious flowers in the tall grasses along the path—the ubiquitous milkwort, bluebells and buttercups, forget-me-nots, mountain pansy, and blossoming pink clover. Tranquillity surrounded her, and yet try as she may, she could not bring peace to her mind. Upon reaching the evacuation site, she stared down into the depression where Mr. Pitney had shown her how

333

to look for artifacts. There was evidence of more recent work, more gaps in the earth where something had likely been discovered. She wondered if he had found his missing link. Surely he would tell her if he had, but perhaps not, now that she was no longer his tutor.

"Father, please help me to stop feeling this way," she murmured, and then realized the unfairness of her request. While God could work miracles, He did not wipe thoughts from a person's mind. Free will was a gift since the Garden of Eden. How could she expect God to extinguish the love in her heart for Mr. Pitney when her mind would not stop thinking about him? And how could she stop thinking about him when she still saw him at Saint Jude's every Sunday? When she could not step out of doors without seeing the Anwyl, knowing he was up there at work?

"You have to do something," Lydia spoke aloud again, this time to herself. And by the time she reached the bottom of the hill, she had a plan.

But her mother and father, awake from his nap, reacted with intense disapproval. "Glasgow?" her father questioned. "Why do you want to go back there?"

"Just for a visit, until school starts here again. I can bring my texts to review and still make myself useful by helping to mark papers and such. It would be nice to see my former students." And there would be students there. *Saint Margaret's* only recessed a month for Easter and one for Christmas, yet still had a waiting list among members of the peerage with too much money and too little maternal and paternal instincts.

"You know what that damp old place did to your lungs. What if you take the pleurisy again, and that far from home? Why, you wouldn't even be able to ride the train back."

"But the summers were pleasant, Papa," she reasoned.

The worry did not leave her mother's normally serene expression. "You plan to stay there the *whole* summer?"

"Closer to two months, Mother. June is halfway over. And I still have to write Mrs. Mitchell and wait for her reply." Mrs. Mitchell was the headmistress and Lydia's mentor for the fourteen years she taught there. "You've nothing to worry about. If I get so much as a sniffle, I give you my word I'll pack my things and catch the first train home."

"That's reassuring, daughter," her mother said, but a question still lingered in her eyes. "But forgive me for asking. You aren't . . ."

"Aren't what, Mother?"

A hesitation, and then, "Running away, are you?"

It would have been dishonest to ask what she meant, and again, dishonest to reply that she wasn't. So Lydia simply replied, "It's something I have to do, Mother."

You have to take that first step went again through Noelle's mind as she brushed her hair in preparation for retiring for the night. How could she take it, when the very thought of Quetin and Meara made her clench her fingers so tightly that her fingernails stabbed her palms? They had hurt her, and no doubt thought her naiveté terribly amusing.

"They're still hurting me," she murmured as the realization struck her. They stood between her and God, robbing her of the peace of mind that she longed to know. And she was the one allowing them to do so!

She set her brush down and studied the image in the mirror. The candle on her dressing table painted her face with a yellow pallor. No innocent victim stared back at her, but a foolish woman who had knowingly involved herself with people who were ruthless with others, even their own families. So why was she so stunned when they turned on her?

And what was more important? Clinging to her hatred, nursing a grudge until it sent bile through her body and hardened her features, or pleasing God, who had mercifully given her another chance?

Pushing out from the table, she got on her knees and rested her chin upon the hands she had clasped upon the bench. Her eyes she closed tightly, and she listened to the night sounds floating in through her open windows. She imagined herself a vessel, filled to the brim with hatred so that there was no room left for joy. *No more*, she thought, and prayed, *Father, I forgive them.*

Yet there was something wrong, something unfinished, for the joy she so longed for did not flood the vessel. And painfully, she discovered that it was not yet empty. Unforgiveness for her family had been stored inside for so long that it had hardened, clinging to the sides. She bit her lip and felt the sting of tears again. She would have thought forgiving Quetin and the others the more difficult, but the family wounds, though they were older, were deeper.

You have to do this, she told herself.

Father, I forgive my family as well. She brought each face to mind. *My parents, sisters, and brothers—all of them.*

The effort had been as strenuous as hiking a mile, and yet now that it was done, she felt strangely relaxed. And clean. Tears that had threatened earlier flowed freely, dripping down onto the upholstered bench until she wiped them upon the sleeve of her nightgown.

Thank you, Father.

She wanted to run through the inn and wake everyone with her news, but instead she blew out her candle and climbed into bed, wearing a ludicrous smile in the dark. She fell into a peaceful sleep, without waking until morning.

*V*icar and Mrs. Phelps had not mentioned avoiding Mr. Clay *completely* as a condition for Noelle's staying at the *Larkspur*, but still, she thought it best to do so. Forgiveness was wonderful and incredible, but it had not halted her steps down the path of introspection. Like peeling the layers of an onion, she was finding out things about herself she had never realized.

One unsettling discovery was that she was quite shallow. It had served her well, or so she had thought, during her time with Quetin. Shallow women lived for the moment, never considering how their actions might affect others or even themselves. To do so might cause pain, and of course pain was to be avoided at all costs. And shallow women certainly did not attempt to direct their thoughts through appropriate channels, as Noelle was suddenly having to teach herself to do.

She figured the only way to do that was to avoid the actor's company as much as possible with the exception of meals. Mercifully he did not sit and glare at her at the table but treated her with the same regard as he did the other lodgers.

He was not in the hall on Wednesday morning, but the Durwins and Mrs. Dearing were, so she took Mrs. Dearing's offer to share her sofa. The two women had needlework in their laps, Noelle's crocheting was in hers, and Mr. Durwin held a small leather-covered photograph album.

"My eldest son, Winslow, sent it from Calcutta," the elderly man told her proudly from the facing sofa. "We haven't seen my grandchildren since our wedding."

"May I have a look?" Noelle asked.

He looked very pleased to get to his feet and hand it over to her. "The girl is Katherine and the boy, William."

"Named after your second son," Noelle commented absently as she admired a photograph of the two children in sailor suits.

"Why, yes. How did you know?"

"I'm not sure," she confessed. Surely she had overheard the Durwins speak of their children. It struck her that she had not forgotten anyone's name in a long time. What had she told Quetin the last time she saw him? *I never forget the name of anyone who's important.* Incredibly, without her even being aware of it, these people had become important to her. She looked up at Mr. Durwin and smiled. "They're beautiful children."

"Thank you. They'll be here at Christmas, my eldest and his family. So they'll have the pleasure of making your acquaintance."

"I'm looking forward to it," Noelle replied before remembering that she had no idea where she would be at Christmas. She was more discouraged than ever about accepting Quetin's support, but if her family refused to take her in—which she expected would happen—how could she possibly support herself?

"Speaking of Christmas . . ." Mrs. Dearing said. "Wouldn't it be lovely to have another Christmas wedding here?" She turned to Noelle. "The vicar and Mrs. Phelps were married shortly before Christmas, and the church was decorated so lovely with garlands and holly."

"Are you thinking of remarrying, Mrs. Dearing?" asked Mr. Durwin.

"Bertram . . ." his wife warned softly.

Catching the glint in his eyes, Noelle realized he was teasing their friend.

Mrs. Dearing took it well. Her turquoise earrings quivered with her laugh. "Not at the present time, Mr. Durwin. I enjoyed my marriage to my sainted Harold, but I am quite content with my life as it is. I was speaking of Mr. Pitney and Miss Rawlins, *and* I suspect you knew that."

The man grinned, and his wife said, "I passed the open door of the library yesterday evening and overheard him quoting poetry to her." She raised a hand to her soft cheek. "Perhaps I shouldn't have mentioned that."

"It will go no further than this room, Mrs. Durwin," Mrs. Dearing reassured her. "I think it's charming. Tell us, dear, does Mr. Durwin quote poetry to you?"

With a shake of the head and mischievous little smile, Mrs. Durwin replied, "Alas, but I'm afraid there are no poems written about hawthorn or foxglove or Saint John's wort."

The laughter that erupted from all three was so infectious that Noelle found herself forgetting her worries and joining in. Why she had ever thought elderly people were dull, she couldn't remember. She had returned the photograph album to Mr. Durwin and was crocheting and occasionally joining in the conversation when the front door opened.

"Good day to you, ladies," Mr. Durwin said, getting to his feet, as Noelle and Mrs. Dearing turned to look.

"And good day to you, Mr. Durwin," Mrs. Phelps answered with

Grace at her side. Mother and daughter wore identical narrow-brimmed straw hats, and Mrs. Phelps' gown and the girl's pinafore were of the same mauve carmeline.

"Don't you both look charming, with those pink dresses," Mrs. Dearing told them after greetings were exchanged all around.

"I can hardly tell you apart!" Mr. Durwin exclaimed, bringing a smile to Grace's somber little face.

"Thank you. Laurel and Aleda have costumes of the same fabric as well, but they're off playing with friends." Mrs. Phelps and her daughter sat in chairs near the sofas. Grace stayed just long enough to be polite before excusing herself to visit Mrs. Herrick in the kitchen. Sarah brought in tea and biscuits, and after they had been consumed, the vicar's wife casually asked Noelle if they could speak privately. This did not raise the eyebrows of the other three, who must have supposed they had business to discuss concerning lodgings or such.

"My husband and I were wondering how you were faring," Mrs. Phelps explained from the chair Noelle had insisted she take, while she herself brought over the bench from her dressing table. She had been surprised when the woman suggested her bedchamber instead of the library, but considered the nature of what they would likely be discussing and was grateful.

Noelle knotted her fingers in her lap. "I have kept all of the conditions so far." Anxious then that she had given the impression that her obedience was only temporary, she added, "And I intend to continue keeping them, of course, because they're pleasing to God, and for my own good and . . ."

"Miss Somerville?" her visitor cut in.

"Yes?"

"Do relax, please? I'm only here to offer my help."

"Thank you," Noelle breathed, feeling some of the tension seep from her shoulders. She drew in another deep breath. "Sunday night I forgave the people in my past. My family included."

Mrs. Phelps smiled. "I'm glad to hear it. Why didn't you tell us?"

"I thought I had burdened you enough."

"Oh, but you haven't. And such news would be just the opposite of a burden. I can't wait to share that with the vicar."

Noelle returned her smile. "I just hope I never take this for granted—feeling clean."

"Just remember to thank God every morning for that cleansing, Miss Somerville, and you'll lessen the chance of that happening. Gratitude gives us marvelous staying power, I've discovered."

"I'll remember that," she promised. But a thought that she had kept buried under activity and conversation all morning rose to the surface again. The smile eased from her face. "I'm still dreading facing Mrs. Clay tomorrow."

"Of course," Mrs. Phelps said with a nod. "But she's the most charitable woman I know. I've no doubt that she'll forgive you."

"That actually makes it more difficult. I regret so much how wretched I've been to her . . . from the very first."

"Indeed? She's never mentioned as such."

Recalling something Vicar Treves had told her, she explained, "It's just the same if your thoughts are ugly. I saw how fine her clothes were and how easy her life was, and allowed myself to get jealous."

Oddly, Mrs. Phelps's gave her a sad smile. "Mrs. Clay has earned the right to an easy life, having spent most of hers in servitude."

Noelle blinked. "I beg your pardon?"

"Didn't you know? In fact, she was the housekeeper here for a year."

"Why, no." If she had felt low for flirting with Mrs. Clay's husband before, Noelle wondered now why God had not struck her dead the minute she knocked on that apartment door. "I'm so sorry," she said meekly.

"I didn't come here to chastise you, Miss Somerville. I came to tell you my husband and I are still praying for you. *And* . . . to talk with you about your future."

"My future?"

"Yes." Mrs. Phelps paused before saying, "May I ask you a very frank question?"

"Yes, of course." Her life was an open book anyway as far as the Phelps were concerned.

Mrs. Phelps's green eyes took on a maternal expression, though she was probably only a decade or so older than Noelle. "It's about your lodgings, Miss Somerville. Don't you think it would be in your best interests to sever that tie completely?"

Noelle had forgotten about *that* page in the book revealing her life. Embarrassed that she had not mentioned the support money at the vicarage on Friday, she asked, "How did you know?"

"Didn't you tell us?"

There was nothing to do but admit that she had held back that bit of information purposely. "I was afraid you would make me leave for certain."

"I see. Then we must have assumed as much when you mentioned that Lord Paxton had sent you here." Mrs. Phelps grew thoughtful. "This is a puzzling situation, Miss Somerville. While some might argue there is nothing inherently sinful about accepting the money, as long as you're no longer seeing him—"

"I don't want it, Mrs. Phelps," Noelle told her quietly, but adamantly.

"Not one penny. But I don't know how to begin to support myself."

"And you're still convinced that your family won't allow you to live with them?"

"I would be very surprised if they did." And almost disappointed, she realized, for as much as she wished to see her family again, she'd found a measure of peace here in Gresham—in spite of making a spectacle of herself. Incredibly, London was losing its appeal. Realizing that Mrs. Phelps was speaking, she apologized for allowing her thoughts to drift. "You said you were on your way to the lending library?"

Mrs. Phelps smiled and shook her head. "What I said was that Mrs. Summers wishes to discontinue her position there as soon as possible. Her age is catching up with her, she says. I've recommended you for the position, and the squire says it's yours if you'd like to have it."

"Mine?"

"Of course, if you do move in with your family later, he understands that he would have to find someone to replace you."

Noelle shook her head in disbelief. "But why would he hire me? I don't even care for reading."

"But you *can* read, can't you?"

"Yes . . ."

"And Mr. Trumble still boasts about his shelves. You have a gift for order that would be put to good use."

"I do?" Coming up with a system for organizing the shelves had been easy, so Noelle didn't think she had done anything that anyone else couldn't do. But a gift?

———

Julia wondered at the disbelief in Miss Somerville's green eyes. Surely she was used to compliments, at least on her appearance. Had the people in her life not noticed that behind that comely facade was an intelligent mind? Did *she* even realize it?

"The squire would give me *wages*?" the young woman asked.

"Of course." However, a serious drawback accompanied the offer. Julia wondered if she would be too proud to accept it. "But I'm sorry to say your wages would not cover the cost of your lodgings here. And to keep the servants and amenities we have, I cannot afford to rent your room for any less."

"Oh dear. Then what good would it do to take the position if I couldn't support myself?"

"You could support yourself. There is an extra bedchamber upstairs."

With a puzzled glance at the ceiling, Miss Somerville said, "You mean the attic? Where the servants live?"

"Yes. But the attic is more comfortable than you may think. There is even a water closet and bath. You would still be considered a guest, and take meals in the dining room, but at a much reduced rate."

Her face gave signs of an intense inner struggle. "What would people think?"

She's very young, Julia reminded herself. Gently, she said, "Is that so important, Miss Somerville? More important than the self-respect you would gain by taking control of your own life?"

"My own life," the young woman murmured thoughtfully, but with no easing of her expression. "But, Mrs. Phelps, what if something were to happen? What if the squire isn't pleased with my work? Or I could contract an illness and not be able to work for a long time . . ."

"And Lord Paxton could tire of supporting you and stop sending money. Every path we take has its risks, Miss Somerville. While I don't believe in making rash decisions, there is a time when we must prayerfully step out in faith. Why don't you pray about this for a little while?"

"I will. Thank you," the young woman replied in an unsure tone.

Well aware of the magnitude of the decision she was leaving Miss Sommerville to make, Julia rose from the chair. "And with that, I'll bid you good morning. Grace and I are on our way to *Trumbles* to look for a birthday present for one of her friends."

Miss Somerville got to her feet and held out a hand. But before Julia could take it, the young woman stepped forward impulsively and embraced her. When they drew apart, Miss Somerville's eyes were shining. "You can't imagine how grateful I am for your kindness," she said in a thick voice. "After knowing everything I've done."

"It's all in the past and forgiven, dear," Julia told her, her own voice altered by emotion. "And I see a promising future ahead for you, Noelle Somerville. You'll be surprised at how gratifying it is to accept God's help in taking control of your own life."

———

As the train wheels began slowing for the last time, Fiona sent a weary but happy smile to Leila Keegan, seated across from her in the first-class coach. "Gresham."

"Aye," Mrs. Keegan said. "It seems we've just left—and yet it seems we've been away forever."

Tom Keegan turned from staring out the window, his flaxen hair almost white in the morning sun. "If you'd ever be needin' someone to go to Ireland with you again, Mrs. Clay, I'd be most happy to."

"Thank you, Tom," Fiona said, and when the boy turned back to the window, she traded smiles with his mother again. A girl from Dublin had won the sixteen-year-old's heart. He had promised to write, and true to his word, he began drafting his first letter while in the boat crossing Saint George's Channel, until seasickness drove him up on deck.

So many things to tell you, Ambrose, Fiona thought, appreciating how nice it was to have someone waiting to hear about her experiences.

And indeed he was waiting, all smiles, along with the rest of the Keegans. As the youngest Irish tot was lifted up into his mother's arms, Fiona was caught up into her husband's. "I couldn't sleep last night for happiness!" he murmured into her ear.

"Nor I," Fiona told him, smiling.

As fond as she was of the Keegans, Fiona was pleased to discover Ambrose had asked Mr. Herrick to deliver the family home in the landau, having borrowed the Phelps's horse and trap for themselves. "Would you care to have breakfast somewhere?" he asked after arranging for her trunk to be delivered and helping her into the seat.

She shook her head. "I just want to go home."

"Home it is, then," he said with a smile and snap of the reins.

On the way she told him of Aileen's wedding, how her family was faring, and of her journey to Kilkenny and back. There was so much news to share that it was only when they were halfway to Gresham that she thought to ask what had been going on in the village while she was away.

He turned to her with a wry smile. "Well . . ."

———

At half-past eleven, Noelle was finally groomed and dressed for the day. She had spent the night in restless sleep, even having to get up once to tuck her sheet back into the foot of her bed. When morning came, she decided she would rather have the extra sleep than breakfast and did not venture out of bed until past ten o'clock.

You can't hide in here all day, she told herself when she became aware of what she was doing. She had no sooner touched her doorknob when a knock sounded from the other side. Noelle opened it.

"Oh!" Mrs. Clay exclaimed with a little jump.

Noelle winced. "I'm sorry!"

The Irishwoman put a hand to her heart and nodded. She showed no signs of the strain of travel in her blue-gray serge traveling outfit and smart Rabagas hat with black ostrich feathers. "I just have to collect my breath."

"Would you care to come in and sit down?"

"Yes, please. But not to sit."

Has he told her yet? Noelle wondered, moving aside to allow entrance.

To her surprise, Mrs. Clay closed the door and turned to look at her. "My husband has told me about your mistake."

Unable to meet the appraising violet eyes, Noelle replied, "It wasn't a mistake, Mrs. Clay. I knew full well what I was doing."

"And that's what I needed to hear," her visitor said in her soft Irish brogue. She stepped forward to take Noelle's hand. "And so it's all forgotten, Miss Somerville."

But that wasn't enough. Noelle forced herself to look up at her. "Am I forgiven?"

"Of course."

"Please say it," Noelle whispered.

Her hand was squeezed as the actor's wife smiled. "I forgive you."

When Mrs. Clay was gone, Noelle had to sit in her chair for a little while. She felt drained of strength, but in a good way. Like a laborer who can finally sit by his fireside after a fruitful day of work. It was the same way she had felt after organizing Mr. Trumble's shelves.

Completely forgiven, she thought on her way downstairs to lunch. She returned the smiles from the dear aged faces at the table, the Clays, and the maids at the sideboard. Had she allowed her impulses free rein, she would have embraced everyone as well. *Except for Mr. Clay*, she told herself and was even able to smile about that.

The next morning she walked across the green and told Vicar and Mrs. Phelps she would be pleased to accept the position at the lending library. That having been done, she went back to the room that would be hers only until the end of June and wrote a brief letter to Mr. Radley.

> Mr. Radley,
>   Please inform Lord Paxton that his support, while appreciated in the past, is no longer necessary.
>   Noelle Somerville

Yet something inside her still wasn't quite right. She realized what it was that evening. All the lodgers and Mr. Jensen were gathered in the hall and in especially good spirits, querying Mrs. Clay about her trip to Ireland, and expressing excitement about the debut of the new pulpit in Saint Jude's in two more days.

"I'm so glad your knee is healed, Mrs. Somerville," Mr. Ellis told her. "It would be a shame for you to miss church on such a special occasion."

There was a chorus of agreement that pricked her heart. For she had not yet set straight the falsehood she had told on her first day in the *Larkspur*. And as long as she allowed them to address her as *Mrs.*, she was perpetuating the lie. *You may as well do it now and save yourself some sleep*, she told herself when tempted to push the thought aside until later. She lowered her crocheting to her lap when there was a lull in the conversation. "If you please, I have something to tell all of you."

"What is it, Mrs. Somerville?" Mrs. Dearing asked, smiling. "Have you some marvelous secret to share?"

"Not marvelous, I'm afraid." Noelle pulled in a deep breath. *Just say the words.* "I'm not a widow. In fact, I was never married."

"Never married?" Mrs. Durwin blinked. "But your husband was a hero . . ."

"He was completely fiction." To Mr. Jensen's concerned look, she quickly added, "I've confessed the same to Mrs. Phelps."

"But why, Mrs. Somerville?" Mr. Durwin asked.

"That would be *Miss* Somerville," she corrected tactfully. "I was told that sympathy would secure me a place here more easily." She restrained herself from pouring out her whole sordid past, because though it was an offense against God and herself, there was no wrong committed against any of them. "And now I must ask your forgiveness."

"And you have it, Miss Somerville," Mr. Clay was the first to respond. Others murmured agreement, and Mrs. Clay smiled across at her. Only Miss Rawlins, seated in a chair next to Mr. Pitney's, looked crushed.

"I was going to base a character on him," the writer said.

Noelle gave her an apologetic look. "I'm sorry."

"But surely you still can, Miss Rawlins," Mr. Ellis told her. "You write fiction anyway."

"I suppose so," Miss Rawlins said, then sighed. "I might have known it was too good to be true. There just aren't many romantic men around anymore."

The smile she then gave to Mr. Pitney made it obvious that she considered him an exception to that statement. Noelle smiled to herself at the happiness on the archeologist's face and thought how glad she was that he had found love. Perhaps she would find it herself one day, but for now, forgiveness was more than enough.

𝒴ou must've left the coffee beans in the wagon yesterday," Mrs. Winters said to Oram when the Sanders males were all at the table for lunch that same Saturday.

Oram swallowed the beef stew filling his cheeks. "I forgot to get some, Mrs. Winters."

She shot him a vinegary look. "You forgot, did you? And me already havin' to dig in the bottom of the crock!"

"I'm sorry—"

"Not half as sorry as you'll be if I have to drink watered-down coffee all week!"

"I'll go," Harold offered. But not because he wanted to spare Oram, who was no better than the rest of them and surely wouldn't jump in to spare him a tongue-lashing. As long as he had to deliver the afternoon milking to the cheese factory anyway, he might as well put off returning to chores as long as possible. And there was always the chance he might happen across Miss Clark.

"Two Sanders in two days?" Mr. Trumble greeted him from behind his counter.

"Oram forgot Mrs. Winters' coffee beans, and she's fit to be tied. If we don't wanter eat porridge all week, I'd best bring her a sack."

"He didn't forget 'em. I told him I was out but would get more in this morning. Didn't he tell her?"

"Nope. But next to Oram, I'm a generous."

The shopkeeper's walruslike mustache twitched. "A what?"

"You know, one o' those real bright people."

"I see. But what you mean to say is a *genial*."

"I do?"

Tapping a temple, Mr. Trumble explained, "I've read through Mr. Johnson's dictionary twice now, so's it's all stored up here to stay."

Harold walked across the lane to chat with Mr. Pool's gardener, Abe Worthy, for a little while, hoping Mrs. Clark would come along. But then

Abe started acting as though he wanted to get back to work, so Harold gave up and went back to the wagon. He wondered if he should drive down Walnut Tree Lane past the Clark cottage, but as everyone in town knew he had no reason to do so, he decided against it. Empty milk cans rattled about in the wagon bed as the team neared the Bryce. He happened to look to his right and saw Lester Meeks standing near an oak at the edge of the green. A girl sat near him on the ground, her arms wrapped around the head she had propped against her knees. Pulling Dan and Bob's reins, Harold hopped down from the wagon.

"What happened?" He recognized that the girl was Phoebe. Her shoulders shook like she was weeping, and Lester's face was pinched up like he was about to do the same.

"She tripped over a root."

"A root, huh?" Harold squatted on the ground beside the girl and touched her shoulder. "Let's have a look, Phoebe."

She raised a teary face and blinked her red eyes at him. "I'm not hurt, Mr. Sanders."

"Billy Casper laughed at her when she fell," Lester explained, pointing off down the green.

"He did, huh?" Raising himself on his haunches, Harold spotted a boy running away from them in the direction of the town hall. "You'd better keep running!" he yelled, shaking a fist. He turned back to the girl and pulled a wrinkled bandana from his pocket. "This ain't too dirty. Blow yer nose."

He waited for her to obey, then asked, "Where are your spectacles, Phoebe?"

"Right here." Sheepishly she took them from the pocket of her pinafore.

"Well, put 'em on."

"Are you going to tell Mother?"

Harold tucked the bandana back into his pocket and rubbed his chin. "Well, that's something I've got to study on. Seems like she'd want to know her daughter is dangerin' her life every time she steps out the door. Why are you so all-fired intent on not wearing 'em?"

Bottom lip trembling, she answered, "I didn't want to be laughed at."

"Is that so? And what was that Casper boy doin', exactly?"

"Laughing," she mumbled.

"Fancy that."

He discovered that the children were on their way to *Trumbles* with a list of goods to have delivered. "You might as well get them now," Harold told them. "Seein' as there's room in my wagon."

Their list was small compared to Sanders standards, and soon he had their sacks of flour and oats, matches, pail of lard, tins of tea and treacle, and a card of sewing pins in the back of the wagon. He allowed them to sit on either side of him on the way home because they were both small enough to fit, and he expected they might like to learn to drive. Dan and Bob didn't care who sat at the reins anyway. After they crossed the Bryce and he had taken the reins from Lester to give Phoebe a turn, he said to her, "Seems like the people you're so worried about laughing at you ain't so nice. Why would you take a chance on doing yourself harm just so's mean people won't laugh?"

"Because it hurts when they laugh," Phoebe sniffed, sitting stiffly.

"Worse than tripping over a root?"

She opened her mouth to answer, but no sound came out. And presently she smiled. "No, sir."

"Besides, you look real bright with those spectacles on."

"I do?"

"Like that lady at the *Larkspur* who writes all those books. You don't see her tripping over roots."

"I wonder what would happen if Billy laughed at *her*?" Lester asked from his left.

Harold grinned. "Well, he oughter not, if he's got any sense. She could just give his name to somebody in one of her books. Somebody ugly, with big warts all over his face."

"Or maybe one big one on the tip of his nose!" Lester chimed in with a chuckle that shook his whole body.

"And green teeth?" Phoebe offered with eyes still on the reins.

"Green as grass!" Harold agreed.

Trudy was sitting on the stoop, playing with a doll, when the horses stopped in the drive. She ran out to greet them, saying her mother and Mark were fixing the door of the hay barn. Harold cocked his head. Sure enough, he heard the sound of a hammer. He gave the lighter items to the three children, then hefted the two sacks across his shoulders and picked up the lard bucket. When the groceries were in the kitchen, he slapped his hands together to get rid of the flour that had sifted through the sack and said, "I s'pose I should see if your mother needs some help."

Out in the barnyard, Mrs. Meeks was holding a board crosswise against the loose planks of the barn door, while Mark held the hammer. With one sweep of his eyes, Harold counted four bent nails. They were miserable carpenters. He would have laughed if they weren't a poor woman and boy trying to do a man's work. But he cleared his throat instead. "Hullo?"

They both turned their heads to look at him. Strands of brown hair had worked themselves away from the knot above Mrs. Meeks' collar, and sweat beaded her face. "Mr. Sanders?" she said.

"I gave Phoebe and Lester a ride home," he explained in case she was wondering.

She smiled and thanked him. Then she flinched as Mark swung the hammer.

"Bent again!" the boy cried in disgust.

"You're holding it too far away from the nail. And you should be hammering from the other side." Harold held out his hand. "Why don't you let me show you?"

Mark looked hurt as he handed over the hammer, so Harold winked at him. "I didn't even learn how to use a saw 'til I was bigger than you." He didn't think it needful to add that a saw was much more difficult to use than a hammer, which he had learned how to use at about age six. It worked, for Mark smiled.

"Now, why don't you go on inside and tend to your groceries," Harold said to Mrs. Meeks.

"But we're keeping you from your own chores . . ."

"Now, don't be worryin' about that," Harold told her, although he indeed did have chores waiting. "We men'll have this fixed in no time."

"No time" took two hours, much longer than he had anticipated. But the door was as sturdy as a new one. For a few minutes Harold and Mark stood there and admired their work. Then Harold said he had to go. "My papa will be mad as—"

Remembering the tender years of his helper, he bit off the next word and replaced it with " a goose with its bill caught in the corn crib."

Mark laughed. "That's mad, huh, Mr. Sanders?"

Smiling, Harold warmed to the subject. "Or mebbe he'll be madder than a mule chewing on hornets."

The boy held his sides. Between chortles, he offered, "Mad as a dog with fleas?"

Harold didn't think that was as funny as his jokes, but he laughed to be polite. "Tell your mother good-day for me," he said as he handed the hammer back to the boy. But he had no sooner reached the wagon when Mrs. Meeks came out of the cottage. She had refastened her hair and changed her clothes, and thanked him with such gratitude in her expression that Harold felt ten feet tall.

"You'll stay for supper, won't you?" she asked. "I've fresh bread and butter, and a fine cabbage soup with some of the ham you gave us."

With a glance at the orange sky to the west, Harold had to shake his head. "Thank you, but I've got to get back."

"Some other time, then," she told him with an understanding smile.

"Yes, some other time." He was just about to hop up into the driver's seat when he told himself that late was late, and no matter what time he showed up back at home, his papa was likely to raise a fuss. Maybe his family had already had supper, and Mrs. Winters wasn't happy about stragglers—even those bringing coffee beans. If he was going to be in trouble, he might as well have food in his belly. He turned around and gave her a sheepish shrug.

"I do admire a hearty cabbage soup, ma'am. Next to fresh bread with butter, that's my most favorite food in the world."

He didn't intend to stay so long, but after the meal the children sat with him at the table and laughed at his jokes while Mrs. Meeks smiled and cleaned the kitchen. Stars were already starting to show themselves in the dusky sky by the time he left.

To Harold's utter surprise, his papa only stopped his whittling long enough to send him a curious look as he came through the doorway. He prepared for bed with the same glow of happiness he had felt before. Not only had he turned a good deed—more than one, actually, because seeing about Phoebe and Lester in town counted—but he had also had a good time. The Meeks looked up to him, something few others in Gresham did. And Papa hadn't yelled at him for missing chores.

"What are you grinnin' at?" Dale asked suspiciously just before Harold snuffed the candle out. "Did that schoolmistress decide she likes you after all?"

"No." But his smile did not leave as he pulled the covers about his shoulders in the darkness. Maybe all this happiness he was having lately was a sign that his luck was about to take a turn for the better. Just maybe it meant that Miss Clark would change her mind as well.

———————

As his family dressed for church on Sunday morning, Andrew walked over to the vicarage an hour earlier than usual. Mr. Sykes and Mrs. Bartley had insisted he not be present when the new pulpit was delivered the evening before. He suspected their reason was due to the same superstition that forbade the groom to see the bride on a wedding day. As much as he disliked superstition, there were times when a vicar just had to be agreeable, and this was one of them.

His breath caught in his throat as he walked up the aisle, for the rich oak glowed like honey in the light slanting through the stained-glass windows. Carved into the front panel was a scene of Christ at prayer in the garden of Gethsemane. Andrew walked close enough to run his hand over wood as smooth as glass. "Thank you, Father," he prayed, his words echoing softly in the quiet sanctuary. Won't the congregation rejoice to have such beauty in front of them every Sunday? Another thought made him smile. *But they still have to contend with my tired old face.*

He turned at the sound of the heavy front door closing. In from the vestibule walked Mr. and Mrs. Hayes. *Not this morning, of all mornings!* Andrew groaned to himself. But courtesy compelled him to call out, "Good morning."

"Good morning, Vicar," Mr. Hayes greeted him. At his side, his wife smiled pleasantly. The effect was astonishing, for it wiped ten years from her face. They were halfway up the aisle when Andrew noticed they were holding hands.

"My sister sends me a special wood polish from London," Mrs. Hayes explained as they stopped in front of him. Her husband handed her the cloth bag he held in his other hand, and she took a cloth and white jar from it. "I thought it might need touching up a bit after being moved."

Staring up at the pulpit, Mr. Hayes blew out his cheeks. "It's beautiful, ain't it?"

"Beautiful," his wife agreed, then gave Andrew a sheepish look. "Truth is, Vicar, I couldn't wait to see it. I shouldn't have mentioned such to Luther, because he pampers me so."

"Well, you deserve it," Mr. Hayes told her.

Andrew smiled and told the two that he would see them in a little while. "Mrs. Phelps may need my help in the vicarage."

"Oh dear." Mrs. Hayes stopped rubbing the cloth in the open jar. "You wanted to be here alone. We've gone and ruined your morning."

"Actually, Mrs. Hayes," Andrew told her, "you've gone and made my morning even better."

———

Harold's good fortune changed for the worse on Sunday. And he had no warning, for the morning was as nice as the night before had been. Mrs. Winters cooked his eggs just the way he liked them and even smiled and thanked him for getting the coffee in town. The sun shone brightly, but the air was not so hot as to make his tweed coat give him a sweat. While he waited at the side of Saint Jude's, a yellow chiff-chaff sang sweetly to him from the branch of a yew tree, sounding like a little bell and fluttering like a leaf in the wind.

The change happened as he was driving the Meeks family home, after passing Miss Clark and her parents on the green. In the wagon bed, Trudy sat on the supply box and tugged on the back of his sleeve. "Wasn't the new pulpit nice, Mr. Sanders?"

Harold, who had just finished telling Mrs. Meeks about the chiff-chaff, angled his head to hear the girl better. "The what?"

"Vicar Phelps's new pulpit."

"It's not just the vicar's, Trudy," Mark said from behind.

That made it a little clearer. Harold reckoned they were talking about something the vicar wore, like a new suit. Maybe his clothes belonged to the church, just like the vicarage did. He twisted his head around to wink at Trudy. "I don't care what he wears, as long as he preaches those good sermons."

The children laughed, which told him he had given the right answer. But when he tried to help Mrs. Meeks from the wagon in front of the cottage, she shook her head and sent the children on inside. They did so quietly, each turning back to look at him before disappearing through the doorway. Only when the door closed did Mrs. Meeks turn to him. Her brown eyes wore a look that Harold didn't understand.

"Is there something wrong?" he asked.

But instead of answering, she said in a quiet voice, "You've been pretending to go to church, haven't you?"

"I go to church."

"Inside, I mean."

A lie rose to his lips, but he was unable to force it out. "Well, not *inside*."

"Why, Mr. Sanders?"

He tried to say Miss Clark's name. However, just like the lie, it wouldn't form on his tongue. So in all truthfulness he said, "I like helping you and the children."

A sad smile drained the brightness from her face. "You're not a believer, are you?"

It was a question, but she said it like she already knew the answer. And Mercy had preached religion to him enough so that he understood what she was talking about.

"I'm aiming to be one day, Mrs. Meeks," he told her.

"I see." Again he saw the sad smile as she folded her work-worn hands over the cloth reticule in her lap. "You've been kind to us, Mr. Sanders, and I thank you for that. But we can't ride with you anymore. And please don't offer my children rides or come to visit."

"But why? The children are fond of me."

"And that's why, Mr. Sanders."

"I don't understand. Ain't it good for them to have a man about once in a while, with their papa being taken from them and all?"

She shook her head and stared down at her folded hands. "Not if he's someone their mother can't consider marryin'. They talk about you all the time. If you come around too much, they're going to get attached to you, and it's going to break their hearts."

This didn't make any sense. Who said anything about marrying Mrs. Meeks? Then it dawned upon Harold that she was thinking that all the attention he was giving her family was because he wanted to court her. *Of course!*

"But why wouldn't you want to marry me?" he asked. Not that he wanted her to, because his heart belonged to Miss Clark. He just needed to know. "Because I don't go to church?"

"Because you're not a believer *and* don't go to church," she said softly, then looked up at him again. Tears were gathered in her eyelashes. "You're a good man, Mr. Sanders. But the Scriptures say a believer shouldn't marry a person who isn't a believer. God's been so good to my family. The least I can do is obey. And my children should have a father who'll set a good example by goin' to church."

With that, she picked up her reticule. Harold had no choice but to help her down from the wagon. He glanced toward the cottage and saw three heads duck from a window. An odd thickness came to the back of his throat. "Well . . . I . . . uh . . . h-hope you'll tell me . . . if you ever need anything," he stammered, shifting his weight on his feet.

"Thank you, Mr. Sanders."

Then to his surprise, she came toward him and planted a quick kiss upon his cheek. "I'll pray for you every day," she said as she stepped backward, tears still shining in her eyes.

"Uh, thank you."

And there was nothing left to do but leave. He swung back into the wagon and picked up the reins. His heart was so heavy that he whistled a tune to try to cheer himself up, but it only made him feel worse. It was the first time a woman had ever kissed him, and he could still feel her lips softly upon his cheek as he neared home.

———

"Wasn't that a moving sermon?" Mrs. Durwin asked at the *Larkspur*'s dining table that same afternoon as the lodgers sat down to a lunch of boiled mutton with caper sauce, roast parsnips, and rhubarb dumplings.

"It was," Miss Somerville agreed.

Mr. Clay, cutting his mutton with a knife, said, "Sermon? My eyes were so drawn by the pulpit that I forgot to listen."

"Oh, Mr. Clay," Mrs. Durwin said with an affectionate smile. "You did no such thing."

Jacob tore off a piece of his bread and wished the conversation would change to something else. The sermon had indeed been moving, but it moved his conscience in a painful direction. For the subject was hypocrisy. As an illustration, the vicar used Ananias and his wife Sapphira's pretending to give to God all of the money they had received for a piece of land, when actually they kept some back. Their sin was not in holding some back—

for as Saint Peter told them, the land was theirs to do with as they wished—but in lying about it so that others would think well of them.

He looked across at Eugenia and winced inwardly while returning her smile. It was ironic that Vicar Phelps had chosen that particular subject, for Jacob had been in torment over his own hypocrisy ever since Friday evening, when Miss Somerville made her stunning confession in the hall. How serene the newest lodger looked now!

You have to tell Eugenia, went through his mind for the hundredth time. Panic quickened his pulse. *What if she despises you for it?* But surely that wouldn't happen. He had won her heart. Weren't they close enough so that he could say anything to her? Often he thought of the two of them spending the future together. Did he really want a marriage built upon a foundation of lies?

In dire need of divine guidance, he prayed silently, *Father, if I should confess all to her today, would you please have her ask me to sit with her after lunch?* Then deciding he should be more specific, so there would be no question in his mind from where the answer came, he prayed, *Outside, if you please.* And just because *outside* wasn't really that specific after all, he added, *In the courtyard.*

After lunch she approached him. "Would you care to sit out in the courtyard for a little while?"

"That would be nice," Jacob replied with mingled feelings of awe that his prayer was answered, and dread over what he had to do.

Soft summer breezes met them as they walked out into the courtyard to take a seat upon one of the benches. Eugenia arranged her plisse wrap about her shoulders and let out a contented sigh. "Isn't the weather just heavenly?"

He sighed as well, but for different reasons. "I suppose so."

"What's wrong, Jacob? Did you not find any artifacts yesterday?"

So seldom did she ask about his work that he hoped her question meant that her fondness for him was increasing. "We found some," he replied, then cleared his throat. "But there is something you should know."

"Yes?" she said with an unsuspecting smile.

"I've been a hypocrite, Eugenia. Just like Ananias and Sapphira."

She actually giggled. "I beg your pardon?"

Nerves as taut as fiddle strings, Jacob confessed how frustration over his own ineptness at reading drove him to hire Miss Clark. He could not look at the woman beside him but stared down at his interwoven fingers, his thumbs circling each other as if they had wills of their own. And then he admitted he had not the soul of a poet, did not even particularly care for poetry, and that it was a labor to learn every stanza. When he had no more to tell, he finally forced himself to look at her. "Will you ever forgive me, Eugenia?"

The anger in her gray eyes caused his stomach to knot. Still, with a voice as calm as if she were discussing the weather, she replied, "I would prefer you address me as Miss Rawlins . . . Mr. Pitney."

"Please . . . if you could just understand how desperately I wanted you to notice me—"

"You led me to believe you were a true romantic, Mr. Pitney."

"I'll do anything to make it up to you," he pleaded.

She shook her head, lips pressed tightly together, before speaking again. "I have to fault myself for turning a blind eye to the cracks I've noticed lately in your facade."

"Cracks—?"

"Glaring ones, Mr. Pitney. And so it doesn't surprise me to learn that you possess the same bland soul as most Englishmen, with their umbrellas and bowler hats and pocket watches."

He didn't understand what that meant and was just about to point out that he did not even own a pocket watch when she rose to her feet.

"Good afternoon, Mr. Pitney."

The remainder of the week passed by as if they had never sat in the garden or courtyard or in the library together, never held hands, never discussed her stories or poetry. If anything, it was worse than the former days, for now instead of treating him with polite disinterest, she simply ignored him.

That was painful enough, but the worst blow came the following Monday evening. He and Mrs. Dearing happened to meet coming from opposite directions on the stairs, and he gathered the nerve to ask her why Miss Rawlins had been absent from meals the whole weekend. "I do hope she's not ill," he said.

Mrs. Dearing gave him a sympathetic look. "Didn't she tell you?"

She would actually have to speak with me then, he thought sadly. "Tell me what?"

"She left for London on Saturday to meet with her publisher. She'll be away most of the week."

"I see."

The elderly woman touched his shoulder. "I'm so sorry, Jacob."

It was the first time she had addressed him by his given name, and he was reminded so much of his mother that a lump came to his throat.

"I feel responsible for encouraging you to pursue her," Mrs. Dearing went on.

He shook his head. "You were just trying to help. Besides, you didn't encourage me to do anything I didn't want to do."

"Perhaps," she said with a little frown, studying his face. "Will you be all right?"

"Absolutely," he replied, even giving her a smile. Then he went upstairs to his room, dropped down upon his bed, and wept between prayers that Eugenia's affection for him would return.

Some time later, when his candle had snuffed itself out in the holder, a passage of scripture roused him out of restless sleep . . . *the truth shall make you free.* He rubbed his burning eyes with the hem of his sleeve. By pretending to be something he was not, he had won Eugenia's heart. But it was at the cost of slipping into a miserable bondage, its chains made up of such links as fear of discovery, self-loathing for his duplicity, and exhaustion from trying to keep the pretense going.

Father, he prayed under his breath. *I'll never be anything but honest from now on.* As an afterthought, he added, *Even if you never make Eugenia love me again.*

*T*uesday, July second was a significant day for Noelle, for she had spent one whole week in the first gainful employment of her life. She was relieved and even delighted to discover that she enjoyed every detail having to do with it. The half-timbered, two-room cottage that housed the lending library dated back to the fourteenth century, the squire had told her, and was one of the first homes in the village. He explained that most of the populace were shorter in those days, which was why people like the schoolmistress Miss Clark had to stoop to pass through the doorway.

By the third day, Noelle had even convinced the squire and Mrs. Bartley that her tiny desk should be moved from the back room to a corner in the front so that she could be accessible at all times to the patrons. And since the Bartleys were so open to that suggestion, Noelle went further and talked them into some chairs and a rug so that the back could be turned into a reading room.

"I've noticed that sometimes people stand by the shelves and read several pages before deciding whether to take a book home," she had told them. While the half-farthing subscription fee was nominal, it still represented a fair portion of poor folks' wages, and they wanted to spend it wisely. They might as well be comfortable at it.

She had decided it would be best to go ahead and move to the attic room at the *Larkspur* before starting her library position, even though the new lodger, a Mrs. Grant from Derbyshire, wouldn't be arriving for another three weeks. Now that she had gotten used to the idea, Noelle decided it was rather novel and even exciting. With her own hands and skills she was providing a living for herself. She likened herself to a nestling falling from a branch but suddenly discovering its wings. And while she found that analogy romantic, she was aware that it was flawed, for she couldn't have gotten anywhere without God's grace and the help of the Phelps and the Bartleys.

The only fly in her ointment was that her family had yet to write. Surely they had received her letter, sent almost three weeks ago. While she had decided to stay in Gresham regardless, being assured of their forgiveness would help heal some of the scars that remained from her wicked past.

At half-past five that Tuesday afternoon she was at her desk printing *Property of the Bartley Subscription Library* on the inside cover of each of a dozen books that had arrived by post earlier, when she heard footsteps on the stoop. She finished printing *Library* and then looked up at the person opening the door. "I'm sorry but the library is clo—"

It was Vicar Treves, his tall frame stooping to enter the room. He approached her desk with hat in hand and an odd expression on his clean-shaven face. "Good afternoon, Miss Somerville."

Noelle flushed at the *Miss*. So he had heard. "How did you know?" she asked, replacing the stopper in the ink bottle.

"Surely you've lived long enough in a small town to know the answer to that one."

She nodded somberly and sat back in her chair. It was good that he knew. She owed him the same apology she had given the lodgers. As for the talkative mother and daughter planning the wedding on the train, she did not feel quite as responsible because she couldn't remember their names and, therefore, could not write to them. She hoped God didn't mind.

"I hope you can forgive me, Vicar Treves. I'm very ashamed."

"I can forgive you for that," he replied, his blue eyes staring down into hers. "But there is something else I'm having difficulty forgiving you for. So I thought we should talk about it."

Again heat came to her cheeks. How had he found out, when the Phelps and Clays were the only ones who knew about the rest of her past? She couldn't imagine any of them breaking their promise not to divulge it. "There is?"

He nodded and held his bowler hat over an empty space on the desk. "May I?"

"Please." When he had put his hat down, she said, "You might as well get a chair from the other room." It would have been more practical for the two of them to go back there and sit, but propriety seemed best served by staying in the front, where she had not yet drawn the curtains.

Bringing a chair to the front of her desk, he sat down and looked at her for a second or two with an expression Noelle could not comprehend. She waited with growing dread for accusations like *harlot* and *doxy*.

But instead he told her, quietly, "You have every right to turn down an invitation for a social outing with me, Miss Somerville. But it is unfair to make a blanket assumption that because your own father neglected your family for his parishioners, all ministers are guilty of the same. If your father had been a neglectful blacksmith, would you assume all blacksmiths were the same?"

Relief came over Noelle, but it was short-lived. He would not be here unless he still cared for her. And she had no choice but to put an end to that, for his sake. "I didn't say all ministers do the same," she protested. "In fact, I distinctly recall mentioning that Vicar Phelps and you were different."

"Actions speak louder than words, Miss Somerville. I was willing to forget about attempting to see you again, but my heart would not cooperate. And so I'm here to say that if you find my personality disagreeable, I shall have to accept that and trouble you no more. But if the only reason you shun my company is because I'm a vicar . . . you need to know that when I have a family, I'm resolved to make them my primary ministry."

"My father would consider that blasphemy, Vicar Treves."

"Then that's his loss, Miss Somerville, and his family's. God ordained the family first. And He did not excuse ministers from training up their children in the way they should go. That involves spending time with them."

"Did Vicar Phelps teach you that too?"

He smiled. "One of the many things he has taught me without even having to speak about it. I can see by his example that if all is right at home, it will be right in the church as well."

She could not help but believe that he was sincere. If only her father had had such a mentor when he was young! Surely things would have been different. But there was no use in prolonging this conversation. "I'm very glad you feel that way, Vicar Treves." *And I envy the woman you'll eventually share your life with*, came into her thoughts. "But I cannot see you socially."

A muscle in his jaw twitched, and the hurt was obvious in his blue eyes. "I'm not so bold as I pretend to be, Miss Somerville. It took days for me to work up the courage to approach you again. If there is something offensive about my character, you would be doing me a great service by pointing it out."

"Your character is above reproach," she told him, truthfully. "It's mine that is lacking."

"Because of the fabrication about your husband? While it was certainly wrong, you did eventually tell the truth and ask forgiveness. I've told lies in the past as well."

Noelle shook her head. Telling him seemed the only way to put an end to his persistence. If only she didn't have to! If only she could boast of an untainted past! Yes, God had forgiven her, but if He had forgiven her for murder, her victim would be just as dead. Some things were simply not repairable.

"I cannot allow you to call, Vicar Treves, because lying was not my only sin." It seemed she could hear her own strained voice coming from somewhere outside of her.

"What do you mean?" he asked, studying her face.

But shame would not allow her to go any further. "Please ask Vicar Phelps for the rest. Say that I insist he tell you."

"Why can't you tell me?"

"Because I would rather drink hemlock."

———————

"You shouldn't try to move it by yourself," Lydia told her father on Wednesday as she followed him from the parlor.

"Not a job for a woman," he said without turning.

It's not a job for an old man either, she thought. If only her mother wasn't visiting Mrs. Alcorn this morning! "Well, then wait until Noah comes over. It takes me almost no time to pack. And I still have three more days, so there is no hurry."

But he shook his gray head and started up the stairs. "I'll have it down before you can say *Bob's yer uncle*."

"How about before I can say *sprained back*?"

Her father simply wagged a finger over his shoulder and continued climbing. Lydia was about to follow when someone knocked at the door. *Please let it be a male, Lord*, she prayed on her way through the front parlor. She was so overjoyed to see Harold Sanders that she could have kissed him—almost.

"Miss Cl—" was all he got out, for Lydia grabbed him by the hand and pulled him through the doorway.

"I need you to help my father bring a trunk down from the attic before he kills himself," she said, propelling him through the parlor. She took his hat from his hand and tossed it to the sofa.

"Uh—all right." At the bottom of the staircase he turned to give her a bewildered look. "Is he up—"

She waved him upward. "Yes, yes, he's up there now." While Mr. Sanders obeyed, Lydia followed until the first landing. Presently the two men came grunting down the stairs with the trunk. She held her bedroom door open for them, grateful that Mr. Sanders had taken the most difficult position, walking backward in front. When the trunk was set down on her rug with a thud, she and her father turned to their caller.

"Thank you," they both said almost at once, and her father shook his hand. It occurred to Lydia only then to wonder why he was here, but it would be rude to ask, and she was more disposed to treat him cordially after the favor he had performed. "Would you care for some lemonade?" she asked instead.

"Uh, no, thank you," he answered, staring down at the carpet. "I were wonderin' if I could speak with—uh, well, with Miss Clark."

"Certainly," Lydia told him. "But I'm sure you won't mind my father along. He's very discreet."

Mr. Sanders blinked at her. "Beg your pardon?"

"Discreet. It means—"

"I think I'll take a nap," Lydia's father said, his eyes shining as he covered a yawn with his hand. "I'm old, you know. Why don't you and Mr. Sanders have your chat in the parlor?"

Lydia almost wished she had allowed her papa to struggle with the trunk himself. But she smiled at their visitor and walked with him out into the corridor toward the staircase. "Very well. But I'm afraid I won't be able to visit for long. I have to pack."

"Where are you going?" he asked as he followed her down the stairs.

"To Glasgow. For the rest of the summer."

"Oh." He said no more until they were seated in the front parlor—Mr. Sanders on the sofa next to his hat, and Lydia in a chair. And even then he stared at her shoes as if working up the courage to speak.

"And what did you wish to discuss?" Lydia finally asked him.

"I came to ask you to be truthful with me about something, Miss Clark."

"Very well," Lydia replied, willing herself not to smile at his overly solemn expression.

He hesitated, and then, "Are you any closer to agreeing to our courtin' than you was before?"

She shook her head. "I'm sorry, Mr. Sanders."

"Do you think you might change your mind one day?"

"Not in a hundred years," she said with as gentle frankness as possible.

"I see." Inexplicably, relief flooded his expression. "Well, I s'pose Seth is right."

"Who?"

"Seth Langford. My brother-in-law. He says it's time to give up trying."

"Mr. Langford is an astute man."

"He's a what?"

"He's bright."

———

"This one just arrived," Noelle told Mrs. Sway on Friday morning as they both looked over the copy of George Eliot's *Middlemarch*. "So you would be the first in Gresham to read it."

The greengrocer's wife dimpled happily. "I would?"

"Unless someone has purchased one from Shrewsbury. But still, you would have read the first *library* copy."

When the woman was gone with the novel cradled in her arms, Noelle sat back down at her desk and picked up the scissors she had borrowed from Mrs. Beemish. Yesterday she had *tsked* at a book returned with two dog-eared pages and wondered if the squire would provide a lettered placard requesting that patrons use bookmarkers. But then an idea occurred to her—wouldn't supplying the markers be more effective? One inserted in each book, showing only fractionally above the pages so as not to make them look untidy in their rows on the shelves. The notion had so excited her that she hurried to *Trumbles* on her way back to the *Larkspur* for lunch and bought a package of colored paper with her own money.

She had just cut out a row of green rectangles when the door opened and Quetin Paxton walked in. He wore a suit of fawn-colored cashmere and carried a silver-tipped ebony cane in one of his gloved hands. Stopping halfway across to her desk, he removed his silk hat. "So . . . it's true. My little rattlebrain has joined the proletariat!"

"Quetin?" Noelle gasped when she found her voice.

"Hello, Noelle."

"How did you know I was here?"

"A housemaid at that inn where you've been staying was obliging enough to tell me. I'm here to take you home, Noelle."

But I'm already home. However she could not stop herself from asking, "What happened to Meara?"

He did not even bother to deny his association with her or to appear surprised that Noelle knew about it. "I got tired of her lifting money from me every time my back was turned." A rakish grin came to his face. "I've your jewelry in the strongbox of the coach. And if we hurry, we can just catch the eleven o'clock to London."

"I'm happy here," she told him flatly, setting down the scissors lest her shaking hands cause herself injury.

"Yes? Well, I have to take a little trip to Paris next week. I hate the thought of traveling alone."

"Paris?"

Making a sweeping gesture with his cane, he said, "But if you're happy here . . ."

Here, she thought, surveying the aged room around her. For the privilege of lodging with servants, she sat in a hut and cut bits of colored paper for dairymen and factory workers who did not understand how to take care of other people's property. What insanity had caused her to think she was happy?

"I'm even considering getting you a larger flat."

His smile was smug—he knew that he had won. And so did Noelle, for she pushed out her chair. He did not move but waited for her to come around the desk to him. There was security in the arms that embraced her, and she relished in it.

"We must hurry," he said after they kissed.

She went with him out to the waiting hired coach, not asking about her belongings. They could be sent for later—she didn't want to face anyone at the *Larkspur*. In fact, as the team of four horses carried them past the inn, she kept her eyes fixed on Quetin's face so that she would not see it. He draped an arm around her shoulders and kept her mind occupied with witty gossip about mutual acquaintances in London. Incidentally he announced that Averyl had decided to move back to the country.

There was a time when such news would have delighted her, but she felt a strange dearth of emotion over it. When they reached the outskirts of Shrewsbury, she became aware of a queasiness in the pit of her stomach. She attributed it to the bumpiness of the road and paid closer attention to Quetin's narrative. By the time they reached the railway station, waves of nausea were rolling through her.

"Is something wrong?" he asked when she hesitated taking the hand he held out to assist her from the coach.

"I just need to walk a bit," she replied.

"Very well. The train is unloading now anyway."

But she felt even worse as they walked on the platform, his arm around her waist to support her while she leaned against his shoulder. She had only been able to shut God and her friends—her only true friends—out of her mind for so long. All she could think about was how hurt they would be when they discovered she had betrayed their trust.

"We can board now," Quetin told her as a sharp whistle pierced the air.

She wound herself out of his embrace and turned to look at him. Had she never noticed the shadows and lines under his self-satisfied eyes? "No."

Quirking an eyebrow, he said, "I beg your pardon?"

"I'm not going with you."

He opened his mouth as if to argue but then closed it and shrugged. "Very well."

Without looking back he walked toward a first-class compartment. He paused at the door, his stance telling Noelle he was expecting her to reconsider and join him any second. *You poor miserable man*, she thought.

Just then she felt a touch upon her shoulder.

"Miss Somerville?"

Noelle turned and gaped at the startled face of Miss Rawlins. It was all she could do to keep from wrapping her arms around her. "Miss Rawlins! I'm so glad to see you!"

"Thank you," the writer replied, her gray eyes bemused behind the spectacles. "What are you doing here?"

"Wishing I were still at my desk." *Please, Father, don't let me have ruined everything!* What would the Bartleys think about her abandoning her post? She remembered then that Miss Rawlins had been in London for most of the week. Noelle's knees went weak with relief. "Are you on your way back to Gresham?"

"Why, yes. Mr. Herrick should be waiting for me. Would you care for a ride?"

"Yes, please!" Noelle told her. Perhaps if she showed up well before the close of day, the Bartleys would forgive her this time. Linking arms with the writer, she did not look again at the train carrying Quetin back to London.

*T*he leather sheath encompassing the blade had blackened and hardened, and Jacob knew he should not attempt to pull the dagger from it. But for the whole two hours that he worked to get it from the ground intact, an indescribable confidence had overtaken him. He wasn't sure how he knew this would be a significant find—he just knew.

"What have you there?" Mr. Ellis asked, walking toward him from the north side of the depression, about twenty feet away.

Jacob held it aloft. "A dagger."

"It must be quite a find. Your face is glowing."

"I think this is it."

"You do?" The older man's steps quickened. When he reached Jacob, he stared with an awed expression at the weapon in his hand. Almost reverently he asked, "May I hold it?"

"Of course."

Mr. Ellis cradled it in the crook of one arm as if it were an infant. With his index finger he wiped away some of the dirt dulling one of several gemstones fixed into the gold handle. "It appears more ceremonial than practical, doesn't it?"

"I wish we could pull it from the case. If it's ceremonial there ought to be an inscription on the blade."

A glint came to Mr. Ellis's eyes but then disappeared. "You know that's not procedure."

"I know," Jacob told him, frowning. "I just hate the thought of having to wait weeks to find out."

"*And* allowing some museum archeologist, who hasn't gotten dirt under his fingernails for years, the first peek at it," Mr. Ellis added with a grim nod.

"Aren't there times when we're allowed to break procedure?"

"Only when the senior associate deems it necessary. But I've never found it necessary to break procedure."

"Never?"

"Not in all my thirty-five years of field study."

Jacob sighed. He had lived his life trying to abide by the rules set before him. Just for once he wished he could be reckless and even defiant. "I suppose you're ri—"

"So I declare it's long overdue, don't you?" Mr. Ellis cut in with an almost wild expression. Before Jacob could speak, the elderly man grabbed the dagger by the handle. There was a crackling sound, and then the golden blade glinted in the sunlight. A hush fell over the two as they put their heads together. Latin words were indeed etched into the metal.

"You'll have to read them, Mr. Pitney," the older man said, handing it over.

Holding his breath, Jacob studied the inscription. He then looked up at Mr. Ellis and smiled. "It was a gift from Vespasian." Which enhanced the value of the find, for Vespasian was Emperor of Rome from A.D. 69 to 79, including the four years Cerealis served as Governor of Britain.

"You say! Incredible! But to whom?"

"Would you care to guess?"

Mr. Ellis put a hand up to his chest. "General Cerealis?"

"General Cerealis," Jacob echoed with a grin.

Letting out a whoop of joy, the older man pounded him on the arm. "I've hoped all my life for a find like this! Just wait until my wife hears—"

But the older man then froze and looked at him with a crestfallen expression. "Oh. Forgive me, Mr. Pitney. The credit will go to you, of course."

Jacob shook his head. "To *us*, Mr. Ellis."

"But you pulled it from the ground."

"And you pulled it from its sheath. We started this together. It could have just as easily been you working this particular spot."

"Are you quite sure?"

"I insist upon it."

Mr. Ellis smiled at him. "Thank you, Mr. Pitney. We've made quite a team, haven't we?"

"Absolutely." Glancing toward the east, in which direction the town lay, Jacob said, "You know, we should put this away at once. Don't you think?"

"I do indeed." The older man's smile grew wider. "And I suspect you can't wait to show a particular young woman."

Again Jacob felt his face flush. But he grinned sheepishly and said, "I'll hurry."

"Take your time, Mr. Pitney. I suspect I'll be singing for joy once you're out of earshot."

With a laugh Jacob replaced the dagger into its sheath and secured it in his coat pocket. He hurried down the footpath, sending small rocks tumbling. His pace did not slow up until he was standing on the stoop of the Clark cottage.

Mrs. Tanner answered his knock. "Hello, Mr. Pitney," she said, wiping her hands upon her gingham apron. "Are you looking for Miss Clark?"

"Yes, please." He automatically glanced over the cook's shoulder. He couldn't wait to see the expression on Miss Clark's face when he told her his news. "Is she here?"

"Why, no. The mister and missus are taking her to Shrewsbury to catch the train to Glasgow."

His heart lurched in his chest. Stupidly Jacob echoed, though he had heard her, "To Glasgow?"

"Well, she'll have to switch trains in Birmingham, you understand."

"Do you know what time her train leaves?"

The cook shrugged. "They left here an hour or so ago. But they're to have lunch at one o' those inns as a farewell, so it ain't likely—"

"Thank you!" Jacob called over his shoulder, already halfway to the steps. *Not Glasgow!* raced through his mind as his boots pounded against cobbled stones. His mind had been so preoccupied over the past two weeks with mourning Miss Rawlins' disaffection that he had not given Miss Clark much thought. How foolish, because now he couldn't imagine Gresham without her!

"Where are ye going in such a hurry, Mr. Pitney?" queried a grating voice from his right as he neared the *Larkspur*'s carriage drive.

"Sorry!" he called back to the lace spinners without slowing down enough even to look at them.

Mildred, the kitchen maid, stood at the edge of the courtyard, throwing a pan of potato peelings out into the shrubberies for the birds. "Mr. Pitney?" she said with eyes round.

"Is Mr. Herrick inside?"

"No, sir. He's down to Shrewsbury, collecting Miss Rawlins."

"Collecting Miss Rawlins?"

"Why, yes, sir. She's been in London."

How could he have forgotten, when he had had to force himself all week not to stare morbidly at her empty dining room chair? But that didn't seem to matter now. Quickly he asked, "Did he use both horses?"

She sent a pointed stare into the direction of the empty paddock before replying, "I expect so, Mr. Pitney."

Jacob went weak in the knees, but this was no time to give into any weakness. He turned and sprinted down the carriage drive. From across the lane one of the lace spinners asked in a more pleasant voice, "Why are you hurrying so, Mr. Pitney?"

"Sorry!"

Fortunately a groomsman was in the stable behind the *Bow and Fiddle*, currying a rust-colored hunter. "Have you a saddle for that horse?" Jacob asked between pants of breath.

Greed washed across the young man's scarred face. "My uncle charges half-a-crown."

"Have him saddled in less than five minutes, and I'll give you double!"

" . . . and so I said to Mr. Wakely and his colleagues, 'With all due respect, you may be shrewd at conducting business, but for you to suggest that my stories are too similar tells me that you're ill-informed about the expectations of readers . . .' "

Sharing a seat with Miss Rawlins in the landau, Noelle nodded absently. The first farms were appearing on the southern outskirts of Gresham. Would she still have a position when she returned to the lending library? *Please, Father . . . one more chance.*

" . . . and he had the *cheek* to declare that if I couldn't display a little more originality in the future, my manuscripts would no longer be . . .'"

"Who is that coming?" Noelle interrupted, craning her neck to the right so she could see past Mr. Herrick. A horse pounded the lane before them, raising a cloud of dust behind. She heard a gasp beside her and turned to look at Miss Rawlins.

"Why, it's Jacob!" the writer exclaimed as she scooted to the edge of her seat.

"Mr. Pitney?"

Miss Rawlins' hand flew up to her heart. "And to think I accused him of not being romantic!"

Noelle turned again to the front. The man rode low in the saddle as if trying to win the Derby. Even in the distance his dark eyes seemed intent, almost blazing. "You mean he's coming for you?"

"Why else would he be flying off to Shrewsbury on horseback?"

That seemed reasonable to Noelle, considering how despondent the archeologist had seemed at the supper table all week. "I wonder why he's not slowing down?"

"He must not have seen me yet." Lips curved into a demure smile, Miss Rawlins sat up even straighter, so that she was almost standing in the moving carriage. Her smile froze in place as she swiveled her head to watch the horse gallop by. "Jacob?" she called, but not loudly enough for him to hear over the thundering hoofbeats.

"You may be right, you know," Noelle said when the carriage was turning into *Larkspur*'s drive. "He didn't even look our way."

The writer, who had sat in silence since Mr. Pitney passed, angled her head thoughtfully. "But of course, Miss Somerville. He was so driven by love to reach the railway station that he fell almost into a trance, his senses unable to absorb anything else." Her expression brightening, she added, "What a wonderful scene that would make! I'll show that Mr. Wakely that I can create fresh pl—"

"Good for you!" Noelle cut in, already halfway out of the landau before it rolled to a complete stop. "Thank you!" she called up to the driver's seat, where Mr. Herrick was tying the reins. She was almost at the end of the carriage drive when it occurred to her that she could have gone around the north wing, or even asked the caretaker to drive her to the library. But like Mr. Pitney, she was unable to turn away from her set path, even to save a minute or two.

"Where are you going in such a hurry, Miss Somerville?" Iris Worthy called from across the lane.

Noelle sent the two women a wave and rushed on toward the crossroads. "Sorry!"

Behind her back she heard Jewel's grating voice. "That's the trouble wi' young folk today. No time to stop and chat."

Not when your life is falling apart, Noelle thought. Presently she spotted a familiar chimney in the distance on Market Lane. A stab of pain found her heart. To think she had been so eager to give it up less than two hours ago! The lending library was not just a place of employment. It was a symbol. Every time the cottage came into her sight, she was reminded that it was her own God-given ability which provided a roof over her head and food on her plate. The confidence that came from performing her job well brought her more fulfillment than being a wealthy man's ornament ever had.

But when she grew closer, the pain in her heart welled to a terrible foreboding. Outside the library sat the squire's barouche and team. The young man clothed in livery at the reins sent her a smile that she was too despondent to return. She went on to the stoop and opened the door. At her desk sat Mrs. Bartley, speaking with a young woman Noelle recognized as a serving maid at the *Bow and Fiddle*.

"Ah, Miss Somerville, there you are!" The squire's wife spoke pleasantly enough, but the blue eyes were sharp, appraising. "Miss Sloane here is seeking *Wuthering Heights*, but we weren't able to locate it."

"That's because it was checked out last Wednesday," Noelle told Miss Sloane, mustering the smile she had not had for the driver outside. "But I'll be happy to hold it and post you a card when it's returned."

The young woman expressed satisfaction with that and left. And then Mrs. Bartley pushed out the chair, got to her feet, and walked around the desk. "Would you care to explain your absence from your post before the lunch hour, Miss Somerville?"

Years of taking liberty with the truth provided Noelle with a ready answer. *Tell her you became ill and had to lie down for a little while*. But the temptation was short-lived. Hanging her head, she replied, "I almost did a terrible thing, Mrs. Bartley."

"You're referring to the gentleman with whom you left in the coach?"

Noelle's chin shot up. "How did you—?"

"Surely you've lived in Gresham long enough to know the answer to that, Miss Somerville. I came to inform you that the rug for the reading room will be delivered Monday. And Mrs. Perkins happened to be out tending her garden. . . ."

"I see."

"And where is the gentleman now?"

"He was no gentleman, Mrs. Bartley," Noelle murmured, shame heating her cheeks. "And he's on his way back to London now. Hopefully to return to his wife."

A slight widening of the eyes was Mrs. Bartley's only reaction. After a short space of silence, she asked, "Does that mean today's episode will not be repeated?"

Noelle shuddered. "God help me, never."

"Very well, then. We'll forget this ever happened."

"Thank you!" Noelle gushed. It took all her self-control to keep from bursting into tears of relief.

Finally the woman smiled. "The squire and I are most impressed with your work, Miss Somerville. We would hate to lose you."

"My loss would be greater, Mrs. Bartley," Noelle assured her.

THE DOWRY OF MISS LYDIA CLARK   *Chapter 45*

*I*f you ask me, Mrs. Tanner's roast grouse is far superior," Lydia's father said as Wellington and Nelson pulled the wagon up Pride Hill toward the railway station after lunch at the *Lion Inn*. There was no room for Lydia on the seat with her parents, so she sat directly behind them on her trunk, which, thankfully, Noah had come over to help load.

"Well, don't go telling her that," Mother warned. "Or the next time you provoke her, she'll be down here asking to hire on."

"Provoke her? When have I ever—?"

Lydia smiled at their banter, but her heart was not merry. *This wasn't a good idea*, she told herself again. Saint Margaret's and Glasgow were her old life. While she would enjoy renewing some of her former acquaintances, exchanging letters would have sufficed. She now feared that absenting herself from any sight of Mr. Pitney would have the opposite effect than the one for which she hoped. Instead of forgetting him, what if she spent the whole seven weeks pathetically brooding over him? *You waited too long to fall in love*, she told herself. *You have a schoolgirl's heart in a thirty-four-year-old body.*

She was so lost in thought that she didn't realize they had arrived at the railway station until the wagon came to a halt on the side of the street. There was a bustle of activity about them as porters unloaded trunks from carriages and wagons and people hurried toward the station for the train presently loading. With a sigh, she stood. Her train was not even due to arrive until half-past one, an hour away. But she still needed to hurry to find a porter before her father got impatient and took a notion to carry the trunk to the platform himself. She became aware then of approaching hoofbeats.

"Someone's about to miss his train," her father pointed out, lighting his pipe.

Her mother sent a worried look up the street, in spite of the fact that the rider was more than likely a total stranger. "I do hope he makes it."

The horse, a rust-colored hunter, only slowed its pace a little to weave

370

around vehicles in the busy street. Lydia's breath caught in her throat as the rider's face became achingly familiar. "It's Mr. Pitney."

"Mr. Pitney?" her parents said in unison.

"Why, it is!" her father exclaimed, rising in the seat. "But what—?"

"Miss Rawlins must be returning from a trip." Come to think of it, Lydia had noticed Mr. Pitney walking home from church alone on Sunday past, but she had just assumed the writer was ill. She prepared to inform the archeologist as he reined the sweating animal to a halt just inches from the wagon bed that she had not seen Miss Rawlins. But he spoke before she could do so.

"Miss Clark—please don't go to Glasgow!"

Lydia blinked. "I beg your pardon?"

He seemed almost maniacal, his dark eyes wild and his hair tousled about his head. The horse, not settled down from its run, stamped and snorted so that Mr. Pitney had to keep the reins taut to keep the animal close to the wagon.

"We found Cerealis's artifact, and you were the first person I wanted to tell. It looks as if we'll be assigned to Gresham for years to come, and I . . ."

It was only then that he appeared to notice her parents, who were turned to face him, for he automatically reached up as if to tip a hat that was probably lying on the side of the road somewhere.

"Good afternoon, Mr. Pitney," Lydia's mother said.

"Good afternoon, Mr. and Mrs. Clark," he said as the old bashfulness overtook his expression. Nonetheless he looked at Lydia again. "And I can't bear the thought of you not being here, Miss Clark."

But I'm only going away for a visit, Lydia started to explain. Her father spoke before she could open her mouth.

"What exactly are you saying, Mr. Pitney? That you want her to come back so you can take some more of those reading lessons from her and impress that writer woman?"

"No, sir!" Mr. Pitney exclaimed with a shake of his head. The motion caused the restless horse to rear a bit, so he swung down from the saddle and, with the reins in one hand, approached the wagon on foot. His dark eyes looked earnestly up at Lydia. "I would like you to come back because . . ."

"Yes, Mr. Pitney?" Lydia said when he hesitated.

"Yes, Mr. Pitney?" her mother echoed.

Resolve replaced the timidity in his expression. "Because I can think of no greater joy than coming home to a cottage every day with you waiting for me, Miss Clark."

Suddenly Lydia felt the need to sit back down. Her mind simply needed time to register everything that had occurred within the past two minutes, so all she could think of to say was, "You found the artifact?"

Looking down to fuss with his coat pocket, he said. "Thank God it didn't bounce out on the way here."

"I didn't realize you could ride, Mr. Pitney," Lydia's mother told him.

He looked up to send her a sheepish grin. "I didn't either, Mrs. Clark."

And then he held out what appeared to be a dagger. He withdrew it from the aged sheath so that Lydia could see the inscription on the blade. "To Governor Cerealis from Vespasian," he explained.

Fearful that she would somehow damage the artifact, even when centuries in the ground had not done so, she took it carefully from his hands. "Incredible," she breathed, turning to show her parents.

"Incredible," her mother echoed.

Her father cocked his head at Mr. Pitney. "You know, after we find that horse some water, we could tie him to the back so you can ride in the wagon with us." He gave Lydia a hint of a smile. "That is, if our daughter is willin' to return."

"Will you, Lydia?" Mr. Pitney asked.

It was the first time he had ever addressed her by her given name, and it warmed her heart. But she had to know one thing. "What about Miss Rawlins?"

"Yes, what about Miss Rawlins?" her mother repeated.

"I wish her well," he replied frankly. His hands closed over the top slat of the wagon's side. "But I was a fool to think that I loved her. And it's you who has found a place in my heart. Please say you'll marry me, Lydia Clark. We've both been alone for too long."

"We have," she agreed, her heart about to burst as she fought tears. "And I will . . . Jacob."

There was a rustling sound in front. Her father began helping her mother from the wagon seat. "Should be a water trough nearabouts," he explained. "We'll look about for a little while."

"May I sit with you?" Jacob asked when they were gone.

"Of course," Lydia replied.

He tied the horse's reins to the back, put a foot in a wheel spoke, and swung himself easily into the wagon. A little of his old shyness seemed to come over him as he approached Lydia, but she smiled and moved aside on the trunk.

"It seems there should be a cat napping between us," he said as he sat next to her.

She smiled and handed him the dagger. "I'm very happy for you."

Holding it across both palms, he said, "Just think, Lydia . . . when Vespasian awarded this to Cerealis, little did he know he would be aiding a romance centuries later." He looked again at her and raised an eyebrow. "We do have a romance, haven't we?"

She nodded. "It appears so."

"Do you find me romantic, Lydia? Even if I don't care for poetry?"

"I think you're incredibly romantic, Jacob."

"Not as romantic as you are. You're the most beautiful woman I've ever met."

She opened her mouth to protest that he didn't have to say such things, that he had already won her heart, but then the devotion in his brown eyes told her that he did indeed behold some beauty in her that she had missed all these years. The tears that had threatened earlier filled her eyes.

"Have I said something wrong?" he asked with brows furrowed.

She sniffed and shook her head. "But I don't seem to have a hand-kerchief."

With a chuckle he dug into his waistcoat pocket. "Isn't this how we got started?"

When she had composed herself, Jacob put away the dagger and held her hand. Lydia appreciated that he was too bashful to kiss her in front of the travelers and porters and people with other business at the station who occasionally sent curious stares their way. She didn't want her first kiss to be a public spectacle. Her parents returned, and after all three horses were watered, Lydia sat with him holding her hand all the way back to Gresham.

He helped her father carry the trunk back into the cottage, this time setting it in the upstairs corridor. As they were betrothed—or at least Lydia *thought* that was what had transpired in front of the station—it wasn't fitting that he should go inside her room. And then he said apologetically that he would have to hurry back to work.

It did happen, didn't it? Lydia asked herself as she accompanied him downstairs. Her parents had bade Jacob good-day and declared their intentions to catch up with some reading. At the door, he turned to smile at her and reached into his coat pocket.

"I was supposed to bring this to the *Larkspur*, but I really must get back up the hill. Would you mind keeping this for me until this evening?"

"This evening, Jacob?" she asked, returning his smile as she took the dagger from his hand. *Yes, it did happen.*

"Why, yes. We should make plans . . . set a date, shouldn't we?" Faint worry came into his brown eyes. "You do recall agreeing to marry me, don't you?"

"I do. Why don't you come in time for supper?"

"I'll be here."

Taking the dagger from her hand, he set it down on the entrance table. He then stepped closer to take her elbows lightly with both hands. Lydia closed her eyes and raised her chin slightly. The kiss was sweet and tender, but with a hint of the passion she suspected had always been hidden under his unassuming exterior. When he was gone, Lydia turned and leaned back against the wall until the spell of light-headedness could pass. Jeanie padded into the room from the back, meowing curiously.

"Thank you for having the decency to wait," Lydia murmured as she scooped the cat up into her arms. Closing her eyes, she said under her breath, *And thank you for answering my prayer, Father.*

From upstairs a voice boomed. "Ly-di-a! Is Mr. Pitney gone?"

She opened her eyes and smirked at the cat. "He is, Papa!"

"Have you seen my—"

"Yes, Papa!" She returned to the entrance table, where the pipe lay next to Governor Cerealis' dagger. *And thank you for men who leave things lying about in the wrong places.*

Mr. Ellis looked relieved to see Jacob. "I was beginning to worry you'd taken a tumble downhill," he said. "Like poor Jack in the nursery rhymes."

"Forgive me." Jacob was truly contrite, despite the fact that he had worn a smile all the way up the hill. "I didn't intend to be gone so long."

"It occurred to me after you sprinted out of here that Miss Rawlins has been away all week. Has she returned, then?"

Miss Rawlins? Jacob seemed to recall seeing her somewhere. Or was that last week? "I'm not sure," was his reply.

Scratching his graying beard, the senior associate looked puzzled. "But wasn't she the reason you left?"

Jacob shook his head. "I went to see Miss Clark. Only she was in Shrewsbury, so I had to go there."

"You mean the schoolmistress?"

"Yes. I've asked her to marry me."

Mr. Ellis's eyes blinked with incredulity. "Pardon my saying so, Mr. Pitney, but it's not like you to act so rashly. Shouldn't you have waited a bit to be sure?"

"I'm already sure," Jacob assured him, his smile returning. "And I've waited for her all my life."

On Sunday morning, for the first time in his life, Harold Sanders talked to God. He did so while riding Bob toward Saint Jude's. There was no sense in bringing the wagon, as he knew better than to offer Mrs. Meeks and the children a ride home. But he hoped Mrs. Meeks wouldn't take offense at his attending church—and actually going inside this time.

And that was where God came in. "Since you're supposed to know everything, you know I'm only doin' this in the hopes that she'll think more kindly toward me," he said softly so that if any unchurched folk were in their gardens, they wouldn't think he had gone mad. Because he spoke aloud and his eyes weren't closed, he didn't know if he should consider himself actually *praying*.

"It's not that I got anything against you—even if you did take my mother. And bein' around good folk like Mrs. Meeks and Miss Clark and Mercy and Seth makes me think that I'd like to be a believer one day too."

But it wasn't right to become one just to win the heart of a woman. Even Mercy had told him that. And he did want to win Mrs. Meeks' heart in the worst way. Even more than he wanted a big farm of his own. If she would have him, he would work his back off to make her little farm provide a decent living for her and the children. Tears stung his eyes just thinking about it.

What he was asking of God was to give him a sign if it was also wrong to attend church for the same reason. "Just give me a sneezing fit or a headache when I get to the door if you don't want me to go through it," he prayed, then added, "Please, sir." He wouldn't be any good to Mrs. Meeks and her children in the future if he was struck with some terrible ailment as punishment for going inside.

He tethered Bob to a post outside the town hall. Vicar Phelps stood in the doorway of Saint Jude's, greeting folks as they arrived. Harold straightened the collar of his tweed coat. His steps slowed as he drew closer to the door. No inclination to sneeze yet, nor did his head feel poorly.

"Mr. Sanders? Is that you?"

With a nod to the vicar, Harold walked over to where he stood. He smiled weakly as his hand was seized.

"I've been told that you've been attending, but I've never been able to see you for some reason," Vicar Phelps said, smiling.

Harold lowered his eyes. God had not shown any sign that he shouldn't go inside, but surely it was terribly wrong to do so with a lie resting on his shoulders. "I never went in," he mumbled.

"Is that so?" the vicar said. But then he smiled again. "Well, that makes me even move grateful to see you here today."

"Thank you." And having had enough chat at the church door for one day, Harold nodded politely, withdrew his hand that the vicar had forgotten to let go of, and walked on inside. Only two people, a man and woman, occupied the very last pew on his left, and they smiled and moved down so that he would have a place to sit.

It seemed the church was nearly filled. While a woman he did not recognize played the piano softly, and Mr. Fletcher the violin, most people sat in respectful silence. In a loftlike section facing everyone else, men, women, and even some older children were rustling pages of books. A few minutes later a hush fell over the whole church as Vicar Phelps walked toward the front. People rose to their feet, and Harold did the same. The people in the loft stood with those same books open in their hands and began singing something that started with the words, "Holy, holy, holy." It was a fine song, Harold thought, as goosepricks tingled his arms.

After Vicar Phelps prayed, the whole congregation took up hymnals and sang "O Word of God Incarnate." He finally felt at ease enough to glance around at the people about him. Across the aisle and three rows up, Miss Clark stood with her mother and papa and the younger of the archeology men from the *Larkspur*. Now he understood why she hadn't wanted to court him. But it didn't matter anymore, and he was even glad she wouldn't be lonely. Loneliness was a terrible thing.

The corner of his left eye caught some motion, and he looked directly in front of him. At first he recognized no familiar backs of heads or bonnets. But through a gap between worshipers, he spotted a grinning Lester Meeks waving at him from about five rows ahead. His mother leaned over to touch his shoulder, and the boy whispered something to her. With a puzzled face she turned and scanned the row of faces before her eyes met Harold's. He was afraid she would show some sign of anger, but she smiled warmly.

Thank you, God, Harold prayed before he remembered he wasn't supposed to.

Chapter 46

*O*n a Wednesday morning one month later, Paul Treves knocked on the vicarage door behind Saint Jude's. Vicar Phelps himself answered within seconds and greeted him with a smiling, "Good morning!"

Paul returned the greeting, noticing the vicar's black suit and hat in his hand. "Do forgive me. Were you about to make calls?"

"None that won't keep." His older friend stepped back from the door and hung his hat on the stand. "Come in, Paul. I'll be glad for the company. Shall I ask Dora to bring us some tea?"

"I had two cups before riding over. It's certainly quiet in here," Paul remarked as they walked into the parlor. Right away he added, "Not that it's ever too noisy, mind you."

"Oh, but Julia would disagree at times. Philip is spending a fortnight in Birmingham with Gabriel Patterson, a friend he met back in boarding school. And Julia and the girls are in Shrewsbury, shopping for a carriage."

"I beg your pardon?"

The older man laughed. "A baby carriage. Did I not tell you that Elizabeth is expecting?"

"No, sir," Paul replied. He was a little astonished and quite relieved that the news did not cause him any sorrow. Indeed, he felt happy for the Raleighs. "I remember how good she was with little Molly and David. She'll make a wonderful mother."

"That's good of you to say, Paul."

"It's good to be able to say it . . . and mean it."

Vicar Phelps smiled. "I knew you would be able to one day."

They chatted then, of news of the diocese, sermons they were in the process of writing, and other ministry-related topics. But as much as he enjoyed talking over these things with his mentor, that wasn't the reason Paul had knocked at his door. And the longer he sat there and delayed mentioning the matter on his heart, the more anxious he was becoming. So during a pause in conversation, he took the leap and bared his soul to one of the few people he trusted to handle it with care.

"I came to ask your counsel, Vicar," Paul began.

The older man nodded somberly, sitting back in his chair. "About Miss Somerville, I trust?"

"How did you know?"

"Just a guess, actually. But it has troubled me for weeks, the look on your face when I told you the truth about her. I suspect you cared for her more deeply than I imagined."

"More deeply than *I* imagined as well," Paul told him. He did not know Miss Somerville well enough to consider himself in love with her. Quality love, such as what his parents and the Phelps enjoyed, took time. All he knew was that over the past month he had thought about her often, in spite of his efforts not to do so. She had repented and turned her life around, according to Vicar Phelps. Paul was to the point where he believed he could forget about her past sins. But would he be acting wisely by attempting to see her again?

He voiced the question to Vicar Phelps, who replied, "It all depends upon you, Paul. We have to assume that if you begin seeing her again, it could lead to courtship and perhaps even marriage, if she feels the same way. But can you forgive her past?"

"Don't you mean *forget* her past?"

His friend shook his head. "While God can and does forget, and it's noble for you to attempt to do so, I don't believe it's possible for a man to totally expunge such a thing from his mind. What I'm asking is if you can forgive what she did."

"But it's not my place to forgive sins that weren't committed against me," Paul responded, perplexed. "She didn't even know me back then."

"If you should happen to marry Miss Somerville one day, then they will have been committed against you. As well as herself and God, of course." Vicar Phelps's hazel eyes were serious, almost grave. "Our sins all too often affect the people in our futures. The woman who frivolously marries a drunkard sins against the children she will bear one day, who will suffer having him as a father. The man who gambles away his inheritance steals from his unborn children, who will grow up in poverty."

"What will she have taken from me?"

"Total peace of mind, Paul. There will be times when you will have to struggle not to think about what she has done. And if you have not forgiven her completely, it will cause a breach between you that can only widen over time and possibly break your family apart."

Paul nodded understanding. He had been in the ministry long enough to discover that most people's unhappiness was a result of seeds planted years earlier. Above anything else on earth, he wanted a home one day

378

filled with harmony and love. "Have you ever witnessed a successful marriage in such a case? Where one partner has had to forgive the other for something of that nature committed in the past?"

"Yes," Vicar Phelps replied, smiling warmly. "And that family is a joyous sight to behold. But I will offer you the same counsel I gave to one of the partners—in this case, the young woman—before they married."

"Please do."

"Repentance is only the first step on a spiritual journey. It is not wise to assume that the person who has turned abruptly from his or her sin has immediately become a mature Christian."

"Of course," Paul agreed. He too had witnessed short-lived *rededications*.

"Then I would advise you to give Miss Somerville a little time to grow spiritually before you consider courting her. For her sake as well as yours. Your courtship will be on a more solid foundation, and you won't have given away your heart prematurely."

That made perfect sense, but Paul couldn't help but feel a twinge of disappointment. Yet he had not sought counsel just to ignore it if it didn't suit him exactly. "I'll do that," he promised.

"Very good." Vicar Phelps glanced at the clock on the chimneypiece. "It's almost ten. This would be a good time to pay her a call at the library. I think you'll be pleasantly surprised."

"But you said . . ."

"I didn't say you shouldn't be friends, Paul. Julia and I were friends before we began courting. You don't want Miss Somerville to forget who you are *while* she's growing spiritually, do you?"

———

In the back room, Noelle read aloud the last page of *The Story of Little Sarah and Her Johnny-cake* to the three women in chairs—one holding a baby—and seven children seated cross-legged on the rug of a rich sapphire blue:

> *The ploughman he ploughed, and the grain it was sown,*
> *And the sun shed his rays till the corn was all grown;*
> *It was ground at the mill, and again in her bed*
> *These words to young Sarah the grandmother said:*
> *"You shall get me a Johnny-cake—quickly go make it;*
> *In one minute mix, and in two minutes bake it."*

Holding up the final page, Noelle allowed her small audience a look at the picture. "And so now Sarah finally has all she needs to bake her grandmother's cake," she told them.

"The story don't say nothin' about eggs," Mrs. Kerns, a cheese factory worker's wife wearing a faded yellow calico, said in a worried tone as she jiggled her baby boy lightly on her knee to keep him from fussing. "She won't be able to bake a decent Johnny-cake without eggs."

"Mayhap she keeps chickens," Mrs. Draper, whose husband worked on a dairy farm, offered as the children began getting to their feet.

Her six-year-old son asked Noelle through two missing front teeth, "Will you read the one about the bluebird again, Miss Somerville?"

Mrs. Draper shushed the boy, but Noelle smiled and put a hand up to her throat. "I'm afraid story time is over, James. I have to save some voice for next week. But you may bring it home with you if you like."

With an eager face he turned to his mother. "Not this time," she said with a shake of her head.

"We have a new policy," Noelle mentioned casually, so as not to embarrass any of the women. "One storybook per child may be checked out at no charge. If you return it within the week, you may choose another and so on."

It had taken all her reasoning abilities to talk the squire into that one. "But subscriptions are necessary to keep the library self-supporting," he had argued. "And we already have the lowest rate in the county."

Noelle's point of view was that very few children's books were checked out anyway, so the loss would be minimal. Most people with means purchased books for their children and handed them down among siblings. And while those with limited means were willing to invest a half-farthing for a thick novel, they considered it wasteful to spend it on a picture book that could be read in a half hour. It was a shame to have such a wonderful children's collection sitting mostly undisturbed upon a shelf. Books were no good to anyone unless they were read.

The Wednesday morning story hour was another of her ideas. Illiterate adults who normally would be too intimidated to step foot into a library— such as the three women present—needed an incentive to encourage reading in their children. Mr. Jones had spread word as he delivered mail, and today's meeting, the second, had double the attendance of the first.

Noelle had no idea where this passion to promote reading in Gresham came from. She still found it difficult to settle her busy mind long enough to become absorbed in a novel. Yet she did enjoy telling stories to her little group, watching their eyes grow large at times, such as when Jack's giant searched for him, and hearing their giggles when Old Mother Hubbard's dog danced the jig. Even the mothers had smiled over that one.

As the women lingered in the reading room to chat, and the children looked through the collection of books she had carried in there with her, she excused herself to see if any patrons waited to be assisted in the main room. She started at the sight of the tall man facing her on the other side of the doorway.

"Good morning, Miss Somerville," greeted Vicar Treves, smiling down at her.

Many times over the past month Noelle had wondered how he had taken the news about her past from Vicar Phelps. While she did not think he had it within him to judge her harshly for the past of which she had repented, she was positive he would have no more interest in seeing her socially. As was within his rights, she had also reminded herself several times.

"Vicar Treves," she said with a polite smile. She did not offer her hand, as it would devastate her if he showed some hesitation in taking it.

But his blue eyes were warm. "I hope you don't mind my lurking about in here. I enjoyed hearing you with the children. What a grand idea—using a library to promote reading."

"Why, thank you." The compliment truly surprised her. But why was he here? Surely there was a lending library in Lockwood. The group from the back came chattering into the room, and she excused herself to move over to her desk to check out books for the children.

"We can come again next Wednesday?" Mrs. Kerns asked.

"*Every* Wednesday," Noelle replied, happy for the question. They left presently, the children turning to wave just before walking out onto the stoop. When Noelle turned away from the doorway, Vicar Treves was walking from the back with a chair hooked on one arm.

"You've changed the place a bit since the last time I was here," he remarked, placing the chair facing her desk. "I like the rug." He went around to hers and pulled it from the desk for her. "May we? I won't detain you from your duties for very long."

As she was getting used to sleeping soundly at night, Noelle figured she might as well hear what he had to say instead of worrying herself with speculation. "I'm very surprised you're here," she told him when they were both seated.

"I needed some time to think and pray. You understand, don't you?"

How well she did. Aware that her past misdeeds were on both their minds, shame threatened to well up within her. *My Father has forgiven me*, she reminded herself and quenched the hateful thoughts.

The door opened, and Helen Johnson, the baker's daughter, came for a book Noelle was holding for her. The girl handed her a small bundle in brown paper, and after dipping a quick curtsy to Vicar Treves, she apologized for having only one chocolate strasse inside. "My mother thought you might like a treat before your lunch."

"Please tell her it was very thoughtful."

"I will." Helen looked pleased but still lingered with a preoccupied expression even when the book was in her hand.

"Is there another book you would like to see?" Noelle finally had to ask.

Twisting a dark braid, she replied, "Miss Clark says I have a very good reading voice, with lots of expression. Do you think I could help you on Wednesdays until school starts?"

"Why, I think that's a delightful idea. That way we could take turns, and I could see about the desk every now and then."

"Oh, thank you!" the girl gushed.

When the door closed behind her, Vicar Treves smiled again and said, "I can recall your misgivings about being here when we first met on the train. But you've made a place for yourself in this community, haven't you?"

"They've made a place for me," Noelle said, returning his smile. She asked if he would care to share the pastry.

He shook his head and apologized for staying longer than he had promised. "I'll get to the reason I came so you can enjoy your treat without me staring across at you."

There was affection in his eyes that should have pleased her, for she had shed her prejudice against ministers as husbands and fathers—even if her own parents had yet to write. And she had learned that contentment and peace of mind could make having only a few material belongings seem like great wealth. But everything within her cried that she wasn't ready for a new romance just yet. She was still in the process of discovering things about herself she never knew and talents she never realized she possessed. If she allowed herself to fall in love, she feared that would again become the primary focus of her life.

But how many times could she discourage the man across from her without his losing all interest? She certainly didn't want that to happen. *Father, I don't even know what to pray for.*

"Miss Somerville, I was wondering . . ." he began.

Noelle held her breath. *Just please don't let me ruin everything.*

" . . . do you think we could establish a friendship?"

She blinked. "I beg your pardon?"

"I have feelings for you that refuse to go away. And frankly, I don't want them to. But I've been made to understand that rushing into courtship isn't always wise."

Tension began draining from Noelle's neck and shoulders. "That makes sense."

"It does?" he asked with a surprised expression.

"Yes. I do enjoy your company. And I've never had a close friend who was a male." She made a face. "Actually, until just recently I've had very few female friends."

"This is new for me as well, Miss Somerville," he said with a wry smile. "I've never had a close friend who was a woman."

"I can see we both have a lot to learn. How should we go about this?"

"Well, we could write."

"Letters, you mean?"

He nodded. "You could tell me all about your workdays, and I could tell you about mine. Our thoughts on different subjects, and so on. We really know so little about each other."

"It would be nice to receive some mail for a change," Noelle told him. "I'm the only person at the *Larkspur* who never gets any."

"Do you think I could bring a picnic lunch here every other week or so? We could sit on the stoop during your lunch break."

"Isn't it the woman's place to provide the food?"

"It still would be," he replied with a sheepish expression. "Mrs. Coggins, my cook, indulges me shamefully."

Noelle laughed. "Then I suppose we have all the rules agreed upon." And this time she had no hesitancy in reaching across her desk to offer her hand. "It's settled?"

"Settled," he said. But then he paused thoughtfully, still holding her hand. "But not quite."

"What's wrong?"

"Is it possible that we could address each other by our given names? As long as we're friends?"

"That sounds lovely to me, Paul."

He squeezed her hand gently. "Thank you, Noelle." Then he left as promised. Noelle went to the window and watched him unhitch his horse from the post. He looked up, smiled and waved, and she waved back.

Early the next evening when Noelle arrived at the *Larkspur* from the library, Sarah told her that there was a letter on her writing table. *He certainly doesn't let grass grow under his feet*, she thought on her way upstairs to her attic room. But the envelope was from London and in her mother's script. Noelle sat on her bed and stared at it for a little while before breaking the seal.

It was quite lengthy, filled with news of her siblings, the servants, and some members of the congregation. Only in the last paragraph was it mentioned that, while her parents were overjoyed to learn of her changed lifestyle and did certainly forgive her, it would be best if she waited a while longer before visiting. Memories were still fresh, her mother explained.

Noelle grieved over the letter all during supper and even the next day while at work. It was the *visiting* part that stung the worst. She had not asked for permission to move back with the family, but it would have been nice had the invitation been extended. But when she went up to her room again, she sat down and wrote, thanking them for their forgiveness and assuring them that she understood. *Just tell me when you're ready for me to come for a visit, and I will.*

From the top of her wardrobe she took down her biscuit tin and put her mother's letter in it. *I should ask Mrs. Beemish for another tin, just for Paul's letters*, she thought. The calendar picture caught her eye, and she took it out and touched it lovingly. If she had not found Truesdale, which had only existed in a little girl's imagination anyway, she had found a place very close to it.

"When did you know for certain?" Jacob asked Lydia on Saturday as they finished their lunch atop a flat sandstone boulder. It was a perfect day to be overlooking the village, warm and breezy, with clouds as white as wool dotting the sky.

Lydia's father and Mr. Ellis, trading jokes and stories of old times, had waved them on. Lydia supposed the two wanted to savor as much as possible of the working camaraderie that had developed between them. Next Monday several archeologists from the Archeological Association would be arriving in Gresham to join the excavation. The trips up the hill—and Lydia and her father had taken several over the past month—would likely be curtailed for fear of getting in the way.

"When did I know what?" Lydia asked after swallowing the last bite of a boiled egg.

"You know. How you . . . felt."

Smiling to herself, Lydia marveled that her fiancé could still get flustered when speaking of their relationship. And some mischievous impulse caused her to reply, "About what, Jacob? Parliament?"

"No, about—" He lowered a dark eyebrow suspiciously. "You're doing this on purpose, Lydia. Aren't you?"

"I'm afraid so."

"You are your father's daughter," he chuckled with a shake of his head.

She dabbed at the corner of his mouth with her napkin. "And *you* have mayonnaise on your face."

"Thank you."

"You're welcome." Brushing crumbs from the skirt of her mauve poplin, Lydia discovered herself to be just as flustered. She folded the napkin and tucked it in the corner of the basket for an excuse not to look at his face. "I knew I loved you the day you lent me your handkerchief. I just wasn't aware that I knew."

384

"What do you mean?"

"Well, I'm not sure if I can explain it." She looked up at him. "All I can say is, when I finally realized my feelings, they came as no surprise. It was like waking up with a fever, and then realizing that for the past few days I'd felt out of sorts."

His brown eyes became teasing. "So, in other words, you equate your feelings for me with an illness?"

"Dear me, no. One hopes to recover from an illness."

Jacob's laugh rang out—so loudly that it seemed the villagers below them should cock their heads attentively and smile. "Beauty and wit. I like that in you."

Now Lydia could feel her cheeks grow warm. Looking down at the hands folded in her lap, she replied, "Please don't make sport of me, Jacob."

"And modesty, too, I forgot to add." He gently took her chin and turned her face so they were looking at each other again. With all seriousness he said, "Please stop trying to deny me the pleasure of telling you how beautiful you are, Lydia."

"It's just that it's not so."

"It *is* so, Lydia Clark, soon-to-be Pitney," he said quietly, releasing her chin.

"Very well," she responded to humor him. And then to change the subject, she asked when he was sure of his affection for her.

"The day Mrs. Tanner opened the door and told me you were leaving. I feared I would never see you again."

"I'm glad you found the dagger when you did." Lydia smiled at him. "One day later, and we wouldn't be sitting here together now."

"I would have gone to Glasgow for you."

"You would have?"

"Absolutely. But I'm glad that wasn't necessary." He leaned back upon his arms, looked out upon Gresham, and let out a deep, contented sigh. "This has been a perfect day, Lydia. I'll miss you and your father coming up to join us."

"And I will as well."

"I almost feel as if we should be reciting poetry to each other." He gave an exaggerated shudder. "Almost."

"Never did take a liking to poems," came a familiar paternal voice from behind.

Lydia turned to smile at her father and Mr. Ellis coming to join them.

"Me neither," agreed Mr. Ellis as Jacob handed him the still-heavy lunch basket Mrs. Tanner had sent up with them. The two men waved aside his offer of the boulder and settled upon the grass with creaks of aged knees. "Most are either sickeningly sentimental or depressingly morbid."

"Surely you don't mean that," Lydia protested.

Her father nodded agreement with Mr. Ellis. "Then give us one that isn't, daughter."

"Yes, Lydia," Jacob told her, his eyes merry with challenge. "Give us one that isn't."

"Very well. I'll just need a minute."

"A minute she needs," Mr. Ellis laughed. "Take all the time you wish, Miss Clark. Just bear in mind that we have to leave here at sunset."

The men chuckled at this bit of wit while Lydia pressed her fingers to her temples and mentally sorted through the myriad of poems she had memorized over the years. Suddenly the perfect one came to mind.

"Very well," she said. "I have one that you'll all enjoy."

"No one dies at the end, does he?" Mr. Ellis asked, causing more male chuckles.

"No. At least no human."

Jacob raised an eyebrow. "I beg your pardon?"

With a smile for each, Lydia began.

> *At River Bryce a tortoise bit my toe,*
> *I danced and roared but it would not let go . . .*

Chapter 47

Six months later on the first Saturday afternoon in February, Saint Jude's lone bell broke the snow-numbed stillness of the village. It was the signal for the congregation to don coats and gloves and, with pinkened cheeks and reddened noses showing between the space of cap and muffler, leave their fireplaces for the joyous occasion of a wedding.

Instead of at the open main doorway, Andrew stood to greet people just inside the nave, allowing the vestibule to be a buffer between the warm air of the nave and the frigid air outside. He had asked Julia to stand with him, and so the Phelps family were the first to arrive besides Mr. Sykes, who kept the stove fires going.

"Here, Grace, your locket is facing backward," Julia said, motioning the girl closer. No matter how much time they gave themselves to dress, it always seemed at least one of the children managed to leave the house needing repairs to his or her appearance. She had the girl turned around in front of her and was squinting at the tiny catch on the gold chain when the vestibule door opened. Laurel and Aleda smothered giggles with their hands.

"Girls!" Andrew scolded in a hushed voice. "Remember where you are!"

"But Philip . . ."

"Philip what?" the boy asked, entering and quickly closing the door behind himself.

Julia smiled and even Andrew let out a chuckle, for Philip's auburn hair stuck out in all directions. He put a hand up to his head and frowned. "It's my cap."

"You're just going to have to spit on your hands and smooth it down," Andrew told him.

"Andrew!" Julia said, shocked.

"Well it's either that or go outside and get a handful of snow. He can't walk around looking like a porcupine."

"I'll go back in there," the boy said, heading back toward the vestibule and sending injured looks to all three sisters, for even Grace had joined in the giggling.

The locket straightened, Julia leaned down to brush a fold from the hem of Aleda's green satin gown, her Christmas dress. The girls then went up the aisle to sit in the second pew, today reserving their usual places in the front row for the families of the bride and groom. Philip came back through the doorway, looking much neater and accompanied by Ben Mayhew.

"My family's on their way," the boy explained, his cheeks tinted pink from either the cold or self-consciousness as Andrew shook his hand. "I thought I would come on ahead and get a good seat."

"Very prudent of you," Andrew observed with a nod toward the rows and rows of empty pews.

After sending her husband a quick warning glance, Julia smiled at the boy. "It was good of you to come, Ben. I realize boys your age don't care for weddings."

"I'm actually starting to like them," Ben assured her.

"And we know what that means," Andrew whispered as the two boys moved toward the front. "I don't care for the idea of Ben and Laurel sitting together. It might give them ideas."

"It's too late to do anything about that, Andrew." Apparently the poetry Ben continued to send Laurel had won her heart. At least he was a decent young man, and if they did indeed marry some time in the future, he would make her a fine husband. *But if he moves her across the country, I don't know how I'll manage her father.*

The door opened, and Elizabeth and Jonathan walked through it. "Hello . . . Papa, Julia!" Elizabeth greeted, looking surprisingly robust for having given birth six weeks ago. They exchanged embraces and kisses, and Jonathan surrendered the blanket-wrapped bundle in his arms to Andrew, who cooed down at the face of his grandson, John Andrew Raleigh.

When it was Julia's turn to hold the newborn, the child stared back at her with innocent blue eyes and worked his tiny bow mouth as if to speak to her. She laughed and pressed a kiss against the soft little forehead. *Why didn't anyone tell me how wonderful it is to have a grandchild?* she thought. But other families could be heard entering the vestibule, and she had to give the baby back to Elizabeth.

"Why don't you sit between Laurel and Ben?" Andrew suggested as they started up the aisle.

"I beg your pardon?" Jonathan turned to ask.

Andrew sighed. "Never mind. I might as well try to stop a moving train."

"What train?"

"We'll explain later," Julia told him. She had just enough time before the door opened again to touch her husband's bearded cheek and say, "This is a joyous occasion, Andrew. Let's enjoy it, shall we?"

"Yes, of course," he said, the crinkles she so loved appearing at the corners of his hazel eyes. "I'll do better, I promise."

"I know you will."

They both turned to greet Mrs. Shaw, who went up to the organ with sheet music under her arm and began softly playing Bach's *Mass in B Minor*. The Reeds, Caspers, Mayhews, and Johnsons arrived next, followed by Mr. and Mrs. Trumble. Everyone seemed to have a comment over the likelihood of more snow.

"I noticed some of those nimble-strategic clouds up over the Anwyl," Mr. Trumble told them with a knowing nod. His wife, the former Miss Hillock of the infants' school, simply smiled serenely at Julia, the message in her eyes clear. *He's still a good husband*.

Seth and Mercy Langford arrived with their children, Thomas and baby Amanda. Ever since the squire and Mrs. Bartley's wedding, Mrs. Langford was asked often to sing at weddings and funerals for all denominations in the village.

The Worthy sisters were dressed in their usual Sunday black, but for the special occasion also wore spring bonnets bedecked with gay silk flowers. If they were not quite suitable for February, there was none present who would have the heart to tell them so. In fact, Julia supposed the village sentries could wear flower pots and geraniums upon their heads without causing so much as a snicker.

"Be sure to notice the lace on the bride's veil," Iris Worthy whispered, her arm linked with that of her sister-in-law.

"Did you spin it?" Andrew asked pleasantly.

Jewel gave him a long-suffering look before they moved away. "Would we be tellin' ye to notice it if we didn't, Vicar?"

Several more villagers came through the doorway, some with children and even two more babies. Mr. Jensen, along with the lodgers and servants alike, arrived from the *Larkspur*—including the most recent lodger, Mrs. Grant, a widow from Derbyshire. Also along was Mr. Kendal, the young archeologist who now occupied one of the family rooms. Since the significant find on the Anwyl, five more archeologists were stationed in Gresham—the other four procuring rooms at the *Bow and Fiddle*.

"I was afraid you would be too busy to come," Julia said to Miss Rawlins, who had just recently signed contracts with her publisher for several more novelettes.

The writer smiled and shrugged. "I simply made myself put down my pen at the last minute. What good is it to write romances if you can't find time to attend the most romantic event of all?"

Next Julia clasped Mrs. Dearing's hand. "How did all of you fit in the landau?"

The woman sent a smile toward Mr. Jensen, who was speaking with Andrew. "Oh, Mr. Jensen didn't want us to have to come in two shifts, so he hired Mr. Thatcher's wagon for the men. Only, we all fussed over who should get to ride in it—it reminded me of the hayrides of my youth."

"Your youth has never left you, Mrs. Dearing," Mr. Jensen assured her, with no lessening of his usual dignity, and he shook a stunned Julia's hand.

Fiona was next, beautiful as usual in a gown of blue velvet. They embraced and Julia whispered, "Did you hear that?"

"They sat next to each other in the wagon as well," Fiona whispered back.

Their shared smiles were in danger of becoming laughter when Ambrose gave them a suspicious look and asked Andrew, "And what are these two plotting?"

"I would just as soon not know," Andrew replied with a feigned shudder.

Julia was grateful for the levity, for she did not want to think melancholy thoughts about Monday, when she and Andrew would be seeing the two off at the railway station so that Ambrose could begin rehearsals for *Sardanapalus* in London. But as much as she dreaded saying good-bye, the knowledge that they would eventually return to the place they considered home always brought her comfort.

"I can't thank you enough for suggesting we hire Miss Somerville!" Mrs. Bartley exclaimed after planting loud kisses upon Julia's and Andrew's cheeks. Her husband, more reserved, shook hands. "Did you know she has talked Miss Clark into beginning Thursday evening classes to teach reading to adults?"

"Subscriptions have increased by almost a third," the squire added, pumping Andrew's hand.

Julia and Andrew had heard those same praises about Miss Somerville from the two many times before, but as they had both had parts in bringing about such good tidings, they delighted in hearing them again.

Mrs. Bartley leaned closer to Julia and Andrew to say in a voice that could probably be heard halfway through the nave, "And I wouldn't be surprised if you're asked to conduct another wedding soon. Miss Somerville asked if Helen Johnson could take her place today so she and a certain young vicar could do some shopping in Shrewsbury. At a jewelers, no less!"

"That doesn't mean they're engaged, Mrs. Bartley," Andrew protested.

Mrs. Bartley gave him a merry wink and took her husband's arm to move on up the aisle.

"What's wrong, Andrew?" Julia asked Andrew in a low voice.

There was hurt in his hazel eyes. "Well, I don't mean to be petty, Julia, but since Paul asked my counsel early on, I should have thought he would have told me they were about to become engaged."

But there was no time for her to reply, for Harold Sanders arrived with his wife of one month, the former Mrs. Meeks. Already Julia found herself forgetting that the four accompanying children weren't his by birth, for he seemed to wear the role of fatherhood as comfortably as one wears a favorite garment. It was a joy to see the family seated together in church every Sunday.

"You're looking radiant these days," Julia said to Mrs. Sanders. Indeed the careworn look about her face had melted away so that attention was drawn to her smiling brown eyes.

Self-consciously, the woman touched the curled fringe above her eyebrows. "Thank you, Mrs. Phelps."

Pride shone in Phoebe's eyes from behind her spectacles. "Aunt Mercy cut her hair."

"And she's wearing perfume!" Little Trudy chirped.

"Papa bought it for her at *Trumbles*," added Lester. "I was with him."

"You don't have to tell the whole church," Mr. Sanders whispered, but with clear affection in his ruddy face. He gave Julia and Andrew an embarrassed grin before the family moved on to join the Langfords in one of the pews.

"Isn't that romantic, how they found each other?" Julia whispered to Andrew.

"Yes," her husband agreed in a preoccupied tone. "But speaking of romance, this wedding cannot happen without certain people."

"They'll be here," Julia assured him. From the pews came the low hum of conversations while the organ and violin played. A baby in front, probably John, began crying for just a few seconds, and she had to restrain herself from rushing up to offer assistance to Elizabeth.

"We were afraid we would be late!" was Miss Somerville's flushed greeting as she and Vicar Treves came next through the doorway.

"The wedding party isn't even here," Andrew groused to the two.

"They'll be here," Julia assured him again, though she was beginning to worry a little herself. She took Miss Somerville's hand. "Did you enjoy your time in Shrewsbury?"

"Paul helped me find a lovely watch and chain for my father's birthday. At a very decent price, too. I'll show it to you tomorrow if you'd like."

"Tomorrow?" Julia spoke before thinking.

Vicar Treves gave Noelle an affectionate smile, then turned to Julia and Andrew. "Would it be possible if we visited with the two of you tomorrow afternoon? We would like to ask your counsel over a certain matter."

"But of course," Andrew replied, putting a fatherly hand up to the young vicar's shoulder.

"Feel better?" Julia asked when they had moved away.

Her husband smiled at her. "Much."

*W*ell, it's that Miss Somerville's fault!" Amos Clark defended to his wife and everyone else present as the wheels of Noah's carriage moved down the cobbled stones of Church Lane.

In spite of her growing concern over reaching Saint Jude's on time, Lydia smiled to herself. Miss Somerville's *crime* had been to show Lydia's father a new book by Mrs. Beeton, *How to Bake and Decorate Beautiful Cakes for All Occasions*, when he had confessed he was growing bored with painting. After some modest but aesthetically successful attempts at birthday cakes, including Lydia's three months ago, he had determined to bake the wedding cake himself.

Lydia had been worried that her future father-in-law, a skilled baker, would be offended when he wasn't asked to do the honors, until Jacob explained to her that a cake would never have survived the train journey from Dover intact.

"Well, you could have at least allowed Mrs. Tanner to help," Lydia's mother said in a voice that gave evidence of an inward battle between strained nerves and her usual self-possession.

"Yes, you could have allowed me to help," the cook echoed. There was no mistaking the injury in her voice.

"*Help?*" Lydia's father uttered the word as if it represented some unfortunate insect squashed against the sole of his shoe. "Did Leonardo da Vinci accept help when he painted the Mona Lisa?"

"da Vinci didn't make his daughter late for her wedding, Papa," Noah, at the reins, reminded him. He twisted in his seat to grin at Lydia, seated between her sister-in-law, Beatrice, and four-year-old nephew, Samuel. "What will you do if it's in the shape of a giant pipe, sister?"

Blessing Noah for the healing balm of mirth against her own strained nerves, Lydia smiled. "I could accept that, only if there was no tobacco used in the decorations."

"Get on with you now!" her father exclaimed, grinning himself. "And I'll have you know, it looks just like one of those fancy wedding cakes in the book. Why, Jacob's father may want to hire me on at his bakery in Dover! You'll see!"

But for this privilege they would have to wait until the reception, for he had assembled the baked sections at the town hall out of fear that delivery in a carriage would undo his hours of labor. And he had arrived at the cottage less than an hour ago with frosting all over his coat and even traces in his beard.

A picture entered Lydia's mind of guests picking gray hairs from their servings of cake, but she did not allow it to linger. She did not even mind the frosty air that caused her to shiver beneath her white satin gown. Today was her wedding day, and Jacob Pitney waited at the altar. Nothing could put a damper on her joy.

———

Most pews were filled, and Andrew had begun to entertain the dreadful thought that the bride or the groom was having cold feet when the Clarks began coming through the doorway.

"Do forgive us for being late," Noah Clark apologized with a meaningful look at his father.

"It was my fault," the older man confessed, hanging his head. "No use in my blaming Miss Somerville."

"I beg your pardon?" Andrew asked but gave him no opportunity to explain. "Is Miss Clark in the vestibule?"

"Aye, with her mother. She refuses to wear a cloak, for worry of crushing her gown. And it's colder in there than a coal digger's—"

"Papa! We're in church," Beatrice interrupted, laying a hand upon his arm, while Andrew shot Julia an amused glance.

"I was going to say *elbow*," the old man said in a wounded tone.

"Well, we should sit now so Lydia doesn't have to wait in there so long."

"I assume Mr. Pitney is in there as well?" Andrew asked. How refreshing it was to find a betrothed couple not bound by silly superstition. But then, Jacob Pitney and Lydia Clark were more mature than the average bride and groom.

His thoughts were interrupted by Noah Clark's query. "You mean he isn't here?"

———

Like almost all inhabitants of the late nineteenth century, Jacob Pitney appreciated the innovations that made life more convenient. He especially appreciated railway transportation, for had he to rely upon coaches, the distance to Dover would severely limit the opportunities for visiting his family.

But today it took all his reasoning to keep from feeling that the *Severn Valley Railway* had acted spitefully toward him, for the train carrying his parents on the last leg of their journey had left Birmingham two hours behind schedule. A cracked wheel-bearing was the cause, his father had explained at the Shrewsbury depot while Jacob hurried them to the barouche that Squire Bartley had insisted upon providing. Fortunately the squire's driver understood his haste, and the team of Cleveland bays had pounded the roadway from Shrewsbury to Gresham.

It was only when Saint Jude's steeple was in sight that Jacob realized, to his chagrin, he had not asked the name of his sister's baby. But not because he blamed his new niece for taking her time about being born. Indeed, he had wired his parents last week, telling them to stay until the baby arrived to be with Gloria, who was rightfully pampered by the whole family, even though she was grown and married. Everyone would have ample opportunity to meet Lydia after school was out for the summer, when he would take her on a delayed honeymoon to include Dover.

"They named her Lydia Rose," Jacob's mother, seated on his right, replied when he voiced the question.

Jacob was both pleased and perplexed. "Lydia?"

"After your Lydia," his father raised his chin from the warmth of his muffler to supply unnecessarily from the facing seat.

"But they've never even met her."

His mother patted his arm, while a smile creased her rosy cheeks. "But we all love her already—just from your letters. And Gloria figured your Lydia must be close to a saint, since you waited so long to pick just the right woman."

Or rather, God saved me from my own stupidity, was Jacob's wry thought. But he smiled at his parents. "You'll love her even more when you meet her."

———

"Should I lower the veil now?" Lydia asked while feeling with a gloved hand for the first tier of lace flowing back from the comb at the crown of her head. Surely Mrs. Phelps would be in any minute to signal time for the walk up the aisle.

"I suppose so, daughter." There were tears in her mother's eyes as she looked up from her diminutive height. "But it's a shame to cover such a beautiful face."

Smiling, Lydia leaned down to kiss her mother's soft cheek. Of course she was just being kind, as was Jacob when he told her she was beautiful—

which seemed to be every time they were together. But it was always nice to hear. The sanctuary door opened and Mrs. Phelps came through it, accompanied by the vicar and Lydia's father.

"What is wrong?" Lydia asked, for all three faces wore the same anxious expression.

"What time was that train to arrive?" her father asked.

"Eleven. Isn't Jacob here?"

Somberly he shook his head, and Vicar Phelps asked if he should send Luke to see if something was the matter. A tiny seedling of doubt entered Lydia's mind, but she forced herself to dismiss it before it could take root. The man who had charged the road to Shrewsbury on horseback to ask her hand would be here.

And sure enough, the heavy door leading from the outside flew open, and Jacob walked through the doorway. He wore his dark suit and a flush across his face. "Forgive me, Lydia, but the train was late," he explained as he held the door for the elderly couple with him.

"You're not to be looking at her, Jacob!" Lydia's mother cried, standing on tiptoe to cover Lydia's face with the veil.

Though she entertained no superstitions, Lydia assisted her mother and covered her face. She said to Jacob's parents while their son closed the door, "I've so looked forward to meeting you both."

Jacob's mother, a tall, pleasant-faced woman with white hair peeking from under a silk bonnet, crossed the small vestibule with her husband following. The older woman embraced her carefully, so as not to crush her gown. "And we've looked forward to meeting you, Miss Clark."

"Please, call me Lydia," she said, then turned to her parents and the Phelps. "And I would like you to meet—"

"Why don't we get the two of you married and then we can sort out all the new relatives?" Lydia's father blurted.

Heat rose to her cheeks, making Lydia glad for the veil. She was startled and relieved when her soon-to-be father-in-law began bobbing his gray head. "That sounds like a fine idea to me."

Over his father's shoulder, Jacob winked at Lydia just before a smiling Vicar Phelps took him by the arm. "Shall we conduct a wedding, then?"

The room emptied of all but herself and Mrs. Phelps as the vicar led Jacob away, and the two sets of parents left for their front-row pew.

"I'll take good care of her," Mrs. Phelps assured Lydia's mother, who clearly would have preferred to stay.

Presently Mercy Langford's clear voice drifted through the door, singing "Love Divine, All Loves Excelling" to the accompaniment of the organ and violin. "Are you nervous?" Mrs. Phelps asked, holding Lydia's hand.

"A little," Lydia confessed. "But mostly grateful."

The vicar's wife smiled. "God's gifts are good, aren't they?"

Lydia nodded, smiling through the lace obscuring her face. "Yes, so good."

And in this fourth decade of her life, she had learned that those gifts which seemed a long time in coming were the most precious of all.

———

"Are you ready?" Julia whispered, easing open the door at the final notes of Mercy's solo.

"I'm ready, Mrs. Phelps," the schoolmistress replied in a voice thick with emotion.

The organist began softly playing Wagner's "Bridal Chorus" with the violin accompanying. Julia nodded. "It's time, then."

Miss Clark's shoulders rose and fell with a deep breath, and she began taking measured steps past her and through the doorway. Not wishing to accompany the bride up the aisle, Julia waited several seconds before easing the door closed and slipping into the back row. Finally she allowed herself a little shudder. She didn't think Miss Clark had even noticed the chill of the vestibule. *Come to think of it, there was an occasion when you didn't either*, she reminded herself, thinking back to a certain December wedding over two years ago.

She grew misty eyed at the joy on Jacob Pitney's handsome face as he stared at his approaching bride. *How dramatically their lives have changed.* What would Mr. Pitney have thought if someone had told him just months ago, when he was too timid to speak to women about anything that didn't involve archeology, that he would soon be standing in front of the village exchanging marriage vows?

And Miss Clark, who had devoted her life to the children of other people. Could she have foreseen at this time last year that she would soon be starting a family of her own?

A snippet of verse from the book of Habakkuk crossed her mind. *I will work a work in your days which ye will not believe, though it be told you.* That not only applied to the couple at the altar, she realized as she glanced around the assemblage in the pews before her. Would Fiona have believed, back in the days when she was scrubbing floors, that she would become the real-life leading lady of a famous actor? Or Miss Somerville, that she would become a respected village librarian? She thought about Mrs. Kingston-Bartley finding love in her advanced years. And Jonathan Raleigh becoming a schoolmaster and new father. Who would have thought a former convict, Seth Langford, would become a successful horse farmer, or Harold Sanders a new believer, churchgoer, and family man?

Her next thoughts turned inward. During her fourteen years as a naive, sheltered London housemistress, she had not so much as daydreamed of becoming a woman of business and then marrying a vicar. *Perhaps it's best you don't tell us these things, Father*, she prayed as her beloved Andrew began the marriage ceremony. *We would lose our sense of awe and gratitude if we could predict everything.*

Another passage of scripture came to her mind and caused her to smile. *I will sing unto the Lord, because He hath dealt bountifully with me.*

"Bountifully," Julia whispered.

More from Lawana Blackwell

Julia Hollis's opulent life in Victorian London shatters when her husband passes away. Now the family's hope rests on renovating an old inn in the quaint village of Gresham. But can she handle everything when boarders begin arriving? And then the eligible new vicar arrives....

The Widow of Larkspur Inn by **Lawana Blackwell**
GRESHAM CHRONICLES #1

Elizabeth Phelps is being courted by a handsome young curate. But while considering his marriage offer, the man she once loved suddenly appears, wanting to prove he's changed and worthy of her affection. As she seeks to know her heart, who will she find has captured it?

The Courtship of the Vicar's Daughter by **Lawana Blackwell**
GRESHAM CHRONICLES #2

The comfortable world of Carley Reed crumbles when she's informed of a substantial inheritance. But moving from California to Mississippi isn't at the top of her to do list—and things get even more complicated when a mysterious murder threatens to destroy the happiness she's finally found.

A Table by the Window by **Lawana Blackwell**

You Liked *The Dowry of Miss Lydia Clark*.... Now Try These Other Regency Era Novels

This new edition of *Pride and Prejudice* offers not only the full novel you know and love but also engaging trivia, lists, notes, facts, jottings, and inspiration from Austen's own prayers and writings on faith—providing an even more memorable experience.

***Pride and Prejudice* by Jane Austen, Insight Edition**

Using Jane's own letters, first-hand accounts, and meticulous research, Christy Award–winning author Nancy Moser transports you inside the life and times of Jane Austen—the loves, disappointments, and victories that shaped the novels that have remained popular for nearly two hundred years.

***Just Jane* by Nancy Moser**

Charlotte Lamb, a fallen vicar's daughter, flees to London's Milkweed Manor and is mortified when a former suitor—a physician her father rejected—is in charge of her care. Yet he's hiding secrets at the manor as well. Determined to protect their loved ones, neither imagines the sacrifices they will make.

***Lady of Milkweed Manor* by Julie Klassen**

I've travelled the world twice over,
Met the famous: saints and sinners,
Poets and artists, kings and queens,
Old stars and hopeful beginners,
I've been where no-one's been before,
Learned secrets from writers and cooks
All with one library ticket
To the wonderful world of books.

DEAD BY MORNING

Leo Martindale's body was discovered outside the gates of his ancestral home, Longford Hall, now a Country House Hotel run by his sister Delia Hamilton and her husband. An accident? Another hit and run outrage? Or is it, as Inspector Thanet of Sturrenden CID begins to suspect, murder?

Books by Dorothy Simpson
in the Ulverscroft Large Print Series:

THE NIGHT SHE DIED
SIX FEET UNDER
PUPPET FOR A CORPSE
CLOSE HER EYES
LAST SEEN ALIVE
DEAD ON ARRIVAL
ELEMENT OF DOUBT
SUSPICIOUS DEATH
DEAD BY MORNING

DOROTHY SIMPSON

DEAD BY MORNING

Complete and Unabridged

ULVERSCROFT
Leicester

First published in Great Britain in 1989 by
Michael Joseph Ltd.,
London

First Large Print Edition
published December 1990
by arrangement with
Michael Joseph Ltd.,
London

British Library CIP Data

Simpson, Dorothy, *1933–*
 Dead by morning.—Large print ed.—
 Ulverscroft large print series: mystery
 I. Title
 823'.914

 ISBN 0-7089-2342-9

Published by
F. A. Thorpe (Publishing) Ltd.
Anstey, Leicestershire
Set by Rowland Phototypesetting Ltd.
Bury St. Edmunds, Suffolk
Printed and bound in Great Britain by
T. J. Press (Padstow) Ltd., Padstow, Cornwall

To Jenny and Ian

1

THANET lifted the edge of the curtain aside and peered out into the dark street. "It's nearly half-past twelve. Where can she be? She's never been as late as this before. And—yes—it's beginning to snow, look!"

Joan joined him at the window. "So it is. The temperature must have risen."

Earlier on it had been freezing hard.

She returned to her seat by the fire. "Darling, do come and sit down, you're driving me mad prowling about like that."

"How you can sit there so calmly I just do not know. She's always home by half-past eleven. Anything can have happened." Thanet, who had seen far more than his share of broken bodies during his years in the police force, blanked off hideous images of Bridget mutilated, injured, suffering appalling pain or even now dying, perhaps. He plumped down beside Joan on the settee and, leaning forward, put his elbows on his knees and his head in his hands.

Joan put her hand on his shoulder. "'Anything' includes perfectly ordinary things like being delayed at work, Tim's car not starting, being held up because they witnessed an accident . . ."

Their daughter Bridget was now nearly seventeen. She had managed to scrape one or two respectable grades in her GCSEs last summer and, always keen to have a career in cookery, was taking a year off to gain some practical work experience in the kitchens of a local restaurant before starting a year's Cordon Bleu course in September. Tim was one of the waiters, and gave her a lift home each night that their stint of duty coincided.

Thanet's shoulder twitched impatiently. "Yes, I know . . . But in that case, why hasn't she given us a ring?" Perhaps Tim wasn't as trustworthy as he had appeared. A married man with two children, he had seemed a decent enough young man, but what if his offer of lifts for Bridget had had an ulterior motive, what if. . . ?

Thanet jumped up and crossed to peer

2

out of the window once more. "It's coming down more heavily now."

The snow was already beginning to lie, mantling the ground with a thin gauzy veil of white. Huge soft wet flakes swirled around the fuzzy orange globe of the street lamp on the pavement outside their house and hurled themselves silently against the windowpane like moths attracted to the light, melting from the contact with the warm glass as they slid down. Thanet peered hopefully down the street. Nothing.

"We should have refused Tim's offer, insisted on fetching her ourselves."

"That would have looked really churlish, as he actually has to pass our house on his way. Anyway, it's ridiculous turning out late every night if we don't have to."

"Better than having to sit here and wonder where she is and what's happened to her."

Joan laughed. "It looks as though you're in for a really bad time."

"What do you mean?"

"Don't look so alarmed! I simply mean that this is only the beginning. We've been unusually lucky up to now but no doubt this is only the first of many, many nights over many, many years when we're going to lie awake waiting for the sound of her return, wondering where she is, if she's all right . . ."

"How can you make so light of it?"

"I'm not making light of it. It's just that I . . . well, I'm a little more resigned to it, I suppose. I can remember how my own parents used to fuss when I was late home after going out with you."

"Do you? Did they? I never knew that." Thanet took her hand, momentarily distracted.

"They certainly did. But I wasn't going to tell you, naturally. It would have made me sound like a little girl, to be fussed over."

He grinned. "The ultimate insult."

"Exactly. And that's precisely how Bridget will take it if she gets home and finds us sitting here like a reception committee." Joan stood up, decisively. "So come on, let's go to bed."

"But . . ."

"Luke! Come *on*."

Grudgingly, he allowed himself to be

persuaded upstairs. "But I'm not going to let it go, mind. If she's going to be late like this she really must let us know."

"All *right*. I'll speak to her about it. Tactfully."

Thanet caught her eye and grinned. "Not too tactfully."

She smiled back. "Agreed."

They had just got into bed when outside in the street a car door slammed. A few moments later they heard the front door close. Quickly, Joan switched off the bedside light. When Bridget had crept past their door on the way to her room, Joan said, "That wasn't all that was worrying you tonight, though, was it?"

Thanet turned to face her in the darkness. There was no point in denying it. "No," he admitted.

"Draco again."

"'Fraid so."

"Why didn't you say?"

"I should think you're sick and tired of hearing about him."

"Nonsense. It enlivens my days no end."

He could hear the laughter in her voice.

"Seriously, though," she said. "What's he been up to this time?"

"That's the trouble, we're not sure. There're all sorts of rumours flying around. Some new campaign he's planning . . . But one thing's certain, it's sure to make life even more uncomfortable for the rest of us."

Just over a year ago Superintendent Parker had retired and Goronwy Draco had taken over at divisional headquarters in Sturrenden, the small country town in Kent where Thanet lived and worked. The new Superintendent was a fiery, dynamic little Welshman who was firmly of the opinion that a new broom should sweep clean as quickly as possible. Suffering under the new regime of regular morning meetings and tighter control, Thanet had grudgingly to admit that under Draco's ever-watchful eye divisional headquarters at Sturrenden had become a much more stimulating place to work. Enlivened by newly-decorated offices and higher standards of cleanliness and efficiency, the place now crackled with a new energy and there had been a gratifying increase in crimes solved and villains safely ensconced

6

behind bars. Draco may not be popular, but he certainly got results.

Thanet sighed. "I expect we'll survive."

As soon as he opened his eyes next morning he was aware of the difference in the quality of the light. There must have been more snow overnight. He hoped that the fall had not been heavy. Snow was very picturesque but it brought problems. However hard the local authority tried, it never seemed to make adequate preparation for bad weather. A mere skim of snow brought its crop of traffic jams and minor accidents; anything over six inches, severe disruption. And of course, there was the cold. Thanet hated the cold and the tip of his nose told him that the temperature in the bedroom was at a far from acceptable level. February was definitely bottom of his personal popularity chart of favourite months. He allowed himself the indulgence of a few more moments in the warm cave that was the bed, then braced himself and slid out, careful not to allow a gush of cold air to disturb Joan who was still sleeping peacefully. He padded across to the window. Might as well know the worst.

Despite his dislike of the inconvenience snow brought in its wake he could not escape the inevitable sense of wonder at its transforming beauty. Beneath its mantle of pristine white, his familiar world preened itself in the first rosy light of a clear winter dawn. He peered at the roof of the garage, trying to gauge the depth of the fall: not more than a few inches, by the look of it. Good. It shouldn't take too long to clear the drive, with Ben's help. And the gritting lorries had been out last night, so the roads shouldn't be too bad.

Three-quarters of an hour later, fortified by the porridge that Joan had insisted on making, he and Ben had almost reached the front gate. Up and down the road warmly-clad figures shovelled and swept drives and pavements. In the road cars seemed to be making slow but steady progress.

Joan appeared at the front door. "Luke? Telephone."

"Finish it off, will you, Ben?"

Ben, thirteen, gave a reluctant nod.

"Sergeant Pater," said Joan, handing over the receiver.

The Station Officer. Something out of the ordinary, then, to necessitate an early morning call, in view of the fact that Thanet was due at headquarters in half an hour or so.

"Thanet here."

"Morning, sir. Just had the report of a body in a ditch at the side of the road, out at Sutton-in-the-Weald. Found by a man walking his dog."

As in his last case, Thanet thought. If you were a dog owner you certainly seemed to run a greater risk of stumbling over a corpse than most.

"You've reported it to the Super?"

"Yes, sir. He says he's going out there himself." Pater's tone was carefully non-committal.

"Ah." Thanet's heart sank. This was new. What was Draco up to now? He remembered wondering, when Draco first arrived, just how long the new Superintendent would be content to sit behind a desk. All that restless energy needed numerous outlets. Thanet hoped that active participation at ground level wasn't going to be one of them. It would be impossibly inhibiting to have Draco breathing down his neck.

"Apparently there's been quite a bit of snow out there, fifteen inches or so, with some pretty deep drifts in places, so it's going to make transport a bit tricky. The Super's put through a request to the Council to clear the road as soon as possible and he's asked for a couple of Land Rovers to be laid on for you. He wants you to meet him here and he'll go out with you."

"I see. What time?"

"Eight-thirty."

"Right, I'll be there. Have you contacted Sergeant Lineham?"

"I'll do that next, sir. I'll arrange for the SOCOs and the CCTV sergeant to come in the other Land Rover, and pick up Doc Mallard on the way. I thought I'd let you know first."

So that Thanet wouldn't be late for Draco, no doubt.

"Thanks."

Grateful that he had already had breakfast and that the driveway was clear, Thanet put on thick socks, wellington

10

boots, sheepskin jacket, gloves and woolly hat in anticipation of hours of standing around in the snow. "I feel like the Abominable Snowman," he said as he kissed Joan goodbye.

She grinned. "You look like him. Here." She handed him a Thermos.

"Thanks, love. Oh, hang on. Better take some shoes, in case. I can't go tramping in and out of houses in these."

"Sure you wouldn't like me to pack a suitcase for you?"

"All very well for you, in your nice, centrally heated office."

Joan worked as a Probation Officer in Sturrenden.

"Courtroom actually."

"Courtroom, office, what's the difference, it'll be *warm.*"

"Stop grumbling," she said, pushing him out of the front door. "Go on, you don't want to keep Draco waiting, do you?"

Thanet rolled his eyes. "Heaven forbid."

As he got into the car he realised that he had been so put out by the prospect of Draco's presence that he had forgotten to

11

ask whether the body was that of a man or a woman.

It was another couple of hours before he found out.

The journey out to Sutton-in-the-Weald had been irritatingly protracted. The first few miles hadn't been too bad but then the snow had begun to deepen and a little further on they had caught up with the snow plough sent out at Draco's request. After that they had resigned themselves to travelling behind it the rest of the way, at a snail's pace. Fortunately a local farmer with a snow-clearing attachment on the front of his tractor had eventually turned up coming the other way and after a certain amount of manoeuvring they had been able to proceed more quickly.

There then followed a long wait for the second Land Rover bringing Doc Mallard and the Scenes-of-Crime officers. Meanwhile, there had been little to do. The body lay in a roadside ditch backed by a high stone wall, only a few yards from the lion-topped pillars at the entrance of the driveway to Longford Hall Country House Hotel. From the road nothing could be seen but the upper surface of a sleeve in distinctively bold black-and-white checked tweed, lying along the edge of the ditch as it had been uncovered by the dog. Although the arm was patently stiff with rigor mortis, PC Yeoman, the local policeman who had been first on the scene, had understandably cleared the snow from the man's face, to make quite sure that he was dead. The rigid features, pallor of the skin and open, staring eyes had told their own tale and thereafter he had left well alone, winning Thanet's approval by erecting a temporary barrier of sticks stuck into the snow and linked by string.

Despite his years in the force Thanet had rarely been able to overcome a dread of his first sight of a corpse, but today, uncomfortably preoccupied by Draco's presence, he had approached the body with no more than a twinge of trepidation and, gazing down at the dead face set deep in its ruff of snow, he felt no more than his usual pang of sorrow at a life cut short. Blurred as the man's features were by snow, it was difficult to estimate his age with any accuracy, but Thanet guessed that he had been somewhere between forty and sixty. Time, no doubt, would tell.

No further attempt had yet been made to clear the snow from the rest of the body. Thanet wanted photographs taken first. Not that he thought this very important. Covered with snow as it was, the body had obviously been placed or had fallen into the ditch before or around the time the snow started. Still, one never knew. It paid to be scrupulously careful and, with Draco taking in every move, Thanet had every intention of playing it by the book.

In any case, the marks in the snow told their own story: a scuffled, disturbed area betrayed the dog's excited investigation of this interesting and unusual find and there were two sets of approaching and departing footprints, belonging to Mr. Clayton, the dog's owner, and PC Yeoman. Thanet, Draco and Lineham had been careful to enquire which were Yeoman's tracks, and to step into his foot-marks when they approached for their brief inspection of the body.

As yet the snow had kept most people indoors and there had been little traffic up and down the road. Half an hour ago a tractor had begun clearing the hotel drive and any minute now Thanet expected someone to arrive and demand an explanation of the activity just outside the gates.

"Where the devil are they?"

Draco, who along with Lineham and Thanet had been stamping up and down the road in an attempt to keep warm, was finding it difficult to contain his impatience. "They should have been here half an hour ago."

"Perhaps Doc Mallard was out on a call."

Draco snorted, two dragon-like puffs of condensation emerging from his nostrils. Short, square and dark and sporting an astrakhan hat and a heavy, fur-lined overcoat, he looked like a Russian statesman awaiting the arrival of foreign dignitaries. The backdrop of snow served to heighten the illusion.

"Like some coffee, sir? I've got some in the Land Rover."

"Thank you. Excellent idea. Should have thought of it myself."

"My wife's, actually."

Thanet fetched his Thermos from the

15

Land Rover and he, Draco and Lineham took it in turns to sip the steaming liquid. Lineham had been very quiet so far, subdued no doubt by Draco's presence. Thanet had to suppress a grin at the memory of Lineham's face when he had seen Draco climb into the Land Rover. The sergeant evidently hadn't been warned.

A vehicle could be heard coming down the hotel drive and a moment later a Range Rover pulled up between the stone pillars. A man and a woman jumped out.

"What's going on here?"

It was, unmistakably, the voice of authority, cultured and self-assured. Its owner, clad in country uniform of cords, thick sweater, Barbour and green wellies, was in his late forties, tall and well built with slightly receding dark hair and slate-grey eyes which quickly summed up the situation and unerringly selected Draco as the person to approach. "What's happened?"

Draco handed the Thermos cup to Thanet and, drawing himself up to his full height, announced, "Superintendent Draco, from divisional police headquarters at Sturrenden . . ."

But the man wasn't listening. He had caught sight of the arm in its boldly checked sleeve and his expression changed. "My God, that's . . ."

He spun around, putting out his hand to prevent the woman behind him from coming any closer.

"What is it, Giles? What's the matter?"

Clear, ringing tones, another Barbour and more green wellies. A beautiful woman, this, a little younger than her husband, in her early forties, Thanet guessed. She, too, was dark, her long hair swept back into a thick French plait, accentuating the classic bone structure of her face. She would look much the same, he thought, twenty years from now.

"I think you ought to get back into the car, darling," said her husband.

She shook off his restraining arm impatiently. "What do you mean, what are you talking about?"

The movement gave her a clear view of the arm for the first time and she gasped. "My God, that's Leo's coat."

Draco stepped forward. "Leo?"

"My brother." Her gaze was riveted to the arm, her eyes appalled. She clutched

17

at her husband, who put an arm around her. "Is he. . . ?"

"Dead?" said Draco. "I'm afraid so. If it is your brother, I'm sorry that you had to learn of it like this."

"But why are you just standing around drinking coffee, for God's sake! Why aren't you trying to get him out? You can't just leave him there!" She grabbed the stick marker nearest to her, tugged it out of the snow and, tossing it impatiently aside, started towards the ditch.

The three policemen darted forward to stop her, but it was her husband who grabbed at her coat and tugged her back. "No, Delia. Can't you see? If it is Leo, there's nothing anybody can do now."

"But it's awful! It's . . . inhuman, just leaving him buried in the snow like that!" She turned on Draco, her eyes blazing. "How dare you!" Her contemptuous gaze swept around the little group of policemen and returned to Draco. "The Chief Constable is a personal friend of ours. I shall report you to him. Immediately!"

Thanet studiously refrained from looking at Lineham.

She turned to her husband. "Come on,

Giles. We'll go back to the house and get something done about this absurd situation."

And with another furious glance at Draco she swung herself up into the car and sat gazing stonily through the windscreen as her husband manoeuvred the Range Rover around and drove off.

"A lady who's used to getting her own way, I presume," said Draco, apparently unruffled. "You're going to have your hands full with her, Thanet."

Just what Thanet had been thinking. Though the prospect intrigued rather than dismayed him. He raised an eyebrow at PC Yeoman. "Who are they?"

"Mr. and Mrs. Hamilton, sir. Owners of Longford Hall. She runs the hotel, he runs the estate."

"There are the others now, sir," said Lineham.

"About time, too," growled Draco.

Doc Mallard's half-moon spectacles glinted through the windscreen as the Land Rover drew up.

"Where the devil have you been?" snapped Draco as Trace, the SOCO sergeant, got out, followed by his team.

Mallard accepted Thanet's steadying hand. "My fault, I'm afraid, Superintendent. Blame it on a doctor's irregular lifestyle. I was out at a confinement. Woman was on her way to hospital, but the ambulance got stuck in the snow. Luckily I just got there in time." He beamed. "Bouncing baby boy, mother and child both right as rain, I'm glad to say. Nothing like bringing life into the world to cheer you up, you know."

"I'm sure." Draco turned to Trace. "Well, let's get on with it now you are here. If we have to stand around out here much longer we'll all turn into blocks of ice."

2

BY the end of another hour Thanet felt as though Draco's prophecy were coming true; his feet were numb, he felt chilled to the bone and he had long since regretted using up his precious flask of coffee so early. Perhaps, soon, they would be able to go up to the hotel and have a hot drink.

There had been much to do. Screens had been erected, photographs of the relatively untouched area of snow had been taken, Doc Mallard had officially pronounced the man dead and then there had been a long wait while the Scenes-of-Crime officers had patiently scooped the snow away from the body, pausing to take samples or more photographs when necessary. Eventually the corpse was completely exposed, proving to be that of a man of around fifty with thinning brown curly hair, dressed in well-cut cavalry twill trousers, Aquascutum sports jacket and the black-and-white checked tweed overcoat. A wallet in his breast pocket contained twenty pounds in notes, various receipts and other scraps of paper and, more importantly, a driving licence and several credit cards in the name of Leo Martindale. It was always a help to establish identification at the outset of a case.

There were no visible marks on the body until it was lifted carefully out of its snowy grave for transfer to the waiting ambulance. Then Doc Mallard had spotted an area of matted blood on the back, left-hand side of the scalp, and there had been some excitement when the SOCOs had found some flakes of rusted paint-coated metal, two caught up in a tear in the back of the overcoat and another on the ground beneath.

"Presumably snagged in the cloth on impact," said Draco as they gathered around to peer at the samples in their plastic envelope. "If so, forensic will find out. Hit and run?"

"Looks like it. Though if so . . ." Thanet was thoughtful.

"What?"

"I was only thinking . . ."

Draco shifted impatiently. "Come on, man, spit it out."

"Well, the injury is to the back of the head, and the tear is on the back of the overcoat . . ."

"So?"

"The implication is that he was struck from behind. I'm just trying to visualise what happened. If he was knocked into the ditch by the impact, you'd expect him to be on his face or his side, or crumpled into a heap, not neatly laid out on his back."

"What are you suggesting? That whoever knocked him down then stopped his car, got out and dragged the body into the ditch?"

Thanet shrugged. "It's a possibility, isn't it, sir?"

"One among many, I suppose. But it is surely equally possible that he could have been thrown into that position by the collision?"

Thanet disagreed. But it would not have been politic to say so. Draco did not appreciate opposition. "I expect we could do some experiments, sir."

"Quite. And then, it's also possible that he wasn't killed outright by the impact.

He could have remained conscious—or regained consciousness—and crawled or staggered to the ditch in order to get off the road, and lain down in it in the most comfortable position, which just happened to be on his back."

This was much more likely. "True."

"Or," said Lineham, contributing to the discussion for the first time, "he could have been deliberately run down."

This earned him a scowl from Draco. Murder investigations were both time-consuming and expensive. "Anyway, if these metal flakes are from a car we shouldn't have any problems in tracing it."

Thanet nodded. They all knew that it was a relatively straightforward matter these days to trace a vehicle from paint samples. Forensic science has reduced it to a fine art.

They all peered again at the largest sample. "Looks like a mid-grey. And definitely going rusty," said Lineham.

"I'll get forensic to hurry it up," said Draco.

"Thank you, sir." There were, apparently, advantages in having the boss along.

"You'd better do a house-to-house, get

the men to check all local vehicles. Radio in for reinforcements. I'm going back to headquarters now."

Another bonus. Thanet suddenly felt a lot more cheerful. Even his toes didn't seem quite so cold.

One of the ambulancemen approached. "We're ready to leave now, sir."

Draco glanced at Thanet. "Might save time if you got Hamilton down from the hotel first, see if he can make a formal identification."

Thanet had every intention of doing so. "Right, sir." And to the ambulanceman, "If you could just wait a little longer . . ."

"Good. Good." Draco gave a little bounce on the balls of his feet, preparatory to departure. The thought of his snug office must be enticing. "I'll take one of the Land Rovers and get it sent back, in case you need it to get off the beaten track. Can I gave you a lift, Mallard?"

"Thank you. Be glad to get back to civilisation." Mallard picked up his bag, brushed snow off the bottom.

"Just one thing, Doc," said Thanet.

Mallard twinkled at Thanet over his half-moons. "Thought you wouldn't let me get away without asking. Time of death, right?"

Thanet nodded.

"Well I'm afraid you're going to be disappointed. In these particular circumstances it's virtually impossible to hazard a guess."

"All the same . . ." pressed Thanet.

"Really, Luke . . . Well, I suppose the best I can do is to say that it must have been some time last night. Say, any time between six o'clock and . . ." Mallard shrugged. "What time did the snow start, do you know?"

"Around half-past twelve, in Sturrenden. Could have been earlier here, of course."

"Well, you'll have to check. But it's obvious that most of the snow fell after the body went into the ditch. Say between six o'clock and four a.m., then, to be on the safe side. Not much help I'm afraid. Sorry, but I have to allow for the fact that it might not have been the accident that killed him. He could have died of hypothermia."

Draco was shifting from one foot to another in his eagerness to be off. "Right, then, Thanet. Keep me informed—in fact, you'd better report in at about five. Interesting to get back to grass roots for a while."

"Let's hope he's had enough of grass roots," said Lineham, gazing after the departing Land Rover. "What now?"

"Better call in for those reinforcements. Tell them to come up to the hotel." Thanet beckoned to PC Yeoman who had kept well away from Draco and was now patiently waiting near the entrance to the hotel drive. "I hope you're not frozen stiff."

"No sir, I'm fine." Yeoman didn't look it. His narrow face was pinched with cold, his nose red-tipped, eyes watering.

"You did well here, before we arrived."

"Thank you, sir." A faint flush warmed the pallor of his cheeks.

"I gather Mrs. Hamilton's brother, if that's who the dead man is, was a stranger to you."

"I knew she had a brother but I've never set eyes on him before. I've only been here two years and he left the village ages ago; everyone assumed he was dead."

27

"Black sheep of the family, was he?" Thanet scented an interesting story.

"I believe so, yes. Pretty unpopular generally, from what I can gather."

"Why was that, do you know?"

Yeoman shook his head. "Not specifically, no. It's just the impression I've got."

"Part of your job will be to find out, listen to the gossip. There's bound to be a lot of talk in the village after this. Meanwhile, nip up and fetch Mr. Hamilton, would you? We'd like him to identify the body. Afterwards, if the SOCOs have finished you can come up to the hotel with us and have a hot drink."

"Thank you, sir." Yeoman set off up the hotel drive at a brisk pace, slipping and sliding on the snow.

Thanet glanced around. "You finished here, Trace?"

"Almost, sir."

"Right. Get those paint samples to forensic as soon as you can, won't you?"

"Yes, sir."

Twenty minutes later the Range Rover returned. Hamilton jumped out and the ambulancemen slid the stretcher out and uncovered the dead man's face. Tight-lipped, Hamilton nodded. "That is my brother-in-law."

"Leo Martindale," said Thanet.

Hamilton looked startled. "How did you. . . ? Oh, I suppose he had identification on him." He sighed and shook his head. "The last of the line." He grimaced. "Sad, isn't it? There have been Martindales at Longford Hall for over two hundred years."

"He was unmarried, then?"

"So he told us."

"You had any reason to doubt him?"

Hamilton looked uncomfortable. "Oh no. No. It's just that . . . Well, I suppose you're bound to hear. He wasn't exactly the most reliable of men."

"I see. We'll need to talk to you and your wife, of course, so perhaps we could now go up to the house."

"Of course." Hamilton glanced at the Land Rover into which the SOCOs were loading their equipment. "You seem to be without transport at the moment, Inspector. I assume that will shortly be remedied but meanwhile may I offer you a lift?"

Thanet would have liked to take his first

look at the Hall in his own time, but it would have seemed churlish to refuse and he didn't want to antagonise the man. Besides, the thought of getting out of the cold more quickly was enticing. "Thank you."

They climbed into the Range Rover and set off up the drive, which was fenced on both sides and wound across open parkland. Before the great storm in October 1987 this would no doubt have been graced by stands of mature oak and beech, but now it was virtually bare, only the odd solitary survivor lifting its branches into the winter sky. Here and there broken and splintered trees still lay about in disarray, testament to the devastation suffered by the whole of this south-east corner of England on that one night. It was said that it would take three generations for the landscape to recover. Hamilton was evidently doing his bit to ensure that it would. An extensive programme of replanting was obviously under way, in the shape of groups of young saplings protected from the depredations of rabbits and livestock by square enclosures of wood and close-meshed wire netting.

"I suppose you lost a lot of trees in the storm?" said Thanet.

Hamilton sighed. "Like everyone else, yes. Around eighty per cent, actually, and, as you see, we still haven't got around to clearing away all the casualties. It's a mammoth task and is costing a fortune so we're doing it bit by bit. We've tended to concentrate on replanting."

The house had just come into view and Thanet was aware of Lineham behind him leaning forward to take a better look. If they'd been alone he knew exactly what the sergeant would have said. "They can't be short of a penny!"

And it would have been true, of course. Longford Hall was not exactly a stately home, but it was certainly the house of an English Country Gentleman; built, he would guess, at the end of the seventeenth or early in the eighteenth century, the rich rose-red of its brickwork enhanced by the mantle of snow which now surrounded it. Its proportions were perfect: the rows of white-painted sash windows, the flat-topped, steeply pitched roof with dormer windows, the stone balustrade running around the roof ridge all combining with the graceful flight of steps leading up to the front door to create a perfect harmony of shape and form often striven for but rarely achieved.

"What a beautiful house," Thanet murmured.

Hamilton lifted an eyebrow, as if surprised that a policeman should appreciate architectural genius. "It is, isn't it. Built by Hugh May in 1675."

And now a Country House Hotel. Thanet wondered how it must feel to have to turn the house that has been your family home for generations into a haven for rich tourists and tired businessmen. He knew that a number of these Country House Hotels now existed but he had never been inside one before. Should be interesting.

They had arrived. Hamilton pulled up in front of the steps, which were being brushed clear of snow by a tall, thin man wearing a padded anorak and a navy blue woollen cap below which his ears stuck out like those of a garden gnome. He gave them a curious glance as they passed, breaking the rhythm of his movements and straightening up to pull out a handkerchief and blow his nose.

"Who was that?" said Thanet in an undertone when they had gone by.

"Byfleet, our handyman-cum-chauffeur." Hamilton pushed open the front door with a proprietorial air and, after stamping the snow off their boots, they followed him into a broad inner lobby that bore no resemblance to the entrance to any hotel Thanet had ever been in before. If he hadn't known it was one he would have thought that he had stepped into a private house. Ranged along the right-hand wall was an orderly litter of gumboots, croquet hoops, umbrellas, walking sticks; exactly as if at any moment members of the family might come out and equip themselves for whichever outdoor activity they had in mind. To the left, a long wooden rail screwed to the wall sported a row of hooks from which hung an assortment of well-worn Barbours, Burberries and tweed caps and hats.

There was no time for more than a quick glance around. Hamilton kicked off his boots and the three policemen followed suit. Hamilton slipped on a pair of shoes he had left beside the door and Thanet, shooting an apologetic glance at Lineham,

33

unwrapped the parcel containing his shoes, which he had removed from the Land Rover before Draco left, and put them on, glad of his foresight. He wouldn't have fancied conducting an investigation in a place like this in the indignity of stock-inged feet. Lineham was no doubt wishing he'd done the same.

Hamilton flung open the inner door and led the way into a spacious hall from which a graceful staircase curled up to the first floor. Thanet blinked, overwhelmed by the assault on his senses. The scent of potpourri and burning applewood hung on the warm air, Persian rugs glowed on the stone-flagged floor, antique furniture adorned with elaborate flower arrangements gleamed with centuries of polishing and everywhere was a profusion of fine paintings, decorative objects and porcelain ornaments. In the distance someone was playing the piano. It was like stepping back in time to a more leisured and gracious way of life.

"Just a moment," murmured Hamilton, and he left them to speak to a young woman seated at a leather-topped desk in the left-hand corner of the room. The hotel receptionist, presumably, the first discreet indication that Longford Hall was a commercial undertaking. As if drawn by a magnet the three policemen moved in the direction of the log fire burning in the huge stone fireplace in the right-hand wall. Two women, one young, one middle-aged, were sitting on the long chintz-covered settee in front of it.

"Say," drawled the older woman, "you poor men look frozen to the eyeballs. Come right on over in front of the fire, and warm yourselves up."

American, by the sound of it. A guest, presumably.

Thanet smiled. "You're certainly in the best place, on a day like this." The warmth of the fire on the backs of his legs was sheer bliss.

The girl pouted. She was in her late teens, small and dark, with the beautifully white even teeth Thanet for some reason always associated with Americans. "Just our bad luck, you mean. We'd planned a trip to Canterbury today. How long d'you think it'll be before the roads are clear?"

Thanet shrugged. "Sorry, I don't know. Could be this afternoon, could be—"

Hamilton approached. "If you'd like to come this way, Inspector, I've arranged for some coffee to be brought. You could do with a hot drink, I expect."

The two women exchanged glances. "Inspector!" said the younger one, scenting diversion. "Does that mean. . . ?"

Hamilton turned on all his charm, gave her a melting smile. "I'm sorry. There's been an accident . . ." And, like a sheepdog herding a small flock of wayward sheep, he urged the policemen towards a door to the right of the stairs. "If you'd like to sit down . . ."

It was a small sitting-room, elegant in blue and gold.

"When you've had coffee I'll fetch my wife."

"Is she very upset?"

"Depends what you mean by 'upset'. Shocked, yes, griefstricken—well I don't think she would pretend to that. After all, until this week she's thought her brother dead for many years now, so you could say she's had time to get used to the idea."

There was a knock at the door and a girl in housemaid's uniform of long black

36

dress, frilly white apron and cap entered with a tray of coffee. Gratefully they all accepted the proffered porcelain cups of steaming liquid. Thanet waited until she had gone, then said, "When, exactly, did she learn he wasn't dead after all?" His fingers and toes were aching now as they thawed and it took considerable self-control not to betray the fact. He didn't want to do anything to distract Hamilton's attention from the conversation.

"Day before yesterday." The muscles of Hamilton's face tightened, betraying the tension their unexpected visitor had caused. He and his wife had obviously not been exactly overjoyed at her brother's resurrection.

An interesting thought crossed Thanet's mind. What if Leo had been the rightful heir to the Longford Hall estate. . . ? Here was a motive for murder if ever there were one. Questions crowded into his mind. He flicked a glance at Lineham. *Take over.* He wanted to think.

"He just turned up out of the blue, without warning?" said Lineham.

Hamilton seemed surprised by the change of questioner. "Yes."

"After—how long?"

"Twenty, twenty-five years. I lost count long ago."

Why come back now, after all these years? Thanet wondered.

"Why come back now, after all this time?" said Lineham.

Hamilton shrugged. "He'd been living abroad for some time, apparently, only returned to England a week ago. Went to the barber's and saw an article on Country House Hotels in one of the Sunday supplement magazines. Longford Hall was featured in it."

Hamilton's tone had subtly changed. Suddenly he had become guarded.

"I saw that article," said Lineham. "Chilston Park was in it too."

This was another well-known Country House Hotel in Kent, notable in that it was owned by the Millers, publishers of the famous *Antiques Price Guide.*

"That's right." Hamilton was obviously relieved to be distracted from the direction the conversation was taking.

But Thanet wasn't going to let him get away with it so lightly. By now he was sure he was right. Leo *had* been the heir.

Another glance at Lineham. *I'll take over again.* They had been working together for so long that this unspoken communication had become second nature to them.

"How long has the Hall been a hotel, Mr. Hamilton?"

"Two years."

"What made Mrs. Hamilton decide to make the change?"

He was rewarded by the answer he expected.

"Her father died four years ago and there was no way she could have kept it on without making it pay its way."

"Was Mr. Martindale aware that his father was dead?"

This was delicate ground. Hamilton's tone was carefully casual as he shook his head. "Apparently not. As I say, he'd been living abroad for a number of years, in the South of France, although we didn't know that at the time. Everything possible was done to try and trace him, without success. Apparently the villa in which he was . . . staying, was very secluded, up in the hills. His hostess was French and they had very little contact with the local community."

39

For "hostess" read "mistress", Thanet guessed.

"So it must have been a considerable shock to Mr. Martindale, to learn that his old home was no longer a private house."

"I suppose so. Though he didn't seem at all put out by the fact."

"Really?" Now if true, that *was* interesting. Had Leo hoped to cash in on all the hard work his sister must have put in to make this place into the going concern it presumably was?

"And of course to learn of his father's death," said Thanet.

"Yes."

An uncomfortable monosyllable. Hamilton must know what was coming next.

"The estate was left to your wife, not her brother?"

"No."

Even more terse.

"So," said Thanet delicately, "there must have been a certain problem of inheritance." He awaited Hamilton's reaction with interest.

But he was disappointed. Hamilton must have prepared himself for this moment for he simply smiled, a bland, meaningless stretching of the lips, and said, "Not at all, Inspector. Sorry to disappoint you, but I'm sure we could all have come to some amicable arrangement. To put it baldly, it's a good-sized cake, there was plenty for everybody."

It depended, Thanet thought, on how large a slice Leo Martindale would have wanted to cut for himself. "How large, exactly?"

"Two thousand acres." Hamilton smiled, the lazy, replete smile of the predator who has caught and eaten his prey. "And the house, of course."

Not to mention its contents, thought Thanet. They alone, from what he had seen of them, would be worth a pretty penny. He wondered how Hamilton's wife had reacted to all this.

As if on cue the door opened and a sleek dark head appeared. "Ah," said Delia Hamilton, "there you are, darling. Sorry to interrupt, but there's a minor crisis. The butcher's just rung to say his van is stuck in the snow. D'you mind if Byfleet borrows the Range Rover for half an hour to go and collect the meat?"

3

AT Thanet's request Delia Hamilton returned after giving permission for Byfleet to borrow the Range Rover. She sat down beside her husband with an embarrassed laugh. "I suppose you think I'm very unfeeling, Inspector, to be worrying about such trivial matters after what's happened. But the fact remains that I'm still responsible for the running of this place and we do have guests. Not many at the moment, fortunately, but still . . ."

She had changed from her outdoor clothes into an elegant tweed skirt, pearls and a smoky-green cashmere jumper the colour of her eyes. Her dark hair was now folded back into a smooth pleat. Immaculately groomed, she looked every inch the country lady, an image no doubt carefully calculated to impress her guests. Of grief there was no sign.

"How many, exactly?" said Thanet, ignoring the spurious apology.

"Only eight. It's usually pretty quiet at this time of the year."

"And they are. . . ?"

"Four Americans—a married couple and a mother and daughter—then there's a family of three and a single man, all British."

Should make the task of interviewing easier, thought Thanet. If it had been a bank holiday weekend, now. . . "We understand from your husband that your brother arrived unexpectedly the day before yesterday, that until then you had thought he was dead."

"Which is why I can't pretend to be devastated now. Leo was dead to me for so many years that it was his being alive I found difficult to take in." The embarrassed laugh again. "I suppose you think I'm pretty hardhearted, but there's no point in being hypocritical about it, is there?"

Thanet made no comment. There had been, he noted, no further word of a complaint to the Chief Constable. Perhaps it had been made and dismissed?

"Could you give us some idea of his movements since he arrived?"

She put up a hand to brush back an invisible strand of hair. "I'll do my best, though we didn't spend that much time together. I still had the hotel to run and Leo seemed quite content to wander around by himself, renewing old acquaintances, no doubt, and revisiting his old haunts."

"If you could just give us some idea . . ."

She glanced at her husband. "Well, let me see . . . He arrived unexpectedly, early on Monday evening, shortly before dinner." She grimaced. "Shortly before we had dinner, I mean. We always dine at a ridiculously early hour so that I am free to be around while our guests have drinks and their dinner later on."

"By 'we' you mean. . . ?"

A glance at Hamilton. "My husband and I."

"There are no other members of the family living here at present?"

"There's Tessa, our daughter, and our son Adam is here at the moment, too. But he didn't arrive until last night. He's away at boarding school but it's his half-term and he spent the first few days of it with a friend. And Tessa was out as usual, she'd been up to town for the day and didn't get back till late."

"By 'town' you mean London?"

"Of course. Look, is all this relevant? I can't see why it matters what we did the night before last, it's last night that matters, surely."

"I'm just trying to get the picture, so bear with me, please. Mr. Martindale gave you no warning of his arrival, you say?"

She shook her head. "No. Just turned up out of the blue."

"It must have been a shock for you, if you had been so certain he was dead."

"It certainly was . . . A nice one, of course."

"Of course," echoed Thanet, hoping the sarcasm was not noticeable in his tone. "Anyway, I imagine Mr. Martindale would have been shown up to his room, when he arrived."

"Briefly, yes. All the rooms are always kept in a state of readiness, so there was no problem there."

"And then you had dinner. That would have been at. . . ?"

"Six-thirty, as usual. It was something

of a celebration, of course, we opened a bottle of champagne. Return of the prodigal and all that."

Thanet couldn't imagine that Leo had really been welcomed with open arms, but they had presumably gone through the motions. "And afterwards?"

"We always have drinks with any of the guests who choose to join us in the drawing-room at seven-thirty. They like that, it fosters the private house image we try to cultivate."

"Did your brother join you that evening?"

"Yes, he did. The idea seemed to amuse him."

"And afterwards?"

She shrugged. "It was business as usual." She glanced at Hamilton. "I believe you did some paperwork in your office, didn't you, darling, and I stayed around, generally keeping an eye on things. Leo went off to the pub in the village. He got back about nine, then disappeared to his room."

"And yesterday?"

Delia Hamilton put a hand up to her head and said irritably, "I saw him around from time to time, but I didn't exactly keep a diary of his movements, why should I? And I did have work to do, you know, this place doesn't exactly run itself." Mention of her domestic duties made her glance at her watch. "Look, can't we hurry things up a bit, we'll be here all day at this rate."

Hamilton stirred. "And I have things to attend to, as well. Do you really need me here any longer? I can't see that there's much I can contribute. I'm out on the estate most of the day."

"I appreciate that, sir, but I'd be grateful if you could stay just a little longer. You might be able to clarify or corroborate what happened last night."

Hamilton settled back in his chair, frowning. "Very well, but let's get a move on, shall we?"

Thanet had no intention of being hurried. "If we could go back to yesterday morning, then . . ."

Delia Hamilton frowned and sighed. "If we must. I'm sure our housekeeper could help you more than I."

"That would be. . . ?"

"Mona Byfleet. She's married to our handyman-cum-chauffeur."

"You saw him outside, if you remember, Inspector," said Hamilton.

"Ah, yes. Perhaps I could talk to Mrs. Byfleet later. But meanwhile . . ."

Delia Hamilton sat up straighter, as if to flex the muscles of her memory, then said rapidly, "Leo had a lie-in, I believe, and breakfast in bed. I saw him mid-morning and he said he was going to wander about, revisit his old haunts, as I said. At lunch he told me he'd been for a long walk on the estate. He said he was going down to the village in the afternoon and I assume he did. Then in the evening we had dinner together . . ."

Some memory was making her uncomfortable, Thanet could tell, by the whitening of her knuckles as her clasped hands tightened, the way she adjusted her position in her chair.

"You, your husband and your brother?"

"That's right," she said impatiently. "Really, Inspector, you do like to dot your i's, don't you?"

"You said your daughter was here?"

"She'd gone off to visit friends again."

48

"In London?"

"No, locally."

"What did you talk about at dinner, Mrs. Hamilton?"

She met his gaze squarely but Thanet saw the toe of her shoe tilt as her toes bunched up in tension. Feet, he found, were always an excellent indicator of state of mind. "This and that." Her chin lifted and her tone was cool. The message was plain. *I don't see that it's any of your business.*

Thanet ignored it. "Such as?"

She shrugged. "Just general chat about what we'd been doing while he was away, what he'd been doing. We had a lot of catching up to do."

Thanet decided not to probe any further for the moment. Later, if necessary, he promised himself. At the moment he just wanted to get the general picture. "I see. And later, after dinner?"

"I didn't see him again after dinner."

"And you, Mr. Hamilton. Did you?"

"See him again?" Hamilton shook his head. "No, I didn't."

"Didn't you think that strange?"

This time they both shook their heads, spoke together.

"Not at all, no . . ."

"Not in the least. Why should we?" This was Delia Hamilton. "This isn't a council house, Inspector, we're not exactly tripping over each other all the time. And there are a number of ways in and out, you could go all day without seeing someone else who is living in the house if your activities didn't happen to coincide."

"Did he say what he intended to do, after dinner?"

More headshakes.

"And you, what did you do?"

The Hamiltons looked at each other. "You drove to the station, to fetch Adam, didn't you, darling?" said Hamilton.

"Yes."

"What time would that have been, Mrs. Hamilton?" Thanet sensed the heightening of Lineham's attention, quite rightly. Any mention of either of the Hamiltons driving anywhere the previous evening could be highly relevant.

"I must have left about twenty-five past seven. Adam's train was getting in at

50

seven-thirty and it takes about five minutes to get to the station."

Thanet remembered what Doc Mallard had said. *Say between six o'clock and four a.m., then, to be on the safe side.*

"So you would have arrived back about twenty to eight?"

"Something like that, yes."

"And you didn't pass your brother on the way, either going or coming back?"

Delia Hamilton's eyes snapped. "Don't you think I would have said so, if I had? I told you, I didn't see him at all after dinner."

"What about you, Mr. Hamilton?"

"I was working in the office. I usually do, in the evenings." Hamilton's eyes narrowed. "Look, why all the questions about what we were doing?" His voice grew a little more strident. "For that matter, now I think about it, why all the questions about what Leo was doing during the day yesterday? What possible relevance can it have? I appreciate that you need to find out about his movements last night in order to discover how the accident happened, but surely it should be enough

51

for us to say that the last time we saw him was at dinner?"

"I'm afraid it's not quite as simple as that."

"Why not?"

"Yes, why not?" said Delia Hamilton.

They both stared at him, waiting for a reply.

Thanet hesitated. How much should he say, at this stage?

"Well?" said Delia Hamilton impatiently.

Thanet shrugged. "A man has died, Mrs. Hamilton, and it's our job to find out how and why. I can't tell at this stage what information might be relevant."

"But it was a simple hit and run, surely," said Hamilton. "Unless you're suggesting. . . ?"

"It's a little difficult," said Thanet carefully, "to see how Mr. Martindale could have landed in that ditch in the position in which he was lying without, shall we say, a little help."

"'A little help'. . ." said Hamilton. "My God, Inspector, you're surely not suggesting that someone *put* him there?"

Thanet shrugged. "I'm afraid I can't say any more at present."

"But—"

"Look here—"

Again, they spoke together. Delia Hamilton deferred to her husband with a glance.

"Are you saying," he said incredulously, "that Leo was *murdered?*"

Thanet was saved from a reply. The door, which must have been unlatched, was pushed open and a head appeared.

"Sorry, couldn't help hearing. Why the surprise, Dad? You always did say Uncle Leo would have come to a bad end."

It was a boy of fourteen or fifteen, though you would never have guessed it from the way he was dressed. Hair slicked down with brilliantine, he was wearing a navy-blue pinstriped suit, white shirt and narrow knitted tie. A white silk scarf hung loosely around his neck and he was carrying a trilby hat tucked under one arm and a silver-topped walking stick. Coming further into the room he posed with one hand on the stick, the other shoved into his trouser pocket.

There were further shocks to come.

"Sounds interesting," said a female voice, and a girl of seventeen followed him into the room. She, too, was apparently making a statement of some kind by her appearance, though Thanet couldn't quite make out what it was. Rebellion against her upper-crust background, perhaps? She sported hair in stiff porcupine spikes, skull-like make-up with hollowed cheekbones and shadowed eye-sockets and an all-black outfit of high heels, tights, sweater and mini-skirt so short that it was more of a frill than a garment.

Thanet sent up a silent prayer of thankfulness that so far Bridget's adolescent revolt had gone no further than a mild flirtation with heavy eye make-up.

With a glance at Thanet Hamilton stood up. "Were you two listening at the door?" he said angrily.

"Oh come on, Dad," said Adam. "Eavesdropping will get you everywhere, you know that." He gave Thanet an amused look. "As in this case. You're the fuzz, I suppose?"

"As you say," said Thanet drily, casting a warning glance at Lineham. The sergeant, ever-sensitive to insults to his

54

superior, had stiffened. PC Yeoman's expression, he noticed with amusement, was suitably wooden.

"Out!" said Hamilton, advancing menacingly on his offspring. But they stood their ground.

"Stop coming over the heavy father, Dad," said Tessa languidly. "We've merely come to offer our assistance, like good citizens. I should've thought you would approve. You're always trying to get us to conform."

"That's enough," said their mother sharply. "You heard what your father said. Off you go. Now!"

Reluctantly they began to turn away. "Just when the conversation was getting interesting," muttered Adam.

Thanet looked at the Hamiltons. "I'm sorry, but would you mind very much if I did have a word with them? They might be able to help."

"Great!" said Adam, dropping his pose and displaying a child-like eagerness to be in on the action.

The Hamiltons exchanged glances.

"How can they possibly help?" said Delia.

"Oh Mum!" Tessa was scornful. "How can he tell unless he tries to find out?"

And without waiting for further permission they crossed to a settee at right angles to the one on which their parents were sitting and sat down, looking at Thanet expectantly.

Hamilton stood up. "I'm going!" he said in disgust. "If you don't mind," he added sarcastically.

Thanet waved a hand. "Fine."

"But I've got to go too!" said his wife. "There are masses of things to be done."

But her objection was too late. Hamilton had already left.

"I don't think there's anything else I want to ask you at the moment, Mrs. Hamilton," said Thanet. "So if you'd prefer to leave . . ."

She shot her children a furious glance, clearly torn between her need to attend to her duties and a reluctance to leave the young people alone with the policemen, for fear of what they would say. "No, I'll stay a little longer."

"He won't eat us, Mum, you go," urged Tessa.

Delia pressed her lips together, shook

her head and settled back into her chair. Her children exchanged glances, rolled their eyes and sighed.

"Oh, *Mum*," said Adam.

"Well now," said Thanet, and introduced himself and Lineham. "PC Yeoman you already know, no doubt."

They glanced at Yeoman and nodded.

"Actually," said Thanet, "I'm not sure whether you can help us much, Adam."

The boy's face fell. "Why not?"

"Well, I gather you didn't get home until twenty to eight last night, so unless you saw your uncle after that . . . Did you?"

Adam shook his head reluctantly. "No. I did go and knock on his door some time during the evening, but there was no reply."

"What time was that?"

He frowned. "Let me think. I had something to eat, then I went up to my room and unpacked . . . It must have been between half-past eight and nine."

"Was the door locked?"

"Yes." A defensive glance at his mother. "I tried the handle because I thought he might have been in the bathroom, and not heard me."

And he might have been, thought Thanet, and locked his door against just this type of eventuality. So they were no further forward.

"And now, of course, I'll never know what he was like."

It sounded like genuine regret. To a boy of Adam's age the mysterious wicked uncle who disappeared into the blue never to be seen or heard of again was no doubt an intriguing figure.

He turned on his sister. "And you can stop looking so smug! Just because you happened to be here—"

"Adam!" said his mother sharply.

"What about you, Tessa?" said Thanet.

But before she could reply there was a knock on the door.

"Come in," said Delia, with evident relief.

A maid entered. "Sorry to interrupt, ma'am, but a lot more policemen have arrived." A glance at Thanet. "They're asking for the Inspector."

"Thank you," said Thanet. "Tell them I'll be out in just a few minutes." He turned back to Tessa and raised an expectant eyebrow. "Did you see your uncle last night?"

"Not last night, no. But I did have a natter with him earlier."

"Oh, when was that?" said her mother sharply.

"I ran into him on my way downstairs yesterday morning, so naturally I introduced myself and he suggested coffee in the conservatory." She rolled her eyes. "He was real dishy."

"Tessa!"

"Well, he was! So smooth and . . . well, he was *in*teresting. I mean, he'd travelled all over the place, seen everything, done everything . . ."

"And everyone!" murmured Adam, *sotto voce.*

"What was that?" snapped his mother. "What did you say?"

Adam and his sister flicked amused glances at each other. "Nothing, Ma, no need for convolutions of the undergarments."

"Adam!"

Lady Bracknell couldn't have put more

disapprobation into those two syllables, thought Thanet.

"I would remind you," she said furiously, "that this is an official interview." She cast a disgusted look at Lineham's notebook. "So just watch what you are saying, if you don't mind."

"Don't worry, Mrs. Hamilton, I have teenaged children of my own," said Thanet. He could imagine Ben's comments if he saw these two. "Couple of *posers!*" Ben would say.

He turned back to Tessa. "Did he give you any details of his activities over the last few years?"

She shook her head and the black spikes quivered. "Not really, no. Just that he'd been living in the South of France."

"Did he say what he'd been doing for a living?"

Tessa gave a shout of laughter. "Work, you mean? You must be joking. Dear Uncle Leo was what Grandmother's generation would have called a lounge lizard."

"Tessa!" Her mother again.

"Oh, come off it, Ma. What's the point of pretending? I'd guess he lived off women, rich widows mostly, I should think."

Delia Hamilton stood up, propelled by the force of her indignation. "That's enough, Tessa! I won't hear your uncle slandered in this way. The interview is over, Inspector. Come on you two, out. And this time I really mean it."

"But Ma," Tessa protested, "that wasn't slander. Slander is false report and that was—"

"ENOUGH!" said Delia. "Just go, will you?"

And this time, they went.

4

"SO what d'you think, Mike?"

They were eating sandwiches provided for them by Mrs. Hamilton while awaiting the arrival of the housekeeper, Mona Byfleet. PC Yeoman had been despatched to the village to help Thanet's men in the house-to-house enquiries, while others had been detailed to locate and examine all the vehicles at Longford Hall in an attempt to find the grey one suspected of running Martindale down. DC Bentley had been allocated the task of interviewing the guests, DC Swift the rest of the staff.

"No one's exactly broken-hearted, that's for sure. Mmm, these sandwiches are good." Lineham lifted the upper layer of bread and peered inside. "Tuna, sweetcorn and mayonnaise, I'd say. Good combination. I'll have to tell Louise."

"If you could drag your attention away from the ingredients of your sandwich, Mike, I'd be interested to hear if you think there might be a case to answer."

"Sorry, sir." Lineham shrugged. "As you would say, it's early days yet. But it seems to me that Martindale wasn't exactly the type to endear himself to people, was he? And there is the question of a nice juicy inheritance at stake."

"Quite."

"It'd be interesting to know whether the matter was actually discussed."

"Exactly."

"I mean, I can't see the Hamiltons being overjoyed at the prospect of going halves in the hotel and presumably the estate, can you, sir, whatever Mr. Hamilton says about there being plenty to go around."

"For that matter, from what we've heard of Martindale I can't really see him being happy to relinquish half of what was rightfully his, however much work his sister and brother-in-law had put in over the last few years."

"No. And leaving the financial aspect aside, I shouldn't think Mr. Hamilton would be too pleased to lose his position as squire, so to speak. He looks the type who rather enjoys the role."

"I agree. It'll be interesting to see what

Swift learns from the staff. In a place like this they'll be pretty thick on the ground, I should think. They might well have picked up some interesting snippets."

"True." Lineham yawned. He was looking tired, Thanet noticed.

There was silence while they finished the sandwiches and mulled over what they had learned.

"About time that housekeeper turned up," said Thanet, draining his coffee cup. He would have liked to smoke his pipe but there wasn't time. He stood up. "Let's go and see where she's got to."

They went out into the entrance hall, which was empty of guests. It was now 1.15 and they were presumably at lunch. A man in formal butler's uniform of black jacket, striped trousers, white shirt and black tie was just disappearing through a door at the far side.

They crossed to the receptionist's desk.

"D'you know if anyone's managed to locate Mrs. Byfleet yet?" said Thanet.

"Yes, we have. She does know you want to see her, she'll be here as soon as she can." An apologetic smile. "A minor crisis with one of the guests. Perhaps you'd like to wait by the fire. . . ?"

"You may be able to help us." Thanet smiled back at the girl, who was in her early twenties, small and well-spoken with a cloud of dark hair and bright dark eyes. She looked intelligent and observant. "Were you on duty when Mr. Martindale arrived, the day before yesterday?"

"Yes, I was."

"It was about 6.15, I believe?"

"That's right. He turned up out of the blue, with no warning. I thought he was just another guest, though they usually book ahead, of course. He asked if we had a room for the night, and I booked him in. Then he asked for Mrs. Hamilton."

"What did he say, exactly?"

"Just said, 'Is Mrs. Hamilton around?' And when I said yes, I could find her if he wanted to speak to her, he said yes, he'd like to. And then he said, 'Tell her her brother is here.' I was surprised. I didn't even know she had a brother."

"Did you see them meet?"

"Yes. When I gave Mrs. Hamilton the message on the phone she sounded very taken aback, then she said, 'I'll be down right away.'"

"Did she seem pleased to see him?"

"Yes, she did. Though . . ." The girl hesitated, then bit her lip.

"What?"

She shook her head. "Nothing."

Thanet guessed that she had noticed a certain falseness in Delia's professed pleasure at her brother's arrival.

"What was Martindale wearing?"

She shrugged. "Sports jacket, I think. And a black-and-white checked tweed overcoat. I remember that because he took it off and laid it across the corner of my desk."

"Did he say anything else?"

She shook her head. "I don't think so. Oh, there was just one thing . . ."

"Yes?"

"While he was waiting for Mrs. Hamilton—just before she arrived, in fact —Mrs. Byfleet came out into the hall from the drawing-room with a young man, and he nodded at them and said, 'Who's that?' So I told him, it was Miss Hamilton's boyfriend. He was just going to say something else when Mrs. Hamilton arrived."

"This young man, who is he?"

"Toby Fever. He's local. His father has a business in the village, he's a haulage contractor."

Not quite Tessa Hamilton's class, thought Thanet. He wondered why Martindale should have been interested.

"Did you see Mr. Martindale talk to him at all?"

"No."

"Or anyone else, for that matter? You must see all the comings and goings, here."

"He passed the time of day with one or two of the guests, that's all. Ah, there's Mrs. Byfleet now."

Thanet and Lineham turned to look at the woman coming down the staircase. Delia Hamilton hadn't been too pleased at the prospect of their interviewing her. "She's not been too well lately, and I don't want her upset. She's . . . well, she's pregnant, with their first child, and she's in her thirties, she's finding it hard going. And I don't want to lose her. She's very efficient and hardworking, she'd be very difficult to replace. It's not easy finding suitable staff for a place like this."

It was true that Mrs. Byfleet didn't look well, thought Thanet. She was, he guessed, about six months pregnant, though her long, dark green dress in some stiff silky material was well cut to conceal the fact. But her narrow face was pale, her short brown hair, despite its good styling, dull and lifeless.

"Mrs. Byfleet?" He stepped forward to introduce himself. "Perhaps we could go into the small sitting-room we've been using. . . ?"

After a brief word with the receptionist she accompanied them back into the little blue-and-gold room, choosing an upright armchair into which she sank with a little sigh.

"Hard morning?" said Thanet with a smile.

"One of the guests had a fall. She's all right, though, thank heaven, just twisted her ankle. She's lying down now. But I shall have to go up and see her again shortly."

"We won't keep you long. We just wanted to ask you if you could give us any idea of Mr. Martindale's movements yesterday."

"Let me see . . ." She passed a hand over her forehead as if to collect her thoughts. "Well, he had breakfast in his room at nine, then I next saw him in the conservatory. He was having coffee with Tessa, Miss Hamilton. Then I saw him go out—for a walk, I assumed. He came back for a light lunch with Mr. and Mrs. Hamilton, then he went out again, to the village, that time."

"He told you he was going to the village?"

"Yes. I was in the hall and he stopped for a chat, said he was going to see how much it had changed. I told him I thought probably very little. That was all. Then . . ." she faltered.

"Then?"

She shook her head. "I was just trying to think. I'm not sure when he got back, but he had dinner with the Hamiltons again."

"And afterwards?"

"I don't know what he did afterwards."

Alerted by some evasiveness in her tone, Thanet persisted. "Did you see him again at all, after he'd had dinner?"

"No."

She met Thanet's eye almost defiantly. She was lying, Thanet was sure of it. But what about? Had there been an incident she didn't want to tell him about, out of loyalty to the Hamiltons?

"Were Mr. and Mrs. Hamilton pleased to see him?"

"Of course."

But there was a note of falsity in the affirmation.

"It was a shock to them, of course, they thought he was dead, it would have been a shock to anyone . . ."

"You didn't see any sign of . . . shall we say, disharmony, between them?"

She shook her head "No." Her tone lacked conviction, but she obviously wasn't going to go back on what she had said. "You like working here, Mrs. Byfleet?"

For the first time a genuine smile gave warmth to her response. "Yes, I do. It suits us very well—my husband and I have a flat over the old stables, he looks after maintenance, and acts as chauffeur when necessary. It's a lovely house to work in, so many beautiful things, and Mrs. Hamilton is a good employer, very fair.

She expects you to work hard, but she works just as hard herself, so you don't mind."

"How long have you been here?"

"Just over three years."

And according to Giles Hamilton Delia's father had died four years ago. She hadn't wasted much time in getting things moving. With an estate like this there must have been considerable legal battles to be fought, in view of the fact that the heir was missing, before she got permission to proceed with her plans.

"And you opened two years ago, I believe?"

"That's right."

"So you helped get it off the ground, so to speak?"

"Yes. Mrs. Hamilton worked like a slave; we all did."

"It must be very satisfying to see it become such a thriving business."

"Oh yes, it has been. We're quiet at the moment, of course, mid-February isn't exactly the most popular time for a break in the country, but we've built up a very good reputation, I think, and for most of the year we're pretty busy."

Which explained why the housekeeper clearly felt such a fierce loyalty to her employer. Having been in on the project since the beginning, she must feel an almost proprietorial interest in its success.

Thanet rose. "What I should like to do now is take a look at Mr. Martindale's room. It's all right," he added, seeing the hesitation in her face, "Mrs. Hamilton has given permission."

"Of course." She rose, a little clumsily, pushing herself up on the arms of her chair. "I'll take you up."

"You've worked in the hotel trade long?" said Thanet conversationally, accommodating his pace to hers as she led them up the graceful staircase.

"All my life, you could say. My parents ran a hotel. Not like this one, of course." And she glanced around at the profusion of expensive hot-house flowers, the oil paintings on the walls, the gleaming antiques and rich variety of decorative objects.

"Forgive my asking, but aren't the guests ever tempted to walk off with any of these?"

"Not the guests," she said wryly.

72

Meaning that the staff were, thought Thanet. Scarcely surprising, really. With so much on display there must be a temptation to think that the odd piece of porcelain or silver might not be missed.

"The guests are usually overwhelmed by it all," she went on. "Especially the Americans. They've never actually stayed anywhere quite like this before and they often walk around in a sort of daze for a day or two, just looking and looking." She gave a little laugh. "It's interesting, in a very old house like this there are bound to be inconveniences you wouldn't find in a modern hotel, but in all the time I've been here I've never had anyone complain. They just accept it as part of the general, well . . ."

"Ambience?" supplied Thanet.

"That's right. They're almost, well, in awe of it, I think, and either complaining or stealing anything would be a sort of sacrilege."

At the top of the staircase they had turned left along a broad landing and at the third door along she stopped. "Here we are. I put Mr. Martindale in the Chinese suite." She pushed open the door and stood back. "And now, if you don't mind. . . ?"

"Ah yes, your invalid. Just one other point before you go. Staff. How many are there?"

"Theoretically there should be thirty in all. I say 'theoretically' because in practice it's very difficult to recruit staff for a place like this, so we're always a few short—we're rather isolated here, you see, there's nothing for them to do when they're off duty, and many of the younger ones can't afford cars, so they get bored and leave."

"So at the moment you're how many, in all?"

"Eight in the kitchen, we're two short there, and seventeen in the house, we're two housemaids and one parlourmaid short."

"So apart from the kitchen staff you have a butler, a footman—"

"A head footman," she corrected him, "then a footman, six housemaids, four parlourmaids, two receptionists, my husband and myself. Then outside there's the gardener—groundsman rather, I suppose you'd call him—and his assistant."

"And how many of those live in?"

"Ten, excluding my husband and myself."

"I see. Thank you, you've been very helpful." Thanet dismissed her with a nod and a smile.

Inside the Chinese suite Lineham looked around and said, "Wow! Some hotel room!"

There was only one word to describe it, thought Thanet: sumptuous. His living-room would have fitted into it three times over and there was so much for the eye to feast upon that it was difficult to take it all in. He pivoted slowly, looking.

Predictably the wallpaper was Chinese, in a pale celadon-green with a delicate design of bamboo and herons etched in cream. On the wide, highly polished oak floorboards lay a silky cream carpet with a green and rose design, and the elaborate hangings of the four-poster bed and the long draperies at the windows were in deeper shades of green and rose. On either side of the bed stood low round tables covered with circular floor-length rose-coloured cloths topped with smaller cloths in creamy lace. Half the room was furnished as a sitting-room, with deep, soft sofas and armchairs grouped around a leaping log fire protected by a brass fire-guard. There were a number of paintings, including two Chinese scroll paintings of misty mountain landscapes and a series of framed prints of ancient Chinese costumes. Various pieces of antique furniture, including a slender writing desk supplied with headed notepaper and envelopes, were scattered around the room. Every-where were small personal touches: apart from the ubiquitous television set and a fine enamelled clock, there were pot plants; two arrangements of fresh flowers, in various tones of cream and pink to match the decor; a small wicker basket of wrapped sweets; a bowl of fruit with plates, damask napkins and fruit knives beside it; a tray of drinks; a pile of books both non-fiction and fiction, the latter all recently published novels; and an array of new magazines.

"Wow!" said Lineham again. "Wonder how much it costs to spend a night in a place like this?"

"We'll pick up a brochure on the way out," said Thanet.

"I'm serious!" said Lineham. "If I started saving now, for our wedding anniversary . . . Louise would love it!"

Thanet rather wished he'd had that idea himself and irritation that he hadn't made him terse. "Come on, Mike, just remember why we're here, will you? Let's see what we can find out about Martindale."

It looked as though Martindale had intended to stay some time. The old-fashioned leather suitcase plastered with airline stickers which had been stowed on top of the wardrobe was large, and the wardrobe and chest of drawers were full of clothes, all expensive if somewhat the worse for wear. As well as a dinner jacket, there were several tailor-made suits and Thanet looked into an inside pocket for the tailor's label: *Filligrew and Browne, Sporting Tailors. Conduit Street 21.9.72.* Quickly, he examined the others. None was more recent than 1981. The shoes, six pairs, all Church's, were well-worn, some of the shirts were beginning to fray at collar and cuffs and the underclothes definitely needed replacing.

"Looks as though he was a bit short of

the ready," said Lineham. "He must have nearly fallen out of that barber's chair with delight when he read that article."

"Quite. Short of the ready but definitely not at his wits' end. If he had been he would have pawned those long ago." Thanet nodded at the objects scattered on the chest of drawers: a pair of silver-backed hairbrushes, silver hip-flask, and gold cufflinks.

"True."

Thanet wandered into the bathroom which displayed the same attention to detail: bowl of potpourri; cut-glass dish of cotton puffs; posy of cotton buds; little basket of toiletries—shower caps, shampoos, foaming bath oil, and a selection of Floris soaps. The towels were thick, soft and in plentiful supply and two luxurious towelling robes with *Longford Hall* embroidered across the pockets hung behind the door. Martindale's possessions were scattered about: razor, shaving cream, badger shaving brush, aftershave, toothbrush, toothpaste. His sponge bag held supplies of paracetamol, Rennies, Alka-Seltzer, and antiseptic cream.

"Nothing much here, Mike."

There was no reply and it occurred to Thanet that all sounds from next door had ceased. Raising his eyebrows he returned to the bedroom to find that Lineham was asleep on the sofa in front of the fire.

"Mike!"

Lineham awoke with a start. "Oh, sorry, sir. I must have dropped off. The fire . . ."

"You did drop off. And I'm the one who's sorry. Sorry that you are so tired you actually fall asleep in the middle of a murder enquiry!"

"We don't know that it's a murder enquiry yet, sir."

Thanet waved a hand irritably. "A potential murder enquiry, then. You know perfectly well what I mean. And stop avoiding the issue."

"I really am sorry . . ."

"It's an explanation I want, Mike, not an apology."

Lineham rubbed his eyes. "It's my brother-in-law."

Thanet gave an exasperated sigh and sat down in an armchair facing the sergeant. "What's that supposed to mean?"

Lineham yawned. "I was up half the

night talking to him. He's having problems with his marriage and he just turned up on our doorstep last night with a suitcase."

"Left his wife, has he?"

Lineham shrugged. "Temporarily, anyway."

"Look, Mike, I'm sorry your brother-in-law is having marital problems and I don't want to appear unsympathetic, but this really will not do, you know. I simply cannot have you dozing off in the middle of an investigation, murder or otherwise."

"Yes, I realise that, sir. It won't happen again."

"Won't it? Leaving the question of your brother-in-law aside, I've noticed that you seem to have been looking very tired lately. So what's wrong?"

"Nothing, sir. Not *wrong*, exactly. It's just that Richard still hasn't settled at school yet. I don't think he gets on with his teacher, she seems to have taken against him. So he isn't sleeping very well, wakes up every night crying, that sort of thing. We take it in turns to get up, but it's pretty tiring, never getting a decent night's sleep. Last night put the lid on it, I think."

"OK, I understand. I've got something similar going on at home myself, as a matter of fact. Ben's just changed schools, as you know, and he's finding it pretty difficult having much stiffer competition. At his last school he could just coast along, but now . . . Anyway, I appreciate your difficulty. But Mike, you're going to have to do something about it. Discuss it with Louise, go and see the Headmaster, but do *something*. And as far as your brother-in-law is concerned, well, I'm sure you'll find a tactful way of ensuring that any discussions you have are before bedtime. Right?"

"Yes, sir, of course. Really, it won't happen again, I promise."

"I hope not. Now, what have you got there? Is that the key to Martindale's suitcase?"

Dangling from Lineham's hand was a tiny key on a leather thong. "I should think so. It was in the toe of one of his socks."

"Let's take a look."

"Ah," said Lineham with satisfaction as it turned sweetly in the lock.

"Now this looks a bit more interesting," said Thanet.

Inside was Martindale's passport and a large brown envelope which looked much handled and which crackled when he picked it up. They sat down side by side on the sofa to examine their finds. The passport didn't tell them anything useful. It had been issued only a year ago and bore no stamps; if Martindale had done any travelling since then it had presumably been in the European community, most of whose member countries no longer bothered to stamp the passports of internal travellers.

There remained only the envelope. Thanet tipped out its contents. These looked more promising: an address book, a bundle of letters and postcards, and another, smaller envelope of photographs.

Lineham picked up the address book and flicked through it. "We're going to have our work cut out if we have to check all these."

Thanet split the bundle of letters in two. "Take a quick look at these, will you? We'll go through them thoroughly later.

Put them in chronological order, if you can read the date stamps."

They were all, they discovered, from women and almost all of them were addressed to hotels or readdressed from one hotel to another. The theme was almost always the same, regret that the sender had not heard from Martindale as she had hoped to, coupled with anxious requests for news of him. Several of them delicately referred to "loans" made to him, and one or two were more strongly worded requests for information about "investments" made by him on the sender's behalf.

"Love 'em and leave 'em was certainly his motto," said Lineham.

"Preferably with a pocket full of cash, by the look of it." Thanet tapped one of the postcards, most of which were of the "wish you were here" variety. "Looks as though this one was the last."

The card was date-stamped 10.11.84 and was a photograph of the Byron Hotel in Worthing. The message on the back read, *Room ready for your return. Roll on the 23rd.* It was signed "B" and addressed to the Hotel Paradis in Nice.

"Looks as though at some point he spent some time in Worthing," said Lineham. "It'd be a good hunting ground for Martindale's type, I should think."

"You're assuming the room she's talking about is in the Byron Hotel. But it could simply mean that the sender was staying in the Byron when she wrote the card, and that the room she's referring to is in her own home."

Lineham pursed his lips. "It could, I suppose. But isn't the other interpretation much more likely?"

"No way of telling. In any case, after this there are no more letters or cards."

"Perhaps it was at the Hotel Paradis that Mr. Martindale met this Frenchwoman he's supposed to have been living with."

Thanet shrugged. "Who knows? But I agree, it's a possibility. Pity there's no indication of who she is or where she lived." He bundled the letters up and emptied out the envelope of photographs. Predictably, these were almost all of women, either alone or with Martindale, posing against varying backgrounds. A few, though, were obviously older, smaller, of poorer quality and with curling corners. Thanet picked these up and studied them more closely. "I think this must be Martindale and his sister, look."

They were recognisably the same pair, both wearing riding breeches and sitting on the steps leading up to the front door of Longford Hall; Delia with a cloud of dark hair framing those classically beautiful features, Leo handsome and carefree, one arm resting lightly across her shoulders.

"And these must be their parents," said Lineham.

Tea on the lawn this time, the man lounging in a deck chair, the woman elegantly erect, caught in the act of pouring tea. They were a handsome pair, and Thanet, always interested in the quirkiness of genes, noted that it was her father Delia resembled, and Leo his mother. He wondered how the Martindales would have reacted to this present situation: with dignity and the famous British stiff upper lip, he imagined.

"Pretty pathetic, really, isn't it?" said Lineham, gesturing at the letters, the photographs.

"What do you mean?"

"Well, presumably this stuff, the stuff that's here, in this room, is all the gear he had."

"I imagine so, yes."

"I mean, someone like him, with his sort of background . . . What went wrong, I wonder?"

"What made him leave it all behind, you mean?"

"Yes."

"With any luck, we'll find out."

But Lineham was right, it was pathetic. And something more, too. Thanet couldn't believe that this small pile of letters represented the sum total of Martindale's correspondence over twenty years or so, or that there hadn't been many more photographs than this. No, in his view, they were the end result of a fairly ruthless weeding-out process. What had been Martindale's criterion? One letter or card, one photograph per woman? What Thanet was holding, he realised, were the trophies of one man's amorous past. He had a sudden, vivid picture of Martindale sitting in a chair, glass of whisky in hand, poring over them with a small, self-satisfied smile on his face. With a shiver of distaste he began to bundle them all back into the envelope. Later he would sort out which leads were worth following up, if any.

There was a knock at the door.

"Come in."

It was one of the DCs, accompanied by a housemaid.

"What is it, Markham?"

The girl turned away and the constable shut the door behind him before saying, with understandable triumph, "We think we've found the car, sir."

Thanet stood up. "Oh?"

"Well, a van, actually, sir. It was parked at the back of the hotel. A 1981 Bedford HA. It's grey, going rusty and we found a couple of threads which look as though they might match the victim's overcoat snagged on a piece of flaking metal just beside the front offside headlight."

"Excellent. Who does it belong to?"

"The hotel, sir."

"Right. Let's go and take a look, shall we?"

5

THANET and Lineham returned to the lobby near the front door to put on their boots. While they were doing so Tessa Hamilton passed through with a young man in tow, presumably the one in whom Leo Martindale had shown an interest. What had Mrs. Byfleet said his name was? Fever, that was it. Toby Fever. Thanet caught no more than a glimpse of him, but there was something vaguely familiar about his features. Could he have a record, perhaps?

As the three policemen stepped outside the young people drove off in a newish Ford Escort, its wheels skidding on the packed snow of the drive.

After the warmth of the house the icy air was a shock to the system and Thanet turned up the collar of his sheepskin jacket, casting an apprehensive look at the sky which had that ominously leaden look which heralds snow.

"Looks as though we might get some more," said Lineham.

"Hope not." Thanet raised his voice to speak to Markham who was leading the way along the front of the house like an eager dog guiding its master to a particularly exciting find. "This van. Who normally drives it?"

Markham slowed down. "Chap by the name of Tiller, apparently, sir. He's the groundsman. This way."

They turned right, along the side of the house.

"Ah, yes." Thanet remembered Mona Byfleet mentioning him. "He's got an assistant, I believe."

"I don't know about that, sir. Someone's gone to fetch Mr. Tiller, he should be there by now. Your Land Rover's back, by the way, sir."

"Good."

They rounded the back corner of the house and a large cobbled yard opened out before them, surrounded on three sides by a range of low, picturesque buildings in brick and tile. At the far side, standing around a small grey van, was a group of policemen stamping their feet against the cold. Amongst them was a man in boots, parka and cloth cap.

"Yes, that'll be him," said Markham with satisfaction.

As they drew closer Thanet saw that Tiller was in his sixties, a burly figure with weatherbeaten face and angry blue eyes.

"Mr. Tiller?" said Thanet.

The man thrust his chin forward aggressively. "You in charge of this lot? What the hell's going on?"

"I'm sure you've heard about Mr. Martindale's . . . accident, by now, Mr. Tiller. We need to ask you some questions. Perhaps we could go somewhere a little warmer? A garage, perhaps, or a stable?"

Tiller stood his ground. "Why?"

Thanet walked around the van and inspected the spot indicated by one of his men. It looked as though they were right and this was the vehicle they were after. A couple of threads of cloth were caught up in a snag of rusty metal. Thanet looked closer. Yes, black-and-white tweed by the look of them. He nodded at Lineham and the sergeant took out a pair of tweezers and a plastic sample bag.

Thanet straightened up.

"Mr. Martindale appears to have been run down by a vehicle and it seems possible that it was this one. As you are apparently in charge of it—"

"Now just a minute. Are you suggesting. . . ?" Head down like an angry bull, Tiller appeared ready to charge.

Thanet sensed the tension in his men. The situation must be defused. He smiled. "I'm not suggesting anything, Mr. Tiller. I merely want to ask you some questions. I'm sure you're as anxious as we are to get at the truth of the matter." He turned to one of the policemen. "Arrange for the van to be towed in, for inspection."

Tiller hesitated, his eyes searching Thanet's face for any sign that he was being misled. Abruptly he turned away. "This way," he said gruffly.

He led the way to one of the outbuildings and pushed open the door. It was a storage shed for gardening equipment, with tools, work bench stacked with flower pots and other clutter, sacks of peat, fertiliser and compost leaning against the walls and several motor mowers of assorted shapes and sizes. It was only marginally less cold than outside.

Tiller leaned against the bench and folded his arms. "Well?"

No point in beating about the bush or attempting to soften the man's mood. Thanet glanced at Lineham to check that he was ready to take notes. "Tell us about the van."

"What d'you want to know?"

"I understand you're in charge of it?"

"Sort of."

"Meaning?"

"Everybody uses it. So why pick on me?" Tiller was becoming belligerent again.

"Please, Mr. Tiller, do understand that I'm not accusing you of anything." *At this stage, anyway.* "I'm merely trying to find out who drives it, when and for what reason, that's all. And the sooner I find out the sooner this interview will be over. So if you could just give me the information . . ."

"Mr. and Mrs. Hamilton, Mr. Talion, Mr. and Mrs. Byfleet, Andy—the lad who helps me. That's it."

Thanet's heart sank. "I see. All of them have keys to it?"

"Yes—except for Andy. He borrows mine, when he needs it. The van stands out there in the yard, and whoever wants to use it uses it."

"Mr. Talion. He's. . . ?"

"The farm manager."

"I thought Mr. Hamilton managed the estate."

"Mr. Hamilton *administers* the estate. It's Jack Talion who actually runs it."

"I see. And where does Mr. Talion live?"

"In Home Farm."

"And where is that?"

Tiller waved a hand. "Over the other side of the Hall."

"And you?"

"Where do I live, d'you mean?"

Patience, Thanet told himself. "That's right, yes."

"Here, in the stable yard. They converted one of the outbuildings," he added grudgingly.

"I see." Thanet did see. This meant that everyone who had keys to the van lived sufficiently close to have had access to it last night.

"So, did any of them use the van last night?"

"How should I know?"

Thanet sighed. It looked as though every drop of information was going to have to be squeezed out of Tiller. He signalled to Lineham to take over.

"What about you, Mr. Tiller? Did you use it?"

"What if I did? I had every right, didn't I?"

"No one is saying you didn't. But in the circumstances . . ."

"Why don't you come right out with it? You think I ran him down, don't you? Go on, admit it."

"Mr. Tiller, as Inspector Thanet has explained, we have no preconceived ideas about what happened last night—"

"Don't give me that guff. In that case why aren't you talking to the rest of them, eh? Go on, tell me why."

"Because," said Lineham with admirable restraint, "we have only just discovered that it is likely to be this particular vehicle that was involved in the . . . accident."

"You did it too, didn't you?" said Tiller triumphantly.

"Did what?"

"Paused before you said 'accident'." His eyes flicked at Thanet. "Just like he did, just now. Go on, admit it, you don't think it was an accident at all, do you? You think it was deliberate."

"Mr. Tiller, can't you understand that at this stage we really don't know what happened? We are, I repeat, merely trying to find out. We shall of course," said Lineham, raising his voice as Tiller again opened his mouth to interrupt, "be talking to all the other people who have access to the van, but as you are nominally in charge of it we came to you first. So if you could just tell us if you did use it last night, where you went and what time . . ."

Tiller was shaking his head in disbelief and shifting impatiently from one foot to the other.

"Very well, Mr. Tiller," said Thanet. "If you don't choose to tell us at present, that is your prerogative. But we must have this information, so if you'd be so kind as to accompany us back to headquarters we can all wait in greater comfort until you are ready to give it to us."

Tiller was nodding his head with satisfaction. "Just as I thought. Arresting me, aren't you?"

"Not at all." Thanet was holding back his exasperation with difficulty. "In fact, if you'd just give us the information we need we'd all be able to get on with our work that much quicker." Then, as the man still remained silent, regarding him suspiciously through narrowed eyes, "Come on, man, let's get it over with. As I said before, the sooner you tell us, the sooner we'll be finished, can't you see that? If you have nothing to hide there's nothing to worry about."

Tiller gave a contemptuous snort and turned his back on them to gaze out at the yard through the cobwebbed window.

Silence.

Then, just as Thanet was about to give up and hand the man over to be taken back to Sturrenden to cool his heels for a while, Tiller swung around. "I suppose you're right," he said reluctantly. "If I've nothing to hide . . ."

Thanet nodded. "That's right," he encouraged.

Tiller hesitated a moment longer. "As a matter of fact I did use it last night. I went to the pub."

The atmosphere eased. "Good," said Thanet.

"What time was that, Mr. Tiller?" said Lineham.

"Half-past eight or thereabouts."

Tiller, it seemed, usually spent Tuesday evenings in the village pub with a woman friend called Sonia Rankle, who also lived in Sutton-in-the-Weald, half a mile out on the Sturrenden road. He would pick her up soon after 8.30 and take her home at around 10.30 before returning to his own quarters at Longford Hall.

"And this was what happened last night?" said Thanet.

"Yes."

"Now think very carefully, Mr. Tiller. Did you, either on your way to the pub or on the way back, see Mr. Martindale at all?"

The answer, of course, was predictable. "No, I did not!"

A thought struck Thanet. "You do

know who I'm talking about, don't you?" To the groundsman Martindale might just have been one amongst a number of guests.

"I know him." Tiller's response was wooden, arousing Thanet's interest.

"You mean, you know him because you've seen him around over the last couple of days, or because you knew him when he used to live here?"

"I'm local. I knew him before."

Thanet strained to catch the overtones in Tiller's voice which, in contrast to all his previous responses, continued to be strictly neutral.

"And you're absolutely certain you didn't see him when you were out last night?"

Suddenly the man's belligerence returned in full force. "I've bloody told you, haven't I? I knew you wouldn't believe me."

"Is there any reason why we shouldn't believe you, Mr. Tiller?"

"No! There is not!"

"In that case we'll get on with our work. Come on, Sergeant."

Tiller unfolded his arms as it dawned on

him that the need to be on his guard was over. "You mean, I can go?"

"Certainly. Thank you for your cooperation."

They left him gazing after them in apparent disbelief.

6

"INTERESTING," said Lineham as soon as they were outside.

"What specifically Mike? The fact that he was so on the defensive or the fact that he clammed up when I asked if he knew Martindale before?"

"Both. I'd say he definitely has something to hide, wouldn't you?"

"No doubt about it. But it won't do any harm to let him stew for a bit while we find out if anyone else drove the van last night." Thanet frowned. "Pity so many people had access to it, though."

"Who're we going to see first?"

"Out of courtesy it'd better be the Hamiltons. We'll start with him, I think. Presumably he is officially its owner."

They went back into the house to find out where Hamilton was and were told that in the afternoons he usually worked in the Estate Office, which was in the stable block at the back of the house.

Retracing their steps Lineham said

suddenly, "So did Mrs. Byfleet, for that matter."

Like the partners in a long-established marriage, able to take up and lay down a thread of conversation without ever having to spell it out, Thanet knew at once what Lineham meant. "Yes. I suspect she's either seen or heard something which she thinks would present the Hamiltons in a bad light."

"She obviously feels a very strong loyalty towards Mrs. Hamilton, at least."

"Quite. That's an interesting point, actually. She hardly mentioned him."

"Don't suppose she sees much of him, it'd be Mrs. Hamilton she works with."

"True."

"There's the office, over there."

Preoccupied earlier with Tiller and the van Thanet had not noticed the tastefully discreet OFFICE sign screwed to the wall beside one of the doors in the stable block. Guests at the hotel presumably shouldn't be made to feel that this was too much of a commercial enterprise.

Hamilton was seated at his desk dealing with paperwork. "Ah, Inspector."

"Sorry to trouble you again, Mr. Hamilton."

"Not at all, I was hoping for a word with you." He waved a hand. "Please, sit down."

It was an attractive place in which to work, thought Thanet as he and Lineham sat down on a couple of upright chairs facing the desk. The original brick stable walls had been painted white, the overhead beams sandblasted to a smooth honey, the old granite floor sets cleaned and polished. Sturdy pine furniture and a huge map of the estate added to the atmosphere of prosperous country living. Even on a day like today the room was comfortably warm.

"I saw your men towing away our van. Do I gather that you think it was involved in the accident?"

"It seems possible," said Thanet carefully. "That's why I wanted to see you."

"Oh?"

"We're trying to find out who drove it last night, and I gather that a number of people have keys to it, yourself included."

"That's true." Understandably, Hamilton's tone was now guarded.

"Did you, in fact, drive it last night?"

Hamilton hesitated only for a moment, presumably realising that sooner or later the truth was bound to emerge. "Yes, I did, as a matter of fact. I went to pick up my daughter from Ashford, at about, oh, it must have been a quarter past eleven."

Well within the time limit set by Doc Mallard.

"She doesn't drive?" Thanet was surprised. He would have expected a girl like Tessa to have taken her driving test soon after her seventeenth birthday, and he wouldn't have thought that there would be a shortage of vehicles for her to borrow, if she hadn't already been given a car of her own. Perhaps she was younger than she looked.

"Yes, of course she does. And last night she borrowed the Range Rover. Unfortunately, when she was ready to come home, she found it wouldn't start. So naturally she rang to ask if someone could come and collect her."

"It seemed to be working all right this morning."

Hamilton shrugged. "It's a bit temperamental sometimes. Last night it was a very simple matter. When I got there I checked the sparking plugs"—he gave a self-deprecating smile—"that's about my limit as far as mechanical failure is concerned. Anyway, I was in luck, one of them was loose and she was able to drive it home."

"You'll understand that I must now ask if you saw your brother-in-law either on your way out or on the way back."

"No I didn't. Anyway, what on earth do you think he would have been doing, wandering around outside at that hour on a freezing night like that?"

Thanet shrugged. "What time did you get back?"

"Around ten past twelve."

"Was it snowing then?"

"It was just starting as I turned into the drive."

"Do you know of anyone else who drove the van last night? Presumably, when your wife went to pick up your son from the station, she would have used her own car."

Hamilton's lips tightened. It was obvious that he had been expecting this. "As a matter of fact no, she didn't."

"She used the van?"

"Yes. The car she usually drives, the BMW, is in for repair. Some idiot backed into it when it was parked in the Stoneborough Centre in Maidstone last week. And of course, Tessa had the Range Rover."

"And the BMW is the only car you have, apart from the Range Rover?"

"Well, there's the Rolls, but that's used strictly for business, to meet hotel guests or ferry them about. It's one of the luxury services we offer. She certainly wouldn't use it to pick Adam up from the station. Anyway, it wasn't here. Byfleet had driven it to Gatwick, to pick up the Americans and he didn't get back till eight."

The door opened and Delia Hamilton came in with a flurry of cold air. "Giles, what's all this I hear—" She broke off when she saw Thanet and Lineham. "Ah, Inspector. Why have they taken the van away? Is it anything to do with my brother's accident?"

Patiently, Thanet went over it all again, the strong possibility that the van had been involved, the necessity of finding out exactly who had driven it last night.

Delia had crossed to stand behind her husband, one hand on his shoulder as if to draw strength from the physical contact.

"Giles, have you told them that I. . . ?" She faltered.

"That you drove it last night?" He reached up to lay his hand reassuringly on hers. "Yes, I have. So did I, if you remember."

She paled, the beautiful bone structure of her face suddenly accentuated, briefly almost skull-like. "Oh my God, so you did. To fetch Tessa." She put up the other hand and pressed her fingers into her temple as if to ease a sudden onset of pain. "I'd forgotten."

"It's unfortunate that so many people have keys to the van," said Thanet. "I understand that apart from yourselves and Mr. Tiller, who presumably uses it most, both the Byfleets drive it and so does the farm manager, Mr. Talion."

"Jack! Oh God, he used it last night too! I didn't bother to tell you," she said to her husband, "because it didn't seem of any importance at the time."

She and Hamilton exchanged a look full of unspoken messages which Thanet tried to read and failed. One thing was certain, however. For some reason the farm manager's name had some special significance for them, in this context. "Jack? Would that be Mr. Talion?"

"Yes." Delia was still looking at her husband. "Just after I got back from the station with Adam someone rang to say that some of our sheep had got out on to the road near the Linklaters' house—that's close to the junction with the Ashford Road," she explained to Thanet. "Jack—Mr. Talion—had walked across from Home Farm to join us for a drink before dinner, he often does, and he said he'd attend to it. Of course, he didn't have his car with him so he went in the van."

"That would have been at what time?"

She shrugged. "Five minutes or so after I got back."

"And that was about twenty to eight, you say? So, say a quarter to eight."

"Something like that, I suppose."

"And how long was he away?"

"I haven't the faintest idea. You'll have to ask him."

"He's been with you long?"

"For years. He was farm manager in my father's time, and stayed on when my husband took over."

"How many years?"

Delia frowned. "I'm not sure, exactly. He came when I was a child. Twenty-five, thirty years, something like that. Again, you'll have to ask him. Or I suppose we could look it up in the records."

"No, it doesn't matter. As you say, I can ask him."

But it was interesting to learn that Talion, too, would have known Leo Martindale before he left the area.

"I didn't ask before, but why, exactly, did your brother go away?"

Delia gave an embarrassed laugh. "I'm afraid my father's patience ran out. Leo was always a bit wild and Daddy was forever having to bail him out of one scrape or another. In the end, after he'd paid off his debts for the umpteenth time, he gave him a final warning: if he didn't mend his ways he would be out on his ear, no allowance, nothing." She shrugged. "Leo didn't pay any attention to the warning and out he went."

"I assume your father therefore also cut your brother out of his will."

Delia looked uncomfortable. "Well no, he didn't. He couldn't. The Hall is entailed."

"I thought most of those old entails were broken long ago."

"Yes, most of them were, in 1925 I think Daddy said. But unfortunately ours was a little more complicated than that."

"In what way?"

"I can't see how all this can possibly be relevant," said Hamilton.

"It may well not be, Mr. Hamilton. But I'd be grateful if your wife would explain, all the same."

Delia Hamilton looked at her husband and he gave a reluctant nod.

"Well, it's a question of something called an entailed trust, actually, and as a matter of tradition the arrangement has been continued from one generation to the next, right from the time Longford Hall was first built. What happens is this. On the twenty-first birthday of the heir, the trust would in each generation be renegotiated so that before anyone actually inherited it, it was tied up for the generation beyond."

"So that if, in fact, the heir ever wished to sell it, he couldn't?"

She nodded. "That's right. Because it would be impossible to know exactly how many children he's going to have until he's dead. It's a very unusual arrangement, but it's what we've always done."

"So you're saying that the trust had been renegotiated with Mr. Martindale on his twenty-first birthday?"

"Yes."

"And once set up it couldn't be broken?"

"That's right." She sighed. "Of course, no one envisaged a situation in which the heir couldn't be found. As it was, obviously someone had to administer the estate so the trustees allowed us to do so in my brother's absence."

"And if he hadn't turned up by the time seven years had passed he would presumably have been assumed dead and the estate would have come to you?"

A tight nod.

No doubt they were all thinking the same thing, thought Thanet. *As it now does.*

"I see. Well, there's just one more question I must put to you." And in the circumstances it was very difficult to think of a way of putting it tactfully. "If it does turn out, as seems likely, that it was your van that ran your brother down, is there any reason why any of the people who have access to it wouldn't be sorry to see him dead?" *Apart from you, of course, with the king-sized motive which you've just handed to us.*

His delicacy was wasted. They were intelligent people and saw at once what he was asking, and its implications. They stared at him, in apparent disbelief.

"Let me get this straight," said Hamilton at last. "I asked you earlier if you were suggesting that Leo might have been murdered. I couldn't believe then that you were serious and I can't believe it now. But you are, aren't you? What you're really asking is whether or not any of these people—including us, I presume, as we also drive the van—had a motive for killing him?"

"This is crazy!" said his wife, clutching her head. "I can't believe what I'm hearing. My brother has a perfectly straightforward accident and before we know where we are we're accused of murdering him!"

"No!" said Thanet. "You're jumping to conclusions. I'm accusing no one of

111

anything at the moment, I'm merely looking at all the possibilities. That is what I'm paid to do. And you must see that—"

There was a knock at the door.

"Come in," called Hamilton, a little too heartily; relieved, no doubt, at the interruption.

It was Bentley. "Sorry to disturb you, sir, but . . ." It was obvious that he had come across something interesting.

Thanet stood up. Clearly he wasn't going to get anything more out of the Hamiltons at present. "All right, Bentley, we've finished here for the moment."

Outside the light was fading and it was beginning to snow. Thanet turned up his collar again and pulled on his woolly hat. No point in freezing in order to look dignified. "What is it?"

"One of the guests told me that he was out for a walk yesterday morning and he saw Mr. Martindale having a blazing row with somebody."

"Who?"

"He couldn't remember his name, though he had heard it—he saw him again last night when they were having drinks

112

before dinner, and they were introduced. Anyway, he says he's the farm manager."

"Talion," said Lineham. "Well well. I noticed the look Mrs. Hamilton gave her husband when his name came up, didn't you?"

"Yes. Was this guest close enough to hear what the row was about?"

Bentley shook his head regretfully. "No, unfortunately. But he did say that there was another man nearby, a tractor driver. Apparently the farm manager and this man were talking when Mr. Martindale joined them. The farm labourer moved a little way away, tactful-like, and soon afterwards the row started."

"But your witness thinks this tractor driver would still have been close enough to hear what was said?"

"Yes, sir."

"In that case," said Thanet, "perhaps it would be a good idea to have a word with him first, before seeing Talion."

He glanced at his watch. Ten to four. With any luck they might catch the tractor driver before he finished work for the day. Presumably the place to look for him would be at Home Farm.

Sam Tiller was crossing the yard carrying a shovel, heading for the storage shed in which they had interviewed him earlier, and Thanet called him over. To get to the Home Farm, they learned, they could either walk through the grounds of the Hall, a distance of about half a mile, or drive down to the road and take the first turning on the left.

With a glance at the leaden sky and the thickening snow Thanet decided to take the easy way out. After a word of thanks to Bentley he and Lineham headed for the Land Rover.

7

"MARVELLOUS isn't it?" said Lineham gloomily as they set off down the drive. "Not only do we discover that six people had keys to the van, but that four of them actually used it last night. And we haven't asked the Byfleets yet." He slowed down as they reached the main road. The red Ford Escort with Tessa Hamilton and her boyfriend inside turned into the drive as he pulled away.

Thanet lifted a hand in response to her wave.

"Those two young Hamiltons could put you off parenthood for ever," said Lineham.

Thanet laughed. "Bit late for that, isn't it, Mike?"

"All I can say is, I hope Mandy doesn't look like that when she's seventeen . . . Anyway, the whole thing seems pretty hopeless to me. Even if we do suspect who was actually driving the van when Mr.

Martindale was hit, we haven't got a hope of proving it. No witnesses, nothing."

"Come on, Mike. It's early days yet. You never know what the house-to-house enquiries will turn up and there's always forensic. If Martindale was actually put into that ditch as we suspect . . ."

"Hmm. Ah, here we are."

He swung the Land Rover into a lane with HOME FARM stamped in black on a wooden sign. There were well-maintained wire fences on either side of the road, with snow piled against them where tractors had no doubt cleared the way. Ahead was a cluster of farm buildings and in a few hundred yards the track divided, one arm entering a drive leading to a red brick-and-tile farmhouse, the other widening out as it entered a broad yard surrounded by barns and sheds.

Over to the left a tractor with a forage box attached was moving very slowly along the wide central aisle of a long cattle shed. Thanet and Lineham walked across, hunching their shoulders and keeping their heads down against the swirling snow. At the entrance to the shed they stopped. On either side were stout iron barriers behind which black-and-white cattle on thick beds of straw were lined up munching the silage feed being spewed out of the forage box into the pens along a narrow conveyor belt.

Lineham wrinkled his nose. "Phew! What a stink! How do these farmworkers stand it?"

"I suppose they're used to it."

The tractor had now reached the far end of the aisle and with a roar it accelerated, described a wide arc in the open space beyond the shed and headed back towards them at a fair speed, its task presumably now completed. They stepped back as it approached and Thanet held up a hand. The driver stopped and switched off the engine.

"Yes?"

The sudden silence was a relief. Thanet stepped forward. "We're from Sturrenden CID." He introduced himself and Lineham. "We're looking into the death of Mr. Martindale, from the Hall."

"Oh yeah." The driver remained firmly planted in his seat, one hand on the steering wheel and the other on the ignition, as if ready to take off again at any moment.

"Was it you who was with Mr. Talion yesterday, when he had that row with Mr. Martindale?"

"Cor, was that him? I didn't realise."

"Would you get down, please? We'd like a word."

With a practised movement the man swung around and jumped down beside them. "Why?"

He was in his forties, Thanet guessed, with the weathered skin of a man used to working out of doors, wearing a bulky ancient parka the colour of mud and an incongruously cheerful bobble cap in red and white stripes. A large dewdrop hung from the tip of his fleshy nose and he wiped it away with the back of his gloved hand. Almost immediately another began to form.

The smell of silage, whether from the forage box, the cattle pens or the man's clothing, was overpowering.

Thanet stamped his feet. "Is there anywhere a bit less exposed where we could talk, Mr. . . . ?"

"Mardy. Jim Mardy. I can't hang about. I got work to do."

"It won't take long."

Mardy hesitated a moment longer and then, without speaking, led the way across the yard to a small shed constructed of tarred weatherboarding and pushed open the door. There were no windows and inside it was very dark. Mardy twisted a switch and a single, feeble electric light bulb strung up on one of the rafters revealed a row of nails on which hung several pairs of overalls and an assortment of scruffy coats. Spaced out around the walls on a floor of beaten earth were a number of bales of straw on three of which lay plastic lunch boxes and Thermos flasks. Mardy crossed to one of the bales, picked up a Thermos, sat down and poured himself a cup of steaming liquid. Thanet and Lineham watched enviously, Thanet making a mental note to make sure that tomorrow, if the case continued, he would come well supplied with hot drinks. Lineham, he was sure, would be making a similar resolution.

Mardy was watching him expectantly over the rim of his mug. Thanet sat down on one of the bales and signalled to Lineham to begin.

Lineham remained standing, shoving his hands deep into his pockets. "We understand that you were talking to Mr. Talion when Mr. Martindale arrived."

"'Sright. Some of the fencing needs renewing, we'd gone to take a look at it."

"What time was this?"

"Just before me dinner break. Getting on for twelve o'clock, it must've been." Mardy wiped away another dewdrop.

"Could you tell us what happened?"

The glint in the man's eye told Thanet that Mardy had now realised the purpose of this conversation. The question was, would he be cooperative or obstructive? It all depended, Thanet guessed, on Mardy's character and on his relationship with his employer, whether loyalty would win over the desire to give an account of the drama.

"What d'you mean?"

The man was playing for time, still hadn't quite made up his mind. Thanet opened his mouth to intervene then closed it again. It wasn't fair to Lineham to jump in whenever the going became sticky.

Lineham had noticed and gave Thanet

an uncertain glance. Thanet looked at the ground. Go *on*.

"We thought you might be able to tell us what the row was about."

Mardy shrugged. "No idea."

"You heard what was said, though."

"Some of it."

"Perhaps you wouldn't mind telling us what you did hear."

Silence. Mardy took another slow, deliberate swig from his cup, then screwed it back on to the Thermos. "Why don't you ask Mr. Talion?"

"We shall."

"In that case," Mardy stood up, "there's no point in me telling you, is there?"

For a few minutes longer Lineham persisted but it was useless. Now that Mardy had made up his mind nothing would shake him.

"Very well," said Lineham eventually. "Just tell me one thing. How long did this conversation last?"

Mardy hesitated, weighing up the pros and cons of answering this question and apparently deciding that it was harmless. "Not more 'n a few minutes."

"And would you say they'd met before, recently?"

Again a hesitation. Then Mardy shook his head. "The other bloke, Mr. Martindale, started off by saying, 'Hullo Talion. Long time no see.'"

"And what did Mr. Talion say?"

Realising that he was imperceptibly being drawn into giving away information he had decided to withhold, Mardy headed for the door. "I gotta get on."

Thanet and Lineham returned to the Land Rover and watched him roar off on his tractor into the gathering dusk.

"I blew it, didn't I?" said Lineham. "Sorry, sir." He thumped the steering wheel in frustration before turning on the windscreen wipers to clear the thin film of snow which had built up while they had been talking to Mardy. "I jumped in too quickly. If I'd begun as I ended, I might have got somewhere."

"No point in worrying about it now. The main thing is, you can see where you went wrong. And those last two questions were very useful."

"I just thought it would be interesting to know how long they'd been talking before the row broke out," said Lineham eagerly. "And whether or not it was the continuation of a recent row."

"Quite. And apparently it wasn't. The implication being . . ."

"That whatever the issue between them, it was a pretty powerful one. I mean, you don't meet someone after an interval of twenty odd years and plunge straight into a row unless you've got a very good reason."

"Also, it sounds as though it might have been Talion who had the grudge. Martindale's greeting sounded friendly enough."

"Mr. Talion now, then?"

Thanet nodded and they drove out of the farmyard and into the driveway of Home Farm. Inside the house a dog started barking as they approached the front door. The barks grew louder and the man who answered their knock made no attempt to stop the noise until Thanet had introduced himself.

"All right, Rhett. Enough!"

The dog, an Alsatian, at once fell silent but remained wary, watching the two policemen for any threatening move.

"You'd better come in."

Talion opened a door to the right of the small hall, switching on the light, and they followed him into a cold gloomy dining-room furnished with heavy oak table and chairs, carpet square and skimpy unlined curtains patterned with orange and yellow flowers. The room looked as though it was rarely, if ever, used and as if no one had cared what it looked like for a very long time.

"What is it?" He was in his sixties, short and stocky, dressed in well-worn corduroy trousers, pullover and tweed sports jacket. He looked like a man who had long ago forgotten how to smile; all the lines in his face drooped and there were deep creases between his eyebrows. He did not invite them to sit down and agreed only reluctantly when Thanet asked if they may. The dog flopped down at Talion's feet and buried its nose in its paws.

The door was pushed open and a woman came into the room. "Who is it, Jack?" She was small, pale and thin, her clothes nondescript, her grey hair pinned back in a meagre bun.

At once his whole demeanour changed

and in a flash he was up out of his chair and putting an arm protectively around her shoulders. "It's all right, Meg, it's only business, it won't take long. You go back in the warm." Gently, he urged her into the hall and through the door at the far side.

"I don't want my wife upset," he said as he came back in, shutting the door firmly behind him. "Her health isn't too good. Heart trouble."

"I'm sorry to hear that."

Thanet was sincere, but Talion gave him a sceptical glance as he sat down again. "Well, what did you want?"

"You'll have heard of Mr. Martindale's death?"

A flicker of—what? Satisfaction? Some even stronger emotion?—in Talion's eyes. He nodded. "Hit and run, wasn't it."

Statement, not question, Thanet noticed. And still no hint of regret, false or otherwise.

"That's what we're trying to find out."

Talion was looking disconcerted. "What do you mean?"

"What I say." Thanet paused. "It looks as though he was knocked down by the

Ford van they use at the hotel as a general runabout."

He watched Talion apparently assimilate this information and remember that he had used the van himself last night.

"So?"

"So naturally we are talking to everyone who drove it last night. As I understand you did."

"Yes, that's true. I did. What of it?"

"Mrs. Hamilton tells us that you had to go to check on some sheep that had got out on to the road."

"That's right."

"You left at about a quarter to eight, I believe. What time did you get back?"

Talion shrugged. "I wasn't away long. Twenty, twenty-five minutes, perhaps."

"So you were back by, say, ten past eight?"

"I suppose. What does it matter?"

"I'm just trying to get a clear picture of the van's movements last night. And naturally I have to ask you if you saw Mr. Martindale, while you were out."

"No, I didn't."

"You'd seen him earlier in the day though, I understand?"

"Who told you that?"

"One of the hotel guests saw you together."

Talion said nothing.

"He said that you were arguing."

Still no response.

"Having a row, in fact?"

"What of it? Aren't I entitled to have an argument with someone without the police taking an interest?"

"Not," said Thanet, "if that someone happens to be killed later on that same day."

Talion stood up and, as if pulled by an invisible string, the dog rose too. "Now just a minute . . . What are you suggesting?"

The dog's hackles were rising, Thanet noticed. "Nothing, Mr. Talion. Merely enquiring. What, exactly, was the row about?"

"It's none of your bloody business!" he snarled.

Lips curling back from teeth, dog and master looked remarkably alike. A low growl issued from deep in the animal's throat.

"That's not true, I'm afraid," said

Thanet mildly. "Everything to do with Mr. Martindale is police business now. A suspicious death means a complete loss of privacy for eveyone concerned."

Talion laid a hand on the dog's head. "All right, boy, it's all right. Lie down." He sat down himself as the dog subsided and for several moments remained silent, staring at the table. Eventually he stirred. "I suppose," he said, "if I don't tell you now, you'll be back, until you get what you want."

Thanet said nothing. He guessed that Talion was remembering that there had been a witness to the argument and, unaware that they had already interviewed Jim Mardy without success, was thinking that it would be best to get in first with his own version.

"So I might as well tell you. Mr. Martindale told me that he was thinking of staying on for good, now he'd come back. I told him that he'd do better to take off again, the sooner the better as far as everyone around here is concerned."

"He was that unpopular?"

Talion shrugged. "Let's just say he had a knack of getting up everyone's nose."

"And that's it?"

"Well, he wasn't very pleased, naturally. Said after all this time we ought to be able to let bygones be bygones. I couldn't agree and said so."

"You make it all sound very calm, very rational. But it wasn't, was it?"

Talion said nothing, just shrugged again.

"Our witness was some distance away, but it was obvious to him that you were having a heated argument."

Talion's mouth set in a stubborn line. "That's all that was said."

Now for the really important part. Thanet didn't think that he was going to get anywhere, but he had to try. "I can't believe that you were concerned only in a general way, for the good of the community. I assume that if Mr. Martindale said you ought to let bygones be bygones you had a personal reason for being so against his settling here again?"

The silence stretched out, became protracted. Thanet waited. And waited.

Eventually Talion stood up. "Sorry, but I've said all I'm going to say." He thrust his chin forward and his voice rose. "And as I said before, it's really none of your bloody business. So get out, will you?"

The dog was on his feet again, barking this time, the fur along his back standing up in ridges.

It was pointless to persist. Slowly, almost casually, giving the dog no cause for alarm, Thanet rose. Lineham followed suit and they left. Outside, Lineham released pent-up breath. "Phew. I thought he was going to set the dog on us in the end, didn't you?"

"Doesn't look as though either of us is doing too well at the moment, Mike."

Back in the Land Rover Thanet looked at his watch. Four-thirty. If he was to report back to Draco as ordered at five they would have to get a move on. And he was chilled to the bone. The thought of home, warmth and hot food was irresistible.

He decided to call it a day.

8

AS usual, however, the lure of home had to be resisted. By the time Thanet had reported to Draco, chewed over the day's findings with Lineham and written up the "detailed, literate and accurate" reports upon which Draco invariably insisted, it was nearly nine o'clock. Fortunately the threatened heavy snowfall had not materialised and all the main roads were relatively clear. Thanet hoped that they would stay that way.

His own street looked unfamiliar, its pavements lined with humps of piled-up snow where householders had tossed it aside to clear their driveways.

Inside the house the warmth and savoury smell of food were like a benediction. He shrugged off his sheepskin jacket and hung it in the cupboard under the stairs, his stomach rumbling in anticipation.

Joan had heard him and came out into

the hall. She was wearing a new jumpsuit which they had chosen together the previous Saturday, in a soft, misty blue which enhanced her delicate skin tones and hair the colour of clear honey.

"Mm," said Thanet as they kissed. "You look gorgeous. Smell gorgeous, too."

"I just had a bath."

"What are you doing?"

"Nothing much. I'm giving myself an evening off."

"Were you watching something you wanted to see, on television?"

"Nothing special."

She led the way into the kitchen, took his supper out of the oven and put it on the table where his place was laid. "I had it on a very low heat but it's a bit dried up, I'm afraid."

"Looks delicious," said Thanet. It was steak and kidney pie, his favourite. "Just what I need."

"I thought of you today, tramping about in the snow. Was it grim?" She knew how he hated the cold.

Thanet grimaced. "This morning was."

"How did you get on with Superintendent Draco breathing down your neck?"

She poured the tea then sat down opposite him and they chatted about the day's events while he ate. When he had finished telling her about the case she sat thinking for a while. Eventually she stirred. "He sounds a pretty sad sort of person. The victim."

"That wasn't the impression I got from the people I talked to."

She shook her head. "No, I don't mean the impression he gave other people, I mean what he was really like, underneath."

"You mean, because I said that no one has yet shown any sign of sorrow over his death?"

"Partly, I suppose. It must be awful to think that there isn't a single person who cares if you're alive or dead."

"We don't know that that's how it was with him. There might be other people, in other places . . . No, well, I admit it does seem unlikely. He was very much a rolling stone, by the sound of it. But if you'd seen the pile of letters—carefully hoarded—

from all his conquests, perhaps you wouldn't feel quite so sorry for him."

"Oh, I'm not trying to defend all that. I'm just saying it must be sad to feel so alone."

Thanet laid down his knife and fork. "He certainly seems to have succeeded in making himself thoroughly unpopular in the area. And now . . ."

"What?"

"I'm just trying to work it out. Yes, I feel as though they're all drawing closer to each other in a tight circle to prevent me from finding out the truth."

"And what d'you think the truth is?"

Thanet shrugged. "No idea."

"You're not suggesting that it was a communal plot to get rid of him!"

"No. Oh no, nothing as bizarre as that. It's just that I'm beginning to suspect that everyone is really rather relieved that he is dead and therefore feels a degree of gratitude to whoever was at the wheel of that van when it happened. So there's a . . . well, a conspiracy of silence, if you like, to protect that person. No one wants to be suspected himself, but he's going to make sure he doesn't point the finger at anyone else. So far the only useful leads we've had are from outsiders." He sighed. "If it continues like that, it'll be hard going. Any more tea in the pot, love?"

She took his cup and he watched her pour it, grateful for a relationship in which each performed such small services for the other when they needed it without a second thought. It had taken them a long time to reach that plateau. For many years he had, while paying lip service to Joan's need for a satisfying career of her own, inwardly been the original male chauvinist pig he outwardly professed to despise. But now . . . He caught her hand, kissed it. He was a lucky man.

"The house is very quiet tonight. Bridget out?" He knew that it was her evening off.

"Yes. And Ben's doing his homework."

"Still?"

They grimaced at each other. The days of Ben's skimping his homework had long gone. The higher academic standards and level of attainment in his new school had seen to that. At first Thanet and Joan had been delighted at his new seriousness over his work but by now they were becoming concerned about it. They'd had enough trouble over Bridget, when she sat her GCSEs, to be concerned lest Ben should go the same way.

"I'll pop up and say hullo."

Ben was sitting at his desk, hunched over his books.

Thanet sat down on the bed. "Still at it?"

"Yes. I've nearly finished."

Ben looked tired, Thanet thought, remembering anew with a lurch of anxiety how obsessive Bridget had become over her work last year, how it had nearly ended in disaster. Questions he longed to ask, things he longed to say, tumbled through his mind but he held them back. He and Joan would stick to their original resolution, to give Ben six months to settle down in his new school before reviewing the situation. He stood up. "Good."

Ben looked up. "There's a chap in my class, Fellows . . . He's asked if I'd like to go ice-skating at Gillingham on Saturday. His brother's got a car."

With difficulty Thanet refrained from asking how old the brother was, how long he'd been driving, how many of them would be going. This was the first time Ben had mentioned a specific friend at the new school. He smiled. "Sounds fun."

Downstairs he flopped down on to the settee beside Joan and told her about the proposed expedition.

"Oh good! I am pleased. I think that's what he's found hardest of all, having none of his old friends at the same school." She frowned. "Though I'd like to have known how long it is since the brother passed his test. Still, as you say, it really will do him good."

"Did you have the chance of a word with Bridget about last night?"

She shook her head. "No. She was in the bathroom, as usual, when I got home and then she came down in a tearing hurry, said she was meeting Diana at seven."

"Where were they going?"

"I didn't have a chance to ask. She was gone practically before I could open my mouth."

Thanet frowned. "I don't like not knowing where she is."

"I know."

"And it's not the first time it's

happened. She's got to realise she must always let us know who she's with and where they're going."

Joan sighed. "I have tried. But she just says, how can she tell me if she doesn't know herself? She says they never decide in advance, just see how they feel when they meet."

"I can understand the difficulty but all the same, it's not good enough. We really must try and work out some system." She could be anywhere, Thanet thought. How would we begin to know where to look for her, if she just didn't come home?

"Perhaps it would be better if you spoke to her, Luke. She's so touchy with me these days. If ever I say anything like that to her she just says, 'Oh Mum, don't fuss', or 'Other people's mothers don't go on like that'."

"I don't care what other people's parents do," said Thanet grimly. "While she's living under our roof we do have a right to know where she is. I'll see what I can do."

"Don't be too heavy-handed, will you? We don't want her saying, 'If that's how you feel I'm moving out.'"

"D'you think she would?"

Joan considered, head on one side. "No, I don't think so. No, I'm sure she wouldn't. After all, on the whole, we get on pretty well. If you think of some of the problems other parents seem to have with their children . . ."

Thanet sighed. "I suppose that's true. It's just that there always seems to be something . . ."

Joan grinned. "At the risk of sounding hackneyed—*C'est la vie.*"

Thanet smiled back. "That's one of the things I love about you. Your truly original mind."

She raised a provocative eyebrow. "What are the others?"

"Which would you prefer?" said Thanet, putting an arm around her. "Demonstration or exposition?"

She snuggled closer. "Oh, demonstration, definitely."

Next morning Thanet set off for work early. There would be a stack of reports to read from Bentley, Swift, and the men who had been working on the house-to-house enquiries, and he wanted to skim through them before the morning meeting with Draco at 8.45. He hated facing the Super's early morning ebullience ill-prepared. He was thankful to note that the temperature had risen and the snow was beginning to thaw. He'd remembered to make two large flasks of coffee but it looked as though it wouldn't be quite as miserably cold today.

Lineham had not yet arrived. Thanet hoped that the sergeant had managed to sort out his problems with his brother-in-law and get a good night's sleep. He lit his pipe, considerately leaving the door open so that Lineham would not be greeted by a smoke-filled room, and settled down to read.

A number of interesting points had emerged.

One of the guests had seen the house-keeper, Mona Byfleet, coming out of Martindale's room at 7.15 on the night he died. This meant that she was, so far, the last person to have seen him alive. Thanet sat back and gazed up at the coils of smoke lazily intertwining above his head, remembering.

"I don't know what he did afterwards."

"Did you see him again at all, after he'd had dinner?"

"No."

And he distinctly remembered knowing that she was lying and wondering why. At the time he had thought that perhaps she had overheard some snatch of conversation, some argument, even, between Martindale and the Hamiltons, but now he wondered. Had she simply not wanted him to know that she had seen Martindale again after dinner? But why not?

Thanet shook his head. No, it was much more likely either that she had been making a routine check on the room or that Martindale had called her in to solve some small domestic problem, and the incident had been so trivial that it had slipped her mind.

He picked up the next report.

The Byfleets claimed that neither of them had driven the van last night, Byfleet stating that he had left the Hall at 5.30 in the Rolls to pick up some guests from Gatwick Airport and had arrived back just before eight. The guests had confirmed this. All very well, thought Thanet. That still meant that apart from the time when

Tiller had been using the van to go to the pub, they had both been free to drive it later on in the evening, if they had so wished.

He moved on to the house-to-house reports.

The landlord of the village pub had mentioned Tiller and Mrs. Rankle, his woman friend, as being among the regulars who had been in that night. They always came on Tuesday evenings, he said, and had arrived at their usual time, around twenty to nine. Also . . . Thanet's eyes widened.

"Morning, sir." It was Lineham, looking, Thanet was pleased to see, somewhat fresher this morning.

"Listen to this, Mike. The landlord of the pub says that Mrs. Rankle—Sam Tiller's girlfriend—always borrows his van some time during the evening to nip home. Apparently she's got a handicapped son and she likes to check that he's OK."

"And did she borrow it on Tuesday?"

"Apparently she went out for a short while as usual, and he assumed that was where she'd gone. She's usually away for twenty minutes or so."

"Wonder what sort of a driver she is. The roads were pretty icy that night."

"Quite. We'll have to go and see her, obviously."

Lineham picked up a batch of reports and sat down. A few minutes later he looked up. "Sir! This is interesting . . ."

It was the report of an interview with a Mrs. Doreen Victor, who lived in the village. She claimed to have seen Martindale (identified by his distinctive black-and-white checked overcoat) twice that afternoon. On the first occasion he had been talking to Mrs. Fever, wife of a local businessman (and mother of Toby Fever, Tessa Hamilton's boyfriend, Thanet wondered?) who had been filling her car up with petrol at the garage. On the second occasion Mrs. Victor had seen him having what appeared to be a heated exchange with Mrs. Rankle, Sam Tiller's friend. Unfortunately they had been on the other side of the street and she had been unable to hear what the argument was about.

"An argument," said Thanet thoughtfully. "You don't walk up to a perfect stranger in a village street and have an argument with her, do you?"

"He must have known her before," said Lineham eagerly. "When he lived here. And she drove the van that night . . ."

"Quite . . . What about this Mrs. Fever? Did the witness have the impression Martindale knew her too?"

"She doesn't say," said Lineham regretfully.

"Did you happen to notice if the petrol pumps at the garage are self-service, Mike?"

"No, I didn't. You mean, there might have been an attendant, who could have overheard the conversation?"

"It's possible. A lot of the smaller garages in the villages haven't switched to self-service yet. We'll check."

Lineham made a note.

Thanet was now glancing through Swift's reports of interviews with the staff at Longford Hall. "Ah, listen, Mike. One of the housemaids saw Martindale having a row with a Mr. Fever—this woman's husband, I presume—at about a quarter past six that evening. She was in the library, checking that everything was in order, and Martindale was there. Fever apparently came barging in and laid into him, telling him to keep away from his wife."

"What did Martindale say?"

"He was very cool apparently, tried to play it down, laugh it off. Said there was no harm in saying hullo to an old acquaintance, was there? Fever nearly went through the roof."

"What happened?"

"Mrs. Hamilton came in and shooed the girl away, so she didn't hear any more."

"So Mrs. Hamilton knew about this and didn't say a word."

Thanet sighed. "It's just as I thought. I was saying to Joan last night, I suspect we're going to have our work cut out trying to get people to talk. Our main hope is through outsiders like this Mrs. Victor, or the pub landlord, and this housemaid."

"They're not exactly outsiders."

"By outsiders I mean people who didn't know Martindale before."

Lineham pulled a face. "You may be right. If so, as you say, it'll be hard going."

Thanet checked the time. Eight-thirty-five. "Let's just glance through the rest of these. I'd like to be up to date before the meeting, and know roughly what our plans are for today."

They hurried through the remainder of the reports. The only other item of any interest was Swift's account of an interview with another member of staff, who had overheard Sam Tiller delivering an ultimatum to Delia Hamilton: if Martindale stayed, he, Tiller, would go.

"Mr. Martindale certainly wouldn't have won a popularity poll around there!" said Lineham.

"No." Thanet shuffled the papers together. "Right, Mike. Go over these again while I'm in the meeting, check we haven't missed anything. We'll have to interview a lot of these people again, see if we can get any more out of them—that's Mrs. Byfleet, Mrs. Hamilton, Mr. Tiller. And we must also try and fit in Mr. Tiller's girlfriend, Mrs. Rankle, both the Fevers and of course this Mrs. Victor, in case she can tell us anything more. It sounds as though she could be an interesting source of gossip, perhaps we ought to try and see her first. So ring and get the interviews set up."

Thanet glanced at the clock again. "Sorry, must dash." One minute to go. If he was late Draco would be furious and they'd waste half the meeting listening to a lecture on the importance of punctuality.

9

THANET made it to the meeting with ten seconds to spare. He slipped into his seat and noted Draco's customary glance at the clock. After murmured greetings all round Draco picked up the sheaf of papers lying exactly in the centre of the blotter on his desk and cleared his throat.

Apart from Draco and himself there were two other men in the room: Chief Inspector Tody, who acted as Draco's deputy should the Superintendent be unavailable; and Inspector Boon, Thanet's long-time friend and colleague. Each was watching Draco in characteristic manner, Tody with an ingratiating half-smile, Boon with an ironic twinkle in his eye.

There was a sense of expectation in the air, Thanet realised. Something was up. He looked at Draco again and yes, the signs were there: the familiar glint of self-satisfaction overlaid by missionary fervour, the almost audible crackle of energy which emanated from him. It looked as though the long-rumoured new campaign was about to begin. Mentally, Thanet braced himself. What now?

"Good morning, gentlemen. Incidentally, I think that we should soon try to amend that state of affairs. There should, if we are to keep abreast of the times, be at least one woman present. That is, however, not what I want to talk to you about this morning. This morning I want to talk to you about a scheme for further improving the efficiency of our police force here in Sturrenden. Oh, I know what you're saying to yourselves."

Draco's Welsh accent was becoming more pronounced, Thanet noticed, a sure sign that he was getting into his stride. He often felt that the Superintendent's style was more suited to the pulpit than the police force.

"You're saying, 'Haven't we had enough changes for the moment? Don't we need —indeed deserve, a bit of a break?'"

Draco brought the flat of his hand down upon his desk, making everyone jump. "No! That is the very moment, I tell you, when standards begin to slip.

Complacency is our enemy. It leads to lazy minds, lazy work practices and, above all, lazy policing."

Draco sat back, tucking his thumbs into the armholes of his waistcoat and deliberately looked at each man in turn. "Now I'm not denying that you've all worked very hard to make this a more efficient force over the last year, and the results show, as I'm sure you'll agree. But I think you'll also agree, when you've heard my new proposals, that there are a number of areas in which there is room for further improvements."

You had to admire the man's enthusiasm if nothing else, thought Thanet. Must remember to give those cards and letters to Swift, he reminded himself, concentration flagging as Draco carried on in the same vein, see if he can track down any of Martindale's old girlfriends. Not that at this stage there would appear to be any urgent reason for doing so, but it was a lead, however unpromising, that ought to be followed up.

Draco was still on his preliminary speech. *Oh, do get on with it, you Welsh windbag,* Thanet urged silently.

He was thinking about Martindale, about how extraordinary it was that anyone could arouse in so many people such a degree of animosity that it could survive apparently undiminished an interval of more than twenty years, when, with a loving glance at the papers in his hand, Draco finally came to the point.

"After considerable thought I have identified the three main areas in which improvements need to be made. Organisation, Delegation and Documentation." He spelt it out letter by letter. "O-D-D. Which, as you'll no doubt realise, spells 'Odd'." He waited for the small ripple of amusement before smiling himself. "Yes, I thought you'd appreciate that. And if the acronym affords the men some light relief, then that's all right by me. I don't in the least mind appearing a figure of fun so long as they buckle down and get on with implementing my proposals. It will, of course, be up to you to see that they do."

He stood up and handed a sheet of paper to each of them. "Here they are. I'd like you to take them away and study them and come back to me tomorrow with comments—constructive, of course. No, don't read them now, there's no time, you'll all be wanting to get back and get on with your work. So, briefly, could we have your reports, please." He sat back, folding his hands over his waistcoat.

Although he made it as succinct as possible Thanet's report was of necessity the longest, the finding of Martindale's body in the ditch being by far the most important of yesterday's events. He wondered if Draco was going to raise any objections to an intensive investigation, but apparently the discovery of the fibres on the van had convinced the Superintendent that for the moment at least Thanet and his team were justified in devoting their energies to finding out exactly what had happened.

"I might even pop out to Sutton myself later on," said Draco, causing Thanet's heart to sink. "You'll be needing to see several of these people again, as well as interviewing new witnesses. I suggest you begin with the chap who barged into the hotel and had a row with Martindale—what's his name? Fever, was it? And with this woman Rankle."

Thanet forbore to say that by now

Lineham should already have a series of appointments set up. If Draco came looking for them, with any luck he wouldn't find them. If this made the Superintendent mad, too bad. Hoping that he wouldn't have to waste too much time in elaborate games of hide and seek with Draco, he made his way back upstairs to his office, where he found Doc Mallard talking to Lineham. As usual the little police surgeon was looking spruce and cheerful and was scarcely recognisable as the sardonic scarecrow of a man he had become after the lingering death of his first wife. Thanet never ceased to marvel at the miracle which remarriage had wrought in his old friend.

"Ah, Luke. Just telling Lineham here that the PM is set for this afternoon. I'll let you know the findings as soon as I can."

"Thanks Doc."

"How's it going?"

Thanet shrugged. "All right, so far. Did Lineham tell you we found the van?"

"Yes. Belongs to the people at Longford Hall, I gather. Does the plot thicken?"

"I'm not sure, yet. It could have been a simple hit and run."

"As non-committal as ever," said Mallard, twinkling at Thanet over his half-moons. "How you ever have the nerve to complain when I can't be too precise about time of death I don't know." He picked up his bag. "Well, I'll be in touch later, then. Happy hunting."

When Mallard had gone Lineham gestured at the paper in Thanet's hand. "Anything interesting, sir?"

"The Super's latest campaign." Thanet handed it over. "Haven't looked at it myself yet."

Lineham took it eagerly. "Thought something was brewing." He grinned. "Does he realise. . . ?"

"Oh yes. ODD. It's his crafty way of taking the sting out of it all."

Lineham, reading, groaned.

"Don't tell me," said Thanet. "I'm not going to read it until I'm feeling stronger."

"At this rate we're going to end up doing so much paperwork there won't be any time for policing. Do you realise . . ."

"Mike, I said, don't tell me. At the moment I don't want to know. Now, did you get those interviews set up?"

"All except the ones with Sam Tiller

and Mr. Fever. I'm still trying to get hold of them."

"Right. You carry on while I have a word with Swift. I want to put him on to tracing some of Martindale's former girl-friends. Are we seeing Mrs. Victor first?"

"Yes. At eleven."

"Fine."

By 10.30 they were on their way. The sky had cleared, the sun had come out and in the town the few remaining areas of blackened slushy snow were thawing fast. Out in the country it was a different matter. Along the sides of the lanes, where the sun had not yet penetrated, the snow still lay in drifts, piled up against tangled brown hedges on which there was as yet no hint of green. In the open fields it had melted in patches, stippling the brown of ploughed earth and tender green of winter wheat with random frostings of white. Tall trees stood winter-stark against a sky the milky blue of opals.

"What I can't get over," said Lineham, pulling into the side of the road to allow a lorry to pass, "is the degree of bad feeling against Martindale. Sam Tiller obviously felt so strongly about him that he threatens to leave if Martindale stays on, Jack Talion tells him bluntly he isn't wanted, this Mr. Fever barges up to the Hall and has a row with him because Martindale passes the time of day with his wife, and even Sam Tiller's girlfriend launches straight into some kind of argument when she bumps into him in the village. It's incredible! Really makes you wonder what he'd done."

"I was thinking the same thing myself, earlier. I'd really like to know just what all these people had against him. And was it the same thing, or did they all have different, individual grudges? The trouble is, I suspect it's not going to be easy to find out."

"Perhaps it doesn't matter, sir. Perhaps it'll turn out to be a simple accident. Someone ran into him by chance—the roads were very icy that night, remember —and couldn't face owning up. So when they discovered he was dead they just dragged him into the ditch and left him there."

"Could be. Though in that case we haven't a chance of finding out what happened unless a witness turns up or someone actually walks into the police station and confesses. Still, we'll just have to see. What did you say the Victors' house is called?"

"Casa Mía. And it's a bungalow, at the far end of the village. There's a For Sale sign outside, apparently."

They were just entering Sutton and Lineham slowed down. Like so many of the smaller villages in Kent it had no obvious centre and consisted of a straggle of houses, a pub, a garage, a church and a village school, now converted into a private dwelling.

The severe shortage of building land in the South-East meant that Casa Mía, like most new houses in rural areas, had been squeezed into what had evidently been the garden of the older house next door. It had been built, Thanet guessed, by someone who had cherished the dream of a villa in Spain and had had to settle for the next best thing. Its Moorish arches and wrought-iron embellishments looked as out of place in this very English setting as a tart at a vicar's tea party.

Lineham parked the car in the road and they got out. The inappropriately tall iron

157

gates were flanked by brick pillars topped with stone pineapples.

"Delusions of grandeur," murmured Thanet.

A curtain twitched as they walked up the drive and Thanet just had time to realise that the doorbell chimes were playing "Home Sweet Home" before the door opened.

"Mrs. Victor?"

The woman patted her towering beehive of dyed blonde hair and gave a coy smile, revealing suspiciously white and even teeth. She was, he guessed, in her late fifties, and many sessions on either sunbed or beach had tanned her skin to a deep, rich brown, unfortunately drying it to the texture of a prune in the process. She was carefully if heavily made up and was wearing unsuitably youthful clothes—tight trousers and flower-strewn sweater. Thanet gave her a warm smile as he introduced himself. She looked exactly as he had hoped she would, a woman with too much time on her hands and little to do but take an interest in her neighbours' affairs.

She peered anxiously over his shoulder

down the drive before inviting them in. "I'm expecting my hubby home any moment."

It was clear that she didn't want the interview to begin until he arrived. In the living-room the Spanish theme continued, with heavily carved furniture in dark oak, incongruously juxtaposed with the ubiquitous dralon threepiece suite, and a garish painting of a Spanish flamenco dancer over the synthetic dressed stone fireplace. Mrs. Victor fussed about, settling them comfortably and insisting on providing them with unwanted cups of coffee. "It's all ready, it won't take a tick."

"Wonder if her husband was due home anyway?" said Lineham, when she had left.

"Or if she rang him after you set up the appointment, you mean?"

"And if so, why?"

Thanet shrugged. "Perhaps she's the little woman type, doesn't feel comfortable unless her husband is at hand to give her moral support."

Lineham's lip curled. "I thought that sort of attitude had gone out with the ark."

"I can't see why you're so surprised at

the idea. There must be thousands of women—Isn't that a car in the drive?"

Lineham half rose to glance out of the window. "Jaguar, E reg. Must be doing well."

Outside in the hall footsteps went past towards the front door and there was a murmur of voices.

Of all the many different aspects of his work interviewing was the one Thanet enjoyed most and it was with a keen sense of anticipation that he stood up as the Victors entered the room.

10

"INSPECTOR THANET?" Hand outstretched, Victor advanced, picture of an honest citizen eager to do his duty.

Thanet experienced in encounters of this kind, sensed a secret bubble of excitement in the man. Was it merely that Victor was relishing the drama of being involved, however peripherally, with the death which must be the talk of the village, or was there something more?

Short and burly with sparse curly hair and copious sidewhiskers, he was formally dressed in dark suit and discreetly striped shirt. Only his tie, vividly patterned in orange and mustard-yellow whorls, betrayed the taste which had bought and furnished Casa Mía.

"The coffee's all ready," murmured his wife, and by the time the three men were seated she had brought it in.

Victor began conventionally enough. "Naturally the wife was wondering what you wanted to see her about." He took a cautious sip of the scalding liquid. "I mean, she told the policeman who called yesterday everything she knew about this Mr. . . . What was his name?"

"Martindale."

"That's right, yes. Which wasn't much. I mean, she'd never set eyes on him before Tuesday afternoon and at the time, of course, she didn't realise who he was. It was only when his coat was mentioned . . ."

"Black-and-white checked tweed," said Mrs. Victor, entering the conversation for the first time. "Very nice, too."

"Yes, Dor, we know that." A hint of impatience, there. He turned back to Thanet. "So. . . ?"

"We just wanted to clear up one or two points, sir. Clarify your wife's impressions."

"I see."

Obviously he didn't, but he pressed gamely on. "Well, any way we can help, of course . . ."

And there was that glint of excitement again, as if Victor was hugging some secret knowledge to himself. Thanet began to wonder if the man's presence had nothing to do with his wife and he was really here because he had a titbit of information to impart. If so, no doubt he would come out with it in his own time.

"Thank you. Now I understand, Mrs. Victor, that on Tuesday afternoon you saw Mr. Martindale twice?"

"Yes." She put her coffee cup down on the low carved oak table beside her and looked at her husband, waited for his encouraging nod. "I had to go to the post office, see, to get some stamps. It's at the far end of the village so of course I had to pass the garage. That was where I first saw this man, this Mr. Martindale. At least, I suppose it was him?" She glanced doubtfully at her husband.

"Tell the Inspector what he looked like, Dor," said Victor, as if encouraging a child who lacked confidence.

"He was in his late forties, early fifties, I should say. Medium height, brown curly hair, going a bit thin on top." An involuntary glance at her husband's own sparse locks before she hastily averted her eyes. "I didn't see him all that clearly then; it

163

was later, after he'd been talking to Mrs. Rankle, he passed quite close to me."

Victor glanced at Thanet for confirmation and he nodded. "Sounds like him."

"I noticed him," said Mrs. Victor, getting into her stride, "because of course he was a stranger and we don't get many around here, we're a bit off the beaten track. So naturally I wondered who he was. Especially . . ." She pulled herself up. "Well, no, not especially, I suppose . . . But anyway, he was talking to Mrs. Fever."

Thanet, intrigued, tried an oblique approach. "Mrs. Fever is a friend of yours?"

"Oh no! It's just that . . ." She stopped, looked to her husband for help.

He sniggered and said, "Fever has a reputation for being jealous as hell. His wife can't so much as look at another man without him going off the deep end, so she tends to avoid little tête-à-têtes with anything in trousers."

Interesting. "You've actually seen him lose his temper over this?" Thanet wondered if Victor had made a pass at

Mrs. Fever himself, and had learnt about Fever's possessiveness the hard way.

"Not exactly. We don't mix much, in the village." He glanced at his wife and gave a bitter little laugh. "To be honest, they're not exactly a welcoming lot around here. Keep themselves to themselves and if you're a newcomer . . . Doreen and me've got fed up with it. We've decided to move back to Maidstone."

"So how did you find out that Mr. Fever was inclined to be jealous of his wife?"

"That was me," said Mrs. Victor. "One day when my car was in for repair I had to go into Sturrenden on the bus and I heard two of the women from the village talking . . ."

"But you can tell by the way he watches her," said Victor. "We've been to one or two dos in the village, the church fête and that, and he never takes his eyes off of her."

"So when you saw Mr. Martindale talking to her on Tuesday afternoon, Mrs. Victor, you were naturally intrigued?"

She nodded. "Yes. That was another reason why I specially noticed him."

"I see. Were you close enough to hear what they were saying?"

She shook her head with a tinge of regret. "No."

"She was filling her car with petrol, I believe you said?"

"That's right. Well, she wasn't actually doing it herself, Bert was. The garage attendant."

"I see." Good. With any luck Bert would be able to tell them more. "And they were just passing the time of day, so far as you could tell."

"Well, I'm not sure. I wouldn't put it quite like that. He seemed to be doing the talking and she was shaking her head."

"As if he was trying to persuade her to do something?"

"Could have been. Something like that, anyway."

"Were they talking long?"

"Just while her car was being filled up. I looked back when I got to the post office and she was just driving off."

"Did you have the impression they knew each other?"

"Oh yes. Definitely."

Thanet glanced at Lineham and raised his eyebrows. *Anything else?*

Lineham shook his head.

"Right, thank you. Now, I assume that it was when you came out of the post office that you saw him again, this time talking to Mrs. Rankle?"

"That's right. When I went in Mrs. Rankle was there, being served. She went out, I bought my stamps and when I went out again there they were, having this argument."

"Where was this? Were they on the same side of the road as you?"

"Yes. He must've crossed over while I was inside."

"How far away from you were they?"

She screwed up her face in concentration and glanced at her husband as she said doubtfully, "Fifty yards?"

"Dor's not very good at distances," said Victor with an apologetic little laugh.

"It doesn't matter. Were they near enough for you to hear what they were saying?"

"Not really, not most of it, anyway. But you could tell they were arguing. And I did hear Mrs. Rankle say, 'How you've got the cheek to show your face here again I just don't know.'"

"She raised her voice, presumably? Yes. Did you hear any more?"

Mrs. Victor shook her head regretfully. "I was sticking the stamps on my envelopes before posting them and if I'd gone back along the pavement the way I'd come, well, I'd have had to pass quite close, you see, and it was so obvious they were rowing . . . It would have been embarrassing, trying to pretend I couldn't hear. And it would have looked a bit obvious if I'd crossed the road just to avoid them. I didn't know quite what to do, so in the end I just stayed where I was and made out it was taking a long time to stick the stamps on."

"Yes, I see." Pity, but still . . . "So then what happened?"

"She went off, well, flounced, really, I suppose you'd say, in a temper. And he came on towards me and went into the post office. That was when I got a better look at him."

"Did he seem upset?"

"Yes, he did a bit. Well, I mean, it'd

be understandable, wouldn't it, after being told to your face you're not wanted."

She and her husband exchanged glances. *We know all about being not wanted.*

"Is there anything else you can recall?"

A shake of the head. "No, I don't think so." Then another glance at her husband, a slight lift of the eyebrows. *Are you going to tell them?*

Might as well make it easy for him, Thanet decided. "I believe you were out yesterday, when our man called, Mr. Victor?"

"That's right, yes."

"So is there anything you can add to your wife's statement?"

"Well there was something, as a matter of fact. Though I don't know if it's of any importance."

"If you could tell us anyway . . ."

Victor passed the tip of his tongue over his upper lip and leaned forward, relishing his moment centre stage. "I was in the pub on Monday night—"

"Sorry to interrupt, but I just want to make sure I've got this straight . . . You're talking now about the night before Mr. Martindale had his accident?"

"Yes."

Thanet remembered Delia Hamilton saying that Martindale had gone down to the pub that first evening, and had got back about nine. "Go on."

"Dor'd gone to her Keep Fit class in Ashford, so I went along for a drink, about eight it must've been. Place was pretty crowded, there was a darts match on. Anyway, this chap was at the bar, by himself."

"Mr. Martindale, you mean?"

"Yep. Though I didn't know it was him, if you get my meaning. At first I thought he was a stranger, just dropped in for a drink as he was passing through the village, then I began to realise there was more to it than that."

"What do you mean?"

"Well, after a while it dawned on me that all the locals, the older ones, anyway, were avoiding him. It was unnatural, like. They didn't look at him and when they wanted a refill they'd deliberately go to the end of the bar away from him."

"How did he react?"

"Just sat there drinking as if he didn't notice what was happening. I wondered if

I was imagining it at first, but after a while I was sure I wasn't and I began to feel sorry for him. I'd just made up my mind to go and stand next to him, have a chat, perhaps offer to buy him a pint, when Sam Tiller came in—he's groundsman up at the Hall."

"Yes, I know. Go on."

"Well, he comes in and goes straight to the bar, to the space next to this man. Martindale looks round and says, 'It's Sam, isn't it? Sam Tiller! How are you?' Tiller looks at him and sort of freezes . . . I swear, if looks could kill . . . Tiller doesn't say a word, just moves away, to the other end of the bar. No one says anything, but all the locals were watching, to see what Martindale would do."

"And what did he do?"

"Just finished up his drink and left."

So, a public snub, thought Thanet. And more than that, a warning?

"What happened after that?"

"Sam paid for his drink and went across to join some of his pals."

"Nothing was said, that you could hear?"

"No. But one of them clapped him on

the back and said something, and they all laughed."

"I see. Well thank you very much, both of you. You've been very helpful."

"There's just one point . . ." said Lineham, as they all stood up. "When you came home on Monday night, Mr. Victor, did you happen to mention this incident to your wife?"

"Yes, I did. Well, like I said, I felt sorry for him."

"I was just wondering why you didn't mention it to the PC who interviewed you yesterday, Mrs. Victor?"

She looked confused. "I don't know. I didn't think . . . He said they were trying to trace Mr. Martindale's movements during the day he died, so I just told him what I'd seen."

"But when I got home from work and heard what had happened," said Victor, "that this chap was dead and the police had been round asking questions, I thought perhaps I ought to tell you. If you hadn't made this appointment I was going to give you a ring."

"Quite right, too," said Thanet. "We need all the help we can get."

In the car Lineham said, "What d'you think, sir? Think Mrs. Fever was an old flame of Martindale's?"

"Possibly. Anyway, it certainly confirms that both Fever and Tiller have some explaining to do, doesn't it? What time is the appointment with the Fevers?"

"Twelve-fifteen."

Thanet glanced at his watch. Twenty to twelve. "Just time for a word with that mechanic first."

11

THE local garage did nothing to enhance the meagre charms of Sutton, being no more than a large weatherboarded hut tacked on to the end of a row of cottages in the centre of the village. At some point the peg tiles had been stripped off the roof and replaced with green-painted corrugated iron. Outside were two antiquated petrol pumps with a notice saying PLEASE HOOT FOR SERVICE, inside was the usual acrid smell of oil and metal.

Business did not appear to be thriving. There was only one car in the workshop and one pair of legs sticking out from beneath it. Bert, presumably.

Lineham advanced. "Bert?" He stooped, peered underneath the car. "Sorry, I don't know your surname."

The legs slid forward, a torso emerged clad in mechanic's overalls, then a head.

"Seller." The man squinted up. "What d'you want?"

He was in his thirties, Thanet guessed, with longish, greasy black hair and pinched ferrety features.

"Police, Mr. Seller." Lineham held out his warrant card.

The man glanced warily from Lineham to Thanet and back again. "If it's anything to do with the business you'll have to wait for Mr. Stake. He's gone into Ashford to pick up a spare part."

"No, it's nothing to do with the business. It's you we wanted to see."

"Oh. . . ?" Seller scrambled to his feet as Lineham introduced himself.

Thanet was intrigued by the overtones of wariness in Seller's voice. Had Lineham noticed?

Seller crossed to a bench, put down the spanner he was holding and wiped his hands on an oily rag.

"We're looking into the death of a Mr. Martindale, the night before last."

"The hit and run."

"Yes. During the afternoon he was seen talking to Mrs. Fever here at the garage."

He was nodding. "That's right. She'd stopped for petrol, and he came over."

"Could you tell us about the conversation, please?"

"Well . . ." He squinted into the middle distance, considering. "I was just starting to fill Mrs. Fever's car when he came across."

"Across the road, you mean?"

"Yeah. He was walking towards the post office, on the other side of the road. I'd noticed him because he was a stranger and we don't get many around here. Anyway, he must've spotted Mrs. Fever because suddenly he stops, looks, and then crosses the road. He nods at me then he bends down and says through the car window, 'It is Yvonne, isn't it?' Well, she looks up and goes white as a sheet. She doesn't say a word, but it's obvious she'd recognised him and he says, 'Yes, it's me. Leo.'

"She still doesn't say nothing, but she opens the door and gets out, and moves away a bit with a look at me as if to say, 'I don't want him to hear this'." Seller grinned. "Out of luck, wasn't she? Hear a pin drop at fifty yards, I can."

"So what happened then?" said Lineham.

176

Seller glanced from one to the other, obviously gratified by their rapt attention.

"The chap runs after her, doesn't he? 'Aren't you pleased to see me?' he says."

"Where on earth have you sprung from, Leo?"

"Oh come on, 'Vonne. What sort of a welcome is that?"

"Why have you come? What do you want?"

"Which question would you like me to answer first?"

"Leo, please!"

"It's quite simple, my sweet . . ."

"Don't call me that!"

"Very well. It's quite simple. I've come home for good."

"Oh God, no . . . But why? Why now, after all these years?"

"Shall we say I recently learned something to my advantage?"

"You mean, you didn't know your father was dead?"

"Not until last week."

"I'd finished filling up with petrol by then and Mrs. Fever asked me how much it was. She paid me and I had to go into the office to fetch her change," said Seller regretfully. "Then the phone rang and I had to answer it. When I went out again he was trying to persuade her to go to tea with him. For old times' sake, he said."

"Did she agree?"

"No. He was still trying to get her to change her mind when she got into the car and drove off. Pretty upset she looked, too."

"Then what?"

"He looks at me, grins, shrugs and says, 'Ah well, you can't win 'em all.' Then he crosses the road and goes on his way towards the post office."

Thanet was surprised that Seller had been so forthcoming. Initially he had thought that Lineham might have problems in getting the man to talk. He remembered Seller's uneasiness when Martindale was first mentioned. Was all this loquacity a smokescreen for something else? He watched carefully as Lineham continued the questioning, and became convinced that the man was hiding something. Seller had apparently worked in the village for only two years and at first had had no idea who Martindale was.

"When did you find out?" said Lineham.

"I mentioned it to Mr. Stake when he came back."

"Mentioned what, exactly?"

"That this Leo character had been chatting Mrs. Fever up."

"And he knew who he was, straight away?"

"Oh yes. Said, 'Leo Martindale back? I hadn't heard. That's a turn-up for the book.'"

"Mr. Stake has lived here a long time, presumably."

"All his life. His dad had the garage before him."

"How old is he?"

Seller looked surprised, shrugged. "Fiftyish?"

Contemporary with Martindale, then, thought Thanet.

"What else did he say, when you told him?"

"Not much. Just said he hoped he wasn't going to start causing trouble again."

"What sort of trouble?"

"He wouldn't say."

Lineham glanced at Thanet, raised his eyebrows.

"Mr. Seller," said Thanet, "did you by any chance mention this incident to anyone else?"

On target! Seller's expression changed and he shuffled his feet, looked uncomfortable.

"Yes, Mr. Seller?"

Seller was still hesitating.

"Let me guess, then," said Thanet. "You thought you might stir things up a bit by telling Mr. Fever, didn't you?"

"He's such a prick!" Seller burst out. "Always throwing his weight about, thinks he's so great! I thought it would do him good, take him down a peg or two. How did I know he'd react like that?"

"Like what? When was this?"

"Outside the Drovers. I went along for a pint, after work. I ran into him in the car park."

"So what, exactly, did you say to him?"

"Nothing much! Just said I'd seen an old friend of his wife's, that afternoon. The man's a nutcase!"

"What did he do?"

"Grabbed me by the collar and said, 'What the hell do you mean by that?'"

"And?"

"I tried to back-pedal, play it down, but he wouldn't have it. He made me tell him what I'd heard."

"And then?"

"He got straight back into his car and drove off."

"In the direction of the Hall?"

Seller nodded sullenly. "Like I said, he's a nutcase."

Thanet considered that after such deliberate malice Seller had been lucky to get away so lightly. He said so to Lineham, outside.

"I should think Fever was much more interested in tackling Martindale, sir. He must have rushed straight up to the Hall to have it out with him."

"Sounds like it. But in any case Martindale was alive and well for some time after Fever tackled him at—what time was it? Six-fifteen?"

"Yes. He had dinner with his sister and Hamilton after that."

"Of course, it's always possible that

Fever went back later. Though that still wouldn't put him behind the wheel of the van."

"We're still not a hundred per cent sure that it was the van, are we, sir? When d'you think forensic will come up with the confirmation?"

"The Super said this afternoon, if we're lucky. If not, tomorrow morning. I'd be very surprised indeed if it doesn't turn out to be the vehicle we're after. Anyway, we'll see what Fever has to say for himself. It's nearly a quarter past, we'd better get a move on."

The Fevers lived in a large modern house set in generous gardens next to the dilapidated range of farm buildings from which he ran his haulage business.

"Wonder how on earth he got planning permission for that," said Lineham as they parked on the wide gravelled sweep of drive. "Bet a bit of palm-greasing went on there."

"Not necessarily, Mike. If you look at the centre section you'll see the brick is older than the rest. I think it's an ambitious conversion."

"Pretty well done, then," said Lineham grudgingly.

Thanet awaited the sergeant's next remark with an inward smile. It came.

"Can't be short of a penny," said Lineham. "There must be money in haulage."

"Thinking of buying a lorry and setting yourself up?" Thanet rang the door bell and this time was rewarded with a rendering of the opening bars of "My Old Man Said Follow The Van".

"Very appropriate," said Lineham with a grin.

The door was opened by Toby Fever, Tessa Hamilton's boyfriend. "Come in."

A good-looking young man, thought Thanet, nagged once again by the feeling that he might have seen him somewhere before. He wondered what the two families thought of Toby and Tessa's friendship. For various reasons, not much, he imagined.

"I'll tell Dad you're here." Toby opened a door to the right of the hall, ushered them into the room then went off towards the back of the house.

It was a large sitting-room, at least

twenty feet square, with windows over-looking the garden on three sides. It had considerable potential, Thanet thought, but whoever chose the furnishings had played too safe with neutrals and pastels; although the thick carpet, heavy curtains and three-piece suite were of good quality the effect was dull and lifeless. Mrs. Fever, he guessed, lacked sufficient confidence in her own taste to indulge it.

"Inspector Thanet?"

For the second time today Thanet was greeted by an outstretched hand. In the case of a man at whom the finger had been pointed, like Fever, such bonhomie invariably made him suspicious.

And Fever himself was a surprise.

It was interesting, Thanet thought, how one could build up an image of someone through other people's accounts of him, and how completely wrong one could be. He'd had a very clear picture of Fever as a great lumberjack of a man, overpowering as much by his physical size as by the force of his personality. Apart from his age, which Thanet guessed to be around fifty, the reality was completely different. Fever was at most five five in height, and wiry as a whippet. He was wearing expensive casual clothes—slightly baggy gaberdine trousers and high-necked cashmere sweater over soft-collared shirt. Beneath the surface affability he was, Thanet thought, distinctly wary.

A woman had come into the room behind him.

"And this is my wife. I believe you did want to talk to her as well?"

Like the Princess in the fairy tale guarded by a dragon, Thanet had expected Mrs. Fever to be beautiful and she did not disappoint him. Well, perhaps not exactly beautiful, he corrected himself, but very attractive, certainly. She was perhaps an inch or two taller than her husband, with a beautifully proportioned figure, a cloud of dark hair and soft deep-velvet-brown eyes. She seemed to exude not sex-appeal but something much more subtle, a fragrant femininity enhanced by the flared suede skirt which flowed about her as she walked, the high-heeled shoes and silk blouse. She might not give her husband cause for jealousy but Thanet could understand his fear of losing her to another man.

They all sat down, Fever and his wife side by side on a settee.

"As you've no doubt realised, we're looking into the death of Mr. Leo Martindale," said Thanet. "And at the moment we're trying to build up a picture of his movements yesterday."

"Excuse me interrupting, Inspector," said Fever. "But why? By all accounts it was a hit and run accident. Surely you ought to be concentrating on motorists passing through the village last night?"

"Among other things, yes, we are. Unfortunately it looks as though it might not be as simple as that. It's difficult to see how Mr. Martindale could have got into the position in which he was lying without, shall we say, a little help."

Mrs. Fever's eyes widened as she understood the implications of what he was saying and her hands, clasped together in her lap, tightened their grip on each other. Thanet saw the knuckles whiten.

Fever's eyes narrowed and he sat forward. "Now wait a minute. What are you saying? Are you implying that it wasn't an accident, that. . . ?"

"We're just trying to find out exactly

what did happen. It's possible that it was an accident, that the driver panicked when he got out to investigate and discovered that Mr. Martindale was dead, moved the body into the ditch to prevent anyone else running over him."

"But it's also possible that he was deliberately run down. That is what you're getting at, isn't it?"

Fever was becoming agitated.

Here we go again, thought Thanet. The interview was already beginning to follow a pattern that had become all too familiar over the last couple of days. "Anything is possible, Mr. Fever. You must see that at this stage we have to keep an open mind . . ."

"Don't give me that guff!" Fever sprang up and began to pace about. "That's really why you're here, isn't it? You heard I had a bit of a barney with Martindale yesterday and you want to pin his death on me!"

Mrs. Fever made an inarticulate little sound of distress then put out her hand towards her husband and said, "Lewis, please."

Fever ignored her. "Well you won't get away with it! If every time two men had

187

an argument one of them is accused of murder, the place would be littered with corpses!"

"We're only interested in one corpse, Mr. Fever, Mr. Martindale's. As I say, we're not yet satisfied that his death was an accident and we are only doing our duty in trying to find out precisely what did happen."

"Duty! Is this what you call duty, coming into a man's home and accusing him of murder!"

"Mr. Fever!" Thanet was capable of showing steel when he wanted to and had no intention of being browbeaten into going away without what he had come for. "I am accusing no one of anything. Would you please sit down and allow us to have a rational conversation, or—"

Fever ran his hands wildly through his hair. "Rational! What's rational about—"

For the second time in two days Thanet was driven to a course of action he normally regarded as the last resort. He stood up. "Very well. If that's the way you want it. I shall have to ask you to accompany us back to headquarters, for questioning."

Mrs. Fever jumped up and grasped her husband by the sleeve. "Lewis, please, they're only doing what they have to . . ."

He shook her off and stood glaring at Thanet.

There was a tense silence and then he plumped down on the settee, folding his arms belligerently across his chest. "I don't seem to have much choice in the matter, do I?"

"On the contrary," said Thanet, sitting down again. "The choice is yours. Here . . . or there."

"Here, there, what's the difference? In any case I have nothing to hide, so for God's sake let's get on with it, shall we?"

In the event, there was little more that they could add to what Thanet already knew. Mrs. Fever confirmed the substance of the conversation with Martindale at the garage, studiously avoiding looking at her husband while doing so, and Fever, keeping his volatile temper barely under control, gave a brief account of his visit to the Hall. His intention, he swore, had merely been to warn Martindale to keep away from his wife, to frighten him off.

"You've all known each other for years,

189

I gather, since before Mr. Martindale went away?"

Fever's face went curiously wooden. "That's right, yes."

Mrs. Fever cast an anxious little sideways glance at him.

"You were friends, at that time?"

"Friends! Leo didn't have any friends, believe me."

"Why not? What did people have against him?" Thanet didn't have much hope of an honest answer and he didn't get one.

"Let's just say he had the knack of putting people's backs up."

And Fever gave a smile that was more a baring of the teeth, reminding Thanet of Jack Talion's reaction.

Thanet stood up. "That sounds like an understatement to me."

They all rose. "Think what you like," said Fever. "That's the way it was. But if you're looking for a scapegoat, Inspector, you won't find him in this house."

"Charming," said Lineham, when the front door had slammed behind them. "D'you think he's our man, sir?"

Thanet shrugged. "As I said before, not

unless we can put him behind the wheel of that van. And even then . . . I don't know, Mike. I suppose I can see him running Martindale down while he was still all steamed up, but not calmly sitting about considering it and going back to do it in cold blood. We'll just have to see. What's next on the agenda?"

"Mrs. Hamilton at 1.30."

It was now 12.45.

"Time we visited the local, I think, Mike."

12

LIKE so many country pubs the Drovers had suffered from modernisation in the sixties and seventies. The ancient floorboards had been covered with heavily patterned carpets, sections of wall faced with synthetic boarding and the bar tarted up with a collection of dangling keyrings. At this hour on a weekday there were only three other customers. The food, however, was good and the beer acceptable.

Thanet took an appreciative mouthful of roast beef sandwich seasoned with French mustard. "What did he say?"

Lineham had been deputed to ask the landlord why he had not mentioned Martindale's ostracism by the locals on Monday night.

"Same old story. 'Nobody asked me . . .'" Lineham loaded his crusty French bread with butter, cheese and pickle. "Think the Super will turn up?"

Thanet grimaced. "Hope not."

Lineham grinned. "Perhaps there'll be a mini crime wave in Sturrenden and he'll be too busy."

"I'll pretend I didn't hear that remark, Mike."

Lineham chewed thoughtfully for a while and then said, "What about this van, sir? Think there's any hope of proving which of them was driving it?"

"Ridiculous, isn't it? Six people have keys and we already know four of them drove it on Tuesday night—as well as Mrs. Rankle, who borrowed it to check on her son."

Lineham ticked them off on his fingers. "Mrs. Hamilton went to fetch Adam from the station at 7.25. When she got back at about 7.40, Mr. Talion used it to check on the sheep that had got out. He took about —how long did he say?"

"Twenty-five minutes or so."

"So he would have got back at around ten past eight. Then it stood idle for twenty minutes or so until Sam Tiller went to pick up Mrs. Rankle. Then at 9.15 or thereabouts she borrowed it . . ."

"Passing the entrance gates of the Hall

on her way. And she wasn't exactly on friendly terms with Martindale, by the sound of it. I wonder what she had against him?"

"Think there's any hope of finding out?"

"Not much, the way things are going. It's like trying to get blood out of a stone, trying to find out why they were all so anti Martindale, isn't it?"

"Never mind. As you would say, it's early days yet."

Thanet grinned. Lineham's unfailing optimism was one of the reasons why he enjoyed working with him. "True. Anyway, you were saying . . ."

"Sam Tiller drove it next, to take Mrs. Rankle home and then go home himself. Leaving the pub at. . . ?"

"Ten-thirty, I think."

"And finally Mr. Hamilton used it at 11.15, to go and pick up Tessa, when the Range Rover wouldn't start. Think that's true, sir?"

"We must check with her. But I shouldn't think he'd risk involving her in lying for him."

"So really its movements are pretty well

accounted for, except for twenty minutes or so between ten and half-past eight and the three quarters of an hour between 10.30 and 11.15. Time enough in both cases for any one of them to have driven it down to the gates and back."

"Yes, but who? Let's see, what did they all claim to be doing between those times, Mike?"

"Mr. Hamilton said he was working in his office during the earlier period. He must have been alone or he would presumably have mentioned that someone was with him. He could easily have slipped out. He and Mrs. Hamilton stood to lose a packet, if Martindale had claimed what was rightfully his. Say Hamilton looked out of the window and happened to see Martindale leaving the house, to go to the pub, perhaps. . . ."

"I doubt that he would have gone to the pub, Mike, after getting the cold shoulder the night before."

"Oh, I don't know. He sounds pretty thick-skinned to me. Anyway, he needn't have been going to the pub. He could have been meeting someone . . ."

"Who, for example?"

"I don't know. I'm only making suggestions, sir." Lineham was beginning to sound plaintive. "He could just have been going for a walk."

Thanet shrugged. "True. All right, Mike, go on."

"So," said Lineham, leaning forward eagerly as he warmed to his theory, "Hamilton sees the perfect opportunity to get rid of him. Everything's quiet, the guests are at dinner . . . He gets to the van without being seen and drives off. He catches up with Martindale at the bottom of the drive and runs him down. He gets out to check that Martindale is dead, then drags him into the ditch so he won't be found by anyone else coming in or out of the Hall gates that night. Into the van, up the drive, back into his study and he's home and dry. It need only have taken ten or fifteen minutes in all. What d'you think, sir?"

Thanet took out his pipe, tapped it, inspected it, blew through it and began to fill it. "Unless it was a straightforward accident, I should think it must have happened like that. But the trouble is, you could apply the same scenario to any one of them. We don't know what Mrs. Hamilton was doing just then, or Sam Tiller, or Jack Talion . . ."

"Or the Byfleets, for that matter," Lineham conceded gloomily. "He's supposed to have got back from Gatwick about eight, so they were both around between ten and half-past eight as well. And the van stands near where they live in the stable yard."

"Unfortunately the van was conveniently accessible to the lot of them," said Thanet with a sigh. "We've got a tremendous amount of checking to do, Mike. It would help if we had some idea what time Martindale was knocked down, but as yet we haven't a clue. After that early dinner, which was over by about seven, no one seems to have seen him."

"Except for Mrs. Byfleet. She was seen coming out of his room at 7.15, remember."

"I know, but it could just have been a routine check. The room might well have been empty."

"We both thought she was lying about something."

"I know. Ah well, come on Mike, drink

up. I don't think Mrs. Hamilton is the type to appreciate being kept waiting."

"Don't suppose we'll get much out of her," grumbled Lineham.

"You never know. We have got one or two cards up our sleeve, remember," though Thanet wasn't feeling too optimistic about the coming interview. Mrs. Hamilton wouldn't easily be manoeuvred into telling them anything she didn't wish to divulge.

In the car park Thanet came to a sudden halt. "It's just occurred to me . . ."

"What?"

"The van. Apart from the twenty minutes or so when Mrs. Rankle used it, it was standing out here in the pub car park all evening, between say 8.45 and 10.30. During that time anyone could have borrowed it and unless they were actually spotted no one would have been any the wiser."

Lineham groaned.

Delia Hamilton was waiting for them in her office, a pleasant, sunny little room tastefully furnished with antiques and country house chintzes.

She rose to greet them. "I hope this won't take too long, Inspector. How are you getting on? Have you found out what happened?"

She was as immaculately groomed as ever, her hair in a smooth chignon today, wearing a simple, elegant dress of raspberry-coloured wool with long sleeves and a cowl neck. Pearls and a beautiful enamelled antique fob watch completed the English country lady image.

"Not yet, ma'am. But don't worry, we shall."

She waved them to two upright chairs already in position in front of her desk and sat down behind it. She raised her eyebrows expectantly. "Well?"

"One or two things have emerged . . ."

"Such as?"

"I understand that there was an argument that night, between a Mr. Fever, who lives locally, and your brother."

"So I believe."

"Can you tell us anything about it?"

"I wasn't present, so no, I'm afraid I can't."

"Can you think of any reason why Mr.

Fever should have been so angry with your brother?"

"I haven't the faintest idea." She waved a hand, dismissing the matter as of no importance. "Fever has the reputation of having what is commonly called a short fuse. I suppose Leo had done something to annoy him. I shouldn't place too much importance on it, if I were you."

"Mr. Fever's wife, Yvonne . . ."

Delia Hamilton's delicately arched brows rose again. "What about her?"

"Your brother seemed to know her. We understand they met in the village yesterday, and he greeted her like an old friend."

"Sutton is a very small community, Inspector. Yvonne Fever has lived here all her life. As children we all knew each other."

"Was there anything special between them?"

"Special?"

"Was she his girlfriend, before he went away?"

Delia laughed. "I wouldn't put it quite like that. Let's just say that Leo was a very attractive young man and I've no doubt that at one time or another he took most of the local girls out. But a special girlfriend . . ." She shook her head. "It wouldn't have been suitable."

Because of the difference in class, presumably. A rather naïve view, Thanet felt. He was pretty certain that if Leo had fancied a girl he wouldn't have hesitated to break the rules. Besides, he suspected that the question had made Delia Hamilton uneasy. Because of Yvonne Fever, or had there been another scandal to do with Leo and a local girl? Sam Tiller's daughter, perhaps, if he had one? Or Jack Talion's?

"So to your knowledge there is no particular reason why Mr. Fever had a grudge against your brother?"

She shook her head. "No."

"What about Sam Tiller?"

"Sam Tiller?" Briefly, she looked disconcerted.

"Someone overheard Sam Tiller telling you that if your brother stayed, he would leave."

A flash of anger, quickly suppressed. At being put in the difficult position of having to explain, presumably. "You shouldn't listen to gossip, Inspector. You can't believe half of what you hear."

"You deny that this conversation took place, then?"

"I didn't say that."

"Or that Sam Tiller did in fact present you with this ultimatum?"

"I'm the one who presents ultimatums around here, Inspector."

"You haven't answered my question."

She hated being pinned down like this, obviously wasn't used to having anyone press her for an answer which she didn't want to give.

"What question was that?" But there was the beginning of resignation in her eyes. She could see he wasn't going to let her wriggle out of it.

Thanet was rather enjoying this duel of wits. "Did Sam Tiller tell you that if your brother stayed, he would have to hand in his resignation?"

"What if he did? What possible relevance could it have?"

"Did he, Mrs. Hamilton?"

Anger sparked in her eyes as she capitulated. "If it's so important for you to know . . . Yes, he did."

But the battle was only half won. Thanet still had to find out what he really wanted to know. "Why was that?"

She shrugged, lifting elegant shoulders. "How should I know?"

"*Do* you know?" he pressed.

"I've no doubt he had his reasons."

"What were they?"

Her self-control was admirable but her fury and tension showed in the unnatural rigidity of her posture, the clenching of the muscles along her jawline.

Thanet waited. Was she going to tell him, would he have to press her further or would she lie? It was, he felt, absolutely crucial that he win this battle. It would be the first crack in the barrier of silence which everyone who knew Martindale seemed to put up when being questioned about the general hostility towards him.

He allowed the silence to prolong itself for a little while longer then sighed. "Mrs. Hamilton," he said gently. "You're not really asking me to believe that if you didn't already know, you wouldn't have asked why Sam found the idea of working for your brother so unacceptable?"

"I'm not asking you to believe or disbelieve anything."

Thanet tried a different tack. "I'm beginning to wonder if you really do want us to find out about your brother's death."

That had stung. Her lips tightened. "You can't fool me, Inspector. You don't believe anything of the sort. You're just trying to goad me into telling you what you want to know. If it's so important, why don't you ask Sam himself?"

"If you don't tell me, I shall. But I assume that as you're so keen to protect him you really don't believe he can be involved. In which case you would be doing him a good turn by telling me, instead of my having to ask him straight out. I assume that it is a matter which has caused him some distress, in the past?"

Still no answer.

"I shan't give up until I find out, you know."

Silence. She rose with an exasperated sigh and went to stand looking out of the window with her back to them.

Thanet waited, glancing at Lineham, who grinned and raised a triumphant thumb. Thanet pulled down the corners of his mouth and shrugged. *We mustn't count our chickens* . . .

Finally she turned to face them, leaning back against the windowsill. Sunlight haloed her hair. "Just why is it so important?"

"We don't know that it is. It's just that it could be."

"Because you suspect Sam of running Leo down."

"It's one possibility among many."

She gave a wry smile and returned to her seat. "Well, Inspector, I can see that as you say you're not the type to give up. As you will have gathered, I don't like talking about my employees behind their backs. In my view loyalty is a two-way process. But I suppose you might as well hear the truth from someone who will give you an unbiased account of it."

And a vested interest in diverting attention away from herself, Thanet reminded himself as she began to speak. But he had won!

"Sam wasn't always in such a . . . well, menial position. He once ran his own farm. It was only a small farm, but it had been in his family for several generations . . . He also had a passionate and life-long ambition, to breed a prize bull. Oh, you may well smile, Inspector, but believe me there was no more serious subject in the world to Sam.

"Well, to skip all the years of trial and error, of complete failure and near misses, and to cut a long story short, in the end he did it. His bull won the prize of Supreme Champion at the Royal Show at Stoneleigh. It's the most prestigious prize of all and Sam was walking on air. Stud fees, he knew, would make him a rich man, but best of all was the knowledge that he had done it, he alone by his own efforts had made it. You understand what I mean?"

Thanet nodded.

"The week after the show my dear brother left open the gate of the field in which the bull was kept. I don't know if you've ever seen one of these creatures, Inspector, but believe me they are massive. It was unfortunate that an articulated lorry happened to be coming along at the time. The bull ran straight out into its path. The animal wasn't killed outright but it was so badly injured that it had to

206

be put down. You can imagine how Sam felt."

"It was carelessness on your brother's part?"

"Oh I don't think it was deliberate, if that's what you mean. But it was carelessness, yes, sheer, criminal, absolutely inexcusable carelessness. My father paid heavily in compensation, tried to smooth things over, but of course it couldn't make up to Sam for all those years of single-minded endeavour. It just about broke his heart, finished him. He couldn't face starting all over again. He let things slide, the money dwindled and dwindled and in the end he went bankrupt. Just about then his wife died and he went to live with his daughter. For years he got occasional jobs as tractor driver or farm labourer, and then when my father died and I decided to turn this place into a hotel I needed someone to look after the grounds. There was accommodation available in the stable block and I felt an obligation to Sam . . . He took some persuading but by then there was friction with his son-in-law and he was tempted, as I hoped he might be, by the prospect of independence. He's been here ever since."

"I see." Thanet did see. Long years of bitterness could shrivel a man's soul. To Tiller the prospect of working for the man who had ruined him would have been unendurable. Faced with having to abandon for the second time the life he had built for himself and presented with the opportunity for revenge he could well have succumbed to temptation.

"Oh, I know what you're thinking, Inspector. It's why I didn't want to tell you. You're thinking that if the opportunity presented itself Sam might well have been tempted to run Leo down. But he's not like that. He's a good man, kind . . ."

Remembering Tiller's defensiveness, his aggression and hostility, Thanet wasn't so sure. He said as much to Lineham, outside.

"I agree. Though how we'd ever be able to prove it, if it was him—" Lineham broke off. "Oh, no . . ."

Thanet turned to look. A police Land Rover was coming up the drive. It was just close enough for him to recognise the passenger.

Superintendent Draco had arrived.

13

DRACO sprang out of the Land Rover and came bouncing towards them across the gravel. Energy emanated from him in almost visible waves. "Ah, there you are, Thanet. How's it going?"

"We're just going to have a word with the groundsman, Sam Tiller, sir."

They waited while two of the guests, a middle-aged couple dressed for a country walk in wellington boots and anoraks, came out of the hotel and passed them, casting curious glances. Then Thanet gave a brief account of the conversation with Mrs. Hamilton.

A delighted smile spread across Draco's face. "That's a new one. Revenge for the death of a prize bull, eh? Thought I'd heard them all, but this really takes the biscuit."

They headed for the stable yard.

"Even if Tiller did run Mr. Martindale down we're going to have a hard time proving it. Have you heard anything from forensic yet, sir?"

"No. I was on to them again just before I left. Usual story, snowed under with work etc. But they promise the results by tomorrow."

Draco was glancing about curiously as they walked. He looked as though he was thoroughly enjoying himself.

Thanet again remembered wondering, when Draco first came, how long the Superintendent was going to tie himself to his desk. He hoped this visit wasn't heralding a new era of involvement on the Superintendent's part in the day-to-day progress of cases in his division.

"There was one point, though." Draco fished in his pocket, produced a piece of paper. "Bentley thought you might be interested to know that Mr. . . ." He consulted the paper. ". . . Mr. Talion had sacked a farmhand a couple of weeks back. Here's his name and address." He handed the paper to Thanet. "He thought it might be useful to interview him, in view of the fact that Talion and Martindale had had a row and you hadn't been able to find out why. He thought the man might possibly know the reason for any animosity between them and if he's still feeling sore he might be tempted to talk. I told him to go ahead. I hope that's OK by you."

It wasn't. Thanet did not appreciate Draco giving his men orders. Who knew where it would end? He swallowed his resentment and said non-committally, "It could be useful." But again, it might not. It depended, Thanet thought, on how long the man had lived in the area and how much he knew about the grudge which Talion evidently harboured against Martindale. Still, he admitted reluctantly, Draco was right, it was worth following up.

The stable yard appeared deserted.

"He may be in the outbuilding where we interviewed him yesterday," suggested Lineham.

They walked across and knocked. A moment later the door opened. Tiller scowled. "Oh, it's you again. What d'you want this time?"

"Another word, if you don't mind. This is Superintendent Draco."

Was that a flash of fear as Tiller glanced at Draco? If so, it was immediately replaced by the old sneering belligerence. "Come to arrest me, have you?"

"Just a word, as I said." Thanet was at his most benign.

Grudgingly, Tiller stood back.

He had been cleaning his tools, sharpening a spade with a whetstone. Not much could be done outside in this weather, Thanet supposed. It was a good time for ensuring that equipment was in good order for the rush of work when spring arrived.

Draco's arrival had given Thanet little time to consider how he was going to tackle Tiller. He felt inhibited by the Superintendent's presence, despite the fact that Draco had tactfully withdrawn into the background and was pretending to examine the tools arrayed on hooks on the walls. With an effort he tried to put the Superintendent out of his mind, pretend that he wasn't there.

He decided to take the bull by the horns. Suppressing a wry smile at the appropriateness of the metaphor he said, "You told Mrs. Hamilton that if Mr. Martindale stayed on here, you would leave."

Tiller leaned back against his work bench and folded his arms. "So?"

"We know why, Mr. Tiller."

A spasm of—what? Anger? Fear?—briefly contorted the man's features. "If you're so clever I don't know why you bother with pretending you want to talk to me. Go on, admit it, you've made up your minds I ran him down, haven't you?" His gaze encompassed all three policemen then focused again on Thanet.

Thanet sighed. "If my mind were as closed as yours, Mr. Tiller, I'd have a string of false arrests to my credit. And that's not the way I work. I repeat, we're merely trying to find out the truth. And I would like to point out that if you were not involved in Mr. Martindale's death it is in your own interest for you to cooperate with us as fully as possible."

Silence while Tiller considered the logic of what Thanet had said. Finally he unfolded his arms and took a pipe from his pocket.

Thanet immediately wanted to follow suit. If Draco hadn't been present he might in fact have done so. Such a small act of sharing a mutual enjoyment could create a common bond and lower the emotional temperature of a difficult interview by several degrees. Once again he cursed Draco's presence.

Tiller was stuffing tobacco into the bowl with practised fingers, taking matches from his pockets. He waited until he had lit up and then, gazing up at the coils of smoke swirling lazily above his head, said, "You could have a point there."

Thanet knew when to keep silent and he continued to wait patiently, acutely conscious of Draco behind him. He could rely on Lineham, but the Superintendent was a different matter. Patience was not his strong point and if he said or did anything at this crucial moment . . . He wouldn't, surely? Thanet reminded himself that Draco hadn't reached his present rank without good reason.

Tiller's gaze slowly descended to linger on Thanet's face. "All right, then. What d'you want to know?"

There was a distinct easing of the atmosphere. But they were not there yet. Slowly now, Thanet warned himself. "We're still trying to check the movements of the van last night. You said you left here at 8.30 to pick up Mrs. Rankle?"

Tiller nodded, puffing rhythmically at his pipe.

"And left the pub at around 10.30, to take her home before returning here?"

Another nod.

"When did you last use it, earlier in the evening?"

Tiller considered, then took his pipe out of his mouth. "'Bout five o'clock. To run Andy home—the young lad who helps me. He usually cycles, but his bike's out of commission at the moment."

"And after that the van stood out in the yard, as usual?"

"'S right."

"Do you know of anyone else who used it, last night?"

Tiller hesitated.

No point in reversing the man's mood and making him dig his heels in again out of mistaken loyalty to Delia Hamilton. "Mrs. Hamilton told us she used it to fetch her son from the station just before half-past seven. Also, Mr. Talion used it to check on some sheep that had got out on to the road, some twenty minutes later.

After that it stood idle until you left at 8.30, so far as we know . . ."

No response.

Thanet tried again. "Do you know if anyone used it either before Mrs. Hamilton or during those twenty minutes between ten and half-past eight?"

Tiller was shaking his head. "Not so far as I know. Someone could have, of course."

"Does your cottage overlook the yard?"

Tiller nodded, eyes narrowing.

"Even if you didn't actually see anyone getting into or out of it, or driving it, did you happen to glance out at any point and notice that it was gone?"

Tiller considered. Finally he shook his head. "Earlier on I was having my tea in the kitchen at the back of the house. Then I watched telly until about eight, when I went upstairs to have a shave and get ready to go out. And it was dark, of course, the curtains was drawn."

Pity. "Did you hear anything, then, while you were in your bedroom? An engine start up?"

"Nah. Had the radio on."

"What about later on, after you got home? Did you hear anything then?"

Tiller started to shake his head again, then stopped. "There was something," he said slowly.

"When was that?"

"Soon after I got into bed. I was just dozing off. Must have been about a quarter past eleven. I heard a car start up."

"Ah, yes, that was probably Mr. Hamilton. Miss Hamilton had borrowed the Range Rover and she couldn't get it to start. Mr. Hamilton went to help her. You might have heard them come back."

"Not me. Went out like a light, I always do."

"What about earlier, before you went to bed?"

Another shake of the head. "Sorry."

Dead end, there. Move on, then, to the more delicate topic of Mrs. Rankle borrowing the van. Would it be best to try to get Tiller to volunteer the information, and risk arousing his anger again if it was necessary to press him, perhaps catch him out in a lie, or to ask him outright? Either way he was likely to erupt. Marginally better, perhaps, to avoid putting him in the wrong.

"I understand that when you and Mrs. Rankle go to the pub she usually borrows the van some time during the evening to go and check that her son is all right. He's handicapped, I believe?"

Tiller's reaction was instantaneous. Ignoring the last question he took his pipe from his mouth and straightened up, glaring at Thanet. "So what? I've got every right to lend it to whoever I like."

"I'm not questioning your right to lend it . . ."

"I should hope not. Because you ask Mrs. Hamilton. Go on, ask her. I wondered about Sonia driving it because of the insurance, see, I wasn't sure who was covered, so I asked Mrs. Hamilton's permission and she told me the cover was comprehensive and I could use it as I liked. 'Off duty you must treat the van as yours, Sam,' she says. 'Just use your own discretion.'"

Thanet held up his hand. "All right, all right. I accept that. I told you, I'm not questioning your right to lend it to whoever you want to lend it to. All I'm trying to find out is whether Mrs. Rankle drove it on Tuesday night."

If Tiller had been playing a game of Statues he couldn't have frozen into immobility more quickly. Only his eyes seemed alive, small black burning coals in an expanse of paralysed flesh. Then a hiss escaped through his slightly parted lips, his left eyelid twitched and he took a deep breath. "Just what," he said through his teeth, "are you implying?"

The waves of antagonism emanating from him were so powerful that it was with difficulty that Thanet stood his ground. "Asking, Mr. Tiller. Not—"

Tiller took a step forward and Thanet sensed Lineham tense beside him. "Just leave Mrs. Rankle out of this, d'you hear me? LEAVE HER OUT OF THIS!"

"That may not be possible, Mr. Tiller."

Tiller made an inarticulate sound that was almost a growl and, bunching his hands into fists, took another step forward.

Lineham also moved forward and Thanet was suddenly conscious of Draco flanking him on the other side. Three against one, he thought. Not very fair. He suppressed a desire to laugh. How impressed the Super must be with his handling of this one!

He was opening his mouth to speak when Draco intervened. "Come now, Mr. Tiller. That wouldn't be very sensible, would it? Assaulting a police officer and all that?"

"Look," said Thanet, humiliated and seething, trying to ignore the fact that Draco had spoken at all, "I can imagine how you feel . . ."

"Can you?" snarled Tiller. "How would you like it if someone you knew died in an accident and before you could turn round you're suspected of murdering him? Or if not you, your girlfriend or wife, perhaps. Just think about it! How *would* you feel?"

"If I were innocent—furiously angry, outraged, helpless, frustrated, hurt, confused, misjudged . . ."

"Well then!"

"But if I were guilty . . ." Thanet allowed the pause to lengthen then said softly, "If I were guilty, then I would put on a good show of feeling all those things, in order to proclaim my innocence."

Tiller stared at him. Then his shoulders

drooped and he turned away. "I can't win, can I? I can't bloody win!"

"You don't help yourself by getting all worked up like this, that's for sure," said Thanet gently. "And I do assure you that we are putting precisely this kind of question to everyone who had access to the van that night. Everyone. Sooner or later the truth will come out. And I meant what I said. If you are not involved you have nothing to fear and everything to gain by cooperating with us in full."

Tiller made a dispirited gesture. "I've told you all I know. But if you want to ask questions about other people you'll just have to go and talk to them yourself, because I can't and won't answer."

There really was no point in continuing. "Very well, Mr. Tiller, I can understand that." Thanet glanced at the others. *Ready to go?* "We'll leave you to get on with your work."

Outside they crossed the yard in a tense, embarrassed silence. After a few moments Draco cleared his throat.

"I owe you an apology, Thanet."

Thanet said nothing.

"I shouldn't have interfered. I was most impressed by the way you handled him."

Apologies didn't come easily to Draco and Thanet felt appeased. "I admit he had me worried for a moment there, sir. I was glad you and Lineham were present."

"Tricky customer. And no fool. With a chip as big as a mountain on his shoulder. If that's the degree of antagonism Martindale was capable of arousing, it wouldn't surprise me in the least if someone grabbed the opportunity to get rid of him. Think it was Tiller?"

"I just don't know, sir. What do you think, Lineham?"

Lineham was pleased to be included in the discussion, Thanet could see, but the sergeant was as undecided as he was himself.

"If Mr. Martindale happened to be walking down the drive when Tiller drove down to collect Mrs. Rankle, well, I could certainly see him being tempted. But I don't know that he would deliberately have planned to do it."

"I agree." Thanet sighed. "If only we had a better idea of Martindale's movements . . ."

"What's your next move, Thanet?" Draco was still being conciliatory.

"I thought we might go and see Mrs. Rankle."

Thanet held his breath, praying that Draco wouldn't say he would accompany them.

They had reached the front drive and Draco stopped. "Right, I'll leave you to it, then, I've got to be getting back."

Relief. "Right, sir."

One foot in the Land Rover, Draco turned. "And as I said, Thanet, well done."

Thanet raised a hand in acknowledgement and watched the Land Rover drive off.

"Think he'll give you a medal, sir?" said Lineham.

He ducked as Thanet threw a mock punch at him and tension dissolved into laughter.

14

"PRETTY uphill work, isn't it?" said Lineham as they set off down the drive.

"I feel as though I'm swimming against the tide most of the time," Thanet admitted. "I can't ever remember a case in which we've had so many hostile witnesses. I just wonder . . ."

Lineham glanced at him. "What?"

Thanet shrugged. "I was wondering if this means we're barking up the wrong tree. That it was after all just a simple hit and run accident."

"I'm not quite with you, sir."

"Perhaps I'm being fanciful, and I don't quite know how to put this, but . . . Well, if someone had killed Martindale, his anger against him would be defused. It wouldn't still be around. But most of these people, they're still so angry it's like handling a lot of unexploded bombs. D'you see what I mean? It's almost as if . . ."

Lineham raised his eyebrows.

Thanet gave an embarrassed little laugh. "It's almost as though their hostility towards Martindale has been redirected, at me."

"Are you suggesting we should abandon the investigation?"

"Absolutely not. In fact, the harder it gets the more determined I become to find out the truth."

"I wonder if there'll be any response to the TVS appeal."

They had arranged for a request for all motorists passing through Sutton-in-the-Weald between the hours of seven p.m. and two a.m. on Tuesday night to come forward.

"We'll just have to wait and see."

"That'll be Mrs. Rankle's cottage, I think."

Lineham pulled up in front of a pair of semi-detached cottages. In the garden of one of them, a youth, warmly wrapped up in rug, anorak and bobble hat, was sitting in a wheelchair parked in front of a rapidly thawing snowman. He was leaning forward and patting it.

"Hullo," said Thanet, smiling.

The youth's head swung around and

Thanet saw that he was much older than Thanet had thought, in his late twenties, perhaps, with the vacant stare of the mentally handicapped. He looked upset, on the verge of tears.

"What's the matter?" Thanet squatted down in front of him.

"No gone." The words were barely intelligible.

Thanet frowned, trying to understand.

"Who are you? What do you want?"

The voice was shrill with alarm. A woman was standing at the open door of the cottage. She started towards him as Thanet stood up.

"Mrs. Rankle? Sorry, we didn't mean to startle you." He introduced himself. "Your son seems upset."

She was in her late fifties or early sixties, thin and slight, with untidy brown hair and a worn, lined face. There were deep creases between her brows and she looked as though she carried the sorrows of the world on her bowed shoulders. She wore no make-up and was dressed in a shapeless brown skirt and fawn jumper matted by many washings. She fished a handkerchief out of her pocket and briskly wiped the young man's cheeks. "He's upset because the snow is melting, aren't you, Vince? You thought it was lovely, didn't you? Come on, we'd better go inside, you're getting cold."

She turned the chair and began to push it across the soggy lawn. It was hard going and Thanet said, "Let us do that for you."

Between them he and Lineham manoeuvred the chair on to the path and in through the front door. Mrs. Rankle went ahead of them, along a short passage. She flung open the door. "In here."

It was a squarish kitchen-cum-living-room, old-fashioned but adequately furnished with central table, china-clay sink, gas cooker and antiquated refrigerator. A small coal fire burned in the black cast-iron grate and there was a wooden armchair beside it, complete with cushion and curled-up cat. It should have been comfortable enough, cosy even, and yet . . . Thanet, ever-sensitive to atmosphere, looked about, searching for clues to his unease. The place felt curiously empty, bleak. Perhaps it was because the room was not only spotlessly clean but immaculately tidy. There was none of the clutter that Thanet associated with living—books, newspapers, magazines, plants, and no signs of any kind of activity on the part of either Mrs. Rankle or her son. What did they do all day in this small bare cell?

Stupid question, he realised. Mrs. Rankle had been removing Vincent's hat and coat and now she went to the huge television set, which Thanet had noticed but not really registered, and switched it on. A gardening expert was explaining how to care for pot plants. Then she manoeuvred Vincent's wheelchair so that it was positioned squarely in front of it. "All right, love?" She ran her hand over his hair in a gesture of affection before turning to Thanet. "What did you want?"

"May we sit down?"

She looked around. "We need another chair." She started towards the door. "I'll get one from the front room."

"No, don't bother," said Lineham. "I can stand." He went to lean against the sink.

"You're sure?" She sat down in the armchair, Thanet in the single upright chair beside the table. Didn't they ever have visitors? he wondered.

"As you've probably guessed, we're looking into the death of Mr. Martindale, on Tuesday night."

He paused. What was the expression that had flitted across her face? Satisfaction?

"And one of the things we're trying to do is piece together his movements during the day." He gave her no chance to ask him why. "You were seen talking to him in the village that afternoon . . . Having an argument with him, in fact."

No response.

"We wondered why . . . Why you were arguing with him, that is." He waited for denial, prevarication, outright refusal to discuss the matter. It would only be par for the course.

She glanced at Vincent who was apparently absorbed in how to take geranium cuttings, her mouth settling more firmly into bitter lines. "No reason why I shouldn't tell you. If I don't, you'll hear soon enough from someone else, I've no doubt . . ."

She gestured at her son. "Leo Martindale did that to Vince."

Thanet was shaken. What did she mean?

"You'd never believe it to look at him, would you, but until he was nine he was a perfectly normal, healthy little boy." Briefly the sour lines around her mouth slackened, then tightened again. "One day, nearly twenty-five years ago, we were visiting my mother, in this cottage. We didn't live here then. We had a council house in Cranbrook . . . While we were here Vince went out to play. We'd told him not to go out on the road but you know what boys are. The first we knew, there was a squeal of brakes and a crash . . . We went rushing out. Vince was lying in the road and Leo Martindale's sports car was slewed across, nose in the hedge."

In a brief, vivid flash of memory Thanet remembered the heart-stopping moment when Ben, aged about nine himself, had been knocked off his bicycle by a tractor. His stomach clenched as it had then and he was not surprised that as she recalled the incident, even now after all this time, Mrs. Rankle's hands were moving in desperate wringing movements painful to watch and her eyes had filled with tears.

She dashed them angrily away. "He'd been drinking," she said bitterly. "There was a girl with him. They were both all right, of course, but Vince . . ." She glanced at him again, immobile in front of the flickering screen. "We thought he was going to die. He was in a coma for weeks, and when he recovered . . ." She shook her head and gave a cynical little laugh. "Recovered! Not a very good choice of word, as I think you'll agree."

What could he say? What did one say, in such circumstances? "It must have been a terrible time for you."

"I can't tell you . . ." She glanced at him assessingly, as if suddenly aware of whom she was talking to, and he could see her wondering whether to continue. Strictly speaking, of course, he had got at least part of what he wanted, the fact that she had a powerful motive for wanting Martindale dead: revenge. He could understand now that look of satisfaction earlier, when he had mentioned Martindale's death. Even if she hadn't been at the wheel of the van herself there must be for her a delicious irony in the fact that he had himself been killed in a road accident similar to that in which he had maimed her son. Thanet knew that he should now go on to question her about her use of the van that night, but something held him back. There was more that she wanted to tell him, he was sure of it. It occurred to him that it must be rare indeed now for her to have the opportunity to talk about the tragedy that had surely blighted her life. The local people must all know about it and would scarcely welcome hearing the same old story over and over again, and she could hardly go up to a total stranger and buttonhole him like the Ancient Mariner.

"It wasn't as though it was over, when he came out of the coma," she said in a low voice. "It was only just beginning. When we found he was permanently brain-damaged and would never walk again, my husband . . . He just couldn't take it, you see. He stuck it out for a couple of years and then walked out." Her mouth twisted and she snapped her fingers. "Just like that. One day he was there, the next he was gone. Leaving me stuck . . ." She pulled herself up. "Not that Vince isn't a good boy, he is. Very loving and obedient, but . . . It's just that there's no relief. You know it's going to go on and on and on, day after day, month after month, year after year . . ."

Her voice was rising and the desperation in her face gave Thanet a glimpse of the endless, unremitting years of selfless commitment she had had to endure. How could she bear it? "Don't you have any help at all in looking after him?"

"A couple of times a year they take him into residential care while I have a break, but that's all. There just isn't enough manpower to give people like me any help on a regular basis, it's as simple as that—especially in a rural area like this. And the fact of the matter is, that so long as you're coping, you'll be left to get on with it."

"And you wouldn't want him to go into residential care." Thanet made it a statement, not a question.

"I've thought about it, often. And I have got as far as making enquiries once or twice when I've been feeling really desperate, but you wouldn't believe the waiting lists, for people in far worse case than Vince. Besides, he's happy here and so long as I'm able to look after him . . .

When you have kids you can't just opt out of your responsibilities when the going gets tough, can you?"

An understatement if ever there was one. Thanet shook his head sympathetically. "Was there a prosecution?"

She grimaced. "Yes. All he got was a six-month suspended sentence and his licence taken away for eighteen months . . . It still makes me mad to think about it. Oh, it wasn't so bad when Mum was alive. Vince and me moved in here with her and she used to look after him while I went out to work part-time. But since she died, ten years ago . . . No one can imagine, who hasn't been through it . . ."

And with no prospect of relief in sight, thought Thanet. It wouldn't have been surprising if, hearing that Martindale was back and faced with the opportunity to avenge the long purgatory of looking after a son born perfectly fit and healthy and now reduced to helpless dependency, she had succumbed to the impulse to run his destroyer down. He hoped very much that this was not what had happened. How could he live with his conscience if she were convicted and Vincent's only prop were removed?

Come on, he told himself. You're not here to judge, simply to discover the truth. And whether you like it or not, that's what you have to do.

Closing his mind with difficulty to the rumblings of his conscience he said quietly, "Mrs. Rankle, I understand you borrowed Mr. Tiller's van on Tuesday night, to come back here and check that Vincent was all right?"

She blinked at the change of subject. "Yes, I always do. It's the only night of the week I go out." She was on the defensive now. "I put Vince to bed a bit early on Tuesdays. He can't move about by himself, you see, so he's perfectly safe. But I do like to check he's OK, halfway through the evening."

"I'm not questioning the care you take of him. It's obvious he's very well looked after, it's just that . . . did you see anybody, on your way here, or on your way back to the pub?"

She frowned, thinking. "Not so far as I can remember. It was very cold, the roads were icy and I was concentrating on driving, I don't drive much, you see . . . Oh!" Her eyes widened as she realised where this could be leading. "Just a minute . . . I was wondering why you'd come. You're not trying to tell me it was Sam's van that knocked him down?"

"We're not absolutely certain yet, but it looks that way, I'm afraid."

"Oh, my God." She glanced at Vincent then shrank back in her chair, looking near to panic.

Thanet saw her throat move as she swallowed convulsively and she put her hand over her mouth as if she were about to be sick. Her eyes above it were wide and staring. If she were acting, he thought, it was a first-rate performance. He sincerely hoped she wasn't.

Then she sat up again, making a visible effort at self control. "You . . ." she whispered, running the tip of her tongue over dry lips, "Surely you're not suggesting. . . ? Oh God, you are, aren't you? You think I might have run him down."

"Mrs. Rankle, I assure you that at this stage we're not suggesting anything. We're merely trying to find out what happened."

A thought struck her. "Sam . . ."

"Several people drove the van that night, Sam included. We're talking to all of them."

Now that she was over the initial shock she was rallying. He could see it in the straightening of her back, the tilt of her head, the hardening of her expression. She was a fighter, he reminded himself. If she wasn't, she would have given up long ago.

"That's why you were asking about the argument." Her voice was much stronger, almost belligerent as she said, "Well let me tell you this. I may have no reason to love Mr. rotten Martindale, but that doesn't mean I'd run him down in cold blood. And in case you're wondering, I didn't knock him down accidentally, either."

Suddenly she leaned forward, eyes gleaming. "You said, 'All of them'. That several people had driven the van that night and you were talking to all of them. Does that include Lewis Fever?"

Thanet saw Lineham, behind her, stiffen.

"What do you mean?" It was scarcely surprising that she should try to use diversionary tactics, but this could be an unexpected break for them. If Tiller had lent Fever the van on Tuesday night they had both kept very quiet about it. Presumably Mrs. Rankle felt no such loyalty to Fever.

"He borrowed the van that night too. He came into the pub, about . . ." She put her hands to her temples, pressed them as if trying to force her memory to function efficiently. "Let me think. It was . . . Yes, it was before I came to check on Vince." The words began to tumble out as she recalled the incident more clearly. "It must have been about, oh, around a quarter to nine. He came into the pub and asked Sam if he could borrow it. He and Sam are old mates . . . He'd just heard his mother-in-law had been taken ill and he wanted to run his wife over to see her."

"Why didn't he use his own car, or his wife's—I presume she's got one?"

"Yes, but Toby had borrowed it. They'd set out in his car, Lewis's that is, but as they were driving through the village he realised he'd got a slow puncture. He didn't want to waste time changing the wheel and he saw Sam's van in the car park at the Drovers so he came in to ask if he could borrow it for half an hour. Of course, Sam said yes."

"Where does his mother-in-law live?"

"Ashford."

So Fever would have had to pass the gates of the Hall on his way. "How long was he away?"

"Only half an hour or so, as he promised. As soon as he got back I drove home to see if Vince was OK."

Outside in the car Lineham said resignedly, "I just don't believe this. How many more people d'you suppose drove the wretched thing that night?"

"The Byfleets?" said Thanet.

"How much d'you bet?"

"I'm not a gambling man, as you well know, Mike. But the way things are going the odds in favour seem pretty high. We need to find out if she actually saw Martindale that night when she went to his room, anyway, so let's go and ask them, shall we?"

15

ON the way back up the drive they passed the middle-aged couple they had seen earlier, returning from their walk, and in the stable yard Adam Hamilton was mooning about, kicking a stone. Thanet scarcely recognised him at first; he had discarded his bizarre outfit of yesterday in favour of jeans and a scruffy sweater—a discard of his father's?—which hung on him in folds and with sleeves so long that they completely covered his hands. He came over as they parked the car.

"Hey, Inspector, how're you doing?"

"Fine, thanks."

"Found out who dunnit yet?"

"Done what?" Though it was clear what Adam meant.

"Oh come on! Bumped off dear Uncle Leo, of course. It's obvious that, as Eliza Doolittle would say, someone done 'im in."

"What makes you say that?"

"Stands to reason, doesn't it? I keep my

ear to the ground and the word is he really stirred things up in the short time he was here."

"And who's the popular choice of villain?"

Adam shrugged. "You pays yer money and you takes yer choice . . . I couldn't care less as long as it wasn't the old man."

His tone was flippant but briefly Thanet glimpsed the fear behind the façade. Adam, whether he knew it or not, was looking for reassurance that his father wasn't involved. Unfortunately Thanet couldn't give it to him, not at this stage. His own tone was correspondingly light as he said, "You think it might have been?"

The boy shrugged, looking suddenly very young and defenceless. "Had a bloody good motive, didn't he?" He rallied, flinging his head back and gesturing theatrically about him. "The old ancestral acres and all that."

Thanet took pity on him. "I shouldn't lose too much sleep over it just yet. As you say, your uncle seems to have stirred up a good many sleeping dogs in the short time he was here and anyway there's no indication yet that it wasn't an accident, pure and simple . . . Look, I wanted a word with the Byfleets. Do you happen to know where they might be at this time of day?"

"Since Mrs. Byfleet's been in pod Ma's insisted on her having the afternoon off, so she might be in the flat. I don't know about him, he could be anywhere around."

"Where do they live, exactly?"

Adam pointed to some windows above a row of stable doors. "Over there. You go in through the right-hand stable, there're some steps leading up."

Thanet thanked him and he and Lineham began to walk in that direction. Adam fell in beside them.

"It's pretty boring hanging around here at half-term. Trust me to be away when something really exciting happened for once. So if I can help at all . . ."

"Go on keeping your ear to the ground. And if you come across anything interesting, let me know."

"Anyone special you'd like me to keep an eye on?"

"Not at the moment, thanks."

Adam looked disappointed and walked moodily away, hands in pockets, in the direction of the house.

"Poor kid. Must be worried sick," said Lineham.

"You noticed, then. Yes. But there's not much we can do about it at the moment."

The door Adam had indicated was propped open with a stone and led into a long building divided off on their left into a series of stalls where horses had once been kept. This end section had been gutted and a sturdy wooden staircase with wide, open treads and a handrail had been fixed to the righthand wall.

"Pretty dark in here," said Lineham. "Wonder if there's a light."

He looked about and found one, just inside the door. He clicked it on and a bulkhead light fitment at the top of the staircase came on, illuminating the door beside it. Byfleet answered their knock and when he saw who it was stood back without a word. He led them through a tiny vestibule into a large sitting-room which ran the whole depth of the building with windows to front and rear. It was, Thanet thought, a delightful room, the sort of room he would be very happy to live in himself, with beams overhead infilled with rough plaster painted a rich, creamy white. Overflowing bookshelves stood between the windows, and the colours in the flowery chintz curtains were echoed in the comfortable, slip-covered armchairs and the patterned rugs on the wide, highly polished floorboards. There were brightly coloured cushions, plants and flowers and, in addition to a small portable television set, there was a modest stereo system and an extensive collection of records and tapes on specially constructed shelves. A bundle of lacy white knitting lay on one of the chairs and a low table with an unfinished game of chess laid out on it stood nearby. On another table stood a beautiful blue-and-white ceramic bowl heaped with odds and ends—some coloured pebbles, a silver nutcracker, a corkscrew, a pocket diary, a brass doorknob, a screwdriver and a pair of pink baby's bootees. Table lamps cast welcoming pools of light. It was a living-room in the best sense of the word, a room for enjoying life. The contrast with Mrs. Rankle's bleak kitchen was almost painful.

"Did you want to speak to my wife?"

"We'd like a word with both of you, actually, Mr. Byfleet."

Up until now Thanet had had little more than an occasional glimpse of the house-keeper's husband and he studied him with interest. Without the bobble hat his ears did not stick out quite as much as Thanet remembered, and the man was younger than he had thought, in his late thirties, perhaps. Divested of his anorak he was even thinner than Thanet expected, a tall, bony, gangling individual whose joints seemed articulated rather than smoothly linked by muscle and tendon. He looked tense, but there was no special significance in that. Most people were tense when interviewed by the police, innocent and guilty alike. And perhaps Byfleet was feeling especially protective towards his wife at the moment, as she'd been having a difficult time with her pregnancy. His next words confirmed this.

"She's having a rest." He glanced at his watch. "But she should be up soon. She asked me to call her at a quarter to four."

The implication was clear. He didn't want to wake her before time. Thanet glanced at his watch. Three-thirty. "That's fine. We can talk to you first, while we're waiting."

They all sat down.

Byfleet looked expectantly at Thanet but as prearranged it was Lineham who spoke. "We understand you picked up some guests from Gatwick last night, Mr. Byfleet."

"That's right."

"You took the Rolls-Royce, I believe."

"I usually do when I'm collecting guests."

"I bet they love it."

"They do seem to appreciate it, yes."

"You're a lucky man. It's one of my life-long ambitions, to drive a Rolls—oh, don't worry, Mr. Byfleet, I'm not hinting. But even a humble copper can have his dreams."

This brought a faint smile to Byfleet's face.

Well done, Mike, approved Thanet. Lineham had done well to get Byfleet to relax even to this degree.

"Anyway," Lineham went on, "you got back at around . . ." He pretended to consult his notes.

"Five to eight," said Byfleet. "Or thereabouts."

"Did you meet Mr. Talion going down

the drive in the van? He had to go and check on some sheep that had got out on to the road about then."

Thanet was sure that Lineham was well aware that Talion had left a good ten minutes earlier.

Byfleet was shaking his head. "I didn't meet anything coming down the drive. But even if I had I wouldn't have known Mr. Talion was driving. It was dark."

Lineham shrugged. "But your head-lights would have been on. You might just have recognised someone. Anyway, if you say you didn't meet anything . . ."

"I didn't."

Thanet missed the next exchange. He was wondering if Martindale had realised that the approaching van was going to run him down. Thanet imagined the scene: Martindale walking through the darkness, the sound of his footsteps crisp in the frosty night. Then, from behind him, the sound of an approaching car, its headlights casting long fingers of light towards the entrance gates. Martindale would have stopped walking, perhaps moved in close to the fence at the side of the road for the car to pass. At what point would he have realised that it wasn't going to, that he himself was its target? Perhaps he never had realised. The tear in his overcoat was in the back. Perhaps he had been hurled all unawares into Eternity. Of course, it was possible that it had been an accident after all. The driver could have seen the pedestrian ahead, braked too fiercely in order to pass him, and found himself skidding on the icy road. And of course the entire incident could have taken place on the main road and not in the drive at all. In any case it was highly unlikely that Martindale would have glimpsed the face of his killer.

Thanet switched his attention back to the interview.

"If you had happened to look out of any of the front windows, would you have been able to recognise anyone crossing the stable yard? How well lit is it at night?"

Lineham had evidently been asking if either of the Byfleets had seen anyone drive the van away.

"Very well lit really. Mrs. Hamilton had extra lights installed when a guest twisted her ankle on the cobbles last year."

"Who is responsible for switching them on?"

Byfleet shrugged. "Theoretically I am. But if I'm not here when it gets dark one of the others will do it."

"Were they on when you got back that night?"

"I think they must have been, or I'd have noticed." He thought for a moment. "Yes, they were."

"Your wife was already here when you got back?"

"Yes. She knew I'd be back about eight, so she came over to finish getting supper ready."

Had Thanet imagined it, or was there a touch of unease there? Any mention of Mrs. Byfleet seemed to disturb her husband. It would be interesting to see them together.

"And you say you sat down to supper straight away?"

In the kitchen, presumably, thought Thanet. There was no dining table in here. Unless they had eaten off trays. He opened his mouth to ask then thought better of it. Perhaps this point had already been covered in the brief snatch of conversation he had missed while thinking about the accident. He mustn't let his attention wander again.

Lineham had noticed and raised his eyebrows. *You wanted to ask something?*

Thanet shook his head.

"How long did you take over supper?"

Byfleet shrugged. "Not that long. Twenty minutes, half an hour perhaps."

So, over the crucial period when the van had stood idle Byfleet was claiming that he and his wife were enjoying a cosy domestic interlude.

Lineham hadn't missed this point. "You usually eat at that time?"

"Generally between eight and half past, yes. By then the guests are usually at dinner, and my wife is free."

"And she goes back over to the Hall afterwards?"

"For an hour or so, yes. From around nine to ten."

"She works long hours."

"She does have the afternoons off. And at least one full day every week."

Delia Hamilton commanded an astonishing degree of loyalty from her employees, thought Thanet. So far he hadn't heard a single grumble about her.

Lineham glanced at his watch. "Well, thank you, Mr. Byfleet. It is ten to four now, so perhaps you wouldn't mind waking your wife?"

Byfleet frowned then stood up, reluctantly. He hesitated then said, "Look . . ."

Thanet and Lineham said nothing, waited.

"My wife . . . She's not been well."

"Yes, Mrs. Hamilton told us," said Thanet.

"I don't want her upset unnecessarily."

A touch of belligerence there.

"We're not inhuman, Mr. Byfleet. We just want to ask her one or two simple questions."

Byfleet looked embarrassed. "I'm sorry. It's just that . . . Well, this baby . . . it's . . . We've been married five years and we'd given up hope, you see, and then . . ."

"I understand."

Byfleet hesitated a moment longer, as if in need of further reassurance, then turned away and disappeared through a door at the far side of the room, closing it behind him.

"Bit jumpy, isn't he?" said Lineham.

"Mm. I can't make up my mind if he's got something on his mind or if it's just that he's concerned that all this shouldn't upset his wife. He obviously feels very protective towards her."

"Understandable, I suppose. They're both getting on, for a first baby, and the pregnancy hasn't been straightforward, apparently."

"Quite. Er . . . I'm afraid my attention wandered for a few minutes back there, Mike. Where did he say they were while they were having supper?"

"In the kitchen at the back of the building."

Thanet got up and wandered over to the bookshelves. He was always interested to know what people were reading. The Byfleets seemed to have pretty catholic taste. There was biography, mostly fairly light, a modest collection of poetry, a whole shelf of non-fiction covering topics ranging from travel to do-it-yourself, and row upon row of fiction, both classical and contemporary. On the bottom shelf, below a row of romantic historical novels, were a few children's books. Thanet squatted to inspect them: Alison Uttley, Beatrix Potter and the once despised but now reinstated Enid Blyton. Smiling reminiscently he picked out *The Famous Five Go Adventuring Again*, one of his own favourites. Inside the front cover was written in neat, carefully rounded script:

Mona Taylor
The Limes Preparatory School
Burgess Road
Brighton
Sussex
England
The British Isles
Europe
The World
The Universe.

He smiled and held it out to show Lineham. "Things don't change much, do they? I remember writing this myself, and I bet you do, too. And so did Ben and Bridget."

"Yes. No doubt my two'll get around to it in due course. Pretty nice place they've got here, haven't they? Bit unexpected, really. For that matter, he's not exactly your typical handyman, is he?"

"Presumably he likes the life. Perhaps they just enjoy working together." Thanet was now glancing at the records and tapes. Popular classics, Gilbert and Sullivan, old pop songs, none of the more recent stuff. He could almost hear Ben and Bridget chanting *"boring"*.

"Taking their time, aren't they?" Lineham was getting restless.

"If she's been asleep she'd have to have a few minutes to collect herself."

"Is the Super expecting you to report in again today?"

"'Fraid so." Thanet returned to his seat.

Lineham groaned. "It's getting beyond a joke. Think he's going to turn up every day, like he did today?"

"I sincerely hope not! I'm trying to tell myself the novelty'll soon wear off."

"It'd better, or he'll be having a mutiny on his hands."

"Now now, Mike. You didn't say that. Or if you did, I didn't hear it. And do stop prowling around like that, you're getting on my nerves."

"You were prowling yourself until a minute ago!" Lineham plumped down on his chair looking disgruntled. "I hate hanging about like this."

"I wonder if they've finished the post-mortem yet."

"Should have, by now."

"Doc Mallard said he'd let us know if there was anything interesting and there hasn't been a word, so it doesn't look as though we're going to get much help there. I'm beginning to think this case might be a non-starter, Mike."

"It's not like you to say that. But I see what you mean. And I agree, there doesn't seem to be much prospect of proving who did it even if we do find out. Still, we've had cases before when we've said exactly the same thing and we've made it in the end—or you have, at least."

"Mm." Thanet was beginning to feel drowsy. If he had to sit in this very comfortable chair much longer he would fall asleep. The first couple of days of this type of investigation were always very tiring. There were so many people to see, so many leads to follow up, so many judgements to make, impressions to absorb. It was fine so long as you kept going, but once you stopped and lost your impetus . . . Abruptly he got up and crossed to the window in an attempt to rouse himself. "They are taking a long time . . ."

"Perhaps they've knotted sheets and climbed out of the window," said Lineham with a grin.

"Ha ha. Very funny." Thanet peered out into the stable yard. The sky had clouded over and once again it was getting dark early. Tiller emerged from his work shed and crossed the cobbles, trundling a wheelbarrow. From here there was an excellent view of almost the entire yard, across to the back of the house. Tiller's house was at the end of this same side and Hamilton's office in the block at right angles. All of them would have had a clear view of Martindale if he had come out of the back door, especially if the yard had been well lit. Thanet said so.

Lineham came across to look. "Yes. And in that loud checked overcoat of his he would have been easily recognisable.

257

But why come out of the back door, not the front?"

Thanet shrugged. "He didn't feel like running into guests in the foyer? It can't be easy, finding your home overrun by all and sundry who feel they have as much right there as you have. Or—"

They both turned as the door opened and the Byfleets came in. Byfleet's arm was around his wife's shoulders. She was wearing the same long dark green dress, her housekeeper's uniform, presumably. Her eyes were still puffy with sleep and she looked alarmingly pale and fragile.

"Sorry to keep you waiting, Inspector," she said with a smile. "I'm afraid it takes me a little while to get going after a rest, these days."

"It really doesn't matter, Mrs. Byfleet. I'm sorry to trouble you again, but I'm afraid there are one or two small points . . ."

"I understand."

She and Byfleet sat down. He took her hand. Side by side Thanet noticed that they were already beginning to acquire that uncanny resemblance sometimes found in married couples who are very close to each other. He had noticed it before and wondered once again exactly wherein it lay. In facial expression, attitude, in tiny gestures or habits unconsciously picked up from each other? Did he and Joan have it?

"It's just that we are still trying to piece together Mr. Martindale's movements on Tuesday, and when we saw you yesterday you forgot to mention that you had seen him after dinner that evening."

He watched the slow tide of colour suffuse the pale, almost translucent skin and wondered if she could remember their conversation yesterday as clearly as he did.

"Did you see him again at all, after he'd had dinner?"

"No."

She shook her head in embarrassment. "I expect you're wondering why I didn't mention it before, but . . ." She glanced at her husband and Thanet saw the grip on her hand tighten as Byfleet nodded.

"It's just that it was so awkward, so embarrassing . . ."

Surely Martindale hadn't made a pass at her, in her advanced state of pregnancy?

"I was just doing a routine check around

the house as I always do at that time, to make sure that everything is in order—lamps lit, curtains drawn, that sort of thing—and as I was walking along the corridor past the Chinese room the door opened and Mr. Martindale looked out. He said he wanted a word with me, so I went in. He . . ." She glanced at her husband again and took courage. "It was horrible! He began to—well—quiz me, about the hotel. He began by asking how long I'd been here, whether I liked it and so on and then he started asking very specific questions about the number of staff, about how many guests we had, about staff wages and holidays and things like that . . . I just didn't know what to say . . ."

She was becoming agitated and Byfleet put an arm around her shoulders again. She shook her head. "I mean, I know he was Mrs. Hamilton's brother, but I just didn't feel he had the right . . . I tried to be polite, or pretend I didn't know the answers but he just persisted . . . In the end I said I was sorry, but I just didn't feel I could give him that sort of information without Mrs. Hamilton's permission, and he said I'd better get used to the idea that from now on I would ultimately be responsible to him, not to her . . . I asked him if that meant Mrs. Hamilton wouldn't be running the place any longer and he said yes, she would, but that he was the owner and everyone was going to have to adjust to the fact. I said that I still felt I would have to get Mrs. Hamilton's permission to give him the sort of information he was asking for. I was a bit nervous when I said it—after all, if he really did own the place, he was my employer and I thought he might be angry, ask if I was calling him a liar or something, but he just laughed and said to go ahead and ask her, that he admired loyalty in members of staff and would see me again when I had spoken to her."

"And did you speak to her?"

"Not immediately. I met a guest on the way, who delayed me for a few minutes, then I found Mrs. Hamilton had gone to the station to meet Adam. Then when she got back she went straight into the drawing-room to have drinks with the guests— she always does, before dinner—and then I had to come back here to get your supper, didn't I, Des, so it wasn't till just after nine that I eventually saw her."

"And she confirmed what he had said?"

"Yes."

"Why didn't you tell me this yesterday?"

She shrugged. "It didn't seem relevant."

Thanet sighed. "I wish people would let me decide what is relevant and what isn't."

She bit her lip. "I'm sorry."

"Never mind, you've told me now . . . We asked your husband, earlier, if he happened to notice the van drive out of the yard during the evening. He said no, but did you?"

She shook her head.

"What about later on? Sam Tiller drove it back from the pub at 10.30."

"I didn't notice," said Byfleet. "Did you, love?"

Another shake of the head.

"And after that?"

She hesitated. "I did hear something . . ."

"When?"

"Shortly after we went to bed. Somewhere around a quarter past eleven. I heard a car start up and drive off, and come back some time later." She gave a rueful smile. "I don't sleep too well these days."

Thanet remembered Joan's restless nights during the latter months of her pregnancies. "No . . . Did you hear one car return, or two?"

"Two, I think."

"And that was when?"

"I'm sorry, I didn't notice. I didn't think it was important."

Thanet rose. "There is just one question I must put to you both. Did either of you, for any reason, drive the van that night?"

They obviously realised the significance of the question. Neither looked at the other as they shook their heads in unison.

"We had no reason to," said Byfleet stiffly.

Picking their way carefully down the staircase outside Lineham said, "Did you believe them, sir?"

Outside Thanet took deep breaths of the clear, cold air. He shrugged. "Difficult to tell. She's so obviously unwell and he's so on edge about her . . ."

"Of course, what she told us does give them some sort of a motive, doesn't it, sir?"

"You mean, they might have been afraid that they would lose their cosy billet if Martindale took over? Bit thin, isn't it? A good housekeeper and chauffeur/handyman can always find a job, surely."

"When she's pregnant and her health isn't too good? Not as easy as all that, I shouldn't think."

"Perhaps not."

As they got into the Land Rover the lights in the courtyard came on. Byfleet was right, the whole area was well illuminated. Had Martindale strolled across this very spot on the way to his death?

As he had said to Lineham, earlier, Thanet was beginning to wonder if he would ever find out.

264

16

ARRIVING home at around 8.30 Thanet was surprised to find Bridget in the kitchen with Joan. He kissed them both, then said, "I thought you were on duty tonight, Bridget."

"Mandy wanted me to swap with her, so I worked the lunchtime shift today."

Thanet nevertheless wouldn't have expected to find her in—but managed not to say so. Bridget led such an active social life. At seventeen she was blossoming into womanhood—face and figure were fast losing the plumpness which had bedevilled her mid-teens and she always managed to look stylish when going out even though her wardrobe could hardly be called extensive. Tonight she was wearing jeans, trainers, a collarless man's shirt and a baggy sweater which practically reached her knees, sleeves pushed casually up to just below the elbows.

He plucked at it. "This looks familiar."

She flung her arms around his neck in mock humility. "I knew you wouldn't mind. You don't, do you?"

"Can't call a thing your own in this house, these days."

"Don't tell me!" said Joan. "We haven't eaten, by the way. We thought we'd wait till nine to have supper, in the hope that you might be back in time. It's ages since we all had supper together."

Thanet beamed. "Lovely." His irregular hours had always meant that family meals were a hit-and-miss affair but when the children were younger he had at least known that if he did manage to get home at a reasonable hour they'd all be able to eat together. But lately, especially since Bridget had left school and begun working in the restaurant, this had become an increasingly rare event. "What about Ben? Has he managed to last out?"

"I stuffed him with baked beans and toast when he got home from school," said Bridget with a grin.

"I'll go and wash my hands, then."

Upstairs he remembered that he and Joan had promised themselves a serious talk with Bridget about late nights and jaunts to destinations unknown, and his heart sank. It would be a pity to spoil the pleasure of an evening together. Perhaps they could put it off to another time? He scowled at himself in the bathroom mirror as he shook his head. No. For his own peace of mind it had to be done. The problem was, how to choose the right moment.

By the time he came down supper was ready.

"This looks good," said Thanet. "What is it?"

Bridget looked pleased. "Chicken with paprika and onions."

"Bridget cooked it," said Joan. "Don't gobble, Ben," she added.

Ben scowled and went on shovelling food in as fast as he could. "I've still got homework to do."

"Don't know how you can taste it when you eat at that speed," said Bridget.

"It's all right for you. You're finished with all that, aren't you? Nothing to do but enjoy yourself these days."

"I wouldn't put it quite like that. I do work, you know."

"Call that work? A few hours a day? I should be so lucky."

"That's enough," said Thanet. "Bridget had to go through what you're doing now, remember."

Ben laid down his knife and fork. "Any pud?"

"All in good time," said Joan. "We're still eating."

Ben pushed his chair back and stood up. "Well I can't hang around. I'll have it in my room, while I'm working."

"You will not!" said his mother. Then, more gently, "Look, Ben, it's ages since we all had supper together. Let's just relax and enjoy it, shall we?"

He gave her a black look. "I'll go without, then!" And he stumped off.

"Ben!" Thanet half rose, then sat down again with a rueful look at Joan. "May as well let him get on with it. I can quite see he finds it difficult to enjoy a leisurely meal with work hanging over his head."

"He's absolutely impossible these days," said Bridget.

"He's finding it difficult settling in to the new school, as you well know," said Thanet. "We have to make allowances."

"But he's always having a go at me! It's my clothes, or my make-up, or I'm taking too long in the bathroom, or—"

"I think," said Joan, beginning to clear the plates, "that his nose is put out of joint."

"Oh, why?"

"Well you used to get on so well together. Now you don't have time for him any more—or so he feels."

Now Bridget was getting cross. She stood up and picked up the other plates, clashing them together in a way which made Joan wince. "What am I supposed to do? Take him with me? Who wants a kid brother hanging around their neck all the time?"

She flounced out and Joan gave Thanet an exaggerated shrug of mock despair. "I always put my foot in it these days. No," she said as he stood up, "don't bother to come out. We can manage."

She and Bridget returned with the pudding, a lemon meringue pie, and the dessert plates. Joan began serving in an uncomfortable silence.

"Look," she said, "I'm not suggesting you should let Ben tag along with you, of course I'm not. But he is going through a bad patch and if you could find a little more time for him . . ."

"But he's always working! And if he's not, I'm out."

Thanet caught Joan's eye and an unspoken message passed between them.

Don't forget we've got to talk to her . . .

I know.

Bridget wasn't stupid. "What was that supposed to mean?"

"What?" said Joan.

"That look. You and Dad looked at each other."

Thanet sighed. There wasn't going to be a right moment to discuss this. Should they leave it? But the subject had come up and if he were realistic, he realised, there never would be a right time for what he had to say. Why did adolescents have to be so difficult? But he refused to give in to moral blackmail and fail to broach delicate subjects for fear of provoking an outburst of bad temper.

"Well, now that you mention it . . ."

Bridget rolled her eyes. "What now?"

"Bridget, I do think that's unreasonable!" Uncharacteristically, Joan was now becoming angry. "How many restrictions do we place on what you do, where you go, or who you go with?"

"Hah. So that's it!" Bridget laid down the spoon she had just picked up, sat back and folded her arms. "Well, let's have it. What have I done now?"

Pleasant family meals were evidently a thing of the past, thought Thanet with regret as he said sharply, "That's enough, Bridget. Your mother and I wanted to have a sensible, adult discussion with you. Please, try to calm down."

"By 'sensible discussion' I suppose you mean you're going to lay down rules that I'm supposed to follow?"

"Well you suppose wrong. I meant exactly what I said, a sensible discussion. That is, a discussion in which both sides put their point of view and a compromise is reached. Now, are you going to listen or are you going to behave like a spoilt adolescent?"

She glared at him. "Oh, so that's what I am now, is it? A spoilt adolescent?" She pushed back her chair preparatory to getting up.

Thanet put his hand on her arm, detaining her. "No, Bridget, wait. Just answer me one question."

"What?" She was still glowering at him.

"Can you honestly say we've been the sort of heavy-handed parents who lay down the law and expect you to accept what they say whether you like it or not?"

Pause. She chewed the inside of her lip, poised for flight yet unable honestly to answer in the affirmative. Eventually, "I suppose not," she said grudgingly.

"Well in that case, can't you at least listen to what we have to say, see if you think we're being unreasonable this time?"

Another hesitation, then he felt the rigid muscles in her arm relax. But she was still sulky as she said, "Go on, then. Let's get it over with."

Thanet paused for a moment, marshalling his thoughts. He had to get this right first time.

"Can you accept that as your parents we're bound to worry about you?"

"Oh, *Dad!*"

"Yes, I realise you must find that irritating. When you're young you don't want to have limitations put on your freedom—

and I want to make it clear that that's not what we're after. We know you, and trust you to be sensible, but at the same time we'd like a little more peace of mind ourselves. So what we're asking is this: if you know you're going to be late, could you give us a ring to let us know, and if you're going out, we would like to know who you're going with and where you're going. That's it."

"But that's impossible!" Bridget burst out. "I've told Mum over and over again! How can I tell you where I'm going if I don't know myself? You don't understand! Say I'm meeting Sue. She may have arranged to meet some other people as well and when we're all together we say, Right, where shall we go tonight? It could be bowling, or to a pub—oh, don't look like that, Dad. It's different nowadays. Everyone goes to pubs and yes, I know I'm under eighteen and I promise you I don't drink alcohol, I really don't, but that's where people get together these days . . . Or we might go to McDonalds or if one of us has a car we might drive over to the Chimneys in Biddenden or over to that Hungarian restaurant in Tunbridge Wells

. . . And you needn't worry about that, either. Whoever's driving never drinks. We make sure of that. We don't want to end up in the mortuary, either."

"Look love, you're wrong in thinking we don't understand. We do. And we do see the problem. We know that that's how things work, and one of the reasons why we've never brought the matter up before is because we really couldn't see any solution to it. But now, well, I think I've thought of a possible answer. But before I see what you think of the idea, I would just like to know if you can understand why we're making a fuss about it. Can't you see that not to know where you are, to think that we wouldn't even know where to begin looking for you if by any chance something went wrong and you just didn't come home—and don't roll your eyes like that! I'm better placed than most people to know just how often these things do happen. If you'd met some of the frantic parents I have . . . But anyway, do you understand what I'm trying to say?"

"I suppose so."

"Well then, this is what I suggest. That you carry on as usual. You meet your friends, you go wherever it is you want to go, with one small difference. That when you get there you make a phone call, just a brief one, telling us where you are. That's all. It need take only a few seconds and it would help us to stop worrying."

"Everyone would fall about laughing!" She mimicked a child's voice: "'Excuse me, everyone. I've got to go and ring my Mummy and my Daddy, to let them know where I am.'"

"Would it really be so impossible? You needn't tell them who you're ringing. Or you can make us out to be ogres if you like, lay all the blame on us. We wouldn't mind . . ."

She bit her lip, thinking about it.

What, exactly, would he do if she refused? Thanet wondered. He had no intention of playing the heavy father and laying down ultimatums which it would be impossible to keep. They never worked and would have a disastrous effect on what he liked to think, despite the present problem, was basically a good and sound relationship.

"Look," he said, as the silence stretched out. "Would you at least agree to give it a trial run? For a week, say? If it didn't work, and you really did find it too embarrassing, we could think again, see if we can work something else out. Or if you've got an alternative suggestion. . . ?"

She shook her head. "I can't think of anything at the moment . . ." Suddenly she capitulated. "OK, then. I'll give it a whirl. Why not?"

The sense of relief was overwhelming. Thanet felt as though he'd just run an exhausting race. "Good! Terrific!" He looked at his untouched piece of pie. Now he would be able to enjoy it. And afterwards, he'd take a slice up to Ben.

He and Joan usually did the washing up together after supper but tonight Bridget insisted on doing it all.

"Go on, relax while you can! I'll bring you in some coffee later."

Thanet and Joan plumped down side by side on the settee. "She's OK really, isn't she?" said Joan. "If you look about you and see the sort of mess so many young people get into, we're very lucky."

"So far."

"So far. It's just that at the moment I seem to get on her nerves all the time."

"Perhaps she's too like you to be able to forgive you your faults at present. She'll grow out of it, later on."

Joan sighed. "I suppose so. Yes. I remember someone telling me once about his daughter. Apparently, in her late teens, she was absolutely impossible, made life hell for them. And a few years later, when she was in her mid-twenties, she was a completely different girl: kind, thoughtful, considerate, a joy, in fact. And she actually said to him, 'You know Dad, when I look back and think what I was like as a teenager, I don't know how you and Mum put up with me.' So when Bridget and I have an argument or I feel I can't do anything right as far as she's concerned, I just remind myself of what he said and tell myself that if I grit my teeth and hang on it'll all work out in the end."

"You're right. I really do believe that." Thanet yawned hugely. "Sorry."

"You're tired. You look tired, actually. Bad day?"

Bridget came in with two cups of coffee. "I'm going to have a bath and wash my hair."

"All right, love. Thanks." He waited

until she had gone, then said, "Not bad, no. But you know how it is at the beginning of a case. And the Super hasn't helped."

"Oh, why?"

"ODD." Which reminded him, he really must take a look at the information sheet Draco had handed out.

"What is?"

"His new campaign. I told you one was brewing. Well, that's it. ODD. O-D-D. Standing for Organisation, Delegation and Documentation. Stop grinning like that. The acronym, I might add, was deliberate. He thought it might afford the men some light relief! Oh, he's cunning all right. Knows how to sweeten the pill. Though in fact—and you may not believe this—he actually apologised to me this afternoon!"

"He did *what*?"

"It's true."

Joan wriggled into a more comfortable position, tucking her stockinged feet up beneath her. "Tell me!"

She was always a gratifying audience. As he talked Thanet thought how much it meant to him to have her there, to be able to share these rare, quiet evenings at home together. He felt sorry for Martindale, who had apparently never known the pleasures of domesticity. No one seemed to mourn his passing—quite the reverse, in fact. A number of people must secretly be relieved or even pleased that he was dead. Thanet wondered what influences had worked upon Martindale to make him the man he was, a man apparently incapable of making lasting relationships or even, indeed, of needing them. Though he did seem to have remained attached to his last, French mistress. Or perhaps it was simply that he had found a comfortable billet and made sure he didn't lose it. Knowing Martindale, that was much more likely. Thanet said so, to Joan.

"Mm." She was thoughtful. "He certainly doesn't sound the most sensitive of souls. Practically everyone he met seems to have had a row with him."

"Quite. At first I thought it strange that people would dive straight into resurrecting old grudges as though they had happened only yesterday, but when Mrs. Byfleet told me how he had tried to pump her, quite unashamedly, it does seem that although he could presumably turn on the charm when he wanted to, if it didn't suit him to do so he really couldn't have cared less if he upset people or not."

"Yes, but we're not exactly talking about trivial matters, are we? Crippling that poor boy for life and destroying his mother's marriage, causing the death of Mr. Tiller's prize bull after all those years of effort, making a pass at a married woman whose husband has a reputation for jealousy . . ."

"He might not have known Fever was the jealous type."

"Even so . . ."

"Then there's Jack Talion, the farm manager. We still don't know what he had against Martindale." Thanet sighed. "Anyway, as I was saying to Mike, I'm beginning to wonder if we're going to get anywhere on this one."

"Oh come on, darling! You've only been working on it for forty-eight hours. And if you gave me a pound for every time I'd heard you say that . . . Nearly every time, at some point in a case, you start having doubts about whether you'll be able to solve it."

"I suppose that's true." Joan was right,

he had to admit it. "But the problem is that this time, even if I do find out who killed him—assuming it wasn't a straightforward accident, that is—I don't see any prospect of proving it."

"And I've heard that before, too! You'll get there in the end, I know you will. You're just tired, that's all. We'll have an early night and you'll feel quite different in the morning, you'll see."

Thanet hoped she was right.

17

AS usual, Joan was right. Although Thanet had lain awake for some time while the crowded impressions of the day jostled through his mind, in the end he did manage a good seven hours' sleep and by next morning his pessimistic mood had vanished. After all, he reminded himself as he squinted into the shaving mirror, he was far from at a dead end. Reports should now be in on a number of enquiries that had been set in motion, including the interview with the farmhand Jack Talion had sacked. Thanet was hoping that this was a local man who would be able to shed some light on the reason for Talion's animosity towards Martindale. Also, the forensic evidence on the van and the results of the postmortem should be in today.

Outside, Thanet's spirits rose further. The sun was shining, the sky was clear and it was several degrees warmer. The last of the snow had gone and they would be able to discard the Land Rover in favour of a car. Lineham would be pleased.

Whistling, Thanet set off for work. But his buoyant mood was soon to be severely tested. In good time when he left home, he was only halfway when there was a squeal of brakes ahead of him and the cars in front braked sharply. Thanet sucked in his breath as there was a dull ominous crunch and his car lurched. The driver behind had reacted too slowly and failed to pull up in time. There followed a time-consuming exchange of names, telephone numbers and details of insurance companies, as a result of which Thanet finally arrived at work only a matter of minutes before he was due at the morning meeting. It was unfortunate that as he hurried in Draco happened to be talking to the Station Officer in the Reception area. The Superintendent's hairy eyebrows elevated themselves in pained surprise, and he glanced pointedly at the clock.

To compound his problem the sight of Draco reminded him that he'd completely forgotten after all, last night, to read through Draco's information sheet on

ODD. He wasn't exactly going to be top of the Superintendent's popularity poll this morning.

Muttering under his breath Thanet raced upstairs to his office, removing his coat as he went. Lineham glanced up, startled, as he burst in.

Thanet tossed the coat on to a chair. "No time to stop," he panted. "Minor accident on the way. No, it's all right, I'm fine. Anything it's absolutely essential for me to know before the meeting?"

Lineham glanced at the papers littering his desk. "Interesting but not essential."

"Fine. See you shortly."

Down the stairs again with seconds to spare. Outside Draco's door Thanet pulled up and paused long enough to take a couple of deep breaths before going in. Once again he was last.

Draco shot him a sideways glance but made no comment. He waited until Thanet was seated then said, "Right, well now that you've had twenty-four hours to think over my suggestions, perhaps we could begin by having your thoughts on ODD."

Thanet slid down an inch or two in his chair, unconsciously betraying his desire to become invisible. Draco noticed and gave him a sharp glance. Thanet sat up again, straightening his shoulders. *Face it like a man*, he told himself with an inward grin, in a Midwestern drawl. And then, with a spurt of resentment, *I have had more important things on my mind.*

Tody and Boon had obviously done their homework. In turn they came up with constructive comments while Thanet continued inwardly to justify himself.

"Thanet?"

"Er . . ." Might as well come straight out with it. "I'm afraid I've been so busy with the Martindale case that I clean forgot you were expecting our comments today, sir."

Draco's nostrils flared. "I see."

There was a brief, pregnant silence before the Superintendent went on, "Well in that case perhaps you could tell us what you have been doing."

Ignoring the emphasis on "have" Thanet launched into an account of yesterday's activities. The others listened, asked pertinent questions and then Draco said, "Anything interesting come in overnight?"

"I'm afraid there hasn't been time to check yet, sir." Thanet was furious. Having seen him arrive only moments before Draco must have known he wouldn't have had time to read any reports. It had been a deliberate ploy to put him further in the wrong. Perhaps the Superintendent was paying him back for having wrong-footed him yesterday. "I was involved in a minor accident on the way to work and there was some delay."

"Not your fault I hope, Thanet."

"No, sir."

"Good. Don't like my officers to be seen to be infringing the law."

The meeting broke up, but Draco called Thanet back. He clasped his hands behind his back and gave a little preparatory bounce, as if to lend more weight to his words. "Look, Thanet, I do understand that you are very busy with this Martindale investigation, but it won't do to let other things slide, you know."

"No, sir."

Bounce. "I don't think you quite appreciate the importance of this new initiative of mine. It doesn't do to let the grass grow under one's feet."

"No, sir."

Bounce. "One has to keep a sense of balance, of proportion. It's so easy to become so obsessed with one aspect of one's work that one lets others slide. Not that I'm suggesting you do that, of course. It's just that one has to be on one's guard against it. . . . Perhaps by tomorrow you'll have had time to come up with some thoughts on ODD."

"I'll try, sir. But . . ."

Bounce. "I'll look forward to hearing them, then. Good. That's all."

Thanet fumed silently all the way back upstairs and into his office.

Lineham took one look at his face and said, "Been having fun?"

"Don't joke about it, Mike!" Thanet reached for his pipe and began filling it, stuffing the tobacco in with angry stabs.

"Bad as that, was it?"

"Let's just say it was an experience I shouldn't care to repeat too often."

With an upsurge of the resentment common among smokers against a world which was making them feel more and more like social outcasts, Thanet lit up. Lineham could put up with it for once.

The door opened and Doc Mallard came in.

"Faugh!" he said, waving his hand to disperse the coils of smoke drifting towards him. "At it again, Luke? How often do I have to tell you—?" He broke off. "Do I detect a chill in the atmosphere?"

"He had a minor accident on the way to work," said Lineham.

"Really?" Mallard advanced, concerned. "You all right, Luke?"

"It's not that," said Thanet irritably. "That was nothing, I'm perfectly all right."

"Sure? You don't want me to look you over?"

"No, no. If you must know, I've just been hauled over the carpet, that's all."

"Oh dear. Our zealous Superintendent on the warpath again. What have you been up to this time?"

Thanet shook his head. "It's not important. Any news for us, Doc?"

"Here's the PM report. I meant to give you a ring yesterday afternoon, but one or two things cropped up . . ."

"That's all right." Thanet knew that if

there had been something important to tell, Mallard wouldn't have forgotten. "So there was nothing unexpected?"

"Not really. It's all there, but shall I give you a quick summary in layman's terms?"

"Please."

"Well, as seemed likely from the tear in the overcoat and the head injury, the victim was struck in the back. My guess is that when the car hit him he was tossed upwards and backwards and struck the back of his head on the front offside corner of the roof."

"That's right," said Lineham. He glanced at Thanet. "The forensic report on the van came in this morning."

"Well, as I say," said Mallard, "the main impact was to the back left side. There was considerable muscle bruising, kidney damage and—this was the worst injury—partial dislocation of the spine. The scalp wound was relatively superficial, a glancing blow."

"So he might have recovered consciousness?"

"He did." Mallard hesitated. "That's the unpleasant part."

"What do you mean?"

"Work it out for yourself. Assuming that he was put into that ditch immediately after the accident . . ."

"Just a minute," said Thanet. "You said 'put'. The spinal injury meant that he wouldn't have been able to put himself in?"

"He certainly wouldn't have been able to walk. He could have dragged himself a short distance, but there were no cuts or abrasions on the palms of his hands. On the other hand, there were particles of dirt under some of his fingernails . . ."

Thanet stared at Mallard, appalled, his imagination at once conjuring up the scene: the injured man in the ditch, a thin mantle of snow covering his face, the gradual awakening, the increasingly despairing attempts to sit up, the dawning consciousness of his situation before the frantic scrabbling of fingernails against the frozen sides of the ditch and the final slide into numbing unconsciousness and death.

"If he'd been taken to hospital right away he'd be in pretty bad shape but at least he'd still be alive. Or if it had been summertime and the weather had been warmer . . . As it was, of course, he didn't have a chance and it's not surprising that he was dead by morning."

Thanet shook his head to try and dispel the grim images lingering on the screen of his mind. "I suppose you still can't be very precise about time of death, in the circumstances?"

"No. But from the rectal temperature and the tests on the eye fluid the findings are consistent with death occurring sometime in the early hours of the morning."

Thanet was still feeling shaken. He took the report Mallard held out. "Well, thanks for coming in, Doc."

"You're sure you're all right, Luke, that you don't want me to take a look at you?"

"No, really. Some idiot behind me didn't brake quickly enough, that's all. The only damage was to the rear of my car."

"It's the inconvenience of sorting it out that's the nuisance," said Mallard sympathetically. "Well, if there's nothing else. . . ?"

Thanet watched him go and then in contrition laid down his pipe. There was no reason why Lineham should suffer because of Draco's unreasonableness.

"Nasty," said Lineham.

"Very. Hardly bears thinking about, does it?" Then, with an attempt at briskness, "Right then, Mike. What have we got?"

"Various bits and pieces. As I said, forensic have confirmed that it was the van that knocked him down."

"Good. Anything else there?"

"Hundreds of fingerprints, of course, all useless. So many people used it legitimately . . ."

"Quite. Never mind, at least we're now certain we're on the right track, and it wasn't just a passing motorist. And talking of passing motorists, anything come in as a result of the TVS appeal?"

"Nothing useful, sir. Of course, it was a bitterly cold night and I suppose most people were at home by the fire, watching television. And it's not exactly a major road, it's mostly local traffic along there."

"Pity. We could just do with an independent witness."

"Doesn't look as though we're going to get one. It's been two days now . . ."

"Don't rub it in, Mike. Anything else?"

"Several things, actually."

"So? Come on, man, we haven't got all day."

"There's an interesting report on an interview with the parlourmaid who served dinner to the Hamiltons and Martindale the night he died. She says she definitely heard him tell them that he was going to be staying on at the Hall and—get this— that he would be establishing his right to sole ownership."

"Really? How did she hear all this? They wouldn't have talked about it openly in front of her, surely?"

"I don't know, sir. I have the impression that people like that think servants are pretty well invisible. But no, they didn't discuss it openly. It's just that she could tell there was a bit of an atmosphere and sensing that there might be some interesting gossip, she eaves-dropped."

"I see. Who interviewed her?"

"Swift, sir. I had a word with him and I gather it took a little while to winkle all this out of her."

"Turned on the boyish charm, I suppose. She was young, I imagine?"

Lineham grinned. "Yes. And pretty."

"Why didn't she come up with all this before?"

"She was off duty the day the body was discovered, so he didn't see her till yesterday."

"So what else did she hear?"

Lineham sat back and grinned. "Only that Martindale informed them that they were welcome to stay on and work for him, if they liked."

"His sister to run the hotel and Hamilton the estate?"

Lineham nodded.

"So much for all that 'I'm sure we could all have come to some amicable arrangement.' And, 'It's a good-sized cake, there was plenty for everybody.'"

Lineham was still nodding. "Quite. It's a classic motive, isn't it? Two thousand acres and Longford Hall."

"It certainly is. I must admit I was a bit suspicious when Mrs. Hamilton told us about Sam Tiller and his bull. Oh, I know she put up a good show of reluctance, but

I'm pretty sure that she still wouldn't have given in if she hadn't had a good reason."

"To deflect attention away from herself, you mean?"

"Yes. Did the girl say how they reacted to the good news?"

"Unfortunately she doesn't know. She had to go and fetch the next course. But she didn't think there'd been an open row about it, judging by their behaviour when she went back."

"I imagine they'd have been too subtle for that, tried persuasion first, or sought legal advice."

"Quite."

"We'll have to talk to the Hamiltons again, obviously. If only we could find out what Martindale was up to after Mrs. Byfleet left him at 7.15 . . . Well anyway, was there anything else?"

"Swift is still trying to trace Martindale's former lady loves. The address book was pretty useless, most of the stuff was way out of date. He thinks it might well take several more days yet. Some of the names were non-starters, of course. Just a postcard, with no address. Some of them were guests at the hotels Martindale stayed in, often some time ago, so it's a long job. Records have been lost or destroyed or the hotel's changed hands, or the women have moved . . ."

"Yes yes, I get the picture. Has he managed to get any positive results yet?"

"Well, some of them were manageresses or even the owners of the hotels, so they're still around. Not surprising, really. Martindale was only fifty and he would have gone for middle-aged widows mostly, I should think. And if they owned hotels they wouldn't be likely to have retired yet. But some of them are now married, so it's proving a bit tricky. Swift's made a list." Lineham shuffled through the papers on his desk and picked out a sheet of paper. "Here we are." He handed it over.

"Mm." Thanet read out the names. "Mrs. Mary Wix in Norwich, Mrs. Elizabeth Johnson in Broadway, Mrs. Jeannette Martin in Eastbourne, Mrs. Brenda Taylor in Worthing, Mrs. Caroline Dempster in Folkestone, Mrs. Kathleen Jackson in Bournemouth." None of them rang a bell. But then, why should they, and what possible relevance could they have? Perhaps

Swift was wasting his time. Thanet said so. "What d'you think, Mike?"

"Well I agree, it does seem an awful lot of time spent to little purpose. I'm not quite sure why you thought it important."

"Not important, just a loose end to be followed up. But if it's going to be as time-consuming as that I'm not sure it's justified." Thanet tapped the report. "Did he actually learn anything useful from any of them?"

"Not really. Reactions varied, apparently. One or two refused to talk. As soon as they heard Martindale's name they slammed the phone down. One—Mrs. Dempster, in Folkestone—was rather pathetic apparently, eager for news and pretty upset to hear he was dead. A couple more said they didn't want to talk about it, they were now happily married . . . No, I agree. I don't think there's much point in wasting any more time on it."

"Pull him off it, then. That the lot?"

"Not quite."

There was a glint in Lineham's eye which Thanet had seen before. It looked as though the sergeant had saved the most interesting item till last. "What have you got up your sleeve, Mike? Ah, don't tell me. That sacked farmhand . . ."

"Right!" Lineham selected another report, opened it. But he didn't hand it over. Obviously he wanted to tell Thanet himself, watch his reaction.

Thanet decided to indulge him. "Well?"

Lineham leaned forward. "Talion's daugher Rose committed suicide when Martindale ditched her."

18

THANET remembered the satisfaction in Talion's eyes when Martindale's death was mentioned, the man's bitter hostility when questioned, the bleakness of the atmosphere in Home Farm, the frailty of Talion's wife, his protectiveness towards her. Had Rose been their only child, he wondered? And had her suicide cast over her home and family a blight from which they had never recovered?

"When was this?"

"Nineteen sixty-four. She was seventeen."

Bridget's age. How would he feel about a man who drove her to suicide? Thanet shivered.

"Explains why Talion was so hostile, doesn't it, sir? Especially when we told him it was the hotel van that ran Martindale down and he knew he'd used it himself that night. No wonder he didn't want to tell us what he had against him.

He must have known we'd consider it a strong motive."

"True. All the same, it doesn't necessarily mean he did it. He might quite simply not have wanted to have what must have been a very painful business resurrected." Thanet sighed. "I must say, Martindale didn't do things by halves, did he? He seems to have left a trail of shattered lives behind him. Sam Tiller, Mrs. Rankle, now Talion . . ."

"We'll have to go and see Talion again."

"Obviously." Thanet grimaced. "He'll probably set the dog on us. But I want to see the Hamiltons first."

"Shall I fix up appointments?"

"No. We'll take pot luck. It doesn't really matter which order we see them in. If we can't find one we'll try another."

It was a real pleasure to drive out to Sutton-in-the-Weald this morning. The countryside basked in the sunshine and it was possible to believe that spring really was just around the corner. Soon now the sheep grazing in the fields would be surrounded by lambs, the woods and hedges misted over with the tender green of young foliage. Thanet loved to watch the progress of the seasons and pitied city dwellers who depended on parks and gardens for visible evidence of nature's annual rhythms.

Longford Hall was at its best today, its rosy brick mellow in its serene setting of park and woodland. Far away over to the right tiny figures toiled on the Sisyphean task of clearing up the storm damage. Thanet wondered aloud if Hamilton were among them.

"Doesn't matter if he is. We can see Mrs. Hamilton first."

"If she's there."

She wasn't, but was due back shortly, apparently. Thanet had noticed Toby Fever's car outside and thought that while they were waiting they might take the opportunity to clear up one or two minor points with him and Tessa.

The receptionist frowned. "I'm not sure where they are. I think they said they were going up to see Nanny."

Nanny! Thanet's ears pricked up. He wondered if, by any stroke of luck, she had also been Delia and Leo's nanny. Sometimes, in families like this one, the nanny became so much part of the household that she stayed on when her charges were grown up and then looked after their children. Such elderly retainers were a dying breed, of course. Today's nannies rarely stayed more than a few years at most, then moved on to fresher and perhaps more lucrative pastures. But in a house like this . . . "Where would we find her?"

"I'm not sure that . . . Oh, I don't suppose she'd mind." The girl laughed. "In fact, come to think of it, she'd probably enjoy it! She's pretty lively still, it's only her arthritis that keeps her confined to her rooms. She's in the day nursery. I'll get someone to show you."

A trim housemaid led the way up seemingly endless flights of stairs and along interminable corridors to a bright, sunny room on the south-east side of the house. At this hour in February the sun was streaming in and Thanet blinked, momentarily dazzled. The room seemed full of people but when his vision cleared he saw that there were only four: Adam, Tessa, Toby and an elderly woman in an orthopaedic wing chair near the fire. The room was comfortably but plainly furnished with sturdy central table and chairs and a number of sagging armchairs with worn loose covers. Adam and Tessa were seated in two of them and Toby was sprawled on the hearthrug in front of the fire, which burned brightly in a black Victorian cast-iron grate surrounded by glazed green tiles with animal motifs. A tall brass fireguard stood in front of it, relic of the days when the room really was a nursery and now presumably retained as a safeguard against the nanny's disability.

They were all clearly enjoying this cosy relaxed domestic interlude. They had been sharing a joke and the faces they turned towards the two policemen were still smiling.

"Inspector!" Adam jumped up. "Allow me to introduce you to the love of my life, Nanny Foster. Nanny, this is Inspector Thanet, that I was telling you about, and his faithful sidekick, Sergeant Lineham!"

Gone were the dandy and the waif. Today Adam was very much the son of the house in cavalry twill trousers, tattersall shirt, old school tie and tweed sports jacket. Which persona would eventually emerge? Thanet wondered. Tessa, too,

303

looked different today. The stiff spikes of hair were now horizontal instead of vertical, sticking out above her ears on either side, as if a mysterious force had visited her in the night, altering their disposition. If anything her mini was even more minimal; the expanse of inner thigh seemed to go on for ever, leaving little to the imagination.

"That's enough, Adam," said the woman, smiling. "The Inspector will think I never taught you any manners."

She was alarmingly frail, her thin body bent and twisted by the disabling disease, her hands as gnarled and misshapen as old tree roots. But there was plenty of evidence that she was well looked after. She was neat and clean, her sparse white hair neatly combed back into a bun. Beside her chair was an adjustable spotlight on a stand and a three-tiered trolley laden with books, magazines, radio, photograph albums, and all the cluttered pill and potion paraphernalia of an invalid's day. Nearby stood a hospital-type table which would swivel across her knees. On it was a half-completed jigsaw.

304

They all settled down, Thanet and Lineham on upright chairs at the table.

"I hope you don't mind us intruding, Miss Foster, but there are one or two minor details we wanted to check," said Thanet. But his mind was only partly on what he was saying. When he'd come in just then and glimpsed Toby from that unfamiliar angle he had once again experienced that curious shock of recognition. He *had* seen the young man before, he was certain of it. But where? Toby was still on the floor but was now sitting up, elbows hooked over knees, leaning back against Tessa's armchair. Thanet glanced at him again and suddenly it came to him. Of course!

"Not at all. The children have told me about you and it's nice to meet you in the flesh, though I could wish it was for a happier reason." Her face was sombre.

"You've been here a long time?" The question was mechanical. Thanet was still preoccupied with his revelation. He realised that Lineham, always sensitive to the nuances of his behaviour, had noticed and given him a questioning glance.

"Forty-six years. I came when Leo was

four." Briefly her face contorted and her lower lip trembled.

With an effort Thanet focused his mind on the conversation. He would think about the implications of his discovery later. Registering her distress he guessed that she was remembering those early, presumably happy days and wondered if this was, after all, a good idea. It was in any case difficult to talk to her as he would wish, with the young people present.

"He had wings and a halo then, didn't he, Nanny?" This was Tessa.

Adam laughed. "Used to bore the pants off us with stories of Ma and Uncle Leo, didn't you, Nanny?"

"All very well for you to laugh, you two, but they were happy days. Right up until your grandmother died."

"Ta-ra-ra, ra-ra ra ra." Adam scraped away at an imaginary violin.

"Adam!" she said sharply and for once he actually looked a little shamefaced.

"You ought to be ashamed of yourself," she snapped. "It's all very well for you, brought up with the security of your mother and father behind you. Your Uncle Leo wasn't so lucky."

Tessa sighed. This was obviously an old theme, retold so often that for them it had lost its impact. "Nanny's trying to say that after Grandmother died Uncle Leo became a Deprived Child."

"He did!" said the old lady. She put her hands on the arms of the chair and shifted herself into an almost imperceptibly different position.

Thanet recognised the signs. She was settling herself into a narrative mood. He hoped none of the young people would sabotage it.

Tessa and Adam exchanged glances. *Shall we go?*

Thanet willed them to leave but to his disappointment they stayed, through sheer inertia he imagined. It was comfortable in here and any entertainment was better than none. Tessa presumably didn't have a job, but what about Toby?

As if he had tuned in to Thanet's question Toby uncurled himself and stood up. "I'd better be off. I'm supposed to be halfway to Maidstone by now and I'll have Dad on my tail. No," to Tessa, "don't bother to come down. I'll see you tonight. About half seven?"

She nodded. "Fine."

Thanet glanced at Lineham and gave an almost imperceptible nod at the door. *Go and ask him.*

Unobtrusively Lineham followed Toby out. Thanet saw that Tessa was frowning. The little exchange had not escaped her.

"Sorry, Miss Foster," he said. "You were saying, about Mr. Martindale. . . ?"

"He was unlucky, that's all. As so often happens, the father favoured the daughter and the mother the son. Leo was the apple of Mrs. Martindale's eye and I'm afraid she spoiled him rather. Over-indulged him. I don't blame her, mind, it was always very hard to say no to Leo. He was such a handsome lad, he could have charmed the birds out of the trees if he'd set his mind to it. But I'm afraid it set his father against him. It was the old story, really, I've seen it so often, the father jealous of the son . . . So when Mrs. Martindale died, when Leo was twelve, he had a rough time."

"In what way?"

"He was shoved off to boarding school for a start," said Adam. "Like poor little me."

308

"You hadn't just lost your mother," said Miss Foster reprovingly. "And you'd boarded at your prep school, too. Leo had been a day boy until then." She shook her head. "Of course, he hated it, just went haywire. Personally, I think his behaviour was so impossible because he was hoping they'd throw him out and he could live at home again. He loved it here. But his father wasn't having that. Every time Leo was expelled he was just sent off to another school."

Lineham came back in and sat down again.

"Every time?" said Thanet.

"Well, it sounds worse than it actually was. He was expelled from three. After that I think it dawned on him that there really wasn't much point, he might as well settle down. But he was never happy. Did as little work as possible and then went to Cirencester, where he started the Estate Management course. Threw it in at the end of the first year and came home, lazed around doing nothing very much. His mother had left him enough for him not to have to work."

"Sounds great!" said Adam. "Wish

somebody'd leave me enough to doss around and do nothing."

"You'd be bored out of your tiny mind by the end of the first week," said Tessa. "I know. I've tried it. I'm off to Art College in September," she said to Thanet, her eyes alight with the first sign of enthusiasm she had shown.

"Good!" he said. "Where?"

"St. Martin's School of Art." There was pride in her voice now.

Obviously he had done her an injustice and he was careful not to sound condescending as he said, "You must be good. It's very difficult to get in, I believe. Fashion?"

"Textile design."

"It's all very well for you," said Adam sulkily. "You've always known what you wanted to do. There's nothing that really grabs me like that."

"Give it time," said Miss Foster, smiling. "Just keep on doing as well as you are at school and who knows, you could end up Prime Minister!"

"Heaven forbid!" said Tessa. "The imagination boggles!"

"I don't suppose," said Thanet, anxious

to lead the conversation back to Martindale, "that Mr. Martindale senior was too pleased, when his son dropped out of college."

"He was furious. Barely spoke to him for weeks. There was always a clash of personalities between them but after that things were worse than ever. Mr. Martindale was a good employer and I don't really like saying this, but he seemed to have this blind spot as far as Leo was concerned; couldn't see anything good in him at all. And that just made Leo behave more badly." She shook her head sadly. "It was a vicious circle, really."

"And once he'd set his foot on the slippery slope . . ." said Adam. He made a sliding motion with his hand. "Oops, it was downhill all the way."

"I've never discovered why he finally went away for good," said Thanet. He'd be interested to hear Miss Foster's version of the rift between father and son.

Miss Foster pursed her lips and shook her head.

"Simple," drawled Tessa. "Oh do stop looking so disapproving, Nanny. If we don't tell the Inspector someone else will.

Can't you see, he's not the type to give up? It happened really because he ran out of money. Grandmother Martindale had apparently been rather unwise and instead of setting up a trust fund from which he had the income until he reached the age of wisdom—though from what we know of Uncle Leo I don't suppose he ever would have—she left him a capital sum outright. He had a whale of a time: wine, women, song, fast cars, expensive clothes, the lot. Grandfather kept on baling him out of debt but when he started betting on the gee-gees it was the last straw. I believe he gave him one more chance and when he finally blew it, to the tune of several thousand pounds—and that was an awful lot of money in those days—that was it. Grandfather did the 'Never darken my doors again' act, and Uncle Leo never did." She shrugged. "We always felt deprived about that, didn't we, Adam, thought our lives had lacked a certain spice."

Adam nodded. "That was why I was so disappointed not to have seen him when he came back. Ah well, that's life, I suppose. Incidentally, Tess, you forgot to put the finishing touch to the scenario. When he went, he took half the family silver with him."

"All right, that's enough!" said Miss Foster. "I let you run on, Tessa, because I could see you were right and Inspector Thanet would have gone on asking until someone had given him the information. But I won't sit here and listen to you running poor Leo down any longer. I know he was bad in many ways but it wasn't his fault. Children aren't born spoiled, you know, it's adults that make them so. And in your uncle's case . . . to be so over-indulged and then suddenly to find himself out in the cold for good . . . I'm not a bit surprised he went off the rails, even if I couldn't approve of some of the things he did. No, I felt sorry for him, still do. He missed so much in life, through no fault of his own. And if you're not careful, Adam, you'll go the same way, with all this smart-Alec nonsense."

Adam jumped up and went to lay his cheek against her hair. "Not true, Nanny! You know that at heart I'm pure gold, right through."

"That's a matter of opinion." But the

smile she gave him showed that she agreed, really.

Thanet decided to change the subject. "Tell me, Tessa, when you drove home that night, did you happen to notice anything out of the ordinary on the way?"

"Such as a body lying at the side of the road, you mean! Honestly, Inspector, you can't really believe I wouldn't have got Dad to stop if I had!" Tessa was scornful and Thanet felt that her opinion of him had just taken a nose-dive. He didn't care, it had just been a way of leading into his next question.

"Of course, your father was with you . . . The Range Rover had broken down, I believe."

"Yes. Infuriating. It was nothing serious, only a loose sparking plug apparently, but I'm not mechanically-minded, I'm afraid. So I rang Dad and asked him to come and fetch me. I knew he'd still be up, he never goes to bed very early. Anyway, he managed to fix it."

Thanet was certain that she was telling the truth. He had never really believed that Hamilton would stoop so low as to get his daugher to lie for him in case someone

314

had seen him driving the van that night. And Mrs. Byfleet had heard both cars return.

"What time did you get back?"

She shrugged. "Soon after twelve, I think. I rather lost track of time, hanging around waiting for Dad."

"Was it snowing when you got home?"

"Yes. It had just started."

On the way back downstairs Lineham said, "We still can't rule Mr. Hamilton out, though, can we? He'd have had plenty of opportunity earlier on."

Thanet sighed. "What did Toby say?"

Lineham waited while a chambermaid went by. "He confirms what Mrs. Rankle told us. He did borrow his mother's car that night, to go to Canterbury on business for his father to discuss a haulage job with a chap who was unavailable during the day. His father was supposed to go, apparently, but then they had that phone call to say Mrs. Fever's mother had been taken ill and he asked Toby to go instead. Toby couldn't use his own car because he was working on it and it was jacked up."

"Cars, cars . . . They seem to crop up

everywhere in this case. Should be just up your street, Mike."

They had reached the head of the staircase and Thanet paused, glancing around to make sure no one was in earshot. Downstairs in the hall the receptionist was at her desk and a group of guests was seated around the fire, a tray of coffee on the table between them.

Thanet lowered his voice. "By the way, I wanted to ask you . . . Did I mention to you that I thought Toby looked familiar, that I had a feeling I might have come across him before somewhere?"

"No, why? Have you?"

"No. But just think, Mike. Doesn't he remind you of someone else in this case? Not all the time, but just in fleeting moments?"

Lineham frowned. "I don't think so. Who?"

"It didn't dawn on me till just now. And then . . . Well, first of all, when we went in, he was lying down, and then he sat up. Both positions were the same, you see, that was what made me realise . . ."

Lineham was still puzzled. "Sorry, I just don't see what you're getting at."

"The first time we saw Martindale, lying in the snow . . . And then that photograph we saw in his room, the one of him and his sister, sitting on the steps . . ."

Lineham's eyes widened. "You mean. . . ?"

Thanet nodded. "I think Toby might be his son."

19

LINEHAM was still looking stunned. "But . . ."

Thanet knew how he felt. The implications were so complicated and far-reaching that it was difficult to take them all in at once. "I'd like to discuss this with you before seeing Mrs. Hamilton. Also, there's a check I'd like to run . . . Let's go outside."

Delia Hamilton was back, apparently. Thanet asked the receptionist to tell her that he had an urgent call to make before seeing her, then he and Lineham went out to the car. There he put in a request for two pieces of information—Toby's date of birth, and the date of his parents' marriage. "As fast as you can, please."

"Will do."

Lineham waited until he had finished before saying, "If you're right, sir, do you think any of them realises?"

"Ah, now that's the million-dollar question. I haven't had time to think about it properly yet, but I doubt that the Hamiltons know. Otherwise they wouldn't be too keen on Tessa going out with him."

"You mean, because they're first cousins . . . Sir!" Lineham's eyes widened in shock.

"What?"

"Do you realise what this could mean? No, perhaps it wouldn't. I don't know . . ."

"You're being incoherent, Mike. Start again."

"Can illegitimate children inherit?" said Lineham.

Thanet could see why the sergeant had looked so thunderstruck. This had not yet occurred to him. If Martindale had been the owner of Longford Hall, and Toby was his son . . .

"I believe they can. Wasn't there an Act, to make it legal?"

"I remember something about it . . . In that case, perhaps the Hamiltons do know," said Lineham. "I should think they're pretty snobbish and I always did wonder if they approved of Tessa going out with Toby. But now . . . Perhaps they actually encouraged it, knowing that it was just possible that one day Toby could be heir to the whole estate."

"Let's not speculate on that one until we're sure of our ground. We might well find that the fact that his mother and Martindale never married would rule him out."

"All the same, I find it difficult to believe that Mrs. Hamilton wouldn't have spotted the resemblance between Toby and her brother before now, if you cottoned on to it as quickly as you did."

"I don't know. For one thing you and I are trained to look for connections, to be actively on the alert for them. And the fact that we are strangers means that we look at everyone with a fresh eye. The Hamiltons will have watched Toby grow up as just another village boy, remember, and probably always accepted him on face value as the Fevers' son. It isn't as if the resemblance is striking—and let's face it, I could be wrong."

But he wasn't—or at least, it didn't look as though he was. A few minutes later the information came through: Toby's date of birth was 9.1.66, that of his parents' marriage 4.8.65.

After their initial elation that it seemed Thanet's hunch was correct, Lineham sobered. "Doesn't necessarily mean he's Martindale's son, of course. He could still be Fever's—or anybody else's, for that matter . . ."

Thanet shook his head. Logically Lineham could be right, but Thanet knew in his bones that he wasn't.

Lineham grinned. "OK, I give in. I've never known you wrong about something like this. So let's see . . . Martindale left in 1965. Right? And if Toby was born in January 1966 he would have been conceived in April 1965. I wonder in which month Martindale left."

"We'll ask his sister."

"In the summer, probably, if the Fevers were married in August. The sequence of events probably went: in April Yvonne becomes pregnant and in June she tells Martindale. That same month Martindale is thrown out of the ancestral home because of his debts—perhaps he was only too glad to get away, in the circumstances! —but Yvonne thinks he's gone away because of the baby, so she marries Fever who is waiting in the wings."

"She might not have discovered she was pregnant until after Martindale had gone," said Thanet. "In which case he might never have known about the baby."

"The question is, did he?"

"And if so, when did he find out? Before he left, while he was away, or after he came back?"

"It's all so complicated," said Lineham with relish.

"I know. It's just occurred to me . . . perhaps you're right, and he did know about the baby before he left. Let's just accept, for the moment, that he did. You remember what the receptionist told us, about Martindale asking who Toby was, when Toby was talking to Mrs. Byfleet? Perhaps there was something about the boy that reminded him of himself as a young man, and made him wonder . . ."

"I don't know." Lineham was doubtful. "Isn't it usually considered rather difficult to recognise a resemblance to yourself?"

"Possibly. But if Martindale knew he had a child, and was on the lookout for him . . ."

"Or her . . ."

"All right Mike, or her, but anyway, on

the lookout; then when he saw this young man of the right age, he could have thought, I wonder . . ."

"It's possible. And then, of course, when the receptionist told him who Toby was, he'd have known this was his son—no, hang on, sir, he wouldn't, would he? Not unless he knew Yvonne had married Fever. And even then he couldn't have been sure—for all he knew, the Fevers could have had several children."

"I think, for the purpose of this argument, we will assume that he did know she'd married Fever and that they'd had no other children. After all, Mike, if he knew she was expecting his baby, he might well have made it his business to keep an eye on her from afar, so to speak, find out what happened to her and the child. If he didn't know, this whole scenario collapses anyway. Still, we might as well follow it through for the moment. So, you were saying . . ."

"Well if he did find out who Toby was, by asking the receptionist, I was just thinking it might have whetted his appetite to get to know him. So I was wondering if, when he ran into Mrs. Fever in the village next day, he could have told her he'd seen Toby and wanted to meet him, make himself known to him, as his real father. Mrs. Victor said it looked as though he was trying to persuade Mrs. Fever to do something she didn't want to do."

"The mechanic said that was because she was refusing to go and have tea with Martindale, Mike."

"But the mechanic wasn't present during the whole conversation, was he? He had to go into the office to get change. After all, it's not the sort of thing Martindale would have been likely to discuss with anyone within earshot, is it? He might just have pretended to have been asking her to go and have tea with him, to fool the mechanic when he came back."

"Mm. Could be, I suppose. All right, let's accept that Martindale was saying that he intended to tell Toby he was his father . . . Let's think. According to the mechanic, it was after he teased Fever about Martindale's encounter with Mrs. Fever that Fever went rushing off—as we know, up to the Hall, to tell Martindale to keep away from her in future. Say Fever then went home and had a row with his wife about it . . ."

"Fever must have known Toby wasn't his son, if his wife was four months pregnant when he married her, mustn't he, sir? If he's as jealous as people say, I expect he would have gone on and on at her until she told him who the real father was, and she may well have thought it was safe to tell him as Martindale had gone away, apparently for good. And if Fever did know Martindale was Toby's father, it would explain why he reacted so strongly when he heard Martindale was back and had been chatting Mrs. Fever up. And then, when Fever went home afterwards and started going on at his wife about her talking to Martindale, in order to distract him she could have told him that Martindale had suggested making himself known to Toby . . ."

"Yes. I always think it must be pretty devastating when someone turns up on the doorstep claiming to be a long-lost son or daughter, father or mother. It must put all the family relationships in a turmoil, especially if the one who is being claimed had been kept in ignorance."

"Of course, in all this we're assuming Toby has no idea who his real father was."

Thanet frowned, thinking. "I don't think he does. After all, if he had known Martindale was his father you'd have expected him to try to make contact with him when he came home, or at least to be affected to some extent by his death, but he seems completely unconcerned by it all. Anyway, assuming Martindale did suggest telling him the truth and Mrs. Fever then told her husband, Fever could have been fuming about it all evening. And then, on his way back from Ashford in the van, if he saw Martindale ahead of him on the road . . ."

They looked at each other in silence.

"It's convincing," said Thanet at last. "But let's remember that at the moment it is still pure speculation and far from the only possibility. But it will be interesting to see what Mrs. Hamilton has to say about it."

They were shown into her office again. Her desk was littered with papers and she wasn't too pleased at the prospect of having to spend more time answering questions. "I hope this isn't going to take long, Inspector. I really have a great deal to do today."

It looked as though she had just been to the hairdresser's. Her hair was loose for once, framing her face and falling to her shoulders in carefully casual waves. It made her look younger and more vulnerable. She was wearing a finely pleated skirt in red wool and a long matching cashmere cardigan over a silky cream blouse with a finely scribbled abstract pattern in red and black.

"No longer than I can help," said Thanet politely. "May we sit down?"

She gestured impatiently. *If you must.*

No point in beating about the bush. "It must have been a shock to you, to learn that your brother intended staying on and taking over his inheritance."

A flash of anger, quickly suppressed. "You've been listening to gossip again, Inspector. Do you enjoy scrabbling around in the refuse of people's lives?"

This accusation had been levelled at Thanet too often for him to be moved by it. "Not at all, Mrs. Hamilton. I'm only too well aware of the fact that after a sudden death, and especially a violent death, people close to the victim are often in a state of shock. To be honest, there are times when I find my work very distasteful."

Recognising his sincerity Delia Hamilton had the grace to look discomforted, but she quickly recovered. "It wasn't that much of a shock, to learn he intended staying on. My husband and I always knew that it could happen. We would have worked something out."

"My information is that Mr. Martindale suggested that you should continue to run the hotel and your husband the estate as his employees, and that you quarrelled about it."

Again that flash of anger before she said coolly, "Then your information is wrong, Inspector, or at least misleading."

"You deny that there was an argument?"

"No. There was an argument, yes, I admit it. But arguments need not end in disharmony. On this occasion I think we managed to get my brother to see that in view of all the hard work Giles and I have put in, it would be a little unfair for us not to benefit by it, at least to some extent."

"You're saying that you reached an agreement?"

"Let's say we were well on the way to it."

"Despite the limitations imposed by the Trust?"

"Despite the limitations imposed by the Trust," she echoed firmly.

No doubt Hamilton would back her up, but Thanet was certain that she was lying.

"Would you mind telling us the terms of that agreement?" He didn't think for a moment that she would, but there was no harm in asking.

"That's out of the question! It was an entirely private matter, and I . . ."

The phone rang and, with a muttered "Excuse me", she picked it up and held a brief conversation about proposed repairs to the roof. After a moment she began shifting papers about on her desk and peering underneath. Then suddenly she tutted as if she had just remembered something, and stopped looking. A minute or two later she put down the receiver and said, "While I think about it, Inspector, I've been meaning to ring up and ask . . . Did your men find a pocket calculator in the van? It's about so big," and she made a window about three inches by two and a half with her fingers. "My name and address are tucked into the inside flap."

"I don't think so, no." Thanet raised his eyebrows at Lineham, who shook his head. "We'll ask, if you like, when we get back."

"I'd be grateful. I really must buy another, it's just a question of remembering, when I'm in town . . ."

"You think you dropped it in the van when you went to fetch Adam?"

She shrugged. "Well, it's several days now and it hasn't turned up anywhere else. I'm lost without it, it's just the right size to carry in my pocket. I've thought and thought and I know I had it just before dinner on Tuesday and that it was missing later on that evening."

"Before your early dinner, you mean?"

"Yes. Anyway, if you'd just check . . ."

"Of course." Thanet caught Lineham's eye. They had already arranged that the sergeant should question her about the two periods when the van had stood idle in the yard.

"You may be interested to know, Mrs.

Hamilton, that it has now been confirmed that it was your van that ran your brother down. We don't yet know whether this was deliberate or an accident, but in any case, as we explained before, it does seem from the position of the body in the ditch that whoever was driving must have moved it afterwards and can't claim ignorance of the accident. So we are questioning again everyone who had access to the van."

He paused.

Delia Hamilton's lips had tightened, but she said nothing.

"We have therefore been trying to draw up a timetable of the van's movements on Tuesday evening. And there are two gaps unaccounted for, when the van was standing outside in the stable yard, unattended. So naturally we are now concentrating on those gaps." He made a pretence of consulting his notebook. "The first is between 8.10 and 8.30 that evening, the second between 10.30 and 11.15. Now, when we first talked to you, you told us that you got back from meeting Adam's train at twenty to eight, but unfortunately Adam and Tessa interrupted us before you could tell us what you did after that. We know, from what you told us subsequently, that you joined your guests for drinks, so if you could give us a summary of your movements from, say, eight o'clock onwards . . .”

"I see. So this is the inquisition, is it?"

"I wouldn't put it quite like that, ma'am."

She stood up abruptly, folding her arms as if to protect herself. "This is preposterous. I refuse to answer any more questions without my solicitor present."

"It's up to you, Mrs. Hamilton. You have every right to do that, if you wish, but . . ." Lineham glanced at Thanet.

Thanet intervened. He knew that the sergeant was asking his senior officer to use his authority to back him up on this.

"Mrs. Hamilton, Sergeant Lineham is simply trying to say that although the choice is yours, there really is no need for you to take this attitude. These are routine questions, which we are asking of everyone who had keys to the van."

"I'm not stupid, Inspector! I appreciate that, but at the same time it does seem to me sensible to protect my own interests."

"Not if you have nothing to hide," said Thanet.

There was a brief silence.

"Very clever, Inspector. By implication, if I still refuse, then I do have something to hide." She sat down in her chair again, an angry, petulant movement, and tapped the polished wood of the desk with one crescent-shaped fingernail. The tiny, repetitive clicking was like the ticking of an alarm clock—or perhaps a bomb, thought Thanet. He watched her with interest. Would she explode?

Suddenly she folded her arms with that same defensive, self-protective movement he had noticed before. "Oh very well. It irritates me to play your game, but when all's said and done, you're right. If I have nothing to hide there's nothing to be afraid of. And as I don't have anything to hide . . . From eight o'clock onwards, you say? Let me see. I know it's only a few days ago, but in a place like this our routine is such that one evening tends to merge into another . . ."

But it didn't take her long to work it out. After the guests went into dinner she had gone along to the kitchen to check that everything was running smoothly. At around five past eight she had gone up to have a brief word with Adam and make sure he had everything he needed before she retired to her room for half an hour. This was her usual practice, apparently, one of the rare periods of the day when she had time to herself, to relax.

"That would have been from, say, ten past eight until around twenty to nine?"

She pulled a face, aware that this covered the first period in question. "Yes."

After that she had gone down to the dining-room to check that all was running smoothly, then watched television with Adam and her husband until ten o'clock. After another trip downstairs she had retired to her room to take a leisurely bath before an early night. She had, she claimed, been in bed by around ten to eleven. She gave a wry little laugh and said, "Hence my irritation just now, Inspector. I suspected that I might be unlucky and have no one to confirm my movements during the two periods in question."

Thanet made no comment. Delia

Hamilton qualified as a suspect in any case, having driven the van during the crucial period. Finding out what she had been doing during those two blank periods was at this stage not as important as it could have been. On the other hand it could prove vital later, if for example a witness was found who claimed to have seen Martindale leaving the house during one of them. "What about your husband?"

She shrugged. "I've no idea. This is a big house, we don't exactly live in each other's pockets. He has a bed in his dressing room and if he's late coming to bed for any reason he sleeps there, so as not to disturb me. He did that night, after going to fetch Tessa."

"So you don't know what he was doing, during either the earlier or the later period in question?"

She shook her head. "You'll have to ask him." She reached for a sheaf of papers, pulled them towards her. "And now, if you don't mind . . ."

"I'm sorry," said Thanet, "we're not quite finished yet."

She gave an exasperated sigh. "For

heaven's sake . . . I'm never going to catch up on my work at this rate."

"One or two more questions about Mr. Martindale. He left the area in 1965, didn't he? Could you tell me exactly when? Which month, I mean."

She frowned. "What on earth d'you want to know that for?"

"Please . . ."

"It was the end of June."

"Can you remember who his girlfriend was, at the time?"

The frown was deeper now.

"The last time we talked to you we asked if Yvonne Fever had been your brother's girlfriend, before he went away . . . We have reason to believe that you were less than frank with us."

"Really, Inspector, what can it possibly matter? We are talking about twenty-four years ago . . ."

"Let me put it this way. Mr. Martindale left in June 1965. The Fevers were married in August. Toby Fever was born in January 1966."

He let her work it out for herself. Delia Hamilton was no fool and he was rewarded by seeing the colour seep out of her face, leaving it chalk white. He saw her throat move as she swallowed.

"You're not suggesting . . ." It was scarcely more than a whisper.

Thanet said nothing. He had his answer. He stood up.

She put out a hand. "No, wait . . . You've . . . Have you . . . Does anyone else know about this?"

"That," said Thanet, "is what we would like to know."

He and Lineham turned to leave but she rose, pulled by invisible strings. "Will you tell them?"

"That depends, I'm afraid."

"On what?"

"On whether it becomes necessary."

She sank back into her seat and he left her sitting at her desk, motionless as a statue.

20

BY comparison with the last time they'd been in, the Drovers seemed positively crowded. There were eight other customers, five of them a group of young men in near-uniform of formal suit, white shirt and sober tie. Salesmen attending a conference nearby?

Sam Tiller was also there, enjoying a lunchtime pint with a couple of cronies. He gave the two policemen a hostile glance before firmly turning his back on them.

Thanet and Lineham waited until they had collected their beer and sandwiches before continuing their discussion. Delia Hamilton's reaction had convinced Thanet that the idea of Toby being Leo's son was entirely new to her, but Lineham was sticking to his guns.

"I think she'll tell whatever lies are necessary to get her off the hook."

"Telling lies is one thing. Changing colour like that is another. I'd say it was virtually impossible to do it at will."

"I don't know. Actors and actresses cry real tears."

"Maybe. But they have years of practice, of thinking themselves into other people's skins, other people's moods. I imagine even the most experienced actor would need at least a few seconds to produce real tears, longer, probably. And she reacted just like that." Thanet snapped his fingers in the air. "One second she was her normal colour, the next she was white as a sheet."

"I suppose so." Lineham was still grudging, reluctant to relinquish his conception of Delia as a devious, scheming woman.

Thanet was shaking his head. "Come on, Mike, you can't tell me she could have faked that."

Lineham took a huge mouthful of sandwich and began to chew thoughtfully. A moment later he made an inarticulate sound.

"What?" said Thanet.

The sergeant's eyes were bulging with frustration as he tried to reduce the quantity of food in his mouth to manageable proportions.

"Serves you right," said Thanet with a grin. "I bet you tell the children never to bite off more than they can comfortably chew."

Lineham swallowed, chewed, swallowed again. "It's just that it occurred to me . . . The fact that Mrs. Hamilton doesn't know Toby is her nephew doesn't mean that Mr. Hamilton doesn't."

Presumably the three negatives made a positive. "You mean, perhaps he does know?"

"Yes. Leo Martindale could have told him."

"And Hamilton didn't tell his wife? I doubt it, Mike. They seem pretty much in cahoots, those two." Thanet took a thoughtful swig of beer. "Besides, come to think of it, I'm not sure why it's especially important anyway for us to decide whether they knew or not. It's interesting, I grant you, but is it relevant to the case? If we're right about this and Toby really is Martindale's son, it could certainly matter whether Martindale himself knew, and also whether Fever knew. But the Hamiltons? I'm not so sure." He paused. "In fact, it could even be a point in their favour. Surely, if there was even the slightest chance of Toby inheriting the Hall the last thing they'd want to do is to get rid of Leo. At least with him in charge they'd be able to stay on, carry on their lives much as before, but with Toby installed there they would presumably have had to get out . . . We really must check whether or not he could inherit."

"So are we going to see Mr. Hamilton now?"

Thanet chewed the last mouthful of his sandwich—ham and pickle, this time— while he considered. "No. I don't think we're going to get anything new out of him at the moment, I think he'll stick to whatever story he and his wife have prepared. If you're feeling brave enough to face the dog, I think we'll go and see Jack Talion next."

"Are you, sir? Feeling brave enough, I mean?"

Thanet laughed. "I'm counting on you to protect me, Mike. What else are sergeants for?"

Privately, Thanet wasn't looking forward to this interview. If Talion's daughter really had committed suicide because of Leo Martindale, it wasn't surprising that Talion had been dead against the idea of Martindale settling down in Sutton again. But that didn't necessarily mean he had killed him and, if not, Thanet hated the idea of reopening old wounds best left undisturbed. On the other hand, if Talion were guilty. . . Thanet sighed. He had meant it when he told Delia Hamilton that he sometimes found his job distasteful.

It took them some time to track Talion down. The farmyard at Home Farm was deserted and when they went up to the house there was no answer to their knock. Thanet shivered while they waited. During the morning the sky had clouded over again, the sunshine become fitful and now, suddenly, a chill wind began to blow.

Thanet turned up his collar. "We'll have to come back later, Mike. Let's see if we can find Fever instead."

They were heading back to the village when Lineham spotted a tractor coming towards them. "Wonder if this chap works for Talion. If so, he might know where he is." He flashed his lights, sounded his horn and pulled up. The tractor stopped and Lineham got out of the car.

"Have you any idea where we can find Mr. Talion?"

Talion, it seemed, was repairing fences and after following the tractor driver's directions they donned their boots and had to plod across two huge fields of winter wheat. It was hard going. The soil, sodden and sticky in the aftermath of the snow, adhered to their boots in heavy lumps and after a few hundred yards it began to feel as though their feet were weighted down with blocks of concrete.

"Should be at the far side of the next field," panted Lineham.

"Mm."

The interlude had given Thanet time to think and he was beginning to wonder if this was a good idea. It was all very well to joke about the dog, but it was distinctly inhibiting to have to watch every word he said in case he provoked a hostile reaction from its master.

"There they are."

They had reached another five-barred gate set into a thick hedge backed by post and wire-mesh fencing. On the far side of the next field were a tractor and trailer and a group of three men working on the boundary fence nearby.

The words were no sooner out of Lineham's mouth when a furious barking confirmed his guess and Talion's Alsatian jumped out of the trailer and began to streak towards them. The two policemen faltered. Would Talion call the dog back?

Talion allowed the dog to get halfway across the field before shouting a command. "Rhett! Stay!"

To Thanet's relief the dog skidded to a halt.

"Rhett! Here!"

Reluctantly, it seemed, the animal turned back and trotted towards its master. Thanet and Lineham exchanged relieved glances before continuing on their way. After a word to the other two men Talion advanced to meet them with the measured stride of a countryman, the dog beside him.

"Sorry to interrupt your work, Mr. Talion," said Thanet when they were within speaking distance.

"Sit!" said Talion as they came up to

him, and the Alsatian obeyed, ears pricked.

Thanet gave the animal a wary glance. This was definitely a bad idea. It was virtually impossible to concentrate out here in the open with the rising wind whistling about his ears and the dog alert to every move. It would have been more sensible to ask Talion to come into headquarters to make a statement. Here, on his own ground, legs planted firmly apart, Talion looked as sturdy and unlikely to bend as one of his own oak trees.

"Well?" said Talion, shoving his hands deep into the pockets of his windproof jacket. His eyes were wary, hostile.

"There are one or two more questions . . ."

Talion said nothing, merely raised his eyebrows a fraction.

"We're still checking on the movements of everyone who has a key to the van."

Still no reaction.

"Could you give us an account of your movements after you returned to the Hall that night."

"Why?"

"A man is dead, Mr. Talion. It has been

confirmed that he was knocked down by the van. We now also know, from the post-mortem, that it was not the impact which actually killed Mr. Martindale. After the incident his body was moved into the ditch where he was found, and where he later died from exposure. This is therefore now definitely a murder investigation, and the movements of every person with access to the van naturally have to come under close scrutiny. So if you would just give us the information we need . . ."

Talion shrugged. "I don't see that it'll help you much, but for what it's worth I went straight home, and spent the rest of the evening there."

"You walked?"

"Yes."

"Which way?"

"Along the footpath which links Home Farm with the Hall."

"Is there anyone who can confirm that you were at home all evening—apart from your wife, that is?"

Talion's expression hardened. "No. And I don't want you bothering my wife, either. I told you, she's not well. You'll just have to take my word for it."

346

"It would only be to . . ."

"No!"

The dog's hackles were up and it again gave that alarming deep-throated growl. Thanet could see the muscles in its front legs bunch as it tensed, ready to spring on command. Time for a strategic withdrawal, he decided. The death of Talion's daughter would, understandably, be a very touchy subject indeed, and even to mention that they now knew Talion had good reason for hating Martindale and therefore a possible motive for leaving him to die would provoke the man even further. Thanet had no intention of putting either Lineham or himself at risk. From now on, if they wanted to talk to Talion it would be on Thanet's terms.

He shrugged. "We'll have to leave it there for the moment, then."

Moving with unprovocative care he and Lineham turned away. They had gone only a few paces when Talion shouted after them. "Remember what I said. Just keep away from her!"

Thanet raised a hand in acknowledgement but did not look back until he and Lineham were safely in the next field.

Talion and the dog had almost reached the tractor and as they watched the animal leaped up to its former position. Thanet could see the silhouette of its head and shoulders above the boarded side of the trailer. It seemed to be watching them.

Lineham grinned with relief. "I was beginning to work out when I'd had my last tetanus jab."

"Yes. Not very clever of me, was it, to interview him on his own ground again. Talk about inhibiting! If there has to be a next time, it'll be safely back at headquarters, minus that dog."

They began to plod back across the fields, collecting more mud on their boots on the way.

"D'you think there will have to be a next time, sir?"

Thanet shrugged. "Difficult to tell. We haven't exactly made much progress with him, have we? But he's got as good a motive as anyone."

"Will we talk to his wife?"

"Not at this stage. No point in provoking him unnecessarily."

"Beats me why people keep animals like that," said Lineham as they struggled on.

"I wouldn't trust that dog within a mile of my kids."

"Ditto."

"Let's hope Mr. Fever is feeling a bit more cooperative."

"It would make a change!"

Back at the car they changed into their shoes, banging their boots on a fence post to remove the worst of the mud then wiping them roughly on the grass.

"Give me a nice warm office every time," said Lineham as he slammed the car boot.

It was a relief to get into the car, out of the wind.

Thanet glanced at his watch. Half-past one. Unless Fever's lunch hour was from one to two, he should be back at work by now. Anyway, if not, the house was only a stone's throw away. "We'll try the yard first."

Most of the farm buildings from which Fever ran his haulage business looked on the verge of collapse. The old Kent peg tiles had been stripped off and replaced with corrugated iron—a common sight since the hurricane, when the value of the old tiles had tripled overnight—and there were ragged gaps in the traditional weatherboarding. Lineham swung in between the open double metal gates which fronted the yard and parked alongside a small brick twin-kilned oast house marked OFFICE, the only building in reasonably good repair. As they got out of the car they became aware of raised voices within. The door was slightly ajar and as they drew closer Thanet put a warning finger to his lips.

"Honest, Mr. Fever, I swear I never—"

"Don't give me that guff! Think I was born yesterday? I been over and over those records and there's no way I can come up with any other answer. If you think I'm going to sweat my guts out supplying easy money for toe-rags like you, you've got another think coming!"

"But—"

"But nothing! I've said all I'm going to say. That's it. Finish. There's your card, there's your money up to date. Now get out!"

Silence, then the sound of a door closing and footsteps approaching. A typewriter started clattering. Fever's secretary starting work after listening to the row?

Thanet and Lineham stepped back as a man emerged. He was grossly overweight, his belly hanging over the waistband of his low-slung trousers, his round moon-face wearing a hangdog expression. After a flicker of surprise at the sight of the two policemen he slunk past them and walked away through the gates, hands in pockets, shoulders slumped.

Thanet knocked at the door and they went in.

They were in a short, uncarpeted corridor floored with scuffed, grubby vinyl tiles. To their left was a closed door, to their right a notice saying ENQUIRIES stuck on to a glass partition through which they could see a girl typing on an anti-quated machine. It was increasingly obvious that however freely Fever lavished money upon his private life, he didn't believe in spending it on his working environment. Presumably most of his business was conducted by telephone and as there was no one to impress he didn't think it worth the expenditure.

Lineham tapped on the glass and the girl looked up, then came to slide a section of the partition open.

351

"Yes?"

She was young and plain, shoddily dressed in a short, tight black skirt and striped acrylic jumper.

"We'd like a word with Mr. Fever."

Her eyes darted anxiously to the door across the corridor. "I'll see if he's free. Who shall I say?"

"Detective Inspector Thanet and Detective Sergeant Lineham, Sturrenden CID."

She looked alarmed. "Yes," she said. "Right. I'll . . . er . . . I'll just go and see."

She came out into the corridor and crossed to knock at the door on their left.

"Come in."

With a nervous glance over her shoulder at the two policemen she opened the door just wide enough to sidle in, closing it behind her. After a brief murmur of voices she came out again, holding it wide open this time. "Mr. Fever can see you now."

Fever was seated at a paper-strewn desk. He cast up his eyes. "This is all I need."

"Trouble?" said Thanet benignly. "I'm afraid we couldn't help overhearing. The door was open."

"Nothing I can't handle." He waved a

hand at a spindly metal stacking chair with a plastic seat. "I'm afraid there's only one chair."

Personal appearance mattered to him. His clothes, by contrast with the tattiness of his surroundings, were again sleek and expensive: creamy silk polo shirt and soft beige suede jacket. His rather sparse brown hair was well-cut, if rather long for Thanet's taste, and a faint aroma of after-shave hung in the air.

"Not to worry."

Thanet sat down and Lineham moved across to lean against the windowsill, taking out his notebook.

"Right, Mr. Fever, now perhaps we can start again."

Fever's eyes narrowed with suspicion. "What d'you mean?"

"Some rather interesting information has come to light since we saw you last."

"Oh?" said Fever, warily.

"Yes. First, it has been confirmed that Mr. Martindale was knocked down by the Ford van from Longford Hall Hotel."

"So?"

"The one used principally by Sam Tiller."

Something flickered in Fever's eyes. Dismay? Guilt? Fear? Impossible to tell. His facial expression did not alter. He had himself well under control. He raised his eyebrows in polite enquiry. *What has this got to do with me?*

"Secondly, we have also learned, from the post-mortem, that Mr. Martindale did not die as a result of the collision. After the 'accident' "—Thanet's voice implied inverted commas around the word—"his body was placed in the ditch where it was found next morning. He died from exposure, Mr. Fever."

"Too bad. But . . ."

The man's indifference infuriated Thanet and, longing to puncture it, he cut in. "We understand that at some point he must have recovered consciousness and tried to get out. Unfortunately his spine was broken and he couldn't." Fever, he was glad to see, was looking shaken. "A very unpleasant death, as I'm sure you'll agree."

"Poor bastard . . . But I still don't see what all this has to do with me."

"Well, as I was explaining, you must see that this is therefore now a murder investigation." Thanet paused, sat back and folded his arms. "We were interested to learn that you drove the van that night, Mr. Fever."

The implication was too obvious to ignore. Fever sat up with a jerk, looking suitably outraged. "Now look here . . ."

"No, you look here, Mr. Fever. You admit, do you, that you drove the van that evening?"

"Well yes. But I had a perfectly good reason . . ."

"So I believe. But that is beside the point. The point is that you did drive it. I think you'll have to admit, it doesn't look good for you. First of all you have a blazing row with Mr. Martindale, telling him to keep away from your wife . . ."

"Why shouldn't I?"

"Then," Thanet raised his voice, cutting Fever off, "only a few hours later, Martindale is knocked down by a van which you admit to driving that same evening."

Fever's face had become suffused with colour and his eyes bulged slightly as he said through his teeth, "I refuse to put up with this." His hand went out to the telephone. "I'm going to call my solicitor."

Thanet sat back, folding his arms. "Do, by all means. But it might be a good idea to hear the rest of what I have to say, first."

Fever's hand hovered above the instrument then fell back. "Spit it out, then, why don't you?"

"It's obvious, surely. Means, motive, opportunity." Thanet ticked them off on his fingers. "I think you'll agree, you had them all."

"Agree! Like hell I will." He gave a cynical bark of laughter. "Motive, indeed. What motive? Just because I told him to keep away from my wife?"

"Partly, perhaps. But I think we both know it goes a lot deeper than that."

Fever was suddenly motionless, his eyes gleaming. "What the hell," he said softly, "do you mean by that?"

"You had good reason to be jealous of Martindale, didn't you, Mr. Fever?"

"What's that supposed to mean?"

"Oh come on, let's not play games. We both know what I'm talking about."

"Do we?"

About to deliver a mortal blow to Fever's pride, Thanet steeled himself. Aggression did not come easily to him and it was only the knowledge that with this particular man he couldn't afford to let up for a moment that enabled him to sustain the attack. And if Fever were guilty, if he had indeed dragged an injured man into a ditch and left him to die, then he deserved all he was getting. But if not, if he were innocent . . . Thanet was well aware that Fever's hostility might well be a defence mechanism to cover up his vulnerability, that the man could have been more sinned against than sinning.

"I must admit that I was a little surprised that a few minutes' conversation in public between your wife and Martindale was enough to send you rushing off to have a row with him . . ."

Fever was very still, waiting.

"And then this morning, of course, I realised why you had reacted so strongly."

The tension in the air was almost tangible.

"What did Martindale say to your wife that afternoon, Mr. Fever, to make you so angry?" Thanet paused before playing his trump card. "Did he threaten to tell Toby that he was his father?"

"No!" With the explosive monosyllable Fever was on his feet, hands gripping the edge of his desk. "Who the hell . . ." he shouted and then, remembering his secretary's proximity, "who the hell," he hissed, "do you think you are, coming here like this, poking your nose into my private life, making irresponsible accusations right left and centre. . . ?" His eyes were wild and flecks of spittle flew in Thanet's direction.

Thanet didn't flinch. "Irresponsible, Mr. Fever?" he said softly. But, although he didn't show it, for a moment he wavered. What if he were wrong?

"Yes!"

"You deny, then, that Toby was Martindale's son?" Thanet held up a hand. "And, before you say 'yes', I must warn you that this is not just idle speculation. We have been in touch with the General Register Office to check dates and so on."

Fever stared at him, the anger gradually dying out of his eyes, to be replaced with despair. Then he slowly subsided into his chair and putting his elbows on the desk buried his head in his hands.

The silence was sufficient answer. Thanet was relieved. At least he hadn't been wrong in this. He glanced at Lineham who gave a satisfied nod.

Thanet waited a moment or two longer and then said, "Look, Mr. Fever, whether you believe it or not, I'm not enjoying this. I don't get a kick out of other people's misery and I'm not here either to make judgements or to broadcast people's secrets unless it is absolutely necessary. I am merely trying to discover the facts but you must see that until I do I can't even begin to decide whether this matter is relevant or not."

Fever was listening, he could tell. Encouraged, he went on. "I've had to be rather hard on you because, as I'm sure you'll admit, you weren't exactly in a cooperative mood. But if we could now have a sensible and rational dis-cussion . . ."

Fever raised his head and looked at Thanet, a long, assessing look. *Can I believe what you're saying?*

Thanet waited, meeting Fever's gaze

squarely and hoping that his expression was suitably frank and open.

After a moment or two Fever sat back, lifting his hands a little way off the desk and dropping them again in a gesture of surrender. He shrugged. "OK. What do you want to know?"

21

AS the tension in the room began to ebb away Lineham shifted his stance and cleared his throat, unconsciously signalling the fact that one phase of the interview had just ended and another was about to begin. Briefly Thanet wondered if highly-charged emotion actually generated its own—what?—static electricity? Magnetic field? He didn't know. He felt depleted, suddenly aware of an ache in the small of his back, always his weak spot. He longed to get up and ease it, to walk about, light his pipe, relax, but he couldn't afford to do any of these things. It was important not to lose the impetus he had won.

Fever, by contrast, had now given up. Slumped in his chair, he was waiting for Thanet to begin, eyes dull, hands clasped loosely across his stomach.

"I'll be as brief as I can. Toby is Martindale's son?"

A tightening of the lips, a nod.

"And you've known this right from the beginning."

Another nod.

"Does Toby know?"

This brought a reaction. Fever straightened up. "No! And I—we, don't want him to know."

"You've brought him up as your own son?"

"Yeah." A wry attempt at a smile. "We always thought if he took it into his head to count up on his fingers, he'd simply work out we'd enjoyed a bit of hanky-panky before we walked up the aisle."

"You had no other children?"

Fever shook his head. "No such luck. So it was all the more important that Toby never suspected . . ."

"Yes, I can see that. All the same, a bit risky, wasn't it?"

Fever shrugged. "Even if he'd been adopted we wouldn't have told him till he was at least four. By then Leo'd been gone nearly five years and as time went on it seemed less and less likely he'd ever come back."

An uncomfortable thought struck

Thanet. "Does anybody else know, or suspect?"

Fever was shaking his head again. "Not that I know of. It's never even been hinted at. There was a bit of ribbing, of course, when Toby was born only six months after the wedding, but we just let everybody think we'd been at it before we should've."

Oh God, thought Thanet. And I've told Delia Hamilton. What would she do, if anything? He shook his head, to clear it. He'd have to think about that later. Ought he to mention it to Fever? No, not now, when the man was being cooperative at last.

"I'm not sure of the legal position of an illegitimate child, but did you ever think that you could be depriving Toby of a fine inheritance?"

"Well yeah, that did worry us, I must admit, but we took legal advice, confidential-like, when old Martindale died, just for our own peace of mind. Anyway, we discovered Toby didn't have no claim at all, in law. According to the solicitor, illegitimate kids can now inherit, but only if the parents are together. To be honest, we was relieved. Having kept it from him all that time . . . And the last thing we wanted was a legal battle on our hands, that sort of thing can drag on for years. Besides, Toby's happy as he is. He's got everything he wants or needs. He's a good lad, we get on well together, he enjoys working in the business with me . . . Nah, we decided ignorance was bliss and to leave well alone."

"You implied just now that one of the reasons why you'd never told Toby was because you thought Martindale would never come back." Now for the important question. "Does this mean that Martindale knew your wife was pregnant by him, before he went away?"

It was clear that the thought of Martindale impregnating his wife was even now, after all these years, painful to Fever. He compressed his lips and shook his head.

"You're sure?"

"Of course I'm sure! We just thought that if Leo did come back he might work it out for himself."

"And did he?"

"No!"

Thanet didn't think he was lying. But

what if, knowing her husband's jealous nature, Yvonne had told Martindale before he went away, but had never had the nerve to admit it to Fever? Remembering Martindale's questioning of the hotel receptionist in regard to Toby's identity, Thanet considered this possible.

Thanet tried to work it out. If Fever truly believed that Martindale had never known and had therefore never been in the position to threaten to tell Toby, the case against him was strongly undermined. Though there still remained his jealousy. Would that have been enough to drive him, on impulse, to murder? Remembering Fever's reaction just now Thanet thought that it might. For Fever to have stepped in and married Yvonne the moment it became obvious that Martindale had abandoned her, it was more than likely that Fever had been in love with her for some time, that he had had to stand back and watch helplessly while she was swept off her feet by the son of the big house. Jealousy was a cruel emotion, a classic cause of murder. In the case of a man like Fever, whose reputation was such that his wife scarcely dared even speak to another man in his presence for fear of provoking an outburst, the reappearance of Martindale, who had once actually possessed Fever's wife, perhaps stolen her from under his very nose while he looked impotently on, could well have reactivated all his original resentment and hatred of the man. Jealousy had certainly driven him to an immediate confrontation with Martindale. Thanet wondered exactly what had been said during that row, how Martindale had reacted to Fever's warning. Could he have laughed at him, thus provoking him even further and sending him away in an even greater rage? If so, and if, later, on his way back from taking his wife to her mother's house in the van, Fever had been presented with the spectacle of Martindale walking along the road ahead of him, alone . . . Yes, it was still possible that Fever was their man.

Thanet became aware that both Lineham and Fever were watching him, intrigued by his long silence. He stood up. "Right, thank you."

Fever came to his feet. "That's it?"

"For the moment, yes."

They left him staring after them with a puzzled frown.

"No point in asking him if he'd seen Martindale later, when he borrowed the van. He'd only have denied it," said Thanet as they got into the car. He wound down the window and took out his pipe, began to fill it.

Lineham was nodding agreement. "He could be our man, though." He smacked his clenched fist into the palm of the other hand. "If only we had some hard evidence against one of them. Just one tiny scrap!"

"I know." Briefly, at the very back of Thanet's mind something flickered. What was it? He struggled to grasp it, drag it out in order to examine it but already it was gone. Had he imagined it?

Lineham was watching him. "What?"

Thanet shook his head. "It's gone." He struck a match, lit his pipe.

"Where now, sir? Hamilton?"

Thanet shook his head. "Not much point. You realise I've put my foot in it there, Mike?"

"By telling Mrs. Hamilton about Toby? I can't see that you've done much harm."

"In any case, it's done now. There's no point in worrying about it, I suppose."

"It'll give them a few uncomfortable moments, I dare say. But I can't say I feel much sympathy for them. They haven't done too badly, have they?"

"I wasn't thinking of them, I was thinking of Toby."

"I shouldn't lose any sleep over it. The Hamiltons aren't exactly about to shout it from the roof-tops, are they?"

"No. All the same, for Toby's sake I think I'll have to have a word with Mrs. Hamilton."

Lineham's expression indicated that he thought Thanet overscrupulous on this point, but he merely said, "So what now?"

Thanet glanced at his watch. Two-thirty. "Might as well go back to head-quarters, have a session going over the papers. There could be something we've missed. And I really ought to glance at the Super's directive on ODD. He'll go through the roof tomorrow morning if I still haven't got around to it."

It was a silent journey back, each of them preoccupied with his own thoughts. Back at the office they wrote their reports on the morning's interviews, then settled down to work systematically through the considerable stack of papers which had accumulated since the case began. They were methodical, both going through each report in turn, in case one of them spotted something the other had missed. In this particular case, when suspects were many and hard evidence against any one of them sadly lacking, it might well happen that some tiny detail which at the time had seemed of no importance could prove to be of crucial significance. The atmosphere in the room was heavy with concentration, the silence broken only occasionally by a murmured comment or enquiry. From time to time Thanet stood up and walked about, conscious that the dull ache in the small of his back was intensifying. He longed to stretch out on the floor, relieve tense muscles of the downward tug of gravity. Instead, he would sit down, pick up the next sheaf of paper and carry on the task.

By twenty to five he had to admit defeat. Nothing of any importance had emerged. Both he and Lineham were bleary-eyed, their thought processes clogged with the mass of information through which they had sifted. He put down his pen, rubbed his eyes, sat back and stretched. Time to glance at Draco's notes on ODD before going down to report to the Superintendent at five. "See if you can rustle up some tea, Mike, while I look at this."

When Lineham got back Thanet was looking much more animated. "Something occurred to you, sir?"

"Not to do with the case." Thanet tapped the ODD directive. "Did you have any thoughts on this, Mike?" He took the cup Lineham was offering him. "Thanks."

Lineham sat down. "Not really. Why, have you?"

"Possibly. Organisation, Delegation and Documentation. Now, the whole point of this campaign is to improve efficiency. Which one of those three would you say is the most time-consuming?"

"Documentation, I suppose."

"Exactly!" Thanet leaned forward across his desk. "Now tell me this. How much time is wasted in the front office looking through the files for, say, a key-holder's card for shop or office alarms that has been put back in the wrong place by some officer in a hurry?"

"Quite a bit, I'd say." Everyone in the situation had ground his teeth over this particular bit of inefficiency, at one time or another.

"Well, why don't I suggest that all that information is put on the computer, instead? It's being done more and more—Maidstone introduced it a couple of years ago, for example. And not only key-holders' lists, but names and updated addresses of station staff, charge cards, details of emergency action plans . . ."

"But if all that information was stored on the computer what happens if you need it in a hurry when the computer operator is away at lunch or, even worse, off sick?"

"Obviously it would mean that everyone in the station would have to be trained to use the computer."

Lineham groaned. He wasn't into computers. "Oh, no!"

"Come on, Mike, don't be faint-hearted. It would all be in a good cause and besides, it wouldn't be too difficult. Not if we got hold of a simple, user-friendly system. Just think how much time it would save in the long run!"

"Well . . ."

"I think I'll suggest it. If Draco doesn't like the idea, then too bad, but at least I'll have come up with a positive suggestion." Thanet glanced at his watch. Two minutes to five. "I'd better go down to give my report."

At the door he turned. "Oh, by the way, while I'm away, give Mrs. Hamilton a ring, tell her her calculator wasn't in the van." This was clear from the report on the van's contents. Thanet had checked. "She must have dropped it somewhere else."

On the way downstairs he was again conscious of that strange, almost physical sensation at the back of his mind. He had felt it before, many times, and it meant that his subconscious had registered something which his conscious mind had not, and the information was trying to get through. Experience had taught him that it was pointless to try and work out what it was. Sooner or later it would surface in its own good time and the best way to speed up the process was to think of something else.

Outside Draco's office Thanet paused, braced himself. What sort of a mood would the Super be in this afternoon? A better one than this morning, he hoped. He knocked.

"Come in."

Draco was sitting in front of an immaculately tidy desk, pens and pencils neatly aligned, in-tray empty, out-tray full, empty blotter before him. He looked relaxed, composed, positively benign. "Ah, Thanet. How's it going?"

Thanet gave a succinct summary of the day's findings, Draco nodding from time to time, putting in a question here and there. It looked as though the session was going to go off without incident and, encouraged, Thanet decided to float his new idea.

"By the way—"

"Just a minute . . ." Draco held up a hand. He was peering out of the window, which overlooked the main entrance to the building and enabled the Superintendent to keep a watchful eye on comings and goings. If anyone sneezed in this building,

Draco liked to know about it. "Sorry to interrupt, Thanet, but who's that?"

Thanet rose and crossed to the window. Walking towards them were two men deep in conversation, one in uniform, the other in civilian clothes. He assumed Draco wasn't referring to Inspector Storey, an old friend of Thanet's now working in Maidstone, and he'd never seen the civilian before. "Sorry, I don't know. Some member of the public coming to—"

"No, no," said Draco testily. "That's Councillor Watford, I know him. The other man, in uniform."

"Inspector Storey. He's one of the instructors at the Police Training School in Maidstone." The words came out mechanically. Thanet was barely aware that he had spoken. He was staring at the two men, dumbfounded.

Of course! Why hadn't he seen it before?

"Wonder what they're doing here," muttered Draco, heading for the door. "Was that the lot, Thanet?"

"What? Oh, sorry, sir. Yes." His suggestion could wait until the morning meeting tomorrow. Besides, he couldn't wait to tell Lineham . . .

He followed Draco out of the office and took the stairs two at a time.

Lineham glanced up, startled, as Thanet burst into the office.

"Mike! Listen to this!"

Thanet watched the light dawn in Lineham's face as he talked.

"I see! Brilliant, sir! So what do we do now?"

Thanet told him.

22

"LET'S hope they haven't gone to bed."

"Shouldn't think so, Mike, it's only ten o'clock."

It was five exhausting hours later. After making the necessary appointment, clearing it with the Sussex police and ringing Joan and Louise to tell them they'd be late home, Thanet and Lineham had set off on the longish drive to Worthing. The interview there had verified Thanet's hunch and presented them with a clear motive where none had apparently existed before. Now they were about to put his theory to the test.

Thanet shifted in his seat in an attempt to ease his back and rubbed his eyes, which were beginning to feel gritty with fatigue. He was glad he wasn't driving. He glanced across at Lineham who still looked relatively fresh.

"I gather you got the problem with your brother-in-law sorted out?"

"Yes. Or at least, he did. Went back to his wife this morning."

"Good."

Lineham leaned forward to wipe the windscreen, which kept on misting up. Since darkness fell the temperature had plummeted rapidly and along the sides of the lane the grass and clumps of tangled undergrowth were encrusted with frost.

The sergeant was driving carefully, leaning forward slightly to peer at the road ahead. "Lucky we haven't had any rain today, or it'd be like a skating rink."

"Mm." Thanet was preoccupied with the interview to come.

"Of course, it still doesn't necessarily mean one of them did it," said Lineham, for the third time.

Thanet realised that the sergeant was merely armouring himself against disappointment. "I'm aware of that, Mike," he said patiently. "But it's a powerful motive, you must admit. And I've just got this feeling . . ."

The gateposts at the entrance to Longford Hall loomed up ahead and Lineham put his indicator on. "Even if you're right,

I still don't see how we're going to prove it."

Ay, there was the rub indeed. "I know."

"I mean, we've no more evidence against them than against any of the others."

Yet again Thanet experienced that flicker at the back of his mind. What was it that he was trying to remember? Was it possible that there was something he had missed, some minute scrap of evidence that could turn the tide in his favour? Not that, if his theory proved correct, an arrest would give him much satisfaction. After the initial excitement over that flash of inspiration he had felt progressively more and more depressed and now he felt only a dragging weariness at the prospect of the interview ahead. He braced himself as Lineham drove into the stable yard and parked. Whether he liked it or not, he had to go through with it. Murder had been done and if one of these two were guilty it was his clear duty to bring the perpetrator to justice, whatever his personal feelings in the matter.

They walked across the cobbles to the

stable block, climbed the indoor staircase and knocked at the door at the top.

It was a few minutes before it was opened by Desmond Byfleet, peering out into the semi-darkness. "Oh, it's you, Inspector."

"May we come in?"

Byfleet stood back to let them pass, closing the door behind them. "We were just about to go to bed." He was in his shirtsleeves, tieless, carpet slippers on bare feet. Without a jacket he looked thinner than ever and more vulnerable, as if with the outer layer of cloth he had peeled off his defences.

"I'm sorry to trouble you so late, but we'd like a word with you both."

"Do you have to see my wife? She's very tired."

Thanet shook his head. "I'm sorry," he repeated. He meant it. "I'll have to talk to her sooner or later. Better to get it over with."

Byfleet hesitated a moment or two longer, apparently trying to make up his mind whether to refuse point-blank, the muscles in his cheeks moving as he clenched his teeth. Then he turned away and flung open the sitting-room door, switching on a light inside. "I'll go and see."

The sight of the cosy, welcoming room reinforced Thanet's distaste for the coming interview. He strolled restlessly about, his gaze wandering abstractedly over the attractive soft furnishings, the books, plants, records, chess-game, bowl of odds and ends on the coffee table. He sat down heavily, his back protesting at the softness of the cushions. "I'm not looking forward to this, Mike." What if he were wrong? He could see the headlines. WOMAN MISCARRIES AFTER POLICE HARASSMENT. He rubbed his eyes, shook his head in an attempt to clear it. It had been a long day.

Lineham had chosen an upright chair which stood in front of a small writing desk. He picked up one of the ornaments on it, a glass paperweight, and peered into it as if it were a crystal ball. "Fascinating things, these." He put it down hastily and stood up as Byfleet entered the room, followed by his wife.

Thanet rose too. "I apologise for disturbing you at this hour, ma'am."

She attempted a smile but said nothing, walking past him to sit on the settee. She was wearing a man's woollen dressing gown, her husband's presumably, loosely tied across her protruding belly. The shade, a drab fawn, did not become her, leaching any colour from her sallow skin and from the lank, lifeless brown hair.

She looked as tired as he felt, thought Thanet. Scarcely surprising, really. If he was right, she couldn't have had much sleep over the last few days.

Byfleet sat down beside his wife and covered her hand with his.

Thanet glanced at Lineham to check that he was ready and the sergeant nodded. *Go ahead.*

"There's no point in beating about the bush, so perhaps it would be best to begin by telling you that we have just come back from Worthing, where we have seen your mother, Mrs. Byfleet."

Mona Byfleet blinked and blindly put out her other hand to her husband who took and clasped it. Neither of them said a word, just stared at him, awaiting the next blow.

"She was naturally very distressed when

she heard what had happened. She realises that you and your husband had no idea, when you married . . . It must have been an awful shock for you."

Thanet paused expectantly. He didn't want to spell it out if he didn't have to.

Desmond Byfleet cleared his throat. "We don't know what you're talking about, Inspector."

Thanet shook his head wearily. "It's no good taking that line, Mr. Byfleet. We know, you see."

"Know . . . what?" Mona Byfleet spoke for the first time, in a near-whisper.

"That your mother told Mr. Martindale and that he must have told you, Mrs. Byfleet, when he called you into his room, the night he died."

"We still haven't the faintest idea what you're on about, Inspector." Byfleet's voice was stronger now. He had obviously decided on the line he was going to take and was sticking to it.

His wife was less certain. She shot him an agonised glance and said, "Des . . ."

Byfleet gave no overt sign of having realised that she was on the point of capitulation. There was no frown, no shake of the head, just a brief exchange of glances. But the message still came over loud and clear. *Stand firm.*

She glanced back at Thanet. *Don't say it*, her eyes pleaded. *Please, don't say it.*

But he had to, somehow, Thanet realised, or they would get nowhere. He sighed. "Perhaps it will help if I tell you a story."

Byfleet clicked his tongue impatiently but his wife, recognising perhaps that Thanet was proposing an oblique approach to the subject in order to cushion the blow, laid a restraining hand on his arm.

"Once upon a time," said Thanet, "there was born in London's East End a girl called Brenda. She had eight brothers and sisters and her father was a drunkard who couldn't keep any job down for more than a few weeks at a time. Needless to say she couldn't wait to get away from home and in 1949, at the ripe old age of seventeen, she married the first man who asked her and moved to the Midlands.

"Unfortunately it wasn't long before she discovered that she had jumped out of the frying pan into the fire. Her new husband was a bully and a brute and not long afterwards, when she was seven months pregnant, he beat her up so badly that the baby was born prematurely."

He had their attention now. They were gazing at him as if mesmerised.

"This was the last straw as far as she was concerned. In hospital she refused to see her husband again and on the day she was due to be discharged she left earlier than the time arranged and, having borrowed the train fare from one of the other women in the ward, came straight to London, leaving her baby boy behind. Being premature, of course, he would in any case have had to remain in hospital for some time but this was, she felt, the only way she could get away from her husband and be certain that the baby would be well looked after. She had had this plan in mind right from the moment of that last, brutal beating and although the baby seemed healthy enough she insisted on his being christened immediately after the birth. In fact, the husband refused to have anything to do with the child, who was brought up first in a children's home then in various foster homes.

"Meanwhile, Brenda changed her

surname and, despite the nationwide appeal for her to come forward, disappeared into the lowest stratum of London's catering trade where employers didn't bother about National Insurance cards and were only too glad to get cheap labour. For some time she washed dishes, waited at tables in the smallest and meanest cafés and then, when she felt it was safe, reverted to her married name, legitimately got hold of a National Insurance card, and began to work in earnest towards furthering the career she had meanwhile decided to pursue. Shrewdly, considering her lack of qualifications, she chose the hotel business. I won't go into the details. It's enough to say that beginning on the bottom rung and by working twice as hard as anyone else, in five years she managed to work her way up to Housekeeper in a smallish hotel. During this period she also divorced her husband. Then, late in 1954, she managed at last to get the kind of job she'd always been aiming for, a post as Housekeeper in a hotel out of London, on the South Coast. At this time she was still barely twenty-three and perhaps it's not surprising that now, for the first time, romance entered her life. It was a small, family-run hotel, and the Assistant Manager was the son of the owners. In due course Brenda and he were married and the following year they had a daughter." Thanet paused. "In a minor way a fairytale ending, as I think you'll agree. Unfortunately, the story doesn't end there.

"In due course first the owner and his wife were killed in a holiday air crash and then Brenda's second husband died, so the ownership of the hotel passed to her. Her daughter grew up and when she left school worked in the hotel with her mother. Although she wasn't exactly antisocial she was never the type of girl to have lots of boyfriends and it wasn't until she was in her late twenties that at last she met a man she liked. He had recently moved down to the South from Birmingham. For some reason—shyness, perhaps?—she kept their association a secret. Finally, when they began to talk of marriage, she broke the news to her mother and asked her to meet him. She was taken aback by her reaction. From the outset, before she had even met him, Brenda seemed prejudiced against him. The girl put it down to over-protectiveness of an only chick and told herself that when her mother met the young man and saw how respectable and hardworking he was she would become reconciled to the idea. Instead, the meeting merely served to harden her mother's attitude. The young man, she insisted, was unsuitable, completely wrong for the girl.

"Naturally, the daughter thought that her mother was being totally unreasonable. But in fact, she was misjudging her. Brenda was against the marriage for quite another reason.

"As soon as she heard the man's name —a fairly unusual one—she had realised to her horror that he could be the son she had abandoned long ago and there was a real possibility that brother and sister were planning to marry."

23

WITH an abrupt, desperate movement Mona turned her head and buried her face in Desmond's sleeve as if ashamed to look Thanet in the eye any longer. Desmond shot Thanet a furious, resentful glance and put his arm around her.

Thanet took a deep breath and attempting to ignore the pity that was churning his stomach said softly, "It would perhaps be more accurate to say, 'half-brother', and it is clear that the young people were entirely the innocent victims of tragic circumstance. Although Brenda had confided the details of that early, disastrous marriage to her husband, she had never told her daughter about it. All that, she had thought, was behind her, best forgotten. Now . . . Well at first, of course, she couldn't be sure that her suspicions were justified. So she agreed to meet the young man and when she did knew at once that he was her son. He was the spitting image of his father. That, together with his name . . . She may have abandoned him, you see, but she'd never forgotten him, and ironically her daughter's name had even been chosen in a rather subtle way to complement his."

Desmond and Mona glanced at each other as they worked out what he meant and the name shivered unspoken in the air between them. *Desdemona.*

"A few questions about his background convinced Brenda that she was right. Now she was in a real dilemma. If she told her daughter the truth, the girl would never forgive her for not having been frank with her from the beginning. If she didn't, her daughter would think that she was against the marriage for far more trivial reasons. Either way she ran the risk of losing the only person she really loved. It wasn't surprising that that night she tried to drown her sorrows in drink, but it was unfortunate that she did so in the company of one of the guests in the hotel, a man by the name of Leo Martindale. He was a confidence trickster who made a habit of preying on lonely middle-aged women and she was his favourite type, the hotel owner who was reasonably well off and might be sweet-talked into parting with some money if he played his cards right.

"In Brenda's case he had got as far as hinting at marriage and had managed to worm his way into her bed. On this particular evening, more than a little drunk and desperate to share her problem with someone, she confided in him and asked his advice. He did in fact tell her that he thought it would be best to tell the girl the truth but when it came down to it Brenda couldn't bring herself to do it. Finally, just when she had screwed up sufficient courage to do so, she found it was too late. Furious at her mother's opposition to the marriage, the daughter had decided to elope. The young people were both over age and there appeared to be nothing to prevent them marrying. For marriage in a registry office couples do not have to produce birth certificates unless they are under 23 years of age, so in all innocence they went through the ceremony and as far as the mother was concerned, just disappeared. Eventually they found work as a husband-and-wife team here, at Longford Hall."

For the first time Thanet addressed the Byfleets directly. "Ironic, wasn't it, that you chose this particular hotel, Martindale's family home. The owner's name, of course, was different, Hamilton, so you had no reason to connect your new employer with the man your mother hoped to marry, and it must have been a shock when he turned up as Mrs. Hamilton's brother . . . And even more of a shock when he told you what he had learned from your mother, Mrs. Byfleet."

Mona was staring miserably down at her lap now, twisting the cord of the dressing gown round and round one finger, releasing it, twisting it again. Still she did not speak and, meeting Byfleet's stony stare, Thanet realised with something like despair that if they chose to remain silent there was absolutely nothing he could do about it. So where did he go from here? He had no stomach for browbeating these people into a confession, they were suffering enough as it was. And, too, there was the possibility that he was wrong and they had had nothing to do with Martindale's death.

Lineham was watching him, aware no

doubt of Thanet's predicament. The silence in the room stretched out uncomfortably.

He had miscalculated, Thanet realised. He had thought that informing the Byfleets that he knew their unhappy secret would be such a shock to them that they would break down and confess, especially if he could do so in such a way as to convince them that he was sympathetic to their predicament. To this end he had put all his ingenuity into devising a way of breaking the news gently—too gently, perhaps. Compassion may have made his efforts self-defeating. In any case, he had not thought beyond that point.

Well, they had reached it and it had got him nowhere.

If only, he thought desperately, he could remember whatever it was that had been eluding him. It was, he was sure, highly relevant. He could feel the knowledge struggling to surface, lacking that final impetus which would bring him enlightenment. He glanced around the room seeking inspiration but seeing only an Eden that was for the Byfleets perhaps forever lost.

It was pointless to prolong the interview. He was about to rise, had actually put his hand on the arm of his chair preparatory to levering himself up when his gaze fell upon the blue-and-white ceramic bowl of odds and ends and, at last, he spotted it.

Of course! That was what his subconscious had registered, the last time he was here!

Despite the pity he felt for the couple still clinging on to the shreds of their dignity, for the second time that day he experienced the unique explosion of triumph which invariably accompanies such rare flashes of understanding—followed at once by doubt.

What if he were wrong?

He longed to put out his hand and pick the object up, his fingers actually ached with the need to do so, to open it, examine it, verify that it really was what he thought it was.

Lineham was now watching Thanet intently. After years of working together he was attuned to even the slightest shift in Thanet's mood and he knew that some-

DBM26

thing of significance had just occurred to him.

Thanet glanced at the Byfleets. They too were watching him, still warily but with the beginning of hope that the worst was over. What should he do? Should he risk making a monumental fool of himself?

His heartbeat accelerated as alternative ways of approaching the subject flashed through his mind.

He took a deep calming breath and exhaled slowly. Then he said, "The last time I was here I asked if either of you had driven the van the night Mr. Martindale died. Now I'd like to ask you again. Did you?"

They did not look at each other but he sensed the unspoken communication which flashed between them before they shook their heads. Thanet waited a moment and then, with a complete change of tone, leaned forward and pointed. "Is that yours, Mr. Byfleet?"

"No. It's my wife's."

Mona twisted to look up at him. She frowned. "No it's not, Des. Mine's back at the hotel, in my office. I was using it this evening and that one's been there for a couple of days. I thought it was yours."

Now it was Byfleet's turn to look puzzled. He leaned forward and reached out to pick the object up, but Thanet put out a hand to prevent him from touching it. Their eyes locked and for a moment there was an unspoken battle of wills between them, Byfleet's hand hovering uncertainly over the coffee table. Then he capitulated, leaning over and pulling towards him the jacket which was lying across the arm of the settee. He patted one of the pockets, put his hand in and took out a virtually identical small black object. Then he looked back at the one in the bowl. *So whose is that?* His wife was looking at it too, but Thanet guessed that she at least now knew the answer and that the question in her eyes was, *How did it get there?*

Now for the moment of truth. Taking a polythene bag from his pocket Thanet slipped it over his hand and then, with care, picked up what he had first thought was a diary, flipped it open. Relief that he had been proved right mingled with regret as he saw the slip of paper tucked into the flap. Even before he carefully extracted it with a pair of tweezers he knew what would be written on it.

Delia Hamilton's pocket calculator had turned up.

Briefly he held out the paper for the Byfleets to read the name and address on it. Their bewilderment was now mixed with apprehension. They couldn't understand why the calculator was important but Thanet's behaviour showed them that it was.

"Where did you get this?" Thanet tossed the question at them both.

They looked at each other. "I really have no idea," said Mona Byfleet. But Thanet could tell that in her husband's mind a memory was beginning to stir.

So Byfleet was their man.

Thanet breathed a silent prayer of thankfulness that at least he would not have to charge a pregnant woman with murder. If she were completely innocent and knew nothing of what her husband had done that night this was going to be a terrible shock to her, potentially disastrous as far as the baby was concerned, and it would be better if she were to leave them now. Perhaps he should insist that she do so. But it was still possible that she was an accessory after the fact. Byfleet was not the sort of man to commit a murder and return home with no sign of distress, and given the closeness of their relationship Thanet thought it highly unlikely that Byfleet would have been able to hold back from telling her what had happened. No, she would have to stay for at least a little while longer.

"Perhaps it would be best if I spell this out. I can see, Mr. Byfleet, that you now remember just how Mrs. Hamilton's calculator got here. On the night Mr. Martindale died she distinctly remembers using it just before she drove to the station to pick up her son. Later, after hunting for it everywhere—as I'm sure you know, Mrs. Byfleet, she realised that she must have dropped it in the van. Mr. Talion didn't notice it when he used the van a little later but you, Mr. Byfleet, I'd guess that after you put Mr. Martindale in the ditch you quickly checked to see if you'd dropped anything and seeing this familiar object on the floor picked it up and put it in your pocket. I also think that you were so shaken by what had happened and in such a hurry to get back to the stable yard before anyone realised that you'd used the van that you scarcely realised what you were doing and later, when you found two calculators in your pockets, simply thought that you must have picked your wife's up by mistake. So you put it in the bowl there and she, of course, thought it was yours, and left it there."

During this brief speech the expression on Mona's face had gradually changed from puzzlement to horrified realisation. Now she looked up at her husband who was staring down at his lap, chewing the inside of his lip. He shook his head in defeat and after a moment Thanet nodded at Lineham, who came forward and delivered the caution.

Mona Byfleet burst into tears.

Her husband put both arms around her and drew her close to him, smoothing her hair. "It's all right, love. Hush. It's going to be all right."

Thanet and Lineham exchanged uncomfortable glances. Thanet longed to get up and walk out, leave the whole miserable situation behind, but duty kept him pinned to his seat. Whatever he did now, sooner or later Mona was going to have to face the consequences of what had happened that night. It wasn't surprising that she had been looking so ill. Ever since she had learned the appalling truth from Martindale she must have been in a state of turmoil, worried sick about the health of a child born of an incestuous union and terrified of the effect of this new knowledge upon their future. And then, on top of that, to know that her husband had committed a murder . . . The last few days must have been a torment for her. What would become of her, he wondered—and of the child?

The ragged sobbing was beginning to abate. Byfleet was still trying to soothe her and now he took a handkerchief from his pocket, moved slightly away from her and began to mop the tears gently from her face. Finally she took the handkerchief herself, blew her nose and looked at Thanet. "You . . . You don't understand. It wasn't the way you think. It . . . It was an accident, wasn't it, Des?" And she gave her husband such a look of love and faith that Thanet could hardly bear to see it.

"It was because I was so upset, you see." She blew her nose again, wiped her eyes and sat up straighter. "He . . . Mr. Martindale . . . was so foul to me."

"When he called you into his room, you mean?" Thanet attempted to make his tone both matter-of-fact and sympathetic. It was important to try to lower the emotional temperature.

She nodded. "It was an awful shock when he turned up at the hotel. I never liked him and he didn't like me—I think he knew I saw through his smarmy ways." She shuddered and made a little moue of distaste. "I knew he'd recognised me, of course, in the foyer." Her voice was getting stronger now as she regained control. It was clear that she wanted to set the record straight, to state the facts in such a way as to present her husband's behaviour in as good a light as possible.

"At first I thought Mum had found out where we were, and had sent him to check up on me. When I left home he seemed to be pretty well dug in there and I'd often wondered if they'd got married. Then when he turned up here and someone told me he was Mrs. Hamilton's brother, I didn't know what to think . . . In any case, I wasn't too surprised when he called me into his room. I was glad of a private word, really. I wanted to find out what the situation was, and if he and Mum weren't together I wanted to make sure he didn't tell her where we were . . .

"At first it was all right. We just chatted, and I was relieved to find he had been living in France and had lost touch with my mother soon after I left. Then it was just like I told you before, he started asking questions about the hotel and when he got on to things that I didn't feel I ought to tell him, I said I couldn't answer any more questions, if he wanted to know he'd have to ask Mrs. Hamilton, she was the boss, after all. He just laughed.

"That's what you think, Mona. Things are going to change around here from now on. My dear little sister isn't going to play at God any more."

"What do you mean?"

"Simply that I've come home to stay. And to claim, somewhat belatedly, my inheritance. So you see, I'm going to be in charge here from now on and I have every

right to ask you whatever questions I choose."

"I'm sorry, I'm afraid I shall still have to talk to Mrs. Hamilton first."

"Think I'm lying, do you? Well I'm not, as you'll soon find out, perhaps to your cost."

"What do you mean?"

"Simply that I could find your excessive devotion to my sister rather tiresome. And if you should find it impossible to transfer your loyalty to me, it might be necessary for me to look around for another house-keeper. You're not exactly the ideal candidate anyway, are you?"

"Because of the baby, you mean? I've never let my work suffer because I'm pregnant. Ask Mrs. Hamilton."

"I wasn't talking about the baby, not exactly, anyway."

"What do you mean, not exactly? What were you talking about, then?"

"I was thinking more on the lines of bad moral influence."

"Bad moral influence?"

"Yes. My God, you still don't know, do you?"

"Don't know what?"

"Why your mother was dead against you marrying Byfleet."

"And then he . . . he told me . . ." Even now, when it was out in the open, Mona couldn't bring herself to say it. She was shaking as she relived what must have been the worst moment of her life. "It . . . Oh, it was horrible."

"I don't believe you."
"Ah, but it's true, my dear. Ask your mother. She'll give you chapter and verse all right. So unless you want the whole world to know the truth about you and your so-called husband, I suggest you remember to toe the line, as far as I'm concerned. Both of you."

Mona was twisting and tugging at Desmond's handkerchief and now there was a small tearing sound as the material ripped. Engrossed in her story, she didn't even notice.

"I ran away, then. I couldn't bear to stay there a moment longer, to see that . . . triumphant look on his face. I came back here and waited for my husband."

She looked up at Desmond. "It seemed such a long time before you got here, but I suppose it wasn't, really." She turned back to Thanet. "He could see at once I was in a state and then . . . when I told him . . . He was so upset . . . and angry because Mr. Martindale had been so foul to me . . . And then, when I told him what Mr. Martindale had said, about the whole world knowing the truth . . . Suddenly he just took off . . ."

"It was all such a shock," Byfleet broke in. "I hardly knew what I was doing. I couldn't keep still, I was walking about, and while my . . . wife was talking I'd happened to glance out of the window and see Mr. Martindale crossing the stable yard, heading towards the drive. I stood there, watching him and listening to what she was saying and, a few minutes later, when she told me what he'd said about telling everyone . . ."

Byfleet's voice broke and he dropped his head in his hands. Now it was Mona's turn to give comfort and she stroked his back, gently, as if soothing a frightened animal.

How was he going to make this arrest with equanimity? Thanet wondered.

Byfleet straightened up again. "In all my life this is the first place I've really felt I could call home. We've been so happy here. Haven't we, love?"

Mona nodded, biting her lip.

"The thought that it was all going to end, that he had ruined it all . . . And my wife was in such a state . . . I'm not trying to excuse myself, but it's true, it really was an accident."

"What actually happened?"

Byfleet was shaking his head. "I don't know what came over me . . . I suppose I just felt I had to do something, anything . . . So when Mona said that, about him threatening to tell the whole world . . . I just rushed out. I wanted to have it out with him at once, then and there. When I got down in the yard he was out of sight and the van was just standing there so I jumped in. I always carry the keys in my pocket. Then the damn thing wouldn't start. It was so cold, that night. . . Anyway, it fired in the end and I went after him. When I was nearing the end of the drive I could see him ahead and I slammed on the brakes. I suppose I left it too late and had to brake too hard . . .

Anyway, the van skidded and went out of control. He'd glanced around when he first heard me coming, and moved right in to walk at the side of the road, but there was nothing I could do to prevent myself hitting him." Byfleet closed his eyes as if to block out the memory.

Mona Byfleet pressed her husband's arm.

Thanet waited.

"It was like a bad dream. It all happened so fast . . . It was over in a flash, in a matter of seconds . . ." Byfleet put up his hands and massaged his temples as if to erase the shock and bewilderment he still felt. "I got out of the car. He was lying at the side of the road. I tried to find a pulse and couldn't . . . I realised he was dead, that I'd killed him . . ." Byfleet shook his head in despair. "I'm afraid I just panicked. I knew that at any second someone could come along and . . . We were near the gates and I thought, the roads are so icy, if I put him in the ditch just outside the gates, it would look as though anyone could have done it . . . So . . . So that's what I did."

"You see, Inspector. It *was* an accident." Mona Byfleet was still holding on to her husband's arm, as if clinging to the wreckage of their life. "The roads were icy and Desmond wasn't drunk . . ."

"It's all true, Inspector. It happened exactly as I've told you, I swear it."

"Maybe so, but I'm afraid it's not quite as simple as that," said Thanet, bracing himself to deliver the blow.

"What . . . What do you mean?" said Mona.

They stared at him with identical expressions on their faces. The likeness between them had never been more apparent.

"If it happened just as your husband told us . . ."

"It did!" broke in Byfleet.

"I believe you," said Thanet. "And if you had immediately gone for help . . ."

"But he was dead!" Byfleet was leaning forward now in his eagerness to convince Thanet of the innocence of his intentions. Then he sat back. "Oh hell, why not admit it, you're right, I know you are. Even though there was nothing to be done for him . . ."

"Unfortunately, that's where you're wrong."

Again that identical expression, an unspoken question in both their eyes. Perhaps they dared not ask it. Suddenly the tension was back in the room, the air was thick with their fear.

Thanet steeled himself. There was no way to soften the impact of what he was about to say and in any case it was true that it was Byfleet's action that had cost Martindale his life. "I'm afraid Mr. Martindale wasn't killed by the collision with the van," he said. "When you put him in the ditch he was still alive, but then it snowed, of course . . ."

He hesitated. Should he tell them that Martindale's spine had been injured, that he had recovered consciousness and been unable to get out of the ditch? No, at this point he couldn't bring himself to do it. They would learn, soon enough.

"So after lying outside all night in those conditions it's not surprising that he was dead by morning," he concluded.

Mona fainted.

24

NOON next day, Saturday.

Thanet laid down his pen, sat back, stretched, then reached for the telephone.

"Joan? It's me."

"Hullo. How's it going?"

"Just finished. I was thinking. . . Fancy an afternoon out?"

"Lovely! Where?"

"What about Rye?"

"Bit chilly, d'you think?"

"Nice and quiet, though. No tourists."

"True."

"If there's anywhere you'd prefer. . . ?"

"No. I like Rye, as you know."

"Yes. That's why I thought . . ."

"Good. That's settled, then."

"What about the children?"

"Ben's going ice-skating in Gillingham, remember?"

"Ah yes, of course. And Bridget? Think she'd like to come?" Much as he loved his daughter, Thanet hoped she wouldn't.

There was so rarely time these days for him and Joan to talk, just to enjoy being alone together.

"She's going shopping with Mandy this afternoon."

"Fine."

"What time will you be home, then?"

"Soon as I can. Twenty minutes?"

Outside on the steps Thanet stopped to inhale appreciatively. It was a perfect winter day: crisp cold air, blue sky decorated with puffs of cotton-wool cloud, and a sun which was doing its best to make you forget that it was February.

By 1.30 they were on their way, with a delicious feeling of escape. Across the Weald the landscapes immortalised by Rowland Hilder basked in the unaccustomed warmth, the bare trees casting long shadows across furrowed fields and empty roads.

For a while they drove in a contented silence, relishing the sense of freedom, and then Joan stirred.

"Feel like telling me how you worked it out?"

Thanet would have preferred to forget about work this afternoon but it was part of the pattern of their lives to have a "post-mortem" at the end of every case and Joan, he knew, would be disappointed if he demurred. "If you like."

He paused, ordering his thoughts. "Actually, believe it or not, it was the Super who finally put me on the right track."

"Really? How?"

"Oh, I don't mean he did it consciously. No, it was just that while I was talking to him, yesterday afternoon, we saw two visitors coming in—his window overlooks the forecourt, as you know. And as you also know, he likes to know every last thing about what is going on in the division. So I wasn't in the least surprised when he said, 'Who's that?' and because I didn't know one of the men I assumed he was referring to him. Then I discovered he was referring to the other chap."

"I don't get it. How did that help?"

"Well, when Leo Martindale arrived at Longford Hall on Monday evening he saw Mona Byfleet, the housekeeper, talking to Toby Fever in the entrance hall, and he asked the receptionist the same question: 'Who's that?' Mona was wearing her housekeeper's dress and the receptionist therefore took it for granted that Martindale would realise who she was and that he must be referring to Toby. So she told him it was Miss Hamilton's boyfriend. Then she said, 'He was just going to say something else when Mrs. Hamilton arrived.'"

"And you think the 'something else' would have been, 'No, I don't mean him, I mean the woman with him.'"

"Exactly. In other words, it was Mona Byfleet who interested him, not Toby, and when I realised that I naturally asked myself why? If she'd been an attractive woman, the sort that Martindale was always on the lookout for, it would have been a different matter, but she's fairly plain and heavily pregnant. So it seemed to me that the most likely answer was that she interested him because he had recognised her and wondered what she was doing there. Until then, you see, I had assumed that the Byfleets couldn't possibly have had any motive for wanting him dead because they didn't appear to have any connection with him, past or present."

"So then you asked yourself what that connection could possibly be?"

"Yes. We knew that Martindale had been abroad for several years but before that, when he was in this country, he tended to move from hotel to hotel, living on any pickings he could glean from women he met, mostly wealthy widows or middle-aged spinsters. They're always the most vulnerable, the most susceptible. Well, Mona didn't really fit that pattern but it did occur to me that her mother might. I knew that Mona had been to school in Brighton and that her maiden name was Taylor—I saw it in the fly-leaf of one of her old books—and then I remembered that one of Martindale's former women friends had been called Taylor and ran a hotel in Worthing, which is near Brighton."

"So you thought, Aha, I wonder if she was Mona's mother and that was where Mona and Martindale met?"

"Precisely."

"But even so, what possible relevance did you think it could have?"

"I didn't know. But if the connection

had been entirely innocent I didn't see why Mona shouldn't have owned up to it."

"Not necessarily, surely. If I became innocently entangled in a murder investigation I'm not sure that I'd be particularly anxious to volunteer information that could connect me with the victim, would you?"

That was a tricky one. "I don't know. It would depend on the circumstances, I suppose. But in this case I just felt that this particular connection could be important."

"Your intuition again."

"Probably."

"I once read that a policeman should never underestimate the value of intuition."

"I think I'd agree with that. Though I know a lot who wouldn't, who are distinctly suspicious of it."

"Why is that, d'you think?"

"Probably because nobody quite understands how it works."

"I suspect," said Joan slowly, thinking aloud, "that although it sounds very vague it's really a perfectly logical process. Without our even being conscious that it's

414

happening, the brain takes note of facts, impressions, expressions, reactions and then assesses them all and comes up with a conclusion."

"I think that just about sums it up. An article I was reading the other day claimed that the brain is infinitely more powerful than the computer and that we only ever use a minute fraction of its potential."

"I'm sure that's true. So anyway, your intuition told you you were on to something . . ."

"Yes. I'd put DC Swift on to checking back on Martindale's women friends and Mrs. Taylor was one of the ones he'd managed to track down, so we rang her up, made an appointment, and went to see her."

They had reached Appledore and Thanet stopped talking while they drove through the picturesque village, pausing to admire a pretty Georgian house built of rose-red brick with a For Sale notice outside.

"My ideal house!" sighed Joan.

"Mm." It was Thanet's too, but a policeman's pay was unlikely ever to stretch to their buying anything like it.

As they turned into the Military Road to Iden Lock and drove along parallel to the Royal Military Canal, Thanet told Joan the sad tale of Brenda Taylor's two marriages and the disastrous meeting of the son she had been forced to abandon and the daughter ignorant of her mother's past.

"Bit of a coincidence, wasn't it? That they should meet at all?"

Thanet shrugged. "Coincidences do happen. And I've often thought that the danger of this sort of thing, the innocent coupling of close relations, is going to become more and more frequent as time goes on. With divorce and remarriage becoming more common, artificial insemination by donor and surrogate motherhood . . . It would be a miracle if half-brothers and -sisters didn't occasionally meet."

"And become attracted to each other for that matter. With all those genes in common . . ."

"Yes. I noticed the resemblance between the Byfleets the first time I met them, you know, but I didn't realise its significance. Just thought how interesting it was that some husbands and wives do grow to resemble each other."

Joan grinned. "D'you think we have?"

He smiled back. "Don't know. I suppose we'd be the last to see it even if we had."

"So, all right, you'd discovered that the Byfleets had a possible motive for the murder. You assumed that Leo Martindale had recognised Mona Byfleet, and had told her the truth about Desmond being her half-brother. Presumably you also thought he must have threatened to blackmail them in some way with this knowledge?"

"I didn't know. I just felt that it was a potentially explosive situation."

"But how did you guess which of them had run him down? Or did you think they'd acted together?"

Thanet shrugged. "Again, I didn't know. At that stage neither of them was even admitting to having driven the van that night and at one point in the interview, I really thought I wasn't going to get anywhere. All along, you see, Mike and I had been saying that even if we did find out who'd actually killed Martindale, there'd be no means of proving it. All the

417

other suspects had admitted driving the van but even so there was no specific evidence, or so it seemed, to link any of them with the crime."

"'Or so it seemed . . .'. There was something, then?"

"Yes. And I knew it. But I simply couldn't put my finger on it. It was just nagging away at the back of my mind . . . Infuriating."

"So put me out of my suspense. What was it?"

Thanet told her about Delia's pocket calculator, picked up in the van by Desmond and mistaken by Thanet for a diary when he first saw it in the Byfleets' sitting-room. "A diary and a calculator can look extraordinarily alike."

"True."

"Though when I looked more closely at it, of course, even without picking it up I could see that it wasn't a diary."

"Bit of a gamble, though, wasn't it? You were only guessing that it was Mrs. Hamilton's."

"I know. I had a few nasty moments there, I must admit. But as soon as I started questioning them about it, it became obvious at once that each thought it belonged to the other and that it therefore belonged to neither. I knew then that I was probably home and dry."

"Because you could then definitely prove that they were lying and that one of them must have driven the van that night —no, wait a minute. Not necessarily, surely. Desmond could still have claimed that he'd picked the calculator up somewhere else, and you'd never have been able to prove it."

"Not really. Because then he'd have *known* it wasn't Mona's. And as I said, they'd both already revealed that each thought it belonged to the other and the only way that could have happened was if one of them had acquired it unconsciously, when they were too agitated to know what they were doing."

"It could still have been Mona, though."

"Less likely, I thought, because Delia had told her the calculator was missing and she was on the lookout for it. But the last place she'd have expected to find it would be in her own sitting-room, obviously."

"So when you'd proved that they'd lied

about having been in the van that night, Desmond confessed?"

"Well it was his wife, really. She just broke down. The past few days had been a terrible strain. I honestly don't think she could have gone on indefinitely, living with the knowledge that Desmond had killed someone. It was only her genuine belief that it had been an accident that had enabled her to keep quiet as long as she did."

"I should have thought that would be the very reason for getting him to own up! After all, no one knew about the connection between her and Martindale."

"I don't think she was thinking straight at the time. Not surprising, really, after what she'd just learned. Her whole future had just collapsed around her ears and I suppose she must have thought, illogically, that if Desmond did own up the truth would come out. But I agree, if he'd only called an ambulance and said it was a straightforward accident, a skid on icy roads, then that would probably have been the end of it."

"I notice you're saying 'she' all the time. Are you implying what I think you're implying? That Desmond either ran Martindale down deliberately or at least knew that he was still alive when he put him in the ditch?"

"Well, I must admit I can't help wondering if he did genuinely believe Martindale to be dead. After all, Martindale alive was an unexploded bomb as far as he and Mona were concerned, whereas Martindale conveniently dead would enable them to decide in their own time and on their own terms what would be their best course of action in the light of what they had just learned. If Martindale were unconscious but still breathing there must have been considerable temptation simply to leave him out in the cold and let nature take its course. And Desmond did move him, remember, put him in the ditch, where he was less likely to be found before morning. And that's what is going to put him in the dock. If only he hadn't moved him, if Martindale had simply died in hospital as a result of the accident, Desmond would probably have got away with it. As it is, because Martindale wasn't dead when he was moved to the ditch we've been able to charge Desmond with manslaughter, on the basis of recklessness in regard to his post-accident conduct."

"You're still on tricky ground there, though, surely. Doesn't it depend whether or not Martindale would have died anyway from his injuries?"

"Doc Mallard says he wouldn't."

"Maybe, but will he be prepared to stand up and say so in the witness box? You know how reluctant expert witnesses are to commit themselves on matters of opinion in Court. And the Defence might well be able to dig up someone to disagree with him. I can imagine a good Counsel having a field day over this."

"The Prosecution too, for that matter. I can imagine them pulling out all the stops, playing on the jury's emotions by painting a horrendous picture of Martindale struggling to get out of that ditch with an injured spine . . . It's something that's going to haunt me for a long time yet."

Joan shivered. "I know. But if Desmond continues to swear that he thought Martindale was already dead when he put him in the ditch . . . Surely, if he can convince the jury of that it would make a considerable difference to his sentence?"

"Yes. If he could pull that off and if there was some doubt as to whether or not the injuries would have been fatal anyway . . . I suppose he could get as little as two years suspended . . . Otherwise he'd get between three and seven, don't you think?"

"Between three and four, I'd say." Joan sighed. "Poor things. What will become of them, d'you think? How is Mona?"

"Still in hospital, under observation."

"They're still afraid of a miscarriage?"

"Yes."

"What will she do? What will they do, even if he does get off?"

"I know."

"What is the legal position of a couple in a prohibited relationship innocently marrying?"

"The marriage is null and void from the beginning, I gather. And in this case there's obviously no question of prosecution because both parties were ignorant of the connection between them."

But in any case, the future for the Byfleets looked pretty bleak. Thanet thought of their pretty, comfortable sitting-room with its evidence of a rich, satisfying life and mourned the bitter blow which fate had inflicted on them. He would never know for sure whether or not Desmond had dumped Martindale in that ditch knowing that he was still alive, but in any case they were to a large extent the innocent victims of a past tragedy not their own and he couldn't help feeling sorry for them.

They were coming into the outskirts of Rye now and with an effort he shut his mind to repercussions of the case. This was a rare treat and he was going to make sure they enjoyed every moment of it.

In summer Rye is always a magnet for tourists but at this time of year it was blissfully empty and they spent the remainder of the short winter afternoon wandering through the steep cobbled streets, gazing in shop windows, browsing in the second-hand bookshops. Before setting off for home they indulged in a cream tea.

In the car Joan settled back into her seat with a smile. "I did enjoy that."

He leaned across and kissed her. "We ought to do it more often."

As they drove through the darkening countryside, ahead of them like a welcoming beacon shone the thought of home, of the pleasure of a leisurely evening together, of drawn curtains, lamp-light, a blazing log fire.

Thanet could think of no better way of spending the evening. He glanced across at Joan's serene profile and gave a sigh of pure contentment. With the case behind him he would be able to relax at last.

He felt at peace with the world.

THE END

GUIDE
TO THE COLOUR CODING
OF
ULVERSCROFT BOOKS

Many of our readers have written to us expressing their appreciation for the way in which our colour coding has assisted them in selecting the Ulverscroft books of their choice. To remind everyone of our colour coding— this is as follows:

BLACK COVERS
Mysteries

★

BLUE COVERS
Romances

★

RED COVERS
Adventure Suspense and General Fiction

★

ORANGE COVERS
Westerns

★

GREEN COVERS
Non-Fiction

MYSTERY TITLES
in the
Ulverscroft Large Print Series

FICTION TITLES
in the
Ulverscroft Large Print Series

By Command of the Viceroy
                                    Duncan MacNeil
The Deceivers   *John Masters*
Nightrunners of Bengal   *John Masters*
Emily of New Moon   *L. M. Montgomery*
The '44 Vintage   *Anthony Price*
High Water   *Douglas Reeman*
Rendezvous-South Atlantic *Douglas Reeman*
Summer Lightning   *Judith Richards*
Louise   *Sarah Shears*
Louise's Daughters   *Sarah Shears*
Louise's Inheritance   *Sarah Shears*
Beyond the Black Stump   *Nevil Shute*
The Healer   *Frank G. Slaughter*
Sword and Scalpel   *Frank G. Slaughter*
Tomorrow's Miracle   *Frank G. Slaughter*
The Burden   *Mary Westmacott*
A Daughter's a Daughter *Mary Westmacott*
Giant's Bread   *Mary Westmacott*
The Rose and the Yew Tree
                              Mary Westmacott
Every Man a King   *Anne Worboys*
The Serpent and the Staff   *Frank Yerby*

WESTERN TITLES
in the
Ulverscroft Large Print Series

NON-FICTION TITLES
in the
Ulverscroft Large Print Series

ROMANCE TITLES
in the
Ulverscroft Large Print Series

The Smile of the Stranger	*Joan Aiken*
Busman's Holiday	*Lucilla Andrews*
Flowers From the Doctor	*Lucilla Andrews*
Nurse Errant	*Lucilla Andrews*
Silent Song	*Lucilla Andrews*
Merlin's Keep	*Madeleine Brent*
Tregaron's Daughter	*Madeleine Brent*
The Bend in the River	*Iris Bromige*
A Haunted Landscape	*Iris Bromige*
Laurian Vale	*Iris Bromige*
A Magic Place	*Iris Bromige*
The Quiet Hills	*Iris Bromige*
Rosevean	*Iris Bromige*
The Young Romantic	*Iris Bromige*
Lament for a Lost Lover	*Philippa Carr*
The Lion Triumphant	*Philippa Carr*
The Miracle at St. Bruno's	*Philippa Carr*
The Witch From the Sea	*Philippa Carr*
Isle of Pomegranates	*Iris Danbury*
For I Have Lived Today	*Alice Dwyer-Joyce*
The Gingerbread House	*Alice Dwyer-Joyce*
The Strolling Players	*Alice Dwyer-Joyce*
Afternoon for Lizards	*Dorothy Eden*
The Marriage Chest	*Dorothy Eden*

NON-FICTION TITLES
in the
Ulverscroft Large Print Series

ROMANCE TITLES
in the
Ulverscroft Large Print Series

The Smile of the Stranger	*Joan Aiken*
Busman's Holiday	*Lucilla Andrews*
Flowers From the Doctor	*Lucilla Andrews*
Nurse Errant	*Lucilla Andrews*
Silent Song	*Lucilla Andrews*
Merlin's Keep	*Madeleine Brent*
Tregaron's Daughter	*Madeleine Brent*
The Bend in the River	*Iris Bromige*
A Haunted Landscape	*Iris Bromige*
Laurian Vale	*Iris Bromige*
A Magic Place	*Iris Bromige*
The Quiet Hills	*Iris Bromige*
Rosevean	*Iris Bromige*
The Young Romantic	*Iris Bromige*
Lament for a Lost Lover	*Philippa Carr*
The Lion Triumphant	*Philippa Carr*
The Miracle at St. Bruno's	*Philippa Carr*
The Witch From the Sea	*Philippa Carr*
Isle of Pomegranates	*Iris Danbury*
For I Have Lived Today	*Alice Dwyer-Joyce*
The Gingerbread House	*Alice Dwyer-Joyce*
The Strolling Players	*Alice Dwyer-Joyce*
Afternoon for Lizards	*Dorothy Eden*
The Marriage Chest	*Dorothy Eden*